A RIYADH RENDEZVOUS

Special Agent Dillon Reece, OSI

BY

DOUGLASS LAIRD DIPPERT

authorHOUSE™

1663 LIBERTY DRIVE, SUITE 200
BLOOMINGTON, INDIANA 47403
(800) 839-8640
WWW.AUTHORHOUSE.COM

First published by AuthorHouse 09/21/05

ISBN: 1-4208-7619-8 (sc)

Library of Congress Control Number: 2005907262

Printed in the United States of America
Bloomington, Indiana

This book is printed on acid-free paper.

Cover Photograph by David Deveson

PROLOGUE

The late model blue sedan pulled slowly through the main gate of Vandenberg Air Force Base into afternoon traffic. Inside, Captain Carl J. Carpton and Chief Master Sergeant Fernando Martinez were silent as they began their journey to a small town near the end of the San Gabriel Valley. As the designated casualty notification team, they were going to visit the home of Airman First Class William Calhoon Crimitin III to tell his family he was found dead outside his apartment in Kottweiller Schwanden, Germany.

"I really hate to travel in the afternoon," Chief Martinez said breaking the silence. There wasn't the expected reply from the officer known as Captain Carl. Both men were members of the 30th Space Wing at Vandenberg. The chief worked in mission support and the captain was a missile maintainer in the wing's maintenance and support flight. This was the captain's first outing as a casualty team member. It was an additional duty assigned by his commander. The old man [1] was prepping Carl for his next assignment as a maintenance supervisor. In that position, he would begin to understand the needs of his people. His only worry as a maintainer was getting the work done. He really didn't have to know the people working for him. In the supervision slot, more and more of the "troops" would show up at his door wanting one thing or another. He would need to understand how to react to each new situation. This team membership will teach him some compassion for members of his unit. His commander knew it was just another stepping-stone in the Air Force work/promotion cycle.

"What say chief? I was lost in my thoughts."

"I understand captain. This is your first time out. It's tough. I've done many of these but each one's different. All you can do is play it out according to your given directions and react as necessary. Anyway, as I was saying, I really hate to be out in afternoon traffic. It just seems to get thicker and thicker each day."

"I know what you mean," Carl replied. "It took me more than an hour to get home the other day. I really dread getting into the LA area."

"Just sit back and relax. Leave the drive to old Fernando." The chief replied with a put on accent as thick as refried beans. "I haven't lost an officer yet." The captain smiled and leaned the seat back for a few minutes of rest as the chief wove his way through southbound traffic.

⁂

"Captain, we're getting into the vicinity. Get out the instructions on how to find this place."

Carl turned as much as his seat belt would allow and reached into the back seat to retrieve his beat up brown bag. Inside were documents requiring signatures by the next of kin. Also inside were instructions how to find the house. The recruiters in Azusa who signed Airman Crimitin up for his current tour of duty supplied them in a call to Carl.

"Dag nab it Captain. Can't you afford a new briefcase?"

The captain held it up for inspection. "What's wrong with it chief? It just has that well used look."

"Well used is an appropriate term. Misused would be even better."

"I've had this thing since I was in college. My wife, well then she was just my steady girl, gave it to me for one of my birthdays."

"Captain! Did you say steady girl? I haven't heard that phrase since I was in high school and that was a long time ago."

"Am I showing my age chief? I'm not the spring chicken you may think I am. I kicked around the computer business before coming into the Force. There were just too many computer geeks out there to land a job worth keeping. However, if you want a good deal on a computer, I'm your man. I can build one from the ground up in little more than a weekend."

"I'll keep that in mind cap but right now we need to get those directions out so we don't end up in San Bernardino."

"Right, let me find them." Captain Carl pulled out the instructions copied down during his conversation with the recruiters. When he told them the news of Crimitin's death, they were surprised. They said he seemed like a good kid and really wanted to be part of the Force. He said the steady job would be good for the family and may lead his brother down the right path.

"OK chief, we're looking for Azusa Avenue. We want to head toward the mountains. The guys said we could take the freeway all the way but if we get off on Azusa, we can stop for a bite to eat. The family is expecting us about 6 p.m. You know, I really don't like the part about telling them we have some paperwork for them to sign. Then we show up in our class A and tell them their son is dead. It just doesn't sit right with me."

"I tend to agree cap but we don't want to break this kind of news to them over the phone. No matter how hard it is, it's best to be with the family and help them any way we can. His parents were the beneficiaries of his insurance policy, so the paperwork issue is really the truth. Since their son was the first family member to join the military, they probably don't expect anything other than a bureaucratic screw up."

"I suppose you're right. Mom always feared that late night visit when dad was flying. He survived his time in Vietnam and then nearly lost his life when he was t-boned by a drunk driver on his way to work. Just doesn't make sense some times."

The pair drove in silence until the captain saw the sign informing drivers on Interstate 10 they were only a mile and a quarter from Azusa Avenue. A cloverleaf exit wraps car and passengers in a circle before depositing them onto the lanes of Highway 39.

"Have you ever been out to this part of the county?" the chief queried

"Only once," replied the captain. "We came out here for a CIF [2] regional football game my senior year of high school. Played the Covina Colts."

"So what was the outcome?"

"I would rather not talk about those dark days," the captain responded with a frown. The chief understood. They probably got their butts kicked and he didn't want to relive the humiliation.

They continued their trek up 39 toward the San Gabriel Valley Mountains. After passing through what seemed like a million traffic signals, they pulled into the parking lot of a steak house for a bite to eat. The time was 1630. They didn't want to arrive at the Crimitin's ahead of their appointment.

After dinner, they continued on 39. In Azusa, they turned onto Baseline and then to Charvers. The Crimitin house was at the end of a cul-de-sac. Each house along the short street was in a differing state of disrepair. The neighborhood was old and definitely showing its age.

"Reminds me of my old neighborhood," the chief sighed as they pulled in front of 1521. Both men had put on their coats as they left the steak house. The chief reached into the back seat for their hats. As they cinched them down, they approached the porch. A hole in the wall with wires sticking out was the only indication of a doorbell. The captain reached through the remains of a screen door and knocked just below the cardboard taped over a hole where the glass should have been.

From inside they heard a female voice shout, "Herman, get the door, I'm still putting on my shoes." The door opened slowly to reveal a frail man they assumed was Herman. Since Herman was not Airman Crimitin's father's name, the captain asked for Mr. Crimitin.

"He ain't home right now," the door opener replied. "He just called from work and said he would be here soon."

Mrs. Sarah Crimitin came down the hallway tucking her white blouse into a dark blue skirt. "Hello gentlemen, come in. Herman, let the men in."

Herman moved away as the captain opened the screen doorframe and stepped into the house. The stale smell of cigarettes and beer hung in the air. A television in the corner was on but there wasn't any sound coming from its location. There was a coffee table in the center of a circular rug. The table was stacked with magazines and newspapers. Next to the table were a well-used lounge chair and a small end table. The couch next to the wall had a throw cover over the seats and an afghan along the back. The threadbare arms spoke about the years of use.

"Can I get you something to drink," Sarah asked.

"No thanks," replied Carl. "Do you know when your husband is going to be home?"

"He should have been home more than an hour ago but he had some favor to do for one of his drinking buddies, so he was delayed." She held both hands in the air and moved two of the fingers on each hand up and down as if putting quotes around the word delayed. "Does he have to sign the papers?"

"Yes he does Mam."

As the words left his mouth, the sound of screeching tires filters through the living room windows. An accelerating engine noise grows closer and closer until it reaches a crescendo outside the house.

"Bill's home," Sarah stated. A car door slammed and then a door at the back of the house shook the windows in the front room, as it was shoved shut. The sound of heavy footsteps preceded the arrival of a hulking man of more than 6 feet and definitely more than 275 pounds.

Sarah began, "Bill, this is, I'm sorry but we haven't even exchanged names." Carl reached out and introduced himself to Bill.

"Captain Carl Carpton, Bill, and this is Chief Master Sergeant Fernando Martinez."

Bill shook hands with both men and then lowered his bulk into the lounge chair. Carl understood why the chair was in its present condition. He and the chief returned to their spots on the couch.

"Mr. and Mrs. Crimitin, we are here to relay some very tragic news. Your son William is dead. His landlord found him. The events surrounding his death are under investigation. We offer you our sincerest sympathy and the services of the Air Force for anything you may need."

Both Sarah and Bill stared in disbelief at the captain and chief.

"Bullshit!" Bill shouted as he jumped from his lounge chair. "I just talked to the boy not two days ago. He said he was on his way to Saudi Arabia on, oh hell what did he call it? A rotation?"

"Yes sir," replied the chief. "The information we have is he was returning to his house after that flight."

Sarah said nothing. The tears were running down her wrinkled face and dripping one by one onto her white blouse. The captain turned his attention to her. "We are truly sorry for your loss."

She looked into his eyes and asked, "How did he die?"

"At the present time, the only information we have is he was found dead outside his apartment. As soon as we have more details, we'll bring them to you. You'll be kept informed during each step of the investigation."

As he spoke the words, the captain felt a presence behind him. He turned to see a boy about 16 or 17 standing in the hallway. Sarah ran toward the boy and threw her arms around him.

"Your brother's dead," she sobbed as she held him tight. The captain noticed the empty look on the boys face as he held his mother.

Chapter One

The soft light of a Florida morning began to show through the bedroom's French doors. The trees lining the lake diffused the rays but no one in the room noticed. The two forms in the draped Victorian style bed were motionless. Dillon Reece bolted upright as the shrill clattering of his phone awoke him from a deep sleep. He reaches across the covered form still motionless next to him and picks up the receiver.

"Dillon here" he mumbles into the mouthpiece of his 1930's style phone.

"Agent Reece?" a cheerful voice on the other end questioned.

"Yes, this is Agent Reece. To whom do I have the distinct pleasure of speaking to at this early hour of the morning?"

"Airman Willis, Sir. I've got Major Littlemore on the line sir."

"Dillon?" Major Littlemore queried.

"Yeah it's me John, what's happened that's so damn important at this time of the morning?"

"We've had a death here under some very suspicious circumstances. You know I would have the crowd here handle this if it weren't for some additional findings. I need your expertise and that sixth sense you always seem to carry with you."

Dillon's close friend filled him in on the situation. "A C-141[3] crew chief[4] was found shot to death outside his apartment. Family notifications are complete and the investigation is just getting underway. Local police are involved gathering evidence and processing documents."

Major John Littlemore had known Dillon for some time. They roomed together during their time at the Air Force academy or "The Zoo," as less reverent members of the Force called the training center. After graduation, they went their separate ways but managed to keep in touch as they continued their Air Force training.

Both men graduated with a schedule for pilot training. However, with the lack of cockpits for pilots during the lean years of the Clinton White House, both went into other career fields waiting their date with undergraduate pilot training and an eventual assignment in high performance fighters. Littlemore went into the logistics arena.

Dillon, on the other hand, used his International Commerce degree for a fling in the field of intelligence collection. Both men completed their respective training and entered their first assignment.

John picked Eglin Air Force Base in Northwest Florida. He designed bunker complexes and then helped the planners develop weapons to destroy the targets. However, the accident changed many things. During an out briefing at a destroyed bunker, John was crushed under a slab of concrete when the portion he was standing on collapsed unexpectedly. He spent months in traction for serious back injuries and a broken pelvis. His recovery was complete but it ended any plans to fly high performance fighters. He decided to concentrate his efforts in the maintenance field.

Dillon completed an abbreviated intelligence-training course at Goodfellow Air Force Base in Texas with additional training at the National Security Agency at Ft. Meade Maryland. Since his schooling was in Commerce, a course was designed to use his studies at the Embassy level for the collection of intelligence material in commercial centers around the world. His selected career path took an unexpected change in direction when his fiancée died in the parking lot of a discount store in Tampa Florida. The event made the instant news as helicopters circled overhead to broadcast the gruesome scene for viewers in the Tampa area. One of those viewers was Dillon. He recognized her car and listened as a reporter described the scene.

"A young woman was killed today, caught in the crossfire of an apparent drug deal gone wrong." The grim faced reporter continued, "No identification has been given to reporters until facts are checked and the next of kin have been notified."

Dillon was out the door. The parking lot was less than a mile from their home. He fought his way to the police line only to face restraint by police officers as he tried to reach his beloved. Once the security forces confirmed his identity and relationship to the victim, he traveled with her body to the morgue. This life shattering experience led Dillon to change the plans he made at the Academy and join the Office of Special Investigation (OSI) in a newly formed Special Interdiction Unit.

Dillon quietly replaced the receiver in its cradle. He reached down and stoked the soft curls on the satin sheet covered form next to him. It had been a long time since he took the bold step of asking a woman to join him in bed. He still missed the woman who agreed to be his wife but knew he must get on with his life. Sonta rolled over and pulled the sheet up to cover her nakedness.

"Something important?" she asked trying to stifle a yawn.

Dillon reached down and ran his fingers through her auburn hair. "Yes," he replied, "I have to be on my way to Germany as soon as possible."

Sonta furled her brow to show her distinct disappointment. "But we've got plans for next weekend," she protested.

"I know, I know but I'll just have to take a rain check on the trip. Why don't you check your schedule and see if you can join me in Munich for a week next month. I know this great little gasthaus in Garmisch-Partenkirchen. The view from the balcony is stupendous and the food is even better. Once I get to Germany, I'll make the arrangements. If you can make it, we can meet in Munich and take the train down to Garmisch. Sonta pouted her displeasure but agreed to try to make the trip to Germany.

⁂

"Sonta," Dillon yelled from the shower, "did you find my boarding bag?"

As Dillon rinsed the shampoo from his blonde hair, Sonta stepped into the bathroom with the boarding bag in hand.

"Is it the blue one with the roll of toilet paper stuck in the corner?"

"Yeah, that's the one," Dillon replied as he stuck his head around the corner of his shower. Sonta was very interested in the roll of toilet paper. "What's this for?" she asked holding the roll up for his view.

"Oh that," Dillon replied sheepishly. "You never know when you are going to need the soft touch of Charmin," he joked as he grabbed the bag from her hands. She grabbed it back and threw him a towel from the heated rack near the tub.

"Don't," she protested, "You're all wet, and we have to get you packed for the trip."

Dillon stepped from the shower and began toweling off. He arranged for pick-up at 0900. He wanted to make a stop on base to do some research into the life of the recently deceased crew chief. Having this knowledge would be a plus when he arrived in Germany. He called the office and talked with the duty agent. Since Dillon was on special assignment with the staff, he didn't have to pull the "duty dog" weekend shift. However, Agent Wendy Lamonge did have the duty and was making calls to arrange transportation for Dillon. First choice was military airlift direct to Ramstein. If nothing were available, he would fly commercial into Frankfurt and get a car from the motor pool at Rhein Main.

Sonta laid Dillon's clothes on the bed. She stood back from her selection for his approval.

"Well," he said as he finished drying his hair, "It's been some time since I've had the pleasure of having my clothes selected by such an attractive valet."

Sonta blushed and pulled the silk robe tighter around her waist. "Why thank you Mr. Reece," she cooed in her best southern accent. "I didn't know you cared."

"Oh, I care very much," Dillon replied as he dropped his towel into the chair and reached for Sonta. As he gazed into her soft brown eyes, he kissed her gently and told her how much he appreciated her being with him. She knew about his loss and never mentioned the situation or queried him about his past.

She met Dillon through a mutual friend. She'd seen him at a Chamber of Commerce function for the March of Dimes. She worked her friend very hard to get the introduction.

She pushed away from his embrace and scolded him. "Oh no, none of that. We have to get you ready and I don't want an interruption by some driver with a waiting staff car. Save it lover boy for our meeting in Munich."

Approving the selection, they both began putting clothes into the suit bag, suitcase, and roll around. He went into his office, pulled his current diplomatic passport from the safe, and slid it into the boarding bag. He also removed the 9MM Detonics, two six round clips and the special travel case he used to transport the weapon on airliners. He returned to the bedroom to see Sonta struggling to close the large suitcase.

"How do you get this thing shut?" she questioned from atop the case.

"Simple." He replied as he placed his hand along the edge of the case and applied enough force to have the two sides meet and latch. "See, simple isn't it?" She shot him a glance that would melt ice. He answered by kissing her on the nose.

Sonta pushed him away and threw his undershirt at him in play. "Put that on and finish getting dressed." Dillon pulled the shirt over his head and finished getting into his travel clothes. He moved his luggage into the foyer and went into the kitchen for some breakfast. Sonta had already poured a cup of coffee and was peering through the breakfast nook window facing the lake behind the house. The sun shown through the thin silk robe and Dillon admired the revelation. He quickly turned to the coffeepot as Sonta turned from the window.

"Are there any fish in that lake? I never see anyone fishing."

I really don't know," replied Dillon. "Since we," he stopped and corrected, "Since I moved into the place, I've been so busy; I haven't taken the time to investigate."

Dillon polished off his normal breakfast of bran cereal, raisins, vitamins, orange juice, and wheat toast. He just finished putting the last of the dishes into the dishwasher when the doorbell rang. Sergeant Bret Walbog was the designated driver. He quickly picked up the bags and headed for the car. Dillon held back the boarding bag and shut the door behind Bret. He turned to Sonta.

"Makes sure you clear your schedule for our meeting in Munich. I'll probably be in Germany for several weeks depending on where the investigation takes me." Sonta reached down and pulled the belt loose on her robe. It fell away from her shoulders and dropped to the floor. She stood on tiptoes to reach his lips and gently kissed him. He drew her close and caressed the small of her back. She stepped away and stood in his gaze. With that final look, he turned and opened the door. Sergeant Walbog was waiting by the car. He opened the back door but Dillon pushed it shut and hopped in the front seat. "I'm not a VIP sergeant; I'm just a guy who needs a ride to the base and depending on what Agent Lamonge has arranged, a ride to the airport."

Dillon looked toward the house and saw Sonta standing in the window. She replaced the robe and blew him a kiss as Walbog put the car in gear and pulled away from the house.

The office building on Tyndall was nothing special. It once held the veterinarian clinic before reorganization placed OSI outside the official chain of command. The Commander at that time decided to punish the agents by reassigning their office space. There was only one small sign to identify the building as their home. Inside, each office was about the same. There were standard Government Issue desks with their gray sides, peeling Formica tops, and broken drawers. Some of the other units on base went to the modular style cubicles but OSI was a traditionalist organization and didn't want the agents feeling too comfortable in their work environment. Dillon stepped into his office, threw his boarding bag on the side chair with the worn seat cover, and pulled out his desk chair with the taped on roller.

Dillon slid the keyboard of his computer out of its storage space and stroked in his password. He entered the Internet to check the Air Force records library in San Antonio. Reaching into his boarding bag, Dillon pulls out the name and identification number of the crew chief. Once into the system, that was all he needed to access a persons entire military record. This one was nothing special.

Airman First Class William Calhoon Crimitin III. Born in Azusa, California on June 06, 1982. He joined the Air Force just over three years ago and served without distinction until discovered deceased outside his apartment. Nothing in his records indicated any type of discipline problems. There were no incidents in basic training, technical school or at his first assignment at Travis Air Force Base in California. So how did this young man end up dead outside his home in Germany?

As Dillon continued to screen records, Agent Lamonge came in and announced that all military flights to Germany were leaving later in the week. Since he indicated a need to get into Europe as soon as possible, she booked him on a flight to Dulles, a connection into Paris and then on to Frankfurt.

Dillon only heard a portion of the discussion because he discovered the reason for young Airman Crimitin being in Germany and not flying the Pacific route out of Travis. The airman volunteered to take temporary assignment to Ramstein. He then applied for and received a permanent change of station move as a swap with another airman.

As Dillon looked up from the computer screen, Agent Lamonge was still standing in front of his desk. "Thank you Wendy," he innocently replied not wanting to give away the fact he heard nothing of what she said.

"I'll be out in a minute. Is Walbog still here?"

Wendy confirmed Walbog was going to take Dillon to Tampa International Airport for his flight to DC. "Is there anything else you need before I head back home?" Wendy asked as she began to back out the door.

"No thanks." replied Dillon; "I just have to print a few things before I leave. What time was the flight?"

Wendy came back to the desk and picked up the piece of paper attached to the tickets she laid on his desk. "It's all right here sir. You leave here at 1330; arrive in DC at approximately 1430. Your flight to Paris leaves at 1805. No problems with any of the connections. You should have plenty of time."

Dillon sheepishly looked down at his desk and saw Wendy had prepared all the documents he would need. "Thank you Mam," he drawled. Wendy turned and left the office. She had a thing for Dillon but knew he just recently returned to the dating game. She didn't want to rush him into anything. She didn't know about Sonta.

He threw the papers into a folder and jammed them into the boarding bag. He stepped into the hall, shut off the lights and headed for the front door. Walbog was sitting in the passenger seat reading the latest issue of

Newsport. When he saw Dillon come out the door, he put the magazine into the glove box and slid into the drivers' position.

"To the Airport James." Dillon joked as he pulled the door shut. Walbog smiled and pulled away from the curb.

Chapter Two

"Excuse me Mr. Reece," the flight attendant whispered as she gently shook Dillon from the peaceful slumber he pursued while crossing the Atlantic. "We're ready to serve breakfast and will be landing in just over an hour. You need to fill out your entry card."

Dillon pulled the mask away from his eyes and let it rest on his forehead, "Thanks" he replied, "I'll get to this as soon as I can get a cup of coffee."

"I'll get you one right now," the attendant responded with a quick turn and a walk down the aisle that drew Dillon's attention. I sure do enjoy flying Business Class he thought as he brought the seat to its full and upright position. He reached into the armrest and brought out the tray table. He pulled the video screen from its hidden compartment and flipped through the selections to settle on the cartoon channel where Daffy Duck was encountering some nasty times from Elmer Fudd. He placed the headset on his ears and began to complete the entry card. How many of these had he completed over the years? That's why he was flying Business Class. It certainly wasn't because the government flew its agents in fine style. He possessed enough frequent flyer miles on five different airlines to upgrade his trip every time he stepped on a boarding ramp. The flight attendant returned with his coffee, a sweet roll, and yesterday's edition of the *Washington Post*. After he completed the card, he sat back, sipped his coffee, and checked into the financial section.

After finishing his coffee, the sweet roll, and a review of his portfolio, he decides to get up and avail himself of the facilities before breakfast. In order to get some stretching done; he walks to the back of the Business section, pulls aside the curtain, and steps into the other compartment.

The lights are still out and only a few reading lights illuminate the area. Most of the passengers are still asleep as the airliner hurries into a new day.

Dillon walks toward the back of the jet where he knows there's a galley and restrooms. After finishing his visit with members of the crew in the galley, he returns via the opposite aisle to his seat. The smell of freshly brewed coffee drifts from the forward galley. It peaks his taste buds and he returns the tray table to a position in front of him to receive the breakfast of scrambled eggs, rolls, jam, cheese, juice, and sausage.

Just as he finishes the last of his jam-covered roll, the captain announces their approach to Charles DeGaulle Airport just outside Paris. As the aircraft begins a slow decent, Dillon watches the countryside become large and more realistic.

Customs in Paris can be troublesome but since he was continuing on to Frankfurt, he didn't have to worry. His bags have tags for the final destination. After visiting the Police office to clear his weapon, he heads for the Business lounge to wait for his flight to Frankfurt.

Dillon spent the morning watching CNN and reading the local English language newspapers. The lounge was very comfortable with showers to refresh and lockers available to store luggage. After taking a combat nap,[5] Dillon visited the duty free stores and selected a couple of Cuban Partagas Lusitanias. He likes a long cigar and one of his friends, stationed in England, told him about this smoke and praised its construction and flavor.

With the announcement for his 1445 flight to Frankfurt, Dillon gathered his bags and headed for the door. The steward approached and handed him a note.

"This just came in for you sir," the man stated as he handed Dillon an envelope with the lounges logo embossed on the front.

"Thank you" Dillon replied as he reached for the message. He stopped for a moment and read the note. It was from Sonta. She missed him already and arranged to be in Germany whenever he wanted to meet. The thought of seeing her again brought a smile to Dillon's face. He slipped the note into the side pocket of his bag and left the lounge. His gate was nearby so there wasn't any rush. With his boarding pass in hand, he ambled down the corridor toward his ride to Frankfurt.

The flight is just about an hour. There was just enough time for another light snack and a look at the *International Herald Examiner*. He was curious about activities in Europe. Since his last assignment was on the other side of the world, he hadn't paid much attention to situations on the continent or in Southwest Asia. After his review of the news, Dillon leaned back in his seat and shut his eyes. Before long, the jet was on final approach. The landing and customs went smoothly. The routine stop by the local constabulary to clear his weapon went without a hitch. John's early arrival and visit to the proper officials cleared the way for Dillon's expeditious processing.

John was waiting outside the police office when Dillon came through the door. It was always good to see him. A special bond kept them close. After exchanging pleasantries, they left the airport and headed for the Autobahn.

"You didn't have to come and meet me like this," Dillon said as they made their way along the highway.

"I know" John replied, "but I knew you would have a million questions about the case and I wanted to tell you as much as I knew before you got started."

John told Dillon to reach into the back seat and get the book bag. Inside were documents relating to the victim, his family, his assignment to Germany, his recent flight records and the autopsy. Dillon glanced at the items and began to read the autopsy.

"Wow," he exclaimed, "they really wanted him dead. One shot to the abdomen and another to the forehead. Not much room for error there. It says both shots were from close range. That's interesting. He didn't live in a bad part of town, so someone approaching him wouldn't draw too much attention. Did anyone hear the shots?" Dillon asked.

"No one heard a thing." John responded. "At least that's the current story and most of the people are sticking to it. The report said he was dead for about five hours before the landlord found him. That would put the time of death around midnight. It just doesn't seem possible that no one saw or heard anything. Our team is still conducting interviews. They'll continue until we exhaust all avenues of approach."

Dillon drifted into his own world as they zipped along the Autobahn. The fields on either side of the road held row after row of grapevines. His wine cellar was lacking the proper balance of American, French, and German wines. There was always room for a case or two of Naha Valley Spatlese or Auslese. The sound of John's voice brought Dillon back to reality.

"I'm sorry John, what did you say?"

John looked at Dillon and repeated the question. "Do you want to go straight to the office or do you want to put your bags in the room and freshen up before you meet the team?"

"I think a visit to the room would be appropriate." Dillon responded. John agreed as he guided the powerful sedan over the crest of a hill and down the other side to the city of Kaiserslautern. Ramstein sat nestled in the valley as a large part of the German Community.

They cut off the Autobahn and headed toward one of the air base's main gates. Both men returned a smart salute from the gate guard. John arranged for a VIP suite in the General Cannon. He knew Dillon would be spending a lot of time pouring over paperwork and having comfortable living conditions was a prerequisite for easing the paperwork nightmare.

John dropped Dillon and told him to take his time getting ready. He would go to his office and make a few calls to the team. He would set up a meeting for 1800 at his office. "I'll have someone come and pick you up just before 1800," John told Dillon as he helped him get his bags out of the trunk and on to the luggage cart.

Dillon agreed and headed for his room. Once inside, he found the accommodations suitable. The living room was comfortable with a couch, wing back chairs, fax machine, big screen TV, and a stereo system. There was a dining area off the small kitchen complete with china and crystal. Great if he planned any entertaining. His passion for microwave popcorn could be satisfied as he spied the latest edition of molecule accelerator on the counter. The bedroom contained a king-sized bed, TV and computer station. There were two telephone lines available. One for regular communications and one hooked into the command post for secure communications. Dillon nodded his head at the impressive arrangement.

He unpacked his clothes and put them into the drawers. He hung his suits, emptied his toiletries into the bathroom, and undressed. He turned on the shower and adjusted the flow. This was going to feel good he thought as he stepped into the spray. As the water beat down on his sandy hair, he thought of the daunting task ahead of him. He just hoped things would fall into place and he could wrap this up in record time. Little did he know the problems he would face!

CHAPTER THREE

Right on time, the driver arrived with Dillon's vehicle for the trip to John's office. The maintenance squadron administrative offices were close to the primary work area. John waved to Dillon as he entered the office.

"Feel more like a human being now?" John asked as Dillon approached.

"I'm always amazed at how much good a nice hot shower does for a man's outlook on life." Dillon replied.

Since Dillon came from the flight line side of the office, he didn't see the other people gathered in the reception area. Having heard the new voice, people began to join both men in the command office. There was Agent Bill Wilmerson, Agent Penny Patterson, and Agent Christina Dean. All had been with the Ramstein OSI office for more than a year. They knew of the relationship between the two men and accepted the fact an agent from outside the command is there to investigate their case. Dillon turned to see them entering the office.

"First, let me introduce myself, I'm Dillon Reece and I've been asked to come and join your team as you investigate the death of Airman Crimitin." He watched their faces for any signs of resentment. The only one to show any was the attractive blonde-haired woman of short stature.

Bill reached out to shake Dillon's hand, "Bill Wilmerson lead investigator on this particular case."

"Hi Dillon, I'm Penny Patterson. I'm not actually working this case now. I just wanted to meet you. I've heard quite a bit about your work at the embassy level. I've always been interested in moving toward that arena. Hope we can talk if the case doesn't take all of your time."

"I'm sure we'll find some spare time to talk about things other than this case." Dillon replied. He turned toward the blonde-haired woman and extended his hand.

"You are?" he queried.

"My name's Christina Dean, Agent Reece. Although you come highly recommended, I don't see why we have outside help. I'm sure we can adequately handle the investigation."

"I'm sure you can," replied Dillon, "but there are some unusual circumstances surrounding this case. People at a much higher pay grade than any of us felt it would be a good idea to get an outside perspective. I'm that outside perspective."

John began to gather some document folders on his desk and politely excused himself from the gathering.

"Just before you got here, I got a call from the old man's office and he wants these letters before he heads for the club. You folks make yourselves at home. I'll lock the doors so all you have to do is let them close behind you. I'll talk with you all later." John threw the folders into his briefcase and disappeared through the doorway.

Since it was late in the day, Christina and Penny excused themselves and returned to their offices. Bill and Dillon sat down in two armchairs located on one side of the office. On the table between them were the latest editions of *Airman* Magazine and various other magazines about aircraft maintenance, both commercial and military.

Bill settled in and began, "I'm sure John gave you a briefing on your ride from the airport."

"He did," replied Dillon, "but I'm interested in what you've uncovered that wasn't in the report."

"Not much to give ya." Bill said. "The local police have been very cooperative with the interview process. We have a liaison officer assigned to the Security Police Squadron. As usual, our security forces are assisting with the investigation. We'll go and meet the commander tomorrow. He's one hell of a nice guy. He's crusty but he knows his business and expects nothing but the best from his people. I know you'll like him."

Bill and Dillon sat in the office and talked for nearly an hour. When Dillon looked at his watch and saw the time, he suggested they adjourn and head for a local eatery for dinner. Bill agreed and pulled out his cell phone to confirm the arrangements with his wife.

"Did they get you the low profile?" Bill asked.

"Oh yea, it's low profile all right," Dillon laughed. "It's a Beemer. What's low profile about that?"

"I expected nothing less." Bill returned. He hesitated as his wife answered the call and he told her about the plans. She must have said a couple of things because Bill did a lot of head nodding and agreeing. When the conversation was completed, he closed the phone, grinned rather sheepishly and returned to the conversation.

"Most of the people who want to have a dependable car settle on one of the local products. The Beemer's are a favorite with stick actuators and mid level management."

"Stick actuators. I haven't heard that one for a long time." Dillon laughed. "I guess when you don't work around pilots you tend to lose some of the quaint terms of endearment we non-rateds have for the anointed ones."

"You're right there," said Bill. "Before I came here, I worked at a logistics center. Fraud, Waste, and Abuse was my mantra. It really took some work to remember what the real Air Force was like when I got here."

"The real Air Force. That's another good one. Everyone seems to think his or her little piece of the pie is the 'real' Air force. I'm still looking for the real force. Here's another euphemism for you to try, zippered suited sun gods. I picked that one up in Florida. Don't know where it started but they sure fit the description. Of course, I'm one to talk. I was supposed to join the elite corps until I made a career change."

"I wasn't going to mention that Dillon but we all know about your loss. It's hard to imagine life without Betsy. We met in college and joined the force together. She works in personnel. Typical Air Force placement. She has a degree in criminal justice and they put her in personnel. I have a degree in accounting and end up in OSI. Can you figure that one out?"

"Has she tried to cross into the cops or our business?"

"We thought about it but with both of us in OSI, we may not be able to arrange our assignments together. With such different careers, we can normally find a place to make an assignment work."

"I understand," Dillon replied. "Looks like you have it all figured out."

"Well so far we do. I just hope it continues to work the right way. I've heard horror stories about some married couples not being able to get anywhere near each other for consecutive assignments. Not something I want to face."

"Well, back to the case. What can you tell me about the circumstances surrounding the shooting?" Dillon asked.

"One thing for sure, who ever did it really wanted to make a statement. Shot at close range with a large caliber pistol. Silenced evidently because none of the neighbors report hearing anything." Bill said while shaking his head in disbelief.

"They may not want to get involved," Dillon responded. "After the police give us their final report, I'd like to go out and talk with some of them on a more informal personal side."

"Fine with me. Oh shit, look at the time. I told Betsy I'd be home to shower and change before we went out." He headed for the front door while Dillon began to shut off the lights. Bill came back into the room opening his briefcase.

"I almost forgot about having these scene photos," he said as he handed Dillon a large manila envelope.

"Have a look at these and bring them to the office tomorrow. I'll tell you how to get there while we're at dinner."

Dillon took the envelope and pulled out the top photo. It showed the body on its back with the blood soaked shirt clearly visible. The wound in the forehead was less evident. The autopsy photos showed much more detail about the exit wound at the back of the airman's head. No doubt, the shooter wasn't playing around. It seems they shot him in the stomach and then put one in his forehead for good measure. The briefcase was lying about a foot from his right hand. It was open and empty. Dillon gave the other photos a cursory look before he got ready to leave.

Dillon just settled himself into one of the lobby armchairs when Bill came charging through the door. "Just as I figured," he said, "Betsy was under a full had of steam when I got home. She likes to plan things and this was an unplanned event. Nevertheless, she'll get over it once she has her first glass of wine. Come on let's go."

Both men stepped out the door and walked toward the light green 7-series BMW. "Damn, Bill I'm impressed." Dillon exclaimed as he stopped in the entranceway.

"Belongs to the wing, so don't get any ideas that I'm on the take. That's the first thing most people say when they see this monster. When I was receiving my in brief, the commander said he had a surprise for me. I was more than surprised when he showed me my staff car. Evidently, BMW had these demonstrators in Munich and offered them to the alliance for use by people with a lot of contact down town. Our office fit the bill so I got what was left of the batch after all the other commanders took their pick. Don't know why one of them didn't take this baby. It drives like a dream and has every perk you can imagine."

As Dillon settled into the soft leather back seat, Betsy Wilmerson turned to him and reached out her hand. Dillon gently shook her hand and raised it slowly to his lips giving it the lightest of kisses. "Pleased to meet you Mrs. Wilmerson, I'm Dillon Reece."

"Oh I know who you are Dillon," she cooed. "Your reputation preceded your arrival."

The restaurant was only a short drive from the base gates. Parking was around back with an entrance covered with vines. Dillon held the door open as Betsy and Bill entered the portal. The heavy wooden door crushed the vines where people leaned against it to keep it open. The smells from inside the establishment were overwhelming. It was a mixture of wine, broiling meat, and pipe smoke.

"Oh man," gushed Bill. "Just smell that food. Makes my mouth water and my senses expand." Betsy gave him a playful push as he stopped dead in his tracks just inside the door.

"Get moving buster or we'll be dreaming about the food and not savoring its excellence."

Dillon was not far behind. He tiled his head back as he drew in breath after breath. "Oh this is really something." He exclaimed. "How many memories come flooding back when you smell something familiar?"

Dinner was exciting. Bill and Betsy knew the owner so the party received special treatment. First courses came with a light wine and then a heartier wine with the main course. Dessert arrived with an excellent Auslese. During dinner, both men avoided discussing the case. Betsy knew they were avoiding the subject on her behalf, so she broke the ice.

"Bill told me you're an expert in drug interdiction and investigation."

Dillon sat back in the booth and furled his brow at his dinner companions. "Just how much has Bill told you about me?" he asked.

"Well," she began, "he told me you were coming to help in the investigation and I did a little investigation myself. Don't forget where I work."

"That's right," said Dillon, "you're one of those pencil pushing bureaucrats that makes my life so difficult when I'm in the middle of an investigation."

"For shame," Betsy gasped feigning distain. "I pride myself in providing excellent customer service in all matters of investigation."

"Oh sure," said Dillon, "It really helps when you're sleeping with the investigator." Bill smiled as Betsy reached to caress the back of his neck.

"I'm sure happy," Bill, sighed.

"OK you two knock it off." Dillon scolded.

Betsy and Bill both laughed as the discussion turned to the pending search for a killer or killers. They set a course of action and made plans to visit the murder scene in the morning. Betsy was actually a great deal of help. Her criminal justice degree was not wasted. Dillon could tell they made an excellent team.

The hour grew late as they paid the bill and left the dinning room. Bill and Betsy dropped Dillon at his room and headed home. Dillon talked with the desk clerk a while before returning to his room. He wanted to review the pictures again before visiting the scene. He showered and crawled into bed. He turned again to the file on Airman Crimitin. The pictures of the murder scene were graphic and detailed. The autopsy report said the cause of death was internal hemorrhaging. Dillon thought that was a bit unusual. He figured the shot to the head was the cause of death. However, the report seemed to indicate the airman was dead before the shot to the head. Why would that be? He looked at the crime scene photos and noticed they didn't really show a large amount of blood. Did that mean he was shot some place else and taken back to his apartment? Did the killer put the shot through his head for effect? All were good questions but were they important or would they add up to nothing? The visit to the apartment may lead to getting some of the bits and pieces put into perspective.

⚜

The man nestled the phone close to his neck as he waited for the receiving party to pick up. The wind was beginning to blow gently against his face. How he hated outside telephones. However, it was the only way to ensure his call wouldn't be monitored. In his business, he knew the importance of keeping what he needed to say away from prying ears. If anyone was listening to his call from this booth, he could easily interfere with their monitoring by turning his head or covering his mouth to prevent lip readers from gaining an advantage. As he was about to drop the handset back into its cradle, a voice on the other end spoke.

"Yes?" was the only spoken word.

"Dinner, conversation, discussion of case, small talk, back to the base."

"Any worries?"

"None at this time." the caller replied.

"Keep me posted." the line went dead.

The man pulled up the collar of his jacket as he turned the corner and headed toward his car. The wind picked up momentum and a slight drizzle began to fall. He picked up his pace as he neared the parking lot entrance. He slipped into the doorway and made his way up the ramp. He didn't notice the van pull away from the curb and head away from the garage. He didn't notice the attendant as he picked up the phone and dialed. He paid no attention as a dark sedan slipped out of a slot 100 feet from his vehicle and in near silence, slowly drove down the ramp. He opened the door of his car and lowered himself into the leather seat. It was then he noticed the note on his window.

CHAPTER FOUR

Agent Dean crossed the lobby and entered the hallway leading to Dillon's room. She wasn't happy with her morning assignment. When she arrived for work, Bill told her she was going to take Dillon out to the murder scene. Despite her vehement arguments, Bill insisted on her getting to know Dillon so she could understand why he was working the case. She was sure no amount of "getting to know" him would lessen her contempt.

She found his room and pushed the brass ringer located in the middle of the door. When there was no immediate answer, she rapped on the door with the palm of her hand. Almost before she withdrew her hand, the door swung open revealing Dillon in his bathrobe with a toothbrush in one hand and a cup of coffee in the other.

"Whoops!" he exclaimed. "Sorry about not being ready, I should have given the office a call to delay your arrival but I really expected to see Bill."

"Sorry to disappoint you," Christina replied, "but Bill had other pressing matters to watch over and decided this morning to send me. I'll go wait in the lobby."

"No, No don't do that," Dillon said, "this place has plenty of room. Fix yourself a cup of coffee."

"I'll do just that," she answered as she stepped into the room and headed for the small kitchen area. Dillon ordered an assortment of rolls for his morning snack. Christina poured herself a cup of dark coffee from the Air Force billeting standard issue Mr. Coffee. They could have sprung for a better coffee maker in VIP quarters she thought to herself as she added sweetener and creamer to her cup.

Dillon came down the hall with his pants and socks on but without a t-shirt. She glanced at him and admired the shape of his chest and stomach.

It wasn't the finely chiseled stomach of a weight lifter but she could tell he carried toned abs under the light covering of fine blond hair.

"Excuse me," he said adding more coffee to his cup. "If I don't get at least two cups before I leave the house, I'm one grumpy bear."

"I understand." Christina replied as she watched him disappear down the hall. He was saying something she didn't catch and she asked him to repeat. She approached the hallway and listened for him to speak. She saw him cross the hall from bedroom to bathroom. He was saying he stayed up late studying the pictures and the initial reports from all concerned. He hadn't realized how late it was and he fell asleep without setting an alarm. He awoke less than a half hour before she arrived at the door.

"What do you think of this whole situation Christina?"

"What do you mean Agent Reece?" she replied.

He stuck his head out of the bathroom door and asked, "Agent Reece? Please, let's not stand on formalities. We're going to be working closely and I would like to think we could be on a first name basis. My name's Dillon."

She hesitated before replying, "And I'm Christina."

"Much better," he said as he once again disappeared into the bathroom and then crossed back to the bedroom

"I'm not really sure what to make of the situation." she began. "It's really a puzzle. From the initial reports, this guy was a straight arrow. No discipline problems and he volunteered to come here rather than stay in California where he could be close to his family."

Dillon came out of the bedroom with his shirt and tie in place and shoes in hand. He threw the sports coat he was carrying on a dining room chair as he pulled one out to sit on so he could put on his shoes.

"I agree," he said. "That's a bit on the odd side. He has an assignment in a place that allows regular visits home and he takes an assignment here. Doesn't make a lot of sense but I've seen stranger situations. It might be a place for us to look."

Christina went into the kitchen and emptied what was left of her coffee into the sink. She reached to turn off the coffee pot since it wasn't one of the fancy ones that automatically shuts off after an hour or two. She instinctively reached for a cloth and wiped small spills on the counter.

"Thanks," Dillon said as he entered the kitchen.

"Just a habit," she said. "I'm one of those neat freaks you read about in your Psych books."

"We all have our crosses to bear," he replied as he rinsed his cup and set it in the sink next to hers. He turned toward her and asked, "Ready?"

"I'm headed for the door," she quipped leading the way out of the kitchen.

Once outside, she led him toward a modest Opal with more than a few thousand miles on the odometer. Dillon slowed as he approached the car and Christina responded to his unverbalized question.

"I don't use the BMW for unimportant trips around town. This is the office heap. We have a couple of them used primarily for short trips. Bill uses his Beemer all the time. I just can't get used to the thoughts of having an office car that I can't afford to buy back home."

Dillon smiled and told her to get pleasure from it while she could. "This place is perk city compared to some of the places I've been. You work hard enough to earn it, so just enjoy."

They strapped in as Christina coaxed the car to life and headed for the gate. The apartment was a 15-minute drive. Dillon sat in silence and enjoyed the warm sun through the windows. He watched the scene change from village, to fields and then back to village. They turned into a side street and immediately began to climb a very steep hill.

Christina negotiated the narrow lane and turned the final corner leading to a steep street with homes on either side. Two houses from the end was the murder scene. Yellow crime tape was visible in one of the trees in a field at the top of the road. A dirt tractor road led from the end of the pavement over top of the hill. A crisp breeze was blowing. It was nothing overwhelming but enough air movement to bring the pungent smells of adjoining fields to his nostrils. He drew a deep breath and looked in the direction they just traveled. It was a steep drop allowing a view of the village below. He looked up and down the street and then turned to Christina.

"OK, explain the scene to me."

Christina headed toward the driveway and stood near the steps leaking to the home's entrance. "He was found lying right here," she said. "The case was found here," pointing to a spot near the rock wall surrounding the yard.

"According to the pictures of the scene, the case was open, correct?"

"That's right," she confirmed. "No sign of forced entry so it was either open or the killer knew the combination."

"Did the police report mention anything about the surrounding area? I don't remember seeing anything in my copies."

"Now that you mention it, I don't recall. Let me check, I've got a copy in the car."

As she returned to the car, Dillon headed past the last house on the street and climbed the tractor road. It was a steep climb covered mostly with small rocks. The tire ruts pointed to use only by farm tractors and not cars. A 4-wheel drive would have no problem traversing the lane but a normal car would face a struggle especially if the road was muddy.

As he reached the top, he saw where the lane joined a dirt track running perpendicular to his path. As he approached the junction, he turned toward a sound to his left. At the edge of the field, he saw a small tractor pull out of a paddock and turn toward him. It was one of those small two stroke types making more noise than providing pulling power. The man at the controls tipped his hat as he passed Dillon and continued down the road to disappear around a corner.

Dillon walked toward the paddock area so he could familiarize himself with the lay of the land. Nothing seemed out of the ordinary but he did want to explore the area another time. He returned to where Christina was looking through the police reports. She was back in the car shielding the documents from the breeze. Dillon opened the passenger door and sat down.

"Anything?" he asked.

"Not much. The report does say the man living across the street heard Crimitin's car pull up and the car door slam."

"Did he mention any other cars?"

"No, that's why I mentioned it. The neighbor was awake at the time. It's not like the car door or the engine noise woke him. His room is at the front of the house but like many German homes, it's like a basement room. The front windows are below ground level with an area dug into the ground to allow light in. It doesn't have a view, just light. His doors are at the back of the house where the ground slops away from the house and everything is on the same level. With the hilly countryside, it's normal to have homes like that. The house that Crimitin lived in was just the opposite. The back rooms are dug into the side of the hill."

"I see what you mean," Dillon confirmed as he looked at the house. "I've seen all that I want to see for the time being. I don't want to bother any of the residents right now. We'll make appointments and visit them another time. Let's head back to the office."

With that, Christina put the reports back in their folders and placed them on the back seat. Dillon closed his door and strapped in. He sat in silence once again as he mentally filed the information just gathered.

As they drove toward the base, Dillon asked Christina about her relationship with the Security Police commander. She said he was a crusty old head but sure knew his business. He was a Master Sergeant cop when he applied for a commission. Selected on his first try, the Air Force showed a burst of brilliance not normally seen from commissioning boards as he was placed back into the Security Police field after his 90-day officer training stint.

He moved rapidly through the officer ranks with selection to major and lieutenant colonel earlier than normal. He recently took command of Ramstein's security force after an inspection team discovered serious deficiencies in several key management areas. The last commander was asked to retire and newly promoted Lieutenant Colonel Karlton K. Krimshank moved from a security support slot at Combat Command headquarters in Virginia, to the hot seat at Ramstein.

Overall, she would categorize their working relationship as very positive. Since he was relatively new to his command position, she didn't have much opportunity to work with him on investigations involving his people however, the support provided by his investigators in all other matters had been very good.

When Christina asked why he wanted to know, Dillon said Bill suggested they visit him sometime today. Since they were out, he thought it would be OK to drop by now rather than get back to the office and try to set something up later. Christina reached for her cell phone, dialed the SP number, and talked to the administrator, Staff Sergeant Jerome P. Johnston. The conversation was short and to the point. The commander was in the office, he didn't have anything scheduled for at least an hour and after checking with him, he would be more than happy to receive the pair of agents at his office. Christina thanked the sergeant and hung up.

Dillon thanked her as they drove on through the countryside. Once inside the base, Christina took a road running parallel to the flight line area. A few minutes down the road, she turned into a parking lot and stopped the car in a slot designated for "Visitors." They went into the building and toward the command offices. As they went, Christina explained the location of dispatch, the investigator's offices, the administrative section, and finally the commander's office. Sergeant Johnston greeted them and made their presence known to the colonel. He immediately asked them into his humble office.

As the commander stepped from behind his desk, Dillon couldn't help but notice the abundance of meritorious decorations adorning the walls of his office. The ones he took notice of were the Bronze Stars and Purple Hearts. Knowing what he did about military awards, the Bronze Stars were awarded for heroic action during operations against an opposing armed force. The Purple Hearts were given for wounds received in combat operations. Dillon was very impressed by the apparent accomplishments of this commander. He may be vertically challenged but no one could doubt his courage in action.

The colonel asked them to take seats located on one side of his desk. He pushed his chair back and turned toward the agents. After polite greetings, the colonel asked what their purpose was. Dillon began.

"During my in briefings with Bill Wilmerson, he suggested I meet with you so when our paths cross during this investigation, we'll have already laid the groundwork for a successful working relationship."

The colonel said he couldn't agree more and was happy they made a stop. They went on to talk about a wide range of things outside the Crimitin case but in some way related. Dillon was interested in current cases involving drugs, suppliers, and possible organizations making a constant flow available.

The colonel pulled some files from a small safe behind his desk and let both agents scan their contents. Each one involved an on going cooperative investigation with the local authorities. After their review, Dillon thanked the colonel and asked for the name of his drug team leader. The colonel apologized for not being able to give him a name. He explained that one of the reasons his predecessor was asked to leave were problems discovered inside the investigative office and specifically with the drug team.

Dillon assured him there was no need for an apology but if he did get a lead man designated, they would like to use him as their main point of contact. The colonel agreed and promised to have a name to their offices as soon as possible.

They continued their conversations covering all types of cases. Dillon glanced at his watch and saw they had been with the colonel for nearly an hour. Both agents rose from their seats and thanked the commander of his time. The colonel thanked them for stopping by and walked with them to the parking lot. He said goodbye and told them he looked forward to working with them.

Back at the office, things were in their normal routine. Bill laid out the conference room with photos, diagrams, files, and boxes to put it all back in once they finished reviewing, perusing, sampling, and reading. Dillon always liked to skip this part of an investigation. He wasn't much for the paperwork if he could avoid it. He liked to operate using all his senses and be where the action was, where it took place or where he figured it might take place.

Dillon stopped by the coffee bar before he walked into the conference room. Christina took a seat at the head of the table away from Bill. With one of the files in hand, she was shaking her head as she read the contents. Bill was looking through a stack of photos placing them into neat little piles on the highly polished conference table.

The table sat on a tile floor that facilitated easy rolling in or out when occupied by a meeting attendee. Around the rest of the room were lesser chairs pushed against the railing used to protect the off-white paint. When Bill arrived at Ramstein, he requisitioned a computer based briefing system. It wasn't state of the art but he used his knowledge of excess equipment procurement to get one that was being sent o the scrap heap by the commanding general. The CPU sat under a small lectern. The keyboard rested on a pull out shelf. The mouse hung in a holster along one side of the lectern. With Ramstein taking on an increased responsibility for airlift and fighter support, the transient population kept his office and the security police hopping at all hours of the day and night. This murder was just another log on the fires. Although his staff may not appreciate Dillon's presence, Bill was ever so happy to see him.

"Back from the scene already?" Bill asked.

"Yeah, there wasn't much to see at the present time," Dillon replied. "We did manage to stop and pay a visit to the security commander. He was very gracious. I don't foresee any problems working with him. He mentioned some problem with his investigation teams so he doesn't have a lead right now. He promised to get one as soon as possible."

"I'm glad you made the stop. I completely forgot about it," Bill said as he picked out another folder and wrote a title across the tab used for identification.

Dillon took a seat and asked Bill, "Do you have papers on the interview with the neighbor? Christina mentioned a few facts from the notes she took but I would like to see the entire interview."

Bill got up from the table and went to a box filled with manila folders. He rummaged around for a brief moment and then pulled one of them from its resting place.

"The name of the interviewee is Horst Hildermann. He works on the base, has a good command of spoken English and from what the police say he's well respected by coworkers and neighbors. He owns the house he lives in but rents out the top floors to Americans. At the moment, the place is vacant."

Bill returns to his seat and hands the file to Dillon. He quickly thumbs through the report and then returns to the first page. He sets the folder and report down on the table and begins to read the entire report. Once finished, he pushes back from the table, leans the chair as far back as it will go and stretches his arms out behind him. He snaps the chair back into an upright position and looks at Bill.

"Doesn't say much does it?"

"No," Bill replies. "I was wondering why you wanted to see that particular report."

"I don't know," Dillon responded. "I can't seem to shake this feeling there was another car there but he doesn't mention hearing one before or after he heard Crimitin come home."

"We know someone was there because we have a dead body." Penny pitched in from the doorway. As she was passing by, she stopped to see how things were going. She listened to the conversation and then put in her two cents.

"No shit Penny," Christina said looking up from the file in front of her. "What was your first clue Sherlock?"

They spent the rest of the afternoon pouring over files, reports, and pictures. All the while Bill was making written notes, Christina was tapping the keys of the conference room computer, and Dillon was making mental notes. Other office staff came and went as they took care of routine business on that day. Bill went out to answer a few telephone calls and order lunch for the sequestered investigators but that was about the extent of his absence.

Bill asked Dillon about his plans for the evening. Dillon said he didn't have any and was really looking forward to getting back to his room for a shower and some TV. The jet lag was beginning to catch up with him and he knew the only thing that would help was a good night's sleep. Bill agreed and said he would see him in the morning.

Christina bid both of them goodnight and headed out the door. They were the only ones left in the office. All the other clerks and agents left during a brainstorming session. Dillon collected his battered case and joined Christina and Penny as they walked across the parking lot to their cars.

"I forgot," he said, "one of you has to take me back to the room." Christina laughed as she too remembered she picked him up that morning.

"I'll drop you," volunteered Penny. "Christina monopolized your time this morning, so it's only fair I get some time with you this afternoon."

Dillon smiled as both women stared at each other.

"OK ladies," he said, "tell you what, why don't you let me buy you both a drink at the club, and then I'll walk home form there."

"OK by me," said Christina.

Penny agreed and they walked to their cars and headed for the club. The place was your typical fighter bar. The three of them drew a few glances as they entered. Both Penny and Christina acknowledged the waves and hellos from more than a few of the zipper suited wonder boys gathered at the bar and the free food table. A smattering of wives graced the arena.

They talked about everything except the case. It was a time to relax and break down barriers on either side. Dillon was an expert and before he headed across the parade ground and back to his room, he won their trust.

CHAPTER FIVE

The next morning Dillon made a brief stop at the office after his ritual breakfast. He told Bill he was going to look again at the crime scene. Bill offered the services of Penny or Christina but Dillon wanted to wander around without having to keep someone else occupied.

Dillon made a quick stop by the exchange complex to get another cup of coffee for his drive into Kottweiller. As Dillon left the base, he pulled the lid from his cup and drew in the aroma of the freshly brewed beverage. He knew it was fresh because he watched the dependent wife of some low ranking airman struggling to make ends meet, put the coffee into the filter and turn on the power. She said it would only take three minutes and sure enough, he was on his way out the door in less than five.

The stereo speakers reverberated with the latest top ten tunes from the local American Forces Radio station. He was just about to cut it off when the song ended and the canned announcement for an upcoming news program pushed its way through the speakers. Dillon decided to catch the latest news having been somewhat isolated during the past couple of days. He adjusted the volume and took a sip of his coffee.

By the time the news ended, he was nearing the outskirts of Kottweiller. He found the turn for the hill but hesitated before turning. Instead, he drove past the street to a place where he could turn around and head back toward the base. He was looking for another road cutting to the left. He found what he was looking for and turned into the narrow street lined with multi-story homes.

The lane was only wide enough for one car until he turned a sharp corner. The street opened to a normal width with beautiful homes on either side. He drove to the end and found an unpaved portion that continued beyond the houses. He dropped the gear lever into low and continued up the gravel roadway. It wandered into a field and past a small enclosure with a cow and two sheep watching his progress. He continued his trek as the road took a sweeping turn to the left. Moments later, he recognized the area. He stopped the car and got out at the intersection. He walked down the road on his left and found himself looking at the murder scene. He returned to his car and stood looking around the fields. He now knew where the tractor disappeared to yesterday. He waked back and forth across the road looking for some type of evidence of a car parked along side the road. All he could find were tractor tracks and evidence that cattle had been that way earlier in the morning.

He reached inside the car for his coffee. It was still hot as he sipped the liquid while walking away from the car. He was a bit disappointed there was no evidence but knew it wasn't a critical point. He returned to the car and continued his drive.

The road seemed to be an avenue for local residents to gain access to various fields. Some were fenced and others were open. He came to a fork in the road. Taking the road to the right, he continued along the path until it began to narrow. Not wanting to get stuck, he stopped, put the car into reverse, and backed to a wider section where he could turn around.

Once again, at the fork, he took the lane to the right. It wandered through a wooded area and then expanded into a wide-open spot of plowed fields, power lines, and hedgerows. He surveyed the scene for a few minutes. It was a beautiful sight so he took time to finish his coffee before turning around and returning to the murder scene.

Not wanting to risk damage to the car, he stopped at the top of the hill and walked down to the house. He stood near where the body was found and made a slow three hundred and sixty degree turn. He just wasn't picking up anything strange or different. As he stood there, Horst came walking up his driveway. He waved to Dillon, checked the front of his house, and walked back down the drive. Dillon returned the wave and started back up the hill.

When he reached the car, he kicked the accumulated mud from his shoes before getting into the drivers seat. As he was leaving the area, he noticed a farmer inside the pen holding the cow and sheep. The man looked up and waved as Dillon drove past. Dillon returned the wave and stopped the car. He rolled down the window and greeted the man.

"Guten Tag, Vegates?"

The man returned the greeting and walked to the fence. Dillon stepped out and walked to the man offering his hand. The farmer shook his hand with a firm grip.

Dillon asked, "Do you speak English?"

The farmer proudly replied in broken English that he did. Dillon was relieved because his German was out of practice. He explained to the man about the death in the adjacent street and asked if he knew anything about it. The farmer said he didn't. He doesn't watch much television and only reads the newspapers when he visits the Gasthaus. Dillon gave him his card and jotted the local OSI office number on the back. He asked the man to give him a call if he or any other residents of the street remember anything out of the ordinary on the night of the murder. The farmer said he would check with his neighbors and get back to him if he came up with anything.

Dillon returned to the car and drove out of the neighborhood and back to the office.

"Hey Dillon," Bill exclaims as he sees Reece enter the office. "Just in time for our jaunt to the club for lunch. Join us?"

"Sure will," Dillon replies. "Let me give John a call to see if he's free to join us." Dillon connects with John and gets a commitment to join them for lunch.

"It'll be a little while," John tells Dillon. "I'm in the middle of reviewing the stats for this afternoon's standup.

"I understand your dilemma John. We'll be at the club in about half an hour. Look forward to seeing you."

"Sure thing Dillon. We haven't had a chance to talk since I drove you in from the airport. See you at the club."

They hung up and Dillon turned to Bill. "I drove all over the area today looking for some sort of track indicating another car was in the vicinity. Nothing was there. I did meet a farmer who lives in the adjacent street. The entrance to the road is probably 1000 yards away from the top of the hill. I didn't notice any tire tracks but that doesn't mean there wasn't a car parked in the road and all of the tractor traffic obliterated the car marks. Asked the man to check with his neighbors and see if they noticed anything. I gave him my card with your number written on the back. He said he would call if he found anything of significance."

⚔

"What do you recommend?" Dillon asked his lunch mates in a general question. Christina said the German food was only so so. It was best to enjoy the local cuisine downtown rather than at the club. Penny was partial to the grilled fishplate and Bill was the meat and potatoes type. So basically, Dillon was left to how own devises on a lunch decision. They continued to look over the menu while the waiter brought out water, sodas, and coffee. By the time Dillon finished looking at the lineup; John was making his way across the room to their table. He took his seat and began to reach for the menu.

"Oh why bother," he said, "I always have the same thing when I come here."

They began small talk as they watched for their waiter to return. After ordering, the conversation turned to the case.

"None of that now," Dillon said. "We came here for lunch and until we finish coffee and dessert, no talk about the case." When coffee was in place and Dillon sent the waiter away with payment and an appropriate gratuity, he turned the table talk back to Airman Crimitin.

He told them about his return visit to the crime scene and his conversation with the farmer. He also explained his firm belief in a second vehicle on top of the hill. He wanted to concentrate some effort in establishing the fact that a second car was there to transport the killer or killers away from the scene.

"The only thing that stands out in hindsight," John began, "was his volunteer status on getting flights to and from Saudi Arabia. Not many of our male crew chiefs want to spend much time there. They're restricted to the base and Eskan village. It's not a place conducive to a young man's expansion of his love life. If there are any ladies there, they're on a rotational basis and their dance cards are usually filled by the time they get off the plane at Al Kharj. When we look at it now, maybe it should have been a flag but what kind of flag. We needed chiefs to make the trips and anyone who volunteered was guaranteed a spot on the manifest."

"Did anyone ever talk to him about why he wanted to spend so much time in Saudi?" Christina asked.

"I'm not sure," replied John. "But I can check into the situation and see if his supervisor ever took the time to have that type of conversation with him."

"That's a good point Christina," Dillon kicked in. "With the traces of coke in his briefcase, we can only make assumptions at this time. He would need some sort of cover story if he were dealing in Saudi. I dread finding out that was his game. That's really a dangerous activity. They chop your head off if they catch you dealing. However, that isn't the issue right now, the issue is we have a dead airman and it doesn't matter how he died, he's dead, and our job is to find out why and by whom."

They continued to trade information for nearly an hour. John looked at his watch and jumped from the table abruptly excusing himself. He needed to finish some paperwork before the commander's standup. He thanked Dillon for lunch and bid farewell to his other luncheon companions. He promised to have the cover story investigated and left the table. Bill, Dillon, Christina, and Penny finished their coffee and headed back for the office.

⚜

"Will," John shouted from behind his desk, "come in here!"

"Right sir," was the reply from the room adjacent to the command office. Senior Master Sergeant Wilber K. Fogerton came striding through the door with pencil and pad in hand. When called into the office, he knew there was going to be some sort of activity for his direct attention, so he wanted to have his note pad ready.

"Whatcha need sir?" he asked.

John put down the folder he was reading and pushed his reading glasses to the end of his nose so he could see his first sergeant over the top of his half frames.

"I need some additional work on the Crimitin situation. I had lunch earlier today with the investigative team. They're interested in why Crimitin was our leading volunteer for Saudi. They're working with some leads but want to know if there was a legitimate reason for this young man to spend so much time in Saudi. Aside from the gold and rugs, I can't see one fucken reason for anyone to spend any amount of time in the desert."

"You're right there sir. With all the restrictions put on us after the bombings, it's a shithole for a TDY⁶. Let me put out some feelers with some of the younger guys and I'll also have a direct conversation with his supervisor."

"Thanks shirt, I'll look forward to hearing what you find. I'll give Agent Reece a call and tell him we're checking into some other avenues for him. That way he doesn't have to worry about grilling anyone over here until we have some credible sources."

John reached for the phone to give Dillon a call. "OSI, Agent Wilmerson."

"Bill, this is John. Tell Dillon I have my first shirt looking into the TDY situation. Should have something for him in a couple of days. I didn't fill the shirt in on all the details but I'm sure he has his ear on the rumor mill."

"Thanks John. Dillon isn't back in the office yet. I'll pass the info along to him when he returns. Take care."

As Bill was setting the phone back into its cradle, Christina came into his office. She carried one of the case files and dropped it on the desk.

"Yes?" Bill asked with a sarcastic tone.

31

"I was looking through the file concerning forensic evidence at the scene. Nothing indicates they ever found the bullets or any casings. Was Crimitin shot outside his apartment, or was he shot elsewhere and brought back to what the killers wanted everyone to think was the crime scene? What happened to Crimitin's car? Was it thoroughly searched? I can't find any significant information about the scene or the car," Christina stated as she flipped open the folder and showed the contents to Bill.

CHAPTER SIX

Dillon set the parking brake as he readied himself to step from the car. Inside the fence surrounding the Security Police impound lot, he could see the remains of several cars involved in local accidents and sitting right outside the little shack erected as an office, was the 1989 Opel belonging to the late Airman Crimitin. Dillon got out and headed for the shack. A civilian employee of the security squadron came through the doorway.

"Afternoon," the man said as Dillon approached.

"Afternoon to you," Dillon replied as he shook hands with the man.

"I'm certainly glad you speak English. My German is way out of practice and I may not be here long enough to bring it back on line."

"I understand," the man said. "I've been working with the Americans for nearly 40 years and I found out early on that my ability to speak English would always be a plus in dealing with other security personnel. However, I do stress the importance of learning at least a few common phrases. The local population always appreciates it if you can order food or ask for prices in the native language." He added emphasis to the word native as he returned the strong handshake offered by Dillon.

"Has the car been here since the incident?" Dillon asked nodding toward the Opel.

"Yes," was the reply. "It was brought here about two in the afternoon. The truck left it and Betsy moved it to that second row over there."

"Betsy?" Dillon questioned.

"Ya, Betsy!" The man replied as he tilted his head toward a huge forklift sitting near the shack. "That's how we move all the vehicles. Some are drivable, some aren't. In this case, we didn't want to disturb anything on the inside, in case someone, like you, wanted to take another look at the vehicle."

"You were right to think someone would return," Dillon laughed. "I'll probably be here more than once to look at the car. I've a couple of questions with no answers. I hope to find some in the car."

"Well have a good time," the man said, "I'm going back into the shack and finish my coffee and newspaper. The keys are inside. Just give me a call if you need anything."

Dillon approached the car and walked all the way around it before opening the driver's door. The inside was relatively clean for a car so old. He remembered his first car. You couldn't see the floor for all the fast food wrappers, cups, and cans. Evidently, Airman Crimitin was a much neater person.

Dillon sat inside the car and took in every inch of the interior. He sat in the back seat and again gave the inside a careful look. After several minutes, he got out, shut all the doors, and went around back. He lifted the trunk and looked inside. Nothing seemed to be out of place. The spare tire was intact and the mandatory emergency items were stowed inside the wheel well. There were no stains on the matting and no discernable odors. He closed the trunk and headed for the shack to thank the guard. After exchanging pleasantries, Dillon walked back to his car and started toward the office.

When he came into the building, Christina literally attacked him as he came through the door. She was so eager to tell him about her findings, he didn't want to disappoint her by telling her he was going to promote the same type of misgivings about the investigation. She talked about bullet casings and how she felt the crime scene investigation was botched. The only relief he got was when Bill came into the office and asked if he had been successful at the impound lot. Christina stopped mid sentence and looked at Dillon. Dillon looked at Bill and grimaced because he knew what was coming.

"Impound lot?" Christina shouted. "Is that where you've been?"

Caught, Dillon thought. "Yes the impound lot Christina, I've just come back from there and what I have doesn't add anything to the investigation. The car is clean. No stains or odors that I can find. I checked the front seats and even sat in the back seat to see if I could discern anything from that perspective. Nothing. I looked inside the trunk and didn't see any stains or," he stopped.

Bill looked at him and waited a moment before asking, "Dillon, what's wrong?"

Dillon turned to Bill and related how he got out of the back seat and opened the trunk. "I just lifted up the trunk lid. I didn't use a key. It was open. Now it may be nothing, or it may have some significance. We need to

34

make another trip out there and check the latches on the trunk. Christina, give security a call and ask them to have the guard meet us out there again. We'll leave here in about 20 minutes. I want you to show me what caught your eye on the crime scene investigation."

Christina came back into the room after talking with security dispatch. She opened the folder and went over detail by detail how things just didn't match up with the violence of the crime. The first shot would have been the one to the intestines. That would have knocked him down and the final shot to the head would have followed. The bleeding from the belly would have killed him. The shot to the forehead could have been a warning to others involved with the Airman.

The type of weapon used expels casings after each shot. No casings were mentioned in the report. There was no mention of digging out bullet fragments from under the body. The reason they knew the type of weapon was the bullet from the shot to the gut was found near Crimitin's heart. It traveled in an upward direction hitting the breastbone and deflecting to near the heart. On its way in, it destroyed organs and tissue causing massive bleeding. The internal hemorrhaging killed the Airman.

Dillon and Christina headed for the car. Christina was in a much better mood since she had the opportunity to explain her findings.

"So how is Penny doing on the review of potential witnesses?" Dillon queried as they left the parking lot. Cleared of her current caseload, Penny worked the witness list.

"Not very good at the present time," Christina responded. "She got called to help one of the other investigators in a child abuse case turned over to us by the hospital. She has a background in family counseling and has a standing order for a call on all abuse cases. Evidently, a relative of hers beat one of her cousins to death. Consequently, she takes that type of incident very seriously. She should be back with us next week." They drove on in silence until they came around the corner and approached the gate.

"Was it Mr. Frankenheim who helped you before?" Christina asked.

"I don't recall getting his name," Dillon replied. "He came out of the office, we shook hands, and I went about my business. I don't think he told me his name." The gate was open and Dillon drove inside the lot stopping just behind the Opel still sitting in front of the shack. Out of the shack came the same old man. Christina waved as she got out of the car and walked toward the guard.

"Hello Conrad," Christina greeted as she gave him a hug and kiss on the cheek.

"Christina," the man responded, "how good it is to see you once again. How have you been? Keeping out of trouble I hope."

"Conrad," Christina exclaimed as she gave him a gentle push. "You know me better than that; I'm always on the edge of disaster."

Conrad laughed as he reached out for Dillon's hand. "Good to see you again so soon. Did you forget something?"

Dillon returned the greeting and explained about the trunk. "You know, I never gave it a second thought," Conrad said. "The trunk was open when it was brought into the lot."

Dillon walked to the car and opened the trunk. Again, he didn't have to use a key. He just lifted the trunk lid. He examined the hooking mechanism on the lid and didn't see anything unusual. When he looked at the catching latch on the body, he noticed a bit of black plastic holding the metal hook away from its over center position.

"Christina, get me an evidence bag out of the box in the back seat of the car please." Christina retrieved the requested bag and brought a pair of gloves for Dillon to use as he pulled the thick plastic out of its wedged position. He dropped the small bit of evidence into the bag and pulled a pen from his pocket. He marked down the time and date of collection and passed it to Christina. She took it back to the car and put it into an envelope.

Dillon continued his examination of the trunk for any other piece of overlooked evidence. Conrad watched from a respectful distance. Dillon sensed he was keeping tabs of everything said and done. He would have to ask Christina what their connection was.

After a few minutes, Dillon finished combing every inch of the small trunk compartment. He turned to Christina and asked if she wanted to give it another look. She agreed taking the flashlight from Dillon to start another look with a fresh set of eyes.

Conrad took a moment to go back inside the shack and come out with cups of coffee for Dillon and Christina. Dillon took his and slowly sipped the hot beverage.

After a couple of minutes, Christina turned to Dillon and said she didn't see anything else out of the ordinary. It was almost too clean for such an old car. Dillon told her he had the same feeling. That's why the trunk not latching didn't seem to be in character with a car so obviously pampered.

With the search completed, Dillon finished his coffee and thanked Conrad for his help. Christina was coming out the shack with a cup of coffee. She stopped to give Conrad a kiss on the cheek. Conrad waved as they backed out of the lot and into the parking area.

"So what's the deal with Conrad?" Dillon queried.

"I met him when I first got here. He was providing security for a crime scene and we just hit it off. Like having a grandfather around to talk with.

He's been working in the security squadron for ages. He started with some other job on base but moved to this security position about 15 years ago."

"Does he have ties to the local police, or is he dedicated to the American style of investigation?"

"I'm not too sure. Let me do some checking on that. Why do you ask?"

"I just noticed him taking an interest in our search. When I found the plastic, he came closer to see what I found. I don't want to face any problems with the locals since they missed the fragment inside the lock."

"I know what you mean." Christina agreed. "I'll let you know if we can expect any problems."

They continued with small talk as they drove back to the office. It was getting near quitting time and Christina said she had a couple of things to wrap up before she headed home. Dillon asked what the custody trail would be for the new evidence and Christina explained how she maintained the local log and where the item would be sent for evaluation. Dillon thanked her as they walked along the sidewalk and into the building. Christina went down the hall to the evidence safe and logged in the envelope. She then returned to her office and added the item to her list. Dillon went into Bill's office and explained what they found.

CHAPTER SEVEN

The investigation pace was slow the following days. Bill concentrated on getting the documents into some semblance of chronology. Penny, after her child abuse case, worked at arranging interviews with individuals who either knew Crimitin or worked around him. Christina and Dillon dedicated their time to establishing an initial pattern of logic to the crime.

With the trace of cocaine inside the briefcase, motive didn't seem to be a problem. It was either a robbery or the airman conflicted with his suppliers. In the drug trade, there is definitely no honor amongst thieves. All his flight records showed his main destination was Saudi Arabia. He logged very little flying time to any other destinations. If he did go elsewhere, it was a last minute call.

He was the chief on all normally scheduled supply flights to Prince Sultan Air Base. Affectionately known as "Al's Garage" for the name of the town adjacent to the air base, Al Kharj. His abilities as a crew chief were improving according to his training records. He progressed through his apprentice training with few problems. He completed upgrade training in a standard time frame. He didn't burn up the process but he didn't lag behind either.

Outward appearances indicated he wasn't using the coke he transported. The question kept coming up. Why was this seemingly sharp troop found dead outside his home with a briefcase that contained traces of cocaine? It just didn't make sense.

Dillon checked records for contents of the briefcase other than the coke. There was nothing special about any of the items. Pens, pencils, a calculator, blank aircrew forms, a couple of letters from home, a pad of paper with the beginning of a return letter, a sports magazine, gum, a ruler, an address book and a small tape recorder. Dillon stared at the list as if trying to wish some magic solution from the items. He held his head in his hands and ran his fingers through his close-cropped hair.

"Christina," he shouted down the hall after walking to the doorway of the conference room and looking toward her office. "Where are the items taken from Crimitin's briefcase?"

After a moment, Christina came into the hallway and motioned Dillon to follow her to a room at the end of the hall.

"We have this office converted into an evidence room," she said as she turned toward the end of the hall. As she walked, she continued to talk.

"Bill didn't want to bother security police with keeping track of all the stuff we gather during an investigation, so he had this office converted into an evidence locker." Dillon was close behind as Christina pulled a key out of her pocket and opened the metal door. Inside was a small area between the door and a wire mesh cage. Inside the cage were gray metal shelves separated only by enough room for a person to slide down each row sideways. If you were lucky, you might have enough room to turn around and look at the shelf behind you.

As they entered the small area outside the cage, Christina grabbed a book located on a small shelf attached to the cage. She opened it and went to the page marked with the letter C. She flipped a couple of pages and ran her finger down the list until she came to the entry for Crimitin. Beside the name was the alphanumerical "F63." She took the other key on the ring and opened the door baring entrance to the cage. Once inside she went to the end of a row with a large letter F painted on a small piece of tin. She entered the space between F and G moving along the shelves until she came to the sixth unit and counted down from the top three shelves. Since it was slightly above her head, Dillon came down the row and on tiptoes looked on the shelf.

"Exactly what are we looking for?" he asked.

"Should be a brown envelope large enough to hold all the stuff from the briefcase. I entered them as one unit when I put them into the room. It should have the number 17 on the outside."

Dillon reached in to drag the envelope from its resting spot. Prominently displayed was a large 17 with a smaller F63 penciled underneath. Also listed were the items inside the envelope. Dillon glanced at the list and confirmed it was the right one as he slid out of the confined space.

"Ever have anything go missing out of the room?" he asked.

"Nothing since I've been here but I was told they did have someone make a bid to get some evidence out of the room to protect a friend. One of the Security Police force got into some trouble and we had the evidence. One of his security pals hatched a lame scheme to come in through the drop ceiling and take the stuff out. He found the airman who installed the security system and paid him a substantial amount of money for the schematics. He knew exactly where alarms were rigged so he figured he could come in from the other side of the firewall, drop down into the room, lift the evidence against his friend, and get away free as a bird. The one thing he didn't plan on was the alarm guy came immediately to our office with the money and the plan. It cost security some long nights but when he came in, they were waiting for him when he tried to get away."

"So none of the alarms went off?" Dillon asked.

"This guy was really good. He didn't disturb any of the sensors. He knew where the stuff was and that he could access it from one corner of the room. He knew we only had motion sensors near the door and windows. I was told he really got a surprise when he came out of the crawlspace next door. The security forces were not pleased to have one of their own attempting such a stunt. He's now serving time with his friend at a military facility in majestic Kansas."

Dillon took the envelope, signed the logbook, and returned to the conference room. The envelope was not sealed. A large black alligator clip secured it. He removed the clip and carefully poured the contents on the tabletop. The pens were standard Air Force issue. The pencils were number twos for ease of reading. The blank aircrew forms were standard 781 issue used for logging maintenance activity on aircraft. Dillon knew any crew chief traveling with a cargo aircraft always kept a few extra forms on hand in case the aircraft binder didn't have enough. The calculator was nothing fancy. It didn't do much more than add, subtract, multiply and divide. The sports magazine was one with a lot of information about soccer teams. The ruler was from one of the local department stores. A place called Karstadt. The gum was sugarless. Dillon returned all the items to the envelope but kept the letters from home, the pad of paper, the address book, and the tape recorder on the table.

He opened one of the letters and began reading. He didn't like this part of an investigation. Even though the individual was dead, he always felt like an intruder into a private location. This particular letter was from his mother. It was written nearly a month before. It was just a letter with information about the immediate family and some of his relatives who had gathered for a picnic at some place called Puddingstone. He made a couple of notes on his pad, refolded the letter, and returned it to its envelope.

The other letter was from his brother. It was a bit more interesting. His brother was telling him how well he was doing in school after his rehab. Rehab.... Now we may have something he thought as he continued to read the letter. There wasn't much else revealing in the letter. He wrote a note to have the brother investigated by a team in California. The beginning of the return letter showed it was intended for his brother. It was just a normal update on his activities. He started the letter during the flight back from Saudi. He didn't get a chance to finish it.

Dillon now turned his attention to the address book. Inside were perhaps 30 names and addresses. The ones in California he surmised were relatives. Most of them were complete with names, addresses, and phone numbers. There were addresses only for a few of them while an even smaller number only had phone numbers. Dillon slowly turned the pages and made notes if he saw anything unusual. The notations with only a first name and no address caught his attention. There were six of them. He made notes about all of them and put the address book back in the envelope.

The tape recorder was one of those very small personal note pads. It had a large speaker/microphone enabling the owner to talk into the recorder using only one hand. The record and playback buttons were located near the top of the miniature machine. Dillon pressed the playback button but heard nothing. He figured Crimitin used the machine for notes on the mission to ensure things were taken care of at home station. He left the table and went down the hall to Christina's office.

"Mam, did we have any small cassette tapes from Crimitin's apartment?" he asked sticking his head inside her door.

Christina looked up from the computer keyboard. "I'm not sure Dillon; let me check the list here. I'm trying to develop a database for the evidence room. I've got the entry list right here," she said as she picked up an accordion folder and looked inside.

"Let me see," she began as she read the stickers on the inside compartments. "Work locker, gym locker, automobile, tool box, crew bags, apartment-kitchen, apartment-living room, apartment-dining room, apartment-bathroom",

"Hold on," Dillon interrupted, "just give me all the apartment lists."

Christina reached into the folder and pulled out the files with apartment-anything written on the tab. There were eight files in the clutch. He thanked Christina and returned to the conference room where he spread the folders on the table. He was looking for cassette tapes. He went through each list but found nothing. He looked at the lists again hoping for find anything similar to his quested item. He found nothing. Crimitin's music collection seemed to be entirely on CD. Not one cassette tape of any shape or form was found in any of the rooms. If he was using the tapes for aircrew messages, why didn't they find least one or two of them in the house?

He returned to Christina's office and asked her to check the work locker listing to see if any micro cassettes were found. She quickly pulled the list and told Dillon there were no cassettes found in the locker. She began to ask what significance there was to the cassettes but Dillon turned abruptly and returned to the conference room.

Christina got up from her desk with a huge stretch and moan as she started out the door toward the conference room. Once inside, she took a place opposite Dillon. She said nothing because Dillon was making notes. Without looking up, Dillon asked, "Questions Christina?"

"Yes but I'll wait until you're finished writing." she replied.

Dillon continued to jot notes. When he finished, he put the pen back into his shirt pocket and looked across the table at Christina. "You'll have to understand that once I get into something, I don't share much with other investigators until I have something solid. I never want to lead others down a path of no return. My hunches sometimes push me down some strange alleyways."

"I've noticed that during our brief working relationship." Christina responded.

"Can you fill me in on your thought pattern concerning the cassettes?" she queried.

"No problem," Dillon responded as he threw back the pages of his note pad to the entry concerning the cassettes. "The small recorder in his briefcase is the type used by many people to keep notes about a wide variety of things. I used to have one when I first came to OSI. It was handy because I have the worst memory in the world. I took it everywhere with me. I would make notes while driving, in every room of my house and while traveling from one place to another. I relied entirely too much on the contraption and suffered when it was stolen along with all my tapes during an investigation in Utah. I made a vow to try and improve my recall abilities and to write my notes on these pads." He held up a small green Government Issue note pad that would easily fit into a pants or shirt pocket.

"I use these and then have them transcribed for the official files at the end of an investigation. I write small so I can get a lot of information in one of these gizmos."

Christina sat nodding her head. "I understand what you mean," she began, "I have a tough time keeping things in order. I rely on notes too. However, I do have the hidden talent of knowing shorthand. My mother insisted I take it so my life as a secretary would be much simpler. Little did she know I would be using it for something so completely different."

"I'm jealous." Dillon laughed. "I don't know any shorthand other than what I invent. Some of the clerks have a real rough time trying to decipher what the heck I'm trying to say."

With that, Dillon and Christina began to brainstorm a few ideas about where the cassettes could be located. They decided a visit to Crimitin's apartment would be called for.

⚜

It took a couple of days to finalize arrangements with local Politzie officials. Christina, Penny, and Dillon were scheduled to meet the investigator at the apartment at 0900. They dutifully arrived with a few minutes to spare. About 0915 an unmarked car stopped in front of the house. Two men got out. One of them walked to Christina's car.

"Agent Dean?" he asked politely.

"I'm Agent Dean," Christina replied as she rolled down the window.

The officer extended his hand inside the frame and introduced himself as Inspector Hanz Ubermann. He nodded toward his companion and told Christina his name was Sergeant Fritz Alfdorn. Christina acknowledged the introductions and began to roll the window back up before getting out of the car. By this time, Dillon and Penny were out and coming around the back of the car to introduce themselves to Hanz and Fritz. Identifications were checked and the team started up the driveway toward the entrance. Once on the doorstep, they rang the bell. A female voice on the other end of the speaker greeted the inspector and buzzed the door open. Once inside Dillon took in the arrangement of the entranceway.

To the immediate right was a door leading to what he figured was a downstairs apartment. A stairway began just past the doorway and ran along the right wall. Behind the stairway was another apartment door with another door on the left. The woman who answered the bell was coming out of the back apartment. The inspector greeted her and introduced other members of the group. All of them followed the woman up stairs to the first floor landing.

"Isn't this a tragedy?" she commented in general as the inspector and sergeant made entrance to the apartment.

"It certainly is," replied Dillon. "We'll try to bother you as little as possible."

"Don't fret about that," she said, "just make sure you find the villain who killed him. He was such a nice person. We never had any trouble from him. We made him part of our family and enjoyed talking."

"We'll do everything in our power to find the killer." Christina said. "Can I ask where you learned to speak English?"

Frau Pffer smiled as she told Christina how she had lived in the United States for more than 10 years when her father was working for an investment bank in St. Louis. She didn't want to be conspicuous, so she worked hard at speaking English without an accent.

"To top it off," she said, "I even developed a mid western accent."

Christina, Penny, and Dillon all laughed with Frau Pffer and bid her farewell as she returned to her apartment. They went through the door into Crimitin's apartment. It was a strange layout. Immediately inside the door was a very wide tiled hallway with four doors, two on each side, leading from the hall. The first on the right overlooked the street. The one on the left overlooked the bottom apartment's patio and a terraced garden with fruit trees and vegetable plots. At the top of the hill were a gazebo type structure and a wooden table with six chairs. One tier down from the top was a water fountain and what Dillon surmised was a small fishpond.

Next on the left was the master bedroom with a queen size bed, dresser, mirror, end tables, and lamps. The view from the window was the same back yard except immediately under the window was the roof section of Helga's apartment. The final room on the right was the bathroom. Nothing spectacular, a tub/shower, sink, mirrored cabinet, toilet, and bidet.

Dillon continued into the living/dining room. It was a rather large area with a pull down lamp over the very German style furniture. Even though it was early morning, the lights were on because the rolladens were down on all windows and doors leading to the backyard and patio. Dillon continued around the corner into the very compact kitchen. A place for everything and everything in its place Dillon thought as he looked around the kitchen area. He turned and joined the others in the living room. He walked to the fireplace and sat down on the hearth.

"Inspector," he began, "who did the initial collection of items from the house?"

"We have a special crime scene team led by one of our senior investigators. All of them are trained in both the United States and Germany. We normally develop the actual crime scene and then move out from there. Since the airman was killed outside the apartment, we were inside in fairly short order. We went through the place with the owners so they could tell us what belonged to Crimitin and what belonged to the apartment. It was fully furnished, so separating his and theirs was fairly simple."

"What did you do about prints?" Penny asked.

"Any place we thought there would be prints we had our technicians work on identifying differences. There were many sets, some good, some bad, and some in between. Typical of any household setting. All of the prints are currently being run through our files, Interpol, FBI, and CIA. We have an excellent working relationship with all our counterparts."

Dillon continued to question the inspector on procedures and policy. He was making sure he didn't offend when he asked the hard questions. He explained exactly what he was looking for and why the absence of cassettes drew his attention.

"After seeing his car and now his apartment, I just feel Crimitin was meticulous in his record keeping. Why aren't there any extra cassettes of his flights?"

They agreed to a systematic approach for searching the apartment again. This time they were looking for the small things. Something out of the ordinary overlooked during the first time through. Dillon saw this done time and time again. Investigators would make a first sweep through a crime scene or other connected location and then go back with finer detail until all possible clues were collected. The search took them until after noon. No cassettes were found. Nothing out of the ordinary turned up. Anything they discovered traced back to the owners. Dillon was disappointed but not dejected. He knew something would manifest itself and lead him to the cassettes. He was working with his sixth sense now. He didn't share his feelings with the others.

Outside the apartment, they bid farewell to Frau Pffer and went to their cars. Fritz asked if they wanted to stop for lunch before heading back to the base. Everyone agreed and Christina followed the inspector and sergeant into Kottweiller. They enjoyed an excellent meal at a place frequented by the town police chief. Once the owner found out who the Americans were, he couldn't do enough to make their stay enjoyable.

Chapter Eight

Dillon spent the next morning reviewing statements of people living or working with and around the victim. He found nothing of interest. The call came in the afternoon.

"Dillon, this is John." the greeting emanated from the speakerphone recently installed in the conference room, "Could you come to the office?"

"Sure John, anything I can bring with me?" Dillon questioned.

"Not this time. I want you to talk with my first shirt. He's been talking with some of the troops and he may have something for us."

"I'll be right there. Just let me finish a few notes." Dillon confirmed.

"I'll be in the shirt's office. Just come on in once you get to this side of the base."

With that, the line went dead and Dillon returned to completing the notes he started. He closed the folder and put it back in the box prominently marked "IN WORK." He picked up the box and slid it between the rows of chairs separating the conference table and the wall until it thumped against the small shredder sitting at the end of the room. He went into Bill's office and told him where he planned to go, shouted a farewell to the others, and left the building.

The drive to John's office didn't take long. Dillon was beginning to feel his way around the base learning all the short cuts. He parked around front and entered the main doors.

At the top of the stairs, he turned toward the flight line and Johns glassed in reception area. He pushed open the door, greeted the clerk, and headed toward the open door where he heard John's voice. The clerk nodded her head and said that the commander and first sergeant were expecting him.

John was sitting on a couch facing the shirt's desk; he was pointing his finger in the air as he concluded making some point. When Dillon entered the office, both men rose to greet him.

"That didn't take too long," John said as he reached out to shake Dillon's hand. "I don't believe you've met the shirt, have you?"

"No sir I haven't" Dillon said as he turned toward the first sergeant to offer his greetings, "I'm Agent Dillon Reece." shaking the oversized hand of the squadron disciplinarian.

"It's a pleasure to meet you sir," the first sergeant replied, "I'm Sergeant Wilber Fogerton, Will to my friends and of course to the Old Man whether I'm his friend or not." He glanced at John to make sure he was smiling. "He's told me a lot about you and it certainly is a pleasure to meet you."

"Don't believe half the stuff this guy tells you," Dillon laughed. "Only half of it will be partially true and the other half will be total bull."

Will offered Dillon a chair on the other side of a coffee table in front of the couch. Dillon sat down as John returned to his spot on the couch.

"Something to drink?" queried the shirt. "I've got some diet sodas, full strength stuff, water with or without and some orange juice."

"I'll have some water with thank you very much," Dillon returned. The shirt turned to a small refrigerator in the corner and returned with a sparkling water, a diet soda for the major and an orange juice for himself. Each man opened the beverage and took a drink before turning to the conversation at hand.

"So what's up?" Dillon began. "You said the shirt had something for me. I'm all ears and no smart ass comments from you John."

"Wasn't going to say a thing Dillon, even though you deserve a shot with an opening line like that. The shirt has been talking with the supervisors to see if they had any information that could help build a trail to Crimitin. Sergeant Carson, the shop chief came up with the name of Doding, Paul S., an Airman First Class crew chief. He got the name from Sergeant Liebtone, Crimitin's immediate supervisor. Evidently Crimitin did a favor or two for Doding." With that, John let the shirt pick up the explanation.

He told a story how Carson put the word out to supervisors during their normal how goes it meeting. The shop chiefs in turn talked with all their people during their morning or afternoon meetings depending on what shift the folks were working. It was quiet until Doding failed a random drug test. Random is what they call it but it's anything but random. If suspicions raise a flag about any person working the flight line, his or her number is sure to appear during a "random" drug screen. Doding was in deep trouble because he tested positive for more than one drug. He immediately lost access to the flight line and during his interview with supervisors; he mentioned having some information about Crimitin. It turns out Crimitin supplied Doding with cocaine a couple of times when Doding was short of cash but long on habit. Crimitin always seemed to have a supply. When Doding asked about becoming a regular customer, Crimitin told him he wasn't a pusher. Doding said he didn't understand that line of reasoning but was happy for the infrequent supply. He didn't give it much thought until Crimitin tuned up dead.

When asked why he didn't come forward with the information before failing the drug test, he didn't have much of an excuse. He just tried to stay in control and out of the limelight. The positive reading on the latest round of drug tests gave him no options.

"How long you been watching this guy shirt?" Dillon asked after the story ended.

"He's been under suspicion for some time. He wasn't one of our sharper troops and was prone to mistakes. Nothing that warranted a test but enough to add him to our list after his latest screw up. As it turned out, he was positive for both marijuana and cocaine. I don't know if we're going to save him, or if we're going to turn him out on the street. That will be the bosses call backed by everyone along the line."

"I know," said Dillon, "we try everything we can and most of the time we get kicked in the face. Can we arrange for a meet with this guy and ask him a few leading questions?"

"I don't see why not." John responded. "He hasn't been formally charged at the moment. Maybe we can get some help out of him if he believes there will be something good at the end of the meeting. I'll be there to put on the official spin and then let's see what the little beggar has to say. I'll set it up for 0900 tomorrow in my office. He'll think it's time for charges and will probably be scared shitless. I do love this job."

"You seem to take a deviant amount of pleasure in shaking down this man." Dillon kicked in as they rose from their seated positions to leave the office.

"I'm right in the boat rowing with you when it comes to drugs." John replied, "But I'd just as soon take him out and shoot him as give him an even break."

With that, the men exchanged handshakes and Dillon left for his return trip to the office. He mulled over the situation and began to formulate his approach to questioning the airman. He'd seen this type of situation provide a wealth of information but he's also seen it develop into a freeze out for fear of reprisal. He would have to make a couple of quick calls to check with the legal beagles and the command structure before he made any promises he couldn't fill.

After he settled back into the conference room with a tall bottle of carbonated water, he made his first call to the Judge Advocate's office.

"Judge Advocate's office, Sergeant Jones speaking," was the very professional sounding voice that greeted Dillon from the other end of the line.

"Sergeant Jones, this is Agent Dillon Reece, OSI Special Interdiction Unit, currently attached to the local OSI office at Ramstein. I would like to talk with one of your prosecutors if you don't mind."

"Is it in reference to a current case sir?" Jones questioned.

"I don't think this one has made it through the bureaucratic maze yet sergeant. It involves a positive test during a drug screen." Dillon replied as he pulled his notes out of their folder. "But just in case, the subject's name is Airman First Class Paul S. Doding. His ID number is 56-34-7896."

"Thank you sir, let me run up the computer, check the files and if we have something on it, I'll get the individual working the case. Just one moment," and the line went silent except for the computer generated elevator music.

"Captain Smithley here, can I help you?" came the tentative voice on the other end of the line.

"Yes Captain, you can," Dillon spoke with his best authoritative tone.

"As you know, my name is Dillon Reece and I'm here on special assignment with the local OSI detachment. I'm currently working the murder investigation of Airman Crimitin. However, that isn't the main reason for the call. As I'm sure your admin man told you, I'm interested in what you have on Airman Doding. He may have some important information on our case and we'd like to use his troubles to our advantage."

"I've got the case file here and there really isn't much in it. The tests were just performed last week and the results were sent to the squadron commander," the captain read from the folder laid out so neatly on his Government Issue mahogany laminated over chipboard desktop, "I don't know where I can help you."

"Very simple," Dillon began. "I've just come from the commander's office and we've agreed on a plan to play good cop bad cop with this young man to get as much information as we can concerning the subject of my investigation, Airman Crimitin. Major Littlemore will naturally be the good cop since that will build credibility inside the squadron and I'll play the heavy. We want to offer him rehabilitation along with non-judicial punishment. We can negotiate with him on taking stripes and money out of his pocket. Since he was positive for two substances, we do believe he'll want to deal rather than end up on the streets, with a multiple habit, and no money. We don't know his story so we don't know how to play our cards at this moment. It may be another case of a kid running with the wrong crowd and getting himself involved too deeply before he realized his situation."

"I seeeee," hissed the captain elongating the eeeee for some time. "I really don't have a problem with anything you're offering. In fact, it'll make our job a lot easier. I do have one request."

"Name it," Dillon quickly agreed.

"Give the ADC[7] a call to clear this with her office. She really takes her job seriously and without her OK, anything we do on our side will land in someone else's office for mediation. I always like to avoid that if at all possible."

"Consider it done. I'm sure I can find her number. Thanks for your cooperation. I look forward to meeting you during my stay." With that farewell, Dillon replaced the phone in its cradle and left the conference room for Christina's office. He stood in the doorway and asked if she knew the number to the area defense counsel's office.

"I sure do but why do you want to talk with that bitch?" Christina replied as she reached for her keyboard to bring up her computerized phone number listing. "She takes her job to heart and has caused us some real problems in the past. I try to avoid contact with her."

"I've heard that she's dedicated to the theme behind her office," Dillon said as he reached for the yellow sticky Christina handed across the desk after writing down the name and number of the ADC.

"We have an inroad to someone who may have information on Crimitin's activities. He just got busted for abuse in a drug screen and we want to offer some assistance in exchange for his help in solving our case. Going to play good cop bad cop," Dillon said as he puffed out his chest, "and I naturally get to play the bad cop."

"I'm so impressed," Christina shot back as Dillon began to laugh. "I'll be waiting to see your costume for the performance."

Dillon continued to chuckle to himself as he returned to the conference room to call the extension Christina just gave him.

"Area Defense Counsel, Sergeant Andre, can I help you?" was the trained greeting from the administrative assistant.

"Yes Mam, I would like to speak with Captain Cannen please. This is Agent Dillon Reece."

"May I ask what this is in reference too?" the sergeant questioned.

"It's a relatively new case concerning Airman First Class Paul S. Doding."

"Thank you sir, I'll get the captain."

Dillon didn't have to wait too long before the captain was on the line. All spit and polish from the tone of her voice. Dillon told her the Crimitin story from the beginning so he wouldn't have to explain it in pieces. When he was done, she asked what she could do for him at this particular time. He paused and mentally reviewed his last words trying to see if his need for cooperation from her office was unclear. He didn't find any fault, so he began to restate his last sentences.

"I need your OK to work with Doding on some type of plea bargain. We want to offer him rehab in exchange for his cooperation. I want to have the commander play the good cop while I play the bad cop."

Silence greeted him after he finished the sentence. "Captain?" he questioned, "are you still there?"

"I'm here. I'm just trying to absorb your request. I've never had anyone come to me before hand and ask for my cooperation. It's usually after the fact and I'm a bit taken aback."

"Well let me assure you I don't want to do anything to jeopardize our cooperative association. I find being up front saves people a lot of time. It's put me in a hot water some times because there are those individuals who can't stand the truth and don't like being hit between the eyes with the obvious. If nothing else, I'm blunt and too the point. I appreciate others who are the same way."

"That's refreshing to know," the captain answered, "I do believe we'll be able to do business."

Dillon acknowledged her cooperative posture and they discussed the finer points of their plan. She offered to be with Doding when the proposition is set before the offending airman. It would give more credence to the offer if defense counsel were there to advise the accused.

When Cannen found out the commander was Littlemore, she was very pleased because all her dealings with John were professional and to the point. The conversation continued until both Dillon and the captain agreed upon ground rules and how things will be run to ensure UCMJ[8] rights are not violated. After they concluded their conversation, she gave John's office a call to confirm the time but found him out of the office. She left a message telling him she talked with Dillon and would be taking part in the meeting.

After his call to the ADC, Dillon called the vice wing, Colonel Fillabee, to give her a down and dirty briefing on their plans. He explained how the initial coordination was done with the JAG[9] and the ADC. She listened intently and asked very few clarification questions after Dillon was done. She offered a back briefing for the wing commander, Brigadier General Carl Quigley, when he returned to the office. Dillon quickly agreed to that proposal because he didn't want to be bogged down having to explain all the details of the case to the wing king. At this time, there were too many loose ends for credible explanations.

After his call to Colonel Fillabee, he made a few notes and prepared to leave the office. He wanted to get back to his room and prepare for the morning meeting. He would call John at home and arrange a time for them to meet before Doding got to the office.

CHAPTER NINE

"Captain, I've got a collect call from a Mrs. Crimitin, do you want me to accept it and pass it into your office?" the fresh faced airman asked as she stuck her head into the maintenance officer's doorway.

"Yes, yes, pass it in to me," the captain responded without hesitation. The multi-line phone on his desk showed a blinking line. It glowed steady as the administrator accepted the charges and passed the call to the captain. The line began to blink again and a buzzer announced the incoming call. "Captain Carpton, what can I do for you Mrs. Crimitin?"

"It's been a few days since I heard from you captain and I was just wondering if there was any news."

"Nothing yet Mam but I'll get with the OSI office here and have them give me an update if they have one, or if they don't, I'll have them contact the lead investigator in Germany. We should be able to get some type of information from him."

"We just want to find out when we can expect to have him home."

"I understand your concern and will make sure I get something for you to work with today," the captain responded. "If I have to visit the OSI office personally, I'll do just that. I'm sure they'll be able to present us with some information. I'll give you a call as soon as I know something."

Mrs. Crimitin thanked the captain and apologized for making the collect call. Carl told her to call collect anytime she needed to talk with him. She hung up and he immediately dialed the local OSI office. He talked with the administrative section. He stressed the importance of getting some information for the family today. The sergeant understood the importance and promised to have the detachment commander call him as soon as she returned from her meeting with the security police. Carl thanked the sergeant and hung up.

He called his admin assistant and asked her to contact OSI in Germany as soon as their offices opened. With the time differences, it was hard to make connections from the other side of the world. He wasn't going to rely on someone else to get the information he needed. He would make the initial call himself to get the ball rolling. They may not want to tell him much on the phone but they'll understand his concern.

His administrator stuck her head back into the Captain's office and told him there was a 9-hour time difference. Carl decided to give them a call from home connecting through the command post. He would have a constant connection and the ability to find the person he was looking for without having to deal with the base operator. He called the OSI office and told them of his plans. He called Mrs. Crimitin to tell her it would be tomorrow afternoon before he heard any information from Germany. She thanked him for his effort.

⚜

Dillon and John talked for more than an hour before agreeing to meet at 0800 in John's office. They would brief the ADC about their plans and get her final approval. They didn't want to violate any rights or privileges of the accused. Dillon read the files again and watched TV for a while. He sipped a glass of single malt and smoked one of the cigars he picked up in Paris. After the smoke, the drink and the movie were all finished; he showered, laid out his clothes for the morning, and rolled into bed. He wasn't prepared for the call.

"Agent Reece," the operator asked. "I've got a call from the command post and they said they were holding a Captain Carpton, from Vandenberg Air Force Base in California on a secure line. Should I put him through?"

Dillon was slow to make any connection between the caller and the case he was working. However when Carpton explained who he was, the connection was clear even at the ungodly hour of 0530.

"Sorry to get you up so early Agent Reece but I've been in contact with the family and our OSI office doesn't seem to have a direct line to your office. I went through the command post and they hooked me into the Cannon. They knew immediately who I needed to talk with concerning the case."

"I left my name and numbers with them in case someone with a real need to find me gave them a call. It was a good decision to go through them.

Not only can we talk on a secure line, they have no problems waking me in the middle of the night."

Carl explained the situation to Dillon in as much detail as he could. Dillon got up to sit at the desk and take notes. He put the desk phone on speaker as he wrote. The scene painted by Carl wasn't unusual for a young single man in the force. He was the first person to join the military with a working class up bringing in a less than desirable location. Dillon asked questions about each member of the family. When he got to the brother, he didn't get as much as he liked.

"You say the boy just appeared down the hallway?"

"That's right," Carl, recounted. "He must have been in a bedroom down the hall because the kitchen was on the other side of the house."

"Can you do me a favor Carl?"

"You name it." Carl verbalized.

"I'm going to need some assistance from your OSI office. I'll need some background on the juvenile records for both boys. Have them contact the city, county and state police to see if there are any serious offenses lurking in their past. Maybe we can make something of why Crimitin was dealing over here. If there's a record of any type of drug offense, the connection can be made."

"I'll give the det. commander a call at home. We'll get it moving in the morning. I'm not sure how long it'll take but will get back to you via e-mail. That way I won't have to wake you up quite so early in the morning."

"Think nothing of it Carl, payback is always my specialty." Dillon laughed as they bid each other farewell. Dillon walked into the kitchen to start coffee. No use getting back into bed. He would watch the news and go through his notes again before the 0800 meeting.

As Dillon entered John's office, the smell of brewing coffee tantalized his senses. On a corner table was a coffee pot, condiments and a box of pastries.

"Still partial to sticky buns?" John asked as he looked up and saw Dillon enter the office.

"Yes you kind gentleman and how did you know I would be looking for a cup of coffee?"

"Just makes sense, Dillon. All the bad cops have a cup of coffee with them to make the suspect believe that at any moment he's going to throw the hot liquid into his face if he doesn't cooperate."

"Damn boy, I hadn't thought about it that way. It's been so long since I played this game, I forgot how much fun it really could be. Thanks for the idea. I'll make sure he sees me get a cup full. That way he'll know it's damn hot."

John came from behind his executive style desk and walked toward the couch. He put a folder on the occasional table and went to help himself to some of the coffee that just finished percolating. Dillon was finishing the rather large piece of German pastry he selected from the open box.

"Whoa there big guy, please leave some for the suspect. These are part of my being the good guy." Dillon and John both laughed as they wandered back across the room to the couch. The men took positions on either end and put their coffee and pastries on the table.

"We should make this room a little more threatening," John said.

"Agree totally," Dillon acknowledged.

"Why don't we put one of the wing backs on one side of your desk, a regular arm chair about three paces directly in front and the other wing back behind the accused on his right side? If there are any bag draggers with them, they can sit on the couch or in the other arm chairs."

"Sounds threatening enough."

"Threatening to who?" questioned a voice from the doorway. John turned to see Captain Mary Cannen entering the office.

"Why threatening to your client, captain. You don't think we want this to be easy for the young man. We want as much out of him as we can get and we don't want to play like we enjoy his extracurricular activities," replied Dillon as he got up from his seat on the couch and approached the Service Dress uniformed defense counsel.

"We didn't mean for this to be a formal affair," he continued as he shook the captain's hand and then stood aside for John to complete the same respectful gesture.

"That's why the major is standing tall in his BDU's[10] and I'm resplendent in my standard three piece suit." Both men watched for some type of sign from the hard-nosed counselor but found none. She continued toward her designated seat and laid her leather briefcase on the table.

"If you gentlemen are trying to ingratiate your way into my good graces, you've made a very poor beginning."

"Well fuck it then captain; let's get down to brass tacks. I wanted to take this little redneck and shoot him at sunrise. However, my compatriot here needs the bastard's assistance in another case. I would rather take the guy, process him for the crime, and send him out on the street. I cannot speak for the Agent but I have no use for drug offenders no matter how dire their story of woe appears to be. There is no place in my Air Force for drug abusing shits like him and especially when I give them the responsibility of ensuring a multi-million dollar piece of aerospace equipment is ready to slip the surly bonds of earth and fly. Any other questions Captain?"

"No sir, I do believe you've covered just about everything. I will inform my client not to cooperate with you in any way. If this is the negative attitude you're going to take, I don't see how the airman can receive a fair deal." The captain reached for her briefcase and began to get up from her chair. Dillon reached across the table and put his hand on her case.

"Now hang on counselor, you haven't heard my side of the story yet and I'm the one who set up this meeting, remember?" He looked into the steel blue eyes of the defense counsel and felt the pull on her case weaken.

"All of us here have a job to get done. You to protect the rights of your client, John to administer punishment for the crime and I'm trying to get as much information out of this guy so I can possibly solve another related case. We all have to cooperate if we're going to accomplish any of our goals."

John rose from his place on the couch and went behind his desk. He was fingering some papers piled on one side. The captain stood from her chair and turned to face the major.

"Sir, I understand your frustration at finding an alleged drug offender in your squadron. I deal with these frustrations every day. I just want to make sure we don't get ourselves into a position where we aren't going to make progress on any front."

"I know that captain but you're forgetting one thing, I'm the good cop. You should be worrying about the other guy. He's the one going to be rough on your client. He's the one who will use the water torture and fingernail removal as a means to his end. I'm going to be bringing this drugged out shit coffee and pastries." The captain stood near the armchair located in front of the commander's desk. She rested her right arm on the back of the chair. She didn't say a word for a moment and then turned toward Dillon.

"He's kidding, isn't he?" she questioned.

"Just the part about the coffee. We don't want him to wet himself during the session." Dillon retorted with a smile. The captain stood in silence as John made his way around his desk to the back of the chair where the captain was transfixed.

"Don't worry captain, you just leave the driving to us, and we'll have this thing over in less than an hour. Speaking of hour, look at the time. We better get down to business and make sure our deal is OK with the counselor."

With that remark, John returned to his spot on the couch and Dillon returned to his place after refilling his coffee. The captain remained mystically attached to the chair in the middle of the room.

"Captain?" John asked, "Are you going to join us?"

Without saying a word, the captain returned to her seat, opened her briefcase, and laid out a folder. She opened it and thumbed through the pages. She pulled out a sheet for each of the men and passed them across the table. The sheet contained a brief synopsis of the life and times of Airman First Class Paul S. Doding. Each of the men took a moment to look at the document while the captain removed her copy and several other documents from their assigned location in her case file. She waited patiently as the two men sitting opposite her committed the information to memory.

"Good information captain, where did you get this?" Dillon asked as he broke the uncomfortable silence. He knew where the information came from; he just wanted to take the captain away from her state of shock after the rough treatment.

"I'm sorry, did you say something?" she asked Dillon as her blank stare into the outer universe suddenly came back to earth.

"Yes I did. I wondered where you got this information on Doding."

"Most of it came from personnel. Other information came from the Security Police files on the man. He isn't an angel but he isn't a mass murderer either. It doesn't say much about his family, so we can't draw any conclusions about what he did before he joined the force. We'll have to get that out of him once we get him in the chair."

"Good enough," John quipped as he got up from his seat, "I'm going to visit down the hall and then get myself mentally prepared for this meeting." With that note, he turned and left the office. When he was gone, the captain turned to Dillon.

"Am I missing something or has the major undergone a Jekyll and Hyde transformation? I don't ever remember him being like that before."

"I've know him for a long time and that's the first time I've actually seen him lose it. However, I do understand his frustration. You were just a target of opportunity. Don't take it personally. You're going to have to work with the man on more than one occasion in the future. You don't want him as the enemy. I can assure you he'll take your advice on matters he feels you're the expert but don't try to cross into his commander's arena. He takes it very seriously and looks upon the members of his squadron as members of his family. He trusts them and they can trust him. When one of the flock breaks that trust, it's a devastating blow. Just don't push his buttons again on a drug case. You'll end up on the losing end."

"Thanks for the advice but I've a job to do also. I'm outside the regular lines of command so I can't be bullied by a commander trying to make a point."

"Don't get your dander up captain. He'll work with you in every case. Just make sure you step lightly when drugs and his squadron are mentioned in one breath. Nuff said?"

"Yes sir," she replied. Both of them gave the room a final look before the appointed hour. Doding would be in the outer office in a few minutes and they didn't want to have him overhear any discussions behind the office doors.

John came back into the room and refreshed his coffee. The First Sergeant brought Doding into the office. Sergeant Fogerton sidestepped to the couch as the airman approached the commander's desk. With a smartly executed salute, he reported in.

"Airman Doding reporting as ordered sir." He held the salute until John slowly raised his hand to return the airman's acknowledgement. After Doding brought his arm down to his side, John sat in his chair, Dillon took his position to John's left, and the ADC lowered herself into the chair behind Doding, as the first sergeant sat in the middle of the couch. The administrator closed the door to the outer office. The scene was set. Standing at rigid attention, the airman waited for the first words.

"Airman Doding," John began, "do you know why you're in my office this morning?"

"Yes sir," was the tense reply.

"Perhaps you can explain it to me?" the major asked as he leaned forward in his seat. He picked up his cup of coffee and took a long slow drink.

Airman Doding, with a shaking voice, began to tell the major about a random drug test for crew chiefs in his flight. He tested positive for cocaine and marijuana. He didn't provide any excuses. He finished with his belief punishment is today and the ADC was there to advise him on his options.

"Thank you airman. Let me introduce the other members of this gathering. You know the first sergeant, Senior Master Sergeant Will Fogerton. The captain sitting behind you is the Area Defense Counsel, Captain Mary Cannen and this gentleman to my left is Special Agent Dillon Reece, assigned to McDill Air Force Base in Florida. He's presently on temporary duty with us at Ramstein. Please stand at ease."

The airman released the tense posture, placed his hands behind his back, and separated his feet to a point just about shoulder width. He continued to look directly at the commander. John looked at the man standing there in his freshly pressed battle dress uniform. He wanted to jerk him across the desk and backhand the son of a bitch but he restrained.

He looked at Captain Cannen and asked, "Captain, what is the penalty for flunking a random drug test?" The captain rose from her seat and stepped beside Airman Doding.

"The penalty can vary sir, from non-judicial punishment under Article 15, or it can include full courts martial with confinement, fines, and dishonorable discharge."

"So if I hear you right, this man could be facing hard time in Ft. Leavenworth, no pay and a discharge that will keep him from working in many segments of our society."

"Yes, sir," the captain replied as she slowly backed toward her seat.

The commander deliberately rose from his seat, placed his clenched fists on the glass covering his desk, and leaned toward the airman. "This might be your lucky day airman. Depending on what you're able to tell us today, I may be very lenient and give you a chance to redeem yourself. I want you to pay very close attention to everything said here today. I want careful consideration on each answer you give to any question posed to you this morning and weigh the consequences before you answer. Am I clear on that?"

"Yes Sir."

"Sit down." With that command, the airman took his seat in front of the commander's desk and waited silently.

After Doding took his seat, John began to ask him a series of routine questions about his activities in the squadron, how long had he been at Ramstein, his last promotion, etc. They were all questions John had answers for but was testing the waters for deception from the airman. He was also trying to get the man to relax.

John noticed Doding clenched his hands together in his lap and was squeezing so hard the knuckles were turning white. When he saw color returning, he knew the man was beginning to relax. He hadn't found any areas where he knew Doding was lying, so he sat back and looked over at Dillon.

"Agent Reece, do you have anything you want to ask Airman Doding before we get down to the legal stuff?"

"Yes sir I do." Dillon returned as he got up from his seat and walked around to the front of the desk. He positioned himself to one side of the desk, placed both hands on the edge, and rested his buttocks in between his hands as he directly faced the ADC. He looked at her for a moment and then turned his head slightly as he addressed the airman.

"Doding, there just isn't anyplace in this Air Force for a drug abusing low life such as yourself." The ADC jumped from her chair and began to protest when Dillon cut her off.

"Don't get up to give me any of your bleeding heart legal crap captain. It's your problem you have the dubious task of defending this type of criminal. I would just as soon take them out to the front gate and tell them to 'Have a nice Day'." Dillon smirked as he let the popular phrase whine out of his mouth. In one quick motion Dillon was directly in front of Doding with his hands on each arm of the straight back chair, his face directly in front of Doding he shouted,

"What in God's name is wrong with you asshole?" With that, John rose out of his chair and shouted at the agent.

"Agent Reece, that's about enough of that. I'll not have you haranguing the airman. If you have questions, please ask them in a civil tone or I'm afraid I'll have to ask you to leave." As he was speaking, Dillon continued to stare into Doding's face. When John was finished, he slowly turned to look directly at the commander standing behind his desk.

In a truly sarcastic tone, he responded, "Sorry sir, I'll try to do better."

With that, he walked away from Doding to a credenza located against the wall. He leaned back against the unit and stared at Doding.

"Let me apologize for the Agent, Airman Doding. I'm not here to harass you; we just have to get some straight answers to some very important questions." He looked at the first sergeant and asked him to get Doding a glass of water. Sergeant Fogerton left the room for a moment and returned with a small paper cup. He offered it to Doding who took it and sipped the contents. He placed the cup on the floor. He again clasped his hands together and sat rigid in the chair. John was writing on a legal pad in the middle of his desk. When he noticed Doding put his cup on the ground, he looked up.

"Airman Doding, did you know Airman William Crimitin?"

"Yes sir," was the short to the point response.

"Tell us about your relationship," the major requested.

Doding began a story that took him back to the day Crimitin arrived at Ramstein. They lived in the same barracks and although they weren't roommates, they did see a lot of each other with time in the day rooms and chow hall. He wouldn't characterize their relationship as best friends but they did have occasion to talk with one another on a daily basis. He knew Crimitin was from California and was stationed at Travis for a while before moving to Ramstein on a temporary and then permanent basis.

Dillon asked if he ever said anything about why he made that move. Doding surmised it was because he wanted to travel in Europe rather than the Far East. Doding continued with details about his family and anything he knew about Crimitin's family. Dillon would be able to confirm that relationship when he heard back from authorities in California.

John asked about the connection with drugs. Doding said he came to Crimitin asking if he knew any dealers. When they talked, Crimitin offered enough powder for a couple of hits at no cost to Doding. He didn't want Doding to believe he was a pusher. He said he was able to get access to a regular supply and would help him out in desperate situations. He said he didn't like to see anyone suffer withdrawal if not ready to kick the habit. He also told Doding if he ever found out he was going into work high, he would turn him into the squadron. Doding made it a point to stay away from Crimitin when they were at work. He did go to work high and that's why he was sitting where he was today.

Just before Crimitin's last trip, they were talking and Crimitin seemed very nervous. When Doding asked why, Crimitin said some big things going to happen in his life and he wasn't sure what the outcome would be. He didn't give too many details but Doding said it was the first time Crimitin ever drank enough alcohol to become knee-walking drunk.

As Doding was talking, Dillon continued to get in his face and question statements he made. He constantly tried to trip him up and get some type of counter productive sentence out of him as he explained one situation after another. If Dillon questioned from across the room, John let him go. If Dillon approached Doding, John would intercede to "protect" Doding. John watched for signs that Doding appreciated his assistance and would watch the ADC to ensure she was playing her part.

It all boiled down to Doding was a friend but he wasn't a best friend. They shared common interests outside work and found some areas to discuss over meals at the chow hall or drinks at the club. Crimitin talked to him on various occasions about dumping the coke but each time Doding recalled, he refused his helping hand. Doding said it was almost like a weird crusade. He knew in a desperate situation Crimitin would come through with a couple of lines but at other times, he would try his damnedest to get him off the shit. He only wished that he'd taken him up on his offer. He wouldn't be facing the problems he was up against now.

Doding did have one very important thing to report. Crimitin always had a supply before he made a trip. Doding recalled a couple of instances when Crimitin returned from a rotation to Saudi and when approached, said he didn't have anything on hand. Before a trip, he always seemed to have the goods. It didn't really sink in to Doding's pea brain until now. He was carrying into the Kingdom. John could see the light come on by the expression on Doding's face. Dillon could tell something was happening because Doding fell silent in the middle of a sentence.

"Just figured it out Paul?" Dillon asked from behind the airman. Silence greeted the question.

"Did you hear me airman?" Dillon shouted from a spot less than a foot behind Doding's buzz cut head. Doding was startled and in one motion, he rose out of the chair and turned to face Dillon.

"Got something you want to say to me, airman?" Doding just stood facing Dillon as he clenched and unclenched his fists.

"Don't do anything you might regret more than the trouble you're already in. You may be on the path to redemption."

"Lighten up agent, Doding you sit back down," John commanded. The ADC got up from her chair and the first sergeant was at Dillon's side almost as quickly as Doding turned around to face Reece. The Airman didn't say a word. He just continued to stare at Dillon.

"Airman!" John commanded, "Sit back down before I come around this desk and help you."

Doding slowly turned to face the major, apologized for his lack of control and sat back down. Dillon looked at John giving him a smile and a wink. John remained stoical. They were too far along to break up a good thing now. John came around the desk and leaned against it as he began to speak with Doding.

"You've been a great deal of help today Airman. You've been able to fill in details about Airman Crimitin that we would have difficulty piecing together. We also know more about you and some of the reasons behind your abuse. All these things put together will help me make a decision regarding your fate. Captain," he began while changing his view to look at the ADC, "I want to offer this man an avenue of redemption. Is it possible for me to send him to rehab, take a stripe, and reach into his bank account for a six month period?"

The captain was out of her seat moving toward the commander. As she reached his side, she turned toward Doding.

"Yes sir, I'm sure we can convince the wing that even though Airman Doding was caught with trace elements of two illegal substances in his system, the assistance he provided today warrants his being given one chance to redeem himself. However, I wouldn't hold out any chance of a second effort by anyone if he were caught again. I would suggest a program of rehab in the United States, followed by routine drug screenings to help him stay clean and an assignment away from his current problems."

"Sounds good to me," John responded, "Agent Reece, do you've anything you want to add?"

"I don't think so major. You've given him the farm and he really didn't provide me with anything other than he had motive and opportunity to eliminate Crimitin for his supply."

The room fell silent. Dillon pulled a trump card out of the deck and threw it on the playing field. He could see the blood rushing up the back of Doding's neck. He wondered how long it was going to take before he would blow up and take away all he earned in the last few minutes. Dillon made the statement to get a rise out of the drug offender. He figured that if he threw it away now, he wasn't worth saving. If he kept his composure after such a blockbuster, he may have a chance at being a productive member of the Force.

John was flabbergasted. He couldn't stop staring at Dillon. They never mentioned any notion that Doding might be a suspect in the case. It never entered his mind. As for the ADC, if looks could kill, Reece would have been a corpse in seconds.

"Well thanks for your input," John sputtered.

"If you have any other surprises, I wish you would share them with us at this time. I don't want to wait until the deal is struck and the wing is processing their approval. If you can provide support for your accusation, please drop it on us now."

As the major was talking, Dillon came around in front of Doding. He stood near the desk but didn't use it for support as before. He just looked into Doding's face. The reaction he got was also one of disbelief and bewilderment. It was the look Dillon hoped he would see. His senses told him the airman didn't have a thing to do with the murder.

Doding was so shocked by Dillon's words he didn't have time to react in a negative way. Dillon thought there might be light at the end of Doding's tunnel and it wouldn't be a freight train this time. He just may be able to redeem himself with John's plan. If nothing positive came out of it for the Force, at least they would have dried out an addict and given him a second chance at making things right.

"No major, I don't have any specifics but I do have my suspicions. I'll continue to follow the leads and if they pan out, you can rest assured I'll put an end to your plan."

"Thank you agent," ended the major.

"Could I ask you to step out of the room? You seem to have a chilling effect on the current situation."

Dillon looked at the major, said nothing, and left the office. When he was gone, John discussed the finer points of the Article 15 action and came to an agreement with the ADC, the first sergeant and Doding. The first sergeant's concurrence was necessary because the right message for the rest of the squadron was very important. If the commander appeared too lenient, the punishment would not have the required effect on others.

The three of them discussed this openly in front of Doding. It wasn't your typical Article 15 preceding but they wanted Doding to understand what a break he was getting and how the commander was the good guy in all of this. He must be seen as fair but serious. After they finished, the first shirt took Doding into his office for some final words. It would be one on one and John was sure the airman would have a full understanding of his situation after the shirt finished with him.

"Will, please ask Agent Reece to come back in."

As Dillon entered the room, John blasted him, "Goddamn it Dillon, what the fuck was that all about?"

"Let me begin by saying I'm sorry I dropped that on you so unexpectedly. That was about the only way I could see to get a rise out of Doding. Apparently, it worked with both of you. We can rule him out of having anything to do with the murder. I believe he was scared enough to tell us the truth. The reaction on his face convinced me he didn't have any more to do with Crimitin's murder than you or I. Again, I'm sorry. It was a cheap shot but I needed to take it."

"When that came out," the captain said, "I began to have my doubts on why I was here. If you suspected him of having anything to do with Crimitin's death, I shouldn't have agreed to this type of meeting."

"No shit," gasped John, "I thought we blew it right then and there."

"Like I said, I'm sorry for the bombshell but didn't our good cop bad cop routine work well? A couple of times I thought you were going to knock me down John."

"You were having too much fun in your bad cop role, Dillon. I was tempted at times but I know you have a little bit of extra training that we maintainers don't get and I didn't want to embarrass myself in front of guests." John chuckled. After all the back slapping and congratulating was done, both men turned their attention to the ADC and finalized the procedures to follow in making the offer discussed a final deal

John looked at the ADC and asked if there was anything else to discuss. As the meeting was taking place, she kept notes on the discussion so no one would have any questions. When she brought all of the required documents to John for signature, she would also present him with a journal on the proceedings. He could file it with all the other documents to ensure no avenue of appeal would be available. Although she was the defense counsel, she was happy to cooperate in a case where the outcome was positive.

After everyone finished his or her input, the captain excused herself and left the office. John and Dillon rose from their seats to thank the ADC for her assistance. The men refilled their coffee and began a discussion of the morning's activities from an OSI and command perspective.

John began, "I just can't get used to the fact of young people using this shit. It totally wastes any potential they might have."

"I agree," Dillon said as he opened the folder on the table in front of him and pulled out his notes.

"Doding was a good student through tech school and his high school transcripts show he isn't a stupid person. However, once he got here, he lost control and let the bullshit put down by his running buddies take over his better judgment. That's another avenue we should have the shirt investigating. We don't want to miss any other abusers. I sure hope this is confined to a small segment of the folks in your squadron. I would hate to think that every 141 I take out of here is being maintained by a dope smoking coke snorter."

John slowly turned his head toward Dillon's location and replied, "Fuck you Agent Reece. It's your fucking job to catch the bastards, so hop to it!"

"I believe you're right my friend. However, the information about Crimitin is puzzling at best. He didn't want to be known as a pusher but was able to provide a supply for an acquaintance when the guy was in need. It all apparently centers on his trips to Riyadh. We could make the bold assumption he was making deliveries and not making pickups. We could again postulate that if he was making deliveries, then the briefcase might have held a large amount of money upon his return. Thus, motive. I wonder if the locals tested it for ink residue."

Dillon finished thinking aloud and began to gather the papers he scattered on the table. John too was picking up his notes and stacking them neatly in front of himself when he turned toward Dillon.

"You do understand this will mean a trip to Saudi."

"I know I know," Dillon quickly replied, "A Riyadh Rendezvous. I've been trying to put that aspect of this thing out of my mind. So far, I've been able to avoid activities in the Middle East. Nevertheless, it now appears that's exactly what is going to happen. We won't understand anything about this apparent pipeline without going to ground zero. Is it really that bad down there the guys are in such desperate need of escape?"

"I can tell you from personal experience," John shot back, "it's a wondrous place if you're only there on a temporary and I mean temporary basis. If you're there more than 30 days, it sucks. Not only is the society restrictive but the forces stationed there are under huge restrictions from the command. After the bombings and such, they clamped down tight on everyone."

"When were you down there?"

"I make it a point to get into locations where my people will be interacting with other support agencies. I always want to make sure I can put a face with a name when I deal long distance with a problem area. With the remote assignment allocation, I make a trip down there once or twice a year. It all depends on the rotation schedule of the commanders."

"When was your last trip?"

"About two months ago. I was asked to support a special mission and took that opportunity to make my rounds of the new boss structure."

"I can tell you this; I'm not looking forward to my trip. I'll expect VIP treatment from your folks."

65

"Yea, right!" John laughed, "I'm sure everyone in the squadron will just be pleased as punch to see a narc on the manifest."

"I would prefer the term 'Mr. Narc' if you don't mind." Both men laughed and continued to talk about Saudi Arabia, the military contacts there and what Dillon might expect when he arrived. They discussed the need for a cover story. Not many people outside their chain of command knew about the drug connection. Dillon wanted to keep it that way and asked John to lay down a thin smoke screen about his purpose for traveling to Saudi. John agreed to get a story circulating that involved the murder but not the drug aspect. Once in Kingdom, Dillon could develop any cover he needed to further the investigation.

CHAPTER TEN

As Dillon came into the office, he asked the admin clerk to get hold of Sergeant Liebtone. Liebtone was Crimitin's immediate supervisor. He might be able to shed some light on a few minor points Dillon still found unclear. Dillon went to the conference room after wishing good afternoon to everyone in the office.

As he entered the room with a bottle of fizzy, the phone rang.

"Yes?" he questioned.

"Sir I have Sergeant Liebtone on the line."

"Thanks put him through."

"This is Agent Reece."

"Afternoon sir, this is Sergeant Liebtone. I understand you wanted to talk with me?"

"That's right sarge, what do you have on your plate later today?"

"Just the normal afternoon routine, sir. What do you need?"

"I need a bit of your time to discuss Airman Crimitin. Where can I meet you?"

"How well do you know the flight line area?"

"Not very well I'm afraid. However, I do know where the maintenance commander's office is located. Can you swing by and pick me up behind that building?"

"Sure thing sir, see you there about 1400 if that's OK with your schedule."

"Perfect, I'll see you then." Dillon hung up and took a long pull on the fizzy water. He would have to get back into his notes and put some questions together for the sergeant. Just as he was reaching in his battered briefcase, Bill appeared in the doorway and asked how the meeting went. Dillon began to relate the morning's activities as Bill took a seat across the table. They talked for some time before Christina stopped in and listened to the finishing portion of Dillon's dissertation. After he finished, they talked about the pluses and minuses.

"Seems like you got what you wanted out of Doding," Bill said as he reached across the table to pick up Dillon's notes.

Dillon took another long pull on his water and went to one of the boxes in a corner of the room. He hauled out a large file with information about Saudi Arabia. He didn't know much about the operation there and wanted to get some data in his working files so he didn't feel like a fish out of water when questioning people about their activities in Kingdom. He was thumbing through the assembled documents when Bill looked up from the notes.

"He didn't want to be known as a pusher?" Bill questioned.

"That's what Doding said. You'll notice the series of question marks after that fact. I really couldn't believe what I was hearing either. If he didn't want to be known as a pusher or dealer, then why was he playing the mule for some syndicate? It all points to someone having something on the boy and we have to find out what that anchor is all about. It was something big for Crimitin to take such a chance."

Bill just shook his head as he agreed with Dillon's summary. For a man to put his career, and in this case his life, on the line, some gigantic pressure was behind his activities. Bill finished the notes and asked a few more questions before leaving the table and returning to his office. Dillon said he was going to take a walk around the building to clear his mind and then head for the flight line to meet Sergeant Liebtone.

⁂

The view from the balcony was magnificent. The shimmering turquoise waters lightly caressed the shore as each small wave unrolled against the rocks. The quiet chipping of a phone interrupted the beautiful scene.

"Yes?" was the question into the receiver.

"They interviewed one of the men in Crimitin's squadron. All I know is the agent was there and the defense counsel. Don't know why they called him in but will try to get some information from the cops. Since defense counsel was with him, they may have some type of file on the guy. I believe his name is Dudeing or Dofing or something like that. I'll get back to you when I've additional information."

As he finished speaking, the line went dead. A waiter approached and delivered a pot of coffee and slice of double-double chocolate cake. He was dismissed with the wave of a hand holding the key to room 1507. The waiter turned on his heel and busied himself adding a large tip to the bill as he strolled back toward the restaurant area. He didn't like being treated with such disdain but he did like the fact this customer never questioned the extra tips he factored in to the bill for such shoddy treatment.

Dillon pulled his car into a vacant slot at the end of a row separating the back of the maintenance building from the flight line access road. As he did, a short stocky man approached him from the opposite end of the row. "Agent Reece?" the man challenged.

"Yes, are you Sergeant Liebtone?"

"Yes sir, come on this way, my truck's at the end."

Dillon locked his car and followed the sergeant toward a small pickup truck with a set of police type lights mounted on top. Liebtone opened his side and reached to unlock the passenger's door. At the same time, he scooped up his clipboard with the daily flying schedule attached, a set of aircraft forms, and some empty manila folders. He reached into the back and placed everything on the small seats located in the extended section of the cab. Dillon got in; Liebtone started the truck and drove toward the entry control point. Liebtone explained how there were a couple of jets to finish before the end of the day.

As they came to the control point, Dillon pulled his USAFE[11] all bases pass out of his pocket and displayed it to the checkpoint guard. As they drove along the flight line, Dillon let Liebtone talk about Crimitin in a very general casual way. He didn't want to ask any questions to lead him down one path or another. He wanted to hear about the airman from his professional mentor. This was the man designated to mold the career of young airmen as they begin what all Air Force leaders hope will be a full time job leading to a retirement check while still in their late 30's or early 40's.

As they traveled, Liebtone would stop at various aircraft lining the tarmac and ask attending maintenance personnel if they fixed specific problems or if they discovered something unreported over the radio net. They talked and drove for more than an hour. After Liebtone was finished talking extemporaneously, Dillon did have a few questions for him. Overall, the sergeant couldn't add much to the investigative picture. Crimitin was a very good troop who would get the job done. He really didn't take any notice of his almost permanent volunteer status for trips in and out of Saudi Arabia.

Hindsight is always 20/20 when reviewing situations that should have made bells and whistles go off in a supervisor's potential problem warning system.

Dillon questioned him about other crew chiefs including Doding. Although Doding wasn't his direct report, he did know about the situation but didn't know about the Crimitin connection. He was very surprised to find out there was any contact at all.

Back at his car, Dillon gave a quick call to the office to check in with Bill. He reviewed the conversation with Liebtone and asked him if there was anything on his pending flight to Riyadh. There were no important messages, so he decided to head back for his room, a shower and then off to dinner with John.

⁂

Monday morning, Dillon was in the office early. He wanted to get things moving toward his trip to Riyadh. Bill started the ball rolling Friday, so the only thing they really needed to follow was the progress of his blanket orders. Late in the day, a call came from the passenger manifest section. He was booked on a flight for Wednesday. There was a stop at Aviano Italy on the way so the transport would be into Prince Sultan Air Base on Thursday afternoon. It was the first flight available that week and if he didn't want to spend the time in Italy, he would have to wait until Thursday night for a direct flight. Dillon agreed to the Wednesday departure.

The next couple of days flew by. Dillon busied himself trying to tie up loose ends before he left the area. He knew Bill would keep him posted while Christina would be doing the meat and potatoes work of the case. It was already Wednesday morning and Dillon was making another call to Sonta. He hadn't been able to contact her and missed her return calls. He wanted to tell her he was leaving Ramstein. Another message on her answering machine as Dillon picked up his bags and headed for the front desk. He settled the bill with his Government Issue credit card and went outside to find Bill waiting for him.

"Morning," Bill shouted as he came to the back of the car to open the trunk. "Thought you might want a lift. Keeps you from having to worry about turning in your car before your flight. Besides, the motor pool came and took the car earlier this morning. You really have no choice but to ride with me." He laughed as Dillon handed him the luggage and got inside the car.

The discussion centered mainly on lines of communication between Riyadh and Ramstein. Dillon would hook into the local e-mail system so

70

the flow of information remains constant. Bill assured him that piecing the puzzle together would be his top priority and that Christina was taking this case as a personal crusade.

⚜

The single ice cube bounced off the side of the Waterford Crystal glass initiating that special ringing noise common only to fine lead crystal.

"What else do you have to tell me?"

"That's the only information I have at this time. He left the Cannon with his bags. Wilmerson picked him up; they spent time in the office before going to base operations. At the moment, we don't know where he's headed because there are several flights out this afternoon."

"Don't be naïve. You know perfectly well his destination. He'll be in Kingdom tomorrow night. Make sure you have our contact notified. We don't want to miss his activities."

"Consider it done" and the line went dead.

CHAPTER ELEVEN

Sarah looked in the mirror and straightened the fluffed out bow on the white scarf she just finished tying around the collar of her plain black dress. She noticed her hat was slightly askew, so she made adjustments and pinned it into place with a couple of unobtrusive bobby pins. She stepped back from the mirror to take in the full affect of the mourning clothes she'd chosen. The simple dress was appropriate. Her son appreciated the simple things in life and really didn't go in for the fancy frills some women wear. She turned from the mirror, stepped into the hall and headed toward George's room. She found him sitting on the edge of his bed, in his underwear, holding a picture of his brother and himself taken during his last visit home.

"George," Sarah began, "why aren't you getting dressed?"

George looked away from the picture and said to his mother, "It just doesn't make any sense. All he wanted to do was help me, and someone shot him. What in the hell did he ever do to deserve that?"

"It's very hard for any of us to understand George. They're still trying to figure out his death. I'm sure the Air Force won't quit searching until they find some type of reason. Until then, we just have to stay close and see to it we keep his memory fresh. Now put the picture down and get yourself dressed. The car will be here in half an hour."

As she turned to leave the room, a loud yell from her bedroom startled her. "Sarah" was the sound bellowing down the hallway.

"Sarah" came the howl once again, "How in the hell do you get this goddamn tie wrapped up?"

Sarah entered the room where Bill was struggling with his bow tie. "Why you insist on wearing this silly bow tie, I just don't know," Sarah said to her husband as she grabbed the tattered ends away from his huge hands.

"Because my son gave me this tie. Now I'm going out to put him in the ground and I just figured it would be right for me to have it on," was the reply from the bulky man standing in front of the dresser in a suit that was much too small for him.

"All right, all right, just keep your hands down and let me work with this thing. You've got it in such a state now; I'm not sure which end is which." Saying that, Sarah pulled the tie from around his thick neck and smoothed out the black cloth. She pulled the tie back around his neck and proceeded to form a beautiful bow under his double chin.

"There, take a look." William stood in front of the mirror and gave an approving smile when he saw the completed project.

"Thanks honey," he sheepishly replied as he reached down, took her chin in his thick hand, and kissed her forehead. For a man so gruff, he did have his moments. Sarah smiled and turned to leave the room.

"Let me check on Herman," she said as she briskly walked down the hall toward the room of William's brother. Herman was a special case. He was living with the family since his accident. He drew a small social security check and didn't cause much of a problem. Sarah found Herman sitting in a chair situated in the corner of his room. He wore the new black pants and white shirt but the tie needed some work. He was holding one of his shoes trying to get a knot out of the laces. As Sarah entered the room, he looked up and smiled.

"Oh Herman, what happened?" Herman just held out the shoe and Sarah took it from him.

"Have you got the other shoe on?" Herman's reply was to hold up his foot showing Sarah the highly polished shoe with the laces neatly tied.

Sarah worked on the laces and quickly undid the granny knot. She held it down for Herman to put his foot in but he grabbed it away and said he would do it himself. Sarah told him to hurry and go into the front room after he was done. Herman nodded his head, returned to the task of getting his shoe on, and tied.

Sarah entered the hall again to see William and George sitting in the living room waiting for her appearance. She went to the window and looked for the car the funeral home was sending. The deserted street held only fading derelict cars gathering dust under the bright California sun.

With Herman's arrival in the front room, all was ready. Sarah kept watch in the window for the arriving limousine. She turned in anger as she heard the distinctive sound of a tab leaving the top of a can. Her wrath eased as the tab removal was from atop a can of soda. She returned to her vigil at the window.

Captain Carpton and Chief Martinez arrived at the funeral home well in advance of the scheduled service. They hadn't encountered the expected traffic on their way from Vandenberg. The ride was relatively trouble free and they found the appointed location in much less time than expected. The captain suggested they adjourn to a nearby coffee shop to wait for the others.

"I'm sure glad they were able to send the airman home so quickly," the captain said in between sips of coffee and bites of Danish.

"At least the lack of information about the case will be overshadowed for the time being by the funeral."

"Right there cap," the chief agreed as he picked sprinkles off the donut he ordered. "I'm just glad there weren't any problems getting the remains released and back here. I do believe the family was suitably impressed with the formal escort. You could tell these people never dealt with the military. The letters from the commanders really set them back on their heels. To think that a four star general would take the time to jot them a note concerning their son was really impressive."

The captain looked over the top of his cup as he nodded his head in agreement with the chief. He continued to sip, as both men were lost in their own thoughts for a moment. They savored a couple of refills and talked about subjects other than the killing and the funeral until the captain said, "The crowds are gathering. The honor guard just pulled into the home. Let's go."

Both men rose from the booth near the front window of the diner and headed for the cashier. The captain told the chief to leave a tip; the coffee and goodies were his treat. The chief threw a couple of ones on the table and walked toward the door. The men crossed the street and walked up to the lieutenant in charge of the honor guard.

"Sir," the lieutenant shouted as he snapped a smart salute. Carl returned the greeting and asked if all was ready.

"Yes sir, we're prepared to provide appropriate honors for the deceased."

Carl smiled to himself as he told the assembled guard where they could find the funeral director. He hoped he never became that gung ho. He watched the guard disappear inside the building. He checked his watch to see how long the wait was going to be. Just as he did, he saw the limousine round the corner and head toward their location.

Both men moved to a spot on the sidewalk in front of the entrance and under the overhanging roof used to protect mourners in case of inclement weather. Today it was protecting everyone from a bright sunny sky. As the car pulled in, members of the funeral home staff appeared out of thin air to open the doors and assist the family. When Sarah saw Carl, she smiled.

"Thanks for coming," she said in a voice barely audible to the captain. Carl nodded as he offered his arm to escort her inside the building. William stepped in behind, George and Herman followed with the chief at the back as the group entered the doors for the final ceremony.

Chapter Twelve

Dillon approached the counter with boarding bag in hand. The technical sergeant behind the desk looked up from his work and greeted him. "Morning sir. Can I help you?"

"Yes you can sarge. I'm manifested on the flight to Aviano. Can you check on it for me?" Dillon responded as he pulled his orders from the boarding bag and laid them on the countertop.

Technical Sergeant Tim Teeds, the passenger service representative at the counter that morning, moved from behind his desk to reach for the set of orders when the phone rang. He excused himself and answered, "Unsecured line, passenger service, Sergeant Teeds, may I help you?"

Dillon watched as Teeds listened to the caller and then responded that Agent Reece was standing on the other side of the counter. He asked the caller to wait a minute and then passed the receiver across the counter to Dillon. The voice on the other end belonged to Sonta.

"We finally get to talk rather than leave each other frustrated notes on answering machines," Dillon heard her say, "I'm glad I checked my messages or I would have missed you."

"I'm surprised you found me now," Dillon exclaimed. Sonta told him how she'd called his room but the clerk said he checked out. The clerk was kind enough to transfer her to the OSI office but one of the administrators said he already left for base operations. Again, she was transferred and this time was successful in locating him.

"That's quite a bit of work just to say goodbye but I'm glad you did. I may be gone for some time and I'm not sure about the communication links in my future location. I may be able to hook into an e-mail account but don't be upset if you don't hear from me for extended periods of time." Dillon

76

could tell by the silence that this type of information was none too pleasing for Ms. Belorn.

"These long distance relationships are hard enough but if this is part of our being together, then I guess I'll have to get used to it." Sonta lamented. They talked briefly before bidding each other farewell. Dillon handed the receiver across the counter and picked up the documents Sergeant Teeds laid in front of him.

"That's all you need. Just put your bags on the scale and I'll take care of the rest. I believe you'll find the aircraft commander down that hall in the weather room. I'm not sure where the rest of the crew might be keeping themselves. Anything else I can do?"

Dillon couldn't think of another need, so he thanked him and headed for the weather room and perhaps a meeting with his driver.

Captain Peter Pullman was at the briefing desk when Dillon entered the office. "Excuse me," Dillon interrupted, "I was told the AC for the flight to Aviano might be in here."

Captain Pullman turned and responded, "I'm the AC, and you must be Agent Reece?"

"That's me, and you're?"

"Pete Pullman," was the reply as he moved from the desk with an outstretched hand.

"Glad to meet you Pete. It's been some time since I was manifested on a flight, so please let me know where I'm supposed to go and what I'm supposed to do. My goal is to be the perfect guest on your trip."

"That's good to hear; some of the boneheads we get to carry really become a pain in the ass. They think we're traveling to point A because they have to go there, not because the Force is sending us there. Why don't you wait by the ops desk and I'll be right with you." With those directions, Dillon returned to the desk where Sergeant Teeds was working and asked where he might find the ops desk. Sergeant Teeds indicated a long counter across the lobby area. Dillon thanked Teeds again and moseyed to the indicated location. Once near the desk, he picked out a chair and lowered himself into the seat to wait for Pullman's arrival.

The wait was a short one. Pete came striding down the hall, across the lobby and over to Dillon. "Just let me get the final documents and we'll be on our way," Pete said as he passed Dillon to approach the desk and the airman working behind the counter.

They spoke in hushed tones until a sudden burst from Pete brought an exclamation of apology from the airman. Pete was heard to say he understood it wasn't the airman's fault, so he shouldn't have to apologize for someone else's mistakes but he did want the man behind the counter to find out the true status and get back to him ASAP. Pete turned to where Dillon sat and took a position across from him. He folded his arms across his chest and sat silent. Dillon ventured to break the ice.

"A problem?" he asked.

"Sorry Dillon," Pete said as he straightened from his slouching posture. "It never fails when I'm scheduled out of here to Aviano. There's always a last minute addition, it's usually a MICAP[12] shipment and we have to wait for delivery and depending on how far along the load has gone, we may have to reconfigure the jet. When they give me an ETD[13], I like to make that time. Gets me in practice for the afterlife of airliners and the bottom line."

"So you don't plan on staying for a career?" Dillon asked as he shifted his weight around in the chair so decoratively covered in blue plastic.

"Oh yeah, I'm in for the long run," Pete shot back. "But when I hit the 20-year point, I'm history. I'll have more than 15 years of flying under my belt and I can find some type of aviation job on the outside. It doesn't matter where or what. If it has wings, some propulsion and slips the surly bonds of earth, I'm there."

They talked about backgrounds and experiences. More than an hour passed before the airman approached Pete.

"The final cargo is being loaded right now sir. I'll get the crew bus for you." Without allowing time for a reply, the airman turned and shot through the doors at the edge of the counter. He stuck his head out a moment later and called for the two men to follow him. Dillon and Pete collected their belongings and headed for the door.

Once inside, they saw the airman at the far end of the hall waiting for them with the exit door held open. As they stepped outside, they bid the airman farewell.

As they drove along the flight line, Dillon marveled at the activity. About half way down the line, the crew bus pulled next to a C-141B Starlifter. As they stepped from the relative silence of the bus, the running support equipment assaulted his hearing. The dash 60[14] was pumping power to the aircraft as other crewmembers scurried about their business. Dillon looked toward the rear of the aircraft to see the loadmaster carefully signaling a K-loader as the driver maneuvered into position. After placement, he jumped onto the ramp and disappeared inside the cargo toting aircraft.

Dillon felt a hand on his shoulder and turned to see Pete standing beside him. Pete put his mouth close to Dillon's ear and shouted, "Here, put these Mickey Mouse ears on before you go deaf." Dillon took the blue plastic muffs from Pete's hand and obligingly placed them over his ears. The offending din muffled as a direct result. He gave Pete thumbs up and followed him into the aircraft's cargo bay. Dillon's luggage was already inside with the bags of other crewmembers stacked against one side of the aircraft with a nearly empty cargo pallet sitting in front of all the others. Dillon put his boarding bag on the pile and again followed Pete up a ladder to the flight deck. On the deck, he greeted Captain Wanda Feelman, the co-pilot and Master Sergeant Bea (short for Beatrice) Goodo, one of the flight engineers. He then stood aside and watched the crew go through their pre-launch checklists.

After a few minutes, the loadmaster, Staff Sergeant Michael Philmont, stepped up and asked Pete to contact ground control and make sure they didn't have any other "stuff" to ship down range for Aviano or Riyadh. Pete obligingly, flicked a couple of switches and spoke to the controllers. He asked the question and listened for an answer. There was a pregnant pause as controllers checked every status board for information relating to anything that might affect the launch of this aircraft for destinations south. Dillon could see Pete nodding his head as he listened to the report.

"Thanks control," was Pete's reply. "We'll be back at you with engine start in a few."

He turned to the loadmaster and told him there wasn't anything else coming their way. Sergeant Philmont told Pete he would button it up and get ready for launch. Dillon followed him as he went down the short ladder into the cargo compartment. He saw the crew's luggage and his large pieces were neatly stored on the front pallet. A cargo net was ready for placement over everything.

Dillon was looking for his boarding bag and when he didn't readily see it, he began a search of the area. A1C Donald Dill was coming down the side of the cargo compartment toward Dillon. When asked about the boarding bag, the airman reached into to a bunk area above their heads and pulled out the bag. He told Dillon he figured that type of bag usually didn't stay on the pallet. Dillon thanked him as the crew chief left the plane to make a final walk around in preparation for engine start.

Dillon settled himself in the web seats and waited for things to happen. Pete called from the deck and asked if he wanted to sit up front. Dillon didn't need another invite. He put his bag back into the bunk area and climbed the steps.

He took a seat between the two pilots and watched as they communicated with each other, the crew chief and ground controllers. When all was ready, they started the first of four Pratt & Whitney TF33-P-7 turbofan engines. Dillon watched Wanda and Pete work in concert reviewing checklists, flipping switches and coordinating with their flight engineer. With the headset Pete gave him, Dillon was able to eavesdrop on conversations between flight deck, controllers, and the crew chief monitoring activities from his vantage point at the nose of the aircraft.

After each engine started, he would confirm a full initiation. After all engines were running at idle speed, he watched Pete put the flight controls through a full range of motion. After the checks were completed, the crew chief unhooked himself from the communications line on the giant airlifter and climbed the ladder to the cargo compartment. Once inside, he buttoned up the door and yelled to Pete that all was secure. Pete received clearance from ground control and eased the throttles forward to get the camouflaged griffin moving toward its launch point.

Once on spot at the end of runway, final checks were made with all locations concerned with launching the mission. After confirming the checks, Pete turned control of the aircraft over to Wanda for the run to wheels in the well. She received final approval from the tower and gently advanced the throttles toward the maximum 20,000 plus pounds of thrust each engine was capable of providing. Slowly the jet began to roll down the concrete strip directly on centerline. It gathered speed slowly but surely until commit speed as Wanda gracefully pulled back on the yoke and coaxed the aircraft into the air. All during this operation Pete was watching every action with the patient look of a father watching his offspring master the complexities of two wheels rather than four. His eyes monitored the gauges and his hands were never far from his controls. He responded to radio calls from the tower and quickly changed the frequency of his radio to the appropriate departure setting. Once there he talked with German controllers to receive headings and information about their departure from Ramstein to their next checkpoint.

The Starlifter rose rapidly to a predetermined altitude and leveled off. After a few more checks with controllers, Wanda pulled back on the controls and began a slow ascent to their final mission altitude. There, she finalized setting and control positions before placing the craft on autopilot. After that was accomplished, she leaned back in the seat and drew a huge sigh of relief. Pete reached over and patted her on the shoulder.

"Not bad lieutenant, not bad at all. I'm a damn good teacher if I do say so myself," Pete exclaimed as he pulled his headset off and turned toward Dillon.

"You've just witnessed this young lieutenant's first in command take-off. I was just along for the ride."

Dillon leaned forward and congratulated Wanda on the excellent job. He told her he thought she'd been doing this for years. Wanda replied it seems like centuries when you're trying to upgrade. They all laughed as Pete told Wanda to take a break. He would stay up front and keep watch over the autopilot. He asked her to give Dillon a cook's tour of the jet. She readily agreed and unstrapped to leave the right seat. Dillon took his clue, unstrapped from his seat and headed toward the ladder. The crew chief gave

Wanda a high five to congratulate her on the excellent departure and then introduced himself to Dillon.

"Airman First Class Donald Dill, crew chief," the young man announced proudly.

"Glad to meet you Don, I'm Dillon Reece, OSI."

Dillon could feel the strength in Don's grip wane as his eyes widened. Dillon didn't let go of the handshake but continued to pump the young airman's hand in greeting. When he felt his point was made, he released his grip; Don quickly excused himself and slipped down the side of the cargo compartment. Dillon made a mental note to get with the crew chief later.

Wanda introduced Dillon to the other flight engineer, Staff Sergeant Colin Caster. This time Dillon didn't get the same type of reaction he got from Dill when he introduced himself. Colin was a recently promoted good old boy from Georgia busy with studies for his next skill upgrade.

Dillon could tell Wanda was very proud of her chosen occupation and assignment. It appeared she knew just about everything concerning the Starlifter. During the impromptu briefing, they made their way to the rear of the cargo compartment. Wanda excused herself after ensuring Dillon had no questions about the equipment and returned to the flight deck. Dillon made his way back up front.

He noticed Dill sound asleep on a pallet with his arms and legs entwined in the cargo netting to prevent his becoming airborne if they encountered any turbulence during the trip. Dillon envied him for his uniform of the day. His flightsuit was perfect for clambering around an aircraft or for allowing a quick combat nap on a cargo pallet. Once Dillon reached the front, he talked with the loadmaster for a while before returning to the flight deck and his vantage point for viewing the passing scenery. They were about to begin crossing the Alps and the weather was perfect. There wasn't a cloud in the sky and the snow capped mountains shimmered in the bright sunlight.

Wanda played tour guide as she showed Dillon their location and planned flight route on a map she pulled from her crew bag. She checked their whereabouts on the aircraft's instruments and showed Dillon their location on the map. Dillon enjoyed the guided tour and the beauty of the terrain. He was amazed at the amount of snow still left on the mountains. The lakes on various valley floors glimmered as the sun reflected off their smooth surfaces. They were almost like beacons beckoning passing travelers to stop and enjoy their sereneness.

Their approach to Aviano was brief. Aviano lies at the foot of the Dolomite Mountains. Dillon remained in his jump seat as the crew prepared for arrival. The approach and landing were as smooth as silk. Pete was in charge for this portion of the trip. Once on the ground, Wanda taxied the jet to the parking ramp, keeping pace with the "Follow Me" truck operated by the transit alert crew. Once the ship was parked, grounded, and chocked, she shut down the engines and logged in the times. By the time Dillon left the flight deck, the giant clamshell doors were opening and equipment to unload the pallets designated for Aviano were approaching the ramp awaiting instructions from the loadmaster. Dillon just shook his head in amazement as he watched the ballet unfold.

After the aircrew completed everything, they boarded the crew bus and headed for their overnight accommodations. Once they showered and changed, Pete called to have a mini-van delivered so the entire group could head for dinner together. The target tonight was Tusee.

The choice of restaurant was an excellent one. The food was stupendous and the atmosphere warm and welcoming. The owner of the establishment came to the table when he recognized the crowd as flight crewmembers. He talked for a while and invited all of them to stay at the hotel attached to his restaurant the next time they were in town. After dinner was completed, he showed them his wall of honor. Patches, flags and pictures of aircraft adorned an area near the cashier. Pete showed everyone where his patch was located and Dillon promised to send an emblem from his office when he returned home. With handshakes and farewells, the evening ended.

The next morning was gloomy and bleak. Dark shadowy clouds hung on the mountaintops like some type of protective blanket, replacing yesterday's bright sapphire sky. When Dillon looked outside, he was not pleased with the prospect of launching into the gray hovering mass.

"Looks crappy outside, have you taken a look yet?" Dillon questioned Pete

"Doesn't make a bit of difference to me," Pete responded. "As long as I'm cleared to taxi, I'll poke the nose of that baby through all the gloom and doom put between me and the clear blue sky."

"I was afraid that was going to be your response" Dillon sighed

"No matter how much flying I've done, I always like to have blue sky at departure and landing. In between I can put up with most distractions but I do like to see where I'm attempting to land and from whence I've come."

"Oh quit your bitchen," Pete laughed.

"I like to play frustrated fighter pilot on days like this. I just have everyone grab something, pull back on the yoke, and wish for the best."

Dillon was hoping Pete's comments were in jest. He knew the 141 was a lot of airframe to try max climbs.

"Just let me know when I can get in the shower," he commented as he left the room and shut the connecting door.

It was only a few minutes before Pete called Dillon and told him the shower was available. Dillon was clearing his belongings and making a few notes. He quickly showered, shaved, and facilitated before dressing in his lightweight tan suit. He knew it was going to be hot when he arrived and he wanted to make a good impression on the greeting committee.

Breakfast with the crew was an informal affair. Small talk about families and friends plus the latest information about restrictions facing them in Riyadh. Until recently, there were no trips into town for shopping, dining, or visiting. They worked, ate, and slept in the confines of Prince Sultan Air Base or Eskan Village. The only redeeming feature of being a 141 crew; they knew the stay in Kingdom would be short.

The forecast for arrival was HOT and haze. Pete made sure Wanda checked and rechecked the frequencies of in route checkpoints and the final destination beacons. He didn't want to end up with interceptors off each wing as he found during one approach into Kosovo. That was one trip he would never forget and he was sure the co pilot on that mission NEVER forgot it either. They finished their discussion as they boarded the crew bus.

When they reached the aircraft, Pete, Wanda, and Dillon climbed the ladders into the cargo bay and then to the flight deck. For more than an hour, the crewmembers went about their assignments until they were ready for departure. Again, Wanda was in command and contacted Aviano's control facility for taxi instructions. Dillon was surprised to see Pete allow Wanda to drive with the weather conditions as they were. He pulled on his lap belt to ensure it was notched tightly. As the bird began to gain speed, Dillon held on for dear life.

When commit speed was reached, Wanda pulled back and the Starlifter broke gravity's hold and leaped off the concrete into the air. With the low ceiling, they were soon immersed in a gray fog. Things were happening fast and Dillon was impressed with the close crew coordination as radio frequencies were changed, headings were checked, and throttle settings were adjusted. Dillon was amazed at how smooth the ride seemed to be. He didn't say anything until they broke out on top of the cloud layer and into bright azure skies.

As Dillon looked out the windows on the left hand side of the flight deck, he could see snow capped mountain peaks shimmering in the sunlight. It was like seeing vanilla ice cream sitting on top of fluffy cotton. As they continued to climb, Wanda put the plane into a steep right turn. They headed down the Adriatic Sea toward the Mediterranean, the Red Sea and into Saudi Arabia. After reaching their cruising altitude, Pete unstrapped and told Wanda he was going to take Dillon down for some coffee.

When they entered the aircraft, Dillon noticed the cargo arrangement had changed considerably. Where the suitcase pallet had been, a very large pallet was located that looked like a portable house. He was soon to discover its purpose. As Pete approached the structure, he reached into a cupboard and pulled out a sleeve of hot cups. He handed one to Dillon and took one for himself. He then reached for a handle and dispensed steaming coffee into the cups. Pete told Dillon the aircraft was going to change missions once it arrived in Saudi. A small contingent of forward deployed troops was heading back to the United States for additional training. They would be leaving in the morning, so the "comfort pallet" was loaded in Aviano.

The remainder of the flight was uneventful. Dillon took some time to talk with other members of the crew about Crimitin but the only one who actually knew him was Dill. Oddly enough, they went to basic training together. Although they weren't in the same training unit, they met briefly during some of the rare free time trainees spent away from training routines on Sunday. When Crimitin arrived in Germany, Dill found out he was coming and volunteered to be his sponsor. They were not the best of friends but did go out with some of the other younger crew chiefs on drinking binges where Crimitin was the designated driver. Then he moved off base and Dill didn't see very much of him except around the squadron. He couldn't put his finger on it but from the time he arrived, he always seemed pre-occupied with something. He wasn't very talkative and Dill wasn't very inquisitive.

Dill really didn't supply any more information than was already in file. When Dillon asked why he acted so odd when they first met, Dill said he really didn't like agents and tried to avoid them. A friend of his was caught in a sting operation and was nearly thrown out of the Force because of an over zealous agent. Dillon listened to the whole story about how his friend was in the wrong place at the wrong time and nearly paid a very steep price for his naiveté.

It was getting near time for their arrival at Prince Sultan. Dillon pulled himself another cup of coffee from the containers and entered the flight deck for the last time. He put on the headset and listened to the conversations between Pete and the controllers. Wanda was busily taking notes to help Pete remember all the instructions. It was a tricky approach highlighted by several changes of direction to keep the aircraft away from the city. Not many non-military Saudis knew of the Air Bases existence and that's the way both the Saudi government and U.S. forces liked to keep it.

CHAPTER THIRTEEN

The intercom buzzer brought Christina back to reality from a daydream about the upcoming festival along the Wine Strassa. Christina hit the button, "What's up Mary?" she asked of the front office receptionist.

"Christina there's a man on the line who won't give his name or location. It's an outside line, so he may not be on the base. Do you want to take it? He just wanted to talk with someone working the Crimitin case. "

"No problem Mary. I'll speak to the gentleman." The intercom light went out and the flashing outside line indicator changed to a steady glow. In an instant, the buzzer again called Christina's attention to the multiline communications device on her desk.

"OSI, this is Agent Dean," was the crisp greeting into the open air of her office as the speakerphone detected her voice and transmitted to the caller. "Can I help you?"

"I hope so," was the reply in a deep very ominous tone. "I'm calling from the American Embassy. I would like to talk with someone concerning an investigation currently underway involving a man named William Crimitin." Christina furled her brow and paused for a moment before replying.

"Well sir, you have me at a disadvantage right at the moment. You know who I am but I don't have any information about you. You say you're from the American Embassy but how do I confirm that point?"

"My name is Cornelius Asterfon. My extension at the embassy is 2435. Please call the embassy, verify that you've in fact reached the American Embassy, and then ask for that extension." Before Christina could answer, the line went dead. Now came the dilemma of should she call or not. She got up from her desk and went into Bill's office.

"You aren't going to believe the call I just got. Some low life says he's calling from the embassy wanting to talk about the Crimitin investigation. He initially didn't identify himself until pressed. When he gave me his name and extension, he hung up."

Bill squinted as he pondered her statement for a moment. "We'll settle this one right away. I'll just dial the embassy, connect with the operator, check about this man's existence, and then hook into his extension." Bill hit one of his speed dial buttons and listened as the tones broadcast from the speaker. The automated answering system kicked into operation and Bill promptly pushed "0" for operator assistance. Once the operator answered, he asked about the existence of Mr. Cornelius Asterfon. The operator verified his name and office extension. Bill closed out his conversation with the operator by asking for a connection with that number.

"Asterfon," was the short answer heard from the other end of the line.

"Mr. Asterfon, this is Agent Bill Wilmerson, Ramstein OSI office. Can we help you with something?"

"Yes you can Bill but first let me apologize to Agent Dean. I assume she's there in your office listening to our conversation?"

"Yes she is."

"Let me get away from the menacing voice and the cloak and dagger stuff. I'm Special Agent Cornelius Asterfon. I work for the DEA[15]. We received information from one of our sources that fingerprint queries were made through various investigative agencies. The results of the investigation were sent to your office. One of the matches was William Crimitin." Asterfon waited for a response but got none. "I would like to visit you early next week if that can be arranged."

There was a brief pause before Bill responded, "Hang on a second," he asked as he pushed the hold button. He looked at Christina and raised his eyebrows in surprise. He quickly consulted his appointment schedule and verified that Tuesday morning around 0900 would be available. He waited a bit longer before disengaging the hold button.

"How about Tuesday at 0900 in my office?" Bill queried of the DEA agent. Without a moments pause, Asterfon agreed to the time and place. He asked for and received Bill's e-mail address to send his particulars and request TDY quarters. He would plan to arrive late Monday and depart on Tuesday afternoon or Wednesday morning.

Bill shook his head as he sat pondering what just happened. "So the big boys are involved in this?" he said as a broad smile erupted across his face. "The plot is going to thicken from now on. Have we heard from Dillon?" he asked.

"Nothing since he left Ramstein," Christina responded as she turned to leave the office. "I'll make sure everyone knows to find one of us the moment we hear from him. Won't he be surprised?"

⁂

The transition to Saudi Arabian air space was uneventful. Wanda performed well and the flight didn't encounter any unwanted escorts. As Pete maneuvered the craft into its approach position, the surrounding landscape was barely visible through a brown haze. Dillon wanted to ask a few questions but with Wanda and Pete fully engaged in their task, he didn't want to interrupt their train of thought. Pete suddenly broke the approach routine.

"This brown crap is a combination of smoke, exhaust and sand. I've seen it so thick we're lucky to see the landing lights. It's a good thing they have the capabilities they have, or I'd be setting this puppy down at some other location."

"I was wondering if this every got any worse," Dillon questioned. "I was hoping to see beautiful downtown Riyadh."

"Doesn't matter if it's a day like today or crystal clear, you wouldn't have been able to see the downtown area from our location. If you want to see a pretty sight, fly into their civil airport in the evening. You fly through total darkness and then the ground lights up as you fly over the city on approach. It goes dark again as you leave the city limits for final into the airport. It's located on the far outskirts of town."

"Depending on what happens during my visit, I may be in and out of here several times," Dillon commented. "I'm sure one of those trips will be on a commercial flight. You know how airlifter's are notorious for providing quality service on an infrequent schedule."

"Bite your tongue," Pete responded as he turned and pointed an accusing finger at Dillon. Both men laughed as Pete returned to the task. Their first approach was turned off before they caught sight of the field. Evidently, the wind direction shifted and controllers wanted the Starlifter to approach from the opposite direction. That approach was successful all be it a bit bumpy. Pete slowed the aircraft directly on centerline and turned over the taxi duties to Wanda. She drove the craft to its assigned parking location and coordinated the mission completion checklists. Pete and Dillon unstrapped and headed for the cargo bay.

"Is someone going to meet you or are you on your own?" Pete asked.

"Tell ya the truth, I'm not really sure," Dillon replied. "I just know the arrangements were made through the Ramstein office and I didn't have enough time to check on the particulars. If there isn't someone here, I'll just stick with you until someone comes to find me. I've really enjoyed the flight and getting back into the Air Force again. Sometimes I forget what's it's really like."

Dillon and Pete watched the clamshell doors open wide allowing an oppressive blast of 110-degree heat to swarm through the cargo area. Pete helped as Dillon threw back the cargo net covering the pallet containing his luggage. Dillon grabbed the cases, slung his boarding bag over his shoulder, and headed for the crew door. Pete went down first and caught the bags as Dillon dropped them out the opening. As he stepped off the ladder, he turned to see two men standing next to a relatively new Toyota Land Cruiser. One of them left the side of the vehicle and approached. "Agent Reece?" he asked as he reached out to shake hands.

"That's me," Dillon replied as he returned the greeting.

"Pleased to meet you sir. I'm Agent Karl Phobie and the man behind me is Agent William Kingston. I'd like to welcome you to Prince Sultan Air Base. Let me get your bags and if you'll follow me to the cruiser, we'll be on our way."

Dillon and Pete watched as the young man grabbed the luggage and headed for the vehicle. Dillon turned to Pete and thanked him again for the ride and the excellent dinner in Aviano. Dillon said to give him a call if he was going to be in Kingdom for a couple of days. They would get together and have dinner. Pete agreed and the two men shook hands before Dillon turned and walked toward the other agents as Pete returned to his job as mission commander.

Agent Kingston was just shutting the back hatch after putting the luggage inside. He greeted Dillon and then opened the door for him. Dillon threw his boarding bag and jacket on the seat and climbed in. It was a welcome relief to feel the cold blast of air from the cruisers air conditioning system. Karl engaged the gears and they were off toward the entry control point.

Once off the flight line, Karl gave Dillon a quick tour of the area and then headed for the main gates. Karl explained that Dillon would be staying at Eskan Village, just outside the main city limits of Riyadh.

Karl took a cell phone from the center console and dialed a number. When the other party answered, the cryptic message he delivered dealt with manifested cargo arrival. Dillon understood that using a cellular line was not a secure type of communication, so the cryptic message definitely dealt with his arrival. Karl listened to the response on the other end and then asked them to notify the attendees that the party was set for later today.

Dillon again made the connection a meeting was arranged and he was the guest of honor.

The drive wasn't as long as Dillon expected. They passed the time talking about things other than the current investigation. Dillon was eager to learn about the exotic places to eat and was a bit disappointed when the first thing out of William's mouth was the location of Burger King. He laughed and told William that wasn't exactly what he was looking for and they spent some time naming all the American fast food restaurants currently taking hold in Riyadh and about some of the others that didn't fare too well.

As they approached the control point for entry into Eskan, Karl asked Dillon to get out his identification. The Saudi guards at the outer gate gave a cursory check of the cards and cleared the vehicle into the second checkpoint where it received a thorough search. Luckily, they didn't want to see inside Dillon's bags. Once the inspections were over, Karl drove to the headquarters building.

As they arrived, Karl parked outside the front doors and asked William to take Dillon's luggage to his quarters. Once the meeting was over, they would walk over and get him settled. Dillon was already out of the backseat with his jacket on when Karl came around the back and William pulled away from the two men. They walked into the building, down a short corridor and into an office. Susan Hugfon, secretary for the commander, greeted the men as they entered. She pushed the intercom button and when a voice on the other end answered, she said Agent Phobie and Agent Reece were in her office.

A very short time later, the door adjacent to her desk opened and Major General Calvin Evantoe came into the outer office. He greeted Karl verbally as he reached out to shake hands with Dillon. "Calvin Evantoe, Dillon. How was your flight?"

"Just fine sir. Had a great crew, a great in route stop at Aviano, and a somewhat interesting arrival in Kingdom," Dillon responded as he returned the strong handshake offered by the general.

"Good, I'm glad the beginning of your trip was satisfying. I hope your stay here will be productive and we can find the underlying cause of this nasty matter. Nothing I hate more than drug involvement in my command. I'm not naive enough to think it won't happen but when we discover it, I want the cancer cut out quickly with the highest possible cost to the perpetrators."

"We're on the same sheet of music sir," Dillon said as he shook his head in agreement. "Nothing would please me more than to ask a few questions, get the right answers and close this investigation down as quickly as I can. However, I know that won't be the case and I want to be only a minor irritant to your operations."

"You won't be an irritant. In fact, I've asked my top people in for a meeting. I want them to know how much I support this investigation and that I'll not tolerate foot dragging or any other bullshit. As requested in the message from Ramstein, the men think you're here on a murder investigation. They're not aware of the other angles involved. Since that's going to be a part of your investigation, only the ones you feel have an absolute need to know will be told."

As the general finished his statement, he turned toward his door and began to say something to Susan. Before he could speak, she cut him off by saying the key players were notified and will be in the conference room in 15 minutes. General Evantoe just shook his head and smiled as he passed through the doorway and into his office.

"Remember Radar O'Riley on MASH?" he asked both men as they took seats in front of his desk and he lowered himself into the high back executive chair behind the desk. "Susan is my Radar. She has things done before I ask and some things done that I don't even know I need done. I trust her implicitly and I'll surely miss her when I leave. Any way, back to the task at hand." The three men engaged in small talk for the time remaining before the meeting.

Susan directed the tea boy to bring in water and soft drinks for the men. The general told Dillon Central Command in Florida gave him information about his investigative expertise. It was only a short time later that Susan buzzed in and announced all the players were in the conference room. General Evantoe got up from his desk and headed for a door on the left side of his office. Dillon and Karl rose to follow.

As the general opened the door, Dillon heard someone call the room to attention. Everyone around the table stood in respect as the ranking man entered the room. After a few steps inside the room, the general told the men to take their seats. As he rounded the table, he greeted the men and asked Dillon to bring a chair to the head of the table. Karl took the first vacant seat he could once inside the room. Dillon obligingly grabbed one of the spare chairs leaning against the dusky paneled wall and drug it to the head of the table.

The general pulled out his chair, stepped in front of it, and addressed the assembled officers. "You all know why we're having this meeting. I would like to introduce OSI Agent Dillon Reece. He's on special assignment from his permanent home in Florida. He arrived this afternoon from Ramstein where the initial portion of his investigation began and is still underway. I expect your FULL cooperation with this man during his stay in Kingdom. If I find out that any of you assembled around this table put barriers in his way, you'll be gone." The general paused for effect.

"With that out of the way, I'll turn this meeting over to Dillon."

Dillon listened to the general's comments and watched the faces of the men seated around the marble-topped conference table. He stood from his seat and began to brief the men on the case status. A few of the men took notes while others just listened. Once Dillon finished sharing the information he was going to share with the men, he opened up for questions.

"Before we have questions," the general interrupted. "Let me introduce the team." He started on his left and proceeded around the room until he ended at the man sitting on Dillon's right.

"Colonel Mohammod Al-Shqah, Saudi Arabian Air Force, Commander Saudi Forces

Lieutenant Colonel Felix Jewstone, British Air Force, Commander British deployed forces

Lieutenant Colonel Felipe Anjou, French Air Force, Commander French deployed forces

Lieutenant Colonel Philip Kilmer, United States Air Force, Commander of US deployed forces

Lieutenant Colonel George Monrose, United States Air Force, Director of J2 Intelligence

Colonel Morse Latamir, United States Air Force, Director of J1 Personnel

Lieutenant Colonel Oscar Owens, United States Air Force, Director of J6 Communications

Colonel Fred Newton, United States Air Force, Director of J3 Operations

Lieutenant Colonel Andrew Johnson, United States Air Force, Director of J4 Logistics

Finally, Lieutenant Colonel Willard Erpack, Detachment Commander, King Khalid Air Base, Khamis Mushayt. Colonel Erpack came up from Khamis because he's been encountering some problems in the maintenance arena and wanted to tie up a few loose ends if they fit into your puzzle."

As the general went around the table, Dillon would look at each man as he was introduced. He would nod his head and offer a brief greeting. Once Erpack was named, the general took his seat and reopened the meeting for questions. At first no one spoke. Dillon glanced around the room and prodded a bit to see if anyone needed any clarification. Finally, Colonel Anjou asked if there was any indication of alliance force involvement. He couldn't see the tie between a dead crew chief, and the French contingent. Dillon agreed in principle with that assessment but wanted to have all commanders involved during the investigation in case a lead brought him into their area of responsibility.

With no other apparent questions, Dillon turned the meeting back to the general who promptly called it to an end. Most of the men came over to shake hands with Dillon and engage in small talk. Evantoe left the room and told Dillon to come into his office when he was finished. Karl and Dillon talked casually with the commanders and after the last one left the room, they went back into the general's office. He was talking with an unknown party and signaled them to take their original positions. Both men sat in front of the desk and waited until the general finished his conversation.

"Well, what do you think of my little group?" Evantoe asked in a non-specific sense so either man could answer.

"I don't really foresee any problems general," Dillon began, "but it'll be hard to keep the drug angle away from them for a significant amount of time. Once they catch wind of that connection, each one of them will know the reason for this meeting and want to have more information than I'm willing to share at this time."

"Well men," the general began as he stood from his chair and walked around the desk. "I won't say that I'm happy you're here. This is a very serious situation and I wish we didn't have to go through this. Just keep me posted on your progress and I'll help you in anyway I can. If you need introductions, let me know. I've contacts with various agencies and if you find yourself headed in those directions, I'll be happy to give you the right names."

Karl and Dillon stood as the general came around his desk. Both men thanked the general for his cooperation and promised to keep him fully informed of any developments. The men exchanged handshakes and left the office.

Once in the reception area, Susan stopped them with a note from Ramstein. It was from Bill. He wanted Dillon to give him a call as soon as he could. Dillon asked Karl if there was a phone in his room to call Ramstein. When Karl said he could, Dillon told Susan he would call from the room and thanked her for the information. Both men left the office and headed toward Dillon's quarters.

Once they arrived, Dillon invited Karl in for his telephone call to Bill. "You never know what he's going to have," Dillon told Karl. "If you're here, I won't have to give you a call later." Karl laughed and agreed to stay. He went to the fridge to check on the water situation. He told William to have some water put in the fridge and was happy to see he took care of the request. He pulled a couple of cold ones out and brought one to Dillon as he was checking through his bag for the Ramstein number.

"Thanks," Dillon said as he found the number and reached for the phone. "I was told to drink plenty of water during my time here. Dehydration sets in very quickly I've been told."

"That's very sound advice. It sneaks up on you and before you know it, you're in the hospital with IV bags hanging all over as they try to hydrate your system. It's not a pretty sight and I've seen it too many times with people who don't follow directions." Dillon told him he wouldn't have to worry about him. He hated hospitals and if a bottle of water would keep him out of one, the H_2O bottle just became his best friend.

Dillon finished dialing and waited for someone to answer. It took a few seconds for the connection and then Penny answered. "OSI, Agent Patterson. May I help you?"

"Penny, this is Dillon. I'm returning a call Bill made to me earlier. Is he around?"

"He's out of the office right at the moment. Did he say what he had for you?

"No, he just wanted me to give him a call as soon as I could."

"Hang on a second; let me switch you into Christina. She might have something. I just came back to the office. She'll be right with you."

Dillon thanked her as he waited for Christina to pick up. When she did, it was on the speakerphone. "Dillon we moved into the conference room so I could use the speakerphone. Since Penny has been out of the office, she hasn't been briefed on the latest development. She can listen in if you don't mind."

"Not at all." Dillon replied as he prepared himself for the news. Christina went into detail about the DEA agent. She explained their surprise at having Crimitin tied to that agency. This could add a completely new wrinkle to the puzzle. She told Dillon they would be meeting with him Tuesday. When they finished their meeting, they would give him a call. If he weren't available, they would leave a message and wait for his return call.

Dillon told Christina he would make himself available on Tuesday in the OSI office. He would catch up on the documentation process and wait for their call. Christina agreed to that arrangement and asked if there was anything they could do for him. Dillon inquired about the interviews and heard they were not providing much information. It seems Crimitin was a loner and not many people got too close. That may have been fine for him but it was really making this investigation a problematic one.

Karl and Dillon talked about the case for a while and what avenues they planned to travel as they began the earnest investigation in Kingdom. Since Karl was nearing the end of his isolated tour, he developed a significant number of contacts in the local community during his tenure. As Dillon collected information, Karl could supplement Dillon's activities with additional points of contact.

Should be an interesting investigation Karl was thinking as he glanced at his watch. "Look at the time," he said. "I promised to be back at the office and bring William up to speed on our meeting. Let me give him a call and tell him I'm on my way." He went to the phone and called William. After a brief conversation, he turned to Dillon. "He wants to take in the Turkish Restaurant tonight if you're up to it."

"Heck yes," Dillon threw in. "It's not like I'm going to be suffering from jet lag or anything like that. I was wondering where I was going to dine tonight. Tomorrow I can get some stuff to snack on here but tonight I'm game for just about anything. What time should we head out?"

"About 1930 will be just fine," Karl responded. "That way, by the time we get to the restaurant, last prayer will be over and we won't have to worry about eating in the dark." By the puzzled look on Dillon's face, Karl could tell he confused the agent.

"I'll explain later," he said as he picked up his case and headed for the door.

"William and I'll be over to pick you up sometime around 1930." Dillon concluded that he didn't have to worry about a thing and said goodbye to Karl. He turned his concentration to getting unpacked and showered before the appointed hour.

CHAPTER FOURTEEN

The buzzer on the captain's phone drew his attention as he tried to figure out why the statistics for this month were looking so shabby. He haphazardly reached over and depressed the flashing button. The administrator him there was a call from an OSI agent. That drew Carpton's attention immediately as he thanked the administrator and reached for the phone.

"Captain Carpton here," he spoke into the receiver.

"Ridgemire on this end captain. I just wanted to come over and give you a briefing on what we discovered on your boy Crimitin. It's an interesting story and one that should have some bearing on the case. You free at the moment?"

Although Carl wasn't the least bit free, he agreed to meet Ridgemire right away. He knew the team in Germany would appreciate the information and he told Reece he would call as soon as they had something to report. Carl turned again to the documents scattered on his desk and made a few cryptic notes on a tattered pad. He used the intercom to call his top sergeant and ask him to make some sense out of the dubious figures for the commander's briefing that afternoon. Carl went and got a cup of coffee to sip before the agent arrived. He didn't have much time to wait.

His administrator stuck his head in the room and announced Agent Ridgemire as he came striding into the office with his hand outstretched. "Glad to meet you Carl. I'm Randy." The two men shook hands and exchanged greetings. Carl offered coffee but Randy declined.

"Had my limit already, thanks." The men went to a small table with four chairs and sat down.

"So what did you find out?" Carl asked.

At the appointed time, Karl and William pulled in front of Dillon's quarters. Since Dillon was watching for them, he came out the door just as William was beginning to walk toward the entrance. He was dressed in casual slacks and an oxford shirt. When Dillon climbed into the front seat, he commented, "Glad to see I didn't over dress. I wasn't sure if jeans were appropriate here."

Karl commented, "When we go downtown, we try to look professional. Although our haircuts normally give us away, we don't want to draw attention to ourselves when we go out in public. With the stark differences in the styles of men's clothes, we know we can't blend in with the locals but we can lessen the attention we do generate by being conservative in the way we dress."

"Is that the reason behind the Land Cruiser?"

"Primarily," was Karl's short answer.

They exited the gates of Eskan and entered a divided highway. Karl cautiously checked every mirror before accelerating to just over 100KPH. He gingerly maneuvered his way into traffic as he settled into the center lane.

"I've found in my time here if you travel in the center, your chances of becoming a target are greatly reduced. You've room to escape on both sides. If you're in the fast lane, you normally have a wall next to you. If you're in the slow lane, you're constantly moving out of your lane to pass diesel trucks bellowing black acrid smoke from exhaust pipes located right at ground level. It just isn't worth the trouble."

Dillon made a mental note not to discuss driving in Saudi with Karl. He noticed William was just shaking his head and smiling as he watched the passing scenery. Evidently, he listens to Karl's ramblings about driving in Saudi during other trips off Eskan. After a few minutes, Karl said they were approaching the Ring Road. The road is appropriately named because when it's finished, it'll encircle Riyadh's entire downtown area.

The central area of Riyadh is a conglomeration of crisscrossing streets, shops, and apartments. A person unfamiliar with the layout can get lost in a snap. However, tonight they were going to avoid the "downtown" area and head for a spot that used to be on the outskirts of town only a few years ago. Riyadh was undergoing a dramatic boom in construction and a person who comes to Riyadh and then leaves for any length of time will find the changes amazing. New shops, new homes, new roads all add to the altering face of this capitol city.

As Karl pulled into traffic on the ring road, he mentioned a couple of places they would visit later. Chop Chop square was one and Clock Tower, its collocated shopping area, was the other. They would head there on a Wednesday night (Saudi Friday) for some shopping and people watching. Right now, they were on their way to the "elevated highway" and transition to another shopping area where the Turkish Restaurant was located.

It only took a couple of minutes to exit the ring road, access the elevated highway, and approach their exit. Along the way, Karl and William gave Dillon a running commentary on landmarks and points of interest. Pepsi circle, the airfield, the Panda Store, Bob's Big Boy, TCBY, the Holiday Inn and the Sheraton, were just a few of the places highlighted as they traveled above the connecting streets crowded with evening shoppers and commuters.

While Karl negotiated the Land Cruiser into the exit lane and off the highway, Dillon noticed a very large complex on his right and asked what it was.

"It's a hospital complex that's been vacant for more than a few years because the government couldn't afford to staff it and maintain its operation. The only new hospitals opening now are privately funded by one big wig, or another," Karl said as he slowed for a right turn onto a street running adjacent to the vacant hospital.

"From what we've been told, and there are any number of stories about this place, the government built it and then stocked it with the latest models of diagnostic equipment. When the oil crunch came, they fell on hard times trying to recruit staff. They just pickled the place, kept it secure, and waited for better times. Those better times just haven't arrived in their estimation. It's been so long, they'll probably have to reequip the joint if they ever open for business. That will cost them another pretty penny. Nothing like Saudi logic when it comes to wasting money."

They came to a light and William pointed to a restaurant called French Corner. "Nice place for a sandwich if you're down in this area at lunch time. In addition, if your investigation takes you into the world of contractors supporting the Air Force mission in Kingdom, a couple of their offices are located toward the end of the block near the Air Force Hospital. We don't have much contact with them because most of their business runs through other channels. You might have more contact than we normally do if you find any connection at Khamis. That's why Erpack was here for the meet and greet. He's been having some problems and can't put his finger on a cause. You may want to talk with him at the beginning to find out what his angle might be."

"Good point," Dillon replied. "If he gets too gabby, it may influence the cooperation of other commanders. People want to help solve murders but

97

they don't like to be forthcoming in a drug case. If someone is flinging crap, they don't want to be on the receiving end."

"I don't think he has made any mention of his suspicions to anyone at this time," William added. "At least he hasn't come to our office for any assistance. We're ultimately responsible for the military activities down there but he's concerned with the contractor maintenance. That's out of our realm of responsibility unless we can tie a military member into some type of illegal activity with a contractor."

"I'll keep all of that in mind as we begin this voyage of discovery. I feel like Captain Kirk on the Enterprise *boldly going where no man has gone before*," Dillon concluded as the group approached a signal light with Karl moving into the turn lane.

"Good analogy Dillon. I'm sure there will be times during your visit to the Magic Kingdom that you actually possessed the ability to have Scotty beam you out because there isn't any intelligent life down here", William laughed as they rounded the corner with a swarm of other drivers.

Dillon watched the tango unfold and was amazed at how they just did manage to stay out of the way when some young Saudi in a brand new BMW came screaming down the road in the right hand lane and wanted to make the left turn with the rest of the crowd. He was nearly T-boned in the middle of the intersection but completed his turn and accelerated down the road.

"Damnation," Dillon exclaimed as the rear lights of the BMW illuminated when the driver nearly rear-ended a slow moving truck. "Does that happen often?"

"All the time," Karl responded. "You have to set your head on swivel when you're out driving. Defensive driving is the watchword of the day. I don't care where in the world you've driven before; you haven't seen anything until you've taken the wheel in Saudi. When you get out and about, just watch for the stupidest thing to happen and you won't be disappointed."

"I can hardly wait," Dillon lamented letting go of the panic bar he tightly gripped during the activity. Karl and William resumed their running commentary about sites along the road pointing out the furniture store with the best deals in town and the Tamimi Safeway store that closely resembled a normal supermarket in the United States. Karl said you could find almost anything you needed but you were going to pay the price. As they passed a large open area on their right, William told Dillon about the bombing in Riyadh. The empty lot was where the terrorist target once stood.

"I can see why this place was put off limits," Dillon commented as Karl pulled into a spot, set the parking brake, and took the truck out of gear.

"The bombing definitely got a lot of attention," William began, "but our government overreacted when they sent all the dependents home. This place is much safer for families than living in the states. You certainly don't hear about kids shooting kids over here. I would love to have my family here. Granted the place does have its oddities but if you have the right attitude, it's a once in a life time experience."

"I'll agree with you there," Karl kicked in. "I would only want to go through this experience once in my lifetime!"

William just shook his head as he left the truck. Karl definitely carried an attitude but he did an excellent job as the lead agent. William just overlooked his prejudicial streak. The three men waited for a clear spot so they could cross the centrally divided street to the restaurant. It was only a two-lane road on either side of the divide but there always seemed to be three cars coming toward them. Two would be in the lanes, and one would be using the space between the right lane and the rear ends of parked cars.

Once the men traversed the gauntlet, they entered the singles only side of the restaurant. In Saudi, single men cannot be in the same eating establishment as families. If you ask why, you'll get as many differing reasons as the number of people you ask. Karl was busy looking for a table where he could put his back to the wall and watch the entrance. He was bitching because he couldn't find one right away. He finally discovered a haven and the men sat down. The waiter promptly arrived, cleared off the table, and brought them an ample supply of fresh bread.

"One of the best parts of this place is the bread," Karl commented as he tore off a large piece. The waiter returned with a large bottle of water and glasses. He also threw down menus for the men to peruse as he attended to other customers. As they made their selection, Karl explained about eating in the dark.

"The first time we came here, we arrived right after sundown prayer. We got our table and ordered. Since it was a weekend night, we took our time working through the appetizers. Once the main meal came, we were engaged in a monumental discussion about cats. Just as I was putting the last bit of lamb into my mouth, the lights went out for final prayer. Diners with previous experience here pulled out their candles, put a light to them, and continued their meal. We sat in the dark until a Brit came over with a spare and illuminated our table. So, that's why I wanted to get here after final prayer. I just don't like to eat by candle light unless there's a chance I'm going to get lucky."

They all laughed and continued the small talk. The meal, as predicted, was excellent. When the bill arrived, Dillon could not believe the total cost. The three men ate one type of food or another for more than an hour and the bill was less than $26.00. Not a bad buy.

Dillon questioned the agents on where he might begin his investigation. Both men suggested a review of their findings before he headed into the field. They all agreed a meeting with Erpack should be arranged as soon as possible. He arrived earlier in the day and would want to leave for Khamis sometime tomorrow. William would arrange to have him stop by the office around 0900 for a meeting. From there, it was going to be up to Dillon to determine how much he wanted to share with the detachment commander.

It was nearly 2300 when Dillon left the pair at his front door. He thanked the men and disappeared into his quarters. The hot shower and cool beverage brought him into a relaxed state as he got out his folders to make a few notes and plan his investigative strategy for the upcoming days.

⊷⧖⊶

The computer awoke from its self-induced state of hibernation as the electronic mail message slipped through the modem to the storage disk. As programmed, the message was received, filed and a response was sent back to the sending party. Once receipt was confirmed, the sending party shut down the lap top computer and stored it away in a lockable filing cabinet next to the desk.

The correspondence was to the point.

From: POCR@totnote.com

To: mainframe@central.com.

Subject: Arrival

Message: INCO[16]. Tracking will begin as soon as moves are made. Report back as necessary.

The receiving computer stored the message and at the appointed hour forwarded it along with other messages to the main frame. From this main computer, access from anywhere in the world was possible. Main Frame didn't like to pick up messages from Totnote. Too many cookies could be laid for consumption by hackers and investigators. Electronic trails were as easy to follow as breadcrumbs in the forest. When MF did pick up the message, its contents were neatly added to the growing dossier on Agent Reece.

CHAPTER FIFTEEN

Dillon left his quarters about 0700 and headed for the building where Karl said he could arrange for some breakfast. He would get one of them to take him shopping tonight so he could stock up on foodstuffs. He was pleased to find the staff could arrange his standard early morning menu. He was a happy man as he walked toward the OSI offices after finishing the meal.

When he walked through the door, Karlotta greeted him with a smile. "Agent Reece?" she questioned as he approached her desk.

"Guilty," Dillon responded as he reached to shake her hand. "Dillon Reece at your service."

"I'm Karlotta Stevensen. I was told to expect you this morning. The others aren't in now, so I'll show you to your office. They have some extra room and decided to make you feel at home."

She turned and went down a short hallway to a room on the left. The room contained a desk, two guest chairs and a wing back chair with end table and reading lamp located nearby. The room even had a TV and stereo system sitting on a bookshelf across from the desk. The desk held, neatly arranged, all the small items the agent could require for business as usual. There was a box of pens, a box of pencils, a battery powered pencil sharpener, a stapler, a staple remover, legal size pads of paper, letter size pads of paper, a multi-line phone, a CPU, monitor, printer and scanner. Dillon was suitably impressed.

"Are you sure this is all for me and you haven't given me someone else's office?" Dillon questioned as he sat his case on the desk's edge and turned to face Karlotta.

"No sir, this is where they told me to set you up. The computer is web ready. All you have to do is get the sign in password from William and then change it to one you'll use while you're here. If there's anything else I can do for you Agent Reece, just let me know," as she turned to leave the room.

Dillon stopped her before she could leave and asked her to call him Dillon during his visit. "I didn't want to take that liberty until you felt comfortable but I see you make yourself at home wherever you are," Karlotta returned. "I'm here to help. So please, Dillon," she began adding emphasis to his name, "just let me know if there is anything I can do to make your stay more enjoyable."

Dillon's mind wandered for a moment as he thought of ways the buxom blond haired green-eyed Karlotta could help his stay become a lot more enjoyable. However, the diamond and sapphire ring on the third finger of her left hand indicated she was a married woman and he followed a personal rule, no matter how much a married woman comes on to him, he NEVER took advantage of the situation. To some of his friends, it was a damn stupid personal rule but one that he followed religiously.

Dillon went behind the desk and pulled out the chair. Next to the phone he noticed a USMTM[17] coffee mug with his name on it. He picked it up and wandered out to Karlotta's desk.

"Point me to the coffee bar?" he asked. She told him where he could find a fridge, microwave, and coffee maker. She just finished putting on the first pot of the morning, so it would be a couple of minutes before he could satisfy the caffeine craving. Dillon returned to the office and began to work on some questions for Colonel Erpack.

Karl and William both stuck their heads in the door as they arrived. Each followed a specific route every morning to retrieve message traffic and check on activities of the night before from the Security Forces. As was the norm, the message traffic was routine and no problems were encountered by security the preceding evening.

When Dillon finished his notes on Erpack, he ventured down the hall to William's office. "William?" Dillon used a questioning tone as he came into the office. "Remember how we talked last night about getting into your files for information gathered during your initial investigation?" William nodded his head to answer the questions.

"How about showing me where you keep those files and I'll begin comparing information with my notes and work on some activities we can all track."

"No problem there," William said as he came around his desk and headed for the office door. "I'll show you where all our files are in case you run across something you have to cross reference. Karlotta has rearranged our filing system into one even I can understand." William led the way down the hall and into a room near the coffee bar. Inside were two rows of file cabinets down the center and cabinets all around the walls.

"Tarnation William, I don't think we have this many files in our Florida office," Dillon commented as he stopped in the doorway.

"Don't be so impressed," William said as he went to one of the cabinets and pulled out the top drawer. "Many of these are historical records sent to us by other units in Kingdom. We have turned into the central repository for investigative reports. They keep all of their stuff on disk and we end up with the hard copies. Many of the ones around the wall store things other than case files. We'll have to find other places to store that crap if we ever get enough cases to fill these center rows."

Dillon said he understood the dilemma and watched as William explained the filing system and where the in progress investigations were located. He pulled two folders out of the file and handed them to Dillon. One of them was marked 'Karl/Crimitin' and the other, not surprisingly, was marked 'William/Crimitin'. Dillon tucked both files under his arm, thanked William, and headed back toward his office. On the way, William told him that Karlotta would be able to help if he ran into any problems.

Promptly at 0900, Lieutenant Colonel Willard Erpack, Detachment Commander at King Khalid Air Base, Khamis Mushayt, came into Dillon's office, followed closely by William and Karl. After the normal greetings and handshakes, Karl and Willard sat in the chairs facing the desk and William took his support position in the wingback. Erpack wasted no time in getting to the point of his being in Riyadh.

"Reece," he nearly shouted as he leaned forward in his chair with both hands resting on his knees, "I know you're here to investigate the death of a crew chief but I've got problems at Khamis that I'm afraid to conjecture as to the cause. It started out with little things but the other day one of my men was almost killed in a damn stupid ground accident that shouldn't have happened if the fucken crew chief was doing his fucken job! I wanted the son of a bitch drug tested because my man said he looked like shit, his speech was slurred, and he had that glazed over look you get when you're drunk or stoned. I went to the prime contractor and asked for a drug test but his smart-ass answer was why test for drugs when they're not allowed in the Kingdom. I almost shit myself. I've known this man for many years. He was one of my squadron commanders when I started in the force but he was giving me some company line crap and he wasn't about to stick his pecker out for anything. Since we had a crew chief on a 141 killed in Germany and we get the head drug investigation agent paying our little piece of the world a visit, I just put two and two together and came up with drug smuggling.

Tell me I'm wrong if you can," he concluded as he sat back in the chair and folded his arms across his chest.

Dillon was sitting back in his chair not giving one hint of reaction while the colonel ranted. With the tirade complete, Dillon paused for a moment and then asked the colonel in very polite terms if he was finished. When Erpack indicated he was done for the moment, Dillon began to speak in very soft tones.

"Colonel, thanks for the vote of confidence on my being the head drug investigator, I hope I live up to your expectations. You're right about a drug connection with the death in Germany." As Dillon spoke the words, Karl and William's jaws went slack. This was supposed to be a closed investigation until connections could be established. That wasn't the case now.

"We have reason to believe the dead airman was transporting illicit substances in his work as a crew chief. We know he made frequent flights into the Kingdom, so we naturally wanted to check on this end to see if we could establish some tie in with activities here and his death. We've naturally kept this part of the investigation away from the public domain. You're the only commander who knows about the connection. I'll trust you to keep it between us until we make a formal announcement to other commanders. If I hear so much as a peep about this part of the inquiry, you'll be the point man on an investigation that will ruin your chances for further promotion. I hope I've made myself clear and to the point." As Dillon finished, he leaned forward in his chair and rested the palms of his hands on the desk. He waited for a reaction from the colonel. He didn't have to wait long.

Erpack jumped from his chair and grabbed the edge of Dillon's desk. As he rose, the other men were on their feet too. "I don't know who you think you are Reece but don't try to intimidate me."

"No intimidation intended colonel. I just made you a promise. If word of a drug connection leaks out, I'll have you up on charges for hindering an investigation. I'll make the charges stick and you'll be finished. We can do this the hard way, or we can do this my way. It's your choice."

The silence in the room was thick as molasses. The veins in Erpack's neck bulged and pulsated as he pondered his next move. He didn't like the agents of OSI and this posture was not adding to their fondness in his heart. Erpack finally spoke.

"Reece, we both have our own views of this situation. My main concern is my men. If I'm forced to work with a bunch of drug-addicted malcontents, I want some help in getting them put on a plane outta here. I really don't care about a contractor's drive for money. I don't want to lose an aviator over something that can be and should be prevented."

"I fully understand your position colonel. Nevertheless, I'm insisting on your understanding mine. Your concerns will be part of our work. I'll personally make a visit to your location even if we don't have a tie in to the crew chief. If I can help you solve your dilemma, I'll certainly do that. However, you must keep quiet about our investigation until a later date. I hope I can count on your cooperation." Dillon extended his hand across the desk.

Dillon hoped Erpack would return the courtesy but he didn't hold out much hope. He was humiliated in front of people he could not control. A pilot's ego was fragile and not easily mended. Dillon was pleased as Erpack slowly reached out and firmly grasped his hand in a return gesture. Both William and Karl breathed a lot easier when they saw the exchange.

"You can count on my silence," Erpack responded. "You let me know when you want to visit and I'll take care of the arrangements. I certainly hope we can put my issues to rest before you go back to Germany."

Dillon assured Erpack they would do everything they could to help him solve what he perceived to be a very serious problem. Erpack turned to William and Karl, bld them farewell and left the office. When they heard the front door slam, Karl exclaimed, "Damnation Dillon, you got some brass balls."

Dillon laughed and said they just witnessed an OSI ploy. "That's why we're all called agents. We don't have to worry about some light bird pushing his command weight around. Our investigations are conducted with complete cooperation and without rank intimidation. I just pulled that out of my bag of tricks and laid it on the colonel. This time it worked well. More than once, I've found it necessary to pull some yahoo aviator's ass in to see his boss if I didn't get the help I needed. Most people cooperate if they believe they have to visit a commanding general."

"I'm impressed," William kicked in. "You were so calm and collected. I'll have to put that into my memory banks for future use."

⚓

Christina pushed the intercom button as the buzzer interrupted her adding notes to her file. Bill wanted to know what time the embassy agent was going to arrive. She told him 0900. He thanked her and the light went out. If he would only look in his appointment book, on his computer calendar, or on the sticky note attached to his corkboard, he would know what time Agent Asterfon would arrive for their meeting. It never failed. He would lose his head if it weren't attached to his shoulders.

Just before 0900, Christina made sure the coffee and sweet rolls arrived in Bill's office. They were going to meet there because the conference room was still scattered with documents, folders, and storage containers of research material. She closed the door to that room as she passed it on her way to Bill's office. Bill didn't look as she entered the room and took a seat in front of his desk. Condiments were on the table behind her. She waited to speak until Bill finished his project. When he looked up, she asked, "You're concentrating very hard. Something I should know about."

"Not unless you want to play second base for my little league team this weekend." Bill laughed as he pushed the lineup sheet across the desk to Christina. "We must play every kid at least one inning during the game. Really makes it interesting. I have some real champs and some real chumps. I know it's only a game but some of the parents think every game is the seventh game of the World Series."

"I forgot you took on coaching a team. Got to build those community service points if you want to stay on the commander's good side." Christina sarcastically retorted as she looked over the lineup to see if she recognized any of the last names from her investigations. They continued to small talk until the intercom buzzed and Agent Asterfon was announced.

Special Agent Cornelius W. Asterfon, Drug Enforcement Agency, was just over six feet tall, mid 30's in age, with a full beard. His wide shoulders were neatly tucked into a tailored suit. Bill knew the game he was playing and didn't feel intimidated by his short sleeve appearance. As Asterfon entered the room, Bill greeted him and introduced Christina. Asterfon was polite but guarded. This was a cat and mouse game played by members of different agencies. Neither side was willing to give much information without getting something in return. Bill did some research on Asterfon, as he was sure Asterfon had on him. It was a sparing game now and Bill was determined to get as much information as he could from the DEA agent.

To show good faith, Bill started the conversation after offering coffee and Danish. Asterfon accepted the offer, sipped his coffee, and ate the Danish as Bill recounted the story of Crimitin's death. He was careful to leave out some important factors and didn't mention anything about the tape recorder. Asterfon listened intently and after asking a few clarification questions, wanted to know what they expected of him. Christina was quick to answer that one.

"We would like to know how a common crew chief's fingerprints get tied into Interpol and the DEA. If you were investigating this man, why weren't we informed of the cloak and dagger work? If you weren't investigating him, how long has he been working for your agency?"

With that statement, Asterfon gave a questioning look at Bill and then asked Christina what made her think Crimitin was working for them? Christina went on to explain how some things just didn't add up in the case. She listed two or three main items that were giving her fits as she tried to piece the puzzle together. Bill knew Christina was stewing about something but hadn't pushed her into revealing her concerns. He knew she would come to him when she had no other avenues to explore. He didn't expect her to lay it all out on the table in front of the DEA man.

"I can help you with a couple of your problem areas. Crimitin was working with us. He came to us a while back with some information about courier operations in Europe. He was a participant in the movement of substance in and out of Saudi Arabia. From what he told us, he was just the conduit through which the material moved from Ramstein to Al Kharj. He made drop offs to three different people, none of whom he knew by name. As usual, everyone took a code name and operated with those references. Anyway, he wanted out and asked if we could help him. He was providing us information on his shipments and we were backfilling with known suppliers in Europe and the United States. Things were beginning to gel but then the information just sort of came to a screeching halt. He was always in contact with us. We didn't want to risk having him seen with one of our agents. We worked with prearranged phone numbers. Each one routed through several switches before it ended in our office at the embassy. When we saw the request through Interpol, we knew something happened. That's when I made the call to your office. I'm sure I haven't answered all your questions but we'll have time to work on this thing together. We want to get the person responsible for this distribution network out of the ball game and hold him responsible for Crimitin's death."

Bill and Christina took their time before making comment. This was a fascinating twist to the game and they knew Dillon would be interested in this development. They continued to talk for more than an hour. They established a means of communication to exchange information about the case. They didn't want to be duplicating efforts if avoidable. Of course, all this work would need Dillon's approval before implementation. Bill was sure Dillon had contact with DEA and wanted to make sure he felt comfortable with the arrangements. Asterfon had some other business in the area, so after the meeting, he excused himself and left the office. Bill and Christina were silent for a while as the magnitude of this revelation became apparent.

Crimitin was an informant for the DEA in an attempt to get out of the drug-running realm. Knowing Asterfon didn't give them all the details, a reasonable person could assume Crimitin was close to "breaking" open the case. The information he collected would have been sufficient for significant arrests but he was discovered and eliminated from the picture. It all fell into place. Now all they had to do was find the information and tie it all in a neat package.

"I hope Dillon's at work," Bill said as he reached for the phone. "He isn't going to believe this one."

CHAPTER SIXTEEN

Carpton depressed the keys that hooked into his superintendent's office. SMSgt Orlando S. Ubar picked up the line, "Yes sir, what can I do for you?"

Although Sergeant Ubar was not formally involved with the Crimitin case, he did know a great deal about the circumstances surrounding the death notification. His captain was one to talk out problems and after the request for assistance came in from Germany, Carpton talked a lot about the situation. "Orlando, did we ever get in contact with Reece in Germany? I haven't heard from him and that seems a bit unusual."

"I haven't followed up on the initial call sir. Let me do some back tracking to see if there was anything we may have missed."

Ubar hung up and went into the administrative office. He checked the phone log for calls to Germany and found calls made each day but Dillon was never in the office. When he asked the administrator if they left messages, the answer was yes but there was never a return call. Orlando thought this was odd, so he decided to make the call himself. Like his administrator, with the time differences, he would make the call through the command post. He told the captain what he discovered and that he would make a call later and talk with an agent rather than the administrator.

It was about 2100 when Orlando called the command post from his home office. He prearranged the call with the duty controllers so he didn't have to worry about getting authorization.

"OSI, this is Mary," was the cheerful greeting from half way around the world.

"Yes Mam, this is Senior Master Sergeant Orlando Ubar calling from Vandenberg Air Force Base in California. May I speak to your detachment commander please?"

"One moment," was the short reply as the line suddenly filled with German beer hall music. Orlando didn't have time to become a fan of the accordions and tubas because Bill picked up almost immediately.

"Bill Wilmerson, can I help?"

Orlando went through his introductions again and explained the situation to Bill. Bill went off the line for a moment as he checked with Mary about incoming calls for Dillon. Once again, Orlando was enjoying the music when Bill came back on line.

"This is mainly my fault Sergeant Ubar. I gave strict instructions about calls for Dillon but they were misinterpreted on this end and the messages were filed for a time when Dillon would give us a call. He's been so busy, he's only been communicating on e-mail, and I just haven't picked up his phone messages. Sorry for the screw up but we'll make sure he gets your information."

"E-mail will be fine if you can give me your addresses, I'll have the captain send both of you the information he has from OSI here." Bill gave him the required addresses and told him he would be looking for his message. After a bit of small talk about Germany and California, the conversation ended. Orlando made a note of the addresses and put them into his briefcase. He gave the captain a call and explained the situation. Carl said he knew there was some reason behind the lack of communication. He bid Orlando good night and told him they would work up a message in the morning.

The next day, Carl and Orlando sent a message telling Bill and Dillon the Crimitin family information. The family was not what anyone would call a sterling example of today's core family. William III faced a few juvenile encounters with the law but nothing that would have kept him out of federal service. Most were typical pranks ending up with community service to clean the mess they created. He was not involved with drugs nor did he associate with anyone caught using or dealing.

William Juniors list showed a record of arrests for drunk and disorderly. He liked his beer and he liked to fight. However, his arrest record came to a screaming halt after he married. He did have one or two minor traffic violations but it appears that a wife and child were enough to keep him out of serious altercations.

His brother Herman moved in a few years ago. He was involved in some type of accident that affected his mental capacity. He could still function but his ability to be on his own was extremely limited. Since living with the family, he improved but not to a point where he could be left to fend for himself.

Mother Crimitin was clean as white silk. She had no record of any infractions with the law including any traffic violations. She was the anchor to which this dysfunctional family clung. The final member, George, was the cause for concern.

He was a problem child from the start. While his older brother ran with one crowd, George didn't find pranksters exciting. He was hauled in for public intoxication at 10 and it went down hill from there. His involvement with drugs is well documented. Court files showed he needed detoxification when he was about 15.

About the same time, William entered the Air Force. His motive was apparently to provide extra money for the family so the rehab program for his brother could continue unabated. Dysfunctional or not, the family seemed to be close knit and this type of activity by big brother William was just out of context. There must be an explanation but nothing in any of the available records could put a beam on the reason behind William's bazaar behavior.

Carl and Orlando didn't know about the other parts of the puzzle. When Bill and Dillon received their e-mail message, it just added another aspect to the reason behind William's activities. However, there were still a few loose ends to mend before they could make a definite connection between his family and supply activities. If they could bring those into focus, the path to solving the case would be much clearer.

⁂

Dillon picked up when the intercom light extinguished. "Hey Bill, how's everything?"

"Could not be finer at the present time. You won't believe what I've got to tell you!" Bill exclaimed as he tried to maintain his composure. He refreshed Dillon on the embassy call and the scheduled meeting. Dillon assured him he recalled the information. Bill went on to explain the meeting and the connection between Crimitin and DEA.

"I had a suspicion of a tie in. To get at the big boys, they were using him but didn't watch him closely enough to ensure he would be alive to testify. I do hate it when something like this happens. I've never lost a witness and I hope I never do," Dillon replied with an exasperated tone. "Did he give you much information about their investigation?"

"Not much at all," Bill expressed bitterly. "However, I do have a few favors owed by guys at the embassy and I'm sure Betty has a few she can pull in if we need them."

"That's good to know." Dillon came back. "I'll make contact with the embassy here during my stay. Hope they aren't too tight lipped about their activities. You can never tell about these diplomatic types. The ambassador sets the pace and if he isn't inclined to help, the entire staff is mute. You wouldn't believe the number of times I've tried to get help from an embassy in some strange and exotic land only to be stonewalled because of diplomatic reasons. Makes my job harder to accomplish and all the while I thought we were working on the same side."

"We know what you mean. I can't count the number of times a lead has sent us to embassy channels and we've run into a brick wall. It's not too bad in Germany but I'm beginning to have my doubts about their true efforts to help after talking with Agent Asterfon. If Crimitin contacted him for assistance, I would have expected him to at least give us a heads up call to ask for background information," Bill recalled.

Dillon supplied Bill, Christina, and Penny with an accounting of operations where DEA was a player. It certainly wasn't a pretty picture. Dillon preferred to investigate without their assistance because they were never cooperative in nature and only wanted to take and hold. When forced to have them as partners, it was a cat and mouse game of information sharing. It was almost as if they were trying to keep score and win some type of investigative trophy instead of concentrating on getting the bad guys.

They continued to share horror stories for a few minutes before Dillon excused himself. He had an appointment with General Evantoe for a how goes it briefing and he didn't want to be late. "This is the first time I've had a one on one with the man, so I don't want to get off on his wrong side. So far, he has been a rock of support and the commanders down here have no misrepresentation about his feelings. Let me sign off and I'll give you a call later this week."

After farewells were completed, Dillon gathered his folders from the small side table he used as a filing cabinet. He was constantly adding and subtracting information in the folders, so it was easier to access the scribbling he annotated on anything from regular note pads to cocktail napkins. He wanted all of the information available in case the general asked detailed questions. Most people assigned to such a command position were satisfied with generalizations but having met the man, Dillon believed being prepared was the best path.

The walk to the general's office was HOT. Daytime temperatures in Riyadh routinely reach more than 100 degrees. The only redeeming quality was the negligible humidity.

When Dillon arrived in the general's outer office, Susan greeted him with a smile and an offer of cold water. Dillon returned the pleasantries and gratefully accepted the bottle of water.

Susan communicated his arrival to Evantoe and the general asked for a couple of minutes. Dillon took a seat on the couch and sipped his water. In less than five minutes, Evantoe was out of his door and walking over to greet Dillon. They exchanged greetings and headed back into the general's office. He asked Susan to hold all calls unless they were from his boss in Florida.

Once inside, Evantoe and Dillon made themselves comfortable in leather chairs situated close to the window. A small reading lamp and end table were located between them. Evantoe adjusted the position of his chair so he could look directly at Dillon and have a view out the window. Evantoe began the conversation.

"Ever been to this part of the world before?"

"Not on any type of permanent basis," Dillon replied as he reached into his case and pulled out the assembled folders. "I've been on investigations where I was part of a team visiting bases for specific reasons but I've never spent as much time as I will here. Now that I'm thinking about it, I've never been into Saudi during any of those trips. We were never involved with anything in the Kingdom before the invasion. After the buildup and war, I was involved with other areas of the world. My trip here is the result of a personal relationship I have with the commander of a maintenance unit at Ramstein. We were classmates at the zoo."

"I'm familiar with your background and your friendship with Major what's-his-name?"

"Littlemore, John Littlemore."

"That's it. Anyway, I naturally did a bit of checking with the folks back at McDill since that's your home station and they have nothing but praise for you, your accomplishments, and your abilities. That's one of the reasons I put the law down so succinctly to my commanders. I didn't want them to take you for just another OSI agent with his head stuck up his ass. All of us have seen them before and only give lip service to their investigations. I wanted no room for any form of misinterpretation during your visit."

Dillon thanked the general for the kind words and promised not to walk around with his head up and locked. Dillon went into a full briefing on current findings. He even mentioned the DEA involvement and his concerns for giving them too much of the pie. The general assured Dillon he would help maintain them at a distance. He did have the name of the Air Force liaison at the embassy. He was sure the man could put him in touch with the Kingdom DEA representative. Both men were sure Germany notified Riyadh and the "bird dogging" would commence. The general figured a preemptive strike would alleviate potential problems and interference. He would give Colonel Rufas D. Vinder a call to talk over the situation.

Dillon smiled to himself as they talked about the "liaison" officer at the embassy. Nothing more than a fancy name for an intelligence officer. Every nation played the game. The only difference is the inherent ability of one nation to have a better collection method than the others. The United States always prided itself on its ability to collect intelligence information. They didn't do well with the dissemination of that information but at least they had it on file.

More times than he liked to count, Dillon would be involved with an investigation and would ask the "intelligence experts" about one condition or another. If they were quick to respond, he ignored the advice. If they took their time to coordinate and affirm the information they provided, Dillon trusted their opinion.

One time Army Intelligence almost got him and some of his compatriots killed during a trip into a "hot spot." The advice was, be prepared but not worry about too much resistance. When deployed, the team ran into fierce fighting and relied on support teams to pull their bacon out of the frying pan. To say the least, his out briefing to the intelligence commander was nothing less than scathing. He almost worked out to have that SOB a part of the next investigation where Army spies assured investigators of "little resistance."

Once done discussing the case, the general began to talk about his time in Saudi. "Let me tell you about the real situation," he said as he dropped his hand into his lap and shook his head.

"I've been here just over a year. After I arrived, I wasn't too sure I would be able to make it to my anniversary. Although my dealings with coalition forces has been nothing but positive, my working relationship with the Saudis really needed some fine-tuning. Now don't get me wrong, there are many fine dedicated Saudis working hard to make their country a decent place to live and work. But the majority of these folks are the biggest bunch of egotistical, boneheaded louts I've had the misfortune to come in contact with." Evantoe paused for affect and any possible reaction from Dillon. When there was none, he resumed.

"I really didn't want to believe the stories I was told by my friends and associates who have been stationed in Kingdom before. They warned me about the driving, the lack of respect for women, the totally closed society, and its resulting problems, the arrogance of the Saudi male, and the general holier than thou attitude they possess. I received my introduction to their driving on my trip from Prince Sultan. I came in before my wife got here and was almost killed getting to Eskan. Some idiot in a Mercedes came screaming around a corner and nearly broadsided us in the middle of an intersection. We were in the right place at the wrong time. Thank God my driver has been here a while and is normally prepared for all contingencies. He made his moves and the Merc ran off the road and overturned. When we drove off, I asked why we didn't offer assistance. The driver said if we were any where around when the police showed up, if they showed up, we would be to blame. No matter the facts, if we weren't in Kingdom, the Merc wouldn't have had to swerve to avoid a collision and wouldn't have rolled over. Even though he ran a red light and flew into an intersection when he should have been stopped, it would still be our fault."

Dillon nodded his head to keep from having to make any comments. He was getting the impression this was cathartic for the general.

"Just before I got this assignment, one of my friends came over for dinner. He just completed an exchange tour with the Navy at their base in Bahrain. While there, he spent some time with our forces in Dhahran. It's just a short drive over the causeway so he couldn't resist checking on some of the rumors he heard. In Bahrain, women work, they drive, and they dress with respect to the interpretive rules of their holy book. He was amazed at the differences in the treatment women receive there and the treatment in Saudi. When you see women out, it's normally always with a male member of the family. That male may only be 10 years old but he's the one driving the Suburban and keeping a watch on mom and his sisters." The general got up from his seat and walked over to a small credenza with a coffee pot and utensils.

"Want some coffee?" he asked. Dillon said yes and the general set about fixing a pot of coffee while he continued his discussion.

"If you ask a Saudi male about the reasoning behind the black garb for their women, you'll get a different answer from each one you ask. Some will say in one fashion or another their holy book directs them to shroud their women. Others will say it's a custom to protect their women from marauding enemies. Another version is to protect the men from having impure thoughts about someone's sister. It's very strange and something I just can't get used too. I have two daughters and I want them to have every opportunity possible for advancement and success in life. Here, a woman has no rights and no possibility of success unless she's a baby machine. Marriages are arranged and the younger you get one the better off you are. One of the guys around here got married to a girl still in school. He's only 28 so the age difference wasn't that large but she was still in school! I just couldn't believe it. He took her to the United States for a honeymoon and I guess all they did was screw.

115

Their first child was born almost exactly nine months to the day after their wedding. You know damn good and well they weren't engaged in anything but casual conversation before they were married. He told me about the meetings they had after this guy's aunt told her friend about his availability and that a union between the two families would be a good thing. He faced more than a couple of meetings with the male members of the family and his intended served tea at most of the meetings. I asked him if she was veiled when they met and he looked at me like I had two heads. He waved his hands at me and said 'Certainly Not' with a flourish. 'How could I know if she were anything but beautiful?' I apologized to him for my lack of knowledge on the subject but then we sat down and I explained the courting rituals of American culture and he was fascinated. Although he was very familiar with America and what it had to offer, he never went there seeking a mate. I do believe all he did was fornicate anything wearing a skirt."

One of the things Dillon noticed was the effect of being a closed society. It was as if some of the young Saudis were longing to have news about the "outside world". Their newspapers were controlled and firewalls limit access to the Internet. Because of this closure, when a young male leaves the Kingdom for any reason, you can count on seeing him blind drunk and acting like a total ass. Alcohol is banned in Kingdom but if you have the right connections and enough money, you can have free flowing spirits of any type at any time. The black market is alive and well in Kingdom.

The general did say that things were improving in the larger cities. Restrictions were coming down and those without the good things in life were learning a lot more about the haves. Those lessons normally precede revolution but he wasn't sure if that would happen here. If it did, he didn't want to be any where around when the people decided it was time to get rid of the monarchy and have some of the oil riches for themselves.

"From what I see, the military is still very loyal to the King. If that wanes, there could be trouble. Since my forte is war making and not diplomacy, I won't venture a guess on the temperature of the desert people still roaming after their goats and camels. This is the way they want it and nothing is going to change. When oil was discovered and the haves became rich, they didn't plan for the care and feeding of the populous. They just set up a self-propagating lineage where becoming a royal assured you and your family eternal riches."

Although the things they talked about were points of concern, the biggest complaint Evantoe voiced about the Saudis was their arrogance. Laws are not made for them because they are *SAUDI*. This arrogant attitude is probably the root of all the other irritants. Traffic laws, no mind, they don't apply to them, they are *SAUDI*. Respect for women, none because they are *SAUDI*.

He related a story where he was in a grocery store at the bakery counter. "There were several people ahead of me so I waited my turn. When the other customers were served, the clerk looked at me for my order. All of a sudden a little thobed blur approached the counter, stuck a 50-riyal note in the air, and shouted SAUDI!!! SAUDI!!! The clerk couldn't see the little guy, just the note above the counter. He ignored the continuing shouts of SAUDI until he took my order. Now this is the best part. By that time, the arrogant little shit attracted the attention of his mother who promptly came over and whacked him on top of the head with her purse." Evantoe smiled at the remembrance.

"If that would happen more often, we wouldn't be facing many of the problems we are face today," the general concluded.

Dillon considered himself a good listener but the ramblings of the general were beginning to get on his short list. It was nothing but complaint after complaint for more than an hour. He needed to figure a way out. During a pause in the general's discourse, Dillon interjected. "Let me ask you a blunt question if I may be so bold?"

Evantoe looked at Dillon and told him to give it a shot. "If you're so damn displeased about being here, why did you accept the assignment? Why didn't you just call it a career and set up a consulting business like all the other generals?"

Evantoe pondered for a moment and then replied, "Good point Dillon. However, I wasn't really pissed off at the assignment. Most of my predecessors went on to much better and bigger things. This was their final assignment before a third star. My wife and I did have one hell of a discussion about that consulting option. If this were a remote, I would be on the streets right now. At this point in my career, we both couldn't see us separated for that length of time. We played the combat tour game during Viet Nam. We figured our dues were paid and we were supposed to reap the benefits now. Two buttons on my shoulders are a direct result of our teamwork. She kept me out of trouble more than once with her sound guidance, so I couldn't see letting her sit at home while I cavort with the rag heads."

Another tirade Dillon thought but he did have a point. "Well sir you've totally tainted my perception of the Saudi Arabian people." He jokingly hung is head in a gesture of despair and wrung his hands. Evantoe stopped his pacing and laughed aloud.

"Of course you know this conversation never took place. I've nothing but great respect for our Saudi brothers and respect their culture to the utmost." Dillon stood up and walked over to the general.

"Sir, if you need to have a vent for your frustrations during my stay, just give me a call. With the support I'm getting from your slot, I'll make myself available at any time. You can count on my discretion in all matters."

Evantoe reached out and shook Dillon's hand. "I knew I could after the first time we met and of course after the background check I did with your folks back at McDill." Both men smiled as they finished their handshake and Dillon moved to gather his files.

"Just keep me posted on your activities and we'll do everything we can to help you bring this puzzle to a swift conclusion," Evantoe said as Dillon walked toward the door. Dillon thanked him, opened the door, and stepped into the outer office. As he shut the door behind him, Susan handed him a note.

"I believe he said his name was Pullman," Susan cooed as Dillon read the note.

"Thanks," he said as he made his way to the exit. "Where is this number?" Susan said she thought it was on the air base but wasn't sure. It wasn't a prefix she recognized. Dillon thanked her again and left the building. It was even hotter than his trip this morning. He welcomed the relief of the OSI offices and another cold bottle of water.

Evantoe decided to give Vinder a call as soon as Dillon left the office. He wanted to give the colonel a heads up to ensure his full cooperation when Dillon made his initial contact with embassy officials. He called out for Susan to get hold of the embassy operator and ring into Vinder's office. It was only a few moments until she buzzed in and told him Vinder was on the line. The general picked up, "Liaison office, Colonel Vinder," was the greeting offered.

"Rufas, this is Calvin Evantoe. How's business this fine day?"

"How you doin general? It's been some time since we last talked," Rufas responded with a friendly tone to his voice.

The men exchanged small talk for a while before Evantoe went on to explain the reason for his call. Vinder listened without interrupting until the general finished. When he replied, his answer surprised the general but it wasn't totally unexpected.

"We didn't have a DEA man down here until this Crimitin guy contacted the folks in Germany. My office got a call from State asking for a secure conference call with the ambassador and a few other key players. Once that was done, we got a new man and he began to work within our system picking up what he could about Crimitin and his activities. I don't really know what he's got into because I've been busy with a few other projects. However, With Reece in Kingdom, I'll get a briefing worked up and wait for him to contact my office. Make sure he comes directly to me. I've been keeping this on a need to know basis. Since the penalties for drug use in Kingdom are very strict, we don't want to have any wild goose chases' taking place and the Saudi's getting involved before we can wrap it all up in a neat package." Evantoe agreed with the colonel's assessment and told him when Dillon made contact with the embassy; it would be directly with his office.

They talked for a while about things other than Crimitin. It was some time since they crossed paths but Evantoe knew Vinder was a man on his way up the ladder of success. In the majority of cases, military commanders in their locale of service do not subject liaison officers to investigation. Nevertheless, Evantoe liked to have a handle on all US military serving in any capacity within his area of responsibility. Vinder was in the job for about seven months and Evantoe knew he could be trusted to keep his word and if he could, keep the general informed of activities that might affect operations. This was the first time Evantoe came to the colonel in an official capacity. He had full faith that future contact with the man would be productive for Dillon and his investigation.

CHAPTER SEVENTEEN

Bill dialed the number for the German crime investigation lab in Munich. The small piece of plastic Dillon took from the trunk of Crimitin's car received local analysis but Inspector Ubermann wanted another opinion before he submitted a report. He sent the evidence to Munich for confirmation of his find. When Bill requested an update, Ubermann gave him the lab's number and asked him to give them a call for a status report. Bill was just getting around to making that call.

Once connected with the lab, it wasn't a simple process to get the update information. There were people to check with and clearances to obtain. Bill thought he was going to get a pot load of information but all he got was a confirmation of the findings from Kaiserslautern. That wasn't what he wanted to hear. He wanted to know what they found. However, the investigators were not going to give him that information because the request was only for confirmation, not conclusions.

Bill sat listening to the very formal reasons behind their refusal to provide specifics. Once the reasoning was completed, he politely bid them farewell and hung up. He immediately dialed Ubermann's number.

"Inspector Ubermann."

"Hanz, this is Bill Wilmerson. I just talked with the nice people in Munich and I really don't have any more information than before I called. They checked with everyone they could check with, told me to hang up so they could call me and confirm my location and even gave me a long dissertation on why they couldn't give me more data than they were providing. I felt abused by the time I hung up."

Hanz asked if they said anything about confirming his findings and when Bill said they had, Hanz was very pleased.

"I asked you to give them a call, because they've been told to give full cooperation to NATO[18]allies in any type of investigation. If I would have given them a call, they would have been very rude, I wouldn't have gotten the information I needed and would face additional waiting time for my report because I had the brass balls to call them and ask a question."

"Ok then," Bill began, "just what are you trying to confirm?"

Hanz said he didn't want to speak about it over the phone, so he would like to meet at a location of Bill's choosing after work. Bill asked him to join him at the club for a drink with his wife. Hanz agreed and said he would be there about 5:15 or 5:30. Bill agreed, hung up, gave his wife a quick call to set it up, and then called Christina to have her come into his office. When she arrived, he asked about the plastic.

"Just what were your suspicions about this bit of plastic?"

"Not many at the time," she began. "Dillon is concerned about the possibility of two cars at the scene. When the trunk wouldn't close and he found the plastic, we bagged it, tagged it, and sent it along to the K-Town lab. Hanz was the one who sent the stuff to Munich."

"I know that but did we have anything other than Dillon's sixth sense working here?"

"No. We talked about finding some type of tie in evidence on the plastic but until you started kicking it around, I haven't given it a second thought. I knew the report would eventually make it back to the office, so it wasn't high on my list of priorities."

"I would have been waiting for the report too but Hanz gave me a call and asked if I would call the folks in Munich. I did that but they didn't do anything but 'confirm' his findings. I'm going to have a drink with him at the club after work. You're welcome to join us for the full story if you want." Christina agreed.

On the other side of K-Town, a man with important information was using a pay phone in a discrete location. When his call was answered, he relayed his message and immediately hung up. His point of contact now knew about the after work meeting.

Bill drove by the personnel offices to pick up Betty. She was waiting for him at the front entrance. When she slid into the front seat, he leaned over and gave her a welcome to the end of the day kiss. They engaged in small talk about her day while on the way to the club. He parked near the casual bar entrance and opened the door for his fetching wife as they entered the domain of circulating aviator sharks.

One of the good things about being associated with OSI was the stick actuators always steered around the girlfriend or wife of an agent. No one was sure how much power the agent would wield to keep her out of harms way. Bill was always thankful for the perpetuation of that barroom myth.

Betty sat at a table in the corner while Bill went and ordered beverages. One of the servers came over and greeted Betty with a warm smile and an offer to get a basket of popcorn from the bar. She said it just finished, so it would be nice and warm. As the server departed, Christina arrived with a drink in hand having stopped by the formal lounge on her way in from the front parking lot. She waved to Bill as she took a seat next to Betty.

"Was that Francy?" Christina asked setting her drink on the club logo embossed bar mat.

"Yes it was," Betty replied. There was a personal reason for the server knowing Betty. She was an active duty airman who recently divorced her husband when she found him cheating with one of his coworkers and classmates. He was banging the bitch in their bed while Airman Francy Zimermon worked her second job at the club to help pay for his college education. Lucky for him she didn't have a weapon handy.

She was a member of the security force administrative staff and trained in the use of deadly force. She maintained her cool and threw the bastard out on his ass. Betty came into the scene because the coworker was an airman and Francy's husband was a Staff Sergeant. Court martial proceedings began for his flagrant violation of fraternization rules but Francy agreed to drop the charges if he was transferred out of Europe. Betty worked with the Judge Advocate's office to make sure that happened.

Bill finally came back to the table with beverages. Again, they engaged in small talk about their day before Hanz appeared at the entrance looking for their table. Bill waved and Hanz headed their way. He made a stop at the bar to pick up a lager. Once at the table he greeted Bill, Betty, and Christina with a hearty handshake for Bill and a warm kiss on the cheek for the ladies. He pulled up a chair and took his place at the table.

He began his visit with small talk about the weather and a few other topics before Bill cut in and asked why he wanted to meet and why he couldn't talk over the phone. Hanz gave a nervous look over his shoulder as he began.

"For some time now, I've been aware of a monitoring operation being run at my headquarters. I normally don't worry about the information getting into other hands but this investigation has wide-ranging implications and I don't want to have any prying ears tuned in to our work. So, if I seem a little hesitant on the phone, trust that the real information will get into your hands before the end of the day. Normally I'll come right to your office with the news. I must protect myself and my close hold investigations from the person monitoring my communications."

"I'm sorry to hear that Hanz. Do you've any idea about who or why?" Bill asked.

"I've got a short list of prime candidates but I don't want to jeopardize this investigation by yanking his ass in at the present time. Once we wrap this thing up, I'll shut all avenues of approach and the circle will be closed."

They talked for a while about cases compromised by internal leaks until Hanz was ready to delve into his news. "When the sample of plastic was sent to our lab, one technician handled it from beginning to end. I trust her implicitly. She ran all the normal tests and did discover a microscopic bit of blood on the evidence. She ran typing on it and found it was the same type as Crimitin. We ran a DNA comparison with a sample held by the coroner's office. When we had the results, I sent all the information to Munich. They worked up their own set of tests and did a comparison with what we sent. Your phone call today confirmed our test and the fact the plastic found in the locking mechanism of Crimitin's car contained a trace of his blood. So we can postulate now that Crimitin was shot at another location, wrapped in a plastic sheet, placed in the trunk of his car, and driven back to his house. There he was unwrapped and placed on the sidewalk. The shooter then left in another vehicle or walked away from the scene. Since no one saw or heard another car, we can assume he walked away with the plastic for disposal at another location."

"Sounds good to me, Hanz," Bill said while making a few notes on a small pad of paper he carried in his coat pocket.

"But what if we find a large plastic sheet among Crimitin's possessions. He could have cut himself when working around the plastic sheet. That would certainly explain the blood."

"Your summation is certainly correct but I would like to think along a more positive line. We're going to find a car with muddy shoes and a large plastic sheet in the trunk. Tie this one up right away."

Both men laughed at that prospect as Betty was trying to get Francy's attention for another basket of popcorn. The Happy Hour buffet line was being prepared and Hanz agreed to stay for snacks. Bill said he would give Dillon a call with the good news. He knew Dillon was suspicious about a second car. Now all they had to do is locate one and hope all the incriminating evidence is neatly stored in the trunk.

CHAPTER EIGHTEEN

Dillon made several calls to the number Susan gave him. No one ever answered. He completed his work for the day and was getting ready to head for the house. Karl asked if he made plans for the evening and Dillon told him he planned to sequester himself with a nice pork steak and a bottle of fine wine.

The walk home was a short one but still stifling hot. Once inside his villa, he dropped his case on the coffee table, reached into the fridge for a beverage, slouched into the overstuffed chair near the couch, and flicked on AFRTS[19] for the news. At that moment, the only thing on was sports and he wasn't interested. He surfed through the channels until he came to a music channel. He put the clicker down and watched the gyrations of some pubescent female as she squeaked out the latest number one song. When the front bell rang, he opened the door and found Peter standing on the other side.

"No wonder I couldn't get you on the line, you're not there, you're here!" Dillon exclaimed as he shook Peter's hand and ushered him into the villa. "So why are you still in Kingdom?" Dillon asked as Peter took a spot on the couch.

"It's not a very long story," Peter began as Dillon walked past him and into the kitchen for refreshments. "We turned over the aircraft to the crew flying the guys out of here to their training. We then got on the board for the next thing smoking north. I talked with the folks back at Ramstein and they told me I could wait a couple of days, or I could come home commercial. Since I talked with other crewmembers in a sort of informal debrief of the mission, one of their biggest concerns was Crimitin. I knew there was more to the story, so I sent all of them home and told Ramstein I was going to take a couple of days INCO to tie up a few loose ends with you. They said they understood and I was to be on stand by for a flight. Told them OK and here I am."

"So what were the concerns of the crew?" Dillon asked. Peter began to tell Dillon how their suspicions of Crimitin grew for some time. Especially Dill. Dillon said he felt there was more to the Dill story than he was letting on.

"I've worked with all of these people many times before. Crimitin was a different kind of bird. Could never put my paw on the reason but he just didn't seem kosher. Did a fine job as a crew chief I never had any complaints. However, when we are INCO, he would turn into another person. I guess I should have intervened and perhaps he would still be with us."

"Hang on Peter; don't even get involved in the blame factor. I believe Airman Crimitin made his own bed of thorns. There were plenty of people in a position to assist but just didn't feel the time was right. It's really a tough call."

Peter continued to relate concerns and how crew dogs would keep checking other people to see if they could add any light to the subject. Dillon was grateful for any assistance he could get especially from the aviator ranks. They continued to talk for a few minutes and then Peter asked the tough question. "Crimitin was moving drugs on board. Wasn't he?'

Dillon paused for a moment before answering. "If we get into this conversation, I'm going to trust you not to discuss it with anyone outside this room. I trust your integrity because of your actions during our trip. Besides, I know who has this information and it would be easy to track down a source for punishment. I've kept the local commanders out of the loop because I don't want to have them interfering if I run into their private domain. The commander has pledged his full support and we've already discussed possible leaks. He would be the one you deal with and I'm sure you don't want to go there."

Peter agreed with everything Dillon said and listened intently while Dillon laid out the problem he was facing. He gave Peter the condensed version, because all the details were only helping to solve the case, not gather information about the case. Once the explaining and questioning finished, Peter told Dillon there was another reason for staying INCO.

"After my discussion with the crew and my unfuzzy feelings about Crimitin, I did some checking around the base for a point of contact to peg my fun meter. I heard about a couple of compounds that host gatherings of men and women for the sole purpose of entertainment. I didn't mention them to you on our trip down here because I knew you would be too busy on the case to partake of such debauchery. However, since my suspicions have been confirmed, we might want to hit one of these places and see if we can dig up a lead or two."

"Well my fellow Sherlock, let's talk some more about these establishments and perhaps I'll take you up on your offer. One never tires of debauchery." The two men sat through another round of drinks and talked about the underground network throughout the Kingdom. If you get the right contacts, you could get anything you wanted. They came up with a plan of attack and agreed to head for one of the spots the next night. They only operated on certain nights and showing up when things weren't happening would certainly be bad form. After setting up their plans, the men watched a bit of television and went down to the centrals for some supper. Dillon missed the call from Bill with the latest development.

⚜

Dillon was on his way from the dining facility to the OSI office when the general pulled up and offered him a ride. Once inside the car Evantoe asked Dillon to come by his office later that day. When Dillon asked what the meeting was about, the general just said he had some things to get on the table. Dillon mentioned his meeting with Peter and asked if he could come over now and they could get everything talked out. The general agreed as they drove to his office.

Evantoe threw his hat into one of the side chairs as he walked behind his desk. Dillon was already at the coffee pot getting things ready for some java. Since they came in the back entrance, Susan stuck her head in the door to make sure it was the general. Once she saw him, she asked if he needed anything. When he told her there wasn't a thing right at the present time, she excused herself and closed the door. Dillon got the coffee brewing and came over to sit in front of Evantoe's desk. Once he was comfortable and Evantoe finished his morning read file, Dillon began to relate the meeting with Peter. Evantoe listened intently and only interrupted Dillon when the coffee was finished and he wanted to get his first cup.

He understood the concern of fellow crewmembers and appreciated the situation Peter found himself confronted with. He was a bit concerned about the two of them heading for a party compound. The general was privy to data concerning the black market trade in liquor and females. He warned Dillon about the type of individuals running the show. Dillon could check the files in OSI for some target names during his evening out. He appreciated the general's concern but assured him he knows all about black market operations.

They continued to talk for a few minutes about things other than the case. Evantoe was on a roll again when Dillon asked about the abilities of the pilots. The general just shook his head and sighed.

"I've never seen a flying club like this one. If you're a royal, you get to be a pilot no matter what your qualifications. Some of these jokers take so long in flight school, we're afraid to upgrade them to their front line fighters. If you can't handle a trainer, how in the hell can we expect them to handle a high performance piece of machinery like an Eagle or Tornado. However, the high time pilot in the Eagle is a Saudi. He's a squadron commander now and just keeps racking up the hours."

"How are his abilities?" Dillon asked. "With all those hours you would think he would be able to teach our guys a thing or two about high performance fighters."

"That would be true if the pilot was an Israeli. These guys just punch holes in the sky most of the time. For example, they have to fly so many sorties at night to keep their qualifications. If it's past official sunset, they get off the ground, fly around for a few minutes, and then put it back on the ground. They lost one of their jets along with the pilot during a night training sortie. The kid just wasn't ready for the mission. Most of them never are. He was disoriented and bunged the jet into the ground. One of the interesting things was he flew the route during the day but hadn't been getting his night sorties when it was actually dark. When the lead went right, he went left, went inverted, and hit the ground upside down. There wasn't enough left of the jet or him to fill a packing crate. The reason we know he was inverted was a bunch of goat herders were having their evening tea and watched him smash into the rocks. Another one of their rocket scientists was showing off for his village elders and put it into the ground after he hit a high-tension wire. His whole family saw him go down in a ball of flames. They just don't think about what they're doing and the possible consequences. They have zero situational awareness. They figure their almighty will protect them. We've already talked about their driving skills. They have none. The have no peripheral vision because of their gutras and they don't use their mirrors, if they're still attached to the car. Just makes me scratch my ass and ask why in the hell did I take this job. But, we've already covered that ground and I'm sure you have some research to complete before your outing tonight."

Evantoe got up from the desk and collected the coffee cups. He went over to the table and set them on a tray. Dillon gathered his case and was waiting to shake the general's hand when the intercom came alive and Susan announced a call for Dillon.

"Agent Reece," Dillon spoke into the receiver.

"Dillon this is Bill, I'm glad I caught you. I've been trying to track you down since yesterday evening."

"Well Mr. Wilmerson, you must have something of importance to tell me. Let me put you on the speaker so the general can listen in too." Dillon reached over the desk and pressed the button for the speaker. He then went through brief introductions so both men knew who was on the line.

"General, I hope Dillon isn't causing too much trouble for you," Bill began. "Once he gets on the trail, he's tough to stop."

The general assured Bill he felt confident that after his time in Kingdom, he would have some solid information for tracking down the perpetrators and the leaders. Bill went on to tell both men about the forensic findings on the plastic.

"Dillon, it appears your sixth sense was working well on the matter of a second car. I just wish we had more to go on than a small piece of plastic," Bill lamented.

Dillon asked Bill to get with the K-Town police and revisit the road at the top of the hill. "I would say that's where the car was parked waiting for the killer, or his partner waited up there for him to drop off the car and body. Since it's only one house from the end of the street, he would draw less attention walking up the hill than back down the street to get in a car someone might remember."

Bill agreed with the reasoning and said he would get with the locals as soon as he could. With Hanz making the discoveries about the plastic, he was sure there would be no resistance on visiting the area again. They talked about a few other points in the case and then hung up. Evantoe could see the information was pleasing to Dillon. When he asked about the plastic, he was told how it was found and why they were so interested to tie in a second car. They could then speculate he was killed at another location and dumped at his doorstep.

Dillon thanked the general for the coffee and conversation. He bid Susan good morning as he headed back toward the OSI office. He wanted to do a bit of research into the local black market hierarchy before his night out. Since the weekend was coming up, he knew he could sleep in the next morning. Peter agreed to pick Dillon up around 2100 for their trip to the California Compound.

CHAPTER NINETEEN

Dillon agreed to meet Pete at the Eskan Community Center before heading into town. Pete knew there would be ample amounts of food at the other compound but it normally consisted of snack food. He wanted to ensure they both put something substantial on their stomachs in case they decided to do some serious drinking after their talks with the main players. It also gave the men time to develop a cover story. They didn't want to raise too much attention on their attempts to gather information about the drug trade.

For this particular exercise, Pete would maintain his persona as the 141 pilot and Dillon would be guised as a pencil pushing personnel type from Florida on temporary assignment at Eskan. Pete and Dillon were acquainted because Dillon flew with Pete on several occasions. Since all the information on Pete's side was true, it would be much easier for him to follow Dillon's lead as he talked and questioned. They would only use first names or no names at all to delay any checking the marks might run on the pair of new players. Dillon already arranged with the folks in personnel to have all questions concerning his employment at Eskan routed through Karl's cell phone.

Dillon didn't share too many of his secrets, just enough for Pete to understand the serious nature of dealing with smugglers. However, from what Pete was able to pick up, this crowd was mainly involved with booze, sex and a bit of the wacky weed. They were betting information about the harder stuff would be available from this crowd.

Pete picked up a late model Suburban to use during his time in Kingdom. It was amazing what the motor pool stashed away in their parking lots. Pete used his aircrew influence to gather one off the ready line. He made a positive impression on Dillon when he pulled in front of his villa.

"Could you find anything bigger?" Dillon questioned as he pulled himself into the front passenger seat.

"Nope," Pete replied," this was the biggest thing on the lot. Don't want to take any chances with the bumper car action on ring road." He smiled as he put the truck into gear and headed for the floodlit gatehouses.

Once through the concrete block maze, he maneuvered his way to the main highway running toward the bright lights of Riyadh. While driving, he asked Dillon to pay close attention to the landmarks. He wasn't sure but if the night was productive, he may have a couple of liquid refreshments too many for a safe drive home.

"So what makes you think I won't imbibe myself?" Dillon asked.

"Not this time," Pete returned. "You'll want to keep your wits about you as we gather information. Getting a snout full would be in fine keeping with my aviator disguise." Dillon just shook his head and laughed as Pete made the transition from access to ring road. They didn't head directly into the city but kept on a vector toward the airport. Dillon watched the numbered exits pass by until Pete put on the turn indicator and thread his way to the ramp for exit nine.

At the stop light, he turned away from the ring road and down a four-lane avenue with no working streetlights. Since there was no moon in the sky, the roadway was pitch black. Dillon could see lights in the distance with their source becoming clear as they approached. A gas station was strategically located next to a brand new Burger King. Just beyond the two businesses situated in the middle of nowhere, was a signal light at the first intersection they encountered since leaving the ring road. Pete hesitated briefly as he checked all directions at the crossing. Although he had the green light, (In Saudi Arabia only one road can traverse an intersection at a time) he wanted to make sure an inattentive driver didn't speed through the red light. Since there were no headlights visible for some distance, Pete made the left turn to the cross street. As he did, a blaring horn assaulted both men's senses as a vehicle blew by them on the right. Neither headlights nor parking lights were illuminated on the small truck.

"DAMN," Dillon shouted as he caught his breath after the narrow escape. "Where... in... the... hell... did he come from?"

Pete was too stunned to respond. He just sat shaking his head for a moment before he answered. "I never saw him and I was looking down the same roads you were. He must have been just out of the intersection lights when I made the turn. Without any lights, he was invisible. Just glad the peckerhead was able to avoid whacking us in the ass.

They continued to drive until Pete started to slow down looking for a road on the right. When he found it, he turned on to a semi-paved lane. In

130

the distance, Dillon could see lights strung along the top of a wall. When Pete told him it was their final destination, Dillon relaxed a bit. If anything came screeching out of the darkness now, it would have to be a dune buggy since each side of the road was dirt and scrub brush. The road they were on dead ended into a dirt road running to the compound entrance. Once they reached the entrance, Pete rolled down his window and gave the Sri Lankan guard the evening's code for entrance. The gate slowly opened and Pete drove in.

The California Compound was typical of most small housing areas catering to westerners. This one was a bit smaller with only 100 villas inside the 10-foot high barbed wire and cut glass topped concrete walled enclosure. As they drove through the electrically controlled gate, they found a wide roundabout decorated with date trees, hedges and rock gardens illuminated with the obligatory lights on a string. In the center was a water fountain or at least it appeared to be a water fountain. There was no water flowing from the rather large gahwa pot perched predominantly in the middle of a round cement pond. It was probably only used for entertaining residents if the compound was fully rented.

Since the Philippine connection took over running the place, only a handful of villas were occupied and the occupants worked for the connection. As the two men drove around the centerpiece, they approached the central facility. This series of buildings is where the festivities of the evening would take place. Pete found a spot to park and backed the truck into a resting place.

"Makes for an easier getaway right Dillon?" Pete joked as he put the truck into park and set the brake.

"If you're worried about a quick getaway, don't set the hand brake and make sure you figure out a way to bust through the front gate with positive ground locks and two inch steel piping crisscrossing the length and width of our only exit."

Pete turned to look at the gates and asked Dillon how he saw that. "Part of the training my yoke pulling associate. When you enter a tight situation, and we aren't sure how tight this one is going to be, always check out the exits. The path you travel on your way in may be the only chance you get to scope your exit. Of course it really isn't necessary for you to commit to memory unless you plan on changing career fields."

"Not a chance of that happening," Pete commented.

The men got out of the truck and left the doors unlocked. Another point for a quick exit. They went around front of the building and through the double doors with blacked out glass windows on either side. Once through the doors, a muscle bound 6-foot plus Filipino bouncer standing in a small enclosure with a curtain-covered wall behind him, greeted both men. He politely asked for the 100 Riyal entrance fee. Once paid in full, they passed through the curtain into another enclosure where a search for prohibited items was conducted. Once that was completed, they were cleared into the lobby area. Soft lights and music greeted them along with an interesting odor combination of perfume, cigar smoke, and beer.

They looked at each other and Pete said, "Let the games begin," as they headed for a set of double doors on their left underneath a sign indicating the "Riyadh Room".

⚜

Bill pulled into the Politzie office parking lot in downtown Kaiserslautern. The inspectors maintained an annex all to themselves. It allowed them space away from the daily routine of a main office. It was some time since Bill visited the office.

As Bill entered the revolving door, he noticed a few significant changes made to the reception area layout. The wide-open space is now encased behind an eight-foot high double pane of bullet proof Plexiglas. A uniformed armed guard sat behind a wide podium with four TV monitors. He controlled access to the space behind the glass with a remote door opener. On each side of the podium was an inlet monitored by a metal detector. All visitors must show a picture ID, have it scanned into a computer and only then were they allowed passage into the office area.

Since Bill was a member of a local police force, he receives a special identification bar code that links him to a computer file containing all his pertinent information. The form for this access document was sitting on his desk under a pile of other forms he planned to review and complete. He put off finishing the form because he knew his visits to this particular office were infrequent. Without this automatic access pass, he called Hanz to vouch for him. The guard screened Bill through the metal detectors and buzzed open the Plexiglas wall door.

Once inside, the place was relatively the same as he remembered. Staircases led up both sides of the room to balconies on each floor where visitors gathered to be met by administrative assistants for each group of investigators. Luckily, Hanz was located on the first floor and his admin greeter was waiting as he rounded the corner from the stairway.

"Agent Wilmerson, I'm Helmut, let me show you to our offices." Helmut turned and walked briskly down the rather narrow hallway to an open door near the end. He stood aside as Bill entered the sparsely decorated room. Of the six doors leading off the reception area, only two showed name plaques over their sills. One belonged to Hanz and the other belonged to Sergeant Alfdorn. Bill walked to the slightly opened door of Hanz's office and knocked on the frame.

"Anybody home," he asked.

"Come in Bill." was the reply.

Bill pushed open the door and found Hanz sitting behind a large executive style desk that had seen much better days. On each side of the room, file cabinets were piled high with stacks of papers and file boxes. A door connecting the adjoining office was the only empty space along the wall. Behind Hanz was a window opened up on to the central courtyard. Hanz got up to greet Bill.

"Good to see you again. How are things going with Dillon?"

Bill began to recount Dillon's activities since his arrival in Saudi. Hanz walked to a small refrigerator stuck under a table and pulled out a bottle of Spatlese. He reached into his desk drawer and found a couple of paper cups for the wine. He passed one to Bill as he continued to fill Hanz in on details surrounding Dillon's activities.

"What do you want to do with the information about the plastic?" Hanz asked after Bill finished his briefing.

"This really points to another car somewhere in the vicinity," Bill said. "We can postulate the killer or killers drove Crimitin home in the trunk of his car. Once there, he was dumped on the ground and the killer took the plastic with him as he left the scene. We have to find out if someone saw or heard another car in the vicinity that night. Dillon mentioned a farmer he met during one of his revisits to the area. We need to talk with that man again to see if any of his neighbors remember anything."

Hanz said he would personally make a trip out there in the morning. He knew exactly where Dillon met the man and would pick his brain again for any information.

CHAPTER TWENTY

As Dillon and Pete stepped through the doorway, a very fetching, buxom blonde-haired woman greeted them with a sweet hello and a copy of a tri-fold pamphlet containing the rules of engagement and locations of various forms of entertainment. The room was set up with a jazz combo currently playing on a small stage in one corner of the room and a disk jockey in the opposite corner ready to take over during their breaks. A dance floor was between both stages. On the floor, couples were slow dancing to the sounds of the quartet. Surrounding the dance floor were candle lit tables and high back booths around the outer walls with small electric lights illuminating the center of each secluded area. On their right was a long bar with two tenders servicing waitresses, waiters, and patrons. Dillon and Pete approached a pair of vacant stools at the bar and sat down. Once they ordered libations, they looked at the brochure.

A greeting on the front page from "Papa Good" welcomed all newcomers and returning patrons. He wished everyone an enjoyable time and pleasant memories. The next page contained a listing of rooms with various types of entertainment. There was one with never ending pornography shows. Another room contained a live sex show with performance times and names of participants in case patrons had favorite couples to view while they engaged in all types of sexual feats. Another room was a key club for couples. Husbands or wives would sign out simulated house keys and at the end of the night would gather for the drawing of pairings for encounters after they left the "club". A small room contained a pair of massage tables where patrons could participate in a "total" body massage. A final room contained a hot tub large enough for one couple. Intercourse was allowed in this tub. The pool and hot tub in the center of the facility maintained a restriction of no sexual intercourse allowed. Nude swimming was allowed but if you wanted watery sex, you needed to wait for a turn in the hot tub room.

After they finished reading the printed material, they turned their attention to the crowd of people. There was a wide assortment of men and women assembled in the dimly lit room. Most of the Asian faces were from Thailand or the Philippines. A few Korean women sat with a contingent of British men in one of the booths. Caucasian women were scattered throughout the room at tables and booths. The men were mostly Anglo Saxon in origin with a few faces of color scattered throughout.

At a table almost directly in front of Dillon and Pete sat four women who were obviously giving both men the once over. Dillon slowly rotated his stool so he was facing away from the women and told Pete, in a discreet manner, they should join the ladies for a bit of conversation. Before he could get the words out of his mouth, Pete pulled his stool away from the bar and up to the table where the three blondes and one redhead readily agreed to have the two newcomers join them.

The first order of business was introductions. The four women were Maureen, from Australia; Monica, from New Zealand; Carmen, from Manchester and Hellen, from Oslo. All were nurses working at various military and civilian hospitals. Maureen and Carmen were supervisors on a ward, while Monica and Hellen were surgical nurses. Dillon and Pete introduced themselves and engaged the women in small talk about the facility and their reasons for visiting. The women agreed their reason for being at the compound was quite simple, they weren't lesbians, and they were looking for a few good men to engage in some simple sexual relations with no strings attached.

The six talked for more than an hour before Dillon noticed a rather strange looking Filipino gent enter the room. There was nothing unusual about his facial features; it was his costume that drew attention. It was like looking at a flashback to the 70's. A pimp could not have dressed any finer while working his women on the street. The man wore a wide brimmed hat with a white band. His shirt featured wide lapels and was open damn near to his navel. The gold necklaces were too numerous to count. They centered on a large gold coin and what appeared to be a chain thick enough to anchor a ship. On each finger of both hands, he sported either a gold ring or a ring with a stone of some magnitude encased in gold. The bell-bottomed pants were covering a pair of shoes with soles nearly two inches thick. Dillon needed to contain his laughter because he felt Papa Good just made his triumphant entrance.

He turned to his companions and was about to ask when one of them just held up her hand and confirmed his suspicions. "That's Papa Good all right. He loves to dress retro. I guess it all goes back to his whore running days in the Philippines. None of us have taken the time to engage him in lengthy conversation because he expects a fuck if you talk with him for any length of time."

"So if Pete or I talk with him, will he expect a fuck from us?" Dillon queried.

"Sorry to tell you this but we do believe he swings both ways, so you may be in trouble," was the reply.

They watched as he gingerly slid in to the only open booth in the room. Once he centered his costumed posterior, four rather shapely Filipino women joined him. Each of them sported a see through blouse revealing the results of enhancement surgery. One of the servers was immediately on the spot with drinks for them all. Papa drew one of those sissy drinks with the fruit and umbrella in a very tall glass. He sipped lazily as his friends engaged each other in low tone conversation. Once the show was over, Dillon asked Carmen to dance.

They moved to the dance floor and took a spot close to Papa's booth. Dillon wanted to be noticed so when he made a move to talk with the headman, he would not be an unknown quantity. As they danced, Carmen waved to Papa and he returned the gesture. Dillon thought that was good for business. He was seen with someone Papa obviously knew.

After a few more dances, Dillon and Carmen returned to the table where Pete was holding his own explaining the finer points of aviation to the enthralled women. He was in his prime. Beautiful women who were anxious to hear all he could say about the macho world of Air Force aviation. Dillon quietly took his seat and agreed with Pete every time he turned to him for support. He didn't want to interfere with the plans he knew Pete was formulating for later activities later on that evening.

Following another round of drinks, Dillon asked Carmen if she could introduce Pete and himself to Papa. When she asked why, Dillon kept to the story about bringing Air Force personnel to the party on a regular basis. When she agreed, Dillon interrupted Pete recounting one of his harrowing experiences involving night vision goggles and low level flying through the hills of West Virginia to deliver a team of Seals on a simulated mission to destroy a hydro-electric plant. Pete politely excused himself and made the women promise not to leave the party before he returned. He ordered them another drink and followed Dillon and Carmen to Papa's booth.

As they approached, Carmen took Dillon's hand and pulled him to the center of the table where she introduced both men to Papa. Papa nodded acknowledgment and introduced his consorts. When he finished,

Dillon greeted them all with "Magan Dang Gabi". Papa Good smiled and complimented Dillon on his Tagalog.

"Don't compliment me too much," Dillon countered. "I can get by with greetings in the morning and evening but after that I'm limited to ordering beers and asking for prices."

Papa laughed aloud and asked the men to join him. Two of the ladies automatically vacated their seats and disappeared. Carmen blew Papa a kiss and returned to her table. As soon as they sat down, drinks arrived. Dillon and Pete toasted Papa, as they tasted the amber liquid. After a bit of small talk about the facility, Dillon posed some questions.

"I haven't noticed too many military personnel in your crowd tonight. Is there some reason?" Papa thought for a while before answering.

"We never had a very large contingent from the American, British, or French forces working at Prince Sultan." Dillon tried not to show his surprise at the base of knowledge this man obviously possessed.

"After the bombings, when everyone was restricted to the base and Eskan Village, there were none. With the restrictions lifted, we are seeing them come back in very small numbers. Since this is a remote tour for the majority of people, I guess it will just take time for the word of mouth publicity to make the rounds. All of the people who used to frequent my establishment have rotated back to their home bases. As I said, it will just take some time."

"We would like to help publicize this place as much as we can," Pete began. "I fly in and out of here on a regular basis. I can act as the informal greeter for your palace of pleasure. I can provide phone numbers and contact points so you can continue to screen participants. I have an inside track to the investigative agencies who might want to prevent our troops from getting involved with sex, drugs, and rock and roll."

As he finished, Papa held both hands above his head with the palms facing out. "Let me make sure you understand one thing right now. If you are going to bring me men and women who are looking for more than sex, booze and maybe a little weed, then you can just keep them to yourselves. I don't allow any type of hard drugs in the facility. I can't control what people do outside the walls but if caught inside, I have my own methods of punishment. You think I am without influence with the local constabulary? It would be very difficult for me to maintain this type of operation without a friendly wink and a nod from the authorities. It may be a costly prospect but then this place is nothing but pure profit."

Dillon listened intently to the words spoken by Papa. When he finished, Dillon looked at him and said, "I'm sure my exuberant friend was just using a euphemism for a good time. However, it's good to know you don't tolerate

137

hard drugs in your facility. We can support the consensual sexual contact between members of the military contingent but we cannot and will not tolerate the introduction of hard drugs into the equation. We don't even want you to supply them with any smoking material. We can sell this as a place where they can get away from the restrictive society outside the gates and relax with friends and new acquaintances. I see the frustrations first hand. If we can find a place for them to let off steam, then we have a contented group of individuals performing their assigned tasks at peak efficiency."

Papa listened intently and when Dillon finished, he asked the two remaining females to join their partners at the bar. After they left, he began telling Pete and Dillon about his experiences with military forces.

His father was heavily involved with bars, whores, and drugs just outside the huge American air base in the Philippines. His father began his trade in the early 60's as the build up for Viet Nam was taking place. He was in the right place at the right time and was able to obtain a series of bars and hotels in the town of Angeles just out side the gates of Clark Air Base. As Papa grew into his late teens and early 20's, he began to take part in the "family" business. He would drive the ladies of the evening to the doctors for their regular checkups. He ran errands for managers of his father's establishments and as he grew taller and stronger, acted as the informal bouncer in case of trouble. He always maintained one of his father's associates nearby. He never carried a weapon but the people with him were always armed.

During Viet Nam, the money flowed and the family became very wealthy. The only problems encountered involved the political situation in the Philippines. The rule of law under Marcos was touchy at best. After the war wound down and the pace of military movements through Clark lessened, the family survived but they weren't rolling in greenbacks as they once were. Changes in the political situation also affected the way they did business.

Papa took over control of all aspects of the operation when his father unexpectedly died of an aneurysm. He reduced the monetary investments in many aspects of the business and totally divested the family support of hard drugs.

Things continued to flourish until 1991 when Mount Pinatubo literally blew away all of his businesses. The Americans were planning to withdraw from Clark and hand it over to the Philippine military but the explosion of the long dormant volcano hastened their departure.

Papa watched the ash cover and destroy many of the buildings where his operations centered. It was a fiasco of the first degree and Papa knew it was time to move his operation to a more lucrative location. He was aware of the large expatriate population in the Middle East and did some preliminary investigations for relocating to the Arabian Peninsula.

What he discovered was an untapped source of revenue for his specialty. With his contacts in the government and his ability to make payments to the right people at the right time, he obtained work permits for a number of his employees and moved to Bahrain. From there he was able to obtain contacts within the Saudi Arabian political structure for a move into Riyadh.

Once that move was made, he set about establishing powerful contacts to protect him from the religious police. Once those protections were in place, he established the facility as it appears today. It was in operation for more than five years and the profitability only grew. He even opened a branch operation that catered to young Saudis so they wouldn't have to resort to the homosexual contacts many of them develop before they become involved in family arranged marriages. Dillon and Pete engaged him in small talk about his current operation but stayed away from getting too involved because they didn't want to scare him away when they got down to the important questions.

They heard the distributor who provided the compound with home made beer and the amber liquid commonly referred to as "brown" was an American named Buzz. With more than 15 years in kingdom, the rumor was he had multiple millions stashed in Swiss accounts. He was due to make a delivery that evening. Dillon wanted to meet him and Papa assured both men Buzz would make an appearance at his table before he left the compound.

After another drink and small talk about the lucrative business of sex, Pete excused himself to rejoin the nurses at their table. "Don't want to mess with a good thing," he said as he excused himself and headed back for the bevy of beauties.

Dillon talked for a while and then excused himself to dance with Carmen and Hellen. Pete left the main room with Maureen and Monica. When Dillon asked where they went, Hellen laughed saying Pete wanted to take a swim but didn't have a suit. The women reminded him the pool was a suit optional type of arrangement, so he immediately asked volunteers to join him. The three of them left the room arm in arm for a late night swim. Dillon just shook his head and grinned.

Just after midnight, Dillon noticed a gruff looking character talking with Papa. They talked for a while and then the man headed for Dillon's table. As he approached, Carmen reached under the table and squeezed Dillon's thigh. The man stood on one side of the table and offered his hand.

"Papa said you wanted to talk with me, Name's Buzz." Dillon stood up and gripped the man's chunky hand.

"Good to meet you Buzz. Let's step over to the bar. I've got a couple of questions to ask." Dillon excused himself from the table and Buzz followed him to the corner of the bar where there were two empty seats.

"Papa tells me you're the supplier of the best brown and home-brew in Riyadh. I don't know if he told you much about my partner and I but we are looking to make this place fashionable again with the military forces. I also understand you have contacts with other locals tied into the drug supply network. I know Papa is hard over on the use of drugs in the facility. I go along with him on that subject but if one of our foreign patrons asks us the question, I want to have some type of an answer. I want to keep the Americans away from all types of drugs but I'm not one to keep the frogs or the brits off the nose candy."

Buzz was listening intently and when Dillon finished, the large man left his seat, put his face up close and personal with Dillon and said, "I don't know who the fuck you are but if you think I'm stupid enough to admit involvement in the Kingdom, you are one dumb son of a bitch".

With that closing statement, Buzz brushed past Dillon and out the door. Dillon turned to watch him leave and then, shaking his head in disbelief, returned to the table where Carmen was waiting and watching the whole development.

"Nice man if I do say so myself," Dillon retorted as he pulled out a chair and rejoined Carmen and Hellen. The waitress passed by and he caught her attention for another round of drinks. When he finished ordering, Carmen began.

"That is one of the nastiest bastards in the Kingdom. Why in God's name do you want to have anything to do with him?"

Dillon didn't want to involve the new friends too deeply in anything that might happen during his investigation, so he tried to play it off with some comment about his brown tasting like shit when he was told it was the best in the Kingdom. He didn't know if they bought the story but asked Carmen why she didn't like Buzz.

"He came into Riyadh some time ago. He set up in Jeddah, moved to Dhahran, and then finally into the capitol. I'm not sure what he does for the Saudis but he always seems to find a job with one company or another. He then sets up his brew factory and begins to rake in the riyals. He has a work force to make deliveries but like tonight, he shows up when there's a payment to be made. The rest of the time, he commutes to work in the back of a 600 series Mercedes. He has tried to get into the sack with each one of us but he just isn't the type we want to play with. That has really pissed him off and he doesn't give us the time of day. Just so he doesn't show up in the hospital for any of us to work with, I guess we can go on ignoring him when we make visits to this pleasure spa."

"That's an interesting story," Dillon commented as he sipped from the tall glass recently placed in front of him. "He really didn't seem like the personable dude Papa made him out to be. I guess we will just have to drink his trash and hope we don't get food poisoning." he finished up by holding up his glass and examining the contents.

Carmen went on to tell Dillon about the special supply of real alcohol Papa stocked for good customers. She was sure he would open the cabinet if the military folks start to return, as Dillon and Pete were promising.

"That's good to know," Dillon said as he looked over at Papa's booth and noticed the old man was watching his conversation with Carmen and Hellen. Dillon excused himself as he went back to Papa's table. He knew there had to be questions about the flare up at the bar. He didn't want to have any misunderstandings crop up as he was trying to gather information. As he left the table, Hellen left for a swim with the others.

"It doesn't appear the conversation with Buzz went too well," Papa said as Dillon lowered himself into the booth next to one of the honeys. She immediately moved closer to him and reached under the table to rub his inner thigh.

"I guess not. He took immediate offense and said nothing nice about me or my parents." Papa smiled, as he knew the volatility of Buzz.

They talked for a brief time before Dillon excused himself and returned to the table. As he sat down Carmen moved closer to his side and reached under the table. "Is that a sock in your pocket or are you just happy to be back at my table?" she cooed as she rubbed the bulge on his inner thigh.

"I had to leave the table before she decided to take matters into both hands." Dillon laughed as he reached down and squeezed her hand. "It's about time for us to go and find our buddies."

They finished their drinks and left a sizable tip for the servers. They went into the reception area and down one of the hallways toward the pool area. Couples waiting their turn in one of the entertainment rooms occupied some of the couches along the way. When they reached the end of the hall, they opened double doors on to the pool area.

A mist emanating from small pipes running under the overhang greeted them as they exited the building. It wasn't enough to get anyone wet but it was enough to cool you off as you stepped into the 100-degree heat. They heard laughter coming from the Hot Tub area and were just rounding the corner near the pool when they saw Pete, in all his nakedness, taking a double bounce on the diving board. He cannonballed into the water close enough to the edge that the resulting splash soaked the naked forms of Carmen's compatriots as they sat on the fabric covered chaise lounges sipping their drinks. They laughed as Pete's head appeared at the side of the pool with a sheepish grin on his face.

"I told you trying to stay dry sipping your foo foo drinks was going to be impossible." He looked over and saw Dillon and Carmen nearing the girls.

"Hey partner, where the heck have you been? Come on in the water's fine." he said as he splashed water their way. Both Carmen and Dillon managed to avoid the soaking spray.

"Keep the water in the pool flyboy," Dillon taunted Pete as they took up seats around a table near the women.

"Are you going in for a swim?" Carmen asked Dillon as she began to unbutton her blouse.

"Not tonight I'm afraid. I really need to get Johnny Weissmuller out of the water so we can be on our way. We have another place to stop tonight."

"I'm really sorry to hear that," Carmen said as she reached behind her back to undo the hooks on her D cup bra. "I was hoping you would join me for a few laps." She threw the bra over the back of the chair where her blouse hung and leaned in toward Dillon to give him a short kiss on the forehead. At this point Dillon couldn't help but notice the lack of tan lines on her natural breasts. After she stepped back from his chair, she slipped out of her skirt and panties to reveal the briefest of tan lines where an apparent thong bikini protected the smallest of areas between her well-defined thighs. Dillon was beginning to regret his earlier statement about having to leave.

Carmen walked over to the edge of the pool and dove in. Pete was out toweling off. He looked over at Dillon and asked, "Sure you want to leave now?"

Once outside and approaching the truck, Pete asked Dillon where they were going now. Dillon laughed and said he wanted to get back to Eskan because he didn't want to spend the night with one of the lovely ladies.

"Next time I'll just give you the keys to go home." Pete said as he opened his door and slid behind the wheel. They made their way down the dirt road before pulling back to the paved surface. As they made the turn to head for the main highway, Dillon noticed a small box van sitting along side the road. As they passed, the trucks lights came on and it pulled in behind them. Pete checked the mirror and asked Dillon what was next.

"Just keep driving." was the advice.

As they approached the corner, the truck pulled around them on the right with its emergency flashers in operation. It pulled back on the road and slowed to a stop. Pete was going to swerve around it and disappear into the night when Dillon told him to stop a few feet behind the truck.

Following his orders, Pete stopped and turned on his bright lights. The passenger side door opened and Buzz stepped out. Since Pete hadn't met Buzz, Dillon told him who he was. Dillon carefully watched the bulky man walk toward his door. He wanted to make sure he didn't have a weapon. He didn't notice anything out of the ordinary, so he rolled the window down to see what the man wanted.

"Good morning Buzz. Did we forget to close out our conversation earlier in the evening?" Dillon asked as the man came within hearing range.

"Don't be a smart ass" was the terse reply. "I didn't want Papa to see I still have contacts in the area you asked about. With his distaste for the hard stuff, I told him I was away from the business. I want to keep my contact with him because he's a gold mine of profit. Everyone associated with his operation makes money hand over fist. He was watching every move we made and when I left with the outburst, I made sure it was loud enough for him to hear. Who's your driver?"

"Buzz, this is Pete. Pete, Buzz," Dillon continued. "So, if I understand, you do know where I can put folks in touch for stuff other than a bit of weed."

"Let's head back for my place and I'll get the names and numbers. I also have a contact down country where they package some of the finest smoke I've every sampled. The operations are separate but I do try to stay in touch with each of them." Buzz told them to follow his truck. He returned to the cab.

They made their way to the ring road and toward the center of town. Within a couple of minutes, Buzz's vehicle signaled a move off the highway. Pete followed. Once on the access road, the truck pulled into a small parking lot next to a furniture store. Dillon and Pete watched as Buzz left the truck and went over to a white Mercedes S600. He opened the door, started the car, and then signaled the two men to follow him.

Once on the access road, they made a turn to a divided road that crossed over the highway. Past some stores and gas stations, they turned into a side street, down a couple of blocks, around a decorative fountain and up to a white wall that illuminated as the Merc approached. The black iron gates slid open as Buzz maneuvered past a guard who appeared from the other side of the gate. He stopped a moment and the guard looked back at the Suburban. Pete drove toward the guard who signaled him to pass through the gates.

Both men were impressed after they entered. Buzz was circling a cobble stone driveway surrounding a garden area with every imaginable type of desert fauna. The centerpiece was a fountain providing water for a pond at its base. Streams ran off the pond and through the garden. They crossed over a bridge that allowed one of the streams to run under the road and into another garden area floodlit with pastel lights on various rock formations. It was rather stunning. As they approached the house, they noticed another of the streams passing under the drive. Buzz was waiting beside his car as Pete put the truck into park and turned off the ignition.

"What do you think of my humble abode?" Buzz asked as the men approached.

"It once belonged to one of the royals. He built it as sort of a zoo complex. Before it was completed, he got some type of a diplomatic post and decided to put it on the market. Some of my connections made the purchase and moved me in as a reward for services rendered. I live here rent-free as long as I maintain their continued good graces. As you can guess, I plan on doing that as long as I can."

"We're in the wrong business." Pete said as they walked toward the ornate double door entrance.

"Instead of defending the world from aggressors, we should be working on a scheme so we can have benefactors like yours."

Buzz pressed a small device on his key ring and one of the doors swung open. Immediately inside the men were standing on glass blocks with the stream flowing under their feet. On either side was a staircase winding up the walls to a balcony area lit with a chandelier that was 25 feet long if it was an inch.

The stream ran from under the entrance way and through a small garden area. On the other side, it flowed over a series of rock falls into a pond surrounded by an entertainment room, a dining room and in the center, a living room. The stream meandered between the entertainment area and the dining room and then split as it passed around the formal living room making it a sort of island. Once the stream rejoined on the other side, it passed under a glass wall, over another set of falls and into a pool more than 150 feet in length. Buzz approached the men as they stood at the railing where the stream ran under the windows.

"Can I get you guys a drink?" Buzz queried as he led them down a nearly concealed stairway on their right. It led to a rather small office area, comparatively speaking, situated in a way the view out the windows was of the waterfall and pond. Both men agreed to join Buzz in a drink as he pulled a bottle of single malt off a shelf at the back of a modest bar area. Once he poured, he showed the two men where they could sit while he accessed his database for the numbers and names of his contacts.

"I know these guys were in business last week. I heard through the grape vine there was some trouble with their supply but they didn't seem too concerned now. Evidently they work with some pretty pure shit and they cut the hell out of it." Dillon and Pete exchanged glances as they waited and listened.

Buzz went over to a floor safe, spun in the combination and pulled out a hard drive, which he installed in what appeared to be a state of the art computer system. He fired up the CPU and adjusted the speaker level. Once he was up and running, he searched a database until he made contact with the information he needed. As he found the names, Buzz pulled a sheet of paper and pen out of a drawer and wrote down the names and numbers. When he finished jotting down the information, he closed the programs, shut off the computer, and returned the hard drive to its spot in his safe. He went back to the desk, picked up the paper and gave the sheet to Dillon.

"These first three are my points of contact for anything hard in Riyadh. They always seem to have a supply but as I said, there's a rumor about their supplier running into some difficulty. If you guys contact them, see if you can ferret out some information. I always like to operate with the latest information. If I come across anything, I'll let you know. Speaking of that, give me a phone number so I can get in touch with you if I run into these guys before you do."

"Since Pete comes and goes more than I do, let me give you my villa number at Eskan." Dillon offered. Once they exchanged numbers, Dillon asked about the contacts. "They only have nicknames?"

"That's the only way I know them. When I asked more about them, I got the cold shoulder, so I gave up and just use their nicknames. HD is a Sri Lankan who is the newest member of the crowd. He's only been connected for about a year. He's used primarily for the movement of smack from their storage area to a customer. It's really one of the riskiest parts of the game but so far, it appears he's doing just fine. The next guy is Floppy. He's an Indian with some big contact points in the government. I'm interested in finding out more about him but with his connections, I don't want to lose my inside track. The last guy is ROM. He's from Bangladesh. He always seems to deal with the numbers. I don't know much more about their operation. I just know you can call any one of them to get a delivery made. The other guys, MD and EB are the contacts downrange for deliveries of smoke. This place is so loose; they have a courier bundle the stuff in a suitcase and bring it down to the big city on a regular basis. I don't know if the folks in Abha are in on the business or they're just stupid."

"I wouldn't want to venture a guess until I get more involved with bringing people together." Dillon said. "I'm not too sure how involved I want to be in the drug aspect of this operation. I'm strictly a sex and booze man. We just wanted to know if customers could make contact if they needed something stronger than a stiff drink and a stiff dick."

Buzz said he understood. He was of the same mind. He didn't use on a regular basis and the only thing he dabbled with was the southern grown hemp. The men continued to talk until they finished their drinks. Dillon said they needed to be leaving. Buzz tried to get them to stay but both men said they had plans for the morning and must go their separate ways.

They thanked Buzz for his gracious cooperation and hoped they would become better business partners in the future. Buzz led them back to the entrance and cleared their exit with the gate guard. The men left the complex and were silent until they reached the ring road. Pete pulled the truck to the curb. "Am I dreaming or did we just hit the jackpot?"

Dillon smiled and said he couldn't have hoped for a bigger cache of information. "I'll give Erpack a call tomorrow. I'm not too sure how to transfer the information to him. Don't want to chance using the compound telephone system. You never know who's on the other end. He wanted me to come down and visit. I may just take him up on his offer and see what he has going on and if his concerns are founded in reality or if he just has a bunch of stupid idiots working for the contractor."

"Not having the opportunity to visit downrange, I can't give you an educated guess one way or the other," Pete replied. "We have contractors at the air base but I don't really have much contact with them.

"I'll touch base with Phobie in the morning. He may have some more information after our initial meeting. I'm not high on Erpack's good buddy list. I came down pretty hard on him to make an impression. Just hope he doesn't hold a grudge too long."

"I don't think Erpack is going to be pissed off too long once he sees the information you have for him. That could really shake up the smoke cartel," Pete commented as he pulled away from the curb and headed for the ring road.

Things were beginning to gel.

Chapter Twenty-One

Hanz and Fritz drove into Kottweiller, drank coffee at the Gasthaus, and discovered the name of the farmer who owned the hill top cattle shed. He was Karl Rasmuller and would be into the restaurant in less than an hour. He always came in after taking care of his morning projects.

True to his habit, Karl came through the door at precisely the appointed hour, went directly to the reserved table in the back corner with a wide view of the entire restaurant area, and took a slow drink from the coffee cup placed on the table just seconds before his arrival. Hanz and Fritz let him enjoy his first cup of coffee in peace. When he was getting a refill, they approached his table.

"Good morning Herr Rasmuller, I'm Inspector Ubermann and this is Sergeant Alfdorn. We're part of an investigation surrounding the death of an American in a street adjacent to yours. I believe my American counterpart talked to you one day shortly after the murder took place?"

Karl returned their greetings and asked them to join him as he began to eat. He recounted the meeting with Dillon and his promise to check with his neighbors about the night in question. However, he apologized for not following up on his promise. He simply didn't believe any of his friends and neighbors would have been awake that time of night, so he didn't make any inquiries. He again apologized for this miscalculation and told the men he would make some phone calls after he finished eating.

Hanz and Fritz were both disappointed at this revelation. They hoped the man would have some small bit of information they could work with concerning another car. Now they were afraid the passage of time would affect everyone's memories. Karl stopped them as they excused themselves to leave. He said he would make the calls right now. Both investigators remained seated and enjoyed another cup of coffee.

After Karl finished his hearty breakfast, he asked for a phone and made the calls right from the table. Most calls connected with wives but one of them found Frank Hildebrand, a fellow farmer, at home. When Karl asked about the night in question, he thought for a moment and then said he didn't have any recollection about late night travelers. Karl continued to make calls until he went through all of his neighbors and friends. He gave the names and numbers of both investigators if the men away at work remembered anything when they returned home. Hanz and Fritz thanked Karl for his cooperation. Karl again apologized for not having taken the matter seriously enough the first time.

As they left the building, Hanz voiced his displeasure. "If someone tells you a murder happened in a street next to yours, you would think a person would take the situation seriously." he fumed.

"I would've been pounding on doors right after Dillon left. How can someone just make an arbitrary decision about something so important?"

"All we can do now is hope one of the husbands was taking a leak on the night in question and heard something out of the ordinary," Hanz finished off as they got into their car for the drive back. As they pulled out and drove down the alleyway toward the street, Karl suddenly appeared waving his hands in the air. Hanz rolled down the window.

"What's the matter Karl?"

"Please come back inside, Frank just called back and asked about the date. He remembers something that might be of assistance." Hanz got out of the car and followed Karl inside.

The phone was off the hook on the table where they sat a few minutes before. Hanz picked up the receiver and spoke with Frank. When he restated the date in question, Frank recalled the evening because it was a birthday celebration for a female friend of his and he was coming home later than normal. Hanz said they would be right up to his house. Both men returned to the unmarked police car and drove up to Frank's house. He was waiting on the sidewalk as they approached.

Greetings were exchanged as the men joined Frank in front of his house. "So you were coming home from a party at a friend's house late on the evening of the murder," Hanz restated.

"I was just approaching my gate when I noticed headlights coming out of the field at the top of the street. Since the hour was so late, I stepped through the gate and waited on the walkway to see if it was one of my neighbors having a problem. The only people who use that road work the fields and tend to their livestock. Just call me nosy. Anyway, as the car approached, it wasn't one I recognized. It was a blue Audi. I couldn't tell you the year or anything else about the car. I just know it was blue and an Audi."

"Did you notice how many people were in the car?" Fritz asked.

"There were two men in the front. I don't remember if there was anyone in the back."

Hanz reached out and shook the farmers' callused hand. "Thank you very much for giving us a call back."

Fritz thanked him also as both men returned to the car and drove up the street to the dirt road. They hadn't visited the area since Dillon left, so they wanted to gather some soil samples to include with other evidence. Since they could now confirm a car was on the hill the night of the murder, they wanted to have every conceivable investigative aid they could gather.

⚜

With the sun slowly illuminating the Eastern sky, Pete dropped Dillon off at his villa. He had to make it back to the air base and check to see if he would be leaving. He wished Dillon good luck on the investigation and promised to keep in touch.

Less than two hours later, Dillon was having a hard time focusing on the dials of his battery powered alarm clock on the bed side table as the shrill sounds of his secure telephone woke him.

Dillon reached in the direction of the irritating noise and picked up the handset. "Yo," he whispered into the receiver.

"Dillon this is Bill. What are you doing in bed at this time of the morning? I've been ringing the office but no one seems to be on duty."

"It's Thursday morning Bill and I endured a very busy investigative night last night. If you care to remember, Thursday and Friday are the weekends in Saudi. What's the good news and I only want to hear good news because I have some hot stuff for you."

Bill explained in detail about his meeting with Hanz and the results of the inspector's subsequent visit to Kottweiller.

"I knew there was a second car." Dillon exclaimed as he slapped his arm into the pillow next to his head. "Whoever killed him drove back in his car and then walked up the hill to his partner. Now all we have to do is get lucky and find the car."

"The K-Town boys are already working that angle," Bill began. "They're running the type of car through their registration data base and will cross check for any problem children. The list may be a long one but at least it's a place to start."

149

Dillon began to brief Bill on the Riyadh visit. He could tell by the excitement in Bill's voice that he was impressed with the findings about the drugs and the three points of contact.

"That really is great news," Bill exclaimed. "How long are you going to try and keep up the undercover work with Buzz?"

"I'm not too sure. I do know I want to make another visit to the pleasure palace for another meeting with Papa."

Bill asked for more details about possible connections between Buzz, the computer nicknamed operatives and Crimitin. They came up with a couple of possible leads to follow. Dillon told Bill about the Khamis tie in and said he was going to make a trip down there to quiet the detachment commander and see if there were any possible reasons to fit Khamis into his puzzle.

"When do you think you'll be making the trip?" Bill asked.

"Not sure at this time. I have to get with Karl to see if he has any ideas on the subject. We haven't discussed Erpack. I hope he's off his high horse. A trip down there will help clear up his potential problem and keep him from screwing up our operation."

After he hung up, Dillon swung his feet onto the carpeted floor and stood up with a long stretch and yawn. He headed for the bathroom, ran a brush through his hair, and splashed water on his face to wake up. He gave Karl a call to set up a meeting later in the day.

The phone rang three times before the machine answered with the announcement Agent Phobie was unavailable at this time. "Karl, this is Dillon. Time is about 8:30. Need to talk with you on some developments from last night. Give me a call; I'll be in the villa." He hung up and dropped back on the bed. He was asleep in minutes.

⚛

The Gray Land Rover left the paved highway to a well-traveled path in the sand. The man behind the wheel cautiously put the drive train into four-wheel mode as he made his way down the path. On either side, rock formations straight from an early space extravaganza dotted the landscape. Spherical rocks lie piled where the forces of nature stacked them millions of years ago as this part of the world lifted from the bottom of the Red Sea and cooled into this forbidding landscape. The stones were dark with some of the largest formations having a very smooth surface as the molten rock flowed from long dormant vents in the earth's surface.

As he pressed on further into the rocks, he kept an eye out for his landmarks. He missed one on a previous trip and nearly spent the night in the desert. This time he was prepared. If he missed his visuals, he would rely on the hand held GPS system he brought back from vacation.

He caught the first visual, made a turn out of the dry riverbed to a track that led him up a rocky pass through the boulders. He was now on a ridge running along side the riverbed. He pressed on for about 15 minutes until he came to the second visual marker. At this point, he made a right turn between two scrub trees protruding from the crevasses of an overhanging rock formation. This path brought him to a grouping of wood and rocks. He stopped the Rover about three feet in front of the formation, got out of the vehicle, grabbed the hook on the winch at the front of the truck and walked over to the tree stump on the left side of the grouping. He pulled aside a rock and attached the hook to a metal frame hidden behind the rocks and wood. He then returned to the Rover, put it in reverse, and pulled the entire formation away from its location. Once there was enough room to pass by, he unhooked the winch drove through, hooked up the rear winch, and pulled the "gate" closed.

He drove a very short distance and stopped beside a large bolder. He scrapped aside the sand and pulled out a box with a cord running from one side. He opened the box, entered a code, closed the box, and replaced it into the hole, which he again covered with sand. The code disarmed a series of remote gun emplacements scattered throughout the rocks which guarded entrance from the outside and escape from the inside. A sensor system controlled each set to detect, target and fire on warm bodies larger than a dog. In the years of operation, the system eliminated four intruders and two attempted escapes. If he forgot to disarm the system, he would be targeted and eliminated in just over 100 yards. The "farm" was a little more than 200 yards up the road.

The farm was a series of small valleys running between rock formations. Each one covered by netting to protect "crops" from the intense sunshine. At the entrance, stood a small cabin to provide protection for "farm" implements and processing of the crop in one form or another. Next to it was another cabin to house the "farmers". They were all TCNs who overstayed their work permits only to be scooped up at a local gathering place for day workers.

Anyone who needs cheap labor can stop there, negotiate a price and working conditions, and take the workforce for a day of labor. Some were picked up and worked all day for pennies. Others were picked up in sting operations and deported. A final group, like these poor souls, would be picked up and placed into slavery circumstances.

Max Delphino, or "MD" to his customers, stopped the Rover next to the work shed. He sat inside the air-conditioning a few minutes and checked the sheet he brought containing statistics of cultivation listed in neat rows that corresponded to the valleys and rows spread in front of him. According to the records, none of the crop was ready for harvesting but the baling material in the back of the truck would be needed very soon.

As he stepped from the truck, he could hear the chugging two-stroke engine pulling the crop's water supply out of a well dug at the far end of row one. It kept a small tank filled with irrigation water. Gravity moved the water from there to each field through a series of PVC piping.

The entire operation was a marvel of modern farming and even more modern security measures. Max and his partner Bernard Estermann, "EB" to the customers, did their homework and were now reaping the benefits. Their Swiss bank accounts were growing exponentially with each successful crop. Ruthless in their pursuit of the greenback, they eliminated many of the workers who helped them install the farm's groundwork. Their bodies were located in a mass grave at the end of the last valley they cleared. Although they didn't participate in the actual elimination of workers, they did authorize and select the ones for death. The others stayed in line by the threat of being killed. The two killed trying to make their way out of the valley was proof enough that trying to make good their escape was a fruitless effort.

Kinkaid Bashir, lead worker at the farm and the only one to have any hope of making it out alive, came out of the worker's shed when he heard the truck stop. MD called him over.

"I brought some baling material and some chow, it's in the back," MD barked at Bashir who turned and called into the shack for others to join him. They began to unload the cargo as MD walked to the field with a crop nearly ready for harvest. He estimated another five to seven days and this cash crop would be on its way to market. Most of the plants were processed into hashish for ease of transport. However, there was still a market for the flowers and leaves processed into rolling material for those addicts who still liked an unfiltered smoke.

Most of the customers were in the big cities of Riyadh and Jeddah. Shipment was easy since most travelers from their region packed everything they needed for vacation into cardboard boxes or huge wrapped packages resembling cotton bales. Since the Kingdom was so tough on drugs, the local constabulary didn't feel a need to screen luggage except for X-ray. With a few clothes packed in for camouflage, they never encountered problems moving their product into the city for sale. They were able to charge sky-high prices because they were the only consistent game in town.

As MD was checking his listings and the condition of the crop, Kinkaid came over and stood silent until questioned. "Whatcha need?" MD tersely asked.

"Sir, there is a box with several bottles of wine and brown. I assume these are to stay in the vehicle?"

"No Kinkaid, they are not to stay in the vehicle. Call me soft in my old age but I decided to bring out some drinks for all of you. You have to make sure they don't get drunk and try to run up and down the rocks. You know what the consequences can be," MD said as he again turned to his review of the crops.

MD finished his review and headed toward the truck. Visits to the farm came every other day. EB and MD rotated the duties because neither of them really liked the tortuous drive. Even in the comfort of their Land Rover, it was tough. Both of the men would be glad when they met their financial goals and could leave the Kingdom.

Once at the truck, MD said a few final words to Kinkaid. Since EB was due out next, he would let him make the final decision on harvesting the crop. He was the farm boy from the midlands of England. MD was from the midlands of the United States but Kansas City is not a small farming community. Finishing their conversation, MD got into the truck and drove down the road. He made his exit to the main road and drove toward town. He could never imagine the problems he would be facing in upcoming weeks.

Karl let the phone ring a half dozen times and was almost ready to hang up when he heard a raspy voice on the other end. "Hello".

"Dillon?" Karl questioned. "I just got back to the villa and picked up your message. Been down at the souks picking up a few trinkets for the wife. What's the news you have for me?" he asked.

Dillon rolled over on his back, looked at the bedside clock, and saw it was just after noon. He told Karl about the previous night's activities. "I made excellent contacts last night. Got some names from this one guy and may have to make a trip to Khamis to shut up the det commander down there. He definitely has the potential for some hash problems but I don't think they're involved with our case. I need some one on one time with him and maybe we can pinpoint a few avenues of investigation for the Saudi police."

"Sounds good to me," Karl replied. "Why don't you come over to the house and we'll discuss what I know about the place over some pizza and beer?" Dillon agreed to the lunch invitation and bid Karl good-by until later. He hung up and remained motionless for a few minutes trying to gain his senses. He always hated waking up to a phone call but in his business, it became a matter of habit.

Dillon made his way to the bathroom and a shower. He made a quick swash at his beard, brushed his teeth, and ran a brush through his still damp hair. He left his villa and made the short trek to Karl's place. There a cold brew greeted him with a promise of pizza on the way. Karl had a CD on his stereo and moved to the sideboard where he installed his small system to turn down the volume. Dillon took a seat in one of the compound provided wing back chairs and propped his feet on a camel saddle. After bringing the volume down a couple of notches, Karl sat in the other wing back, put the long neck down on the table separating the two men and asked what information Dillon collected the night before.

"Met with Papa Good, the old Filipino who owns and runs a pleasure palace known as the California Compound. He introduced me to a guy named Buzz. As you may know, Buzz is the one who supplies Papa with beer and wine."

"I've heard the name but with our supply of the real stuff, we haven't taken the opportunity to meet him. He hasn't been involved in any of our serious investigations," Karl responded.

"That's good to know. At least if we meet him together, he won't know your business. Anyway, Buzz was making a delivery. Papa sent him to me and we talked for a moment. When I made a move into information about drugs, he got into my face, denied any knowledge, and then stormed out. When Pete and I left the compound, he was waiting for us on the access road. He explained his behavior as a ruse to continue the game he was playing with Papa about his non-involvement with hard drugs. He led us to his mansion, and I do mean mansion, where he gave us the names of people involved with the cocaine business and the hash trade. The three we have to concentrate on are ROM, Floppy, and HD. From what I gathered, they are TCNs who were drop points for Crimitin. Buzz knew there were recent problems with their delivery system but wasn't sure what the problems were. He also gave us MD and EB in the Khamis area. They are the major suppliers of hash and marijuana. We need to set up a trip as soon as possible. What's the quickest way to get there? Any military flights?" Dillon wondered.

"We have some and the Saudi's are supposed to have a 130 parts run but both are hit and miss at best. The contractors have a Lear making daily runs to all the bases but you have to be related to the pilots or one of the high up muckty mucks to get a ride with them. Besides, we don't want to draw attention to your visit. Best bet is to fly commercial. They have two or three flights everyday. I'll take care of getting you booked on a flight. When do you want to go?"

"Let's make it Sunday," Dillon answered. "That way I can go, spend a couple of days, and be back for the weekend. By then I'm sure to have a pile of paperwork to sort through and can use the weekend to catch up."

"Done deal. You'll have a full day with Erpack to get him pointed in the right direction." Just as Karl finished, the doorbell rang.

"Pizza's here," he shouted.

As Karl headed to the door, Dillon headed for the kitchen to get plates, and pick up the utensils already set on the counter. He grabbed a roll of paper towels and headed back toward the living room.

"It ain't Pizza Hut but it's sure a suitable substitute," Karl said as he laid two boxes on the coffee table. He switched to the movie channel where an old black and white murder mystery was just beginning. With pizza boxes open and brews in hand, the two investigators settled down for an afternoon of relaxation as things developed in other locations.

CHAPTER TWENTY-TWO

When she heard the front door buzzer, Helga hurried to the kitchen from her back yard where she was tending her strawberries. She pushed the intercom button and greeted the unseen person outside her front door. A very courteous man identified himself as Sergeant Henrick Hoffen of the Kaiserslautern police. With him was Sergeant Alfred Jater. When Helga inquired what she could do for the gentlemen, Henrick asked if she received the call from headquarters about their visit. Helga said she received no such call. The two men discussed the lack of effective communications in the office and then asked Helga if she would mind if they looked at Mr. Crimitin's apartment. Since Helga certainly didn't mind another police visit, she pressed the release latch for the door and then stepped into the hallway taking her keys off the hook as she went.

She greeted both men and asked for some identification. Both presented cards with their picture, names, rank, and badge number. Once she was satisfied, she led the way to the second floor and the door to Crimitin's apartment. Both men thanked Helga for her cooperation and entered the apartment. Once inside they put on the rubber and cotton gloves each man carried in his coat pocket. First on was the rubber under glove and then the cotton gloves over them. This method prevents leaving latent prints through the rubber gloves as they searched the house.

They started in the small bathroom immediately to their left. For the next two hours, they methodically searched each room of the apartment moving in a clockwise direction from the bathroom, to the first bedroom, to the master bedroom, to the living room, to the back patio, to the dining room, to the kitchen, to the second bathroom and to the final bedroom. The men looked in every closet, under each bed, in every kitchen cabinet and tested every tile and brick for one that may be loose or removable. Net result, nothing.

Both men were frustrated and tired as they dropped on the living room sofa. Just as they did, there was a knock at the door. Both men jumped up with Henrick walking down the wide tiled hallway to the front door. He put one eye up to the peephole and saw Helga waiting outside with two glasses of amber liquid. He pulled off his gloves and opened the door to let her inside. She brought them some very cold apple cider. Henrick thanked her and pushed the door shut with his foot as she went down the stairs. He brought the glasses to where Alfred waited and handed him a glass as they discussed their lack of results.

They brainstormed for nearly half an hour before they agreed there was no place in the house they overlooked. Alfred got up from the couch and walked into the dining area. He stood with his back to the window and the front street as he looked toward the terraced back yard. He mentally examined each room as he sipped the cider. He finally said, "If he left anything here, we are never going to find it".

"I'll have to agree," Henrick replied as he walked to the brick fireplace. "Maybe he was smarter than we give him credit for. Maybe someone else was helping him and they have the tapes."

"I really doubt it," countered Alfred. "He was too much of a loner and we haven't been able to find anyone who really knew him. I guess we'll just have to keep digging until something appears. Let's get going." He picked up Henrick's glass and headed toward the door.

Henrick finished checking the fireplace one last time. He made sure the doors leading to the backyard and patio were secure. He followed Alfred out the door and down to Helga's apartment. She answered the door and asked if they were finished. They said they were and thanked her for the cooperation and cider. She set the glasses inside on a small end table and went with the men as they left the house. They walked down the driveway and got into their car. Helga waved as the men drove away.

⚜

Bill stepped into the hallway and turned toward Christina's office. He wanted to pay a visit to Crimitin's house. When he got to her doorway, she came out of the evidence room at the end of the hall. "Need something Bill?" she asked as she locked the door.

"I was going over the list of evidence and remembered what Dillon said about giving the residence another visit. Let's see if we can set something up with Helga. I can make myself available whenever she can arrange time for a visit." Bill said as he turned and headed back to his office.

Christina said she would have one of the administrators make contact with Helga and set something up. She went to her office, buzzed TSgt. Lenny Ikemann, lead administrator, and asked if he would make contact as soon as possible.

Hanz pulled his pass out of its protective covering as he entered the building. The guard greeted him as he traversed the maze of metal detectors and bulletproof doors leading to the entrance area, stairway, and his office. Picking up his distribution and mail as he passed the administrator's desk, he sifted through the envelopes and found nothing requiring his immediate attention. He threw the personal mail on a chair next to the police issue briefcase he used to transport documents between offices and personal items home in the evening. He reached into the small refrigerator, selected a sparkling apple juice, and took a long drink. He set the bottle down on a coaster emblazoned with the emblem of Baltimore's police department. It was a conference souvenir from an anti-terrorist meeting held on the banks of Maryland's Chesapeake Bay. He was reaching for a folder on the corner of his desk when his pager began to vibrate. He looked at the number and saw Bill was calling. He picked up the phone on his desk and dialed Bill's direct line.

"OSI, Bill Wilmerson."

"Bill this is Hanz. You just vibrated me?"

"Yeah, Hanz. Can you join me for lunch in my office?"

"I would love to Bill but I just got back to the office and have a pile of nuisance paperwork to forge my way through before the end of the day. Have to take a rain check on the offer."

Bill's tone was still upbeat as he restated the offer. "Hanz I must insist on your being my guest for lunch. I have something very special prepared and I don't want you to miss this opportunity."

Hanz thought his attitude was puzzling. It was a bit out of character for Bill so he kept up with the play-acting. "OK master chef, what time do the festivities begin?"

"As soon as you can get over here. We look forward to your arrival."

Hanz hung up and leaned back in his chair. What was going on? Bill seemed a bit out of sorts. He pushed the folders back into their original positions, finished off the sparkling apple juice, picked up his briefcase, and headed for the door. He told his administrator he was going to Ramstein and the OSI office. He would be there if they needed to get hold of him. He left the office, went down the stairs and out the door.

He pulled into the visitor-parking slot outside the OSI office, locked his case in the trunk, and went through the front door. As he was greeting Sergeant Ikemann, he heard Bill shout his name. He continued down the hall and into the conference room doorway. As he stepped through, Bill looked up from his notepad.

"I've got a very short question to ask and depending on your answer, we may have a very large kink in our operation. Did you send a Sergeant," Bill paused to check his notes," Hoffen and a Sergeant Jater out to visit Crimitin's apartment this morning?"

There was no noticeable hesitation as Hanz replied in the negative. "I've never heard of either man."

"Goddamn it. I was afraid that was going to be your final answer. I never heard of them and when I checked the list you gave me, I didn't see either of them in your division or any other division. Let me fill you in."

Bill began to tell Hanz about his desire to pay another visit to the apartment and that he asked Christina to make the arrangements.

"Sergeant Ikemann made the initial contact and when he asked about a convenient time, Helga said she had visitors that morning. The call passed to Christina who took down the information about the men. She didn't recognize the names so she brought them to me. I checked my list and couldn't find the men in any division or subsection. I made a call to Helga and without trying to upset her, asked a couple of questions about the men. Her answers didn't give me a warm fuzzy feeling."

Hanz ran his fingers through his thinning hair and shook his head.

"Since you have a breach in your office, I didn't want to put the news on the wire services", Bill finished off.

"I'm glad you played it the way you did." Hanz replied. "We'll want to collect as much as we can from Helga and the apartment. Let's head out there now and see what we can pick up on first glance. I'll get the crew to check the place over once we make an initial visit." Bill agreed as he pushed papers inside a folder and dropped them into the file box at his feet.

Both men left the conference room with Hanz going down the hall to the front office and Bill making a stop at Christina's office to tell her where he was headed. He then picked up his case and went out the side door to his car. He drove around the side and into the front lot where Hanz was waiting with four way flashers illuminated. The small dashboard mounted police beacon would light up once he left the base confines.

The drive to Helga's took less than half the normal time. Hanz pulled into the steep drive with Bill parking in front of the walkway. As Hanz reached for the entrance buzzer, the door swung open. Helga was standing on the other side. Both men greeted the landlady and followed her up stairs to Crimitin's door. She opened it and led the way inside. The three of them stood in the tile hallway looking into each room. Nothing seemed to be out of place. They obviously wanted everyone to believe they were truly police officers and not thugs.

"Looks like they didn't tear the place up." Bill began. "Helga, what can you tell us about their demeanor?"

Helga related they were both very professional and were in the apartment for more than two hours. They never asked her for anything. Bill and Hanz walked into the living room looking for something out of place. Helga stood in the entranceway and watched. Bill went to the patio door and abruptly turned toward Hanz.

"We might as well stop here," he said as he pointed to the brass plate surrounding the door handle.

"They were wearing some type of gloves." Hanz came over and examined the spot Bill was pointing too.

"You're right; they were wearing something to conceal their prints." Hanz agreed. The brass plate showed a smudge spot where one of the men pulled the door shut as he went outside. The smudge was noticeable because it wiped off some of the material used to check for prints during initial evidence collection after Crimitin's death.

Both men turned from the door with disgusted looks on their face. When Helga queried about their concern, they invited her to join them in the living room. She sat on the couch as Hanz dropped into an armchair and Bill sat on the hearth. After a moment for reflection, Bill asked Helga to go systematically through the sequence of events surrounding the morning visitors. Helga paused to gather her thoughts before beginning.

She told the investigators how the men appeared at her door and asked if she knew about their pending visit. How they were upset because the communication line bogged down. How they went into the apartment, closed the door, and spent more than two hours on what she can only surmise was a complete search of the apartment. She told how she brought them something to drink and after bringing the glasses down to her apartment, they left.

"You brought them a drink?" Hanz asked getting out of his seat.

"Yes I did," Helga replied. "I thought they were police. I wanted to be courteous." Bill rose from his spot on the hearth and now stood on the other side of the coffee table.

"When you gave them the drink, were they wearing gloves?"

"Gloves?" she questioned. "No he wasn't. The man who came to the door when I knocked did not have gloves on when he took the glasses from me. He didn't have any on when they brought them back to my apartment just before they left."

Bill and Hanz could not believe their luck. Perhaps the tide was turning in their favor. Hanz asked Helga where the glasses were at this moment. She told him in her kitchen. They asked her to lead the way.

Once downstairs, Helga showed them into the kitchen. She was looking for the glasses on the sink. They weren't there. She stood with hands on hips puzzled by that fact. Then she clapped her hands together when she remembered putting them on the end table behind the front door where she kept her outgoing mail and car keys.

She led the way back down the hall and was about to pick up the glasses when Bill asked her to wait. He turned to Hanz and asked if he carried a superglue kit with him. Hanz said he didn't. Bill then asked Helga for a pair of tongs and a cardboard box. Helga retrieved the tongs from a drawer in the kitchen and took Bill to a small storage room where she kept a few boxes for mailing purposes. Bill selected one the approximate size of the glasses and returned to the hallway table. He folded back two of the boxes flaps and notched the remaining flaps just wide enough to fit inside the mouth of the glasses. He carefully picked up each glass with the tongs and placed it inside the box away from the sides. He folded the flaps down so the notch fit inside the opening of the glasses. The other flaps were closed and taped down.

"Not bad," Hanz said as he watched the final touch of Bill's evidence collection technique. "Where did you learn that?"

Bill explained how Dillon related an incident with a beer bottle at a crime scene. He transported the bottle back to the office in a manner similar to the one he just completed with the glasses. It protected possible erasure of latent prints on the non-porous surface of the glasses. Now all they could do was hope for the best when they used the superglue technique back at the office. This was a great find and they would keep their fingers crossed for adequate prints. Before they headed to the office, Bill asked one final question.

"Did you happen to notice what type of car they were driving?"

"Yes I did," Helga replied immediately. "It was a blue Audi sports model."

⚜

Buzz brought both hands up to his forehead and drew them back over his balding dome. He turned around and sat down on one of the steps leading out of the pool. He rubbed his ample abdomen as he recalled past years when he could swim lap after lap and only be mildly winded at the end.

He shifted his sitting position when he heard Lola call his name as she came down the steps toward the pool. In one hand, she cradled a phone and in the other, she held a small cigar.

"There's a business call for you. I brought the hard line phone." She swayed over to a chaise lounge, knelt on the cushions, and pulled open the door of a small cabinet. Inside was a phone jack where she hooked the line as she set the phone on top of the cabinet. Buzz stepped out of the pool and toweled off. Lola turned and as she reached out to caress him through his Speedo, she kissed his chest and told him she would be back later to join him in the pool. Maybe working out turns her on Buzz thought as he sat on the lounge and picked up the phone. "Buzz here."

"Buzz this is Papa."

"Papa! This has to be a first. To what do I owe the distinct pleasure of having you give me a call at home? I hope there isn't a serious problem with my product?"

"As usual Buzz, your product is quality and everyone seems pleased. It gets them as high as they want to fly. I'm calling about my new patrons. I'm a bit concerned with their story and was wondering if they tried to contact you after you left my place."

"You're my first call today Papa. The guy I talked to wanted to know something about drugs and you know I'm not in that business. You said visitors. Was there someone with him? When I talked to the guy you pointed out, he was only with one of the regulars. There was someone else?"

"Yes, a pilot. They want to get involved with bringing the military back into the establishment. As you can imagine, I'm all for the added clientele but I don't want to have them bringing unwanted attention to the compound. You know how stories get started and I don't want to be making additional protection payments."

"I understand your concerns but why do you think he would contact me?"

"Please Buzz, give me a little credit. I didn't just fall off the delivery van yesterday. I know you have contacts in the drug line and are just playing the part to keep me happy. I know you have cut down on your drug connection but you still keep your hands in the pie. I would imagine you've the names and contact points for most of the movers in Riyadh. I have trusted you to keep that connection away from my operation and I appreciate your support for my personal position." Buzz paused a moment before replying. Papa's knowledge level interested him.

"Let's just keep our partnership on the same level it is right now. You're a good customer and I don't want to jeopardize our relationship. Let me do some checking into the situation and I'll give you a call when and if I discover anything." Papa thanked him for his cooperation and hung up. Buzz slammed the phone into the cradle and lay back on the chaise.

"That crotchety old fuck," he said aloud.

"Which old fuck are you talking about," Lola asked from a chair next to the pool.

"That shithead Papa. He's had me figured for some time now. I should have given him more credit but we aren't in the same business, so I really wasn't worried about putting him out of the way. We rather complemented each other. Now he wants me to check into a couple of Air Force types. I tried to show him last night I didn't want anything to do with them. Oh well, just as long as we keep our mutual respect for each others operation, I guess I can live with the humiliation of being cross checked by a Filipino."

"Were those two with you last night the ones Papa is concerned about?"

"That's them. Papa doesn't want any large influx of military types to cause undo attention to his operation. He surely doesn't want any drugs involved. I guess I'll just have to make contact with the guys and see if I can squeeze some information out of them."

As he was finishing his thought, Lola got up from the chair and moved toward the chaise. She put one leg on either side of Buzz and lowered herself on top of his Speedo. She pulled the tie loose on her robe to reveal her well-sculptured nakedness. She put her hands on his shoulders and leaned down to kiss him on the forehead. As she did, Buzz put his hands underneath her rounded buttocks and stood up from the lounge. Lola wrapped her legs around his waist and pulled the robe from her arms as he carried her to the steps and into the pool. As she held on with arms and legs encircling his neck and waist, he pulled off his Speedo so they could partake of watery pleasures other than swimming.

CHAPTER TWENTY-THREE

Bill burst into the office and as he streaked down the hallway toward the conference room he shouted, "Christina!"

"William," was the reply.

"Come to the conference room. I have something very important to show you." Bill and Hanz were just entering the conference room when Christina asked if Penny was invited. "Certainly, I didn't see her car outside, so I didn't think she was in the office."

"It's in the shop," Penny said as she came out of her office and joined Christina and the others in the conference room. They took standing positions across the table from Bill. Hanz pulled out a chair and was in the process of sitting down when Bill, standing straight as an arrow with both hands on top of the cardboard box sitting on the table, began.

"We have just made a grand discovery." He opened the flaps of the box and pushed it across the table toward the two investigators.

"Oh goody," Christina exclaimed as she gave Penny a playful poke with her elbow. "The gas station is now giving away custom glasses with a fill up." Hanz covered his mouth to stifle a laugh.

"No Miss Smartass, Hanz and I picked these up from Helga's house. The two men who visited this morning used them. We're hoping they didn't put on the gloves they were using when they searched the house as they drank from these glasses. Helga said the man who answered the door when she brought them upstairs and when he returned them to her apartment wasn't wearing any gloves. If we're lucky, and I mean very lucky, we'll be able to put names with our mysterious visitors."

"The best part of the equation is Helga saw the car they were driving," Hanz added. "It was a blue Audi sports model."

"So fill us in on all the details," Penny asked as she and Christina sat down.

Bill pulled out a chair and sat at the table. He began with his desire to visit the house again and unfolded the story from there. Christina and Penny sat and listened in stunned silence.

"Now we have to figure out how to keep this find away from the inside source in my office", Hanz began. "I don't want to put the glasses into my system for identification if it can be helped. Do you guys have a source for checking the prints?"

Bill agreed with Hanz on keeping their find out of the German system. With Asterfon monitoring Interpol help, they decided to send the evidence back to the Army lab in Georgia and let them handle the identification in strictest confidence. They would be able to process the glasses and obtain identifications using interconnected computer systems. No one outside the lab or OSI channels would know anything about the queries or the results. It took much longer but no one on the team wanted to take the chance of having this bit of evidence compromised. They wanted the phony cops to believe they got away with their little ploy.

"Christina, I'll let you take care of shipping the glasses to the lab." Bill said as he pulled the box back to his side of the table.

"From their packaging, I will guess you didn't have your superglue kit with you?" Penny asked.

"Correct assumption. I didn't think about it this morning as we rushed out of the office. If you want to go into the evidence room and bring our kit here, we can get this out of the way."

Penny retrieved the kit sitting it at the end of the conference table near an electric outlet. "I don't remember the last time I used this thing," Christina said as she removed the masking tape.

Inside were the tools necessary to superglue fume the glasses. First, she pulled out one of the small tubes of superglue from a self-sealing baggy. Next, she picked up a roll of aluminum foil and a roll of masking tape, setting them both on the table. Penny removed a coffee cup warmer and a smaller cardboard box. Christina reached inside the larger box for a coffee cup still inside. Penny took the coffee cup and went down the hall to heat up some water. While she was gone, Christina put the cup warmer inside the smaller box and ran the cord through a hole cut in the side. She then fashioned an aluminum foil tray and set it on the cup warmer. On another piece of foil, she pressed down her thumb to give them a control print. This would provide some type of assurance the fuming was completed. When Penny returned with the hot water, they placed it next to the cup warmer inside the box. Both glasses were carefully placed near the cup warmer as a small amount of superglue was added to the aluminum foil tray on the warmer. Penny then ran a strip of tape across the top of the box to seal in the fumes. Since they were fuming two glasses, they let the process run for about 15 minutes before shutting off the heat and opening the box. They brought in a fan to circulate the air out an open window as they pulled the tape off the small box. The test print was clearly visible as were several prints on each glass.

"Hot Damn," Bill exclaimed as he looked inside. "We may have hit pay dirt!"

"This really looks good," Hanz added as he looked inside the cardboard chamber. "Let's just hope they have something to match those prints."

"Good work ladies," Bill said to both investigators. "I haven't seen such clean results in some time. Most of the time I can't see the prints I'm trying to save until after they come back from the lab. Let's get some pictures for our files and send a set on with the glasses. I believe we have some shipping containers in the evidence room. Make damn sure we secure then so they don't rub off the prints in transit."

Before the end of the day, Christina and Penny catalogued the evidence with pictures and computer entries, packed it, and transported it to the overnight delivery company of choice. From the offices in Landsthule, the pack goes to Frankfurt and an early morning flight back to the United States. Guaranteed delivery by noon the next day.

Christina gave lab personnel a heads up email message to inform them of the delivery company and tracking number.

After Penny and Christina departed the conference room, Bill and Hanz turned their focus toward trying to figure why the two men they are tracking for Crimitin's death would take such a risk and search his apartment. "I'm *fully* convinced at this juncture Crimitin had some type of personal record of his activities and these two were sent to find what ever it is and bring it back to the boss," Bill began as he rose from his chair and headed for the door.

"I'm headed for the coffee bar, want anything?" he asked.

"Not right now," Hanz replied, "But I will join you for a change of scenery." The two men walked in silence to the coffee room. Since the carafe was nearly empty, Bill dumped the remains into the sink and began preparing another pot.

"Let's hope for the best and make the bold assumption these two didn't find anything more than dust when they searched the place," Hanz said as he took a place at the small table situated in the middle of the room. "We're looking for micro cassette tapes, so they could have found them and just slipped them into their pockets as they were leaving. We could be facing the loss of very important evidence. Being realistic, with each passing day I hold out less and less hope we will ever find the tapes, if they really do exist. We may be chasing after our tails. He probably kept some type of a journal which is hidden in a safe deposit box in Switzerland."

As the words came out of his mouth, both men realized what was said. No one checked with the family to see if there were any personal items stored at their home in California.

"The Crimitin's!" they said in unison.

"Let's make the call," Bill said as he got up from the table and headed toward the conference room with Hanz right behind him. Bill called the command post. He wanted to make the call over secure lines. Within a couple of minutes, he was talking with the duty controller at Vandenberg.

"Good morning, this is Agent Bill Wilmerson calling from Ramstein Air Base in Germany. I was wondering if you could connect me with the duty OSI agent."

"One moment sir." was the brief reply. Bill heard the line clicking as the connection went through. No elevator music on this hold button.

"Agent Moankat," was heard in a drowsy tone.

"Sorry to disturb your sleep, this is Agent Wilmerson calling from Germany. We need your help on a case currently under investigation over here."

"Hang on just a second; let me get to the desk and some note paper." The line went dead as the agent in California's early morning hours put the agents in Germany on hold. His voice was much clearer when he picked up the line at his office desk.

"OK, now *who* is on the line?"

"Agent Bill Wilmerson, Ramstein OSI."

"My name's Sidney Moankat, Bill. What can I do for you at this early hour of the morning?"

"We're working a murder investigation over here and the victim was a California boy who ran afoul of some pretty nasty people," Bill began to explain. He brought Sidney briefly up to speed with the California connection.

"I don't have any information on the case. However, I do remember Randy Ridgemire providing some information about the case during one of our weekly meetings. I'll get with him and find out what he knows. What are your specific questions?" Sidney concluded.

"The most important item is any information about a journal, micro cassette tapes, or a safe deposit box. We believe this guy had information on the cartel and was about to bring it home when he was killed. We haven't been able to locate notes of any type but we do know he had a micro cassette tape recorder with him when he died. There was a blank tape in the recorder

167

and we don't think he was carrying his evidence around with him. We've been over the house from top to bottom and today we find out our suspects paid a visit to his apartment. We hope they didn't find anything we missed." Bill finished up.

"Sounds like you have your hands full," Sidney said as he pushed his note pad to one side of his desk and leaned back in his chair.

"I'll talk with Randy today and see what we can find. I'll give you a call through the command post when we have something to report. If there is a safe hiding place with the family, I hope it contains what you're looking for."

"Thanks for the help. We'll press on over here and hope you guys come up with the silver bullet." Bill responded to Sid's offer of assistance. The two agents exchanged phone numbers and other pertinent information before disconnecting. As Bill returned the phone to its cradle, Christina came in the door with a cup of coffee in each hand.

"Thought you might want this," she said as she sat the cup with Bill's name down in front of him.

"How did you know," Bill replied.

"Simple enough. The pot was just finishing its brew cycle and your cup was sitting next to the pot. I heard you talking in here so I just figured I'd be out of character and bring you a cup."

"Glad you did," Bill began. "We just had a brain wave strike both of us as we were putting things in perspective. Since we aren't having any luck finding his hiding place here, we thought there might be a connection with his family in California." Bill went on from there to tell Christina about the recently completed call and the offer of assistance from their fellow agents in California.

"What's next?" Hanz asked as he reached across the table for the folder with Helga's name written in red ink across the front.

"We need to bring Dillon up to speed as soon as we can. I want to make sure he has all the information he needs as he prods the players in Kingdom. You never know. The leader of the pack may be located in Riyadh. At this point anything is possible," he finished saying as he reached for the phone.

Again, he went through the command post for a secure line. He listened as the phone in Riyadh rang three times before Dillon's machine answered with a not available message. Bill stated his name and time of call before hanging up.

"He's not home now. I'm sure he'll give me a call when he gets back. The next thing we should do is make contact with Helga and tell her we are the only ones she should deal with. We don't want to alarm her but she does need to know about the two phony cops." Bill concluded as he pushed the phone toward Hanz.

He quickly dialed and waited for her to answer. After the cordial greetings, he told her the two men who visited her that morning were not from his department as they proclaimed. She asked if she should be fearful and Hanz assured her everything would be under surveillance from now on. Regular patrols would be in her area looking for the same car. If she saw the men again, or if they contacted her in any way, she should get in touch with his office as soon as possible. She sounded relieved as they ended their conversation. Hanz said he would visit her later in the afternoon. She thanked him and hung up.

"How'd she sound?" Bill asked.

"She sounded very nervous at the beginning but after I told her about the patrols and such, she seemed to calm down a bit. I'll stop by and explain about the patrols we will run and give her your number and all of my numbers so she can contact one of us if there are any further visits."

Hanz asked for a couple of the investigative folders and Bill pulled them from their file boxes.

When Hanz finished his review, he pushed the folders to the corner of the table nearest the file boxes. He turned off the lights as he went out the door to the hallway. Christina was just coming out of her office. "Hello, I didn't know you were still here."

"I just went over some of the files and was getting ready to head for Helga's house. I just wanted to ensure she understood we would be watching her house from now on."

"Give her my best. I'll make it a point to clear any visits I want to make with you or Bill," Christina said as Hanz reached her spot in the hall. They both continued to Bill's office.

"Visits to whom?" Bill asked as Christina came into the office and took a seat in front of his desk. Hanz stopped just inside the door.

"Helga," Christina said.

"I'm on my way out there now," Hanz added as he reached in his pocket for his car keys. "I'll give you a call later and let you know how everything went. I want to make sure she feels comfortable with the situation." Hanz waved good-by as he turned to walk toward the front parking lot.

<hr/>

Dillon opened the door and let Karl step into the coolness of his villa. Karl had two plastic bags in each hand containing a few rations for the weekend. The men planned to bar-b-que that evening. Dillon followed him inside as he picked up the box of liquid refreshment. If they had to plan strategies, they wanted to be relaxed. As they went into the kitchen, Dillon noticed messages on both machines. The local one showed two calls and the secure line had one. After setting down the groceries, Dillon twisted the cap off a long neck and returned to retrieve his messages. He started with the secure line and heard Bill. The local line was a hang up and Buzz. Dillon wrote down the number Buzz left and went back into the kitchen to pick up some snacks before returning the calls.

The first call was to Buzz.

After their escapade in the pool, Buzz and Lola retired to a small cabana near the pool for a nap. When the phone rang, Buzz reached over for the mobile and as he did, Lola shifted her naked backside away from Buzz so he could answer the call. "This is Buzz," he mumbled.

"Buzz, this is Dillon. You called earlier?"

Buzz sat up and as he did, Lola fell from the lounge. She grabbed her robe and covered up as she reached into the small fridge and pulled out a sparkling water. She offered one to Buzz but he declined as he spoke to Dillon.

"I got to thinking after last night we might want to talk a bit more about our possible business arrangements. I might have some additional contact points for your clients."

Dillon's sixth sense was aroused as he paused before answering. "Sounds good to me Buzz. What did you have in mind?"

"I'm partial to Chinese food right at the present time. My tastes change from time to time but I have been frequenting a place call Lai-Lai. It has a great buffet Wednesday and Thursday night. We can meet there tonight and put some more information on the table."

Not wanting to be rushed into anything, Dillon put Buzz off. "I can't make it tonight Buzz. I have several projects on the burner and only being here on a temporary basis, I can't afford to take any personal time right now. Actually, I just laid in some food for the rest of the weekend. I'm going to hunker down in the air conditioning and finish off at least two of these things before Saturday morning. I appreciate the offer. How about we make it for next Thursday and I'll try to get hold of Carmen." Dillon finished.

"You must have read my mind. As you were so skillfully putting me off, I thought it would be nice for companions of the opposite sex to join us. Always makes dinner more interesting." Lola looked at him as she finished her drink.

"Sounds great. Can I get back with you later this week to finalize a time?" Dillon asked.

"Just give me a call on this mobile. I don't use it for business, just personal calls." Buzz said as he got up from his lounge and walked over to where Lola was sitting. She reached out and caressed him as he concluded the call. "I look forward to hearing from you."

"OK Buzz, talk with you later this week." and Dillon hung up.

"That was interesting," he said as he turned to where Karl was standing.

"Buzz wants to meet and discuss additional names. It just doesn't feel right. I put him off until next week. I'll need some help getting additional information on him if it can be arranged."

"We'll work on it," Karl said as he came over to the couch and sat down.

"I can't guarantee we'll have much on him. The local authorities are more interested in protecting special interests than they are on catching the bad guys. However, when they do get a wild hair up their ass and pull in drug dealers or murderers, their justice is short, sweet and to the sharp point of an executioner's sword. They don't mess around. You're found guilty and the appeal process is just a rubber stamp of the verdict. They take you out in the main square and chop off your head."

"I was told about their justice system. Is it only effective for foreigners or do they make Saudis pay the same steep price?" Dillon asked as he unscrewed the caps on another couple of long necks.

After taking a long pull on his beer, Karl explained. "We keep tabs on these things for the commander and we see Saudis facing the same type of punishment. They do have a system we refer to as blood money. Once convicted of a crime, the victims' family can elect to have the perpetrator's family pay cash for his release. If they don't, off comes the head. There was one guy convicted of a killing and the victim's family wanted more than one million riyals. It took some time and some stays of execution but I do believe the guy's family came up with the money."

"That's one hell of a system. However, some of the people around here have told me they just aren't afraid to be out on the streets at night. The only thing scaring expats now is Al Qaeda and car bombs."

As he was reaching across the coffee table, the secure line began to ring. "I'll bet that's Bill trying to connect again." Dillon went to the small desk holding both phones and recording machines. He picked up, "Dillon here".

"Well, well, well. It's good to see you finally returned." Bill quipped.

"I was out shopping. I brought in some supplies for the weekend. We're formulating a plan of attack for my visit, as they call it downrange, and what we're going to do once I return," Dillon replied. "I hope you have good news."

"Sit yourself down my friend. What I'm about to tell you will roll your socks down." Dillon took Bill's advice and pulled out the desk chair. He took another sip of his beer as Bill began to relate recent activities. The look on Dillon's face must have been one of total shock because Karl went into the kitchen and brought Dillon another brew as he drained the one in hand.

His first words of reply were "You have got to be shittin me? Why is it I'm sitting in the desert and you're getting all the hits."

Bill just laughed. "I can't say it was all due to brilliant detective work. This just fell into our laps. Hanz is talking with Helga right now. We don't want her to be afraid of staying in her own house. I'm just thankful they didn't see a need to eliminate Helga. She's been so cooperative up to now. Hope this doesn't change anything."

"Knowing Hanz, he'll be able to put aside any fears she might have. If there *are* leaks in his office, they will also leak out the increased security measures. I doubt the two men will make a return visit. Is Hanz going to have her look at mug books and give us a sketch?" Dillon queried.

"We didn't talk about that; I was too excited about getting the glasses. I'll give him a call after we finish and find out his plans. A sketch would be a handy item at this time. Once we match the fingerprints we can compare the items for a positive identification."

"That's all good in a perfect world. We can't hope for everything," Dillon cautioned. "We can be sure these two are only goons for the bigger operation. They may be the intermediaries between the supply and the demand. We still have to confirm they're the killers."

"Please let me bask in the potential," Bill laughed. "Are you getting a surge of foreboding?"

"Let's just play on the cautious side of optimistic. I've seen good things in an investigation go to hell in a hand basket right before we make a big snag. This information is grand but keep it in perspective. Let me fill you in on my end of the equation."

When Dillon finished, Karl questioned, "You looked like a deer in the headlights there for a while. What's the grand discovery?" Dillon told him the latest from Germany.

"That's some great information but my sense of perspective tells me these two are very professional and won't leave too many clues lingering around. I would say they won't be able to do anything with the prints," Karl stated.

"Willing to put some riyals on that perspective?" Dillon asked as he returned with two more long necks.

"Oh please, let me show my complete arrogance by wagering on a hunch!" Despite his skeptical attitude, Karl agreed to dinner at a restaurant of the winner's choosing. The only stipulation, it must be in Riyadh since no airfare was included in the wagering process. The men exchanged a handshake to seal the deal as they returned to planning Dillon's trip to Khamis.

⚜

The fax machine on the small table next to a window overlooking the harbor came to life after two rings. The message was short and too the point. The two female agents, referred to as Frick and Frack, took something to an overnight delivery service in Landsthule. Destination unknown, contents unknown. No way to find either answer because the item was kept out of Politzie channels. Again, reason unknown. It may have nothing to do with their current dilemma but the sending party wanted to ensure any activities out of the ordinary were reported for the files. After the message finished printing, it ended up in a read file on the large mahogany desk situated in the center of the room. The view of the harbor was breathtaking with the twinkling lights just beginning to illuminate the calm water as the sun slowly disappeared behind the mountaintops. Standing on the balcony one could hear the gentle clanging of metal sail fasteners as they stuck the masts of sailboats anchored in the harbor or tied up at the docks. It was a tranquil setting only disturbed by the distressing news.

Chapter Twenty-Four

Sidney Moankat came into Randy Ridgemire's office with cup of coffee in one hand and a note pad in the other. "Randy, you got a minute?" Randy turned from his computer screen and gestured for Sid to have a seat.

"I got a call from a guy in Germany who wanted me to check on a," he paused and looked at his notes, "Crimitin family. I understand you made some contact with them?"

Randy leaned back in his chair and thought for a minute. He reached into the desk's file drawer and pulled out a log of contact points. He ran his finger down the list until he came to Crimitin and next to it the name of Carpton, Carl J., Captain, 30th Maintenance Squadron, Ext. 6789. Next to it was a reference number referring Randy to one of his file cabinets. As he pulled the designated drawer, he began to recall his involvement and started to brief Sid on the Crimitin's and Captain Carpton.

"That's why the name didn't ring an immediate bell. Carpton gave me a call about a background check on these folks. We didn't play much of a part. Called the county sheriff's office, the highway patrol, and Azusa police. They all ran checks and sent me written reports. I've got them all right here," he said tapping the folder he removed from the cabinet. He opened the file and looked at the name list.

"The guy who called you, his name Wilmerson?"

"Right! He wants us to get with the family to see if the boy left anything with them. A key, a journal, a package, cassette tapes or anything else. He didn't go into all the details but I'm going to make the broad assumption he was murdered for information but now they can't find anything and they thought his family may have it stashed away for him."

"I would say you're on the right track." Randy said as he wrote down Carpton's number.

"There was another guy involved with the notification and follow-up. His name is Martinez. Let me see what I have on him, yes here it is, Martinez, Fernando, Chief Master. Works over in personnel." Randy wrote the chief's number and handed the sticky note to Sid.

"Let me know if you need anything else."

Once back at his desk, Sid called to talk with Carpton. The administrator said the captain was on temporary duty downrange and before Sid could ask another question, Sergeant Ubar was on the line.

"Senior Master Sergeant Ubar, can I help you?" questioned the maintenance superintendent.

Sid paused slightly before answering. "Yes sergeant, this is Special Agent Moankat, OSI. I was calling for the captain. Your admin man said he was TDY downrange."

"Right sir. Should be back at the weekend. Anything I can do for you?"

"Actually there might be, do you know anything about Crimltin?"

"Just the fringes. The captain told me the basics of the situation but since he wasn't assigned to our unit, I didn't take the time to investigate any further than he wanted to share with me."

"I understand," Sid replied. "Know anything about Sergeant Martinez in personnel?"

"If you mean the chief, I know him both professionally and personally. We've been stationed together several times. He's really a great guy. I'm sure he'll have much more information about the family than I have. Do you have his number?"

"Yes I do. I'll give him a call. Please let the captain know I called. Have him touch base with me next week. I may have some additional questions for him."

"Will do sir. Is there anything else I can do for ya at this time?"

"Thanks, you've been very helpful. I'll talk with you later," Sid finished. He made a few notes and then punched the speaker button on his phone as he dialed the chief's number.

"Personnel, Chief Martinez." came blaring through the speaker as Sid reached for the receiver.

"Hello Chief. I didn't expect to hook right into your office. I expected your admin man. This is Agent Moankat from OSI."

"Greetings," the chief replied. "Actually you did get my administrator. I was just passing her desk when the phone rang and by habit, picked up the line. She's on the other side of the room getting a briefing ready. What can I do for you?"

Sid gave the chief a brief synopsis of what was happening with the Crimitin's and the reason behind his call. Chief Martinez was very forthcoming with the family information. They agreed it would be best to visit the family in person rather than trying to get anything out of them over the phone. The chief offered to set up a meeting with the family for later in the week. Sid agreed and gave the chief his contact numbers. Sid asked if the meeting was set up for next week, get Captain Carpton to join them. He felt it would be more comfortable for the family if there were two people on their side when they faced questioning from an official Air Force investigator. He certainly didn't want to frighten the family into thinking they may be in danger from the people who murdered their son.

⚜

"OK, here it is," Karl proclaimed as he tore a sheet of paper from a pad on the telephone desk.

"This is what you have to choose from for your trip south. From Riyadh to Abha, we have a flight at 0430 getting you there at 0610. Problem there, it doesn't go on Sunday, so you would have to change your departure day." Karl paused and looked at Dillon for some type of response. Receiving none, he continued.

"The next flight is 0700 getting you there at 0835. Flight number is Sugar Victor 1831. Not sure what type of equipment it will be. Most of the time they fly Airbus 300's to and from Abha. They do occasionally put in an MD90 but those are rare. I have you coming back on Tuesday afternoon, departing at 1755, and arriving here at 1925. I'll pick you up at the airport and you can take me out to pay off the bet you're going to loose."

"Yeah right," Dillon said as he grabbed another handful of cashews.

"Just be sure you have sufficient funds to make restitution on your losing effort." Karl came around the edge of the couch, sat down and picked up his beer.

"Make my reservations on the 0700 flight. I don't want to change the day for my trip. I don't want to be stuck down there over the weekend. I want to be back on Tuesday night as planned. If Erpack wants to see me again, he can get his ass up here. I didn't come in Kingdom to help him solve his dilemma. Since I'm fairly sure his problems are not interconnected with our case, I'll give him what I have and turn him loose to smooth over his own rough patches."

176

Dillon looked at Karl for some reaction.

"Reservations are made. Tickets will be delivered to the office Saturday morning. Since they don't have business class on these craft, you're in first class both ways. Just makes the flight a little more bearable. You get free fruit juice in first class," Karl added as he smiled to himself. He took the flight before and knew what Dillon would be facing.

"How efficient," Dillon commented. "Should we call Erpack now or wait until Saturday?"

"Probably should give him a call now so he can arrange for billets. I know Khamis has a few VIP quarters. Let's see if he puts you in one. You already have an all-base pass from RSAF, so there shouldn't be any problem getting on or off the base if he feels it's necessary. Let me give him a call now," Karl said as he returned to the telephone table and picked up the secure line. "This way you won't have to go into any detail about your visit until you see him."

Dillon agreed. He didn't relish getting into a big conversation with the colonel. It was going to be tough enough to spend any time with the cantankerous stick actuator.

"I'll need to get in touch with Vinder once I get back. Try to set something up for Wednesday if you can. I can bring him up to speed on Khamis activities at the same time."

"No problem," Karl replied as he added the meeting to his list of things to coordinate and arrange.

"We'll have all the information we can on Buzz and set up a lunch time meeting at the Embassy. Rufas shouldn't have any difficulties making that happen. You did want to meet with the DEA man too, didn't you?"

"Good point. Add him to the meeting agenda. If Vinder wants to meet with me separately, have him set up a time for the DEA guy. I'll take my cues from him since he's the one working closest to the man." Dillon tipped back the long neck and drained the remaining brew. He stood up and stretched before heading for the kitchen.

"I do believe I've had enough for the present time. How about you Karl? Care for another?"

"Not right now," was the answer Dillon received from Karl as he added the finishing touches to his list.

"Let me review my notes and then we can finalize our planning before we settle down for the John Wayne western coming on in a few minutes." Karl finished his review and the two men discussed the ways and means of getting things done.

On the other side of town, Buzz was sitting in his office watching the landscapers work the fauna, which protects the pool area from outside views.

Buzz was waiting for a return call from some of his contacts in the police force. He wanted to find out if they knew anything about the visitor from Florida. If Papa was concerned, he should look into the situation. He didn't have to wait long. It was less than two hours since he made the calls to his contacts from poolside. One of his well-compensated captains called him back just as Lola was bringing him a tall Cuba Libra and a few snacks.

The captain made some calls to his contacts within Eskan and Prince Sultan Air Base. At the present, there really wasn't much to report. He manifested on a 141 out of Ramstein through Aviano. He was met by two men in civilian clothes and taken to Eskan. None of his activities drew the attention of anyone in particular. He was going to try to find out who met him. Perhaps that would lead to why he was in Kingdom.

There was no information on his traveling companion. He was a 141 pilot who flew in and out of the Kingdom on a regular basis. He never drew any attention to himself during any of his visits. It did seem a little strange he would show up at Papa's place as part of a 20-question seminar. However, he would keep checking that angle also.

During the remainder of the afternoon, he received a couple of additional calls with the same information. Nothing out of the ordinary. Buzz felt relatively secure in meeting Dillon later in the week.

⋈

Helga walked Hanz to the end of her driveway. The conversation and the reassurances Hanz was able to give Helga made her feel much better. Hanz reminded her with the extra patrols, they probably wouldn't reappear in the neighborhood. Nevertheless, that didn't mean they wouldn't follow her when she went shopping or visiting. Helga said she wasn't afraid of leaving the house if she needed to. Hanz again gave her all of his contact numbers and Bill's card so she could call either of them with information about the investigation or with questions about her personal situation. She thanked him again, gave him a hug, and turned to go back inside the house.

Before leaving Kottweiller, Hanz drove up the road the killers used. He wanted to look at the scene so he could advise shift supervisors what they might discover during their patrols. When he was on top of the hill looking down at Helga's street, he called Bill to fill him in on the details of their conversation. Since there was nothing sensitive about their discussion, Hanz

178

felt he could talk over the open cellular airwaves. However, Bill had some additional information for him and asked if he could stop by for an update.

He left the confines of his drivers' position while talking with Bill. When they finished, Hanz leaned against the hood of his patrol car as he took in the grandeur of the scene. The peak of the hill afforded a panoramic view of the town and surrounding countryside. It was picture postcard viewing. The afternoon sun was just at the right angle to give each tree a special tint. The deep tones were breath taking even for a hardened police investigator. He could just make out the glimmer off a small lake on the outskirts of town. He remembered his youth, as they would gather at the lake for summer swimming parties. How did he get from there to here? Oh well, he thought, enough of this soul searching. He had a meeting to attend so he had better be on his way.

CHAPTER TWENTY-FIVE

In order to catch the entire Crimitin family at home, they set a meeting for Saturday. Agent Moankat met Chief Martinez and Captain Carpton at the appointed location for an early breakfast before leaving for Azusa. On the way, Sid was able to quiz Carl and Fernando about the entire family situation as they saw it. He appreciated their candor as each man gave his opinion of why the Crimitin's son was found outside his apartment with two very large bullet holes in his body.

Surprisingly, the ride was relatively uneventful except for one small delay as police cleared a fender bender at one of the numerous intersecting freeways winding their way in and around the LA basin.

As the chief wheeled the staff car into the cul-de-sac, Sid took notice of the dilapidated condition of homes and vehicles. "That junk heap is still there," Carl said as they passed a late model Ford collecting dust under the afternoon sun.

"If we came back here a year from now, that car would still be there," the chief added as he pulled up to the house at the end of the street.

Herman, sitting on the stoop, looked up from his comic book as the car stopped. When Carl got out of the passenger's door, Herman recognized him and scooted through the torn screen door and into the living room. Before they were halfway up the walk, Sarah appeared in the doorway holding open the screen doorframe as the three men entered. Inside, the same stale cigarette and beer smell greeted the men. The room was arranged in a similar manner to their first visit. As they walked into the dimness, William was getting out of his lounge chair. He extended his meaty hand in greeting first to Carl and then the chief. When he reached for Sid's hand, he introduced himself and waited for Sid to reply before releasing his grip. Sid could feel the power of the man as he pumped his arm.

Sarah was standing near the kitchen as she watched everyone take their seats. Before they began talking she offered sodas and ice tea. Each man stated his preference as she disappeared into the kitchen. Carl began by telling William, Herman, and George what transpired since the last time he talked with Sarah. He paused as she returned to the living room with a gray plastic tray, a silver bowl half full of ice cubes, a miss matched collection of fast food restaurant give away glasses, several sodas and a glass pitcher of ice tea. After every one made their choices, Carl continued to fill in the gaps. Once he was done, he turned the conversation over to Sid.

Sid began by telling the family about current happenings as best he knew them from the briefing Bill gave him during their telephone call. As he was talking, he made an effort to look at each member of the family. He was trying to observe any glimmer of understanding they might have. There wasn't much there. When he got to the part about the tape recorder and journal, he held high hopes one of them would flicker to life with recognition of an important finding. No reaction from any of them.

Sid was internally frustrated as he finished the talk with a question. "Did William leave anything with any of you that might lead us to a stack of tapes or a journal?" Each member of the family looked at one another with blank stares. This was going nowhere. Sid continued to ask leading questions only to meet the same empty looks. The men were in the house for less than an hour when Carl interceded to break the questioning.

"I do believe we have taken this about as far as we can. Why don't we call it a day and if you remember anything, you can contact us at Vandenberg."

Sarah was quick to agree. She was getting up from her spot on the tattered couch when William slammed his large hands down on either side of the lounge chair.

"Sarah, this has got to stop. We can't go on facing the threats. They've already killed one of our sons. Are we going to let them get away with terrorizing us for the rest of our lives? These men will see to it we're protected. All we have to do is trust them. You know the captain and the chief can be trusted. Now we have one of the investigators in our home asking for our help. I say we give it to them and quit acting liked chicken shits!"

"William!" Sarah admonished as she watched the big man get up from his chair. The three Air Force visitors were watching the action unfold. It was exactly what Sid wanted. It took Carl and the chief by surprise.

"I'm sorry Sarah but I may look and act like one dumb son of a bitch but I can't be feared of some snotty nosed drug pushers. They KILLED our son and I want to have some revenge," the big man raged as he approached Sid who by now was up and standing on one side of the small coffee table. Sid held both hands up in front of himself as William approached.

"Let's just take this one step at a time," Sid began. "You will have your revenge if we can put these criminals before a court. Let's sit back down and discuss."

William stopped on the other side of the table. He was clenching his fists in alternating patterns. The veins in his neck were pulsating as the sweat broke out on his forehead.

"It's just gotten too much for me to put up with. I have never backed down from a fight in my life and I won't let some coke snorting shithead get the best of this family. They have already damaged my brother, killed one of my sons, and are now threatening George. We need your help." Sid looked into the large man's face and saw the tears welling up. He surmised crying was not one of the attributes a person would associate with a man like this but he could see William was near the edge of a total breakdown.

Sid asked William to sit back down. Without turning, William retreated toward his lounge and when the back of his legs hit the chair, he dropped like a stone into the well-worn seat. He took the back of his hand and wiped away the wet lines where tears spilled over and followed the pull of gravity down his creased cheeks falling finally on to his shirt. Sarah came over to his chair and stood in front of him as she ran her fingers through his tangled hair.

"I was beginning to worry all of this pushed you to the breaking point. If it had to happen, I'm glad it happened today. It's probably the right time and the right place. We can't live in fear. They have hurt us enough and it's time to hurt back."

Sarah turned and looked at the men standing opposite her. "Please sit down gentlemen. This may take some time." Sarah returned to the couch as Sid, Carl and the chief retook their seats. Sarah, being the most articulate of the family members, began to relate a story beginning when William's brother Herman was nearly killed with a batch of bad crack.

He was always a hell raiser like his brother. They were in many a fight in their younger days but when William married Sarah, he nearly eliminated the rough and tumble aspects of his life. Not saying he would back down from a fight but he didn't go around with his brother instigating altercations. Being married and a father seemed to calm him down. However, his brother didn't have anything or anyone to put the skids on his extracurricular activities.

At first, it was just the booze and the whores. He would run the bars and get into fights at least twice a month. He spent time on probation for fighting and public intoxication. William tried to help him cut down on the sauce but each time he thought the end of the tunnel was in sight, he would have to go bail Herman out of a poky in some small California town. It seemed like a never-ending battle. However, booze wasn't the only thing keeping Herman strung out.

As time went on, William and Sarah began to notice changes in Herman. He became moody and withdrawn. They were too busy concentrating on their sons to worry too much about brother dear. When they got a call from the Sheriff's office saying they found Herman unconscious in his car along Angeles Crest Highway, it was too late for intercession.

Herman was in a semiconscious state for nearly a month. When he regained some semblance of capability, brain damage was discovered during a series of routine tests. After considerable state funded rehabilitation, William and Sarah brought him home to continue care giving. During the intervening years, Herman progressed remarkably well. He was able to care for himself and was much less of a burden than he was when he first came to the house.

Even with the considerable turmoil surrounding his uncle, George was too weak to resist the slick talking pusher who located another victim after nearly killing a steady customer. As long as pushers have someone on the string, they seem content

When Herman fried his gray matter, the pusher knew who to approach. During the course of his association with Herman, he was able to collect a wealth of information about the family. The one person in the family unit who may want to partake of his special service was George. William the third was a hell raiser but he didn't seem to be the type for drugs. William junior was just too big to approach. However, George was another case.

Picked up on drinking charges, he was running with the right crowd for a pusher's purposes. If he could foster a relationship with George, he might be able to get a toehold with the group.

The plan worked well. After some casual meetings with George and his crowd for some hard drinking, the drugs arrived. At first, it was a difficult sell. George resisted because of his uncle. He was suckered into believing Herman overdosed on something other than the crack he was being offered. After some relentless pressure, he submitted to an experiment and was lost to the pipe. It wasn't long before all of his low life friends were hooked and partying with crack supplied by the same pusher who nearly killed George's uncle.

Lucky for George, William noticed the changes in his personality and activities. He tried unsuccessfully to get George away from the drugs and his situation. He took the final step when he went to their mother with the unnerving news. Total shock would be an understatement. William picked the right time for the parental notification. George was out with his drugged up friends and when he came into the house, the entire family accosted him.

Too stoned to offer any credible resistance, he was pummeled by William junior. The only thing to stop the beating was William stepping between his father and brother. The shouting went on throughout the night. George began to pull out of his stupor about dawn. His father was still under a full head of steam. He pulled his brother into the room and used him several times as an example of what can happen to an idiot on crack.

After this initial intervention, William junior collapsed into his chair as Sarah and William took George to his room and continued the lecture. By now, George was a jumble of tears and sobs. He straightened up enough to realize the trouble he was in and was rightfully fearful of his father. He begged his mother and brother for help. They naturally were prepared to offer him redemption but it was going to be expensive. Not only expensive to George himself but financially to the entire family. No matter what, they would find a way to get him off the pipe and back to reality.

The next few months were tough on the family. They were able to get detoxification help through William juniors insurance. Once the money and program were exhausted, they began a continuous search for help to keep him on the right path. Some were more effective than others were but the fear of a brutal beating from his father was probably the one thing to keep George away from the pipe.

Sarah wanted to get him into a program in nearby Glendora. It was directly primarily at high school age addicts to keep them off drugs, away from gangs and in school. The only problem was the cost. Although the program did receive some state funding and private donations, there was still a cost for each attending member. The Crimitin's went to their savings to ensure George was able to attend all the required meetings and activities. However when the money became critically short, William made the decision to enter the military.

He toyed with the idea for some time but felt his presence was needed at home to help with his brother. When money became an issue, he talked it over with his parents and then secretly discussed the matter with his brother's counselors. All were in agreement George needed the continued support of a structured program to keep him away from his habit. The family saw tremendous results and felt they could trust this particular group of counselors and former addicts to keep their son and brother alive. The decision made, William Calhoon Crimitin III became a member of the United States Air Force.

After basic training and technical training in a specialty commensurate with his mechanical abilities, William was assigned to Travis Air Force Base,

184

California. Close to home and family. He was able to provide the continued support for George as he kept up with his program of stability. At this point, the family begins to lose touch with the full story.

⁂

Shortly after his arrival at Travis, William received a strange phone call. As the winner of the Travis Air Force Base Special Services new arrival drawing, he was eligible for one of five prizes donated by local community merchants. First place was an all expense paid cruise to Baja California. Second place was a wide screen television complete with surround sound. Third place was an 8mm movie camera. Fourth place was a set of pots and pans. Fifth place was a $25 gift certificate from K-Mart. The only requirement was confirm his mother's first name and the town he listed as his home of record. The caller told him he would be notified at a future date what prize he won. The prize notification never came. What did come was a visit from a very nasty individual who made William an offer he could not refuse.

One balmy weekend evening, William was out with a few friends at one of the local meeting places for young ladies of the community and young airmen from the base. While concentrating on a lovely lady sitting next to him at the bar, a short stocky man with a very bad complexion, thinning hair parted in the middle, horn-rimmed glasses, and a really ugly Hawaiian shirt under a well-worn sports coat tried to strike up a conversation with the newly minted crew chief. William was not amused or interested. When the man pushed a picture of William's mother under his beer glass, it got an immediate response.

"Where did you get this?" William demanded.

"Not for you to know," was the short reply. "I need to talk with you right now. I'll be outside." The little man turned and headed for the door.

William made a quick apology to the puzzled woman and left a few steps behind. Once outside, he came up behind the man, grabbed him by the shoulder, and spun him around. When he did, he was looking down the barrel of a very large pistol complete with silencer.

"Don't touch me again or I'll drop you where you stand," the craggy faced man spit out at William. "Follow me." He turned quickly and walked to the edge of the parking lot under one of the lamps used to illuminate the car dealership next door. As William leaned on a red pickup truck, the man stood near the chain link fence separating the two businesses and began to speak.

185

"I represent a group of venture capitalists who need your assistance in opening a relatively untapped market. These business associates know your family and the *problems* you and your loved ones have been facing. It was a tragedy what happened to your uncle. However, a business cannot be held responsible for faulty products. Caveat Emptor, applies in every business deal. Although not pleased by your brother's departure from his group of friends, we can understand his desire not to utilize our product any more after discovery by your rather large father. Survival is always paramount."

"You pissant drug dealing fuck," William shouted.

"Now calm down William. Name calling will get you no bonus points with the organization."

"What do you mean calm down? I'm not going to be threatened by some drug pushing shit like you. I'll just warn my family to be on the watch and report your ass to the police."

"Do as you like my young friend but let me show you some additional photos that may change your mind." The man reached into his coat pocket and pulled out a small stack of photos showing every member of his family going about their daily routine. Each one showed a small bull's-eye imprinted on their heads.

"If we are able to get these photos, what chance do you think you have on warning them to *be careful?* A high-powered weapon with scope and silencer will bring them down one by one. You will be the last to go. Once we start, you will be the only one who can stop us from finishing the job at hand."

William was dumbfounded. He had no reply. He just stared at the photos. After a moment, the dealer spoke. "Since I've made such an impression on you, let me tell you what we expect. We want you to leave Travis and get an assignment in Europe. We don't care how you do it. Just make it happen. After you get there, one of our associates will contact you with further instructions. Please, don't be a stupid man. Just follow our instructions and your family will survive this speed bump in your life."

He took the photos from William but handed one back. A picture of his mother leaving the local supermarket with a bag full of groceries. The target was on her forehead. "Just remember my promise."

The man turned, walked out of the parking lot, and disappeared down a side street. William stood stunned. It was a few minutes before he gathered enough composure to go back inside and tell his friends he was leaving.

It was several days before he went back to work. He made visits to sick call feigning some type of abdominal distress. He just needed some time to think. Once he returned to work, he began his quest for temporary duty in Europe and finally a permanent assignment. The stage was set for the drug running connection.

"After what seemed like a very short time", Sarah continued as she took a small sip from the soda can Herman brought from the kitchen and set down beside her, "William began to fly in and out of someplace in Germany."

"Ramstein?" Sid questioned.

"I don't remember. All of a sudden, he told us he was reassigned to Germany, rather than that base up north. When we asked why, he just said it was better for his career to be flying in Europe. We didn't question anything he said because we really didn't understand the workings of the military. We just kept hoping George would follow his brother into the Air Force and the structured life William found. Little did we know the torment he must have been facing."

"Once he was established there, let me ask this question again, did he make any trips home or send you anything for safe keeping?" Sid asked the family members.

"He came home just before he moved and then one time for Christmas. But I don't remember him leaving anything here." William stated as he looked to the other family members to back him up. They were all shaking their heads in agreement. William left nothing for safekeeping during any of his visits. Carl got up from his seat and was pacing. After some additional questions, he asked Sid to come out to the car with him. He asked the chief to check on personal services the family received so far.

Once outside, Carl walked slowly toward the car with Sid at his side. "Have you noticed Herman?" he asked.

"Noticed what?" Sid asked.

"The other three are paying attention and taking part in the conversations. Herman isn't doing a thing."

"Well shit Carl, he's brain damaged. What the hell do you expect?" Sid stressed as he turned to go back inside.

"No wait. With all the contact I've had with this family, I know him just a bit better than you do. He may be brain damaged but he isn't brain dead. I have seen him in action and he knows exactly what is going on and probably has answers to many of our questions. We have to find some way to get a reaction out of him."

"What do you have in mind?"

"I'm not really sure but let me ask a few questions during the remainder of our time here."

Both men returned to the living room. The chief was still talking with the family about personal services received since the death notification.

When he finished, Sid was eager to see if there was anything connecting the family with the people who committed the crime. William answered.

"Since the funeral, we've had several phone calls from a man making threats. He said George was an easy target the first time and they would get him hooked again. They knew their shit handicapped Herman so they didn't really care about him. They wanted to make sure we kept our mouths shut. Goddamn, we don't really know anything. We know George got involved with drugs but we didn't know William was involved. He went into the Air Force to give us enough money to keep George under treatment and in school. Now they have us afraid for our lives. I won't be pushed."

Sid agreed and told him to count on a call from this man after their visit. He wanted them to play along with the threats. Their story would be an update on the investigation in Germany. Nothing more, nothing less. They could say the investigation was progressing but they weren't any closer to finding out who killed William than they were right after it happened. The family members agreed Sarah would be the one to pass along the information. After they finished discussing their story, Carl asked if he could stick in a couple of questions.

He began with George and asked specific questions about relationships and rehab. He moved to Sarah and asked about trusting a helping hand and parenting. He asked William about the relationship with his namesake and if they ever kept secrets from other family members as part of a bonding ritual. He then turned his attention to Herman.

He spoke in a soft voice as he tried not to be intimidating. He talked about promises made and keeping things safe. He told Herman William would want him to help wherever he could to find the people who took him away from his loving uncle and family. Carl continued to ask pointed questions all relating to how William would want each family member to help anyway they could.

The entire time, Herman held his head in his hands and stared at the floor. One time when Carl paused before asking Sarah another question, Herman raised his head to look directly at Carl. His eyes filled with tears. They began to run down his cheeks as he stood and headed for the hallway. The others were silent as they followed.

When Sarah, Sid, and Carl reached the doorway of Herman's room, they saw him standing in the center sobbing. They didn't say a thing. They just watched. After a moment, Herman went to his dresser and pulled out one of the bottom drawers. He turned it over dumping the contents on to the floor. Taped to the bottom of the drawer was a small white envelope. Herman pulled it from its hiding place. He dropped the drawer on the pile of clothes and turned toward the people standing in his doorway. He held the envelope out for Sarah. She took a couple of steps toward the still sobbing uncle and retrieved the envelope from his grasp. When she did, Herman turned and laid face down on his bed where he continued to sob. George came into the room and went to his uncle. He sat down next to him and laid his head on his back as he grabbed the man's shoulders to hold him close.

With the envelope in hand, Sarah, Sid, and Carl returned to the living room where William was still sitting in his lounger. "What the hell is going on," William demanded.

Sarah looked at him and held up the envelope. "It appears William didn't feel he could trust any of us, so he left something with his uncle." She turned to Carl. "How did you know he was hiding something?"

"I'm not sure. Call it a hunch," Carl began. "Since I've known you folks, I noticed Herman may be slow but he doesn't seem to miss a great deal. He just didn't seem to be paying much attention today. I just can't explain it. I told Sid and he agreed to let me ask a few pointed questions. I'm just lucky Herman reacted the way he did and gave us the envelope."

"All we can do now is hope there's some connection between what William wanted to protect and his connection with the drug runners," Sid said as he reached for the envelope. Sarah was so stunned by the last few minutes she didn't realize how tightly she was gripping the envelope. Sid took it by an edge and pulled it from her hand. They would want to test everything for evidence.

He took his pocketknife and sliced open the top seam. Inside was a piece of folded cardboard. The fold was held closed by two pieces of tape. He cut the tape and unfolded the cardboard to reveal a key. The key was the type used to unlock safety deposit boxes. Brass colored with a long stem.

"I don't expect to find much on this," Sid said as he opened his briefcase and put the evidence inside. We'll take it back to our office as is and see if we can pull any prints off the envelope, cardboard or key.

Sarah took her seat again. She stared blankly across the room at William who stared back. Both of them were mildly shocked to say the least. The chief turned from the window and walked over to a spot just behind and to the right of William's lounge. Carl took one of the kitchen chairs, turned it around so he could sit and rest his arms on the seat back. Sid remained standing in the middle of the group.

"I can't emphasize enough how critical it is that you keep this information secret," Sid stressed.

"If the man making the threats on your lives finds out we have taken this key away from your house, he may have no reason to keep you alive. You may become targets for elimination."

"I'll be damned," William said as he got up from his chair and went over to where Sarah was sitting.

"Like I told you earlier, I have never backed down from a fight and I'm not about to start now. We may not be as educated as some folks but we do know when someone is giving us good advice and will certainly follow your directions." He was now standing beside his wife gently rubbing the back of her neck as she held her head in her hands.

Sid could see she was sobbing silently. He knelt down in front of the distraught mother.

"I know there isn't a thing we can do to make this situation any easier," Sid whispered as he put his face close to Sarah.

"But you can trust the OSI and the Air Force as a whole to do everything we can to bring this tragedy to a close."

Sid stood and held out his hand to bid William good-by. "Carl or I will be in touch with you as soon as we have more information. I can only hope this key opens more than a safe deposit box." Sid closed his briefcase. Carl and the chief shook William's beefy hand as they headed for the door.

Once they were back in the car and headed down Highway 39 toward the interstate, Carl broke the silence. "So what can we expect from this safe deposit key?"

"First we have to make sure it's a safe deposit box key. Not having taken a close look at it, I don't know if it has any identification marks to associate it with a manufacturer or bank. I'll turn it over to the lab boys for determination. I'll just wait for the results. I'll keep you guys apprised of the findings. I can see you've become personally involved with the family."

"This is the captain's first experience with this sort of thing," the chief said as he signaled for a turn.

"I try not to get personally attached to a grieving family but this case is my first experience with a murder notification. I feel such empathy with the Crimitin family it's hard not to become attached to the situation."

"I have to agree with the chief," Carl said as he turned in his seat to look at Sid sitting behind the chief in the back seat.

"I'll have to stay detached from the family if I'm going to be successful at providing assistance in a crisis. I guess that's why the Old Man put me in for this detail. He wants me to have compassion for the families but be ready to stand outside the crisis to provide help. I just feel these people are due as much as we can do for them since their son was murdered."

"I wouldn't worry about this one," Sid replied to Carl. "It was your connection with the family that brought out the Key. I don't think anyone is going to find fault with your compassion in this situation."

The Air Force trio was gone from the Crimitin's house less than an hour when a phone on the kitchen counter rang. Sarah answered and listened intently before answering.

"We didn't have anything more to tell them than we have told you already. Why can't you just be satisfied and leave us alone. We don't know anything about William's activities in Germany and we can't give the Air Force anything we don't have. Just let us grieve and get on with our lives."

She paused as she listened and then added. "They gave us an update on the Germany investigation and asked if we needed anything. That's all there was to their visit." She abruptly hung up.

"What did he say?" William asked

"Same crap as always but he did know the Air Force was here," Sarah told him as she walked toward where William was standing in the kitchen doorway. She put her arms around his waist and buried her face in his chest as she began to cry.

"I just want this to be over and done with. We've buried our son and I want to concentrate on saving our family."

"All we can hope for is a break with the key Herman gave them," William said as he held her close. "Things can't get any worse."

The man parked at the end of their street put the car in gear and headed for the Foothill Freeway. His part of the game over, he would report and wait for further instructions.

It was late when the three men made their way back to Vandenberg. Sid thanked the chief and Carl for their assistance. He promised to keep them appraised on the investigation and asked them to give him a call if either heard from the Crimitin family. He went into his office to make a couple of preemptive phone calls and to super glue treat the envelope, cardboard and key before heading home. Getting the location of the bank holding William's safety deposit box was important but it didn't require any activity until Monday morning. He would find the best place to send the key and then have it overnight delivered it to the suggested location. He figured the FBI would be the place his superiors would recommend. Their database on manufactures was one of the most extensive in the world. If the key could be matched, they were the ones who would make the connection. He just hoped this whole exercise wasn't a wild goose chase.

He decided to send a note to Bill in Germany and tell him what he found. Sid was sure the investigators would be interested in the threats being handed to the Crimitin family and the safe deposit key. There could be no doubt now about the reasons behind William's sudden transfer and involvement in the movement of drugs. They threatened his family and he was only doing what he thought was best for their protection. Why he was eliminated from the picture was the question now facing everyone. Sid wasn't privy to the entire investigative file so he wasn't aware of the DEA connection established with the embassy in Germany. However, being the astute investigator he was, looking for a journal and tapes would soon lead him to surmise there was some sort of record keeping taking place. With the continued threats from the bad guys, it would appear they were also interested in records.

Since Sarah put a death grip on the envelope after Herman gave it to her, Sid didn't expect to find much. He was right. The envelope held only smudges and partials. The cardboard held only one good set and he put those down to William. There was nothing on the key. Disappointed but not discouraged by the results, he headed for the house.

CHAPTER TWENTY-SIX

Karl came into the office sorting through some of the distribution and mail he picked up during his trip from the house. He kept some of it in his hand and laid the rest of it on Karlotta's desk. "I'm expecting someone to deliver tickets for Dillon. Go ahead and sign for them. He's traveling down south tomorrow and may not be in when the tickets get here."

"Who may not be in when the tickets are delivered? Dillon asked as he came into the reception area.

Karl turned and told Dillon the tickets were due this morning. "Karlotta will sign for them and get them into your office."

Karlotta smiled and handed Dillon the latest edition of *Stars & Stripes*. He bowed in thanks and started toward his office. He threw the paper on his desk as he passed on his way to the coffee. After pouring a cup, he went to Karl's office and asked about the gathering of information on Buzz. Karl told him William hadn't given him any kind of report on his findings thus far. Dillon wanted to have as much information about his adversary when they met following his trip to Khamis.

William came in from his rounds and when he stuck his head in the door to wish them good morning, Karl asked him to come in. "What's the latest on Buzz?" Karl asked. William asked for a moment as he dropped off his case and got himself a cup of coffee. When he came back, he took a seat by the door and began to relate the facts from a folder retrieved from his office.

"Let me start at the top and you may not believe what I am about to tell you but Buzz isn't his real name," William said as he winked at his coworkers.

"His name is Cedric A. Brakenful. Born, June 2, 1952 in Olympia Washington. Been kicking around the Kingdom for some time now. Always has some kind of fancy titled job that allows him maximum freedom to establish contacts and keep up with his brewing business. Right now, he's working for Saudi Arabian Investment Corporation. One of the royals heads the thing. I really wouldn't expect the boss would be involved with Buzz in his other enterprises but one will never know. Anyway, he works as the New Contracts Administration Manager. I have a job description coming our way."

"OK, let's just hold on for a minute. We only started to talk about this last week. How did you get such information so quickly?" Karl queried.

"Actually it was just a stroke of luck. I knew where he worked because I just happened to see one of his delivery trucks stopped by the side of the road. The driver was talking with another man who was standing by a little run about with the logo of this investment group on the door. I wrote down the name and then called asking for Buzz. With the grace of the almighty, they hooked me into his extension. He wasn't in, so I dialed back to the operator and asked to speak with their HR office. Once there, I asked to speak with the supervisor, told them I was from the American Embassy and was doing a follow-up on a visa application. The person on the other end asked what I needed exactly and I said his passport number. The one given on the application didn't bring up any information on Buzz. When he asked where the visa was for, I told him it wasn't for Buzz; it was for someone who was using him as a point of reference to enter the United States. He bought it saying the number was wrong and gave me the right number. With the right number, I called my point of contact at the embassy and in the time it takes to punch in his number, I had the information. I just continued to shoot the breeze with this HR guy and when I told him I was looking for a contract administrator at the embassy, he *offered* to send me the job description."

"You devious little shit," Karl said as he came from behind his desk and shook William's hand. "Remind me to watch my back. Before I know it you'll be knocking on my office door asking me to leave so you can move in."

William laughed as he returned Karl's handshake. He assured him there were no plans for a palace coup. As he told both men, it was just a matter of blind luck with everything falling into place after a few phone calls. With the information from Buzz's passport, he sent for complete reports based on social security number and last known stateside address. He would be doing some follow-up as soon as he could. Karl asked for a copy of the information. William pulled out a copy with Karl's name at the top and one for Dillon. He closed the folder and left for his office.

"What have you decided to do with the situation at Khamis," Karl asked.

"One of the biggest things I have to do is get the Air Force working with the contractor if they feel there's a problem to be solved. I haven't dealt much with FMS[20] contracts but I made a couple of calls over the weekend and asked a few pointed questions. It appears sales through the government only ensure payment by either the contractor or the United States. For instance, in this case, the Saudi Arabian government wanted to buy F-15s. All contracting is done through the United States government with McDonnell Douglas. MAC then built the aircraft and delivered them to the Air Force who in turn sold them to the Saudis. Of course, most of this is just on paper. When a jet comes off the line, a US Air Force pilot picks it up and delivers it to the Saudis. FMS is good for the contractor but bad for the customer. Along the line, people are taking their pound of flesh. With a straight commercial contract, the customer can set the tone but the guys working the line are at the mercy of a foreign employer. It's almost like indentured servitude."

"Interesting. I wondered why there are so many US military and civilians working here who weren't part of the training package. They must be part of the FMS contract maintenance."

"That might be true but there's a group of other programs which support a wide range of treaty and international agreements. Would you like a lecture on the economic influence of the gulf region on international commerce? I just happen to have one prepared from a course I took at the academy."

Karl dodged the lecture but did say he would trade information after he returned. Dillon agreed and turned to leave Karl's office. He stopped in the doorway to ask Karl if he made contact with Colonel Erpack to ensure there was going to be someone at the airport in the morning to pick him up.

"When I talked with him over the weekend, he assured me transportation would be at the airport to pick you up when you arrive."

"Very comforting but knowing his attitude, he may just leave me standing there."

"After your first encounter, I don't think he has the balls. He may be a rotten shit but after you two went toe to toe, he knows exactly where you stand and I don't believe the man wants to get in the way."

"Your tickets are here," Karlotta purred while setting a Saudi Arabian ticket folder on the corner of Dillon's desk. "All you have to do is sign this voucher and you're on your way."

Dillon looked up from his computer screen and thanked her. He signed the voucher and moved the tickets to a spot next to his case. He didn't want to forget them when he left in the afternoon. He took a moment to talk with Karlotta. Karl came by and offered to refill coffee. Karlotta bid them both good afternoon as she left the office for lunch. Both men watched her leave.

The remainder of the afternoon was spent sending and answering messages and checking information on the operation at Khamis. With a 0700 departure from Riyadh, he would have to leave Eskan very early in the morning. The international airport was located on the opposite side of town about 30 clicks outside the ring road. Twenty years ago, the airport was right on the edge of Riyadh but the town grew exponentially and engulfed the airport. It's now a military base.

✳

Dillon put the finishing touches on his packing. Since he was only going to be down south for a few days, he used his roll around and boarding bag. He left his pistol with Karl since he knew the Saudi authorities would not look kindly on an expat carting around a 9MM. William was going to pick him up around 0500. Since he held his ticket and boarding pass, he would be able to process directly through immigration and into the gate waiting area.

Before hitting the sheets for a few hours sleep, Dillon called Sonta. She wasn't home and he didn't want to leave a message so he made a note by the phone to give her a call when he returned. He pulled the roll around off the bed and took it into the living room to leave by the front door. Walking over to the credenza, he took a glass and poured about three fingers of single malt. Picking up the remote, he turned on the television to see the news. The reporter was just beginning to relate the devastation of some small town in Kansas following a tornado.

The knock on the door startled him. When he answered, William was standing on the other side. "Ready?" he asked. Dillon just stared at him.

"As a matter of fact, yes I am. Do you think the flight attendants will mind me in my boxers?" Dillon laughed as he stepped aside to let William enter.

"I just got an e-mail about our mutual friend Buzz. I didn't want to wait until I picked you up for the airport, so I brought it over on my way home. I think we're going to be able to get significant help from this man." William handed Dillon the message as both men took seats on the couch. Dillon muted the newscaster and read the mail.

"It seems our Mr. Buzz, alias Cedric Brakenful, real name Lumir Barak of the Israeli Baraks, is a fugitive from several states where he apparently ran internet scams. The alias of Brakenful was concocted over the net with phony birth certificates and other supporting documents. The Feds figured he went underground in the United States. They didn't figure he made his

196

way to of all places, Saudi Arabia. If he's doing a brisk business with the Saudis, they sure didn't know he's Jewish." Dillon smiled as he read the news and began to formulate a plan to get the maximum amount of cooperation out of Mr. Barak.

"Isn't this a bit of interesting information?" Dillon said as he went back to the credenza to pour another single malt. "Can I get you a libation?" he asked William.

"No thanks," William declined. "If I'm going outside the confines of Eskan within 12 hours, I don't imbibe. I will have a diet soda though. I thought you would appreciate the information. That's why I brought it over. I'll answer the notes in the morning and put off the hounds. I know they will be after as much information as I can provide concerning Mr. Barak. You don't know off hand if we have an extradition agreement with the Saudis do you?"

"Why do you think the scammer ended up here? What a great place for a Jew to hide. Up close and personal with the Arabs. I bet he laughs his ass off every night as he lays his scheming head down in his richly appointed mansion." The men continued to discuss their good fortune for a few minutes before William looked at his watch and declared it was time to leave.

"See you in a few hours," he said as he went out the door. Dillon downed the remaining whiskey and headed for bed. With big plans for the next day, he wanted to be semi-rested before locking horns with Erpack.

⚔

"Shit," Bill hissed as he stared at the ringing telephone. "It better not be anything to take me out of this house."

"Answer it William," Betty directed. Bill reached over and picked up the receiver.

"Wilmerson"

"Good morning Mr. Bill," came the bright greeting from Christina. "Have you been into the office e-mail this morning?"

"No Mam, since you have the duty, it's your job to check messages and notify other office personnel of anything important. So! This had better be *important*. My coffee is getting cold."

"I do believe you will be interested in my call. I just picked up the mail and we got a note from an Agent Moankat in California. Evidently he made contact with the Crimitin family concerning any journals or tapes."

"Tell me more Christina. You have my undivided attention."

197

"Don't get too excited Bill, they didn't come across any notes or tapes, but they did come up with a safe deposit key. They are sending it out for identification. Let me read the note on how they found it." Christina read the details about the uncle holding the key and retrieving it from its hiding place. She also related how they were threatened.

"That's wonderful news," Bill said as Betty asked what was so wonderful. Bill held up his hand for quiet as Christina read the rest of the note. When she was done, Bill thanked her and hung up. He then told Betty about the find.

"I've got to get hold of Dillon. Where did I put the number?"

"It's in the other room on your desk," Betty said as she got up and crossed the room to the bathroom. Bill was out of bed and on his way down the hall before he realized he took off the robe he wore while preparing breakfast. Oh, what the heck, he thought, it's my house, and if I want to run around naked, I'll just do it. He was trying to connect with the command post when Betty came in holding his robe.

"Put this on Tarzan. Jane doesn't like the sight of your naked butt so early in the morning." Bill took the robe and swung it around his shoulders. His connection was routed to several locations with no luck of finding any of the agents. He left messages at each location.

CHAPTER TWENTY-SEVEN

Dillon was putting the final touches on his cereal and toast when the tones of the front door bell signaled the arrival of his transportation. Still chewing on the brown bread toast with a strawberry preserve topping, he answered the door.

"Good morning Dillon. All ready?" William asked as he stepped into the villa.

"Just finishing breakfast," Dillon replied as he turned back toward the kitchen to close everything down. "At this hour of the day I can't be real sure if it's a good morning or not. Can I get you a cup of coffee?"

"I'll get it," William said as he reached into the cabinet for one of the simple ceramic mugs provided by the compound. "I just wolfed down a pop tart for my breakfast. I'm not too good in the morning, especially the early morning. I'm just glad there wasn't any room on that 0430 flight."

He poured a cup from the maker and asked if he could refill Dillon's cup. Dillon held out his mug as they polished off the remaining coffee. William turned off the coffee maker and took a sip of the hot beverage.

"How long a ride is it to the airport?" Dillon asked while following William from the kitchen and into the living room.

"As you've discovered since your arrival, it all depends on traffic. If we don't have any accidents to bypass, it's only about 45 minutes. If I drop into warp drive, we can be out there in 15. However, they're beginning to crack down on speeding in the Kingdom. It's the biggest killer of all. I try to avoid confrontations with the local police if I can avoid it. Since you have your boarding pass, we can get out there just before boarding. Should not be a problem."

Dillon finished his coffee and waited for William to finish his. He picked up the mugs and took them back into the kitchen. William was waiting at the door with Dillon's bags in hand. Dillon came over and opened the door. They stepped into the oppressive morning heat, put the bags in the car, and headed for the gate.

Once through security, they joined the relatively light traffic flow heading toward the city. Following the sign, they made their transition to the ring road. At the exit for Dhahran, William negotiated the congestion as vehicles from the left lane were trying to exit on the right.

"They never seem to plan ahead for an exit," William grumbled while slowing to a crawl.

"It's like they're asleep and all of a sudden, their exit jumped up out of the desert and bit them on the ass. If I don't come out of this assignment with anything else, I will have gained experience as a defensive driver."

Dillon smiled and said he understood.

As the words came out of his mouth, a jet black BMW with only its parking lights illuminating the front of the car blasted past in the breakdown lane. If William were a few millimeters farther to the left, he would have lost the side mirror. Both men sat in stunned silence. The rear lights of the sedan disappeared around a slight bend in the highway.

As they continued, William pointed out a few of the local highlights. There was an amusement park, a new school, Imam University (training center for their religious leaders), a high-rise commercial center with apartments and shopping, an upscale western compound that had been targeted by a deadly terrorist attack, and an ever-expanding section of land development for the growing population.

"I'm not really sure what the purpose of this overpass is," William commented as they approached a well-lit, gaudily decorated segment of concrete spanning all lanes of the airport approach road.

"They put it up during their centennial year. I was told it was in celebration of the glorious victory by their King but I never looked into it any further. Nice piece of work though." he finished as they passed under the multicolored arch.

They were now in what appeared to be the middle of nowhere. There wasn't a light visible except for the lights strung along the highway. The center divider was hedge and tree covered. As they wound their way up an overpass, the lights of the international airport glistened in the distance.

"That's a pretty sight," Dillon commented.

"I'm always amazed at how many lights the Saudi's can put in one location. Lucky for them they have cheap electricity," William said as he moved into the exit lane for the departure area.

King Khalid International Airport is one building with four interconnected terminals. The first one they passed was unused. The next three dealt with in country departures, Saudi Arabian Airlines international flights and then all other airlines. Departures are on the upper level. William pulled to the curb, put on his emergency flashers and turned off the engine. Dillon was out getting his bags from the back seat. William locked the truck and came around to offer assistance.

"Let me pull your case. That way you can get all your papers out before we get to the checkpoint."

William took the handle of Dillon's roll around case. "I don't know what it is about emergency flashers but as many times as I've come here for one reason or another, if I park and leave them on, I don't get a ticket. They must have some significance I just haven't figured out."

He led the way to the electronic eye controlled sliding doors opening to the ticketing area. A large counter in the center contained one harried agent trying to satisfy the needs of 10 Saudis. Each one waving a ticket and shouting instructions.

"Patience is not a virtue in this country," William said while leading Dillon around the counter area to one of the clearance checkpoints. "What gate do you have?"

"The boarding pass says 35," Dillon responded while looking for some type of gate directions.

"Here's the drill. You show your boarding pass to the man at the counter. You then take your bags and send them through the x-ray machine. What I usually do is put all of my loose change, rings, watch, pens, and whatnots inside my boarding bag. These scanners are extremely sensitive and I've seen westerners nearly strip naked to clear through the gizmos. Anyway, after you get your bags back, you just go around that customer service counter," William told Dillon as he pointed to a counter on the other side of the gauntlet. "Gate 35 is straight behind that counter. Can't miss it."

True to the explanation, on the other side of the counter was a walkway leading over the arrival area and straight to gate 35. Dillon was impressed with the water fountains and plants decorating arrivals. Departing passengers could look down on the waterworks from their second story vantage point.

As Dillon would discover on his return to Riyadh, disembarking passengers went down stairs to the baggage claim area. For international travelers, immigration was the first stop followed by customs. All areas where interspersed with plants and waterfalls. A very impressive sight. Dillon took in the view before reaching the waiting area for gate 35. He found a seat near the windows and gate. Having a first class ticket would mean he didn't have to fight his way on board to ensure space in the overhead compartment. He was warned about the amount of packages some of the Saudis brought. With just under an hour before departure, he watched the comings and goings of service crews as they scurried about loading an Airbus at the next gate.

Dillon was surprised at the number of passengers arriving for the flight. He didn't realize Abha was quickly becoming the vacation spot of choice for Gulf Coast States. Saudi Arabia began a campaign to open up their formerly restricted tourist program. The gates weren't opened for westerners but they were attempting to attract other Arabs to visit some of the sights in the Asir Region.

Continuing to people watch, Dillon noticed two airline agents opening the gate desk as several of the men occupying space in front of the counter questioned them. Guards took up positions inside the red ropes cutting off access to the Jetway doors. As he was watching the guards, flight attendants and crewmembers came up the stairs from arrivals. At the same time, Dillon saw the Airbus moving into position.

Less than 10 minutes after the crew entered the jet, one of the agents announced boarding. Dillon gathered his case and bag as he walked to where the man was collecting boarding passes. He haphazardly tore Dillon's pass and handed him the jagged stub. A rush of hot air greeted Dillon as he entered the Jetway. At the jet's door, one of the attendants checked his stub and ushered him to his seat in First Class. Dillon stored his case in the overhead and put his bag underneath the seat in front of him. He settled into his window seat and graciously accepted the offer of orange juice from the flight attendant. He enjoyed the cool beverage as the remaining passengers boarded the wide-bodied jet.

Shortly after their scheduled departure time, the door closed and the Jetway moved away. The tug used to bring the jet into its parked position, now pushed it away from the terminal and on to the taxiway. Once there, the engines cranked, the crew chief signaled the pilot all safety devices were removed and the craft was ready for flight. Since departing traffic was light at this time of the morning, the airliner slowly taxied toward the end of runway.

As it taxied, the normal safety announcements were made to keep passengers informed on how to buckle their seatbelts and retrieve their life vest from under their seat in case they made an emergency landing in a long forgotten ocean smack dab in the middle of the desert. One additional item not heard aloud too often on American carriers was a prayer to the almighty for a safe trip. Once the asking for divine guidance finished, the captain turned the jet on to the active runway and launched into the dust and smog clouded morning skies.

One of the flight attendants brought a light breakfast of rolls and fruit. Dillon took the offering and sat back to enjoy a cup of coffee. It was less than 90 minutes to his destination. He read one of the English language newspapers as he continued to glance out the window at the changing desert scenes some 5 miles below him.

With getting up before dawn, Dillon slipped into a Combat Nap. He awoke when the flight crew announced their approach to Abha. Dillon looked to see the terrain changed from desert to steep mountains with sharp cutting valleys. The pilot put the jet through several positioning turns as he brought the craft in line with the runway. Dillon saw the edge of the mesa where Abha is situated as the plane made a final gentle turn.

He noticed a fort like structure perched on the very edge of the plateau. Below the fort a road clung precariously to the sides of the gorge, as it made its way down the valley to what he assumed was flatland along the Red Sea. He knew the approximate location and terrain of his destination but wasn't ready for the cragginess.

The crew adjusted the plane's configuration for landing as the flaps extended and the gear lowered. They were passing over scattered homes not appearing to be in any type of prescribed development. There were a few roads cut up and down the hills but nothing seemed under construction. They crossed over a dual highway, more rocks and then over the approach lights. The touch down was smooth despite the warnings William gave him. Evidently, the wind wasn't a problem in the morning. Thrust reverse engaged, the jet slowed to taxi speed and pulled off the runway to the only taxiway in view. The drive to the designated parking spot in front of the terminal was a short one.

Dillon got up to retrieve his case from the overhead and his bag from under the seat in front of him. The exit door opened and the pleasant coolness of morning mountain air greeted the passengers. It was a stark change from what they left behind in Riyadh. The passengers began to leave the aircraft so Dillon followed his fellow travelers down the stairs, to the parking ramp and into the arrivals area.

As he was coming down the stairs, he noticed a 747 sitting in front of an adjacent building and another Airbus next to their aircraft. He was surprised to see such a large plane at a one-runway airport.

Since he didn't have any checked luggage, he went straight for the exit doors. He saw the colonel waiting behind a rather large crowd of kissing and hugging Saudis. Dillon excused his way through the throng and offered a greeting to Erpack. The colonel looked like any other foreign contractor standing in the waiting area. Erpack returned the greeting and led Dillon toward the parking lot.

Once outside, Dillon followed Erpack as he thread his way through the crowd of people loading bags into cars from a previous arrival. They crossed the access road, passed through the waiting line of airport taxis, and entered a two-tier parking lot. Using the stairs to the second tier, Erpack approached a Suburban, unlocked the doors, and climbed in. Dillon swung his bags into the back seat and joined Erpack up front.

When they made it out of the lot, the exit road led them past the cargo section, fire department, an abbreviated maintenance area and finally through the guarded gates of the airport. In Kingdom, every civil airport doubles as a military facility. In this particular case, King Khalid Air Base moves emergency landings to Abha's airport during contingency operations. During the Gulf War, allied forces were a permanent fixture at the civilian facility.

"Despite the confrontation during our first meeting, I'm glad to see you," Erpack said as they crossed the final barriers.

"I can't say I was pleased when I got the call about your visit but maybe we can put this thing to bed and I won't have to worry about some dope head killing one of my men. I was out of line when we met in Riyadh. I was under a full head of steam and you took the right approach to bring me back to reality. I won't say I liked being dressed down in front of others by some pencil pushing investigator but it did have the desired effect. Made me think about how I would react if placed in your shoes. I would have taken the same approach. I hope we can work out the differences."

Dillon wasn't going to question the reasons behind the semi-apology; he would accept it at face value. "No need to worry. In my line of work a person has to use whatever card in the deck he feels is appropriate for getting the job done. In our case, the games are done and we can get on with solving your problems."

"Enough said. Let me point out some of the high lights along our way to the base." The colonel began a running commentary about points of interest. Before they reached the main connecting highway, Dillon saw a conference center, fairgrounds, exposition center, family restaurant, printing plant and more than a dozen little carts lined along the roadside at regular intervals.

"What are those?" Dillon questioned.

Erpack just laughed as he began to explain. "I don't know what it is about the Saudis and camping out. Maybe it goes back to their migratory roots but every evening, especially on weekends, these roads are jammed with people sitting on blankets in the dirt or on the sidewalk watching the runway. Don't ask me why, I have yet to figure it out. They come here in droves and just sit by the road and munch corn from these little stands. Anywhere there's an open spot; you'll find a group of Saudis with a pot of tea on an open fire. Sometimes they have a television hooked into the car so they don't miss their favorite soap opera."

"Soap Opera?" Dillon said raising his eyebrows.

"I'm being facetious," the colonel laughed. "It's just another one of the wonder points about living in this region. I'm told there's a large tent contingent near the Peace Program compound in Riyadh where they camp on the weekends. They drive their cars and trucks up to a tent complete with satellite dish and spend the weekends communing with their past. Strangest damn thing I've ever heard of. However, it is their country and we are here to help."

"That's what everyone keeps telling me," Dillon replied. "I've only been here a short while but it certainly has been an experience."

By now, they reached the main road connecting Abha with Khamis Mushayt. Abha is the "county seat" for the Asir Region. They have their own prince who's making a valiant effort at opening the region for expanded tourism. As Dillon experienced on his flight to Abha, there seems to be a wide range of people taking advantage of the cool weather and differing landscapes.

"I don't know how you feel about Saudi drivers but I just hate to be out on the road with them. Lucky for us they gave us this armored Suburban. The only things I worry about are the water trucks. If one of the little pick-ups hits us, he'll just bounce off. These water trucks are another thing."

Dillon agreed with him as he related a couple of the stories about driving in Riyadh. They compared stories for a while until they pulled up to a stop light. Next to them was one of the dreaded water trucks. Erpack and Dillon were in the left lane next to the left turn lane. The water truck was in the right lane. A car was in front of them.

On the left and right, cars pulled up to the intersection so they could jump ahead of the cars in the driving lanes. Dillon watched the entire thing. When the light changed green, everyone broke from his position like horses out of the starting gate. The guy on the left cut in front of the car ahead of them so he didn't smash into the center divider on the other side of the intersection. The car on the far right had an easier time as he only needed to beat the water truck across the intersection before the small strip of asphalt he was traveling on turned into an even smaller strip and then disappeared all together. When the truck began to pull out, their Suburban vanished in a thick cloud of black smoke. Luckily, the car in front of them passed through the intersection so Erpack didn't have to worry about running over him.

"Damn that's nasty," Dillon commented.

"You've got that right. I believe all the truck manufacturers in the world dumped the smoke belchers in this country. You don't see one rig here that doesn't blow thick smoke when they start or accelerate. That one's a Mercedes. They're the worst offenders. I don't think you could find an anti-pollution rule on the books. They just don't seem to give a shit. Diesel is cheap and they don't care about mileage rates. To make matters worse for fellow travelers, the exhaust pipes don't point up in the air; they're right at ground level so they blow right into the cars next to them as they start. Luckily, we have a good air conditioner."

"I guess it's the same way in Riyadh," Dillon replied. "They may not have the same number of water trucks on the road but they do belch the black smoke. I did notice some expensive cars running around the capitol. Lots of Mercs and BMWs. Just in my short time here the Toyota pickup seems to be the vehicle of choice."

"You've got to remember just a few years ago this section of the Kingdom was part of Yemen and these folks were chasing goats and camels through the hills. They didn't have roads and didn't have vehicles. Since their attempt at civilization, the little truck has replaced the camel. The biggest problem is they still think they're in the wide-open desert riding herd. You'll see them cut in and out without regard to anyone. I just sit back, get up to the speed limit, and let the mayhem take place around me. Thank goodness for Uncle Sam's overreaction by providing us Armored Annie," Erpack added as he affectionately patted the dashboard.

"What's on the agenda?" Dillon asked as they continued on their way.

"First stop will be the air base. I want you to meet a couple of the key players so you know what I'm dealing with. Once you meet them, I'm sure you'll understand the problems I face on a daily basis. Then we can head back for the compound or begin our discussions in my humble office complex."

"Sounds fine with me. What have you told people around here about me?"

Erpack looked at Dillon with mock astonishment. "Told people about you? They don't even know you exist. After the tongue lashing you gave me, I wasn't going to say a goddamn thing about you. I've got a retirement check to protect."

"Glad the tactic worked," Dillon smiled as he replied. "We can just give them some BS about me coming up for a staff assistance visit. The all-base pass should help the situation. I'm told they aren't given to just anyone."

"Most of the staff can get them if they push the right buttons. As I'm sure you have discovered this place is run by whom you know, not what you know. They have some of the dumbest bastards running a program they can't even spell but daddy is somebody and that's their ticket."

They continued their drive toward the air base as Erpack resumed his role as tour guide. The rock formations fascinated Dillon. The region formed millions of years ago by volcanic activity that literally pushed the ocean floor straight up. The "escarpment" was the edge of the erupted area. Abha sat on the edge with Khamis Mushayt sitting a few kilometers inland. The drive to the Red Sea was only about three hours long. Many of the men went snorkeling or scuba diving at least once a month. Special beaches were set aside for use by westerners. They didn't have to face the restriction of keeping women in abayas while swimming. Dillon listened intently as Erpack showed him the newest hospital, shopping center, grocery store, and medical consulting clinic.

"One of the things that really grabs my attention," Erpack said as he rounded a corner to access another divided highway, "is the number of showrooms for bathroom fixtures. Beautiful bathtubs, sinks, and toilets for a population that craps into a hole in the ground. It just doesn't make much sense. What kind of a toilet fixation do they have? Also, gas stations, there must be one gas station for every five cars in the area. Moreover, they keep building them. If it isn't a new toilet store, it's a new gas station. Now they're building children's clothing stores. Must be the result of some baby boom. It's just fascinating to watch."

As Dillon began to reply, a small white flash passed on the right and attempted to pull into the space in front of their truck. It wasn't big enough for a skateboard. The Saudi driver, realizing his error, abruptly cut back to the right, on to the shoulder and around a bus. Dillon grabbed the panic bar as Erpack reacted to the situation.

The truck disappeared into the line of traffic as Erpack indicated a lane change. "Let me show you a monument built to the sterling Saudi intellect and after such a demonstration of their driving ability, I'm sure you'll appreciate the irony." He joined the flow of traffic into an access lane with a concrete monument in a small park like setting.

"That's what we affectionately refer to as the Saudi brain." Dillon looked at the monument. It consisted of concrete pillars with a very large bolder encased in the middle.

"A stone brain covered in concrete is how we look at some of the Saudis we deal with. If it ain't their way, it's no way. They operate from a stone mentality. If you ask anyone what it really stands for, no one can seem to find the right words. Guess our interpretation will have to suffice."

"I'll try to remember." Dillon said as he released the panic bar. They were now on the main road known as "military road". It led to an access road to the air base and to the main gates of the army training facility. If travelers followed the road without turning, it leads directly to Najran formally owned by Yemen and a stopover point on the ancient spice routes through the area.

At the "crown", an intersection hosting a billboard type apparatus over the road with a large crown encircling a picture of the King, Erpack turned off the main road and on to the base access road. They passed under two simulated F-15s perched on their tails holding a sign announcing welcome to King Khalid Air Base.

One inside, Erpack carefully observed the 60KPH speed limit. "I've been caught once and all of my men have been caught at least once," he said as a Saudi air force type passed on the right.

"Of course the speed limits don't seem to apply to Saudis!" They continued on their way passing through a couple of roundabouts.

"Gifts from the Brits. I'm just glad no one in the states noticed this method of traffic control. We have accidents in these every week. One guy doesn't want to give way to the other and they smash into each other just to prove a point. Knock on simulated plastic," he said as he rapped his knuckles on the dashboard, "we haven't had anyone hit yet."

"Don't they follow the rule of the person in the roundabout has the right of way?"

"Please!" Erpack exclaimed as he negotiated his way around another traffic circle. Once on the other side he moved into the left lane and made his exit off the road into a parking lot. He pulled into a spot reserved for "USMTM", put the truck in park, and turned off the engine.

"Welcome to my humble home away from home", he said opening his door to leave the truck. Dillon followed to the side door of a building directly in front of their parking spot. Inside he found a sparsely decorated room with temporary dividers providing separation from what Dillon assumed was non-military offices.

At a desk in the center of the room, a Saudi was playing a game of solitaire on the computer. He minimized the screen as the colonel approached.

"Dillon, I would like you to meet my government relations coordinator, Abdullah Al-Kahfanny." Abdullah stood to greet Dillon.

"Dillon is down from Riyadh on a staff assistance visit. He has some staff experience I want to pick apart for our detachment." Kahfanny continued to hold Dillon's hand in greeting.

"But I wasn't aware of a pending visit," Kahfanny stated to Erpack.

"It was a last minute thing, my friend," Erpack replied as he headed for an open door in a corner of the room.

"I'll fill you in on details later. He has an all base pass, so there really wasn't any requirement for your services." The colonel stood aside so Dillon could enter the office. Once inside, Erpack shut the door.

"Worthless, nosy, piece of shit," he hissed as he went around his desk and took a seat. Dillon lowered himself into one of the tattered metal armchairs facing Erpack's desk.

"While you're here," Erpack warned, "don't tell that man anything. I trust him about as far as I can throw him. He tried to screw me with some trusted information I shared with him after I first arrived. I haven't confided in him since that time. He only gets what I want him to have and that's all. He spends most of his time playing computer games and trying to nose into everyone else's business."

"Point made," Dillon acknowledged. Erpack left his seat and went to the door. He pulled it open a bit and asked Abdullah to get both of them some coffee. He left the door opened slightly so he could watch Abdullah after he returned from fetching the coffee. He didn't want the man listening at a closed door. Both men would have to speak in hushed tones to prevent Kahfanny from overhearing their conversation. "Let me tell you a bit about the people who work for me", Erpack resumed the conversation after returning to his desk chair.

Major Earnest W. Abelman, call sign "Honest Abe", a pilot with nearly 15 years of experience in the Eagle. Abelman was the quasi deputy commander for the detachment. His formal title was lead trainer but he did serve as the det commander when Erpack was not around.

Next in rank order was Major Sid S. Trouter, call sign "Fishhead". He was a newly minted field grade officer getting his remote tour out of the way, so he could concentrate on getting a spot in the Pentagon rotation. He set his sights on bigger and better things. He was single so he could keep his life focused on becoming the youngest Air Force Chief of Staff in the short history of America's aerospace team. Fishhead was a pilot with a good deal of time in the Eagle but he spent more time kissing the butts of commanders with staff jobs to ingratiate himself to folks he thought could do him a favor later in life.

Last of the pilots was Captain Winston E. Millenhoff, call sign "Smokes". With more time as a lead than Fishhead, he was concentrating on being a better pilot rather than being a better staff worker.

The only Weapons Systems Officer was Captain Stephen P. Spocker, call sign "Vulcan". Their recently promoted administrator was Technical Sergeant Fred D. Cander. Call sign "Candyman".

Erpack, call sign "Pacman", explained all aviators picked up call signs when they first entered pilot training. Most stuck to them throughout their careers. Fred carried one because they used radios to keep in touch when traveling outside the compound or air base. Since the Saudi bombings and a declaration of the area as hazardous, all the vehicles were equipped with two-way radios. One of the base stations was in Fred's office and the other was a mobile for relocation to the "duty officer" on weekends.

Their conversation came to a stop as Abdullah came into the office with two cups of coffee on a battered silver tray. He sat the tray on the edge of Erpack's desk and began to take a seat on the couch when Erpack stopped him.

"Sorry Abdullah but this conversation has nothing to do with Government Relations. I'll give you a call if we get into your area of expertise." Abdullah nodded his head and left the office.

"He called the tea boy, had him bring the coffee over to his desk, and then he brought it in so he could try to weasel his way into our meeting. I wish there was some way to get rid of his ass but I've been told he's connected and that's all there is to it."

Erpack continued to give background information on his aviators and the situation, as he perceived it. "I would like to speak with each one if that could be arranged?" Dillon asked.

"No problem there," Erpack responded as he reached into one of the desk side drawers to pull out the flying schedule. "I was on the schedule for today but Abe took the mission. Let me see what we've got here," he mumbled as he looked at the flying and training schedule. "Do you want to speak with them individually, or as a group?"

"Individually would be best. Let's me find out what each of them thinks without feeling any peer or command pressure."

"That will take some time but it can be done. I'll bring them into the office this morning and then we can meet with the ones we miss at my villa later tonight. By the way, that's where I've got you bunking down."

"Sounds good to me," Dillon agreed. Just as he did, Erpack called out Fred's name as he saw him come into the office. Sergeant Cander came to the door.

"Yes sir?"

"Fred let me introduce you to Dillon. He's here on a staff assistance visit and wants to talk with the guys about a wide range of things. Can you arrange to have them stop by here this morning?" Fred stepped into the room and greeted Dillon.

"How ya doin sir?" Fred asked as he shook Dillon's hand. He looked over to Erpack and asked if there was any special time Dillon wanted to see the other men.

"Just have them stop by as they can. We'll be here most of the morning and then head back for the compound just after noon prayer. I want to talk with the major and the Boeing boy sometime before we leave. Check to see if they're going to be in this morning."

"Right sir. See you later Dillon." Fred responded as he disappeared around the corner into his office.

"Fred's a good man. Just put on tech. Going through one hell of a nasty divorce. He may sign on to stay longer than his year. As a remote, this is paradise. The only thing missing are the bars and whores outside the main gate but there are plenty of nurses to go around and you know we can get our rations from the commissary. Life is good," Erpack sighed as he leaned back in his chair and sipped his coffee.

"Any further incidents since the near catastrophe?" Dillon queried.

"Just the non removal of a gear pin on launch. End of runway crew found it when they were giving the jet a final go over before taking the active. The streamer was clipped off. More than likely one of the Saudi crew chiefs took it for his car keys. We see them downtown all the time. I do believe there's a massive black market for the damn things."

Erpack kept up a steady stream of minor and major problems discovered in one situation or another. Dillon began to see why the man was so frustrated at the situation. He shouldn't have to face a drunk or stoned crew chief trying to launch one of his men on a mission. The only people with access to alcohol are government employees through special arrangement with the embassy and Saudi government. The ration is strictly controlled and if rule violations are found, military members can be dishonorably discharged. Civilian employees are terminated for cause preventing future employment with any government agency.

"As I'm sure you've discovered since your arrival, bootleg booze is alive and well in the Kingdom. Rumors around here have a guy producing stuff on the compound that tastes like quality Bourbon. He even imports wood chips for flavor. Sells for 100 rips a bottle."

"I was introduced to black market booze in Riyadh. Part of our cover story as a matter of fact."

"If that's part of your story, I won't go any further," Erpack said raising both hands and holding them in front of him across the desk. "I don't have a need to know and what I don't know can't hurt me, or so they say."

Dillon asked if it be worth his time to talk with Fred. Although he didn't actually have any professional contact with the contractors, living on the compound did serve as a conduit for personal communication. Erpack thought it was a good idea and called Fred to join them in the office. "Have you finished contacting all the guys?" Erpack asked as Fred came into the office.

"Yes sir. Just hung up from talking with Vulcan. All of them said they would be glad to talk with Dillon. They'll try to get back here before you guys leave. If they can't make it, they'll contact you on the radio to set up a place and time."

Erpack asked Fred to take a seat and explained about Dillon's "staff assistance" visit. He was looking into problem areas for contract negotiations. Erpack looked to Dillon for disapproval of the story and receiving none he continued. What Dillon needed were instances of poor maintenance or situations where contractor personnel didn't follow established procedures and put safety at risk. When Fred asked for an example of what he meant, Erpack mentioned the gear pin incident. Fred nodded his head as an indicator of his understanding. He thought for a moment and began to discuss three instances.

Both Dillon and Erpack listened as Fred explained in no detail what bothered the aviators. Two of the instances Erpack was aware of and knew Dillon would be fully briefed by the other members of his team but one of them was a new situation.

A scheduled mission called for munitions delivery to the range located near the air base. On board each aircraft of the four ship package was a full load of MK-82, 500LB high explosive bombs. Each one fully fused and ready for delivery on simulated targets scattered around the range. Everything was normal until Fishhead was going through a series of checks before departure. His Saudi student in the back seat said he was getting a fault indication for the munitions. After a couple of minutes troubleshooting the apparent problem, Fishhead called for maintenance assistance. The crew chief got with dispatch who called the specialists to respond. Within a minute or two, the maintenance crew arrived at the hardened aircraft shelter and approached the jet.

Once on the headset, the specialist made a preliminary assessment of the problem and told the pilot he needed to access the cockpit switches. To do this, one engine must be shut down. Before Fishhead could shutdown, the specialist took off the headset, handed them back to the crew chief, walked over to where the boarding ladder was stored, and approached the jet with the engine still running. Luckily, for the specialist, the crew chief saw him and ran over to keep him from getting too close to the engine air intake. He could have been sucked into the engine and killed when his body reached the rotating blades. Before the canopy opened, there was much discussion between Fishhead and the crew chief about allowing the specialist to approach the jet.

As he reached the top of the ladder, Fishhead asked him a couple of simple questions and didn't get a warm feeling about the man's condition. When he couldn't fix the problem by adjusting switches, Fishhead aborted the mission and sent the other three ships on their way to the training ground.

Fred told the two men those were the only instances he could remember at the time. Erpack asked the date of the Fishhead incident with Fred giving him an approximation of the mission but he could check the old flying schedule to give him an exact date. The abort would be listed.

As it turned out, the situation happened while Erpack was in Riyadh meeting Dillon for the first time. When he returned, the guys stayed away from him with their problems because they could tell something fired him up and he needed time to cool down. Once a couple of days passed, Fishhead just forgot to tell him about the experience. Erpack told Dillon he would get with Fishhead to find out any additional details about the problem.

"Let me call the major's office to see if he has a minute or two to talk with us. If for nothing else, it makes him feel important knowing all the visitors we have up here. Since you're staying with me, he didn't have to approve any special housing. However, that doesn't mean he's unaware of your visit. The guy is really connected. He's a member of the ruling tribe in the region. Uncles, brothers, grandparents are all entwined to the ruling prince and his entourage. We always have to watch our step for fear of offending one of his relatives. We just try to keep him informed and let him play his cards."

"I'll keep that in mind," Dillon said as he reached for his cup of coffee. "I certainly don't want to offend any Saudi officer. They all have friends in Riyadh and a couple of phone calls could cause problems."

"You are *so right*," Erpack agreed while dialing the major's number. The Indian clerk answered.

"Raja, this is colonel Erpack. Is the major available?" Erpack paused while listening to the reply.

"Good. I have a visitor I want the major to meet. We'll be right over." He hung up and rose from his chair.

"Let's go. He's there right now but will be leaving in about half an hour for a meeting with the base commander. We know he won't miss that one so he can't keep us talking forever. Prime opportunity to make our escape."

Dillon followed Erpack out of the office, down a narrow passageway with a wall on one side and temporary partitions on the other. They approached a door, which Erpack unlocked as they stepped into the contractor side of the building. This was the place where Saudi or American employees handled the majority of government relations and personnel items. They continued to walk through a set of double doors, into an entrance area and into the other section of the building housing the RSAF contingent. Raja greeted them and ushered them inside the major's office.

213

As they entered, Major Al-Kawaji asked the colonel and Dillon to take seats in the two armchairs located directly in front of his desk. Between the chairs was a small end table with three or four neatly arranged books of one type or another. The one on top was a "coffee table" book about Florida.

Behind Saeed a wall filled with photos of himself in uniform or national dress with a wide range of what Dillon assumed were visiting dignitaries. There were a few faces Dillon recognized as members of the Desert Storm team and commanders of Central Command, and various fighter squadrons. Since King Khalid hosted F-117 Stealth aircraft during the war, it would only make sense the major would have contact with many of the key players.

On the major's left was a computer keyboard with a very large flat screen monitor. Obviously hooked into the web, MSN displayed prominently across the screen with scrolling stock quotes and the latest news. Connected to the computer table was a smaller table holding a fax machine, two multi-line phones, and a cellular phone charger. Adjacent to the table was a bookcase filled with binders. Some of them showed Arabic writing while others showed English. Some of the English listings were for contractor personnel policies, Air Force directives concerning Foreign Military Sales, manning documents, and aircraft status reports. There was a door in the far corner leading to a conference room. Dillon could see a few chairs against the wall. There was a map of the air base, a collection of models, plaques from various organizations and directly behind the colonel and Dillon, a cabinet holding more mementos of the major's career.

Since their entrance, the major took two calls. He pushed the intercom button, gave directions in Arabic, and told his guests they wouldn't be disturbed again. He then offered tea or coffee. Erpack and Dillon both requested tea. He again used the intercom to order the "shai". They continued the small talk until the requested beverage was carried into the office and placed close to each man.

"Dillon is here on a staff assistance visit at my request," Erpack began. "He's currently attached to USMTM in Riyadh. When I was there earlier this month, he offered to visit and gather information on the maintenance problems we've been experiencing. You recall the instances I'm referring too?"

The major nodded his understanding of the question and the situation.

"With the experiences of the air force team working with your forces," Dillon interjected, "I want to talk about what they notice and perhaps come up with a common thread. None of these men are junior aviators. All of them have seen good and bad maintenance. When the colonel came to Riyadh and talked with the folks up there, they felt it would help the situation to have an outside perspective on the problem."

"Have you had any problems with the Saudis?" the major asked.

Dillon looked to Erpack. The colonel hesitated before answering. "None that have come to my attention at this time. All the problem situations have involved contractors."

Erpack would tell Dillon later the reason they didn't have any problems with the Saudis was you could never find one when there was work. In each squadron where contractors were supposedly training members of the Saudi Air Force, when it came time to launch jets, the only people available were the contractors. Now their expertise was being questioned.

"I'm very concerned about the problem you're investigating. Squadron commanders have approached me with some instances involving some of our senior pilots. The students don't have any idea what is supposed to be happening with maintenance. When they pull the handle to start the jet, they want it to work. If it doesn't they could care less. They are too concerned with time in the air, not time on the ground. I'm going to put something on the table which could or could not be of relevance." He paused for effect.

"There is a rumor floating around the ranks about the abuse of certain native products which produce a state of euphoria. I believe your compatriots refer to it as wacky weed. It's chewed and produces an effect similar to marijuana. If contractors have picked up the habit from some of their Saudi counterparts, I'm afraid it may be affecting their work. You might want to look into that aspect of the problem somewhere along the way."

Both men rose from their seats and reached across the desk to shake the major's hand as they prepared to leave. Neither man spoke until they were back in Erpack's office. "Wacky weed?" Dillon asked.

"I'll have to do some checking on that one," Erpack replied.

"Does it have anything to do with the stick I see them chewing on and rubbing their teeth?"

"I hope not," Erpack replied. "I've tried it. It's called a swake and they use it like a toothbrush. Tastes like shit, so I didn't pick up the habit. It has some kind of anesthetic effect. Rubs the crap off their teeth and deadens them from the effect of their cavities. Some of the guys around here have the worst teeth I've every seen. Absolutely black. I can see why they want to have something to kill the pain. I don't believe it affects the brain, just the area they rub it on. They certainly aren't the Crest generation."

Since the major mentioned the Saudis chewing the substance, it didn't appear he was aware of the possible marijuana connection. Dillon wondered if he should bring him into the picture or leave him on the outside until things in Riyadh were completed. He decided to continue his work with Erpack and make a decision before he left Khamis. One plan of attack could be to have him search out possible connections between the initials EB and MD.

Were they name initials? Was one of them a doctor? Could they work in the same shop? All sorts of possibilities presented themselves for investigation. Once some leads developed, he could have William come down in an official capacity to bring all the investigative entities on line for a final assault. He would continue to concentrate on Crimitin.

"Fred, you in the office?" Erpack shouted.

"Yes sir," was the reply.

"Come in here a sec, will ya?"

Fred was soon at the doorway. "We just came out of the major's office as part of our little staff assistance effort," Erpack began, "and he mentioned something chewed by the Saudis we Americans refer to as wacky weed. Ever hear of it?"

"Wacky weed?" Fred puzzled. "Right off the top of my head I can't say I've ever heard that term used. However, I can tell you Sergeant Weberton would have a better handle on that situation. He has more contact with the guys on the line than I do." He turned toward Dillon to explain.

"My main job is to keep the administration of the training mission in one line. He works for the logistic center. He not only has contact with the guys at work, he parties with them at the compound. They dive the Red Sea and generally hang out more than I do. He's single and runs the nurses."

"Sounds like he may be a good place to start," Dillon said as he got up. "Where does this guy hang his hat?"

"Logistics support is located in a trailer behind this building. Let me give him a call to see if he's in his office. He spends a lot of time at what he calls coordinating. Actually, he screws off more than any senior NCO I've ever met. He's been stationed at every one of the detachments in Kingdom. I don't know why someone hasn't caught him at his game. However, I'm only the technical sergeant. I'm not paid enough to figure out such things. Let me get off my soap box and make the call."

After he left, Dillon commented on how displeased Fred was with the senior non-commissioned officer next door. Erpack agreed to give the Riyadh logistics folks a call next week. However, if the Saudis are getting some extra benefits from this glorified supply sergeant, they may not want to close the door on him. Erpack related to Dillon how during his time in Kingdom he witnessed some worthless individuals keep their jobs because of the extra services they provided. Then there were the folks who converted to Islam in order to protect their positions.

"These folks are called 'MOCs' or Muslim of Convenience." The colonel stated. "They convert, take a Muslim name, get a different identification booklet, and then sit back on their ass just daring the managers to take any action against them. If ever approached, they pull out the Islamic identification

216

and wave it in their face. One individual was so derelict in his duties, even the Saudis looked to get rid of him. However, he held a pair of cards to play. First, on the table was his racial background followed closely by his Islamic faith. When he was facing imminent dismissal, he made a preemptive visit to RSAF headquarters claiming he was being discriminated against because of his race and religion. What he neglected to tell the command structure was the initial call for his dismissal came from his Saudi supervisor and not the American managers. When the general said he didn't have to worry about losing his job, the man returned to his base. When the deception was discovered, the general couldn't go back on his word, so he transferred the man. It would save face and get him away from the people he deceived."

Fred came back into the office and told the men Sergeant Weberton went to the store to pick up some cases of water for the snack bar he ran for the benefit of what he called his "retirement fund".

"Have his admin guy give us a call when he returns. I would like to touch base with him before we go back to the compound." Erpack asked Fred while he reached for his phone.

"I'll just give the Boeing boys a call to see if they have time for us." He listened while the Sri Lankan answered the line. "Yes you can help me. Is Horace at his desk?" Erpack queried. "He is. Good enough. I'm on my way over." He stood while hanging up. "Let's go!" Dillon followed him out the door and down the same small hallway. The turned into a small "reception" area and approached an open door in the corner. Erpack gave a light rap and waited for an acknowledgment.

"Horace, you got a minute?" The man sitting behind an executive style desk looked up from the papers he was reviewing and motioned the men into his office.

"Always got time for you Will. Have a seat." Erpack and Dillon took seats in front of the desk.

"What can I do for you this morning? Horace W. Abercrom, Colonel, USAF Retired. A full-fledged card carrying member of what Peace Sun employees know as the "Colonel's Club". Retired from the Air Force one day and working for a defense contractor the next. Used by contractors for their long list of contacts with decision makers throughout the Air Force. Most had command experience in a fighter wing and some time flying combat in Viet Nam. However, a Viet Nam era commander was getting older and harder to find. Now the combat experience was coming from Desert Storm and the Balkans.

Abercrom worked for a couple of other companies before ending up with the Peace program. Each one of his positions was eliminated during contract negotiations. He only landed the manager position with Boeing because of contacts in Riyadh.

Following a consolidation of programs, Boeing set about eliminating duplicate office functions. One of his old time friends was placed into a "Vice President" position and saved him one more time from dismissal.

Erpack would later tell Dillon about the change in attitude when the former manager was fired. He conflicted with the Saudis for trying to implement a few subtle changes. However, the hierarchy did not favor the changes. He was "reassigned" to Riyadh and then cut loose from the program. When Abercrom was appointed, Erpack said the community was relatively shocked. Since his investiture, morale suffered and he was content to sit back and collect a paycheck. The incident Erpack faced with Abercrom not initiating an investigation into possible maintenance under the influence was just the crowning glory.

"Horace, this is Dillon." Erpack introduced. "He's here from Riyadh looking into the problems we've been having with some of the maintainers. He's on the contracts side of the house and wants to make sure we're getting what we paid for."

"Problems?" Horace began with raised eyebrows. "What are you talking about?"

"Don't go there Abercrom. You know goddamn good and well what I'm talking about. You've hired a bunch of drunks and druggies. My detachment has suffered some of the shoddiest maintenance I've every experienced in all my years flying fighters. When I brought it to your attention, all you did was poo poo me. That's when I asked for some help from headquarters. Dillon's the help and if you aren't careful, you'll be looking for another job and this time your buddies won't be able to save your ass!"

"I resent the inference," Abercrom stuttered leaning forward in his seat and putting both hands on the edge of his desk.

"I really don't care what you resent," Erpack fired back. "I'm tired of you sitting back on your ass and not taking any action on serious problems. You didn't even fake an interest. Your only comment was there couldn't be a drug problem here because drugs are illegal in the Kingdom. What a crock of shit. They're illegal in the states and we have one of the biggest drug problems in the world."

"Gentlemen," Dillon interjected. "Let's keep a modicum of civility. We're here to locate and solve problems, not create wars. Both of you please sit back and release from the cocked and loaded positions. We aren't going to make any headway if you keep sniping at each other."

Dillon got up from his chair to close the office door. The outbursts garnered the attention of a few TCNs and Saudis in the small waiting area.

Dillon wanted to keep things as private as possible. This wasn't helping the situation at all.

He didn't return to his seat but took up a spot behind Erpack in front of a couch situated under a picture of the first Saudi F-15 to leave the St. Louis plant. He began to give Abercrom a brief explanation of how he came to provide a bit of outside staff assistance in what Erpack perceives as a major problem.

"From what I've been told, there's something going on with the maintainers. We need to find what it is and eliminate the problem. If the problem is home brew, then we have to cut down on the source. If drugs are involved, there must be a source. It could be local; it could be outside the area. That has to be determined so we can request Saudi intervention. We've made initial contact with the PSPO[21] and he's aware of some problems. What he suspects is a local concoction the Bedouins chew for a buzz. If he suspects anything else, he isn't sharing it at this time."

"You've got to understand my position," Abercrom began to make excuses for his lack of concern.

Erpack cut him off, "I don't have to understand anything other than I came to you with a problem and your fat ass refused to investigate. That's all I need to know."

Dillon interceded again to stop the bickering. He felt the meeting was going nowhere. "Let me tell you what's going to happen. We'll call this meeting quits right now. I can't see where we're going to make any headway with you two in the same room."

Dillon was now standing by one side of the desk facing both men. "I'll get back with you later today or tomorrow. Will, let's get back to your office and see if we have any messages."

He waited until Erpack got up and headed for the closed door. Once he opened it, Dillon nodded to Abercrom as he too left the room. Once back in Erpack's office, Dillon shut the door and leaned against it shaking his head in disbelief.

"What!" Erpack exclaimed. "I'm not allowed to say anything?"

"Not the way you went about it. If we're going to get any cooperation out of the man, you can't go around spitting on his dinner plate. If I get a chance, I'll go back later and see what he has to say in his defense. It appears he just doesn't want to run afoul of the Saudis and will go to any length including denying a problem to keep a paycheck coming in."

"It's not only a paycheck for him," Erpack added. "His wife works on the compound and he certainly doesn't want to lose that bit of loose change. I'm not sure what she does but I know she doesn't have permission to work. One of those under the table arrangements."

"Not really any of my concern," Dillon countered. "Just let me do the talking from now on if you want to stay around. I only have a couple of days to give you a path to follow. As I've told you, and I hope you understand, I'm not in Kingdom to help you solve your problems. I'm here on a murder investigation and once I leave your company, I'll have the right guys give you a hand. Are you tracking along with me?"

Erpack was sitting on the edge of his desk. He gave no recognition of the question other than a nod of his head. "Good, I'm glad we're on the same path. Let me see if Fred got a call from Weberton." He opened the door without turning and stepped into Fred's office to see if there was a call.

Fred held the receiver on one shoulder as he typed notes on his computer. "Right sir, I'll make sure we get the changes made on the radios. Anything else?" He bid the caller farewell and hung up.

"If it's not one thing, it's another. Now they want us to change all the transmitters in our radios for a newly developed encrypted type. Sounds like a monumental waste of money to me. But then again, I'm not paid to make those types of high-level decisions. Whatcha need?" Dillon asked if Vernon returned from his buying trip.

It was a short walk from Fred's office to the office of Sergeant Weberton. He was a member of the Logistics support team. Direction for the groups in Kingdom activity came from Warner Robins AFB just outside Atlanta. A civilian in the grade of GS-12 was assigned to the base but like the military, he couldn't bring his family. Result, no one wanted the spot on a permanent basis and the program suffered with a series of temporary duty assignments. As he came around the corner of the building, he saw a man in jeans and T-shirt pouring some dry cat food on the sidewalk. Just out of his reach sat four "Saudi cats". It was obviously time for their daily feeding. As Dillon approached, the man turned toward him.

"Excuse me," Dillon said, "I'm looking for Sergeant Weberton".

"You've found him." the casually dressed man replied. "I just came back from a shopping trip and haven't changed into my BDU's yet." He offered his hand in greeting.

"Glad to meet you. Name's Dillon. If you don't mind, I'd like to talk with you a bit about your knowledge of the contractors?"

"Don't mind at all. Let's go inside before the beasts attack for not moving out of the way quickly enough." He stepped away from the food just dispensed and the four felines moved swiftly to make short work of the pile.

Dillon followed him into the building and to his office. Inside the walls held plaques, pictures, and certificates.

"Coffee?" he offered. Dillon agreed to a cup and followed down a hallway past an empty conference room and a couple of empty offices.

"These belong to our resident engineers. One of them was an active duty captain. The other is a contractor. The captain just left for another assignment. We aren't sure if we're going to get a replacement. Most of the contracted construction has been completed. With the money crunch, no one is betting on them getting anything else started."

As he finished speaking, he picked up a cup off the sink drain board and offered it to Dillon. He then poured from the standard issue Mr. Coffee pot sitting next to the sink. Inside the small kitchen was a microwave oven, a refrigerator, a table and four chairs, boxes of bottled water, a storage cabinet and a wall sized bookshelf affair filled with every conceivable type of junk food. There were six kind of chips, 10 varieties of candy bars, four different brands of cookies, and a dozen packages of miscellaneous snack cakes. Quite an assortment of stateside products. All were for sale at prices ranging from one to five riyals.

"Care for a snack cake to go with your coffee?' Dillon declined as Vernon picked up a "Tiger Cake" on his way out the door. Once back in his office, Dillon took a seat against the wall opposite Vernon's desk. He was again admiring the array of memorabilia situated around the office.

"Seems like you've been here a while." Dillon said as he leaned over to read the small brass plate on a very elaborate presentation statuette of two F-15s.

"You're right there. I've been stationed at each one of the bases. Started at Dhahran, moved to Taif and ended up here about two years ago. Since I'm single, I don't have to worry about not being able to have my family with me. I've really learned to enjoy the area. This has to be the best of the assignments. I love to dive and with the Red Sea only a short drive away, I'm in paradise."

"I'm glad to see someone is getting something out of their time here," Dillon responded. "I've heard some horror stories about the assignment. I must admit most of the complaints are from guys who left their families but this really isn't a bad place for a remote assignment. It could be a lot worse."

"That's for darn sure. What can I do for you?" Vernon asked as he took a sip of coffee. Dillon explained the reason behind his visit. He stuck with the story about being a contracts guy investigating possible problems with the contractors and the lack of corrective action by the prime contractor and subcontractors. The men continued to talk for nearly half and hour about one subject or another. Finally, when Dillon figured he heard enough of the background information, he asked the pointed question.

"From our conversation, it appears you have a great deal of contact with the contractors in one form or another. You dive with them; you run the compound bars and shoot darts with them. What can you tell me about a drug connection of any type?"

From the facial reaction, Dillon wasn't sure if Vernon knew the question was coming or not. He sat behind the desk with little physical response. As Dillon asked the question, Vernon sipped from his mug. He slowly lowered the beverage to the desk before providing the carefully structured reply.

"Why do you believe I would have any knowledge of drugs in the Kingdom? Aren't you aware of the severe punishment for dabbling in that shit?"

"I'm well aware of the consequences. However, basing my question on the contact you have with the contractors, you might have picked up information others have missed." Vernon carefully pondered his next move as he took another slow sip of coffee. Dillon too was making mental notes on where he would take the conversation depending on Vernon's answer.

"Well Dillon, I'm afraid you're going to be disappointed. With all my contacts, I don't have any knowledge of any illicit use of banned substances."

Dillon looked down at his coffee cup as he sat in front of Vernon. He slowly turned the mug in his hands before raising it to his lips to drain the last of the liquid. When he finished, he rose, stepped up to the desk, and placed the mug near Vernon's name plaque.

"You're right Sergeant Weberton, I am disappointed. Just let me give you a little food for thought. Down in the coffee room you seem to be running a very lucrative side business. It would be interesting to see where some of those products came from. I'm sure you can't find them in the local grocery stores. I would also be interested in finding out what you do with your ration of liquor. I'm confident a brief search of the records would indicate you are dealing the booze or you have one hell of a drinking habit."

Dillon rested his closed fists on the desk. "Let me calculate this. You're a master sergeant with what 15 or 16 years of service?"

"Eighteen." Vernon corrected.

"Eighteen years service! That is great. Only two more years until you can sit back and draw a nice retirement check from Uncle Sam." Dillon leaned toward Vernon.

"Well let me assure you of something. If you are bull shitting me about your knowledge concerning contractors and drugs, you will never see a retirement check." Dillon stared into Vernon's eyes before turning to leave the office. He half-expected Vernon to call him back but it didn't happen. Dillon left the building, stopped to pet one of the cats waiting for another handout, then returned to Erpack's office. He wasn't sure if the ploy would work but it was the only card left to play. He wasn't going to be in town

long enough to try other tactics. He hoped the direct approach coupled with veiled threats would serve the purpose.

Erpack was just coming out of his office when Dillon came around the corner. "How'd it go with Vern?" he asked as he went into Fred's office and dropped a letter into the in basket sitting on the corner of a rickety fold up card table.

"Too early to tell. I played a trump card because I'm pressed for time. Hope it works."

"I'll keep my fingers crossed. That guy has connections all over the Kingdom. I would be very surprised if he had anything to *do* with the drug scene but if there's one out there, he'll have a point of contact." Just as Erpack finished speaking, the door leading to the parking lot opened and Fishhead entered the office area. Dillon turned around when he heard the door open. Erpack introduced the two men.

"Tell ya what; let me pick up a few papers I need to drop off at the training squadron. That will leave my office open for your talk."

The three men entered Erpack's office while he gathered the papers. Once he slipped them into a small leather case, he bid the men good-by and left the building. Dillon shut the door and both men took seats in front of the desk. Dillon again repeated the story of why he was at Khamis. Fishhead listened and then unloaded when asked if he noticed any problem areas with contractors.

He offered examples of incident after incident all centered on a hand full of crew chiefs and specialists who tended the jets. Some of them Dillon thought were just petty but he let the man rant on for more than an hour. Dillon feigned great interest by taking notes while Fishhead raved. Once he was done, Dillon checked his notes and asked a few questions. He was hoping Fishhead was done ranting and could answer the questions in a short to the point fashion. After a few minutes, the men were finished talking. As they shook hands, Dillon opened the door to let Fishhead exit. Erpack was propped back in a chair reading the latest edition of *Stars and Stripes*.

"You two all done?" he asked.

"All done for right now," Dillon replied. "I told him if there's anything else he wants to make a point about, I'd be staying at your place."

Fishhead waved as he went down the narrow hallway into the contractor's area. Erpack checked his watch and said it was time to head for the compound. The other guys were flying or in class. They would have to be contacted later in the day. Before leaving, Erpack checked with Fred to insure there were no messages. The men left the building, got into the Suburban and headed for the compound.

CHAPTER TWENTY-EIGHT

The small van turned off one of the main streets crisscrossing Riyadh to a side street no wider than an alley. There would have been ample room except the locals park on either side of the street without regard for anyone trying to use the road. Some cars parked parallel to the street while others nosed in to spots not quite large enough for a bicycle.

The driver slowed to a crawl, pulled in the side mirrors, and picked his way through the maze. Once this initial labyrinth was negotiated, the road widened and the van's speed picked up accordingly. A few side streets further into the neighborhood, the van stopped in front of a wrought iron fence with decorative frosted glass blocking any view through the gate. Each iron bar topped out with a sharpened point. The glass continued past the top of the bars and then curved slightly toward the street. Not obvious to casual observers, the frosted glass was laminated, more than three inches thick and bullet proof up to 50-caliber.

The concrete block fence connected to the gate was more than 15 feet high. What isn't visible from the street is the electric grid running along top of the fence. When activated, there was enough current running through the grid to render a strong man unconscious. Picking up the access phone, the driver keyed in his code, waved to the security camera now pointed toward the van and greeted the person talking with him from inside the walls. He hung up and waited for the gates to swing open. There was a moment's delay as the multiple layers of blocking devices inside the gateway deactivated and lowered out of the way.

Once the gate swung open, the van pulled into the compound and parked to one side of the front door. As the driver stepped from the van, he could hear the gate swinging closed and the barriers activating to their locked position. Inside the fence was an array of crosshatched razor wire running from the top of the block wall to a point about 10 feet out from the bottom of the fence. The recently planted Morning Glories were beginning to climb the wire toward the top. Nice camouflage the man thought as he opened the van's rear door to remove the briefcase and wooden crate. On his earlier departure, the crate's compartments held small brown envelopes containing zip lock bags of cocaine. The briefcase was empty. Now the roles reversed. The crate was empty and the briefcase was full of Saudi riyals and US Dollars.

He kicked the door shut and headed for the villa's entrance. He sat the briefcase on the stoop as he opened the door. A blast of cold air greeted him as he walked into the tile floored entrance hall. To his right was a living room area used for relaxation by the villa's occupants. On his left was a stairwell to the second level of the house. Beyond was a hallway to a small washroom, a laundry, exit to the carport, and finally the kitchen. From there, you could access the dining room and back through to the living room. Sliding glass doors from both the living and dining rooms opened on to a covered patio area with a small pool and waterfall/garden area. A separate wall dividing it from what would have been the servants' quarters surrounded the yard. In this "home", the area served as armory, garage and final assault/escape route.

In case of police intervention in their lucrative activities, the men would fight until everyone was located in a solid concrete room near the back wall of the compound. Once inside, they could access an escape tunnel leading to an adjacent villa complex. Located inside those walls were two armored 4-wheeled drive vehicles complete with rations, gas, and munitions.

The dealers devised a rather unique method of hiding their purpose. Both vehicles parked in a structure closely resembling a normal garage. However, during renovation of the villa for their specific purposes, they removed the concrete blocks from the wall and replaced them with a thin wooden structure. Viewed from the street, the new wall looked like every other wall along the residential street. However, if required, the men would use the escape tunnel to the vehicle parking area, load the vehicles, and drive straight through the wall. Once outside they would separate and head for desert locations outside Riyadh. Satellite communication would be established for a later rendezvous. It was quite an elaborate setup none of the men every expected to use.

Rajmohamed took the box into the kitchen and left it by the door. He went back to the stairs and up to the second floor. At the top of the stairs opened a large area normally used as a sitting room for the four bedrooms. This one converted into a processing area. This was the action center for the operation. The pure cocaine, cut by several levels, was weighed, and placed in zip lock bags to "preserve freshness". The men always got a laugh out of the correlation. Abdunn Almany was sitting at a desk in the center of the room working on a spreadsheet. When Raj reached the top of the stairs, he looked his way and asked, "How did things go?"

"All contacts were made and the goods were delivered with full payment received. All we need to do is count the proceeds to double check." Raj set the briefcase on a small table next to the desk. Al made a few final entries to the sheet, closed the application, and opened another sheet for balance of payments.

When deliveries were made, they were done in public areas. Since they were the only game in town for main supplies, they could dictate terms. No late night deliveries to out of the way locations. They delivered in the morning or early afternoons to restaurants, juice bars, shopping centers, or any other facility, which allows relative safety for the deliveryman. Thus far, the operation was very successful. The men weren't even concerned about losing their main supply source. They cut the product efficiently enough to keep ample supplies on hand to last for several months.

Raj dialed the briefcase combination and began to take out the cash. Each bundle numbered to correlate with the bin holding the goods. Since they considered themselves nothing more than businessmen, they held their prices at the same rate for regular customers. As new contacts were made, the prices would fluctuate slightly. They didn't want anyone to feel they were being gouged so their hard feelings might result in unwanted contact with enforcement agencies. However, as all good businessmen in a community did, they developed a friendly and profitable liaison with the local constabulary. Any incursions into their area would have plenty of advance warning.

When deliveries were made, the amount for collection was listed in each compartment. Contact would be established, the cash would be exchanged, verified and then delivery would be made. Sometimes Raj would arrange to meet several contacts in a mall. It made the delivery process so much easier and he was all for simplifying his workload.

Al picked up each bundle, checked the amount to be collected from his computer sheet, and then counted the cash. Once verified, he would make an entry on the sheet, which transferred automatically to another worksheet to update the running balance on hand. It took them about half and hour to count, verify and log in the morning's receipts.

Once completed, Al put the packs back in to the briefcase and headed downstairs. He went out the back door, around the pool and out through a gate which led to the "safe" room. Inside the room, he unlocked a door closing off the stairs and leading to the tunnel. At the bottom of the stairs was another door allowing actual entrance to the tunnel. Also along the wall was a large safe door controlled by two combinations and two keys. Al and Raj retrieved the keys from around their necks and dialed in their separate combinations.

Al swung open the door and stepped into the vault. He set the briefcase on a small table located in the center of the room, opened the case, and pulled out the day's receipts. When receipts reached a certain amount, they transported the money to several banks in the city for deposit. Standing orders with each bank directed them to transfer money out of the Kingdom when the balance reached a certain amount.

Al made sure each deposit brought the balance over the designated amount so a transfer would be initiated. The funds would normally end up in off shore accounts in Jersey, the Caribbean, the Emirates, or a numbered account in Switzerland. After the transfers, electronic notification went up the line until it reached the designated level. At that level, a computer, consolidated receipts and disseminated funds to various operating locations throughout the world. Each working group received capital to allow continued operations. It was an electronic wonder and one they believed would be very difficult to trace.

Garmat pulled the chair away from it's resting spot next along the railing protected wall where it stopped the last time he got up from the computer desk. The castors glided silently across the seamless marble tile floor as he readjusted the high back chair closer to the desk. He pulled out the keyboard so he could type in the latest informational message to the boss. He wasn't sure how the news would be received. Not having anyone around to watch Dillon's movements would not be a welcomed change in plans. When Garmat was notified about Dillon's departure from Riyadh, he quickly checked his list of contacts. Since the Khamis/Abha area was so remote, they hadn't probed the necessity of beginning a regular supply route to the area. Consequently, there were no established points of contact. He knew the folks in Riyadh kept busy with regular customers in the capitol, Jeddah and Dhahran. Unless they wanted to face the required outlay of bribes, they would just stay out of the backwoods.

As was normal procedure, he sent the message to a holding area which at the appointed times during the day would send the message through a scrambling device, along electronic pathways through several forwarding stations to the boss. If the message were marked urgent, the powerful computer would notify the boss by means of a paging device. The message could then be received from a remote computer, or if the boss was home, from the main computer. He selected words carefully as not to upset the one person in the organization that could reach out and have him killed almost immediately. He followed directions without question and was always successful in completing any requests.

As Garmat was getting ready to send the message, Alfred came into the office. "Have you heard back from the boss yet?"

"Just getting ready to send the message now. Take a look at this and tell me if you think it will be too upsetting." Alfred came over to the desk so he could see the screen. He reviewed the message and proposed a paragraph saying they suggested to Riyadh that they send a contact man into Abha. It would put the onus on the Saudi connection and take the spotlight off their operation. Always spread the wealth when facing the main man's wrath.

When the message to the boss left the hard drive, Alfred moved Garmat out of the way so he could surf the net a bit about an upcoming vacation to the Mediterranean. He was planning to rent a 40-foot powerboat for an extended tour of the northern Italian coast. This hic up with Crimitin and the OSI agent put his plans on hold.

He only negotiated two web sites with boat listings when the "You Have Mail" icon flashed on the screen coupled with the computerized voice announcing the same thing. He called Garmat who was in the living room watching soccer with a small bottle of Eiswein.

"Garmat! I believe we have an answer." Both men hoped the message would be a while in its transmission phase before having to face any adverse response.

"Shit, I was hoping it would take some time to get through," Garmat said as he came into the office carrying his wine glass in one hand and a slice of cheese in the other.

"I guess this one time we hit all the gates and the boss just happened to be writing poetry when the note came in. Let's see what he has to say."

Alfred clicked the icon and the mailbox opened. The message was short. Their instructions concise. Ensure the group in Riyadh reestablished contact with Dillon right now. Both men sighed in relief. They successfully dodged the bullet and put the work on Riyadh. Having Dillon wandering around without someone from the group watching, unsettled the headmaster. The instructions to reestablish contact as soon as possible better put fear into their hearts or they would suffer the consequences. TCNs were a dime a dozen in Riyadh and the money paid for their services would buy an entire village in their home countries. Elimination would slow the flow of goods but it wouldn't stop it. When an edict issues, it's expected to be followed without hesitation.

⁂

EB reached into the side pocket of his Italian leather briefcase, pulled out the spreadsheet listing fields, and projected harvest dates. Each field took a little more than a week to harvest and process. Since all the processing happens at the farm, the product leaves the property in shipping condition. Under discussion today was the quantity of product and packaging requirements. If the goods were destined for local markets, the packages were small and ready for purchase. If they packed for delivery to another location, the bundle was camouflaged with clothing and wrapped as if it was being sent to India or Bangladesh. The review process at Abha was simply an x-ray by unconcerned police. If it didn't look like a bomb, they didn't pay much attention. Who in their right mind would try to ship an illegal substance via Saudi Arabian Airlines?

"Let's put this crop into local packages," MD said as he looked at the projected harvest date.

"I don't know if you've checked the warehouse but the supply is getting a bit thin. Need to bolster our ability to provide the locals. Don't forget we have the holiday coming up and the boys will have a few days off to imbibe. I don't want to be caught without enough goods for delivery."

"No problem there," EB responded. "We can process this entire field for local if you want but according to the file, we do need to move at least one bale to Riyadh."

They agreed on the plan and talked about the logistics of getting the required material to the farm. MD made the last trip, so EB planned on loading the 4-wheeler and heading out. Checking the list, he found only a small number of items still missing from the processing line.

After they completed their conversation, he went into the large shed attached to their offices and put the items in the back of the truck. Later, he would make the trip and deliver the items to Kinkaid, give him instructions for processing, and check the other fields.

MD left the offices and headed to the compound. They met each day on their way from the air base. They purchased a small compound through one of their Saudi contacts. The only thing they worked on in their respective compounds was computer records. They didn't even send electronic mail from their homes. All contact was made from the office. So far, the plan worked and the protection paid was well-spent money.

Their "compound" consisted of a house, a small storage building, a pool, tennis court, a garden, which they let go to seed and a covered parking area. Since neither of them lived there, they didn't bother putting furniture in any of the rooms. If they needed air conditioned storage, they used one of the extra rooms. Most of their supplies were kept in the storage building.

When needed, they packed one of the four wheelers and took the material out to the farm. They tried to keep a low profile in the sparsely populated neighborhood. The Saudi who got them the villa was told they wanted a place off the compound for discreet meetings with "others". Being a westernized Saudi, he didn't question their motives. With a nod and a wink, he made the right payments to the right people and purchased the property for them through one of his associates.

The only thing they did to the place was have an electronic gate installed so they didn't have to leave their vehicle when entering or departing. They also added a satellite communication system in one of the upstairs bedrooms. With the extra height to a wall used to hide the cistern on the roof, they were able to hide the dish from outside eyes. The nearest neighbors were three lots away so they didn't have to worry about anyone looking in on their activities.

MD could tell EB was itching to get out of the business and into retirement. It was beginning to rub off on him. They never really discussed how they were going to end their partnership. Since profits were equally split and deposited in separate accounts, there wouldn't be any problems about who should get what. They went into the project knowing the end would be brief. Now each man was nearing his "projected" nest egg and it was probably time to discuss an ending point. It certainly would be a surprise to both men when someone outside their group would set the date.

⚓

Sunday meant brunch at the club after Episcopal services on base. Bill was clearing out of the bathroom so Betty could move in for her beautification process. He was toweling off his head as they passed in the hall. She stepped aside and let him pass.

He went into his office to take a quick check on his e-mail account before leaving the house. He keyed in the password and logged onto the military controlled network.

There were five new messages. The only one to peak his interest was from OSI headquarters. They were confirming his request for a special investigation team to give the Crimitin apartment another visit from a different perspective. With the killers paying a visit, they may have left some minute piece of evidence.

With the problems facing the local constabulary, this collection of evidence remained strictly in Air Force channels. The message told Bill a team was already in Europe tending to some other business. The lead agent was SA Budmere Baker with SA Cathy Clanmire the other member of the special team.

Bill clicked the print button, took the finished product from the printer's holding tray, and slipped it into his case. He would have Christina finalize things tomorrow. He closed the session; picked up his towel from the back of his chair and headed for the bedroom where Betty laid out the pants, shirt and tie she wanted him to wear. Just as he was pulling on his boxer shorts with the South Park characters emblazoned on the cloth, the phone rang. He pushed the speaker button.

"Agent Wilmerson."

"Bill, Christina. Have you checked your e-mail this morning?"

"I just finished reading the note from headquarters about the team arriving on Tuesday or Wednesday. You can pick up the ball and run with it to use a tired cliché."

"I just wanted to make sure it was going to land on my plate before I went off and made arrangements."

"You have most of the information for them to read, so I didn't want to step in the way. You might want to send a note to the duty officer to see if they can give you a bit more information about their arrival."

"I know. They didn't tell us how they would be arriving, when they would be arriving, where they are right now or anything else. Just confirmed your request."

"That's typical of headquarters. They only tell you what they feel you have a need to know and then they only tell you part of that story. Giving the duty dog something to do on a Sunday will break up the afternoon. Ask for an early A.M. reply to our side of the pond. That way they have to get some action taken today."

"Will do," Christina affirmed. "I'll update you on progress when you get in."

"Thanks," Bill replied. "We're on our way to church and the club. Will we see you there?"

"Not today. I'm entertaining tonight and as normal, my personal life gets the back burner for my professional life. Aren't you glad I'm so damned dedicated?"

"Don't try to wangle any complements out of me Agent Dean, and don't try to get me away from the fact you are entertaining tonight. Anything serious? Anything we need to plan for, like a wedding reception?"

"Quit yanking my chain. This is our first date. We both love Monty Python, so he's bringing over a couple of tapes to watch. Simple dinner, snacks, and movies. Nothing MORE."

"Just checking," Bill responded. "You have a grand time tonight and I'll see you in the morning."

"Who was on the phone?" he heard Betty ask as she came back into the bedroom.

"Just Christina checking the e-mail traffic. The team I asked for will be here next week and she is going to handle their arrangements," he responded as he turned to see his wife drop her terry cloth bathrobe on to the floor and bend over to get into one of her dresser drawers.

"Where's my snapping towel when I need it," he shouted as he scrambled for the towel he dropped on the floor.

"Quit your crap William," Betty admonished. "Just continue to get dressed."

CHAPTER TWENTY-NINE

"Want the nickel tour?" Erpack asked as they pulled out of the parking lot.

"OK by me," Dillon replied. Erpack turned toward the flight line's access control. After showing their line badges to the security guard, he waved them through the gates. Once inside, Erpack began a running commentary on buildings and their intended purpose. They drove to the hardened aircraft shelters where the majority of U.S. contractors worked. As they were approaching one set, an F-15S taxied out of its parking spot and past the two men. It was an impressive sight.

"Fun to fly?" Dillon asked.

"You can bet on that," Erpack responded as he waited for the Eagle to pass. He then proceeded to show Dillon the inner workings of the shelters. It was a thing of beauty for maintenance. In shelter refueling, banks of moveable lights for night work, hydraulic pressure lines, self-generating electrical power and fire suppression systems were all integrated into the shelter. If the Saudis ever went to war, this was the place to fight.

There were offices, sleeping quarters and a small kitchen area. The maintainers and pilots could be self-sustaining in one complex for a considerable time.

"There isn't a base in our Air Force with such facilities. None of our NATO allies have anything like this either. I know, I've flown out of quite a few during my time in Europe," Erpack commented as he turned the Suburban back toward the entry gate.

"I really hate the fact these contractors are getting high and then launching my guys out on missions. No telling what they might have missed on preflight. There are so many nooks and crannies in these shelters, they could be snorting or smoking as we drive by. I just hope what ever you have up your sleeve will work on catching these bastards."

"I hope so too," Dillon agreed as he watched an Eagle lift off from the runway and head for the range.

"If we can find the suppliers, it won't be too hard to close them down. I can't see them wanting to face the punishment served out by the Saudi government." They continued their drive toward the control point as Erpack concluded the nickel tour. Once outside the gate they proceeded down the base's main road and out the front gate.

Once at the compound, Erpack went directly to his villa. He would call the dining facility and have some lunch delivered. Much nicer to have a cold beer with their burgers. He pulled the truck into the drive but left it short of the overhanging sunshade.

"If I pull it in all the way, I can't get out of the drivers door. Have to park it out here. Damn thing is so big I don't want to chance taking off the roof rack." Dillon laughed as he followed Erpack into the kitchen.

"Let me show you where to put your gear," Erpack said as he motioned Dillon to follow him through a den area and into a hallway leading to three bedrooms. One to the left was the master bedroom with a computer room in the middle. Erpack pushed open a door at the end of the hall and told Dillon to put his stuff on the bed. He then went back down the hall and into the kitchen. He picked up the portable phone from the counter and dialed the dining facility. A couple of Sparky Burgers with some fresh cut fries would go well right now. Once he finished placing the order, he pulled two long necks from the fridge and handed one to Dillon.

"Got to be cocktail time someplace in the world. Cheers." Dillon commented as he took a long pull from the ice-cold brew.

Erpack started toward the den when he stopped and turned toward Dillon. "I said to you before I didn't believe Vern had anything to do with drugs. What's your take on the guy?"

"He may be a shyster but I don't think he would be into anything to get himself killed. He knows how to make a buck but he doesn't strike me as the type to dabble in drugs. For his sake, I hope I'm right." Erpack nodded in agreement, as he dropped into one of the armchairs facing the wide screen television. They talked for a while before the doorbell rang.

"Damn that was fast", Erpack said as he got up from the chair and reached into his pocket to retrieve the wad of Riyals he always carried. When he opened the door, he was surprised to see not the deliveryman but Vern.

"Why Vernon, what a pleasant surprise. I thought you were the delivery man."

"Sorry to disappoint you colonel, is that number cruncher here?"

"Yes I am," Dillon responded as he came around the corner into the entrance area. "What can I do for you Sergeant Weberton?"

"May I come in?" he asked.

"By all means," Erpack responded with a slight bow as he stepped out of Weberton's way indicating passage into the living room with a wave of his hand.

"Please step into the parlor." Both men followed Weberton into the cozy living room where they took seats opposite their visitor. After a moment of awkward silence, Vern spoke.

"First off, I'd like to know what's in this for me."

"I don't follow," Dillon questioned. "What are you looking for?"

"What are you going to do for me if I did have some information about drugs and contractors?" With raised eyebrows, Dillon looked at Erpack, pursed his lips, and nodded his head as if a revelation was forthcoming.

"I tell you what sergeant," Dillon began as he leaned forward and spoke very slowly.

"If you *have* information tying contractors to the use of illegal substances, the colonel and I just may be able to keep your happy ass out of jail for the black marketing scheme you have going. So choose your battlefield very carefully. You're too close to a retirement check to be fucking around with this type of situation."

He continued to lean forward for effect before slowly sitting back in his chair. He could see by the expression on the veteran's face, he made an impression. Now they just need to wait for his reply.

"You fucking number crunchers are always the same. Try to save a penny here or there with a lack of big picture understanding. I'm not doing anything different from the Saudis. They are always running some type of scam with equipment earmarked for one program or another. I saw one invoice where they ordered two Towncars from Lincoln. Both of them went to brothers of the program director. I'm just a small time operator at the end of the pipeline trying to make an honest buck."

"Spare us the song and dance Vern. We aren't interested in your sad state of affairs nor are we interested in how corrupt the Saudi Air Force appears to be. All we care about is the quality of maintenance being done on jets my pilots strap to their ass on a daily basis." Erpack rose from his seat during this tirade and stepped toward Vern who got up from his spot on the couch.

"Calm your shit down colonel. Once Dillon made his position abundantly clear, I really didn't have any choice. I didn't understand the gravity of the situation. I know there are drugs around but I didn't know the contractors were boneheaded enough to toke up and work. It's obvious you're pissed off, and I don't want to risk losing the retirement check."

"You're still not out of the woods," Dillon interjected.

"If the information you have is substantial and the contractors are caught and punished, then you're home free. If what you give the colonel is crap, then you're on the line."

"All I can give you is what I pick up from the guys around the pound and when we go diving. I've seen some of them smoke a joint or two in the evenings at the Red Sea. At least they're smart enough not to get high and then dive."

"My congratulations to their sterling behavior. What do you know of a supplier?

"I've heard two names mentioned in connection with supply and demand," he began as he sat back on the couch. "One is Doc and the other is Ebby. I've never met them nor seen any transactions. I guess they figure a government employee couldn't be trusted to keep his mouth shut about drugs. Anyway, a few people get stoned on a regular basis. I can put out a few feelers to see if I can get more information if you want."

"All we want you to do is keep your eyes and ears open. Don't do anything different. Continue to run your scams like there's nothing changed. If you can give us a name rather than a nickname, get in contact with the colonel. I'll be turning over my report to the investigative agencies in Riyadh. They'll be the ones to decide a course of action. Do you have anything else?" Dillon finished.

"Not now," Vern began. "But I just want to make sure I'm not going....." Dillon held up his hand to stop any further conversation from the sergeant.

"All I can say is you're not on the colonel's hit list. We were talking about you while we waited for our food. His main concern is protecting his people and my main concern is ensuring the customer doesn't have to worry about his contractors coming to work stoned. You'll have to make your decisions about where you want to go with your activities on your own at a later date."

Vern began to speak again but was cut short by doorbell clatter. "That should be the lunch delivery," Erpack stated.

"Time for you to go sergeant. We didn't expect luncheon guests." Vernon followed the two men to the door. Erpack swung the door open for a greeting by one of the dining facility waiters in white shirt, bow tie, and black pants holding a plastic bag with four foil-wrapped plastic containers inside. Vernon began to speak but was stopped by Erpack with a shake of his head. He made his exit pushing the waiter aside as he stepped through the door. Erpack and Dillon watched him head down the walkway and into the street.

"Sorry about that," Dillon said to the waiter. "He isn't too happy right at the moment."

Dillon reached for the bag while Erpack was sorting the money situation. He tipped the waiter generously for his abrupt treatment and bid him a good day. He shut the door and joined Dillon in the den.

"Where do you keep the napkins," Dillon asked from the kitchen.

"Napkins?" Erpack responded. "This ain't no fancy smancy restaurant, just pull off a couple of paper towels." He could hear Dillon chuckle as he pulled towels from a rack hung underneath the cabinets.

"Grab another couple of long necks, will ya?" Erpack requested as he unwrapped the burgers and fries. Dillon sat the beer near Erpack and picked up his meal.

Dillon was draining the remainder of his beer when Erpack asked, "What do you make of Vern's information?"

"Gives us a place to start. Can you get a listing of all the contractors?"

"In normal circumstances, that wouldn't be a problem. I'd just go to Abercrom and ask for a listing. However, with the problems I'm causing for him, he may not be too cooperative."

"On the flip side of that coin," Dillon began. "He may want to appear very cooperative once he took the time to reflect on our allegations. I don't think he wants to show up in any formal report as being uncooperative during an investigation. Especially when a new guy shows up to work in your admin office."

"A new man?"

"I figure the best way to get the information we need is to have a man up here working on your problem. He will have all the information we gather during my stay and he can slide in undercover. I'll call Ramstein and get them to send someone to Riyadh within the next couple of days. When I get back I'll brief him on what we discover and he can be on his way here as a new administrator. He'll be able to shape what he feels is necessary to end this and get the Saudis in for an assist. If we don't invite the host nation to participate, it may look like we don't trust their abilities."

Erpack smiled. "What abilities? The only thing I see is a concerted effort to stay away from responsibility. Don't rock the boat is their motto."

"Be that as it may," Dillon responded. "They are the host nation and we need to have them on our side. Despite our philosophical differences, we will do the leg work and then bring in whatever fire power we deem necessary to close down the operation."

Dillon was certainly right in his assessment of the operation. Having worked with host nations in other ops, he knew sorting out the corrupt officials and getting the assistance of the right people was always necessary.

When he worked undercover, he was able to determine the good the bad and the ugly in most situations. He always formulated his plan of attack before breaking his cover to local officials. All Dillon wanted to do now was give Erpack a plan of attack, recruit an undercover agent, and get back to his pressing business in Riyadh.

"Have you got a secure line in the villa?" Dillon asked.

"As a matter of fact, there's one in the computer room. From what I understand, there was hell to pay in getting a line installed. You can't handicap the det commander by not having communications available at his quarters. I guess no one wanted to outlay the initial costs of getting the lines laid and the satellite hooked up. It's the green phone on the printer desk."

Dillon left the den and went to the computer room. One of the past commander's went to great lengths to have the room converted into a quasi-command center. Since they were always in the same house, a predecessor put shelves along one wall, installed extra phone jacks and phone lines, and built a desk/storage unit. It was very functional.

Dillon rolled the chair from its location near the computer desk and picked up the DSN[22] line. He dialed the special access code, waited for the signal, and then dialed Karl's number in Riyadh. Once Karl answered, Dillon explained the situation and asked for an agent from some European location to expedite his arrival.

"I would like to have him there before I get back in town. I know that's a tall order but there has to be some agent in Europe with time on his hands. When you talk with Bill, tell him it's his challenge for the week."

Karl assured Dillon he would be on the line as soon as they hung up. Dillon needed some additional information on personnel working at Khamis and the contractor situation in Kingdom. He didn't fully understand the relationship of Boeing and the Saudi Air Force. He wanted to have the information to work with when he briefed the agent before he sent him into the fray. Karl took down the requests and told Dillon the information would be waiting for him when he got back to Riyadh.

Returning to the den, Dillon untwisted the cap on the long neck Erpack sat by his chair. "Get the balls rolling?" Erpack asked as Dillon dropped back into his seat.

"I hope so. It's a tall order to get someone away from their job and over to Ramstein as quickly as I want them. Couple that with trying to get them on a flight to Riyadh and you have an almost impossible situation. However, knowing Karl and William, it's just the sort of thing that gets them going. They both love a challenge and I've just laid a significant quest in their ballpark. If they don't get it all done by the time I get back, it won't be for lack of effort."

238

"I haven't had much contact with them. After getting my ass chewed in front of them, I'm not hot to talk with them any time soon. I do remember William seeming to be a firebrand. He should go far."

They talked about Khamis when Dillon snapped his fingers. "I just remembered a question I wanted to ask you," he said as he pointed a finger in Erpack's direction.

"When I was getting off the plane this morning, I noticed a 747 sitting on the ramp. Is it normal for them to fly up here with a jumbo jet?"

Erpack laughed as he started to tell Dillon about the jet. "As you have seen, this place is getting to be an Arab vacation spot. It's great for the local economy but the summer months are crowded. The royal family owns the jet. They converted one into a mini-flying palace. All the trimmings. They don't want to feel unroyal during the flight. Several of the royals have homes up here. They bring all the relatives for the summer months and then head back for the hot climates when school starts. The first time I saw a jumbo sitting on the ramp, I was shocked too. The place just doesn't seem big enough. However, the runway is more than 10,000 feet long and that's plenty of room to put one of those on the ground and get it back in the air again."

The men watched a bit of news on the local cable channel before returning to their discussion about the situation at Khamis. Dillon was intrigued by the apparent lack of concern from the prime contractor. Erpack said the human resources manager, an ex-Army type, was a by the book lout who could be counted on to give the people the hardest time possible. He wasn't familiar with the term "customer service". He viewed the contractors as irritants in his extended vacation. If they needed help, his immediate response was "aisle or window". With each passing conversation, Dillon could tell Erpack carried no respect for any of the Boeing hierarchy. He was soon to find out other members of the USMTM team felt the same way.

⚜

Christina reached in the refrigerator and picked up a small blue plastic container with her special glaze for baked sausage. One of the bad points she discovered about an assignment to Germany was the food. There was too much of it and every bit was excellent. Conrad gave her this particular glaze recipe. On several occasions, he invited her to his house where his wife prepared something scrumptious to eat. One of the visits included a sausage appetizer Christina adored. Conrad explained the sauce was a family favorite. He shared the secret ingredients with her because he felt she was family. Each time Christina entertained, she prepared the treat. Today it would be the centerpiece of snacks she fixed for the Monty Python film fest.

Her date, Captain Albert Evermann, promised an ample sampling of local wines for the afternoon. He lived just two blocks from Christina, so imbibing in good German wine would not be a problem. Christina built a tolerance for the local vintages but needed to limit her enjoyment today since she was on weekend duty and would have to respond if called.

Christina agreed to this afternoon of movies because she met Al away from the normal pickup locations. She literally bumped into him at the local supermarket. She wasn't paying attention to where she was going and pushed her cart into his as she came around a corner. She quickly apologized in German but he didn't understand. A conversation ensued and the rest is dating history. Al worked in command headquarters as a logistics specialist. Now he was working with NATO munitions but was on the short list for movement to the Inspector General traveling team. It would give him a chance to visit throughout NATO on compliance inspection tours.

Christina pulled the baking pan from the oven and sat it on top of the stove. She then added liberal amounts of glaze to the partially baked sausages. After she was done, she returned the pan to the over and cut down the heat. Another 20 minutes or so and they would be done. She made a final check on the remaining snacks and was satisfied her work was complete. The next step was a shower and the wait for Al to arrive. She wandered down the hall to her bathroom pulling off the robe and apron she used while fixing the snacks. A warm shower followed by a quick blow dry and a selection of comfortable lounge clothes and she was ready for the afternoon.

At the appointed hour, the buzzer on the speaker connected to buttons at the front door, announced the arrival of her guest. She unlatched the front door by pressing the release mechanism. She stepped on the landing and called down to Al as he entered the small reception area at the bottom of the stairs.

She lived on the second level of a four-story apartment building. There were four apartments on each floor. Single military members occupied most. Since the apartments were only one bedroom, there wasn't any room for children. This was one of the deciding factors when Christina was looking for a place to live. The bachelor accommodations on base weren't to her liking, so she took this place for the duration of her stay in Germany. It was a convenient location to town center and allowed her the freedom of being able to walk to most of the main shops.

Al came up the stairs carrying two heavy gauge plastic bags. One contained the wine selection for the afternoon and the other contained a selection of what he considered the finest of Monty Python.

"Good afternoon, Mam." he said as he reached the landing where Christina waited. He held up the two bags, "I kept my part of the bargain. I'm ready for the show to begin." Christina laughed as she took one of the bags from his outstretched hand.

"And things are ready in the main showing room." she quipped as she turned and headed back into the apartment.

"Follow me into the kitchen," she said as Al closed the front door.

"I want to check on the final item being prepared for today's menu." She placed the bag she was carrying on the counter since it contained the videotapes and asked Al if the wine needed chilling. He responded it was perfect for consumption. Christina reached into the oven and pulled out the glazed sausage as Al took one of the bottles and searched for the opener he dropped into the bag on the way out of his apartment.

"I know I put an opener in here somewhere," he said as he peered into the dark green bag. Christina sat the pan on the stove and was reaching into a side drawer when he found the small two-piece opener he obtained from one of the local vintners. They engaged in small talk about the wine choices as Christina put the finishing touches on the sausage, the veggie plate, the Doritos, and the corn chips. When all was finished, they carried the goodies into the living room where she prepared the coffee table with candles, flowers, and placemats.

Al told her he was impressed and helped her arrange the food. He poured a sample of the wine for her to taste and once she approved, filled the glasses. He gave her the first tape of the afternoon and she quickly slipped it into the player. The wide screen monitor flickered to life as the opening credits passed in review. It was at that precise moment her phone rang.

"Shit," she whispered under her breath.

"What say?" Al questioned.

"Nothing," she replied. "I'm on call this weekend and was hoping for a quiet afternoon. Let's just hope it's nothing to take me away from the scheduled programming."

"I'll cross my fingers and hope for the best," Al responded as he watched Christina cross the room to a small desk nestled in a corner near a window overlooking the apartment building's small garden area. Christina picked up the cordless receiver to answer. "Hello."

"Agent Dean?" was the reply. Christina grimaced as she shook her head in a disappointed manner. "This is Agent Dean."

"Christina this is Karl Phobie calling from Riyadh. I've been trying to get hold of Bill but each time I get his answering machine. I've left messages but he hasn't returned my calls."

"It's the holy day here Karl. I know you keep different hours down there but we are traditionalists up here and Sunday is a day of rest and church. Bill and his wife are regular attendees at the Episcopal Church in town and then their normal practice is to head for the club and brunch. What can I do for you? I've got the duty this weekend."

"That's what I found out from the base operator when I couldn't get Bill on the line," Karl recounted.

"I was talking with Dillon earlier and he's got a short notice request. He needs to find an agent for a special assignment down here. He wants the agent in place by Wednesday. That's why I was trying to get hold of Bill. Dillon asked me to call him direct."

"So the request is for an agent to come down there and work with Dillon?"

"Actually, the agent would be assigned to another location. I can explain in more detail if you can give me a call on a secure line."

"I can do that unless you want to speak directly with Bill? He should be home at any time."

"I don't think that's necessary. Dillon wanted to get this thing rolling as quickly as possible. If you got the duty, you can pass along the information after we talk. It's nothing earth shattering but we're working on a short fuse. The faster we get hold of headquarters and have them check availability, the quicker we can get someone identified and moving this way."

"Agree with your assessment Karl. It won't take me long to get into the office and give you a return call. Give me your secure number and I'll be on my way." They exchanged numbers and ended the conversation.

"Doesn't look good for the film festival", Al lamented as he walked toward where Christina was finishing up her notes.

"Just some activity on a case we're working. Another added twist to the plot."

"I know better than to ask questions. You OSI types are very good at keeping secrets. I played softball at my last base with one of the agents. We would talk after an investigation ended and I would be shocked at the amount of work each case carries. However, it does have its drawbacks. Like our present situation."

"It doesn't mean the afternoon is a bust. Instead of an afternoon of film watching, we'll just have to make it an evening," Christina said as she reached out for his hands. He took hold of her tiny fingers and raised them to his lips.

242

"I look forward to the resumption of our film frenzy," he replied as he gently kissed the back of her hands.

They quickly cleaned the room putting everything into storage for the moment. Christina walked him to the door and told him she would give him a call when she got back to the apartment. After he left, she threw off the lounging clothes and slipped into a comfortable pair of jeans and a sweatshirt. She grabbed her bag off the counter and the keys off a hook near the front door. In minutes she was clearing her way through the gates of the base and on toward the office.

The call to Karl clicked through without problems. She listened intently as Karl explained the situation to her. It was fascinating how quickly Dillon was able to formulate a plan of attack and set things into motion. Now all they needed to do was locate an agent, get the agent to Ramstein, arrange for transportation to Riyadh, and do it all in two days. Not an impossible job but one requiring some immediate action. This wasn't going to be a job done in a vacuum. After her talk with Karl was completed, she dialed the number of the headquarters coordinator for all OSI activities in Europe. One of the distinct advantages of working at Ramstein was the availability of decision makers. She would drop this bomb on him and let it work from there. She knew Bill wouldn't be upset if she got the ball started down this very short hill. Time was of the essence and since she was the duty officer, it was ultimately her responsibility to take immediate action on situations. She could back brief Bill later.

The number she called was a pager. She entered her office number and name so Dick would know who was calling. Dick W. Famington was on staff for about a year. In Europe for more than eight years, he started in England, moved to Italy and then to Ramstein. Christina liked him because he was straightforward.

She didn't have long to wait. She was just coming back into the office from getting a soda when her phone rang. "OSI, Agent Dean."

"Christina, this is Dick. What can I do for you this fine day? I hope you know you interrupted my preparations for a scrumptious bar-b-qued steak. I just put ...."

"That's just fine Dick but I have got some urgent business and I need your help."

"Fire away," Dick said as the tone in his voice turned from carefree to serious.

Christina set out the details of the request as much as she could over an unsecured line. Dick wanted to meet with her to pick up the finer points of the request. She glanced at the clock on the wall and told him she needed to make contact with Bill and then run by his place. Dick lived on base with his wife and two elementary school age children. He agreed with the plan and signed off.

Christina called Bill's cellular to coordinate a meeting. Luckily, Bill and Betty were still at the club finishing off brunch and some after meal conversations with another couple they knew from church. Bill told Christina to come over for a cup of coffee and she could brief him on the problem. Christina agreed and hung up. She closed the office and headed for the club. She found Bill and Betty waiting for her in the lobby. They walked back into the dining area and took a table near the rear of the room. They ordered coffee as Christina began to lay out the dilemma faced by Dillon and the investigators in Riyadh.

"They're right not to have one of their people go down to Khamis. Their faces may be known and that wouldn't be good. I'm sure Dick has someone in mind for the job. I'd be real surprised if he didn't have a name while you were talking with him."

"He wants me to stop by his place and give him all the inner details," Christina said as she picked up her cup of coffee. "I told him you were first on the list."

They finished their coffee and walked together to the parking lot. "Where can I find you later today?" Christina asked just before heading toward her car.

"If you need me, I'll be at home," Bill told her.

The housing at Ramstein is apartment style surrounding a central courtyard with playground equipment and bar-b-que pits neatly arranged near an array of concrete picnic tables. Dick was lucky. His assigned quarters faced a very nice central courtyard. The residents of adjoining buildings took the time to maintain the facilities for others to use. There were always kids playing on the swings and slides. Most weekends saw parties given by one family or another. Today Dick was fixing the main course for three other families. Most of the parental meetings came through the kids. With the diversified jobs, most friendships came from the children interacting. Christina pulled into one of the vacant "visitor" slots in front of the building and walked up the single flight of stairs to Dick's second floor apartment. Dick greeted her at the doorway.

"Good to see you Christina. It's been some time since we had the opportunity to talk. Can I get you a glass of wine?"

"No thanks," she replied as she followed Dick into the kitchen. Nan, Dick's wife, was cutting a salad at the kitchen table. The women exchanged greetings as Dick continued his preparation of the steaks.

"Just let me turn these babies over in the marinade and we can go into the living room." Once he finished his chore, he motioned for Christina to lead the way. They sat on the couch as Christina began to detail the happenings in Saudi and the need for an immediate response. Dick clarified a few points and then told Christina he knew the perfect match for the assignment.

"Name of the agent is J.R. Lopez."

"I'm not familiar with the name. Where's he working now?"

"J.R. is not a man. J.R. is a woman working at a small detachment in Belgium. She's been notified of a pending assignment so we sent her replacement in early. I was going to bring her up here for a couple of weeks to get the lay of the land. She has a move to a liaison agent slot with the Army in Schweinfurt. The incumbent doesn't leave for a couple of months, so we can move her to Riyadh without any problems."

"Without problems? She's going in to work a drug case in Saudi Arabia. You don't see the problem?" Christina asked.

"I know about the archaic way women are treated in the kingdom but she is the best person for the job. She's been involved with other drug investigations before she came to Europe. I've talked with her and she understands the difficulties she may face with Saudi law enforcement but she is more than willing to take the job. She's already packed her furniture and sent it on to Schweinfurt. She's packing her bags as we speak. She'll be up here tomorrow afternoon. You can get her on the log run to Sultan and the rest is history."

Dick seemed very pleased with himself for being able to get someone selected on such short notice. It was fortuitous J.R. was up for an assignment. She did have drug investigation experience and most agents understood host nation sensitivities very well. Christina just shook her head without making another comment. She asked for the particulars on J.R. so she could make flight arrangements. Dick went to a desk in the corner of the living room and pulled a sheet of paper from a binder. He handed it to Christina as she stood up from the couch. Everything she needed was on the sheet. She could get J.R. on the first flight out.

Christina thanked Dick for the extra effort. Although she held huge reservations about sending a woman into Saudi, she didn't say another word. Dick invited her to stay for dinner but Christina politely declined. Once back in her car, she headed for the terminal to arrange for passage to Riyadh.

Luckily, there was a flight Tuesday. She booked J.R. under official orders, jotted a few notes on the sheet of paper so she could recall the flight number and projected arrival time in Riyadh. She then headed off base. Using her cell phone, she gave Al a call and told him to be waiting at her apartment. She was on her way.

"What in the hell was I thinking when I agree to take this assignment?" Juanita Rene Lopez proclaimed aloud as she stood in her disheveled bedroom.

"I hate when I do this to myself. I'm always so eager for a new challenge; I neglect to factor in the dull mundane subjects like getting packed."

She laughed and reached for the glass of dark Belgian beer sitting on the dresser. In the time she spent in Belgium, she acquired a fondness for the thick dark liquid.

When Dick called earlier in the day, she practically jumped through the phone lines to accept the assignment. It was a few years since she involved herself in undercover work but she was always ready. The last time was in Central America as part of a program at Howard in Panama. She began to remember those days and the enjoyment she got when the lines of supply were broken. Since Dick couldn't explain much over the phone, she was eager to meet him at Ramstein and pick up the full story. She turned back to the job at hand. Only a few hours remained before she needed to be on the road.

CHAPTER THIRTY

"Are you planning on leaving the compound any more today?" Erpack asked Dillon before he turned the cap off another long neck.

"I don't have any reason to revisit the base until tomorrow. We can wait until all the guys pay us a visit and then I'll have a better feeling for whom I need to talk with. Right now we have to take a look at the manning documents to see if we can tie in the nickname with an actual person."

"I'll work on that through one of my backdoor contacts," Erpack said as he reached for the phone. Just as he did, the front door bell rang and he started to go answer it. Dillon told him to make the call and he would get the door. When he opened the door, Captain Stephen P. Spocker was standing on the stoop. When he saw Dillon, he began to apologize for having the wrong house.

"Looking for Erpack?" Dillon asked. When Vulcan gave him an affirmative answer, Dillon introduced himself and invited the man inside.

In the den, Erpack was heard talking with some unknown person. Dillon ushered Vulcan into the living room and explained the situation to him. He listened intently and when Dillon asked if he could comment about the situation, the only thing he wanted to know was if his comments were going to be attributed to him later. When Dillon assured him, all comments would be taken in the strictest of confidence; it opened the floodgates for the stick actuator. He pulled out a small green pocket sized U.S. Government spiral notebook and turned a few pages. He then began a tirade about the "shitty" maintenance done by contractors. It wasn't every time he flew but it was more than he ever wanted to experience.

Dillon listened to the information provided but was finding the complaints were just about the same as Fishhead. There was a definite pattern and one he hoped could be exploited to their advantage. He needed a plan of attack and the arrival of his "administrator" to tackle the situation. During the remainder of the afternoon, Honest Abe and Smokes paid visits to the villa. Their stories all contained the same common threads. It was just an accident waiting to happen and they were right to be concerned about their safety. Each one aborted training missions on more than one occasion because of shoddy maintenance. Dillon understood why Erpack was under such a head of steam when he visited Riyadh.

Arrangements were made for everyone to meet at the "party" house later that evening. The party house was a villa specially set up for military gatherings. The centerpiece was a wide screen projection TV hooked into one of the satellite systems. There was room to store the commissary goods brought in from Jeddah and a bar area where they kept their rations. In the yard was a shed set up to keep all the MWR[23] gear. This included their small sailboat, a zodiac boat for diving expeditions, diving gear complete with oxygen regeneration system, deep-sea fishing gear, camping gear, and four sets of golf clubs.

A bar-b-que pit was build behind the villa for parties hosted by Erpack as the senior military representative at Khamis. There was even a pit for roasting whole pigs. That was a special treat for many invited guests since pork is not available in the Kingdom for common folks. If you know the right cabbie to contact in Jeddah or know the place in Riyadh for the "special" club sandwich, you can satisfy your taste for pork.

For a remote tour, the boys of Khamis were living the life of Riley. Steaks on the barbie would be the fare of the evening. Plenty of liquid refreshment and Cuban cigars. One more perk of the assignment. Hand rolled Cubans out of Jeddah. Dillon looked forward to the evening.

The next morning, all of them met for breakfast at the dining facility before heading toward the base. The topic of discussion was the preceding evening's festivities and the results of several games of chance and agility engaged in throughout the gathering. Dillon's success at agility contests was not unnoticed.

"Not bad for a pencil pusher" was heard many a time during the evening. After breakfast and coffee, each man departed the compound for King Khalid. Since Erpack was on the flight schedule, he would head for the squadron. He suggested Dillon tag along with Fred for his ride. Dillon agreed knowing it would give him another opportunity to question the administrator without having the boss around.

During their drive, Dillon engaged the sergeant in small talk before asking a pointed question. When he did, Fred went silent for a moment. "Look sir, I'm not really sure who you are but I find it hard to believe a

248

number cruncher from anywhere would be asking the type of questions you ask. This whole drug situation is something I never figured I would have to face in Saudi Arabia. Drunks, drugs, and hookers. What a paradise. It's like my dad told me his remote assignments used to be like but he was fighting a war. I'm just here trying to make the time pass until I can get on to another assignment. I was going to extend because my marriage just fell apart but with all this shit going on, I need a change. I don't want to be hassled and I don't want to get involved with any of the fact finding you're doing. I just want to spend my time and get the fuck out of here. This is one scary place and I'm just going to keep my head down and hope for the best."

Dillon made no immediate comment. He let Fred drive on for a moment before he replied.

"I understand your situation. I won't pry any more. As for whom I really am, I'm just an administrator tying to make sure the United States Government is getting what they paid for."

Dillon figured a little white lie at this time wouldn't hurt the situation too much. He couldn't afford his OSI connection to become common knowledge in the Air Force community. He was forced to trust the commander's in Riyadh but trusting the guys on the line would be risky.

Once they reached the Peace Sun building, Fred opened their side of the building and let Dillon into Erpack's office. Dillon wanted to contact Karl to see if he was notified about a selection for the assignment to Khamis.

The phone in Karl's' office rang three times before his voice mail picked up. Dillon left a quick message and hung up. He got himself a cup of coffee when the phone rang in Fred's office. He was mixing the concoction at the coffee bar when Fred called his name.

"Dillon, this is Karl on the line. Want me to pass it into the colonel's office?" Dillon told him yes and hurried back to the seat behind the desk shutting the office door behind him.

"Karl," Dillon spoke into the receiver. "I just got off the phone. Did you pick up the message or are you just calling to tell me you've solved the Crimitin case?"

"No such luck I'm afraid. I just got my first cup of caffeine and was checking my weekend distribution."

"I just wanted to know if you heard anything from Ramstein on a selection for the Khamis work."

"Nothing this morning. I haven't checked e-mail yet but I would expect them to give me a call. As soon as I have something, I'll call you. Use this same number?"

"That'll be fine. The admin guy will find me. I'm not going to far from this office this morning. Have to talk with the head contractor. Erpack and

I spoke briefly with him but didn't make any forward progress. Erpack is so pissed off he can't see straight. Frankly, I don't blame him. He's trying to teach a bunch of pilots' combat tactics and they're more interested in sipping tea or just poking holes in the sky. He shouldn't have to worry about the status of his jet."

"Is this one of the people you want me to check on?"

"Yeah. I want to have some background info on the top guys before our man gets in place. Better to be aware of the sticking points."

"Agree with you there," Karl responded.

Dillon took a long sip of his coffee as he went over his mental filing system. A morning meeting with Abercrom led to the question; was he involved with the drugs? Is his involvement why he was making the choice to ignore the situation? All possibilities.

Dillon left the office and told Fred he was going to the other side. He wanted to find out when Abercrom was due into the office. The secretary stood as Dillon came around the corner. Dillon was greeted very politely with a slight bow from the middle-aged man. Dillon inquired when Abercrom would be in the office. The response was any time. Normally the site manager was in the office around 8:30. Dillon thanked the man and asked for a call when he arrived. The little man again bowed slightly as he said he would come over personally to get Dillon.

Dillon went back to the USMTM side of the partition, fixed another cup of coffee, and sat back down in the colonel's office. This time he sat in front of the desk where he could lay his notes on the coffee table.

There must be a common thread to the dereliction of duty facing the instructors. Dillon's senses weren't picking up anything. With the nicknames of Doc and Ebby, there must be a connection. Once they gathered a listing of contractors, they could try to piece the puzzle together. Dillon went on to make additional notes when there was a knock at the door. The little man from next-door asked Dillon if he was free to meet with Mr. Abercrom. Dillon followed the man back to Abercrom's office. As Dillon entered, he pushed the door shut behind him.

"Have a seat," Horace offered as Dillon stepped up to the desk and shook hands with the site manager.

"Thanks," he replied lowering himself into one of the straight back chairs in front of the desk.

"You and I need to have a little one on one discussion about the problems Erpack sees with your contractors. Drugs and drink are too very serious problems when it comes to operating a multi-million dollar fighter. He feels there's a problem but hasn't been able to get any cooperation from your side of the office. When he brings the problem to our attention, we have no other choice than to investigate the allegations. You just seem to be sticking your head in the sand. We can't have that type of attitude and that's exactly what I'm going to tell the people in Riyadh when I return."

"Is that a threat?"

"No. It's a promise. I never use threats. If I tell you something is going to happen, you can take it to the bank. From what I have been able to gather in my short time here, you are ignoring a very serious problem and the United States Government will not tolerate such blatant disregard for aviation safety. Your attitude of there couldn't be a drug problem in Saudi Arabia is just nonsense and if the tune doesn't change soon, you'll be a prominent player when the FMS contract awards to another company. I don't think Boeing would be too pleased with the prospect of losing all this profit."

Horace sat behind his desk staring at Dillon. His calls to Riyadh about this guy went unanswered. No one in the Boeing chain of command heard of the guy and no one on the military side of the house was giving up any information. It was as if the guy just appeared without any type of history attached to his visit. That worried Abercrom. If you can't find out information about a person, all the threats or promises may come true. If you know what is behind a person, you can normally figure out the validity of what they have to say. Without knowledge, Horace could base his actions on nothing but the persona of the man sitting in front of him. The persona he saw scared the shit out of him. He firmly believed, for whatever reason, this man held the power to make his promises come true. He could just feel the connection.

"You're going to have to give me some time." Horace stuttered. He paused to clear his throat hoping the stutter wouldn't be so noticeable.

"I'll have to discreetly get the message to my main office so they know what is going on."

"Please don't try to bullshit a bullshitter. You've already been on the phone with them trying to figure out just who the hell I am. I can guarantee to be your worst nightmare if you don't begin an investigation of what's happening with your contractors. I'm on a plane tomorrow. You best get with the people you feel required to check with and get off the fence. You are either going to be part of the solution or you're going to be named as part of the problem. It's your choice to which side of the report you fall on. I really don't give a damn. I'm here to do a job and make a report back up the line. As they used to say on *Dragnet,* just the facts, Mam. Just the facts." As he finished, he stood up to leave. Horace stood up too.

"Can't you give me some time?"

"Time for what? This isn't brain surgery Horace. There is only one path to take. You don't have a long decision process here. You either come across with some cooperation, or your time here will rapidly draw to a close." Dillon turned toward the door.

As he opened it, he paused long enough to bid Abercrom a fond farewell for the benefit of the secretary. He didn't want to give the impression he was leaving under anything but wonderful conditions.

"Thanks for the information Horace. I know the general will be very pleased. I'll make a point of telling him myself about the sterling program you're running down here." Dillon left the door open as he headed back for Erpack's office.

Dillon was disappointed he didn't get the type of cooperation he hoped for from Abercrom. He thought the man would be more forthcoming if Erpack wasn't with him. Without his immediate consent to help, Dillon played the hardass one more time. It didn't bother him but he would like to have someone cooperate the first time they were asked without having to apply pressure.

He knew Abercrom would not like being the reason for a company as large as Boeing to lose a source of income as large as the Saudis. McDonnell Douglas milked this beast since the early 80s. Before Mac D, it was Northrop and any number of other companies involved with selling the Saudis the latest and greatest hardware of all types. When Boeing acquired McDonnell Douglas for its fighter building capability, they also acquired the profit margin of McDonnell Douglas Services Incorporated. Erpack told Dillon the company made 12 percent on everything they bought for or sold to the Saudi Air Force. Dillon was sure the investigation would be getting all the assistance it needed when the new man arrived to sort out the wheat from the chaff.

As he was sitting in Erpack's office, Fred came in with an envelope. It was addressed to Fred. "Note inside says to give this listing to you," he told Dillon as he handed him the envelope.

Dillon reached inside and pulled out a spreadsheet with pertinent data on every member of the Peace Sun workforce. As he flipped through the pages, he commented to Fred, "This will certainly keep me busy the rest of the afternoon. Hope we keep the coffee hot."

"I'll keep you fixed up. Just let me know whatcha need," Fred commented as he left the office.

Dillon sat the pile of papers on the table and ripped out of piece of binder paper. He made a few notes of possible combinations to look for as he went through the listing. He would be happy for once to see Erpack come through the door. This time he could be part of the solution and not part of the problem.

"Morning Randy," Sid greeted his coworker as he passed by the open door on his way to his office. With a wave of his hand, Randy returned the greeting as he entered his password for the secure military e-mail system. Sid came back down the hall and asked if Randy needed a refill on the coffee. He did and joined Sid as they went to the coffee bar. When they came back Randy noticed the "You have Mail" icon flashing on his screen. He clicked it open and saw a message from the FBI.

"Sid," he called out. "Got a message from the FBI."

Sid came through the door and positioned himself at the corner of Randy's desk so he could see the message as it appeared on the screen. Simple and to the point. The key was in fact a safe deposit key. Manufactured by the Carlton Key Company of West Piedmont, Montana. Carlton Key also assembled safe deposit boxes under the "Safe Box" label. This particular batch was purchased by Anderville Construction of Cucamonga California. The boxes and supporting keys were for use in the construction of a small family owned bank in Covina California. The bank, 1st United of Covina, consisted of three branches. One on Citrus, one on Hollenbeck and the third on Azusa.

"Good news," Randy exclaimed as he hit the print icon. "Now all we have to do is find out which branch has the box and we're in like flint."

"That is a stroke of luck," Sid agreed.

"Knowing where the family lives, I'd be willing to put my money on the Azusa branch. It would be right on his way toward the freeway. I'll work on getting a court order to open the box. I don't want to rely on the good graces of the bank to give us access without a court order. I'll give the JAG a call right now and see what they can do for us."

He took one of the copies Randy printed for his files and left the office. It would be a simple matter to get the cooperation of a local judge once the JAG explained the situation. Sid found working lawyer to lawyer was always the simplest way to get anything from that side of the enforcement equation.

His initial contact with the lawyers was very positive. They would start working through their channels and should have the order processed within a couple of days. Sid told them it was fine and to contact him if they needed any additional information for the judge. They would provide all the file information including family contact points.

He gave Carpton a quick call to tell him the news. He was glad this part of the puzzle fit into place. He asked to be included when they decided on a date to visit the bank. He would make contact with the Crimitin's to

253

let them know about the key and give them an approximate time line for a return visit.

"Don't be too specific with the date just yet," Sid cautioned.

"I'd be willing to bet they are being watched or monitored by the other side. We don't want to play our hand until we're ready. What I'd like to do is make the determination of which branch is affected, get the bank management on board and then set a time and date to meet the family. Make the lead time as short as possible."

Carpton agreed to the plan as he hung up. He would tell the Crimitin's about the key identification but nothing more. Like Sid, Carl hoped this was an important clue to solving the case. In reality, it would be just another piece of the puzzle.

Dillon stood up and stretched. He picked up the sheet of paper where he made some notes concerning possible combinations of letters and names tying into the nickname of Doc or Ebby.

Dillon was rubbing his eyes when Erpack came in the door. "Sleepy are we?" he quipped as he went around the desk and sat in his chair.

"Damn right," Dillon answered.

"Paperwork is one part of any investigation that sticks in my craw. I know its all part of the game but I don't have to like it."

"Well let me get a cup of coffee and I'll help ya out." Erpack told Dillon as he left the room for the coffee bar.

Dillon and the colonel worked for another hour or so before they decided to head back for the compound. They would get the other men over to the house for a brainstorming session. While there, Dillon would tell them about the new administrative man coming to work with them. Although he didn't want to finger the man as an agent, he deduced they would make the connection soon after his arrival. They already knew Dillon's connections with investigative agencies so it would only make sense someone with the power of law enforcement behind them would be next in line for a visit to Khamis.

The next morning Dillon packed for his return trip to Riyadh. The evening of discussion between the men was very productive. They came up with several possibilities for the nicknames. Most of them dealt with the first and last or first and middle initials of men working on the project. Each one would be checked by federal and state agencies for involvement in any drug schemes. However, Dillon really didn't expect much of a discovery from the search. Job requirements in Kingdom included a security clearance of Secret. Anyone with documented involvement with controlled substances would be eliminated during their security investigation. He also wanted the men to put together a listing of the maintainers they suspected of using drugs. There were many ways to determine their guilt or innocence with or without the assistance of Mr. Abercrom.

With a 1755 flight for Riyadh, the men would spend most of the day going over notes from the previous night.

"Have I told you about the Saudi bypass?" Erpack asked as they left the villa.

"Saudi bypass?" Dillon pondered for a moment. "I've heard the term but I haven't seen them used up here."

"I'll point them out on the way in. You just won't believe the stupidity of these guys. Moreover, most of them are in the military. Either the Air Force or the Ground Forces."

As they drove, Erpack pointed out some additional points of interest. "Right behind this wall is what they call the truck souq. It's a conglomeration of shops selling everything under the sun. There are a couple of vegetable places, grain sales, candy shops, and dates. Dates by the thousands. Have you seen how they package their dates?"

"No," was the short reply.

"You've got to see this," Erpack said as he signaled for a lane change and wheeled around the center divider at the signal. He made a right turn on to a semi-paved section of road which passed by a warehouse which stored packaged drinks. Dillon could see the vegetable sales and various other open market type sales taking place under a metal-framed sunshade.

Erpack turned down a lane flanked by open fronted shops containing candy boxes of varying shapes, sizes, and flavors. At the end of the row sat refrigerated trailers some with their doors open revealing cases of candy and fruit drinks. Erpack slowed as he advanced toward an intersection between the buildings and trailers. He crept forward looking down the intersecting road for any approaching vehicles.

"Almost got t-boned right here one time. Some idiot flew down this road with crates of chickens. He was gabbing on his cell phone and didn't see me until the very last minute. He slammed on his brakes and a couple of the crates flew over the cab and crashed on to the hood of his truck. He was one pissed off little man. I just drove off. Better to leave the scene of a near miss rather than argue."

As he finished telling the tale, he made a right turn to another traffic aisle. As Dillon looked at these shops, he saw they contained nothing but metal cans, plastic containers of all shapes and sizes and box after box of dates. As they slowly crept down the aisle, the men sitting behind the tables sipping tea would call out to them offering samples of their wares.

"But they all sell the same thing," Dillon commented as they reached the end of the shop fronts.

"I know," Erpack returned. "How can they make a living when all of them have the same stuff at probably the same relative price? I buy dates but I buy them at one of the fancy shops downtown. I just couldn't bring myself to dig out dates from a metal can after it sat in the sun for days on end. Call me different but I'd have to be pretty hungry before I would venture into that Arab delicacy."

By this time, Erpack reached the main road on the other side of the souq area. He brought the truck down the access road in front of the various carpet stores and back on to "military road".

As they approached the first light on their way, Erpack slowed slightly in an effort to be "caught" by the light. It obliged by changing from green, to yellow, to red. After it made the final change to red, four cars sped through the intersection.

"Another reason not to be the first one off your mark when the light changes." As he was speaking, a car pulled around them on the right, made a right turn at the corner, went down the block a few hundred feet, made a u-turn around the center divider, cut through a parking lot, and rejoined the road on the other side of the intersection. Dillon watched the entire thing as Erpack explained the moves.

"That's one type of bypass," he said as their light returned to green. He cautiously followed the surrounding cars through the intersection. At the next light, he pulled off the road to give Dillon a complete view of the show.

When the light changed to red, the drivers would swing on the paved section of parking lot bordering the right side of the roadway. They would streak through the parking area to rejoin the main road further down. They didn't decrease their speed; they just swerved to avoid head on collisions with cars in the parking lot. Dillon remained silent as he shook his head in disbelief. Erpack just chuckled as he put the truck in gear and rejoined the others on their way to work.

MD was coming out of his villa when he heard the phone ring. Before running back inside, he listened to the number of rings. After the third ring, the line fell silent. He knew it was EB calling. When he reached his office, he would make a quick call to see what he wanted. MD was luckier than most. His office was in a small compound adjacent to the main housing area. His commute was a short one.

"Assalam Alaykum" was the greeting given by the Saudi sergeant who controlled access to the phone. MD returned the greeting and asked for Estermann. In passable English, the NCO asked him to wait a moment. MD could hear the man call for EB across the shop floor. It was only a moment before Estermann came to the phone.

"Estermann," he spoke into the line. "EB, this is MD. You called?"

"Sure did. I need to see ya later today. Is 1400 OK with you?" MD took a quick look at the calendar he kept on his desk to confirm he was free. The only thing on his calendar was a meeting at 1000. He told EB it was fine. Since they always met at the same location, there was no need to agree on a place.

Chapter Thirty-One

"I'll get the coffee while you see if the Major is available," Dillon told Erpack as they entered the office area. Erpack took the short walk down the hallway, unlocked the door, and stepped into the contractor's area. As he did, the HR manager, Oswald F. Booker, greeted him. This forced Erpack into being civil to the man as they were practically face-to-face.

"Mornin Willard," was the greeting given by the short, white haired, bespectacled man with a widening ink stain in his pocket. Erpack hated to be called Willard by people he didn't like. They always seem to add a twist to the pronunciation.

"Morning Oswald," was the polite reply.

"You might want to check the cap on your pen." Erpack commented as he pointed to the dark blue stain on the other man's shirt.

"Shit," Booker exclaimed as he pulled the cap less fountain pen out of his pocket. Turning away from Erpack, he stomped off toward his office. As he disappeared into the doorway, Erpack waved and bid the man "Have a nice day!" He then continued his walk to the Major's office chuckling the entire way.

He greeted Sajah and asked if the major was available. Erpack already knew the answer. It was before 0900 and he was positive the major wasn't in the office. He was right as Sajah confirmed the major wasn't in the area. Asking for a call when he did arrive, Erpack went back to his office where Dillon just finished coffee preparations.

"Not in yet?" Dillon asked as Erpack sat on one of the couches in the outer office area.

"It's not 9 yet. He's never here before nine. Sajah is very good about protecting the man. He's been here more than 10 years. I just can't believe

258

any man would leave his family for that period of time. I can understand a year or two at the most but 10 years!" Erpack took a sip of his coffee as Dillon took a seat in one of the chairs.

"Do you have anything for me to say when the major does get here?" Erpack asked Dillon.

"Not really. I don't want to give him too much information at this time. I'll wait for the new man to make his in roads. I'll just let him know the information we've collected does warrant additional time. I'll politely ask again for his assistance and assure him he'll be fully informed of our activities."

When Dillon spoke those words, Erpack cocked his head Dillon's way and squinted. "You are kidding aren't you?"

"I'm not kidding actually; I just have a different opinion of what fully informed means."

"I see. You will explain your opinion to the man coming down here won't you?"

"You can rest assured your new administrator will be fully informed of the current situation. All you have to do is provide support."

Erpack mockingly mopped his brow. "Thank goodness. I'm beginning to believe you guys will be able to conclude this shit. I just hope it doesn't take too long."

Dillon told him he couldn't rush the process. It may take a short amount of time and then again, it may take much longer than his Riyadh investigation. It all depended on what leads were formed and how they panned out in the end. No one could predict how long an investigation would take unless the clues to solving the case were precise and abundantly available.

Dillon began to tell Erpack about a case he worked in Japan when the back door swung open and Al-Kahfanny walked into the open area. The conversation ceased as they greeted the man and exchanged morning handshakes. Dillon and Erpack retreated to the office. Once inside they continued their story swapping until they needed refills for their coffee. With their cups recharged, they turned their attention to the list of possible problem children. They busied themselves adding notes behind each name when they heard a light knock at the door. Erpack looked up to see the major standing in the doorway.

"What a pleasant surprise major. Please have a seat," Erpack invited as he motioned toward an empty chair.

"You came to see me earlier?" the major addressed Erpack.

"Sure did sir but all I was trying to do was arrange a time for Dillon and I to visit. He's on his way up north this evening and he wanted to brief you on our staff assistance visit."

"Agreeable with me," the major replied as he shifted around in his seat so he was facing Dillon. "What have we discovered?"

Dillon went into no great detail about the visit. He wanted to make the major aware a problem did exist and they would be some additional investigation done by other agencies. The customer was not getting value for money and there needed to be a few changes. He did mention, in a round about way, his conversation with Abercrom. When Dillon mentioned the name, the major lowered his head and with his left elbow on his knee, he rested his head in the palm of his hand. Dillon paused.

"Ever since that man was placed into that position I've had a bad feeling. I just don't know if he's to be trusted."

"I've got a few words to say about that major," Erpack began but after catching a glimpse of Dillon staring at him, he changed the ending.

"After we gather all the facts concerning the contractor's performance, we can have a meeting and discuss what I feel are some pretty important issues." Dillon smiled as Erpack diplomatically ended his planned attack on Abercrom. Dillon was in no mood for listening to a tirade on the man.

The major agreed and began to ask a series of questions which Dillon delicately answered in an effort to keep certain information away from the project officer. He didn't want some aspects of the "visit" revealed. It didn't matter what country you were dealing with, GIs tend to talk, and talk could be hazardous to the ongoing investigation. Each answer appeared to be a satisfactory judging by the major's body language. Dillon was pleased Erpack didn't put his two cents into the equation.

"Anything else?" Dillon asked when the major paused.

"No Mr. Dillon, I do believe you've answered all the pressing questions. How have you enjoyed your visit to our paradise?"

"Well sir, let's just say it's been an interesting experience. I hope to make a return visit for some site seeing rather than staying so busy with military business."

"Yes you should. We have some great places to see and you can count on the weather being much nicer than the desert climate you have to endure in Riyadh." The three men talked for several minutes about places to see and things to do in the Asir region. The major drained the remainder of his tea, shook hands with the men, and left the office.

"I get a good feeling about the man. I just hope my Arab senses are acting along the right lines," Dillon commented as he came back in the room with a fresh cup of coffee.

"I really have no opinion at the present time. The major's educated and has been working with US forces for a number of years. His deputy is cut from the same bolt of cloth. I have more contact with him because the major is normally away from the office. I go in to bullshit with the captain on a regular basis. Do you have any problem with me bringing him in on the picture?"

"I'd clear it with the major first," Dillon cautioned. "You know the hierarchical structure they have. Knowledge is power and I'm sure the major, for all his better qualities, is still a tribal elder when it comes to having information as his power base."

"You're right there," Erpack agreed as he pushed his empty coffee cup to one side of the desk. "Where were we?"

Dillon and Erpack continued to go over the personnel roster adding notes and comments to a growing list of possibilities. "You don't think a dependent is involved do you?" Dillon asked as he looked at the listing of wives and children.

"Without the ability to transport ones self from point A to point B, I would tend to doubt it. It would involve another person to provide transportation, which would widen the circle of people with knowledge about the operation."

"Agree. I just wanted to make sure we're in harmony. There may be others involved with the distribution but I think the main players are employees. Just how many remains one of the items we're going to sort out."

While Dillon was making comment to Erpack, Fred came into the office and put distribution into the black plastic "in" basket. Erpack nodded as Fred left the room. "Let me see what the wide world of government correspondence has for me today."

He picked up the first of at least a dozen "US Government" envelopes, unwound the thin red string securing the covering flap, and peered inside. He continued the same procedures as he read the correspondence and placed the documents in an active or file category.

"Damn," he said as he looked into one of the remaining envelopes. "Forgot about these folks," he commented as he pulled a roster for the school and its teaching staff out of the paper container.

⚶

As MD pulled into the compound, he could see EB already arrived. He pulled close to the villa so the truck was in the shade of the building. EB came out the front door and approached the truck before MD could get out.

"I don't know what it is," EB began" but I'm having bad feelings about the operation."

261

"I tell you what," MD retorted, "let me get out of the truck and we can talk about it."

EB backed away from the door and MD got out. He asked EB to explain. The men went to the front porch and sat on the stoop. EB began a story of how he felt watched and on the verge of begin caught. It was causing him to be suspicious of people he dealt with on a daily basis and that wasn't good.

"Is there anything specific you can point to with some assurance or is this just your ever present paranoia appearing once again?"

EB turned toward MD and leaned away from him questioning, "Just what the fuck do you mean?"

"We've been over this time and time again." MD began as he kicked a stone away from under his foot "You were telling me almost on a daily basis you were being followed or watched. It almost ended the operation at one point. I just didn't want to hear about some mystery man following you to the farm or watching you as you came to the villa. However, I must admit, you have been a lot better the past few months. I just hope this doesn't develop into a constant thing."

"Well excuse my fucking ass," was the short reply as EB rose from the stoop and stood in front of MD. "I really didn't think it bothered you. You and your counselor background! I figured I could talk with you and perhaps you could help. I'm fucking sorry you were bothered by my concerns."

MD raised his hands above his head to signal capitulation. "Just hang on. It did bother me and as I said, it almost ended this thing. I figured with your paranoia acting up, you were bound to make a mistake and we'd both be in hot soup. I did use my counselor training to try and understand. As the complaints diminished, so did my concern about your vulnerability to error."

EB had no immediate reply. He was pacing a small path in front of MD. As he walked, MD was flicking small stones from the area between his feet. He figured EB just needed a moment to align his thoughts. After several laps, EB stopped directly in front of MD where one of the small stones MD was flicking hit the toe of his shoe. It popped up and landed behind the laces.

"You don't have to throw stones at me too," EB said as he reached down to retrieve the pebble from its resting place. "Your verbal lashings are enough."

"Maybe it's time we get out." MD began as EB returned to his place on the stoop. "My financial goals are more than satisfied. I've just been upping my expectations each year."

EB laughed and told his partner he was in the same situation. He would never be able to spend all the cash he accumulated. MD admitted he was growing weary of the constant worry. The penalty facing the men if discovered was harsh. The potential for disaster was enough to cause paranoia.

"Let's plan to put this thing to rest by the end of the year," MD said as he threw his flicking stick into the flowerbed next to the stoop. "We can maximize production and put the product into its most profitable form. We can begin to eliminate any surplus we may have in supplies and then each of us can decide if we want to stay on in Kingdom, or if we are going to give notice and depart."

EB didn't answer for a while. He just rested his elbows on his knees with his head in his hands. When he did answer, he didn't lift his head. He just spoke toward the ground.

"You always know something good is going to end but I'm afraid of being caught and taking those final few steps in chop chop square. I think it's time."

"Your fear is not unfounded," MD agreed as he put his hand on EB's shoulder. "And I agree. It's time."

<hr>

"Randy, I'm headed over to pick up the JAG and take him downtown for the court order. They said it would expedite the process if one of the investigators were there as the judge hears the situation. Evidently, he's very pro military and likes to keep up with investigations. He's near retirement and they believe he's looking for some part time work with the base after he leaves his state position."

"Sid," Randy called as he remembered a question. Sid replied from down the hall and again appeared in the doorway. "Did you get hold of Carpton?"

"Sure did. He was happy about the news. He sure has taken an interest in this family. He's going to have a tough time on casualty notification if he works this hard with all of them."

"This one's special because it's a murder. He'll find his level after a few trips."

"You're probably right." Sid agreed. "We'll make contact with Carpton and the family after we get the order in hand and we've talked with the bank. Carpton knows the family is being monitored and we don't want to put them in a difficult position. I want to give the bad guys no time to react to our moves. Once we find what's in the box, we can give them a story to play for their minders."

"Sounds like a plan. Just keep me informed and let me know if there's anything you need from me before you visit the bank."

"Will do," Sid replied with another wave as he left Randy's office.

The JAG's office was only a short drive. One of the lawyers was waiting on the front steps for Sid to pull up. It would be a simple matter to get the order signed once the judge heard the full story about the family and the sons' situation. Within two hours, Sid obtained the order and was back in his office. He waved the order at Randy as he passed.

"Quick work," Randy commented.

"Like I told ya, he's interested in keeping his hand on Air Force work after he retires. He's a real buff. Pictures of him and past commanders of the base are all over the walls in his office. Even some Sec Defs are there. The man has connections. I'm just glad he's on our side." Sid went on to his office after a brief stop in the coffee room for a soda. When he got to his desk, he put in a call to Carl.

"Carpton," Carl spoke into the receiver.

Carl, Sid here. We're in business. I just got back from downtown with one of the legal beagles and we have our court order. What I'll do now is make initial contact with the bank management and set up a date to visit. How's Thursday for you."

"I'll make myself available. Just let me know what time and I'm there."

"Great. Do you want to bring along the chief?"

"He's going to pass on this visit." Figures there will be enough people there *helping* the situation along."

"I'll let you know when we're going to leave the area. Randy is going to come along this time."

"Sounds good to me. I'll be waiting for your call with the time and place to meet. I'll talk at ya later." Sid completed the call as he pulled the address and phone number of the main office for the 1st United Bank of Covina out of the case file folder. The president's name was Don Holtz. After one ring, the call was answered. "First national of Covina, Don Holtz office."

"Yes Mam, this is Agent Sidney Moankat calling from the Air Force Office of Special Investigation, Vandenberg Air Force Base. Is Mr. Holtz available?"

"One moment please." was the reply. Sid listened to the dreaded on hold music with a few bank commercials tossed in for added effect. He went through two commercials before the music ended and Mr. Holtz answered. Sid reintroduced himself to the bank president and began to tell him the nature of his call and some of the background. He didn't go into much detail because frankly it just wasn't any of the president's business. He only gave him enough information to justify the court order. The president listened silently and when Sid finished, his only comment was, he needed to talk with his legal department before agreeing to a date for opening the box. Sid agreed but said the day was fixed. It must be Thursday. The main investigators were leaving the state on Friday and needed to inventory the contents of the box before they left. Sid figured a small lie would expedite the matter. Mr. Holtz told Sid he would have an answer for him before the close of business.

After he finished, he went to Randy's office and told him of the arrangements. "Did you get the feeling he was going to be a problem?"

"I don't think so. His legal folks ought to know by having a court order for access to the box we have already done our homework and aren't relying on the good graces of the bank to open it up. They will want copies of the document and all the other paraphernalia. I'll make sure we have a complete file for the bank so they can justify their actions. I didn't mention the family was going to be there. I was saving it in case they came up with some excuse."

"Good ploy. I'm looking forward to the trip." Sid went back to his office and called the JAG to get official copies of the order. They told him the procedures and he arranged to get it done. He wasn't going to let some small technicalities delay getting into the box.

⚜

Christina paused in the doorway before coming into Bills office and dropping into one of the chairs in front of his desk. Bill was checking e-mail and waited for her to speak. She just sat silently. Bill thought, OK I'll play your game as he continued to scroll through his mail. Finally she spoke.

"Why are some of our coworkers such raving assholes?" Bill continued to watch the screen for a moment before he turned toward Christina to reply.

"Could you be a bit more specific with your complaint Agent Dean?"

"I just finished a conversation with Agent Budmere B. Baker. He's one of the biggest nincompoops I've ever met. Excuse me, ever talked too. I haven't experienced the distinct pleasure of actually meeting him yet. I can hardly wait."

"So what's his major malfunction?" Bill queried.

"It's attitudinal. It's as if he's doing us a favor by gracing our humble operation with a visit. I sure hope he's worth the money."

"I did a bit of checking on the man and he should be worth the time and energy we put into getting him here and into the crime scene. His findings and testimony have been important parts of several high visibility cases in the

265

past. He's very concise and doesn't miss a thing when it comes to gathering evidence. He's one of those guys who found a niche and stuck to it."

"What about his cohort, Clanmire?" Christina asked.

"Not much on her. She's relatively new to the program and just hooked up with Budmere. He has a tendency to go through partners rather rapidly."

"I can understand that!" Christina laughed as she got out of the chair. "I wouldn't be working with the jerk for more than an hour. His attitude sucks. I just hope I can contain myself when we meet."

"I have complete confidence in your ability to act as a total professional, Agent Dean," Bill stated as he placed his clasped hands on the desk in front of him. "I know it's only an act but you're getting so good at it!"

"Funny William, very funny." Christina responded. "I'll go prepare the bastard traps for strategic placement in my office. I can only hope he doesn't trip."

Bill sat with his hands still clasped on his desk as he watched Christina leave the office. He just smiled to himself and shook his head before returning to his in basket. He knew Christina would provide nothing but the finest of professional assistance to the man. However, he hoped no imaginary lines in the sand were crossed. He also knew she would cut him at the knees if he trod over one of the lines. Bill waited a few minutes before ringing Christina on the intercom.

When she answered, Bill asked if there was any agreement on when the two agents would be arriving at Ramstein.

"I'm sorry Bill, he just got me so riled with his attitude I forgot to tell you. Right now plans are to have them on the base sometime Wednesday. Still don't know where they are but they would be arriving by car so they can't be too far away. Do you want me to put them up at the Cannon?"

"No," Bill responded. "If he's got an attitude, just fix them up with regular quarters. I don't want to feed his ego too much."

Since they were going to be working downtown, Christina arranged to have them booked into a contract Gasthaus in Ramstein village. With agent housing accomplished she placed another call to Karl. She hadn't been able to get hold of him for the notification on J.R. If she didn't talk with him this time, she would just leave a message about arrival time and name of the passenger. The flight J.R. was booked on was a direct flight. No in route stops at Aviano. The phone in Riyadh rang three times and Karl's voice mail answered. She left the flight number, arrival time, and the name, J.R. Lopez.

CHAPTER THIRTY-TWO

"Do you want to stop someplace along the way to pick up a bite to eat?" Erpack asked Dillon as they got into the truck.

"No, lunch was enough for me right now. I've got a bet riding with Karl about some evidence collected in Germany. Loser has to buy dinner tonight."

Fred went to pick up Dillon's boarding pass earlier in the day. Since Dillon was traveling with only carry on luggage, it made the transition through Abha's airport much easier. Erpack gave Dillon a brief tour of the thriving metropolis of Khamis. They took a back road in to the town center. Erpack showed Dillon the abundance of gold shops and tailors. As was the case in most Saudi cities, specialty shops grouped together. They passed furniture stores, paint stores, plumbing shops, lighting stores, electrical shops, sporting goods stores and clothing stores all along the main route out of the city center.

"Makes shopping much easier," Erpack noted as they passed through the last signal light in city center. They were now on the main Abha road headed for the airport.

It was only a short time before they approached the exit for the flyover to the airport. The two-lane road widened to five lanes. As Erpack signaled for an exit on the right, cars wanting to pass on either side surrounded him.

They made the transition from main road, over the bridge and on to the road leading to the airport. Dillon again saw the corn stands but this time they were open as families gathered for their nightly ritual of plane spotting. Some of the folks already started fires in preparation for the cool of the evening and the cooking of tea. Erpack just smiled as he drove toward the entrance to the airport proper.

"Do I need to escort you through the maze?" he asked as they slowed to pass over the barriers.

"Not unless you believe there's a reason I can't make it myself?" Dillon said as he reached into the seat behind him for his boarding bag. "I've got my passport, my travel letter, and my boarding pass. Once inside, where do I check through?"

"You'll have to put your bags through an x-ray machine at the door. Once that's done, just follow the wall on your right. It'll lead you to the security guys. They will check your papers and then pass you on to another x-ray machine for hand carried items and the metal detector. Trust me, if you have one small item of metal, it will sound off. I have yet to make it through Abha without taking everything out of my pockets; taking my shoes and belt off and I still set the thing off. You've less than an hour before flight time. That is if the big bird is on time. Saudi Arabian is well known for diverting domestic flights for the convenience of the royals."

"I'll keep my fingers crossed none of them want to make a quick trip anywhere this evening." They were now in front of the terminal. Erpack put the truck in park and turned on the flashers. He opened the back window so Dillon could retrieve his roll around.

"Thanks for the visit," Erpack began as he reached to shake Dillon's hand. "I hope by now you understand the shit I was facing and why I went off the deep end when we first met."

"I won't say the incident is gone and forgotten but I will say I have a much better understanding on the gravity of the situation and I can promise you our organization will be taking a closer look at solving the problem. The first step is getting you an admin man," Dillon said winking at Erpack.

"Received and understood," the aviator replied.

Dillon picked up his bags and stepped on the curb. Just as he did, a policeman approached Erpack and gestured for him to move the truck. Dillon noticed Erpack nodding politely but not responding since the policeman evidently spoke no English. Dillon waved as Erpack dropped the shift into drive and pulled away from the terminal. Pulling the handle out on his bag, Dillon walked into the building, put his bags through the x-ray machine, and found the security checkpoint. With no problems encountered there, he proceeded to the final x-ray and metal detector. Just as Erpack said, he set it off with the metal in his belt. Once removed and placed on the tray, he cleared the detector without another hitch.

The departure lounge was one big open room. Since there is only one gate, travelers don't have to worry about missing their flight. A small snack stand supplies stale sandwiches, cold sodas and hot tea. The "first class lounge" consists of three couches, one chair, and a coffee table. The tea or coffee is free. Dillon steps into the lounge to find the occupants all smoking in a no smoking area. He decides against joining them and instead ops for one of the blue plastic chairs connected to each other near the front of the room. He passes the time by watching a couple of Saudi children playing hide and seek with their father.

About half an hour before departure time, the flight is called and Dillon joins the line for single members of the flight. Once outside he walks down the gently sloping sidewalk to the tarmac. He crosses the short distance to the steps leading to the front door of the Airbus. An attendant at the foot of the stairs checks his boarding pass and allows him to climb the steps into the first class section.

Once the passengers boarded the aircraft, it taxis to the end of runway and immediately takes the active for a launch toward the west. Once airborne the craft makes a sweeping right turn. When it leveled off, Dillon had a great view of the escarpment form his vantage point on the left side of the plane. He watched the scattered houses pass underneath the plane as they climbed into the evening sky. He did notice a rather large facility sitting right at the edge of the mountain. He noticed it because there was a very large dome on one of the buildings. He surmised It was the Intercontinental Hotel Erpack mentioned during one of their talks on the Asir region. Shortly after passing the complex, the plane made another turn to the right as it headed north and its final destination, Riyadh.

⚔️

Horace got up from his favorite chair in the den when he heard the front door bell ring. When he opened the door, Oswald Booker was on the other side of the screen door. Horace pushed open the screen as he greeted his HR manager. "This is unexpected Oswald. What's up? No crisis I hope?"

"Not unless you consider some guy snooping around asking questions a crisis."

"You mean Dillon?"

"That's the one," Oswald said as he followed Horace into the den.

"Have a seat. What have you been able to find out about him?"

"Nothing and that's what scares the hell out of me. You know damn good and well he's going to be checking on us and I'm just afraid of what he might discover. You know my record in Kingdom isn't the best."

"I know Oswald but since you've been up here we haven't faced any repercussions over the detention. You were probably right when you said it was the captain you conflicted with up at KKMC[24]. You should have known

269

he was going to make trouble for you after you didn't carry out the tasking he gave you."

"I would have but…" Horace held up his hand to stop Oswald.

"Let's not go over that crap again. You were given this spot to hide you and so far, it's worked. Can I get you a drink?" Horace asked as he got up and headed for a room adjacent to the den. This being the "managers" house, one of the previous occupants spent RSAF money to have a 12-foot extension added across the entire width of the house. The three quarter length windows looked out on the carefully manicured garden area. Horace went over to a credenza and opened one of the cabinets.

"What's your poison? I have bourbon, scotch, a small amount of vodka, some brown and I do believe my brew should be about done out in the shed. I can get some if you like."

"I'll have a bit of the scotch if you don't mind," Oswald said as he approached the back of the room to look out at the garden.

"You want it neat or with water?" Oswald said he would like some water with it. He stood silently until Horace came back into the room and joined him by the window.

"You know we may have to cooperate with this guy if they take him seriously in Riyadh. If Erpack has been complaining up the line, it may be in our best interest to show some concern in these dope heads we have launching aircraft."

"Probably 100 percent true," Oswald agreed as he took a sip of the liquid cut with water and a couple of ice cubes. He stared into the glass as he swirled the contents around and around.

"It just amazes me no one in Riyadh has a handle on the guy."

"The game isn't over yet," Horace consoled the man standing next to him.

"I'm still working a couple of angles. I just hope they pan out before he gets his act together." The men continued to gaze out the windows and sip their drinks. Their concerns were genuine and rightfully so. Dillon was not going to give up on this matter. He had seen enough during his short stay to be concerned.

Oswald drained the remaining liquid in his glass and turned toward Horace. "I appreciate all you have done for me since I got up here. I know I'm not qualified to be in the position I'm in and I have made a few stupid mistakes during my time. However, with all said, I'm not going to take the fall for some dope heads on the line. If I find the supplier, I'll turn him in sooner than spit."

"I would expect nothing less," Horace commented as he led the way out of the room and into the kitchen. Oswald set his glass in the sink and leaned back against the counter resting his hands on the rounded tile edges. Horace continued. "I feel the same way. I just want to make sure this man has the influence he insinuates. Let's just keep our heads straight and we should be just fine."

"I hope so." Oswald shook hands with Horace and walked toward the front door. He pushed open the screen and turned to say goodbye. "Thanks for the shot. I forget what the real stuff tastes like after a while. I'll see ya tomorrow." Oswald cut across the lawn and walked up the sidewalk toward his villa.

"Shit," Horace muttered to himself as he gently shut the door after Oswald. "I was afraid that chicken shit Army puke would cave," he continued to complain as he went back to pour himself another stiff drink. "I'd better tell Doc what's up."

⚔

"Welcome to Ramstein Agent Lopez," Dick greeted as he came from behind his desk to shake hands with the fashionably dressed woman with the shoulder length black hair, dark brown eyes and perfect smile. "I'm Dick Famington. I'm the headquarters point of contact for OSI matters here in Europe. I'm sorry I missed you when you processed for your work in Belgium.

J.R. slowly stopped returning the handshake until Dick noticed he was doing nothing more than holding her hand. He abruptly pulled back like some schoolchild caught holding hands with his first girl friend at recess.

"It's a pleasure to meet you Dick. I just can't believe you picked me out of all the other agents in Europe."

"Well like they say, timing is everything. You were at the right place at the right time and now you are being given a chance to excel. From what I'm being told, you're on a non-stop flight from here to Riyadh this afternoon. Agent Christina Dean from our local office has handled all the arrangements. I'll give her a call and have her come over."

"Don't bother her. I know how hectic offices can be. Just point me in the right direction and I'll find her." Dick agreed and after some talk about the assignment in Belgium and her follow on to Schweinfurt, Dick escorted J.R. to the door of his office. "Whom will I be reporting to when I'm there?"

"The lead agent is Karl Phobie. He has one other man there with him but his name escapes me at the moment. He's a junior agent and will probably be the one you have most contact with in getting set up." J.R. left

271

the headquarters for the base OSI building. She found Christina and made herself ready for the trip to Riyadh.

❈

Dillon slowly sipped the orange juice as he watched the desert landscape pass. Since he was told about the beauty of Riyadh from the air, he was looking forward to seeing the city lights as they approached from the south. He wasn't disappointed. As he saw a few smatterings of light from scattered homes, a discernable road system became noticeable. The system was well lit but without residences. Next to pass under the craft was an industrial area with large warehouse type buildings and smoke stacks belching some type of combustion byproduct. Then more street systems but this time there were homes located along the streets. The layout was geometric with large roundabouts giving some semblance of traffic control.

As Dillon was not familiar with the city or airport approach routes, he just watched the panorama unfold beneath him. They passed over what he thought was the central area of Riyadh. Then the lights began to fade as the jet passed away from the city and into the desert. A couple of banking turns coupled with the announcement of their approach to Riyadh's international airport led Dillon to settle back in his seat for landing.

With the Jetway was on his side of the aircraft, he watched it maneuver into position. The majority of first class passengers got up from their seats and proceeded to grab their bags from the overheads even before the jet stopped moving. Since he was in no hurry to make a connection, he paused to watch the frantic rushing, pushing, and cell phone calls. Once the throng moved away from his row, he retrieved his bags and made his way through the crowd, down the Jetway and into the terminal.

Since baggage claim and exits were downstairs, he followed the crowd to the stairway and escalator. As he shuffled along, he noticed all the faces watching disembarking passengers from their vantage point in the departure area. Most were Filipinos, Indians, or Deshies with a scattering of Anglo faces among the throng. As Dillon boarded the escalator, he was disturbed by a commotion above his head. Some of the awaiting passengers were being pushed aside by a man hell bent on getting to the front for a better view.

At the bottom of the stairs, Dillon continued to follow the crowd but paused to admire the flora and waterfalls he'd seen when he left Riyadh. It was interesting to see how the area was designed to appear like an oasis in the barren desert setting. Once on the other side of the baggage claim area, Dillon saw Karl waiting behind the crowds.

272

"How was the flight?" Karl asked as he reached for Dillon's boarding bag.

"Very nice. Not a bump anywhere along the way. This is some place from the air. What a beautiful sight."

"I'll have to agree. The first time I flew in commercial, it totally caught my attention. This place has grown by leaps and bounds. I don't know where all the people are coming from but they sure are crowding into the capitol."

They were passing a small snack stand adjacent to one of the exits when Karl paused. He reached into his pocket and pulled out his stash of riyals. "Let me give you some ones. Buy me a bottle of water and get something for yourself. I'll go down and get the truck. Meet me right outside those doors." Before Dillon could protest, Karl shoved the bills into his hand, slung the boarding bag over his shoulder, and was heading down the escalator directly beneath a large green sign with a white car embossed in the middle.

Dillon went to the kiosk and ordered two waters. He waited until the two Saudi youths who pushed their way past him as he approached the counter were served their tea. Once his transaction was completed, he headed for the automatic doors and the heat of the Riyadh evening.

⁂

Helga pushed the laundry basket with the side of her foot as she maneuvered it out of the bathroom into the hallway. She just emptied the hamper into the basket and was getting ready to do her bi-weekly batch of laundry. The kettle on the stove was beginning to sound off as the water inside came to a rapid boil. She smiled at the thought of having a nice cup of chocolate while she waited between the washing and drying of her clothes. She went into her intimate kitchen and shut off the burner under the water. Her cup, a small spoon, and the chocolate were laid out on the counter next to the stove. By the time she returned, the water would be just right for her first cup.

She picked up the basket and walked down the hall to her front door. Once outside she approached the door to the laundry room located near the garage. She propped the door open with a decorative brick strategically placed by the door for that purpose. She reached into the basket and grabbed a handful of clothes sorting them on the floor into whites, colors, and delicates. Once the sorting was done, she reached for her bucket of soap located on one side of the divided shelf above the washer and dryer.

On one side, she kept her laundry products and on the other, the tenants kept their supply. As she felt the weight of the small bucket she used for ease of access, she remembered her supply was very low. Nice time to remember Helga, she thought to herself. There was just enough for the first load. She didn't want to make a special trip out so she reached over on the tenant side and grabbed a box of the local supermarket brand from the back of the shelf. She pulled back the flap and noticed the box was nearly half-full. More than enough to finish today's wash. She set the bucket on the washer top and tipped up the soapbox to empty the contents into her container. The last thing in the box to fall into her bucket was a small plastic bag sealed with duct tape. Inside the clear bag, she could see a small box. She held the soapbox at arms length to see what free gift was being offered by the manufacture. There was nothing listed. Puzzled by her find, she dropped the package into the pocket of her apron set the controls on the washer and headed back to her apartment for a nice cup of hot chocolate.

CHAPTER THIRTY-THREE

As Dillon negotiated his way through the electronically controlled double doors leading to the passenger loading and unloading area in front of the terminal, numerous vehicles passing rapidly by the building created the only hint of air movement. He walked toward one of the circular roof supports to wait for Karl. Across the street was the impressively large airport mosque. The steps leading to the entrance were lit in preparation for last prayer of the day.

Arriving passengers from various points around the Kingdom were busily loading their luggage into waiting taxis or the trunks of vehicles brought to the airport by relatives or business associates. An airport police tow truck was moving into position at the rear of a late model Mercedes to remove the sedan from a point blocking one lane of traffic. A policeman slipped a ticket on the windshield just before they towed the car to the police lot.

While Dillon leaned against the concrete support pillar observing his surroundings, a man came running out of the terminal almost colliding with the automatic doors before they slowly slid open. Dillon noticed him as part of his peripheral vision when the man approached the curb. At first, the man looked to his left and then rapidly to his right. When he saw Dillon, he noticeably calmed down. The man turned to his left and slowly walked away from Dillon's position. When he was about 20 feet further up the sidewalk, he paused and turned toward the building. Dillon continued to monitor the man's location for the few minutes before Karl pulled into view.

As Dillon opened the rear passenger door to put his roll around on the seat, he asked Karl to look at the man. Dillon closed the back door and got into the passenger's seat next to Karl. He asked Karl to watch the man's reaction as they pulled away from the terminal. Karl said the man walked quickly to where they left the curb, pulled out a pen and wrote something on the palm of his hand.

"He took down our license number," Dillon commented as he pulled the seatbelt from its stowed position and fastened it across his lap and chest.

"Why would he do that?" Karl asked while negotiating the exit lanes, which lead to the airport's access road.

"I'm not sure," Dillon replied as he related the story of the man's arrival outside the terminal. As he finished he fell silent for a moment and then exclaimed, "Shit, I thought the guy looked familiar."

Dillon turned slightly to look toward Karl. "As I was getting off the flight, I was watching the people getting ready to board the plane for the return trip to Abha. Nothing out of the ordinary until I was riding the escalator down to the baggage claim area. There was a commotion along the rail and a man pushed his way to the front of the crowd. It was that man."

"That guy?" Karl questioned. "Are you sure? Why would he be outside the terminal if he was waiting to take the Abha flight?"

"Good question Watson! Since he seemed to be so interested in our vehicle and he just kept standing around the terminal once he saw me waiting outside, let me make the bold assumption he knows who I am and wants to know who picked me up."

"Oh horseshit!" scoffed Karl. "Why would a guy getting ready to take a flight to vacation land be so interested in you?"

Dillon didn't reply immediately as he pondered the situation. Why indeed? If it was the same man, and Dillon was now 100 percent sure it was, who was he and why was he so interested? It could have a connection with the cartel. Was he a main player or just one of the lackeys? Was he on his way to Abha for some specific business purpose or did he just happen to be traveling for a break away from Riyadh? Dillon doubted the latter. The man had a purpose for traveling and Dillon's sixth sense said he was the subject for the travel. When the man saw the subject of his travel getting off the plane, he became excited and faced a quick change of travel plans.

"Halala for your thoughts," Karl quipped as he merged the Suburban into the flow of traffic heading away from the airport's bright lights.

"Just trying to put some sort of spin on the guy. I get the feeling I was the reason for his travel and when he saw me coming off the plane, his plans took a drastic turn."

"I've been warned about your sixth sense," Karl replied as he checked his mirrors for a lane change. "Let me change. I wasn't warned, I was told you get feelings about things and nine times out of 10 they're spot on."

"Thanks for the vote of confidence," Dillon laughed. "I guess I'm going to have to keep my *feelings* to my self before I lose all credibility."

"Don't worry about the credibility aspect until they ship you off to some remote office with the title of assistant. You'll know you screwed the pooch."

"So what did we find out about the fingerprints?" Dillon asked. "Who's on the hook for dinner?"

"It's going to be a Dutch treat. Our friends did leave some excellent prints on the glasses but no one came up with any identification. All our sources have been played out. If they have a record, the normal investigative agencies don't have a file on them."

"I'm not surprised," Dillon replied. "They seem to have gone to great lengths to prevent leaving any prints but loosen up at the end of their search. We'll just have to keep the prints and glasses on file to match them against the men we pick up. I just know we're going to get a break eventually. It's out there waiting for us."

They continued with non-related conversations until Karl began to move toward the right side of the highway and exit 10. He successfully made the transition from ring road to a divided cross-town road. He picked a spot in the center lane to traverse the distance between the exit and King Abdulaziz Road. Well before the signal light at Sahara Mall, he turned on his left turn indicator and began a slow move toward the left lane. He turned at the light and stayed in the far left lane.

"We've got to make the next left turn and if I get into the center no one will let us make the turn." Karl commented as he again flipped on the turn indicator. At the Tamimi Safeway corner, he made his turn and pointed to the restaurant as they passed it on their left.

"We make a U-turn at the top of this street. There's no other way to get over there. They've got another street planned but it hasn't materialized yet." Karl came to the end of the central divider and wheeled the truck around the concrete abutment as he headed back toward the "Mexican Connection".

Pulling into a parking spot right in front of the dilapidated doorway with a sign posted "SINGLES"; Karl slipped the truck into park and set the brake. Dillon looked to his right and saw another door with the "FAMILIES" sign. Between the two signs was a large picture window with dark red curtains haphazardly hanging on a cafeteria rod. The hand painted display on the window announced "Mexican Connection Restaurant -- A Mexican Fiesta". The "i" in Mexican was in the form of a saguaro cactus wearing sunglasses. As Dillon began to unsnap his seatbelt he looked over at Karl, "I hope the inside is better than the outside!"

"It isn't", was the reply. "But the food is first rate." They sat at a table near the back of the room facing the door. Dillon let Karl order since he was the culinary expert of the moment. The owner of the place came out and greeted the men as if they were old comrades. The first non-alcoholic beer was on the house. The owner joined them for appetizers and suggested a new dish for them to try. As usual, no talk about the case during dinner. When they finished the last course and were sitting back to enjoy a cup of thick Turkish coffee, Dillon asked about notifications from Ramstein.

"Are you sure it was him?" Raja asked.

"Positive. He came off the plane from Abha and was met by a guy driving a Suburban. I got a partial license plate so we can check the registration. Anyway, I took a closer look as he went down the escalator and I'm absolutely sure it was the same guy. I had some trouble getting out of departures but was able to get to the street before he was picked up."

"Did he notice you?"

"I don't think so. He was leaning against one of the pillars out front and I made like I was looking for a ride. He didn't appear to pay much attention to what I was doing. When his buddy showed up, he just got into the truck and they drove off."

"Get back here as soon as you can. I'll get a message ready to send up the line. What ever the reason for his being in Abha must not have been too important or complicated. He was only gone a couple of days," Raja commented.

"Well he's back here now. I've got to go back inside and cancel my ticket. I'm sure they're looking for me. Glad I didn't have any luggage to check. That would have really screwed them up. I'll be back at the villa as soon as I get off their passenger list." Abdunn disconnected the cellular link and dropped the phone into his briefcase.

Raja pulled out the keyboard and composed a short message to Germany informing them of Dillon's return to Riyadh. He was relieved Abdunn didn't have to make the trip. He didn't have full confidence in his abilities. After he completed the draft, he went to the kitchen to make a cup of tea. He would wait for his co-worker to get back before he sent the message.

Abdunn scrambled to the front of the line and explained the situation to the harried clerk behind the counter. Having just finished dealing with a very irate Saudi with two wives and six children in tow, he was more than happy to handle a request as simple as Abdunn's. Within minutes, he was away from the counter and into the adjacent underground parking lot. He threw his case into the back seat, retrieved the parking receipt from over the visor, and was on his way back to the villa.

When he arrived, Raja pulled out a photo of Dillon for Abdunn to confirm it was the man he saw getting off the plane from Abha. "Please don't give me any shit about who I did or didn't see. It was this man and that's my final answer."

Raja said he just wanted to make absolutely sure before they notified their minders. With the tone of the boss's message, he didn't want to face punishment for a missed identification. Both men went to the computer room. Raja read the note he prepared and when Abdunn agreed to the content, he cut and pasted the text into his e-mail account and sent the message along their scrambled lines of communication.

In Germany, Garmat came into the living room and sat on a footstool near the coffee table. He reached for his glass of wine as he read the note just received and retrieved from the e-mail account. "It appears our boys in Riyadh have been able to pull their wurst out of the fire. Evidently their man came back from, let me see here," he paused as he scanned the note. "From Abha".

Leo sat his glass on the table and reached for the note. "I was hoping they would be in the hot seat a bit longer. Sure takes the pressure off us. Did you send this along the line?" Garmat acknowledged sending the note along their lines. Nearly halfway around the world from the wine drinking in Germany, a system remote station flickered to life as the note made its way into a storage location on the hard drive.

The late morning sun enclosed the deck in a warming overcoat of brightness. In its place overlooking the harbor area, the deck afforded occupants an extensive view of activities engaged in by members of the yacht club and accompanying residents of the exclusive housing area. On this particular morning, the deck's only occupant was too busy to notice any activity other than the words printed on pages of documents on the cabana table near the deck's railing. Detailed on the documents was information concerning the Crimitin family. Of particular interest was the last bit of information about the visitors and subsequent phone conversations. Something was about to happen. A possible interception plan is required to ensure any incriminating information didn't stay in the hands of authorities. A few phone calls later, the plans were completed and the pleasant view of the harbor could once again be enjoyed to its fullest.

⚔

"Notifications from Ramstein?" Karl began as he took a sip from the small cup holding the hot, deep dark Turkish blend. "I really haven't had

279

a chance to talk with them but I did get an e-mail detailing some of their activities. It did have the name of the guy on his way down here." He paused as he took another sip of his coffee.

"Someone with just initials for a first name. I remember the initials, J.R. like Ewing from the TV show. I didn't bring the notes so I'll get the last name for you when we get back to the villa."

"Does Lopez ring a bell?" Dillon asked as he leaned toward Karl's side of the table.

"Yeah, that's it, Lopez. Do you know him?"

"Nope, I don't know him, I know her!" Dillon flatly stated as he sat back in his chair and downed the remaining liquid in his coffee cup.

"Her?" Karl questioned with a look of astonishment.

"Juanita Rene Lopez, OSI Agent assigned to Howard Air Force Base in Panama the last time I saw her," Dillon concluded as he raised his cup toward the waiter in a quest for more coffee.

"We worked a rather large movement case during the final phases of our tenure in Panama. She's one hell of an agent and her ability to blend in with the locals was instrumental in getting the case closed with the arrest of an entire chain of command. Quite an accomplishment for her. But I thought they were going to pull someone from Europe?"

"Evidently she didn't make much of an impression on you or you would have kept in closer touch. She's been working in Belgium. They tapped her for a liaison assignment with the Army in Schweinfurt. Dick, our USAFE contact man, pulled her in early and sent her to us. I just naturally assumed it was a guy. Now I'm worried."

"Don't. She's an excellent agent and once she gets the lay of the land, she'll bag this thing in quick order. When's she due in?"

"She's leaving Ramstein today. Should be on the ground in the morning, if the 141 doesn't breakdown somewhere along the line. I've arranged to have her met by transportation and brought over to the commander's office. Less connection with us. We can meet her there and provide briefings. Depending on how much you two have to reminisce about, we can have her on the way down range on Thursday or Friday." Karl concluded.

"Sounds like you've got it handled. I'll pull my notes together and put them on disk. She can hand carry the initial stages with her and set up in one of the villas on the compound. Have you worked the all base pass?"

"In works as we speak. We have an inside point of contact with all the right stamps and forms. All we do is supply a picture and he can fix one up in the morning." Karl and Dillon were alone in the restaurant, so they talked about the work at Khamis and the Crimitin case. They finished off the Turkish brew and swapped insults about the fingerprint results. They each paid their bill, bid the owner goodnight, and headed into the evening's heat.

Karl tried to engage Dillon in small talk but each time Dillon was lost in some thought process not shared with Karl. He was thinking about the investigation and the presence of J.R. Lopez. He remembered the final assault on the fortified compound. J.R. and Dillon stationed themselves at the foliage-covered exit of a tunnel leading away from the mountain top complex. Having been on the inside for some time, J.R. discovered the tunnel while on rotational guard duty. Once the assault began, the plan laid out by the kingpin of the trafficking ring was to pull more than 5 million dollars out of his safe and make his escape through the tunnel with his wife and children. His escape was cut short by Dillon, J.R., some tire spikes and a Humvee with a turret mounted 20MM cannon.

Dillon not only remembered the investigation and the rush of the final capture, he was remembering the soft brown skin of Juanita and the sweet smell always emanating from her hair. They spent time together after the capture completing the subsequent mountains of paperwork always required after an investigation wraps up. He recalled the dinners after filing reports and the lovemaking in any available space they could find. She was an expert. He especially remembered the last time they were together. Their passion was intense and after they finished exploring new sexual territories, they fell asleep to the sound of tropical rain clattering down on the metal roof of their room.

When Dillon awoke, Juanita was gone. There wasn't a note and when he called her office, he was told she left two days ago for a new assignment. Since her specialty was undercover work, Dillon knew better than to delve any further into her location. She made the effort of telling the office staff she was leaving so she could spend uninterrupted time with him. He certainly appreciated the deceptive tactic and smiled as he again recalled the passion and technique of the woman.

"What are you grinning about?" Karl interrupted.

"Does J.R. know I'm here?" Dillon asked.

"I'm not sure what they told her in Germany. As I said, we haven't had any contact with her so we couldn't tell her a thing. Is that why you're grinning? Surprising her?"

"Yeah, that's it," Dillon replied as the thought of Juanita Rene again filled his mind. "It'll certainly be a surprise!"

CHAPTER THIRTY-FOUR

"Agent Dean?" questioned the man standing in Christina's doorway. Christina looked up from the document she was reading. The man in the threshold was more than six feet tall with dark brown hair. His mustache was Poncho Villa style drooping past the corners of his mouth. It was bushy with a few gray hairs noticeable along the edges. His hair was combed straight back and came to rest slightly below his collar. He wore an opened collar shirt with a floral design. His chino pants were well worn. The ensemble was topped off with deck shoes and no socks.

"May I help you?" Christina asked without getting up from her desk.

"Yes, Yes you can. I need to know where I can set up my operation and if quarters have been set up for my stay. I'm Agent Baker. Budmere Baker." Christina stared at the man in disbelief. Not in a million years would she have pictured the agent in this style. "Agent Dean? Did you hear the question?"

Christina stood up behind the desk asking Budmere to take a seat. "Is Agent Clanmire with you?"

"She's checking the contents of your exchange. We've been rather busy these past few weeks and haven't had the chance to stock up on the finer things in life. We know you have a large complex here, so that was the first thing she wanted to check. I've got a few things to buy myself, so I told her I'd pick her up at the snack bar. I hope that doesn't create a problem?"

"No problem at all. I'll just follow you over there and then take you to your quarters in Ramstein Village."

Before Christina could say another word, Budmere asked, "We're not staying at the Cannon?" Christina paused and thought; boy, this guy has done his homework. He knows the VIP quarters and expected to be set up there. Got to be careful here.

"No, I'm afraid not. Our lead agent asked me to put you closer to the investigation. We have a very nice contract Gasthaus in Ramstein Village which is only a short drive from the site of the investigation in Kottweiller."

"Where is Agent Wilmerson? I need to discuss this matter with him."

"Bill isn't here right now so I'm afraid you'll have to deal with me. I'm your designated point of contact for all activities and unless I'm not doing what I'm told to do, my arrangements are final." Christina waited for the expected response but didn't get what she expected.

"Thank You. May I use a spare office to check my e-mail?" Now Christina was stumped. She expected a tirade from the pompous ass but when it didn't materialize, she stumbled in her reply.

"Ah, certainly..... you..... can. Right this way." she stammered as she came around the desk and to the hallway. She led Budmere to an adjacent office and showed him where the laptop connections were located. He thanked her and began the process of hooking up his communications link. Christina didn't pause to help; she knew he didn't need it. She just went back to her office to call the Gasthaus for confirmation of room availability. The agents arrived a bit earlier than she expected so she didn't want to show up in the village and not have rooms available. The owner said that by the time they arrived, the rooms would be ready. Christina thanked him and went back to reading the reports on her desk.

In less than an hour, Budmere appeared in Christina's doorway. "All finished?" she asked getting up from her chair. The only reply was "YES". "OK then, let's be on our way to the Gasthaus. Where are you parked?"

"Where else? Outside the front door."

Christina paused before answering, getting a full count of 10 in before her response. "I'm parked out the side door. I'll pull into the parking lot and follow you to the exchange. You can then follow me to the village. Is that all right?" There was just a nod of his head as Budmere turned toward the front door. Christina checked with the admin office and signed out on the board. She pulled into the front parking lot to find Budmere anxiously waiting by the lot's exit. She dutifully followed him to the exchange and watched him leave his car and walk briskly to the snack bar without waiting for her. Christina took her time entering the dining facility as she window shopped along the way. Don't want to seem too anxious she thought.

When she came in the door, she spotted Budmere at the salad bar. He was preparing a small plate of condiments for a snack. In a corner of the room, a woman stood up and waved. Evidently, he described her to his companion. She joined the woman at the table.

"I'm Cathy Clanmire," the woman greeted Christina as she reached the table. "Bud gave me your description in case he wasn't finished getting his snacks before you came in. As I'm sure you've found during your *brief* encounter with my coworker, he's a bit rough around the edges."

"Christina Dean," was the return. "That's a nice way to put it." Christina laughed as she pulled out one of the bright yellow plastic chairs. "He does have a way about him."

"He has a tendency to go through partners like water off a ducks back. I took this job to learn his techniques. He's really one of the best at crime scene investigation. The last guy to work with him lasted less than a month. I've been in the hot seat nearly twice that long and might be able to last six whole months." Cathy stated proudly with a wide grin.

"In one statement you've answered a couple of the questions I had for you. All I've got to do now is make sure the maestro has all the tools necessary to complete his assignment." As she finished, Budmere joined them. Cathy and Christina chatted as their companion concentrated on his snack. When all was finished, they left the exchange and headed toward Ramstein Village.

The Gasthaus was one block off the main street at the far end of town. It afforded the investigators easy access to the village proper and not much confusion on how to reach Kottweiller, the next village along the road. Christina pulled to the front of the house and parked on the street. Budmere pulled into the drive and parked near the front entrance. The owner, Klaus M. Otterman, came out and greeted the trio as they approached the door.

As they went inside, Christina watched Budmere survey his surroundings. Both of their rooms were on the first floor at the back of the building. After the formalities of registration were completed in the owner's apartment, Klaus led them up the stairwell to their rooms. Each was tastefully decorated in pine with queen size beds situated under a large picture window overlooking the gardens and fishpond at the back of the property. There was a small kitchen area just inside the entrance with the bathroom along the adjoining wall. A small writing desk, dining table with two chairs, a couch, and side chair were also available for the occupants use. Christina kept watching Budmere for some sign of disapproval.

"I'm sure you want to see where you'll be working, so I'll just wait downstairs with Klaus while you freshen up." With a wave, Christina followed Klaus to his apartment/office at the front of the house. Christina knew Klaus for some time. She met him while arranging billeting for some visitors shortly after her arrival in Germany. She could trust him to provide the best of German hospitality while understanding the nature of their business. Some times the guests came and went at very odd hours of the day and night.

In just a few minutes, Budmere and Cathy joined them. Klaus explained breakfast would be served in the small dining room at the end of the hallway each morning from 6 a.m. to 10 a.m. He asked for preferences and took notes on their responses. Handshakes were exchanged as they left the house to head toward Kottweiller. Christina suggested Budmere drive so she could explain the way and he could ask questions about the route. He paused before agreeing.

Out of Ramstein Village and on to Kottweiller was a short transition. They negotiated the hill and pulled in front of the house. They sat in the car for a while as Christina explained the scene to them. Cathy was taking notes while Budmere listened. When she finished, they left the car and walked up the hill to where everyone figures the second car was waiting. Budmere was nodding his head as he surveyed the environment. After a few minutes, Cathy put her notebook away and headed down the hill with Christina. Budmere stayed at the top of the hill for an extra couple of minutes before joining the ladies in front of the house.

"Can we get into the apartment now?" Budmere asked.

"Not this afternoon. No one could tell me when you were going to arrive, so I arranged to bring you out here as early as you want in the morning. How long do you think the investigation will take?"

Budmere said he couldn't be sure without getting inside. "Normally it would be a day to survey the scene, decide on techniques, and then proceed with the actual collection of any evidence. For an apartment this size, two maybe three days and we can be finished. Of course that's based on working 10 or 12 hours a day for those three days."

CHAPTER THIRTY-FIVE

Dillon met Karl and William for breakfast early the next morning. He spent the preceding evening going over notes from Khamis so he could consolidate everything on one disk for J.R. With a bottle of single malt whiskey and a Partagas Lusitania cigar, the time was productively spent. Having worked with J.R. before, he knew she would understand some of his approach for solving the problem. He could also have William make an appearance if necessary. Dillon was very confident J.R. would be able to identify the players involved with the Khamis supply and turn them over to Saudi authorities.

As Dillon was coming out his front door for the short walk to the dining facility, Karl pulled up. Dillon waved and turned to lock the door's deadbolt. He came around to the passenger side and got into the cab. "Chauffeur service. Can't beat that." Dillon commented as Karl dropped the truck into gear and pulled away.

"Just been out making the rounds and decided to swing by to give you a ride if you were still here. I got a call from PAX service at Sultan. True to form, the 141 with J.R. on board diverted into Aviano for a cargo pickup. Sounds like something similar to your trip. The dispatcher wasn't exactly sure what the cargo was but he assured me the delivery is set for today. I told him I was waiting for delivery of forms and they were supposed to be on that flight. I didn't mention J.R."

"It's probably a good idea to distance ourselves before she gets to Khamis," Dillon agreed. "I don't want to handicap her before the games begin."

Karl pulled into the parking lot just as William was coming around the corner from his villa. The men exchanged greetings and went inside.

When they finished, Dillon asked for more coffee and queried Karl about arrangements for getting J.R. to Khamis.

"As it stands now", Karl began. "We haven't made any final reservations. There are several flights headed south each day so it won't be a problem getting her down the road. Whenever she arrives, transportation at Sultan is primed to pick her up and bring her here. I checked with Susan in the boss's office and there are no meetings scheduled for the conference room anytime today. I'll have my point of contact give the folks at Sultan a call so we can be notified when the bird arrives."

The agents left the facility and went to the OSI office. They made coffee and filed into Karl's office to discuss tomorrow's meeting with Buzz.

"I'm not getting a good feeling about this guy," Dillon began. "We're lucky William found out so much usable information. No matter what kind of game he's playing with us, we have the trump card. I just hope I don't have to play it tomorrow. I would like to string him along a bit longer before we lower the hammer."

"I don't think he's going to try anything at the moment. He's probably trying to get on your good side for the business you can bring in. Face it; he's a businessman first and foremost. No matter his business can get him chopped, he's still a business man." Karl took a sip from his coffee after finishing his assessment of the situation.

"We'll be able to tell more about his motives after tomorrow's meeting. You're taking someone with you?" William asked.

"Got her number right here," Dillon said as he reached into his shirt pocket and pulled out a hospital business card.

"I've got to finalize arrangements with Carmen and then give Buzz a call to find out what time we should rendezvous. Have either of you guys eaten at this place?"

"You're going to Lai Lai's?" William clarified.

"That's the one. Buzz said they have a killer buffet. I hope he's right. I'm a sucker for good Chinese food at a reasonable price." Dillon listened to suggestions about how to handle Buzz made by the two men but knew exactly how he was going to handle the Jew in Arab clothing. Buzz held an agenda and Dillon was part of his master plan. All Dillon needed to do, in the course of the evening, was figure out what part he played, and determine if he could turn it to his advantage.

Since J.R. was going to be late, Dillon suggested a cancellation of their meeting with Vinder at the embassy. Karl said he would make the call and reset the meet for Saturday. Dillon wasn't too sure how much good the meeting was going to be. He was going to ask for NSA assistance in locating the bad guys. The National Security Agency, headquartered at Ft. George

G. Meade Maryland, was never anxious to lend their expertise to a project outside their span of control. With the FBI, CIA and NSA competing for the title of 'Most Improved Spy Organization' he hoped a big find such as drugs in the Kingdom would give them a boost during budget negotiations. They could bring in the State Department and feather their nest with a diplomatic connection.

Dillon was just glad he only dealt with military politics. His diplomacy during investigations was limited, so when he ventured in the world of 'real' diplomacy, he always got a knot in his stomach. He didn't like to banter with diplomats. During most operations, he avoided them like the plague. In this case, he was going to ask for embassy assistance because he knew the colonel's connection with the NSA and NSA owned the ECLIPSE system. He needed their help to bring this thing to a speedy resolution.

He walked back to the villa and showered. He gave Karl a call to see if they heard any information about the 141's arrival. "Funny you should ask," Karl replied. "I just gave my guy a call and he said they didn't have any information about the jet's ETA. He's going to give the folks at Aviano a call to see if the damn thing has launched yet. Once we have departure time we can guesstimate the arrival here."

Dillon told Karl he would be in the villa taking care of some business. After hanging up, he brought his laptop to the table, connected the phone line to the modem, opened his communications program, pulled up Sonta's phone number and with his wireless headset in place, he began to dial her number in Florida. He stopped midway through the process to check the clock. It was very early morning on the east coast so he decided to postpone the call until after dinner. He just disconnected the line from the computer and reconnected it to the phone when the instrument rang. Karl greeted Dillon and told him the jet was inbound with an ETA of 1500. That would put J.R. into the conference room about an hour later. Karl was going to get another call when the jet was actually on the ground so the men agreed to finalize their meeting time based on the wheels down call.

J.R. was enjoying all the attention lavished upon her by the members of her crew. She was traveling in the guise of a Master Sergeant. The crew insisted on making her an honorary member by getting her issued a flight suit for the trip. Before they left Germany, the loadmaster used a connection to get her the garment. Always prepared, he slapped a couple of unit patches on her shoulders and created a makeshift nametag for her. On their approach to Aviano, the aircraft commander invited her up front for a view from the jump seat. Now, as they approached Prince Sultan, she was on the flight deck again for the approach and landing.

The weather was cooperating and no changes to course were required. The Starlifter slid out of the dusty sky and floated to a touchdown on centerline of the white concrete strip. The follow-me truck picked them up at their turn off point and led them to the parking ramp. J.R. jumped into the crew van with the others as they departed the jet for ops. Before leaving, she stripped off the flight suit and returned it to the loadmaster. He pulled off the patches and gave them to her as a reminder of the trip. J.R. told them it was her first flight on a 141. She didn't like to deceive them but she was traveling as an administrator so she couldn't tell them she jumped out of one during another operation. Once inside a motor pool driver located her and threw her bags into the trunk. They were out the gate and on their way to Eskan.

"She's on the ground," Karl said as he pulled a sheet of paper from the printer and hung up. William was standing in the doorway and said he would give Dillon a call. Karl picked up his notebook binder and headed for the front office. He told Karlotta where they would be and went into William's office. William was still on the phone.

"Right, she's on the ground and on her way here. Karl and I are headed for the old man's office right now. We'll get everything set up. See ya over there."

Dillon hung up, closed the folder he was working with and stood up from the desk. He stretched both arms over his head and took a deep breath. Well Miss J.R., he thought, let's see how you've changed over the years. He scrapped everything off the desk into his case and left the villa. The walk to the command office was a short one. He greeted Susan as he came into the villa and went directly to the conference room. Susan would remain in the office until J.R. arrived. She would usher her into the commander's office and then would leave for the evening. All was prepared for the briefing.

The general was in his office surfing the web when Susan buzzed his intercom. "Yes Mam?" the general questioned. He knew it could only be one thing. "Sir, Sergeant Lopez is here to see you."

"Send her in." In a moment, the office door opened and Master Sergeant J.R. Lopez stepped into the office, walked smartly to front of the desk, popped a sharp salute, and reported in.

"Sir, Sergeant Lopez reporting as ordered." General Evantoe watched the woman as she entered the office. He was impressed with her military bearing and professionalism. He returned the salute and asked the sergeant to have a seat.

"I'll dispense with the bullshit. You have an idea of why you're here. I'm here to tell you if anyone you run across gives you too much trouble and they wear the uniform of the United States or any other allied uniform, I want to know everything about the incident and I can assure you the situation will be solved. I don't like drugs and I won't tolerate them in my command. If the contractors at Khamis are putting our aviators at risk, I want it stopped, and I want it stopped NOW!" he stressed as he slapped his hand on the desk for emphasis.

Very impressive show of force J.R. thought as she pondered her response. The general continued.

"You were requested because we have some very big fish to fry in Riyadh and at this time I can't afford to send any of my agents to Khamis to end this shit smoking fiasco. You've the lead and when you conclude your business, and I stress when, not if, you'll receive the accolades deserved."

J.R. told the general she wasn't looking for accolades. She explained how the rank of Master Sergeant was chosen so she would outrank the current administrator at Khamis. She would be able to fit in better if it appeared she was there to lend some leadership to the detachment's administrative function. When they finished with the question and answer period, the general got up from the desk and asked J.R. to follow him into the conference room.

As the door opened, the trio of agents rose from the chairs around the conference table. "Agent Lopez, I'd like you to meet my two agents and the specially assigned agent working the other case I mentioned a moment ago. This is Agent William Kingston," William stepped over and shook J.R.'s hand.

"This is Agent Karl Phobie," Karl waved from the other side of the table.

"And finally, Agent Dillon Reece." There was no sense of recognition from either Dillon or J.R.

"Gentlemen," J.R. greeted as she pulled out a seat next to William. The general strode to the end of the table where Dillon was still standing. "Get this thing off the ground as soon as you can so we can concentrate on the bigger problem. Remember, you have my full support." The general then returned to his office and shut the connecting door.

"Shall we take our seats?" Dillon asked as he pulled out the high back chair used by the general during meetings. Dillon took the lead as he explained the situation to J.R. Since he was in Kingdom because of another case, he would let Karl be the focal point for all activities. He would naturally be available for consultations should the need arise.

The discussion was a lively one after Dillon finished. J.R. had questions about personnel and how aggressive she could be with Erpack. Dillon gave her those directions. Karl and William filled her in on the chain of command in the Boeing organization. Their efforts to gather important information about the subjects paid dividends.

Abercrom, a retired Air Force colonel, was a card-carrying member of what technicians in the program called "The Colonel's Club". Before Boeing bought McDonnell Douglas, thus acquiring McDonnell Douglas (MDS) services, MDS was very partial to hiring colonels as they retired from the active rolls. They used their contacts to gloss over some of the problems a large manufacturing company might face with their complex product. Abercrom originally hired into the Kingdom with another company and was let go for one reason or another. He secured the manager's spot by knowing other club members holding positions of authority in the Boeing hierarchy.

When the team read the information sheet on Abercrom, Karl wondered aloud how the man ever made colonel. He didn't have the right credentials for anything. Then the connection was made. He was married to the former Sally Ann Kutchins, daughter of a past Air Force Chief of Staff, General Leon W. Kutchins. If his sponsor was that high in the food chain and he didn't make star rank, he was really a screw up. A sponsor guarantees you stardom unless you're such a pitiful manager the sponsor can't protect you from your own ineptness.

Oswald Booker was an Army reject from copters. He came into the kingdom as a mechanic on the newest McDonnell Douglas helicopters sold to the Saudi ground forces. He worked along the Iraqi border but lost his job when they transferred routine maintenance on the aircraft to another company. Again, because of connections, he was able to secure a spot in the wide wonderful world of Human Resources. He floundered around at various locations staying one-step ahead of a pink slip. One finally caught up with him in Riyadh at a headquarters position. He stepped on his crank too many times for the Saudis to ignore and they changed his position to a Saudi national. Once again, through some devious methods, he wormed his way into the "manager" position at Khamis. No one seemed to care he didn't have a shred of qualification for the job. The only people who really did something about it were the staff and they voted with their feet. Every one left for other positions rather than face Oswald and his incompetence.

The last member of the troika under heavy discussion was a man referred to as the Maintenance Superintendent. According to what they could find on the man, the Saudis liked him, thus his position of "authority". He was a retired enlisted man who spent his entire career in munitions. He worked in the Kingdom since the Peace program began. Learning the system quickly, he was able to move from position to position until he was the only one left standing after a rather vicious round of cost cutting and position elimination. J.R. would be able to use him for leads into problem children within the maintenance complex. Most of the information they gathered concerned his foreign-born wife. She was reputed to be the madam of a high-class ring of "wives" serving as prostitutes for the local workers and Saudis. Since this was not part of the problem, it was just an interesting side road J.R. may be able to exploit to her advantage.

Once the round table discussion of key players was finished, the four investigators adjourned to the dining facility for some dinner and conversation about things other than criminals and crimes. When dinner was over, Karl offered to take J.R. to her villa. William excused himself to head back for the office and Dillon told the group he was going to visit with the general for a while and then retire for the evening.

Dillon's discussion with the general went very well. He wasn't subjected to one of the general's tirades about the Saudis or their way of life. Dillon was thankful. He returned to his villa, showered, slipped into his robe, poured himself a glass of single malt, and settled on the couch for some television. After a few minutes of relaxing, there was a knock at the front door. Dillon wondered who it might be as he rose from the couch and meandered to the door. Knowing William, Dillon surmised the determined agent discovered something during his time in the office after dinner and just wanted to get Dillon's spin on the problem. Dillon was surprised to find J.R. standing on his threshold as he opened the door.

"Good evening," Dillon began. "This is an unexpected surprise."

"Unexpected?" J.R. asked. "You didn't think I was going to leave the area without some time to catch up on happenings in your life did you?"

"I had my doubts," Dillon replied. "Please, come in," he asked as he stepped out of the way. "After our last meeting I wasn't sure how you wanted to handle the situation. I was going to let you set the standard, like you always do, and I would just follow your lead."

"When I came into the room and saw you at the end of the table, my heart skipped a beat. Why didn't you contact me after Panama?"

"I could be asking the same thing," Dillon responded as he walked over to the cabinet where he kept his rations. "Can I get you a drink?"

"Please," she replied.

"Still on the same, Vodka neat with a twist?"

"How gallant of you to remember. That will do nicely, thanks." Dillon retrieved a glass from the shelf above the cabinet and poured three fingers of Vodka into the glass. He reached for the lemon he purchased earlier and scrapped a bit of the rind into the glass.

"You just happened to have a lemon in the cabinet?" J.R. asked tilting her head in a questioning manner.

"Let's just say I'm always prepared for contingencies," Dillon responded as he came across the room to where J.R. sat on the couch. Dillon picked up his glass from the side table and proposed a toast. "To successful investigations and renewed friendships." They touched glasses and sipped their beverages.

"I see you're still taking the same poison. Single malt?"

"Right you are. I was surprised to find an ample supply of the nectar when I arrived in Kingdom. They have some local brews and stouter mixtures but that's another story. Let's begin with your tale and then if I'm totally satisfied, I'll fill you in on my life."

J.R. began at the end of their past relationship. She explained how her next assignment was a deep cover job in Peru. She didn't want to involve Dillon because after having worked with him on the Panama situation, she felt he would be worried about her safety if he knew anything about the investigation. She opted instead for a disappearing act and possible reconciliation after she came out of the project. When it was all over, additional projects immediately cropped up and she honestly didn't have a free moment before going back into another investigation. As she was telling Dillon the broad story about her activities, she'd moved closer to his side of the couch. When she finished, she took his hand in both of hers, raised it to her lips, and gently kissed the back of each finger.

She looked at him and asked, "Am I forgiven?"

Dillon hesitated for a moment before making a sweeping move off the couch. "Another drink?" he asked as he walked briskly to the cabinet.

J.R. came over and threw her arms around his neck. "I had no choice but to take the path of keeping you in the dark about my activities. After working with you and making love to you, I didn't want to put any pressure on you by having to worry about where I was or what I was doing."

She took her arms from around his neck and dropped them to the tie on his robe. She pulled it free and embraced his nakedness. She looked up and welcomed his lips to hers. After a long passionate kiss, she pulled back and unbuttoned her skirt. She let it drop to the floor revealing her well-sculptured legs. The oversized shirt she wore covered her thighs. She slowly undid the buttons and pulled it off her shoulders letting it drop to the floor behind her. There she stood in all her Latino loveliness. She was even more striking than Dillon remembered. He reached out and swept her up in his arms. He kissed her forehead as he turned toward the bedroom. He laid her gently on the bed, turned on the bedside lamp, and pulled the robe from his shoulders.

"All is forgiven", was all he said as he came to her. Their lovemaking was as exciting as he remembered. J.R. was thrilling and Dillon knew some of her secret passions.

Dillon opened his eyes to see the display on his bedside clock indicating the time as 0200. He rolled from his side of the bed to embrace J.R. There was no one there. He sat up in bed and called her name. There was no answer. He threw back the covers and was about to get out of bed when J.R. came back into the bedroom holding a sandwich in one hand and a soda in the other. She finished chewing the bite of sandwich already in her mouth, held out the snack toward Dillon, and asked, "Wanna bite?"

"I certainly do but not of the sandwich." She came close enough to the bedside for him to reach out and pull her close. He pressed his face against her warm stomach and playfully chewed on her tanned skin.

"Enough already," she protested as she gently tapped him on the head with the soda can. "Let's save some of this passion for after we solve the cases at hand. You do remember how much fun celebratory sex is between us." Dillon held the cheeks of her buttocks as he leaned his head back.

"Oh yeah, I remember. Our celebration is when we have wonderful sex and I wake up in an empty bed. How exciting. I can HARDLY wait." He squeezed her backside as she pulled away from his grip.

"You don't keep much around here in the way of snack food."

"Most of the stuff I buy is specifically chosen for special purpose events. Like a lemon." he laughed getting up from the bed. He headed for the doorway and the kitchen. J.R. obliged the show with a catcall whistle as he flexed his backside while leaving the bedroom. Dillon pulled a small bottle of water out of a case he kept near the fridge. He unscrewed the cap, threw it into the trashcan and was about to head back for the bedroom when J.R. came down the hall to the living room.

"Leaving so soon?" he asked as she picked up her blouse, slipped it on and began to button it.

"Sorry stud muffin. I have to meet my minders this morning and I would like to appear as having gotten a bit of sleep. It also wouldn't look too good if I'm seen by either of them coming out of your place just before breakfast!"

"Karl is aware I knew you in the past but he doesn't know anymore than we worked together."

"Even more reason to keep our distance right now. I don't want him to think you enlisted my assistance so you could satisfy your carnal needs in a less than hospitable sexual environment for a single male. You're still single, aren't you?"

"J.R.! Do you believe I would be unfaithful to a spouse?"

"Just checking the ethics button," she laughed. "I remember the questions you strategically asked me before we made love the first time. I'm glad to see there is one knight in shining armor left in this futile world."

294

"At your service," he vowed with a sweeping bow. He set the water on the coffee table as J.R. was slipping on her shoes. He cradled her face in his hands and gently kissed the tip of her nose.

"It is really good to see you again. Not only for the GREAT SEX but also for knowing you're safe and alive. You always drifted in and out of my thoughts. When I would go looking for you, even using my official capacity, your cover stories were always so tight no one seemed to have any idea of your existence."

"I'm alive and well, thank you very much." She reached around, grabbed his butt, and pressed herself against him. They kissed and without another word between them, she pushed away, turned to the front door, and was gone into the early morning darkness. Dillon walked to the front window and watched her walk down the street toward her villa. He certainly WAS glad she was alive and well.

CHAPTER THIRTY-SIX

"McDonalds, you want to meet at McDonalds?" Sidney gasped. "I was hoping for something a little more exotic."

"Sorry," Randy lied. "I just want to get on the road and Macs is definitely the quickest."

"I hope Carl protests!"

"Don't hope too much. I've already called him and he's going to meet us there. We'll leave your car and his car in the parking lot. I checked out a staff car so we could be on the road early. Meet you there at 0500", Randy finalized as he hung up before Sidney could catch his breath for another round of protests. Sid resigned himself to the fact of breakfast at McDonalds.

The next morning was a bright one. As the sun rose slowly over the Coast Mountains it began to burn off the ground fog that clings to the coastline on cool mornings. Sidney, Carl, and Randy rendezvoused at the undignified hour, downed a quick meal, and headed south. Sidney scouted another route to the area that saved them some time. They would arrive in ample time for their meeting with the bank president, the bank's legal team, and the Crimitin's.

William took the day off so he could be at the bank with the Air Force team and Sarah. When Carl called and told them the time, William was concerned about trouble from the people watching their house. Carl listened and after giving William a rough assurance all would be well, he immediately called Sidney to confirm everything was prearranged and they didn't have to worry about problems from the other side. Sidney couldn't give him that assurance. In fact, he told him they expected trouble and if he wanted to stay away, he was well within his rights. Carl said he would be with them all the way.

"William," Sarah shouted down the hall from the living room. "Are you ready yet? If you don't shake it, we're going to be late and you know how I hate to be late for an appointment."

"I'm coming," William responded as he came out of their bedroom with one arm in his jacket sleeve.

"I still don't see why I've to wear this stupid tie. I'm not going to be a banker; I'm just going to see a banker."

"Quit your bitchen," Sarah admonished. "I don't want you lookin like a slob. Just do this for me. We can only hope this visit to the bank will be an end to our loss. We won't have to worry about being watched and harassed."

She turned from the window to look at her husband. She had picked the clothes and laid them out on her side of the bed. William slept until Sarah was finished in the bathroom. She woke him with a cup of coffee and toast. She took the same snack in the living room as he showered and started to get ready.

"You look wonderful," Sarah praised as she adjusted the knot in William's striped tie. "Let's get going."

Sarah and William went out the back door after saying good-by to Herman. George already left for school. They pulled out of the drive and headed down the cul-de-sac toward the connecting street. They made the left turn on their way toward Azusa Avenue. The occupants of the SUV hunkered down when they saw the Crimitin family car pull out of their drive. They watched them head for the main street leading out of the housing development. When there was sufficient distance between them, they followed.

Using the new shortcut to Covina reduced their drive time. The Air Force team arrived well ahead of their appointment. Fortunately, or unfortunately depending on your point of view, there was a *Denny's* located directly across the street from the First National Bank of Covina. With their approach from the east, they were on the right side of the divided highway to access the parking lot. The three men decided to wait for their appointment in the comfort of a booth where they could watch for the Crimitin's arrival. Sidney was very pleased with the decision. He enjoyed the never empty pot of coffee offered by the establishment and he could wolf down a modified Grand Slam breakfast. As it turned out, there was sufficient time to finish eating and go through two pots of coffee before their appointment time and the arrival of the Crimitin's.

"There they are," Sidney said as he stood up from the booth. "You two head over and I'll pay the check."

He waited for a protest but received none. The men decided to leave their car in the parking lot and make their way by jaywalking across the four-lane highway to the bank. They were going to take their time getting back to Vandenberg, so access to Interstate 10 would be easier from their current side of the street.

Randy and Carl left the building and crossed to the bank's parking lot. As Sidney came out the front door after paying the bill, he noticed two men arguing in the parking lot. One of them was inside an SUV and the other was standing on the passenger side stressing some point to the other man. When Sidney came out, the man inside the truck saw him and waved his hand in front of the other man's face. The shouting stopped. Sidney thought this a bit unusual but didn't put anything to it other than they didn't want strangers to be a part of their dispute. He made his way across the street and into the bank.

Randy, Carl, Sarah, and William sat in a small reception area on the right side of the bank entrance. A decorative silver tray sat on a small table between them with a hot pot, cups, creamer, sugar, and sweetener. The receptionist came over and offered Sidney a cup of coffee but he declined.

The intercom on the receptionist desk buzzed. The manager requested the groups' presence. Donald Holtz was standing beside his desk as they filed into his office. He greeted each one with his name and listened as they returned the favor. He returned to his chair after everyone took a seat on the couch, love seat or in one of the chairs situated in front of his desk. Before he sat down, he turned to the man standing in front of a chair near the manager's computer table.

"If I might introduce the bank's legal advisor, Martin Lowenbac. Could I have a copy of the court order?"

As the words came out of the manager's mouth, Sidney was excusing himself as he stepped out of the office into the reception area. He left his case near Sarah's chair while they were waiting. As he came out of the office, he noticed the man who was arguing with the driver of the SUV sitting at the new accounts desk across the lobby. He noticed him because he wore a windbreaker with "Los Angeles Rams" emblazoned across the back and down one sleeve. Since the Rams were now in St. Louis, it was something he noticed. He retrieved the case from next to the chair and returned to the office.

Sitting the case on the table, he dialed the combination, pulled open the top, and withdrew two copies of the document from a folder marked, "Court Order". He already gave a copy to the Crimitin family. Both bank authorities took a moment to scan the document before making any comment. The lawyer was first to speak.

"Of course we'll want to make an itemized listing of the contents," he said as he sat the papers on a corner of Holtz's desk.

"We have no problem," Randy commented. "We want to make this as simple as possible for the family." He looked over and nodded to Sarah.

"If there are no further comments, let's go to the vault and open the box," the legal advisor said.

Holtz rose from his black leather high back swivel chair and led the group across the lobby to a short hallway leading to a secured gate. Inside the gate were two cubicles on either side of a small anteroom. Entrance to each cubicle was near another locked gate allowing access to the rows of safety deposit boxes arranged along the walls and down the center of the room. At each end of the center row of boxes, sat a small metal table for customers who didn't need the privacy of the cubicles to view their treasures.

Randy watched Donald put the passkey into the bottom lock on box 4694 and turn it 180 degrees to the left. He stepped up to the box and inserted Crimitin's key into the top position and rotated the key 180 degrees to the right. The lock clicked freeing the box from his position along the wall. Randy pulled the long narrow box out and turned to set it on the metal table directly behind him.

"Sarah, William, would you be so kind," he asked stepping out of the way. Sarah and William came closer to the table. They paused before lifting the lid. William's hand was visibly shaking as he brought the lid from its resting place on the box to an upright position leaning against the wall of the boxes along the center row. Everyone leaned in for a better look.

"Well an inventory won't be a problem," Sidney quipped. Inside the box was a white legal sized envelope with a large ornate wax seal with the letter "C" prominently displayed in the deep red wax securing the flap.

"May I?" Sidney asked Sarah and William. Both parents stepped back as Sidney slipped on a pair of gloves and reached into the box gripping the envelope by one corner. He laid it on the metal table with the seal side down.

The envelope, addressed to Sarah and William Crimitin, was a standard legal size holder. Again, Sidney asked permission before attempting to open the seal. He pulled a letter opener from his case and slipped it into the small opening at the corner of the flap. He slit the envelope in one quick move. He dropped the opener back into his case and pulled open the envelope. Inside was a folded piece of paper and a key. He removed the paper, leaving the key inside, unfolded it and began to read the hand written words.

"Dear Mom and Dad," he stopped and held the letter toward Sarah. She hesitated before reaching for the note. She held it at arms length so she could read without her glasses. William looked over her shoulder as they both read the note in silence. When they finished she gave the note back to Sidney. Tears were brimming up in her eyes as she turned to William, put her arms around his waist, and buried her face in his chest.

"Ok for the record," Randy said as pulled a micro recorder out of his coat pocket, flicked the unit on, and looked to Sidney for comments.

"The safe deposit box contained one wax sealed envelope addressed to William and Sarah Crimitin. Inside the envelope was a note to Mom and Dad and a key with no apparent markings. Contents of the note unknown at this time. Since the contents don't affect the bank or its responsibility toward their client, the investigative team will read the letter later. Witness the letter was given back to Special Agent Moankat by Sarah Crimitin."

Randy looked to the Crimitin's for comment and then to the bank manager, legal advisor, Carl and Sidney. With no comments from anyone, he asked Sidney to bag the envelope, the key, and the note in separate evidence bags. Sidney complied and placed the bags into his case. The safe deposit box was returned to its position in the wall with the keys removed in reverse order from its opening. Randy took his key and returned it to its evidence bag. He dropped it into Sidney's case. He looked toward Sarah to see if she'd regained her composure. She was dabbing the tears from her eyes with the end of William's tie. William put his arm around her shoulder as the group began to file out of the secure room. They went down the short hallway, across the lobby and back into the manager's office.

Randy asked if the bank wanted to have the tape-recorded message given to them now or could they wait for a full transcript of their visit within the week. Donald said he had no problem with receiving a full report if the legal aspects satisfied the lawyer. Martin agreed to the arrangement. Everyone exchanged farewells as the Air Force team and the Crimitin family left the bank.

Once outside they talked for a while about what was going to happen with the letter. Since Sarah and William were the only ones to read the note, they told the investigators and Carl what it contained. Briefly, it was a note to say goodbye. William knew if someone other than himself was reading the note, he ran into some trouble.

Sarah told the men her son said goodbye in the note. He hoped he hadn't caused them too much trouble and his efforts to help keep his brother in treatment paid dividends. The note was undated so they couldn't tie it to one particular visit from their son. As they told the investigators before, he hadn't been home too many times since he joined the Force.

"We can tie that down by checking the bank records on when he rented the box. They'll also have a record in the vault when he made access. That won't be a problem," Randy said. "They'll know exactly when he put the note in the box. That may correlate to other happenings in Germany."

"One unusual thing," Sarah began. "There are some letters under his signature. I don't recognize them at all. I thought they might be x's and o's for kisses and hugs because by the time I got to the bottom of the note my eyes were tearing so much I could hardly read."

"You're right," William agreed. "I saw them too but they just didn't sink in as anything."

"Well let's take a look," Sidney said as he put the case on the hood of Crimitin's car, dialed in the combination, and opened the case. He pulled the evidence bag with the note out and turned it over so they could see the written portion. Before putting the note in the bag, they opened it so it could be read without having to handle the document.

At the bottom of the page, directly under the signature, were the letters RNZOANW. Sarah and William again stated the letters meant nothing to them. It wasn't a family code or the initials of family members. Carl said he used to sign his notes with KYWAY for "keep your wits about you". Randy chipped in with TTFN or "Ta Ta For Now". None of them could come up with anything for the unusual combination.

"Let me write them down for you and if you come up with anything, give us a call," Sidney said as he pulled one of his business cards out of the brass holder he carried. He jotted the letters down on the back of the card and gave it to Sarah.

"If you come up with an idea call any of the numbers on the card. There's even a toll free number to the office."

Sarah and William thanked the men for all their work. "Remember," Randy said. "You're still being watched. Keep us informed if you're harassed any more. These guys are going to make a mistake soon and we'll be able to get the authorities to provide some relief. Until they make that mistake, there's not much we can do. I don't expect them to harm anyone in your family but we have to be careful with the information you've access too. That's why we took the precaution of telling you about this meeting at the last moment. Don't want to give them anything more than we have too. I expect they're watching us right now."

Randy was correct about being watched. From the same booth the Air Force team occupied earlier, the two men from the SUV were carefully observing the meeting in the parking lot. They paid particular attention when the evidence bag came out of the case. "There's the pay dirt," one of them said. "We need that bag for the boss."

"Thanks for coming," Sarah said to Carl as she reached for his hand. "You've been wonderful through this whole ordeal."

"You're more than welcome," Carl replied as he held her small hand in both of his.

"Make sure you keep me posted of any problems. I've a direct line to these guys and we can help solve any problem you might encounter." He went to the passenger side of their car and opened the door. William was already taking his place behind the steering wheel as Sarah got in.

William and Sarah pulled out of the parking lot and headed up 39 toward their home. Carl, Randy, and Sidney waved goodbye from the curb. The next test was getting across the street without being hit. When they made it to the center divider, Sidney suggested a visit to the restaurant for lunch.

"I've got a much better place to stop," Randy said. "I know a place in El Monte that serves the best homemade Mexican food this side of Mexico City."

"That's a pretty tall boast," Carl chided as they made their way to the car. "I happen to be an expert on Tex-Mex and a wide variety of California styles. Let me be the judge of quality."

"Care to make this interesting if it isn't the best Mex food you've ever eaten?"

"No problem. Let's keep the wager in the food category. If this doesn't measure up, I'll buy lunch and then treat all of us to dinner at that new seafood place on the docks." Sidney liked this kind of wagering. He let Carl and Randy battle it out and he got a free lunch and dinner out of the deal.

The men got into the staff car and headed toward Interstate 10. They merged into the light traffic and took a spot in the center lane. They talked about the morning activities and the need to have the unusual letters investigated for meaning. When they got back to the office, they would send a note to Germany and Saudi. It was better to have more than one brain working a problem and they all agreed this might have some significance.

After a few minutes of travel, Randy started edging toward the right lane and the exit for El Monte. As they came to the signal light at the bottom of the exit ramp, Randy slowed to make a right turn. As he did, the trio felt a bump at the rear of the car. Nothing serious, there was no crashing glass or violent movement of the car. The men all turned to see who hit them and saw a rather large SUV. Sidney immediately recognized the truck as the one from the restaurant parking lot. He leaned over to see the passenger and sure enough, it was the same guy who argued with the driver and came in the bank.

"Randy," Sidney gasped as he reached over and tapped on the center console. "They didn't damage our mobility did they?"

"I don't think so," Randy responded.

"Then trust me on this, floor this puppy and get us back on the freeway." Since Randy only put the car in park without stopping the engine, he dropped the gearshift into drive and smashed the accelerator. The passenger opened the door of the truck and used the widow sill to steady a very large bore pistol at the retreating sedan. Luckily, for the Air Force team there wasn't any traffic in the intersection between them and the freeway entrance on the other side. The squealing tires created a trail of smoke helping prevent the shooter from getting a clear shot. None of the men knew how many shots he took but one of them shattered the back window showering minuet chunks of laminated glass into the back seat.

"You Ok?" Sidney yelled to Carl over the noise of the accelerating engine and windblast coming through the shattered window.

"Just scared shitless," was the reply from the hunkered down maintainer on the floor of the back seat. Sidney told Carl to stay low as he ventured a look out the empty window frame to see their adversaries were not going to give up easily. They too were on their way up the ramp.

Neither of the agents drew a weapon from the armory for this routine trip. Since the vehicle was from the motor pool neither of the men carried a personal weapon with them either. They were out gunned and out powered. The economical sedan would be no match for the speed of the new SUV. Randy would have to rely on his high-speed chase training to elude the pursuing bad guys.

Randy put the training to good use as he weaved his way through the lanes of traffic. The volume of vehicles was increasing as they approached the downtown interchanges. This maze of concrete overpasses and underpasses was confusing to motorists on a good day. It was doubly disconcerting when being pursued. Randy continued to weave and dodge preventing the larger truck from getting along side for a close in shot or a forcible removal from the freeway with a well-placed ram using the trucks large bumpers.

"Where are the Chippies when you need them?" Sidney asked as they rounded a sharp curve and headed along the breakdown lane to stay ahead and out of range. Just as the words came out of his mouth, he shouted again, "Eureka! See the flashing lights?"

"Sorry Sid but I'm a bit occupied at the moment!" Randy was too busy watching the rear view mirror and approaching traffic to see the flashing lights on the right side of the roadway. They were now traveling in the center of a six-lane stretch of freeway heading toward Santa Monica.

"Get over to the right. There's a traffic stop up ahead," Sidney told Randy as he began to maneuver his way toward the right lane and the welcome flashing lights.

The occupants of the SUV also saw the flashing lights and when Randy made a move to the right, they made a move to the left in order to avoid any assistance the Air Force trio was going to obtain from the highway patrol officer. Randy noticed the SUV was not making the same moves. He slowed down and as he passed the patrol car and traffic offender, he slammed on the brakes and slid to a stop.

The officer was crouched down on the passenger side of the other car as the sedan sped past their position. Sidney was first out. He sprinted toward the officer who stood up and put her hand on the butt of her pistol.

Still in his dress blues, Sidney slowed his approach. "Officer, we have just been shot at and pursued by a dark blue Ford Explorer. He's still on the freeway headed toward the beach. We need your help."

By this time, Randy was out inspecting the damage done to the rear of the car. The patrol officer gave the speeding offender a break by telling him to slow down as she let him leave. "Did you happen to get a license number on the truck?"

"No officer, I'm afraid I didn't," Sidney replied as he turned and called out to Randy.

"Randy did you happen to catch the license plate during the high speed chase?" he asked with a bit of sarcasm in his voice.

"Sorry Sid, I was a little busy to take notes." As he turned back to his survey of the damage, he heard a voice from the back seat.

Carl peered over the glass covered rear deck and out the shattered window. "I got a partial on the license plate," he said.

They spent the rest of the afternoon filling out reports with the CHP and hoping they would call in with a pickup on the SUV. However, even with a partial on the plate, they weren't able to put anything together. It would take some time to get a listing of the vehicles and be able to eliminate the ones not fitting the description. It was late evening when they finally finished the required paperwork. Sidney was first to remind the others they missed the Mexican feast Randy promised.

"I just don't see how you do it," Randy laughed. "Food is foremost on your mind and you weigh nothing. Wish I had your metabolism."

"That's not true. My dedication to God and country is always at the forefront of my life," Sidney replied with a smile as he placed his hand over his heart in a mock salute. Randy pushed him off the curb and suggested they grab a steak at the Western style restaurant across from the CHP offices. The men strolled to the entrance and a bit of relaxation after an excitement-filled afternoon.

CHAPTER THIRTY-SEVEN

Klaus retrieved the coffee cup from its spot next to the edge of the wooden tabletop where Budmere placed it after banging it on the sugar bowl to get Klaus' attention for a refill. Steam rose from the hot coffee as Klaus poured another cup for the investigator. His partner requested and received breakfast in her room. Budmere pulled off a corner of his toast and swiped it through the egg yellow quickly coagulating on his plate in the cold air. With no thanks given, Klaus left the table and went back to the small kitchen adjacent to his office. He hoped whatever business the two people had in town, they would quickly complete their tasks and be on their way. He couldn't remember a time he met such a disagreeable person.

Budmere was just about to bang on the sugar for another refill when Cathy came into the room. "Christina called. She's on her way off base. She said she'd meet us at the house. She talked with the landlady yesterday evening and told her we would be coming over this morning."

There was no reply from Budmere. He just nodded his head. He picked up his knife and scrapped the remaining cream cheese from the corner of its foil wrapper, spreading it on his last bite of sweet roll. He popped it into his mouth and without a word, got up from the table and headed for the door. Klaus stuck his head into the room and said good-bye to Cathy as she followed Mr. Personality to the car.

The drive to Kottweiller was a quiet one. Cathy admired the fields still covered with a light ground fog. They made their turn up the hill and pulled in front of the house. Budmere got out and went around to the trunk where he pulled one of his kits from its spot, shut the lid, laid the case on the closed trunk, and began an inventory of the items neatly arranged inside the case. It wasn't more than five minutes before Christina pulled around the corner, passed by Budmere and parked in front of the driveway. Cathy got out and went to greet Christina as she came up the walkway.

"Morning Agent Baker," Christina cheerfully greeted the lead investigator. He barely looked up over the top of his open case.

"Let's go see Helga," Christina whispered as she led the way to the front door.

Helga unlatched the door without answering the bell. When Christina and Cathy entered, she was coming out of her door to meet them. Christina introduced Cathy and told Helga there was a very grouchy man coming to join them. Helga just shook her head in an understanding way as she led them up stairs. They propped the front door open so Budmere could get in without having to ring the bell. He came into the apartment about five minutes after the women gained access. Christina explained the layout of the place and then excused herself as she followed Helga downstairs.

"I'll give you a call later today just in case our friend gives you any trouble," she assured Helga.

Christina rolled down her windows and returned to the base via one of the back roads so she could enjoy the sights and smells of morning in Germany. When she got back to the office, she stopped by Bill's compartment to tell him she was back. He asked her to come in and look at a curious message from the boys in California. She took the printed e-mail and leaned against the credenza as she read about the gunplay and unusual letters on the letter discovered at the bank.

Bill picked up his coffee cup and headed for the door. "Coffee?" he offered. Christina affirmatively nodded her head as she continued to read the note.

When Bill returned, Christina moved to one of the chairs in front of his desk. "Well," she began. "It looks like things are beginning to heat up. This is some serious shit." She raised her coffee cup slightly in a thankful manner to Bill.

"That's an astute observation." Bill laughed. "Heating up is a mild way to describe what happened. I'm just glad no one was hurt. I sure hope they find the guys who created the excitement. We might be able to get some information about the operation over here."

"What do you make of this?" Christina asked as she handed the note back to Bill.

"I haven't got a clue. Some type of anagram would be my first guess. It could be the initials of something over here. The possibilities are immense. Dillon got a copy of this note too. I'll give him a call and see if he's working a solution. With his luck, he probably took one look at the letters and put it all together."

"He's that type," Christina agreed as she left Bill's office for her own.

Bill picked up the secure line and pushed the speed dial for Riyadh. First, he connected to Dillon's home phone, then office phone but he never did connect for a conversation.

⁂

"We got a call at the station telling us about a car fire in an alleyway between the warehouses on 52nd street. We responded and found this truck fully engaged. We knocked down the fire, prevented the spread to adjacent buildings, and then began to mop up. When we were checking for hotspots on the truck, we found the remains. Since the police backup hadn't arrived, we called for some assistance." The fire chief concluded as he turned away from the Harbor Division detective to check on the close down operations.

With a car fire, there's always the possibility of explosion and spread. He responded to the call with three of the four vehicles from his station. He would leave one pumper at the scene while the rest of the trucks would return home and go back on status.

"You got any more questions for me detective?" the chief asked as he started to back away toward his truck.

"Not now chief. This comes into our arena now. As soon as we get the coroner out here and the truck picked up, I'll send your guys back to work." Detective Jose Gonzales said with a wave of his hand in a farewell gesture.

Jose walked to where the back of the truck was opened during mop up operations. Inside were two badly burned bodies. It appears they were wrapped or covered with heavy plastic sheeting. Melted plastic covered the charred remains. The smell was offensive. Jose covered his nose and mouth with his handkerchief as he surveyed the scene. He walked around the vehicle to see if there were any other bits of interesting evidence available for his use.

As he approached the passenger's side door, he reached to pull the handle. Before he could touch it, he felt the heat still radiating from the metal. He called one of the firefighters to open the door with a gloved hand. Jose peered at the interior of the vehicle. Noticing the keys were still in the ignition, he mentally put things in order. Killed in another location. Wrapped in plastic to prevent bodily fluids from leaving evidence. Driven to a location some distance from the scene of the murders. Set on fire to hinder the investigation. Typical gang tactics. He would enlist the help of his fellow detectives in the gang section of LA's police force to see if there were any wars pending or happening.

If this were gang related, it was a damn serious sign, he thought as he came around front of the truck. Thank goodness for the raised letters on

California license plates. Even with the paint burned off the plate, Jose was able to read the numbers. He was just finishing his inspection when the coroner's van pulled up.

The driver got out and came over to Jose. "Aw shit Jose, not crispy critters. If I'd known they was crispy, I'd given this to someone else. You know how I hate crispy critters. They leak all over the place and most the time fall apart before we gets them back to the doc."

As the man was complaining, Jose motioned him to follow toward the back of the truck. As they approached the doors, the smell became stronger.

"Dat's another thing. Dey always smells like shit."

"Are you done bitchen?" Jose asked Leroy Wilkerson, senior coroner's aid for the county of Los Angeles.

Leroy just stood in silence looking at the coming task. His partner, Billie Thorndike, or Little Bill as he was affectionately known, came around back of the truck pulling two gurneys.

"Odds and evens for who gets to climb inside," Billie said.

"Don't give me that crap," Leroy shot back. "You know damn good and well you can't get your huge white ass into the back of that truck. I gets the honor of pushing them out the back. Man I hate this part of the job. Why couldn't they just stuff them in a dumpster in one piece?"

Leroy went back to their truck to get coveralls and gloves for both of them. When he came back, they set about the nasty task of transferring the corpses from their location in the burned out truck to the gurneys. Once they made sure they hadn't left any bits and pieces in the back of the truck, they put the remains in their van and left for the coroner's office.

As they were about to leave, Jose reached one of his cards toward Leroy. "Man you don't have to give me another one of your cards. I gots your number memorized. You're by far my best customer. I'll make sure the doc gives you a call as soon as he determines the cause of death. I'll bet you dimes to donuts it wasn't smoke inhalation!"

Jose just laughed as the van left the alley. He was walking to his car when the police wrecker arrived. It was one of those with a lifting device to hoist the remains of the truck on to the flat bed of the wrecker. They would take the truck to a central forensics lab for analysis. This time when he handed the driver one of his cards, the man took it. He never dealt with Gonzales before so the card would come in handy when the specialists got finished with their investigation.

Jose walked back to his car and pulled a panatela out of the glove compartment. Just another day, just another homicide.

CHAPTER THIRTY-EIGHT

Dillon hung his towel over the doorknob as he came out of the bathroom. Still having to shave, deodorize, and apply what he referred to as smelly stuff, he padded his nakedness down the hall to the front room. He wanted to give Carmen a reconfirmation call before going into his final preparations. Just as he was about to pick up the phone and dial, it rang. Magic, he thought. Perhaps his cosmic thoughts about Carmen registered with her on the other side of town and she was connecting with him. That couldn't be, he never gave her his number. He picked up the receiver, "Dillon here".

"Dillon, William. Just wanted to make sure you didn't need an escort tonight. This will be your first time on the road and Karl doesn't want you to get lost."

"Thanks for the vote of confidence," Dillon replied. "I'm pretty sure I can handle the directions but it may be a good idea to have you in the area. Let me put some thoughts together and I'll give you a call before I leave."

"Fine with me," William agreed. Dillon pressed the flash button and waited for the dial tone. He checked the number on the business card and pressed the touch pad. After two rings, Carmen answered. "Hello."

"Carmen, this is Dillon. Just wanted to make sure we're still on for tonight. Hope you haven't been called in to work?"

"As a matter of fact, they did want me to come in tonight but I was able to talk my way out. It always helps to have a couple of deep dark secrets on the head nurse." She laughed.

"Sounds exciting. Anything I would be interesting in learning?"

"Not unless you're keen on dykey religious zealots. Maureen and I caught her providing special services for one of the younger nurses. Now don't get me wrong, she's one of the finest administrators I've ever worked with. She's just a little fruity in the confines of her own home. We were a little lit one night and came barging in her front door quite unannounced. We caught her and the new recruit in a very compromising position and I do mean position. I'll fill you in on details after dinner.

"I'll meet you at Lai Lai's about 8:30. I won't have my driver return. The only honorable thing you can do is provide an escort for me on the way home."

"One escort at your service," Dillon quipped as they said good-bye. He returned to the bathroom for a finish his preparations. Once he completed the routine, he called William. He'd decided it would be a good thing to have backup near by in case of a problem with Buzz. Since they both were to be escorted, Dillon didn't expect any problems but his sixth sense was picking up some contrary vibrations about Buzz and the real reason for this meeting.

"William, Dillon here. I'll take you up on your offer of accompaniment with one condition."

"And that condition is?" William asked.

"I get to lead the convoy. I'll show you two my sense of direction is as finely tuned as my typing speed."

"Excuse me?" William questioned. "Am I missing something?"

"Just pulling your chain my friend. What are you going to do while I'm enjoying dinner?"

"I'll be enjoying dinner too." William replied. "As in all restaurants, there's a family side and a single side. With the buffet style, both sides meet in the middle to serve themselves. When you're getting ready to go, come over to the single side and walk around like you're surveying the place. When I see you, I'll make my way back to the car."

"Carmen wants me to take her home, so that's where I'll be headed after dinner. I wouldn't expect any problems from Buzz after we leave the place."

"No problemo," William agreed. "Hope you have an interesting night with Carmen. From what you described after your first meeting, I'm looking forward to seeing her in person. Who knows, after you leave, there might be hope for little old me."

"Quit whining," Dillon scolded. "If you're good, I'll even put your name into contention. See ya in a while," and Dillon hung up. Just as he settled down with TV clicker in hand, the secure line began to flash. Mumbling under his breath, he went to the phone.

"Dillon here," knowing it was going to be a call from Germany.

"You're sure a hard man to find," Bill prodded. "Where you been all day?"

"Hither and yon, here and there. Just trying to stay one step ahead of your calls," Dillon shot back.

"Have you checked your e-mail lately? We got some information from the boys in California after they visited the bank. They ran into some trouble with a couple of thugs after they finished their business. Evidently, our adversaries are getting desperate. They took a few shots at the guys and then chased them damn near to Santa Monica."

"So what was in the box?"

"Nothing but a letter to his parents. However, at the bottom of the note, under his signature, were the letters RNZOANW. It didn't make any sense to the guys in California and it didn't make any sense to Crimitin's parents. It isn't a code they use between family members and it doesn't appear to be the initials of any organization he would be associated with."

Dillon grabbed a pencil from the Lazy Susan type apparatus he got as a special gift from one of the local bookstores. "The letters again were, RNZO...?"

"ANW," Bill completed. He paused while Dillon looked at the letters.

"Means nothing to me at this juncture but we're just beginning to put all we have into one neat pile. I'm on my way to meet the guy who has the drug connections in Kingdom. I think he's acting on orders from others. I'm going to play him along because we made some very interesting discoveries about his background. It'll come in very handy as we get to the short strokes of this investigation."

"Sounds like a short hair pull to me," Bill commented.

"That's exactly where we'll grab him when the time comes. Anything else for me?"

"NO. Just check your mail. I'll talk with ya later this week," and Bill cut the connection.

Dillon hung up and yanked the line from the back of the instrument. He pulled his laptop from the drawer and hooked up the communications line. He logged into the system and pulled up his mail. The note from California *was* very interesting. He stored the messages he wanted to print later in a file on his hard drive and deleted the others. He wasn't going to bother trying to decipher the letters right now. It was time to head for William's and the bright lights of the big city.

⚔

Jose pulled into an open parking spot at the rear of the division's building, put the sedan in park, and swung his bulky frame out of the car. His right

311

knee still gave him fits if he didn't keep it exercised on a regular basis. The bullet shattered kneecap almost cost him his career if it weren't for the strides made in sports medicine during the past few years. With a complete knee replacement, he was back to work in less than six months. However, he was still bothered by the injury because he didn't follow the doctor's orders by exercising and keeping his weight down. He managed to put on a few extra pounds during the intervening years. He pushed open the back door and strolled down the linoleum-covered hallway to the front of the building. Just on the other side of double swinging glass doors was the designated location for the desk sergeant. After pushing open one side, Juan looked for the man in charge.

"Needles on duty?" he asked the clerk sitting near the front desk.

"Yes sir," was the reply.

"I need to talk with him for a minute. Have him give me a call in my office."

Just as he finished his request, Kristo Pinneyman came through the front door. Kristo was a large man at more than six and a half feet tall and weighing more than 325 pounds. Unlike Juan, his weight was distributed proportionately across a barrel chest, biceps that strained the openings of his shirtsleeves and thighs requiring specially made pants to accommodate their bulk. He was the most intimidating member of the force and prided himself on his ability to take control of front desk situations that sometimes became unruly.

Juan gave him a wave. "Out bench pressing a Pinto?" Juan asked as the blue suited weight lifter came around the corner of his desk.

"Not at the moment. Had to make due with one of those new VW bugs," he laughed as he reached to shake Juan's outstretched hand.

"What brings you to my domain?" Juan explained the afternoon discovery and asked Needles to check with the gang unit and any of his other contact points in the neighborhood to see if they could tie in some sort of connection with the deaths and perhaps a drug deal gone wrong or a turf war forming.

Kristo promised to keep his eyes and ears open for any information. Juan knew he could count on getting the information as soon as Kristo gathered anything. He recommended Needles for a promotion to Detective but withdrew it when asked by Kristo. With an undergraduate degree in criminal justice, an advanced degree in law and a second graduate degree in Human Resources, Kristo liked the front desk and wanted to stay in place. Juan admired the honesty and told Kristo he would resubmit the recommendation any time he was ready to move up.

312

On the way to his office, Juan checked with his chain of command and shot the breeze with other members of the detective section. He passed the word to them about the truck and the bodies. With all the players notified, he went to his office to attack the stack of paper he knew was piled into one of the plastic trays marked "urgent", "maybe" and "ignore". The second and third trays were always empty.

Further along the highway system at a CHP office not far from the Santa Monica freeway, a typist retrieved paperwork from the Captains out tray. She set about sorting the important items for immediate dispatch, delayed dispatch, filing, or shredding. Located in the delayed dispatch file was a request to all departments for assistance in locating a blue Ford Explorer with the partial California license plate number of 138_ _ M. Suspects were armed and considered extremely dangerous.

In another beachfront community, an impressively detailed color photo of a burning SUV was being scanned into a computer file. Once the photo scanned, a chilling note was added to the bottom of the photo. "DON'T EVER LET ME CATCH YOU FUCKING UP A SURE THING!" The photo was sent along communication lines to several destinations around the world. It was designed to ensure compliance with future orders. There would be little doubt it achieved the desired outcome.

CHAPTER THIRTY-NINE

Dillon reached for the cell phone as it chirped to life on the passenger's seat. "Yes?" was the only response made into the communication device. Knowing the Saudi Government monitored the transmissions, the agents were careful about what they said over the airwaves. The voice on the other end belonged to William.

"Congratulations. We can now trust you to find your way downtown. You're on your own about getting back to the villa."

"Thanks for the vote of confidence. I'll check in tomorrow." Dillon broke the connection and turned off the phone. He opened the glove box and tossed the leather-incased instrument inside. He just passed the spot where *Wendy's* was once located and made the right turn off Olaya Street. Since this was his first time in the area, he proceeded slowly causing much anxiety for local drivers who used the approach road as a shortcut between Olaya and the ring road.

He saw the ornately decorated entrance to Lai Lai's on his right and took the first opportunity to pull into a parking spot. As he approached the entrance, he heard his name called. As he turned in the direction of the voice, he noticed a man waving his hands in the air. When Dillon made eye contact, the man cut between two cars and opened the door of a nicely appointed *Lexus*. From the back seat, Carmen stepped into the red glow of the restaurants neon lights. Dillon smiled and waved as she stepped on to the sidewalk.

"I'm glad you got out of the car," Dillon said as he reached for her hands, raised them to his lips, and gave each one a short kiss. "I sure didn't know who this guy was."

Carmen laughed, turned to the man, introduced him as her driver, and then told him not to wait; her escort would bring her home.

As the couple approached the "family" entrance, the doors opened and a Filipino in black pants and a Chinese style high collar red shirt greeted them. He bowed deeply as they made their way through the doors. Once inside another similarly dressed man with menus in hand greeted them. Dillon asked if a Mr. Buzz arrived. The man showed recognition of the name but said Buzz had not yet arrived. He was to escort them to their table and provide drinks until he did arrive.

Dillon and Carmen followed the man past individual dining areas to a door at the back of the facility. He opened the room to reveal a good-sized round table with four chairs placed equal distance from each other. In the middle of a lazy Susan apparatus on the table was a very ornate centerpiece with a dragon as the main portion with rock and flowers added for effect.

As the man pulled out a chair for Carmen, Dillon asked where the men's room was located so he could wash his hands before the meal. A doorway on the other side of the room was indicated as the location for both the men and women's washrooms. Dillon excused himself and indicated they would like Saudi Champagne.

Once inside the washroom, from an inside coat pocket, he pulled a small device that indicates the presence of electronic bugs. It appeared like a pager so he would be able to use it even if Buzz arrived before he returned to the table.

Buzz hadn't arrived when he returned but the Saudi Champagne was in place. Carmen removed her deep blue abaya to reveal a very elegant floral patterned dress with long sleeves. Dillon complemented her on the dress and offered to pour the Saudi concoction. It was a mixture of fresh fruit chunks, ginger ale, apple juice and mint leaves. It was very cold and refreshing.

Dillon and Carmen were engaged in small talk when he reached into his coat pocket and pulled out the scanner telling Carmen he was "vibrated". She laughed saying those things come in handy some times. Dillon asked not to have the details as he read the LCD screen. It showed an electronic bug was located within one meter of his present location.

He was right about Buzz. There was another motive to his meeting and someone was going to listen to the conversation. He would keep with the pencil-pushing story and hold back on his information about Buzz. Others may not know of his Hasidic connection and he didn't want to blow an opportunity to capitalize on his vantage point.

The waiter knocked on the door and requested permission to enter. Carmen acknowledged the request and the waiter stuck his head in the door to assure the guests were satisfied with the level of service thus far. Dillon and Carmen exchanged questioning glances before Dillon answered. "All's in order at the present time." The waiter thanked them and was about to leave when Dillon stopped him.

"Before you leave, I'm impressed by the simple nature of your centerpiece. Does someone here design them or do you use an outsider?" The waiter said he really didn't know but would check with the manager. With a slight bow, he backed out of the door.

Carmen and Dillon returned to their conversation. In a couple of minutes, the manager knocked on the door to announce his presence. He told Dillon members of his staff normally construct simple centerpieces. This particular one was delivered earlier in the day with a request for it to be used for their specific gathering. When Dillon inquired for the sender's name, the manager replied there was no indication of who sent the piece. Dillon thanked the man as he left the cubicle.

"It's an interesting ornament," Carmen commented as she spun the lazy Susan around to admire the entire piece. "The dragon actually looks like he's coming through the forest looking for something."

Oh he's looking for something all right, Dillon thought. "That's why I asked about the builder. Shows some imagination. If I entertain while in Kingdom, I may have to use the same person. I really like the way its head is cocked as if listening for the knight in shining armor to ride up and rescue the damsel in distress."

Carmen reminded Dillon this particular creation was an imaginary Asian dragon and not an imaginary European dragon. "A Samurai may slay the beast but I don't believe there were knights in shining armor rescuing anything in China."

They both laughed at the truth in that statement. Dillon pondered the origin of the item for a moment. Did Buzz arrange for the decoration or was someone watching them both. Interesting conjecture. Perhaps he would be able to pick up some clues from the evening's conversation.

Before long, the door to their space opened and Buzz stood in the threshold. "Dillon, good to see you again." He came in the door; sat down a small cooler he was carrying in one hand and stepped around the table to greet Dillon. As he moved out of the doorframe, Lola entered the confines of the room. Her burgundy abaya was decorated with sequins in various swirling designs. The door shut behind her.

"Good to see you too. You know Carmen."

"Yes I do. Carmen, how are you?"

"I'm fine Buzz. Always a pleasure."

Buzz smiled at the reply knowing it was all Carmen could do to be in the same small space with him. He tried too many times to get into her knickers and failed each time. He turned to his companion and introduced her. "Dillon, Carmen, this is Lola." As he finished the brief introduction, as if on cue, Lola pulled off the abaya to reveal a bright red mini-skirt, sleeveless blouse and apparently, no undergarments. Dillon thought, how interesting. Carmen thought, slut.

The four sat down and Buzz pulled open the container he brought with him. Inside were two bottles. One of single malt, the other Kentucky bourbon. "Might I interest you in a libation?" Buzz questioned his dining companions.

When Carmen asked the origin of the drink, Buzz assured them it was the real stuff and not some of the local brew. Having to trust his word, Dillon and Carmen both opted for single malt. When Dillon took his first sip, he knew Buzz was telling the truth.

When finished with their drinks, Buzz suggested they wander to the buffet and begin the feast. As Lola was about to leave the protected confines of their dining room, Buzz reminded her to put on the abaya. Although he was pleased to show off his companion, he didn't want some zealot calling the religious police and ruin the evening. Carmen knew her attire was proper, so her shroud stayed on its hanger.

The buffet was everything they were promised. The food was plentiful and well prepared. Even the ladies made more than one trip through the line. Buzz and Dillon seemed to be in some sort of unannounced competition. Both men thoroughly enjoyed the food and drink. Dillon quit after one more drink but Buzz kept up the pace.

Once they finished dinner and dessert, Buzz began to ask simple questions about Dillon's background and his relationship with Peter. Dillon was ready with the answers. His undercover work really paid dividends during this type of operation. He makes up a persona and then without missing a stroke, keeps in tact all aspects of his alter ego. As the questions became more pointed, he stopped Buzz during one of them.

"So what's the third degree about?" he asked staring directly into Buzz's now bloodshot eyes.

"I approach you with some simple requests for information and now I'm the subject of an inquisition. Just what are you after?"

Buzz held his hands over the table. "Just hang on a minute. You have to appreciate the situation I'm facing. You swagger in here asking the type of questions you were asking and I begin to get suspicious. You could be an undercover cop."

No expression crossed Dillon's face. He was careful with the inflection his voice carried in his answer. He didn't want their minder to make any assumptions. "I'd like to thank you for inviting me for this wonderful meal. That type of questioning tells me the evening is over."

He turns toward Carmen. "Ready?"

"Wait" Buzz protests. "I won't apologize for my question. You have to admit your dropping in at Papa's and asking leading questions is somewhat odd. Just what are you expecting to get out of this situation?"

"That's one I can answer," Dillon responded. He got up from his chair to help Carmen put on her abaya and turned to face Buzz.

"When I find the type of action I can profit from, I'll be making my requests. Getting people into Papa's and having information about various types of entertainment is all part of the package. As in any business arrangement, you'll just have to trust the new guy to provide the promised services." Dillon leaned toward Buzz putting both hands on the edge of the table.

"Let me make this perfectly clear, I don't like to be second guessed. I've an agenda to follow and will stick to it with or without your assistance. You can add to your profits or sit on the sideline. I really don't care. But don't question my motives or methods."

Without hesitation, he again turned his attention to Carmen who was standing silently by his side. She put on her abaya and was ready to leave. As they pushed open the door, Dillon turned to Buzz, "Thanks for dinner".

Dillon and Carmen left the restaurant and got into Dillon's vehicle. As they were leaving, Dillon stopped in front of the singles side, excused himself, and left the truck. He stepped inside the building and was back out in a few seconds. When he got into the truck, he turned to Carmen to explain. She put her hand over his mouth. "After that little speech, you think I want to know your methods or motives? Not on your life."

Before she could remove her hand, Dillon kissed the palm as it lay against his mouth. When she took it away, he just smiled. Other than the meal, the evening was a total bust for Dillon. With discovering the bug in the centerpiece, he couldn't really attack with his information to gain total support from Buzz. He would have to plan another avenue of approach.

Carmen asked Dillon to turn left at the next intersection. It would take him to the right road. She said it was the quickest way home. Once he made his way through the maze of side streets and recklessly parked cars, he tuned on the approach road and finally to the highway. Carmen was right about the quickness of the trip. Within a few minutes, Dillon was taking an off ramp. At the top, he turned to cross over the highway. Once over the bridge and thorough the signals at the other side, it appeared they were headed into the desert.

"Am I sure you know where you're going?" he asked.

"Just watch out for the potholes," Carmen cautioned as they bumped over a small crevasse in the road.

"See those lights in the distance on the right?" Dillon looked in the direction she indicated.

"That's the hospital. We live right behind it at the Kingdom." Dillon continued down the road and followed her directions when she told him to turn.

He approached the gate and when the guard saw Carmen in the seat with him, he cleared access without hesitation. She lived near the central facility. She showed him where to park and was out of the truck before he could shut off the engine. She waved for him to join her as she took the sidewalk in front of her through what appeared to be a large bolder protected path. Dillon followed. Carmen was waiting just on the other side. The path continued through a garden area and wound up at the side of a freeform pool complete with waterfalls, mood lighting, palm trees, and rock formations.

"Impressive," Dillon commented as he went to the side of the pool. When he turned back toward Carmen, he saw she dropped her abaya on a table next to a chaise lounge, pulled up her skirt, sat on the lounge, and tucked her well-shaped legs beneath her.

"Wanna take a swim?" she asked.

"That would be nice but I neglected to pack my suit and I just have this feeling the staff and management of the facility would front about me skinny dipping in their masterpiece."

"For the record," Carmen cooed, "I wouldn't mind the view at all." By this time, Dillon came back to where she was sitting. He leaned down and placed a gentle kiss on her forehead. He stood up as he heard someone approach. It was a waiter from the restaurant. He asked if they wanted any refreshments. Carmen ordered single malts for both of them. Dillon took up residence in a lounge next to Carmen.

"Single malt?" he asked.

"Since this place is owned and operated by one of the Saudi royals, we do get certain perks. We have an international population with specialists of various types serving on staff. On the weekends, we have access to the real thing, so to speak. Now it's only on weekends and only in the central facility area. None for home consumption.

"That's still not a bad deal. So why do you frequent the other compound?"

"Like we told you and Pete, it's strictly for the sex. We don't date most of the men here because they're all married. We aren't dykes, although I do have a feeling Hellen has experimented. As for the single gents at the hospital, we would wear out the western ones too quickly and none of us are into Asians. Now it's not to say the western gents don't get lucky occasionally but we like variety in our life and the compound offers us that variety. At this time in our lives we aren't looking to get married and raise families, so this is the best place in the world."

As she was explaining her philosophy, the drinks and a few snacks arrived. Dillon paid for the refreshments and left a rather substantial tip on the tray. "Keep them coming," he asked.

When the waiter left, he raised his glass to Carmen and toasted, "Here's to variety, the spice of life!"

CHAPTER FORTY

J.R. came down the steps from the first class compartment of the Airbus and followed the crowd toward the baggage claim area of Abha's airport. The office in Riyadh presented her with a rather fancy abaya to use while in Kingdom and keep as a souvenir of probably one of her strangest assignments. She claimed her luggage and headed out the only doorway into the reception area. Can't get lost here she thought. She scanned the waiting crowd of thobe wearing greeters until she saw a man holding a hand written sign "J.R.". She pushed her way toward him and as she was coming through the crowd, he saw her and approached from his place near the door.

"I sure hope you're J.R.," the man said as he approached. "If your not, I'm in deep trouble with some husband."

J.R. smiled. "No problems to be faced, I'm J.R. Lopez."

"Will Erpack," the colonel replied.

"Let me get that cart for you. It'll be easier for me to make our way back to the truck." Erpack took the handles of the cart and headed out the front door, down the ramp and into the parking lot.

Once they reached the truck, he opened the doors and put her cases on the back seat. Dillon warned her about Erpack and advised her to listen intently and then carry the investigation in her own manner. He told her about their initial meeting and the subsequent "apology". She trusted Dillon's insight to the man and would act accordingly.

She listened and listened and listened. Some of his points were salient to the situation, as she knew it and others were out in left field. She nodded her head as if taking all of his suggestions into consideration. She knew this initial blast of information would be repeated during her assignment. She could take notes later and sort out the good from the bad.

In between suggestions, Erpack once again acted as tour guide during their trip to the compound. Having never been in this part of the world, J.R. found the moon type landscape interesting.

Erpack arranged for a villa near the other administrator to keep with their cover of her being at Khamis to help. He sidestepped the busy body questions of the Indian housing clerk in the HR office. He was a nosy little man who wanted to have as much information about happenings on the compound as he could muster. Knowledge is power in this society and this guy played "I've got a secret" to the maximum extent possible.

Once at the villa, Erpack gave J.R. a stack of papers on various aspects of the case. J.R. already knew the information from the notes Dillon provided. Since it was still early in the day, J.R. wanted to take some time for review before heading to the base early the next morning. She politely got rid of Erpack, pulled a long neck from the fridge, dropped on the couch, and dug into the stack of information.

In Riyadh, Dillon was putting the final additions on a sandwich that would rival the masterpieces of Dagwood Bumstead. Wheat bread, skinless chicken and turkey, some green peppers, lettuce, one slice of tomato, a thinly cut dill pickle and a bit of pepper. A gastronomic treat is one way to face the labor of paperwork. When he came across the mail from Germany with the strange letters, he set it aside for additional work after the mundane work was completed. He would enjoy putting his analytical abilities to the test once again.

William gave him a call later in the day with the information J.R. made a safe transition to Khamis. Before she left, she indicated a desire to limit contact during the initial stages of her work. Once she got the lay of the land, she would provide secure messages about her progress. Dillon said it was typical of J.R. He told William not to worry about the lack of words between her and Riyadh. When she felt it was necessary to provide progress reports, she would make the calls. William said he would follow those directions and asked what Dillon planned for dinner. With some steaks out, he was going to contact Karl to see if he wanted to have a dinner meeting about their visit to Vinder at the embassy.

"Count me in," Dillon answered. "What time?"

"Let me hook up with Karl and I'll give you a call. You gonna be at your villa?"

"Unless I take a run at the gym. However, that doesn't appear to be in the cards today," Dillon laughed.

He returned to the paperwork with thoughts of steak on the barbie making the rest of the afternoon bearable.

"...and that was my introduction to the grandiose investigator known to us all as Budmere Baker." Christina finished explaining the circumstances surrounding the arrival of Budmere and Cathy. Bill didn't notice any complaints about Cathy during the heated conversation.

"How's the other investigator?"

"Cathy? She's just on the team to pick Baker's brain cells for a learning experience. She told me she already outlasted her predecessor. Evidently, Baker goes through them like grease through a goose. I would never be able to put up with his crap!" Bill just shook his head as he watched Christina drain the remainder of her coffee.

"I know you better than that," he said as he came around the corner of his desk. He leaned against the edge and told Christina a story about an investigator he knew during his early days in OSI. The bottom line to the story was he learned a great deal about the business from an old crotchety bastard no one liked. It wasn't worth battling the guy, so Bill just made like a sponge and sucked all the information he could out of the old fart before he retired. It certainly made him a better investigator, manager, and leader.

"Gee thanks dad," Christina quipped. "Get ya some coffee?" Bill grabbed his cup.

"So, besides your intense dislike for the man, what has he discovered during his examination of the apartment?"

"I really couldn't tell you right now. He said he would need a couple of days. That would mean today would be the last day. He didn't talk with me yesterday and I haven't called Helga today. Let me do that to make sure they're working and then I may run out there for an update."

Both investigators filled their cups and returned to their offices. Christina sifted through the in basket and then pulled up Helga's number. The phone rang twice before Helga answered.

"Helga, this is Christina from the base. How's everything today?" That question opened Helga up for a long discussion of village happenings. This discussion took place every time Christina called. She didn't mind and it helped with her German. Although Helga spoke English, Christina always greeted her in German and then would carry on with the conversation in German for as long as she could keep up. Some days Helga would forget she was talking with Christina and would have to slow down so she could understand. After a while, Christina interjected a question into the conversation.

"Did the investigation team show up this morning?" Helga told her the pair of them showed up exactly at the agreed time and were busy at work. Christina thought it was typical of a man like Baker to be on time every time. No delays in his world. She wondered how he coped with the world of "scheduled" airlines. She would love to be a fly on the wall when he faced a delay of several hours. She bet it drove him crazy

"That's good news," Christina said. "Maybe you can get back the use of your house." Helga told her there was no hurry.

"You haven't seen the car or those two men around town have you?" Helga answered neither the car nor the men made a return visit. Christina was thankful. Getting the apartment back to its landlord would certainly make it appear the investigation had turned to other areas.

Budmere told Helga they would finish in the afternoon. With them at the apartment conducting the investigation without any apparent problems, Christina didn't see a need to make a visit. She was pleased with the situation. The less she interacted with the disagreeable man the better she liked it. She would busy herself with the stack of review paperwork and give him a call just before she headed home to see if he was going to work the next day. Although it was Saturday, she would make the office available to the team for final reports.

Cathy and Budmere were hard at work in the apartment. They photographed, dusted, treated, lifted, gathered, and categorized all types of "evidence" during yesterday's 12-hour marathon. Today they were going over a few remaining areas and then, a Budmere quirk; Cathy would sit and listen as Budmere talked aloud in a one man brainstorming session. For all the excellent training she was picking up during her stay with Budmere, she would not be adding this one technique to her repertoire. During the session, she wasn't allowed to comment on things said by Budmere. She could take notes and after the "session" was completed, she could ask clarification questions. She asked a question once and faced a 15-minute tirade on just how asinine her query was. Since that day, she hasn't made the same mistake.

Cathy could tell the single brainstorming session was about to begin. Budmere maintained a ritual that kicked off when he started to put the equipment back into its cases. They were at the packing up stage now. Just as they were beginning the process, the cell phone rang. Christina was on the line checking their immediate needs. Cathy also learned not to interrupt the process once it began. She told Christina the collection process was complete and they were just cleaning up. They didn't need anything now and would give her a call at home if they needed anything later that day or in the morning. By the time Cathy finished talking; Budmere retrieved the "storming liquid" as Cathy referred to it and took a seat on the couch. With eyes closed, Budmere took a few sips of the liquid and began the session.

Behind the house, Helga was puttering in her garden. There was a potluck dinner at the church and she volunteered to bring a large pot of vegetable soup. To give it the special Pffer zip all her parish friends loved, she gathering up a few herbs from the neat rows growing at the top of her terraced backyard. On her way down from the top terrace, she gathered in a few vegetables fresh from the ground. She placed them in one of the wicker baskets she carried. As she reached the bottom terrace, she set them on the edge of the stone wall surrounding her small patio. She didn't want to take a chance of falling if she missteps on her way down the short flight of stairs.

Once on the patio, she retrieved the baskets, washed off the dirt under the faucet, and brought the fruits of her labor into the kitchen. She sat the baskets on the sink and was about to begin soup preparations when the doorbell rang. On the other side of the front door to her apartment were Budmere and Cathy. They thanked her for her cooperation and said their investigation was completed. She walked with them to the door and bid them farewell. She stood in the doorway until they were in the car and gave them one last wave before going back down the hall to her apartment. She grabbed her apron off the hook near her refrigerator. The apron seemed heavier than usual and once she put it on, she reached into the pocket and pulled out the forgotten package.

Why didn't she remember to give it to one of the agents? She placed the package on the counter and reached for the phone. She called both numbers Christina gave her but both of them went unanswered. She hung up promising to call before she went to dinner. She returned to the task at hand, vegetable soup.

As Budmere and Cathy were leaving the house, Cathy called Christina. Since it was just about closing time, they wanted to know if anyone would be in the office. Christina told her if they needed the office, she would wait for them. When Cathy relayed the information to Budmere, he paused and then in a manner so untypical of him, said they would not need the office space this weekend. They would see Christina on Monday morning bright and early. Cathy paused before relaying the information to Christina.

As she began to speak, Christina interrupted her. "I heard. Are you sure your sitting in the car with the same man I've come to know and love?"

Cathy laughed which drew a sideways glance from Budmere. They made plans for Christina to pick Cathy up later for a night on the town. Cathy readily agreed since their last assignment held gruesome details and there was nowhere to blow off steam. She told Christina she would be waiting for her in the kitchen of their Gasthaus. By the time they finished their conversation, Budmere was pulling into the parking lot.

Hurried with the preparation of her soup, the calls from friends making sure she was bringing her masterpiece to the dinner and the final hasty preparations of hair and makeup, Helga forgot to make her call to Christina.

CHAPTER FORTY-ONE

Dillon, Karl, and William sat around the small circular table in a corner of the dining facility. Dillon moved a small vase with the accompanying saltshaker, peppershaker, and toothpick holder from their location in the center of the table to the placemat on his right. The vacated space was well utilized by the men as they sat their coffee cups, extra dishes with pancakes and syrup, toast and condiments in front of the plates holding their eggs and bacon. "I'm glad to see we all have a healthy appetite this morning," Dillon commented as he reached for his cup of coffee.

"I don't know why," Karl responded. "But since I arrived, I have this ability to eat one of these breakfasts every Saturday morning. I don't come down to the buffet on weekends, I just hold off until Saturday and then scarf down before heading to the office."

"And the bad part about it," William began, "he brings me down here and I'm forced to partake of the same type breakfast."

"Right! I noticed how he was twisting your arm as we ordered," Dillon observed.

The men talked about the weekend and their leisure activities. Dillon was careful not to divulge any details about his evening with Carmen. Karl and William both tried in varying ways to find details about Dillon's activities after his meeting with Buzz. Dillon made comment about the luxury of the compound and how the occupants were able to access liquor on the weekends. After a while, they gave up trying to slip Dillon into compromising his nocturnal activities. The subject for discussion then turned to the afternoon meeting with Colonel Rufas D. Vinder.

"So what kind of a guy am I dealing with?" Dillon asked as he poured another cup of coffee from the large silver hot pot recently refreshed by the dining room staff.

"For one thing," William began, "he's one smart son of a bitch. Undergraduate work at M.I.T. Graduate work at Stanford and then the Air Force sent the guy to Harvard through AFIT[25] to get his doctorate."

"So what you're telling me", Dillon began with a smile. "Don't go toe to toe with this guy on an educational resume basis?"

"Funny, Dillon. Very funny," William replied shaking his head. "I just wanted you to know this guy has the book learning but we aren't sure where his street smarts are. Although we've had dealings with him, we haven't worked as closely with him as you will. Can't give you any reading on how he might react to the request for NSA assistance. The guy has a sponsor too. He's only been in the Force a little over 16 years."

"I'm not surprised," Karl interjected. "With all the money the Force spent on the guy, I'm surprised he doesn't have stars on right now. He destined for bigger and better things."

"At 16 years there would be too many bull colonels boiling over if he got promoted to star rank without having spent at least 20 years in uniform. When he gets his first star, watch out. He'll climb right through the ranks until he's ready to take over as chief of staff and then chairman," Dillon surmised.

"Is he a stick actuator?" Dillon asked.

"Let me see," Karl answered as he reached for the tattered briefcase leaning against the wall under the mini blind covered window. He pushed himself away from the table and sat the case on his lap. Once opened, he sorted through a few folders until he came to one marked "Embassy". Inside were biographies on key players currently assigned to Riyadh, Jeddah, and Dhahran. He arranged them in alphabetical order so finding "Vinder" was easy. Straight to the bottom of the pile and one up. Only "Wilson" was further down the stack.

He pulled out the paper, placed it on the table next to his pancake plate, shut the case, and sat it back on the floor. "Let me see what we have here", he began as he picked up the biography.

"Nope, this guy has never slipped the surly bonds of earth as a stick actuation member of the Force. He has always been a member of the intelligence collection community." He looked up from the paper with a furled brow as he sat the sheets back down next to his plate.

"But that doesn't make much sense. I've never met a liaison officer who wasn't a pilot. That's normally one of the prerequisites to land one of these cushy jobs at an embassy."

"You're right there," Dillon agreed. "But with his credentials, he must be in place as a training exercise. His collection knowledge and analysis work is probably coming in handy with all the happenings in the Middle East. I'm surprised he could find time to entertain us."

The men continued to discuss the biographical data as they consumed another pot of coffee. When it was drained and the men finished the remaining portions in their cups, they left the facility and walked to the office. Mary was in place and greeted the men as they arrived.

"Coffee gentlemen?" she asked as they filed past. They all laughed as they turned down her kind offer. Karl said they were finished with coffee for the present time.

"Had one of those breakfast meetings with all the trimmings and pots of coffee I would assume?" she commented with a tilt of her head.

The remainder of the morning was spent clearing paperwork. Dillon dropped into the chair behind his desk with a thud. He couldn't remember the last time he indulged in such a breakfast extravaganza. Glad Karl doesn't do it every morning. He just pulled files from his case when the intercom light flashed. He depressed the speaker button. Mary announced a call from Bill in Germany. He thanked her and pressed the small button next to the steady illumination of line one.

"Bill! What are you doing up at this hour of the morning?"

"I wanted to make sure I talked with you before you headed out on another adventure."

"Have you collected your e-mail and made a decision on the lettering sequence?" Bill referred to the letters Crimitin left in the note to his mother.

"Just beginning to work on that," Dillon said. "Let me see if I can move it to the top of the pile so I can send you anything that might pop into my head." As they continued to talk about various subjects, Dillon sorted through the pile until he came to the mail with the odd letters. He pulled it out of the stack and sat it to one side of the desk. "Anything on our associates?" referring to the agents searching Crimitin's apartment.

"Funny you should ask. Talked with Christina last night and the weekend was declared off limits. From what she said, it was very out of character for the top man. No results from them yet. Will get back to you when we have something."

Dillon said he understood knowing the personality of Budmere. He agreed it was a bit out of the ordinary but every human being faces a point of diminishing return. Perhaps Budmere reached his and needed some recharge time before heading to the next investigation.

When Dillon hung up, he picked up the note with the letters. RNZOANW. One word? Two Words? One repeated letter to correspond with the N. This shouldn't be too hard he thought as he scribbled the alphabet on a piece of scrap paper. He looked at it briefly, jotted another alphabet below the first one, and promptly spelled out the clear text word SOAPBOX. A very simplistic transference of letters. The most basic of sliding scale encryption. He didn't want to brag but this was too simple. He knew the others would have the same quick solution to this perceived problem.

He pushed the solution to one side of his keyboard so he could send it along secure lines to all the addressees on the note. He was sure it would be a confirmation of their findings. Besides, it was Saturday and none of the other investigators involved with the case would be in for business until Monday. Dillon continued to sort through the notes he accumulated and place them into their corresponding file folders. William came to the door and told him they would be leaving about 1300. They never knew how long the ride to the embassy would take and then processing into the building was always a thrill. It was 1100.

The American Embassy is located Riyadh's "Diplomatic Quarters". It was designed to give embassy staffs a semblance of security but as William expounded, was really designed to keep them under tight control. He carried on a nonstop conversation about the situation and how the Saudi government controlled access to and from the embassies. He found it rather bothersome to know the great Seal of the United States was held hostage behind a contingent of Saudi Armed Forces. As he was going on and on, Karl caught Dillon's attention and gave him a knowing wink. When William paused during a lengthy discussion of security problems, Karl asked if he felt the bombings in Africa would have been prevented if the host country provided sterner security measures. That stopped the lecture mid-stream. They drove on in silence.

Colonel Vinder's office was located near the ambassador. Once the men cleared through the Saudi security forces, identified themselves to the Marine guards, were scanned, probed, and scrutinized, they were allowed to enter the building. Once inside they made their way to Vinder's designated location. Since they were a few minutes early, the men were provided refreshments until the colonel returned.

About 10 minutes to three, Vinder came into the reception area. The coat to his tailored three-piece suit was open and revealed a watch fob of some magnitude. As he came in the door, he pulled the attached chronometer out of the watch pocket and checked the time. "I'm not late am I?" he asked the men as he walked toward them.

"No sir, we were early. We never know how long it's going to take for the transition from Eskan to the quarters. We always allow for the inevitable traffic accident or an over protective security force. Today we had none of that and arrived in short order." Karl stood from the couch and greeted the colonel.

"Good to see you again. It's been some time since our last visit."

"Yes it has. Of course, that's a good thing. If I see you two it means there's a problem and I don't like to deal with problems." Dillon made a note on that comment. He must delicately approach his situation or face the real possibility of Vinder not helping because he didn't like to "deal with problems". William and Dillon came around the table as Karl was greeting the colonel. Karl turned to them and made introductions.

"Sir, you remember my trusted assistant, William?"

"Yes. How are you William?"

"Just fine sir. It has been quite busy since our last visit. Good to see you again."

"And this is Agent Dillon Reece, on temporary assignment to USMTM from McDill."

"Mr. Reece's reputation precedes him. Good to meet you Dillon."

"Good to meet you sir. I hope the reputation didn't scare you off." Dillon replied with a smile.

"Didn't scare me but it did peak my interest. Get your cups and come into the office." Vinder turned and headed for the open door behind the administrator's desk. The three agents followed. Once inside Dillon was impressed with the lavishness of the decor. He stopped as he entered the door and looked around the room.

"Well I can see I picked the wrong career to pursue," he commented.

Vinder went around the corner of his double wide teak desk and was looking at some notes in the middle of his blotter. He looked up when Dillon commented.

"Not bad for a boy from the projects," Vinder replied. Dillon smiled in return. Vinder pulled a note pad out of a drawer and came back around the desk. He motioned the men to take seats around an octagonal coffee table along one wall of the room.

"I don't know if you've had the opportunity to visit any high ranking Saudi military officers but their game appears to be bigger is better. I've seen some of the most outrageous office decorations during my travels around the Kingdom. This office is set up for the liaison officer to show off. We didn't want any of the generals I deal with to get an opinion my position was any less important than the ambassador. I deal with all of the military requests and activities. Takes the burden off the boss and lets him get on with the business of diplomacy."

"Sounds interesting," Dillon responded. The administrator came into the office with two waiters in trail. One of the men carried a tray with coffee and necessary flavorings. The other man held a tray of assorted pastries.

"Another perk of the job." Vinder said as he picked up the pot and poured himself a cup. He drank it without condiments.

"With a complete kitchen on the grounds, we get the best of both worlds. All the American cooking we can take plus a quality bakery." He now reached for one of the pastries and placed it on a plate near his pad of paper. The other men refreshed their cups.

"It is about time for afternoon tea," William surmised as picked up one of the goodies with lots of frosting and cherry topping.

"Glad I didn't have any lunch today. I was still stuffed from breakfast," he laughed as he took a taste of the flaky crust. Karl explained the breakfast meeting and the reason for William's comment. Vinder was just finishing his taste treat as Dillon began to explain the reason for their visit. The colonel raised his hand to stop Dillon.

"When Evantoe called, I promised a briefing on what we had. Do you want to go over the information now?" Vinder asked.

Dillon turned to Karl and asked if he wanted a briefing now or later. Karl said they would wait until later. He nodded to Dillon who turned back toward Vinder. He began again to detail the problem, activities in Germany, and the Kingdom tie-in. The codenames of the operatives were mentioned and Vinder made note. Dillon also mentioned activities at Khamis and how another agent unrelated to their operation was handling them.

Vinder took notes but didn't ask any questions. When Dillon was done, more than 30 minutes after he began, the colonel asked Karl and William if they had anything to add. Neither man did. Vinder picked up his note pad, leaned back in the chair, and crossed his legs. He read for a while as the agents talked between themselves about the benefits of afternoon tea. After a few minutes, Vinder sat the pad on the table and leaned in toward the men.

"I know you gentlemen are here for my assistance. What can I do for your investigation?"

"I'll skip the platitudes and cut right to the core of the matter. We know the Kingdom contacts are using code names, computer connections, and cellular phones. We want NSA assistance to pick up the communication links and provide us with inside information concerning the cartel and their operations. It isn't being run from Riyadh and I doubt it's being run from the contact points in Germany. This is a mighty big operation and we need to gather enough information to close down the entire process. We don't want to leave any of the tentacles on this monster alive and capable of regeneration. Once we kill the limbs, we want to be able to deal a deathblow to the heart of the operation. Right now your guess would be as good as mine as to where the headquarters of this operation is located. We've had contacts in California, Texas, Delaware, Germany, Italy, and the Kingdom. We need information from the ECLIPSE system." Vinder stopped taking notes and looked across the table at Dillon.

"ECLIPSE? I'm not sure I understand what you mean."

"Please colonel. Give me enough credit for knowing the capabilities of the system if I could tell you the name. You have the code names, now all you've got to do is match them up with collected data and we're on the track home." Vinder continued to look at Dillon after his statement. He was quickly formulating a snappy response but then thought better of the situation. He was told Dillon is no nonsense when on a case. His request for assistance needed to be taken seriously.

"Well Mr. Reece," Vinder began. "Let me form a report on our conversation and pass it along the lines to my superiors. I should be able to give you an answer next week."

"Not good enough colonel. You have the ability to get the duty officer back at mother state department. That person, being politically correct, can get hold of your boss who can get hold of his contact at NSA. With the time differences, I do believe you can have an answer for me by the close of business tomorrow. At least that's what I'm expecting. Anything less will be a disappointment all along my chain of command."

Vinder just sat looking across the coffee table at Dillon. Dillon took a chance by matching wits with this over achiever. He figured to out challenge him if he didn't have the street smarts to make an end run around the bluff.

"Tomorrow, close of business. I'll give you a call at Eskan." It worked, Dillon thought. Now let's play it off as if I expected nothing more.

"I understand you have a new member on staff. Is the man from DEA available?" Dillon asked.

Vinder said he figured the agents might want to talk with him so he was standing by for a call. He went back to his desk, pushed the intercom, and in a moment was talking with the agent.

"Could you come down to my office now? Your compatriots need to speak with you." Vinder continued to sit behind his desk looking at his notes. He didn't say another word until the DEA man entered the office.

Drug Enforcement Agency Special Agent Christian B. Nelsum came into the office with a laptop under his left arm. Even though it was the end of the day, his tan pants carried a razor sharp crease and the open collared

333

shirt appeared freshly pressed. He walked directly to where the OSI agents were seated. As he approached, Dillon rose for introductions.

"Agent Christian Nelsum," the man began as he reached for Dillon's hand. "On temporary assignment from Frankfurt."

"Dillon Reece, Christian. Good to meet you. Let me introduce the other members of our group. This is William Kingston and the other distinguished gentleman is Karl Phobie." The men exchanged greetings as Nelsum took a seat across the table from the OSI agents. Small talk preceded the exchange of information.

"The colonel indicated you would like to have a briefing on what we've found thus far on our end of the investigation. I must admit it isn't much. We were sort of hoping you guys had the inside track and would be able to fill in the blanks."

"The more information we have the better off we're going to be," Dillon said.

"We were a bit surprised to discover there was an agent assigned down here," William commented as he opened his note pad. "You said this was a temporary assignment from Frankfurt. Who sent you down here?"

"Frankfurt's agent in charge is Cornelius Asterfon. When he found out about the Crimitin situation, he arranged to send me on site to help in anyway I can. I've a feeling there's more to the story than what I'm being told, so please excuse me if there are few blanks in the background information I was able to obtain. Asterfon is tight lipped about investigations unless you're intimately involved with the situation. I was working other cases and didn't really know much about this case until he called to give me this assignment. It's really a typical bureaucratic stovepipe situation. One hand doesn't know what the other is doing and consequently we spin our wheels on a number of occasions."

"We'll trade horror stories some evening over a drink," William said. "Being the junior guy on the team, I can empathize with that bureaucratic situation. I'm just glad these two guys have kept me in the loop on."

Christian opened the laptop and was going to have the men look at the on board screen when Vinder stopped them.

"Wait a second. No need to squint at the screen. Let me show you another perk of the position." He reached into his bottom desk drawer and pulled out an interface cord. He threw it to Christian who hooked it into his laptop. Vinder turned around and pushed a couple of buttons on a control panel behind his desk. Across the room from where the men were sitting, a screen appeared from a recessed post in the ceiling. From a spot several feet in front of the screen, a trap door type apparatus lowered and the lens portion of a projector aimed its electronic eye at the screen. Vinder came to where

Christian was sitting and slid a panel on the wall to a locked open position. He hooked up the interface cable and told the DEA man to progress with the briefing. The screen illuminated with Christian's desktop setup. He entered the PowerPoint address and the introduction screen flashed into view. From there it was simply a matter of flowing through the slides explaining each one in as much detail as the investigators required.

When they finished, Dillon was not too impressed. He knew the DEA was never on top of their game but he didn't expect this many holes in their information. "Thanks for the data Christian. What I would like to propose is a joining of efforts. I know the DEA is usually against such a union but in this particular case, I do believe it would benefit both operations. If you're the one to uncover a major drug operation in Saudi Arabia, just think how much that will do for your promotion opportunities." Dillon saw a positive reaction.

"I'll have to keep my superiors in Frankfurt informed of the operation," Christian flatly stated.

"Of course you will. Don't want them to feel left out," Dillon agreed. They talked for a while about the case and how they enlisted the assistance of Colonel Vinder. Dillon wasn't sure if the youngster knew Vinder's connection to the wonderful world of intelligence collection but he wanted him to know Vinder was a player. He would only give the man from DEA a limited amount of information concerning the finer points of the search.

Vinder remained behind his desk during the briefing. Once Nelsum left the office after offering hearty thanks for use of the projection system, he came over to the agents and sat down.

"From what I've seen of Nelsum, he's a go getter. He's very enthusiastic about his work and I believe you can trust him to give you his best effort."

"Thanks for the assessment," Dillon replied to the unsolicited vote of confidence.

"We came here to solve a murder. The trafficking is secondary to our main purpose. We're not glory hounds seeking recognition for our efforts. We're here seeking justice for the slain airman. The DEA can take all the credit for the collapse of this cartel if we're successful in identifying the main players. I believe our governmental side of this investigation will make more than a few points with the world community if they help bring an end to a drug running scheme at the center of the Muslim world."

Vinder spoke of the ambassador and his need to be kept abreast of the situation. "You're well aware of my background," Vinder restated. "I'll give the man only what I feel is absolutely necessary to keep him informed. I don't want him dropping a big one on the king during one of their meetings. Once we're ready to solve, I'll fill him in on details."

"Totally agree on that point," Karl responded. "Since Dillon is concentrating on the murder, we'll keep you informed on what we find with the cocaine connection."

Vinder excused himself and went back to his desk. He pushed one of the intercom buttons and spoke with the ambassador's assistant. "I told the boss I would see if he had time for a visit once we were done with our business," Vinder told the men as he held his hand over the receiver.

"Still here," he replied to an unheard question. "He does, ...Good. We're on our way."

The four men left the office and walked the short distance to the ambassador's suite. They spent more than an hour talking about a wide variety of subjects but avoiding the investigation. It was a diplomatic visit designed to introduce the key players to one another. When they finished, Vinder escorted the men to the entrance and said goodbye.

As Dillon was shaking Vinder's hand, he reminded him once more, "Tomorrow, close of business!" Vinder didn't reply. The only acknowledgement was a slight nod of his head.

While clearing the maze of security, the men engaged in small talk about their meeting with the ambassador. As they approached their vehicle, Nelsum got out of a car parked across the way from theirs.

"Gentlemen, can I've a moment of your time?" None of the men spoke as Nelsum approached. "I didn't want to say anything in front of the colonel less he thinks I'm a glory seeking bureaucratic. I haven't been with the agency very long and the reception I got in Frankfurt was less than thrilling. I'm prepared to provide all the assistance of the agency if necessary. I see this as a giant boost to my career potential. I'm dedicated, educated, and ready to work. All you need to do is give me a lead and I'll give you results." As he finished, the trio of investigators exchanged glances before Dillon replied.

"Thanks for the information. I can't guarantee what type of role you're going to play but I'll tell you the DEA has never been a faithful companion. On more than one occasion, they have nearly busted a long investigation by trying to horn in at the finishing line. I'm perfectly willing to share the case with you and assure you all the glory you gain will be earned." Dillon turned to join Karl and William in the truck.

"Oh by the way," he said turning back toward Christian. "The colonel basically told us the same thing right after you left the office. We'll be in touch." Dillon turned and got into the passenger side of the truck. He waved to the dumbstruck agent as they pulled out of the parking space and drove away.

CHAPTER FORTY-TWO

"Absolutely, send her right in," Captain Wilmerson spoke into the intercom. She got up from her desk to greet her visitor.

"Francy, good to see you again. What brings you to my side of the world?" They shook hands and Betty offered her one of the seats in front of her desk. Betty sat in the other chair.

"Well Mam," Francy began in a nervous tone. "I've begun to date again."

"Wonderful," Betty interrupted. "There's got to be at least one other good guy out there. I know I found one." Francy smiled at the statement.

"Yes, Mam. Anyway, I've been seeing this Airman from the security squadron. This weekend we went to a concert in Frankfurt. The concert was on Saturday, so we drove down Friday night for dinner. We agreed to take one of my friends, with one of his friends so we could get two rooms and I didn't have to face the inevitable sexual games. I like the guy but I'm not ready to share a bed with him," she flatly stated. Betty nodded in an understanding manner.

"So, we had a real nice time on Friday. Dinner and drinks at the hotel and then we went to a club that caters to Americans. The next day we were going to spend sightseeing around town before the concert. When David came down for breakfast, I noticed he was a bit groggy. I knew it wasn't from the beers we drank because we didn't have that many. He seemed to come around during the day and by concert time, there didn't seem to be any problem. At the concert, I found out about the grogginess. He's a pot smoker. During the concert, he and his buddy lit up and offered some to us. Buffy and I don't use, as you know, so we declined. It didn't seem to bother him and the guys proceeded to get stoned. They really enjoyed the concert getting down in the pit and dancing up a storm. Buffy and I just watched. The hotel we stayed at was within walking distance of the concert so we didn't have to worry about driving. The next morning, or should I say afternoon, we met for brunch and they still looked stoned. I drove home."

Betty sat without comment waiting to see if Francy added anything. Francy just sat with her head lowered as it was during her story. Betty reached and patted her knee.

"I do believe we can scratch these two losers off your list of potential good guys." Francy looked up and smiled at the captain.

Betty got up from her chair and went around her desk to sit down. "Who are these two fine gentlemen?"

"The guy I've been dating is David Durowe. He's a Senior Airman. The other guy is Paul Benrod. I don't know what rank he carries." Betty wrote down the names. She turned her attention to Francy once again.

"I appreciate you coming here. I know it's tough to try and fit into a crowd when the crowd is involved with drugs. I'll turn these names over to the proper authorities and let them take it from there. No one will know you're the one involved."

"Right!" Francy exclaimed. "They'll be able to put it together when these guys get pulled in."

"I'll pass along your concern to the right guys. You just keep up the good work and stop by anytime you want to talk. You know I'm always here." Francy got up, reached across the desk, and shook the captain's hand.

"Thanks for your time." She stood back, snapped a salute, turned, and left the room. Betty dropped back into her chair and let out a sigh. If Francy didn't have bad luck, she'd have no luck at all she thought. She reached for the phone and speed dialed her husband. "OSI, Sergeant Bower, can I help you?"

"Willie, this is Betty. Is my husband there?" Betty used Willie's first name to be on the casual side with this conversation. Although it was a business call, she always asked for her husband and not the agent. Made all of the people in the office feel more like a family than a military unit.

"Yes Mam, I'll put you through." Willie answered.

Without answering the intercom, Bill picked up the flashing line. "Agent Wilmerson."

"Bill, Betty."

"Hello my dear. How's everything in the wide world of personnel?"

"Are we meeting today for lunch at the club?" Bill replied he didn't feel like dining at the club today. He felt more like a burger at the exchange. A time was agreed upon and they bid farewell. Betty returned to the work at hand and Bill went to check in with Christina.

"Anything out of the inspector's cubby hole?" he asked nodding his head in the direction of Agent Baker's temporary workspace.

"Nothing so far this morning. He came in with nary a word. Cathy said hi but after she went into the room and closed the door, she hasn't even come out for a coffee refill."

"I see," Bill responded rubbing his chin in a thoughtful manner. "I really don't want to knock on his door, he's such an asshole." Christina's eyes widened.

"Who's an asshole," Budmere asked from behind Bill. Without missing a beat, Bill turned to greet Agent Baker.

"Morning Budmere. Oh, we have a crotchety old fart who works with one of the commanders. Always has his door shut when you go to see him. You never know if he's hittin' the hooch or hittin' on some young lady. It just ticks us all off so we try to avoid knocking on his door."

Nice try Bill, Christina thought. I won't ever believe Budmere bought it.

"Interesting set of circumstances. I hope you don't have to deal with the man very often."

"No thank goodness. We only have to see the man on very special occasions."

Tie game. No fouls called. We move into overtime, Christina said to herself as she watched the two agents spar in her office doorway. "You need anything Agent Baker?" Christina asked trying to spring her boss from a sticky situation. Bill stood out of the way so Budmere could enter the office.

"Yes, I've put my report on disk. All I need now are your requirements on format, letterhead and the like."

"We've got the right man here," Christina replied nodding her head toward Bill.

"All we need is an original on your letterhead with an original signature. Made a dupe of the disk and let us keep it along with any other pertinent notes you think we might need in the future. It'll all become part of the Crimitin file."

Without reply, Budmere left the office and returned to his workspace. Christina looked at Bill. "Nice save." Bill just shook his head as he sat in one of the office chairs in front of Christina's desk.

"By the look on your face I knew he just appeared out of the darkness. We need to tie a bell around his neck so we know where he's at." Christina just smiled as she pulled some papers out of the stack on her desk.

"Have you checked your mail this morning?" When he said no, she handed him a note from Dillon.

"Soapbox. Just how did super sleuth come up with that one?" Christina told him to read on. "A simple sliding alphabet scale," Bill read from the copy. "Oh please! Why didn't we come up with the solution?"

"We were trying to reinvent the wheel," Christina began. "We were looking in a different direction and Dillon came at it from another perspective. Guess all that spy training comes in handy once in a while."

"I suppose you're right," Bill responded dejectedly. "I must admit he's one hell of an investigator. I'm learning a lot from just watching his methods." Christina agreed. Now the two began to compare information about the word SOAPBOX. Christina checked the inventory and found nothing resembling a soapbox. Actually, no laundry products were listed on the inventory at all.

"Do you remember a washer in the apartment?" Bill asked.

"I was thinking the same thing," Christina replied as she left her desk and headed for the door. "Let's check with Budmere and see if he remembers a washer anywhere in the apartment." Bill followed Christina to the visitor's office.

"Excuse us," she said as she pushed the partially opened door up against the cylindrical rubber stopper and walked into the room. Budmere looked up from the laptop and Cathy stopped stacking papers on a small side table. "Do you remember seeing a washer in the apartment?"

Budmere looked at Cathy and began to shake his head in a negative reply. "No I can't say that I remember a washer in any of the rooms we investigated. The kitchen didn't have enough room and the bathroom was fairly compact too. Cathy?"

"None," was the short reply. Bill and Christina thanked them and returned to Christina's office.

"That just doesn't make much sense. You know the family doesn't take their laundry out, so where's the washer?" Bill pondered. Christina remembers looking into the garage during one of their visits when the garage door was open and there wasn't a washer or dryer visible.

"Let me give Helga a quick call to see where Crimitin did his laundry," Christina said as she picked up the phone to dial Helga. When the connection was made, it rang half a dozen times before Christina hung up.

"It doesn't appear she's home. I'll try again later." Bill agreed as he checked his watch. He didn't want to be late for his luncheon meeting with Betty. As he was getting up to leave, Cathy appeared at the door with a report binder and a 3.5 disk.

"Budmere asked me to give you this so you could check it and make sure it meets your needs. He's on line checking his mail."

"Thanks Cathy," Bill responded as he took the binder and disk. He turned to Christina and laid the items on her desk. Bill offered Cathy a seat, which she took, excused himself and went back to his office.

Christina and Cathy talked a bit about the case and what discoveries were made during their two-day search. The place was full of prints but most of them were identified. Some fibers on the door leading to the patio area were the most promising item. Budmere said they looked like cotton. Could have been from a pair of gloves. They would have to wait for the final lab results but at least they would have them on file in case they came up with comparison material. They went over the report and opened up files on the disk so Christina would have a working knowledge of its contents. Before they realized it, nearly an hour passed. Christina looked at the standard Government Issue clock hanging from an exposed nail on the wall next to the door.

"Whoa, look at the time. I've got a meeting with Penny at the commander's office about one of her cases and I need to call Helga." Cathy got up to leave but Christina stopped her.

"Don't leave yet. Let's see about the laundry arrangements and maybe Budmere will have an idea." Christina pushed redial. It rang only twice before Helga answered.

"Good morning Helga, its Christina. Have a minute?" Helga said she was always happy to talk. Christina was going to try and limit the conversation today. When she asked about laundry facilities Helga said the tenants did their laundry on a rotating basis. Monday, Wednesday, Friday for one apartment. Tuesday, Thursday, Saturday for the other apartment. No washing was done on Sunday. Helga did her laundry in the evenings since the entrance to the room was near her apartment at the back of the building. Christina asked if she was going to be home the rest of the afternoon and Helga said she would.

Before Helga could add another word, Christina excused herself and bid her goodbye. Helga was somewhat taken aback by the abruptness of the process but figured Christina was busy with the investigation. She placed the receiver back into its spot on the table next to the ornate candy dish containing the duct tape wrapped package. She snapped her fingers when she saw the item. She would try to remember to give it to Christina when she visited later in the day.

Christina looked at Cathy with a smile. "We may have hit gold," she exclaimed as she explained the information. Cathy agreed it was a good lead and asked if she could come along when Christina visited Helga. Christina quickly agreed. They both went to Bill's office and told him the information and then Cathy relayed the message to Budmere. He was still on line

341

communicating with headquarters on their next assignment. Surprisingly he complemented the women on their find. Cathy was almost too stunned to reply.

"Thanks," Cathy stuttered as she left Budmere to continue his communications with headquarters. She hoped he would have information about their next assignment before she came back from Helga's house.

CHAPTER FORTY-THREE

Jose pushed his chair back from the computer keyboard and rolled over to the bottom right hand drawer of his desk. He grabbed the battered handle and opened the drawer. Inside was his stash of snacks to sustain his concentration during hours of paperwork. He just selected a package of chocolate covered cupcakes when Needles approached.

"Have you seen this information on the burned out truck?" he asked laying a sheet of paper on Jose's desk blotter.

"I haven't had time to check distribution this morning. What's the down and dirty," Jose asked as he unwrapped the cupcakes. He offered one to Kristo knowing he would turn down the offer.

"Over the weekend we got in a report of a shooting incident on the Santa Monica involving some Air Force special agents and a vehicle matching the one you're involved with. Partial license plate matches and there were two occupants when the shooting began."

"Interesting," Jose mumbled with a mouth full of cupcake. He paused to finish chewing the snack before he spoke again. "Is there anything else?"

"Nothing more. Let me give the chippie desk a call to see if he can shed a bit more light on the situation. I'll just tell him we may have found the vehicle. Let's see how accommodating he wants to be."

Jose agreed to the idea and picked up the incident sheet. Needles was right, there wasn't much information. He would be interested to find out what the hell was taking place on the Santa Monica freeway involving the Air Force and some shithead gang members.

Needles made copies of the dispatch keeping one at his desk. He put on the speaker headset he used to keep his hands free for note taking and dialed the CHP office number. The desk sergeant answered.

"California Highway Patrol, Sergeant Kasey."

"Kasey, this is Pinneyman, Harbor Division. You got a minute?"

"Right now, got a few. No one in the office and none of the phones are blinking. What's up?" Pinneyman explained how they received the dispatch about the freeway shooting. He said the vehicle they were looking for was involved in another incident. It was now in police custody.

By the tone of his voice, Kasey knew Pinneyman was only telling him a portion of the story. He didn't pry because it wasn't his place to try and get the full story. He would simply turn the information over to the person in charge of the incident and press on with his day. He took down the phone numbers for the desk in San Pedro and the office phone of Detective Gonzales. He read back the information adding emphasis to the words another incident so Pinneyman would know he realized he wasn't getting the full story. Pinneyman understood the game and after agreeing with the message, he complemented his CHP counterpart on his full understanding of the situation. He pushed the intercom for Jose and relayed the information to him.

At the CHP office, Kasey placed the note in the distribution box of Lieutenant Ackedawn. She was working a split shift so she wouldn't be in the office until after noon. He also clipped a copy of their original dispatch and the numbers for the OSI office at Vandenberg.

Sidney came through the door of Randy's office and plunked on the Government Issue simulated leather couch. Randy was writing on a notepad and greeted his fellow investigator without looking up. Sidney returned the greeting and waited until Randy looked up from the pad. "I checked all my messages and e-mail. I don't have anything on the truck. Did you get anything?"

Randy said he hadn't checked yet but would do it right then. Sidney picked up Randy's coffee cup and headed for the coffee pot. He pulled one of the spare mugs off the shelf and filled both. He returned to Randy and set his mug next to the computer keyboard. "I don't have anything on e-mail from the CHP but I do have some questions from headquarters and one from Germany. Let me open up the headquarters' note and see what they want."

He read the contents of the note aloud so Sidney could hear. It was nothing more than a request for a full report on the incident.

"Like we weren't going to send them a full report," Sidney commented as he took a long drink of his coffee.

"I don't really think we need a reminder from the home office about telling them all the details of the incident. Hell I've been in the field longer than that pinhead Younger has been an agent and he has the audacity to send us a note to ensure we tell headquarters the full story?" Randy fumes as he punches the mouse to have a copy of the note printed.

He sits in silence until both copies of the document have slid into the printer's tray. "Let me give you this friendly reminder from headquarters," he hisses as he hands a copy of the note across his desk. Sidney moved from the couch to a chair in front of the desk while Randy was fussing about the reminder. He took the paper and read the information again.

"Do we have anything on the key?" Sidney asked. Randy again reviewed his in box and said there wasn't anything on it yet. It may be a day or two even with the high priority they tried to place on discovering what the purpose of the key was. Both men still felt it was another safe deposit key from the shape and size. However, it didn't appear to be the same manufacturer as the first one in Covina. This one was a bit more ornate in design and complexity of keying. They would just have to wait until the lab was able to produce some information on the key and its intended use. The men talked about some other cases currently on their plate and were about to break up the impromptu meeting when the intercom buzzed to life. The administrator asked Randy to pick up line one. It was a CHP lieutenant. Randy asked Sidney to sit back down.

"Agent Ridgemire, can I help you?" Lieutenant Crystal Ackedawn and Randy exchanged pleasantries before getting down to the reason behind the call.

"We had a hit on the truck. Seems like the Harbor Division police have the truck impounded for involvement in another incident. I picked up the note when I came in and wanted to give you guys a call before I did anything with the folks in San Pedro."

"Appreciate the call," Randy replied. "Mind if I put you on the speaker? Sidney's in the office with me." Crystal didn't mind and the conversation continued between the three law officers.

"Did they mention what type of incident the truck was involved with?"

"No, and that had me puzzled. Normally we give other agencies as much information as we can but this time there wasn't much. I asked my desk sergeant about the conversation and he said there's more information. He knew the other desk sergeant was just giving him the tip of the iceberg. I guess they have this unwritten code not to interfere if not invited. He just took down the basic information and the numbers for the Harbor Division office and a Detective, hang on a sec, a....detective....., here it is, Gonzales. I would bet he's the lead on the incident. Can't help you with any information on him or the station. It's not one of our neighbors so we don't have regular dialogue with them."

"I understand," Randy states. "just how do you suggest we proceed?"

"Tell ya what," the lieutenant offers. "Let me give the guy a call and see what I discover without letting him in on too much of the situation. I'll try to see if they picked up any prints from the truck. They didn't indicate they had the men, just the truck."

"Sounds good to us," agreed the OSI team. "Give us a call when you're done. One of us will be in the office all day," Randy says as he gets a nod of approval from Sidney. "Thanks for the information, talk with ya later today."

"Hot damn," Sidney exclaimed as he stood from his spot in front of the desk. "We may be cookin' now."

"Let's not get our hopes up. You know damn well the truck is not going to be registered to the guys who shot at us. It's going to be stolen or registered to some dummy company." Sidney reluctantly agreed. It would be too much of a good thing if the truck led them right to the culprits. However, he wasn't one to be pessimistic.

"I'll go back to my office and make sacrifices to the evidence Gods for a full set of prints and the owners' registration." Both men laughed as Sidney left. Little did he know they had more than fingerprints to work with.

Crystal had some paperwork to process before she took an opportunity to give Jose a call. She had answers to most of her questions when he answered. "Homicide, Gonzales."

"Detective, this is Lieutenant Ackedawn, Highway Patrol. I understand you've got a truck impounded that we have a bulletin out on."

"Yes we do lieutenant. It was involved with a homicide," was all the information Jose was going to provide. The two representatives of different agencies floated around the subject for a while before Jose tired of the game and asked a blunt question. "So what were these Air Force types doing on the Santa Monica with people in this truck shooting at them?"

"For that answer detective, you're going to have to ask them. Since you and I aren't going to make any headway playing the games we're playing, let me contact the others involved and have them give you a call direct."

"Sounds reasonable to me," Jose quipped as he ended the call. Crystal sat for a while before giving Randy and Sidney a call. She really hated to deal with homicide dicks. They were always so secretive and conniving. She finished with a couple of deep breaths and then called the OSI offices at Vandenberg.

The office administrator answered and passed the call into Randy's office. "Hello Lieutenant. I do hope you have some good information for us."

"The one bit of information I can tell you with absolute certainty is the truck was involved in a homicide. This Gonzales guy works homicide in Harbor Division. He wasn't very forthcoming with information about the type of crime or exactly where it occurred. He wanted to talk with you guys. I didn't give him your number because I know he would become a pest. My suggestion is to give him a call and visit his domain. You may be able to pull more info out of him if he feels comfortable at home."

Randy agreed. If they asked to see him at Vandenberg, he would feel like a fish out of water. Randy and Sidney would give the man a call and see what he would pass along over the phone. If they couldn't get much out of him, they would take the time and pay a visit to San Pedro. Crystal offered any assistance her office could provide. Randy thanked her for the offer and promised to be more up front with information they discovered after talking with Jose.

Randy and Sidney played a game of cat and mouse with the detective. They didn't want to reveal too much about their investigation without getting some type of cooperation in return. They danced around the subject like couples in a ballroom competition. Randy finally said they weren't going to get anywhere and suggested a meeting, in San Pedro, with all information put out on the table for review by all the players. Jose agreed so a date, time, and place were arranged. Randy and Sidney could only hope the detective would be as accommodating as they planned on being.

CHAPTER FORTY-FOUR

"Anything from Vinder?" Carl asked as he came into Dillon's office.

"Late yesterday, like after normal duty hours, I got a call from an embassy staffer. Vinder didn't even have the gonads to call himself. The staffer said Vinder asked him to pass along a very short message. The message: all arranged. When I asked the guy if there was anything else, he said there wasn't and the colonel would be in contact with us in a few days. Short, sweet and too the point. I hope he doesn't try to play hardball. I do hate to push a colonel around," Dillon finished with a sly smile and a wink.

"On the subject of information, do we have anything on the key they found at the bank?"

"I haven't gotten anything. Let me check with William." He returned in less than a minute.

"He doesn't have anything either. We may want to tweak them to see if there has been anything on the key. You did send along your possible solution to the anagram didn't you?"

"Just what do you mean by possible solution?" Dillon asked in an accusatory tone.

Both men laughed as Carl left for the administrative area to check on messages there. Dillon picked up the secure line to call Bill. It took a moment or two before he heard the connection click through and the phone begin to ring. "Agent Wilmerson."

"Bill, Dillon. Just calling to check on your progress. Did you make anything out of the soapbox reference?"

"You must be physic. I was just going to give you a call before I headed for lunch with Betty. She called with some information but didn't want to talk about it over the phone. I don't know if it relates to our investigation or another one in the office. I'll e-mail you this afternoon. Anyway, we kicked the soapbox reference around for a while and then Christina and I realized there weren't any clothes washing materials on the inventory. Then we thought about a washer and dryer and came up with the notion there wasn't a place to wash clothes in the apartment. Christina called Helga and found out the washer and dryer are in a room near her apartment. They alternate washing days for the different apartments. Christina and Cathy are making a trip there this afternoon to check it. We can only hope the soapbox reference has something to do with the wash room."

"That sounds reasonable," Dillon commented. "Let me know what you find. Have you heard anything from the California connection?"

"Nothing," Bill responded. "I was hoping this key would be as easy to identify as the key for the safe deposit box in Covina but I guess that would be too much to ask for. I'll send them a note and ask for a progress report."

Dillon recounted the Vinder connection and the indicated cooperation with NSA. "I know some of the players at Meade. If I suspect a cold reception, I'll play those trump cards. I didn't want to burst Vinder's bubble by insinuating I would be checking on his effort. I'll just spring it on him all at once. That'll be interesting to watch him squirm." With no further information to share, the men talked about personal issues for a while and then broke the connection. Bill headed for lunch with Betty and Dillon went to brief William and Carl.

The luncheon venue selected by Bill and Betty was the golf course snack bar. Since both of them dabbled in the game, they enjoyed visiting the course during lunch to watch the people who managed to slide away from work to play the course. The lunchroom overlooked the short 10th hole from tee to green, the 11th tee, and the 18th green. Bill backed the Beemer into one of the available slots and went to open Betty's door. She gave him a kiss on the forehead as she got out.

"So when are we going to play the course again?" Bill asked. "We've both been so busy lately we haven't taken much time for a nice walk in the woods."

"Speak for yourself, nature boy. I'm not the one who carries a chain saw as part of my club selection," was Betty's retort.

Once inside the clubhouse, Bill went and ordered their burgers and sodas. Betty chose a table in the corner with a nice view of the course. Before their meal came, Bill wanted to know why the secret meeting?

"Do you remember Francy?" Betty asked.

"Isn't she the waitress at the club?"

"You're right, she's a waitress at the club, but she's also an Airman working in PMEL[26]. I helped her in a very difficult personal situation and she has

349

come to me on a couple of other occasions just to talk. She trusts me and I believe our talks have kept her in service. When her marriage fell apart, she nearly asked for a discharge to get away from here. When we talked about where she would go and what she would do, she really didn't have a good answer." Betty paused as the waitress brought their drinks and setups for their burgers. "Anyway,"

"Is this all going somewhere?" Bill interrupted.

"Hang on," Betty scolded. "I just want to fill you in on details so when you hear what she said you'll take it seriously. She wouldn't come to me if the story weren't true. ANYWAY! I got her to change her mind about leaving the Force and Ramstein. We did manage to get rid of her ex and the prospect of being in Europe seemed to please her. We've had some good discussions but I wasn't really prepared for the one today." Betty picked up her diet soda and took a drink. She turned away from Bill to watch the players on the 10th tee shoot for the green.

"Well," Bill questioned.

"Oh," Betty sarcastically replied, "I have your attention now?"

"Yes, yes, yes," was the response as Bill leaned forward. Betty took another sip of her soda and recounted the talk. Bill was very interested in the fact both the men were in the security squadron. He just sat back and shook his head when she told him.

"I'm beginning to believe the old adage if you want some dope, all you have to do is visit the Security Police barracks." The waitress brought their burgers and asked if there was anything else. With nothing additional from either of them, she sat the bill on the table and left them to their conversation. Bill asked a few more questions about the relationship, how they came to be dating, the other female airman, and if Betty was sure this wasn't just a setup to cover up use by Francy. Betty assured her investigative husband Francy could be trusted on this one. If she were lying, Betty would help process her immediate discharge papers. They finished lunch and sat for a while nursing their sodas as they watched and commented on the play of afternoon golfers.

Bill dropped Betty off and went directly to the Security Police offices. He wanted to get the ball rolling on these two lowlifes as soon as possible. He knew the problems bringing Krimshank to the commander's position but hadn't pried into his area of responsibility unless asked. Who knows, he thought, maybe these two will be able to add something to the Crimitin investigation.

He pulled into the parking lot and took a space away from the entrance. Once inside he greeted the desk sergeant and the force members he met on his way to Krimshank's office. "Sergeant Johnson," he hailed the administrator as he came in the door. "Is your boss available?"

"Afternoon sir," was the reply from the sergeant. "He's on the phone right now. Have a seat and I'll tell him you're here." Bill thanked him as he took a seat on the couch. Sergeant Johnson opened the commander's door and slipped inside. He wrote Bill's name on a small post it note so he could stick it on the dial of the phone. He didn't want to interrupt the commander during this call to security headquarters at the Pentagon. When he came out of the office, he offered Bill a soda or coffee but Bill declined recounting the lunch he just finished at the course. It was only a few minutes before the colonel came out to greet Bill.

"Well, well, well. It has been some time since you graced my humble abode Agent Wilmerson. What brings you to my neck of the woods?" Bill got up to shake hands with the security force leader.

"It has been some time sir but in our business that's a good thing."

"I suppose you're right there," Karlton replied as he ushered Bill into his office. Since Bill was making an unscheduled visit, Krimshank felt there was a problem so he shut the door as he followed Bill into the room. The men exchanged small talk before Bill got down to business.

"Betty and I just had lunch at the course. She brought me some disturbing information about a couple of your troops." He reached into his coat pocket and pulled out a napkin with the course logo embossed in one corner to read the names Betty provided.

"The two men are Senior Airman David T. Durowe and Staff Sergeant Paul N. Benrod." Bill retold the tale Francy gave Betty. Krimshank leaned back in his chair as he listened to the narrative. When Bill finished, the security force commander sat upright and put his hands along the edge of his desk.

"I'll tell you those two names don't surprise me. As you know, I was sent here because of problems discovered during an inspection. One of the biggest problems was our drug unit. We relieved the lead investigator. Durowe is still a member of the unit because we feel he can connect us with a supplier in this area. I've asked for and been told I'll receive some outside assistance. I was just on the phone coordinating with Washington on where assistance would be coming from. It may be a joint OSI security force effort or it may be an in house search. The big boys haven't really made up their mind yet. I'll tell you this; Dillon's name was mentioned during the conversation. His reputation is certainly well known around Air Force law enforcement agencies."

Bill agreed and said it was an education so far in their joint effort to find Crimitin's killers. The men continued their conversation about a possible effort to cut out the drug problem in the security squadron. As they finished, Krimshank assured Bill any decision made by higher headquarters would be coordinated with his office.

"I never held a doubt," he replied to the colonel's statement. The men parted company with Bill returning to his office and the colonel heading out for a meeting with the USAFE commander.

When Bill got back, he went to Christina's office to inform her about both meetings. As they were talking, she entered the names into her database to see if there were any OSI related incidents with either of the men. The only thing showing was a couple of domestic violence cases involving Durowe. When they finished both investigators went to Penny's office to check on her records about the domestic violence incidents. Since they were not within the past year, Penny didn't have full recall about the problems. She went to the files and pulled out the folder containing all the reports.

"Senior Airman David Durowe, Security Police. There was a series of incidents involving the couple. We were called when the wife reported to the emergency room with a cut on her forehead," Penny read from the report. "When the duty dog visited her in ER, she mentioned other incidents. She said all the problems were minor but David did have a violent temper. She never mentioned drugs or alcohol. Of course you always suspect those in a violence case." They talked about the case file, the subsequent divorce, the custody case and kept it out as an addendum to the Crimitin case. Bill said he would bring Dillon into the loop the next time they talked.

CHAPTER FORTY-FIVE

"We should be coming up on the exit," Randy commented as they passed the city limits sign for San Pedro. Sidney dialed the station house phone. Needles answered and gave them final directions to reach the office. He told them they were only a few minutes away.

"Watch for the Channel exit," Sidney called out as he broke connection with the station.

"We get off there, keep to the right, and make a right turn at the first corner. That road dead-ends into John Gibson where we make a left. He said the office is just past the on ramp for the Harbor on the left side of the street."

The directions Needles provided were complicated but spot on target. Sidney and Randy pulled into a visitor spot in the parking lot. As they came into the office, Sergeant Pinneyman came to greet them.

"Welcome to San Pedro gentlemen. I've told Detective Gonzales you're here. He's waiting in his office." They followed him down the hall. He rapped lightly on the partially open door and waited for Jose to ask them in before he slipped the door out of their way.

"Gentlemen," Jose greeted as he stood up behind his desk pushing his chair back against the well-worn wall. "Welcome to my humble hacienda. I trust the trip was a pleasant one?"

"Very nice, thank you. We didn't have to content with the majority of traffic and there weren't any accidents along the way so it was a very pleasant ride." Sidney replied as both men took seats in front of Jose's desk. Pinneyman was still filling the doorway.

"Would you like some coffee?" Jose asked. Both agents said it would be fine with them. Needles nodded and emptied the doorway.

"I don't know if she told you but I invited the CHP lieutenant to join us. Since her office was the one to send out the bulletin, I figured it would be best if we all talked about the situation you two faced and what we have to add." Randy and Sidney voiced no objections on including the lieutenant in their conversation. There was a knock on the doorframe as one of the administrators brought in a wooden tray with a hotpot of coffee, cups, and condiments. He sat it on the corner of Jose's desk, poured the steaming liquid into the mugs embossed with the department's logo and passed them to the agents.

Since the CHP representation was missing, the talk centered on things other than their prime reason for visiting. No more than 30 minutes passed before Pinneyman was again at the door. This time he brought Lieutenant Ackedawn. Greetings exchanged, coffee poured, and the conversation quickly turned to the main reason for their visit.

Jose started by telling them how he became involved with the vehicle. He reached into a document tray marked "HOLD" and pulled out a folder, which he placed on the desk blotter. He pulled the alligator clip off the side and opened the folder. Inside were documents and photos. He pulled duplicates of the report out and gave each of his guests a copy. He paused as they read the contents.

"So the truck was set on fire between the buildings and when the fire department responded to douse it, they found two bodies in the cargo compartment?" Randy commented as he finished reading the narrative.

"That's about the size of it," Jose replied. "We figured it was gang related so I told all the local players to watch for any kind of movement on a turf war. Nobody had anything of significance happening at least according to some of our plants and informants. When we saw the bulletin, we became very interested on how this particular vehicle would end up in our jurisdiction with two corpses?" Randy said that was a fair concern. They became involved with the men near Covina and this was quite a distance from where they made contact with the CHP.

"So what caused the demise of these two?" Crystal inquired. Jose pulled the autopsy sheet from the file and handed it to her.

"Looks like an execution to me," she commented after reading the report and handing it to Randy. "Hands bound behind their backs and a large caliber weapon used to put one round through the back of their head." Jose then handed her a set of the scene photos and the autopsy photos.

"They weren't messing around were they?" was her only comment after looking at the glossy color photos.

354

"The truck was filled with flammable liquid and then torched from down the alley. Whoever did this didn't really care about leaving the can of gas for us to find. It came off the back of the truck. Kind of a makeshift jerry can arrangement. The owner of the truck rigged it for use in the desert. Anyway, after the guy doused the truck, he laid a trail of gas to a spot near the end of the street, threw a match into the stuff, and then, we assume, left the scene. Hell with all the buildings around, he could have been watching the whole thing."

"So," Sidney began. "The truck was duly registered to some decent citizen but was reported stolen."

"Correct there but the twist is the truck was missing for more than two years. The registration was totally bogus. The only way we found the owner was through a VIN check. It came up with the name of Yardley N. Nott of Lancaster, California. The truck he lost was a different color but when the lab guys went over it, they found several layers of paint. Seems like they would use the truck for something and then paint the son of a bitch over and over again."

"So who were these guys?" Sidney asked as he placed the papers on the desk and picked up his coffee mug. Jose pulled another set of documents from the folder and handed them across the desk.

"The first guy is Patrick Elohrock. Small time criminal. Caught in some fencing stings selling stereo equipment. However, his record has been clean for at least five years. Not even a traffic ticket."

"I guess not if he was driving a hot truck!" Crystal laughed.

"The other guy is Poindexter Xylodu. That's his real name. He has several aliases but that's the one his mommy gave him. He's been a bit more active than his partner has. Grand theft auto, armed robbery, breaking and entering, possession and one charge of attempted murder that didn't stick. Like Patrick, he's been clean for about six years. What ever game they were involved with seemed to keep them off the streets."

Randy and Sidney combined efforts to explain the situation, as they knew it. Jose sat and listened without asking a single question. The lieutenant also sat in silence since this was the first time she heard the entire story as it related to the Vandenberg OSI office and their involvement with the Crimitin family. When they finished, Jose asked about the key and if they met with any luck identifying a use. Randy said he expected some type of results very soon. Both the agents felt it was another safe deposit box key but not from the local area. It may have come from his time in Northern California or it could be from a box in Germany. They would just have to wait until the other investigative labs finished their work.

"Well that seems to put my biggest concern about a turf war to rest. I was worried we would be finding more of these burned out trucks around the city. However, I'll put out a note to all players telling them we have a possible motive solved, we just don't have the triggerman, nor do we have the torch. Is that alright with you folks?" Jose questioned. The lieutenant and both agents agreed to the plan but wanted to ensure as little as possible is mentioned about the breadth of the investigation.

There was certainly some type of tie in to the local community but until they gathered more information, they didn't want to tip their hands. Jose agreed and even offered to send them an advance copy of the note before he put it on the street. Randy thanked him for the offer. The four investigators continued to talk until it was about lunchtime. Jose offered to take them to lunch at the Omelette and Waffle Shop before they were on their way back home. Randy and Sidney wanted to see the remains of the truck so lunch would be the perfect precursor to the visit. Crystal needed to head back for her office but agreed to partake of lunch before hitting the road. Jose said the place was on Gaffey, so he would lead the way.

As they entered the "place where old friends meet", Jose waved to Mona, one of the owners. "We're not too late for lunch are we?" he questioned. She said they just made it under the wire but Jose was a regular customer so the lateness of his arrival wasn't significant.

"What's the recommendation of the day?" Sidney asked. Jose said he was steadily making his way through the entire menu as he patted his expanded waistline.

"I haven't found a bad item on the menu. It all depends on what you want in your omelet or on top of your waffles." The law officers made their selections and fell into discussions of similar problem areas facing the three distinctively different types of agencies. When they finished the talking and eating, Jose left a significant tip to compensate for their late arrival and departure. Mona waved as they left the building.

As they were bidding farewell to Crystal, Jose asked her to keep in touch for any assistance the CHP could provide on locating the connection between the truck and the killer. After she left, Jose led Randy and Sidney to the impound lot. There wasn't much to see but they did confirm the burned out hulk was the same truck used to chase them along several miles of the Southern California's convoluted freeway system.

"We may not want to search too deeply for the reason behind the execution. I really don't think they expected us to run like we did. Their orders were probably very specific and when they screwed up by not getting the contents of the safe deposit box for their boss, he sent a message to all the players," Randy said as he turned away from the charred remains.

"You could be right there," Jose agreed. "In my time on homicide, I've seen a lot less reason for having someone whacked. If gang related, they may not like the way you looked at one of their girlfriends. If it's drugs, they're just out to ensure the elimination of all competition. That's why we originally thought this might have something to do with gangs. We've never seen the burning trick but we have seen similar executions."

CHAPTER FORTY-SIX

Christina wheeled around the corner and up the hill. She called before leaving the base to ensure Helga was home. As the two agents pulled in front of the home, Helga was just coming out the front door. She waved as Cathy and Christina got out.

"Good afternoon," Helga called as she pulled the newspaper and advertisements out of the mailbox attached to the house at the top of the driveway. As the two agents approached, she turned and greeted each of them with a kiss and hug.

"It's good to see you both again," she said leading the way back through the doorway. She made her way around the stairs, opened the door to the laundry room, and then left the two investigators to complete their search while she went inside her apartment to fix a suitable beverage.

Both agents entered the room. Before pulling anything off a shelf, they made a visual inspection of the area. Helga used the room not only for laundry but also for storing a wide variety of cleaning supplies. With the small size of her apartment, she didn't like to waste space on seldom-used items. On specially built shelves behind the two agents were cleaning materials of all descriptions.

On a shelf near the bottom were five boxes of soap powder. All unopened. On the divided shelf over the washer and dryer were open boxes of soap. Starting on the left, Cathy pulled one box off the shelf, pulled back the lid, and looked inside. Nothing. They moved down the shelf and looked inside each of the open containers. Each inspection resulted in the same conclusion. There just wasn't anything in any of the soapboxes. Disappointment showed in the expressions displayed by each agent.

"I guess I had my hopes up too far on this long shot," Christina said as she shoved the last box back on the shelf.

"It really would have been too good to be true if we found something of significance in one of the boxes," Cathy added. "We just need to expand the search for a soapbox associated with Crimitin. Maybe it's not a large laundry soapbox. Maybe he's talking about the small kind used to carry bath soap when you travel. Maybe it's in a soapbox he used to wash his car. We can't be dejected at this point. We'll just have to keep looking."

Christina agreed with the points Cathy made. This was just the first place searched. She really wasn't ready to accuse Dillon of getting it wrong but she would really get a kick out of pushing his buttons if nothing came of his "discovery".

The ladies shut off the light and pushed open Helga's door. Christina called her name. In response, Helga invited the agents in for coffee. The coffee, cups, condiments, and cookies were neatly arranged on an ornate silver tray. As Cathy and Christina entered the tiny room, Helga indicated they take a seat on the couch across from her chair. She poured the steaming, richly brewed blend into their cups.

"So did you find anything additional?" Helga queried.

Christina said there wasn't anything new in the room.

Helga handed the cups across the table and offered the plate of cookies to each woman. "Remind me," she said. "I've got something I want you to take with you when you leave." She then turned the conversation to happenings in town.

Bill pushed the button for Christina's intercom. When she didn't answer, he called Penny. "Did Christina go out to Helga's?" he asked.

Penny replied both Cathy and Christina made the trip. "Why do you ask?" she queried.

"I just picked up my mail and the boys in California reported a major discovery. I just wanted to share the news with her." Penny said she wanted to hear the report. She came down to Bill's office where he proceeded to tell her about the truck and the bodies.

"That's interesting news," Penny agreed. "If they can tie up the knot on who put these guys away, it would certainly add significant pieces to our puzzle." Bill agreed and the two of them talked for a while before Penny left the office. After she left, Bill gave Dillon a call on the secure line. He found him home fixing a snack.

"Just getting ready to have a bite to eat before heading back to the office," Dillon greeted.

"Have you looked at your mail today?" Bill wanted to know. Dillon said he checked earlier in the morning but had not checked this afternoon. He'd been arranging files in preparation for another meeting with Vinder. He wasn't getting the type of cooperation he expected, so he was going to pay a surprise visit to the colonel and place some additional emphasis on his prior request for assistance. Bill proceeded to report the findings in California. It tweaked Dillon's interest.

"That certainly adds to my theory of a California connection. We knew they were watching the Crimitin house but we couldn't be sure if they were just some flunkies or if there were some power hitters out there. This points to a significant operation on the West Coast. Evidently, the leaders of this particular pack of dogs didn't appreciate getting into a shooting war with the Air Force. The poor dupes who thought they were just doing a good job ended up dead. It was probably set up as a warning to others in the group and a side note to us if we discovered they were the same guys who shot up the car."

"What do you mean by a side note?"

"It could be a note to tell us the main players of this ring didn't appreciate what these two did. If they eliminate them and make it obvious to law enforcement it was a purposeful killing, they may believe we'll look kindly upon their actions. We weren't meant to be shot at and they cleaned up their own act."

Bill agreed in some sort of twisted way the theory made sense. "But you don't think they believe we'll give up looking for additional information, do you?"

"They know the locals will keep on this for a while but they probably don't believe the Air Force will keep on top of the situation. We have to make sure we keep our finger on the pulse without being too conspicuous." Bill said he understood and would keep in touch with the office in California.

"Just make sure you info me on any mail you send. I do like to kibitz." Bill laughed as he settled with Dillon on how to proceed.

"You mentioned Vinder earlier." Bill solicited. "Isn't he providing as promised?"

"I just have a feeling he isn't being as forthcoming as he can be. I know the cloak of secrecy the agency places over any significant involvement they have in a foreign country. Everyone knows we spy, no one knows how well we accomplish the task. With Eclipse, we can get right to the nitty gritty of their communications. If he's really having trouble-making things happen, then I'll just have to pull a few of the strings I've tied to the boys at Fort

Meade. However, before I take him out of the game, I want to make sure he understands what I'm going to do because it'll affect the way he operates in the future."

"Sounds ominous," Bill commented.

"It's so ominous Colonel Vinder may want to consider a change in careers. I do believe the Salvation Army is recruiting," Dillon finished with a slight laugh.

"Can I interest you in another cookie?" Helga offered as she slipped to the edge of her chair, picked up the plate, and reached it across the table. Cathy and Christina both eyed the selection as they each picked a different type of cookie from their last choice. They just refilled their cups with the remaining coffee while Helga reported on all the happenings in the village and invited the women back for the next potluck supper at the church. She winked at Christina as she told her about all the eligible men who came to the dinners. As she finished with a statement about the upcoming holiday celebrations, she sat up straight and slapped her hands together. It startled both agents.

"What's the matter?" Christina asked.

"I almost forgot again," Helga responded as she got up and headed into the hallway. "You just wait here. I found something the other day and I haven't got any idea what it is," she said as her voice faded away down the hall.

She returned a moment later with the duct tape wrapped package. She handed it to Christina. "This dropped into my bucket of soap the other day when I was doing laundry."

Christina held the object between her thumb and forefinger as she examined the outside wrapping. She could see flecks of laundry soap attached to the edges of the duct tape. She was almost afraid to ask the obvious question.

"Helga," she tentatively began. "Where did this fall from?" Helga recounted the story about how she ran out of laundry detergent and didn't want to take the time to visit the store since she really didn't need anything else, etc. etc. After what seemed like hours to Christina, she finally got around to the point. "So I pulled out a partially used box young William had at the back of his shelf and when I poured the remaining soap into my bucket, it fell out on top of the heap."

Eureka, Christina thought as she sat the small package down on the table before getting up to give Helga a thankful kiss on the cheek.

361

CHAPTER FORTY-SEVEN

Dillon picked up the portable phone and settled into the cushions of his couch. He checked the small piece of paper just retrieved from his briefcase and carefully dialed the number. After only one ring, Sonta answered.

"Greetings Mr. Reece. It's good we have this opportunity to speak with each other."

"At least give me a chance to apologize for my lack of verbal communication," Dillon countered. "I've been very busy as I explained in my notes. By the way, thanks for the new e-mail address. I kept wondering why my last few notes came back as undeliverable."

"I changed providers so I went to one of the standard e-mail accounts. That way I don't have to change addresses if I change providers again." Sonta began to fill Dillon in on details of her charitable activities and what was happening in the local area. Dillon listened intently only interrupting if he didn't recognize a name or activity. Sonta continued for some time before she paused.

"I'm sorry; I do tend to ramble on when I get on a roll. What's been happening in your world and I don't want to know anything about your work, just your recreational activities if you have any time for such things."

Dillon began telling her about some of the dining establishments when he was disrupted by the doorbell ringing incessantly. He got up from the couch and made his way to the tiled entrance area. The bell continued to ring until he pulled the door open to reveal William on the other side with his finger on the button. He began to speak but paused when he saw the phone up against Dillon's ear.

"Excuse me my dear, the pizza delivery man is here," Dillon said sarcastically. William remained silent as Dillon stepped out of the way and waved him into the living room. Sensing the urgency of William's visit, Dillon arranged for another calling time and bid Sonta goodbye. He returned the phone to its place on the desk. "I hope this is good," he said turning toward William.

"Karl has been trying to get hold of you. He wants us at the office for a conference call with Germany on the secure line. Evidently they have something big and they want us to have the information as soon as possible." Dillon went back to his bedroom, slipped into his shoes and pulled on a shirt. Both men were out the door and into the truck parked curbside. The ride to the office was short with Karl greeting both men as they came into his office.

"Christina gave me a call when she couldn't get through to your place," Karl said to Dillon.

"What's the big deal?" Dillon questioned.

"She really didn't explain her excitement. She just wanted to get all of us together for what she called very good news," Karl returned. "I'll get her on the line now."

Karl connected into the secure communication link and dialed the number for Christina's office at Ramstein. The call transferred to the conference room where Bill, Christina, and Penny were gathered. After exchanging greetings, Christina could hardly contain herself any longer. She began with the anagram solution and how nobody remembered any washing facilities in the apartment. She told about their visit to Helga and the disappointment of not finding anything in the laundry room. Then the news about the coffee, cookies, and duct tape package.

"Here's what we have." Christina began. "A voice from beyond."

She pushed the play button on the micro-cassette recorder placed close to the speakerphone. The voice was youngish. The recorder identified himself as William Crimitin, Azusa, California. From there on, the story unfolded of the meeting in California, the threats to his family, the move to Germany and the blackmail scheme to keep him running drugs into the kingdom. The agents sat in disbelieving silence. How could their luck run so good? Here's a confession from the victim so motive wasn't a factor any longer. He was going to turn evidence over to the DEA in Germany for a promised immunity deal and an assignment back to California. After the first tape finished, Dillon asked Christina who else knew of the tape.

"Just the agents here and now you guys," Christina replied.

"Does that include Budmere and Cathy?" Dillon queried. Christina replied it did.

"Of course this is a great bit of evidence but if we all calm down, it leaves more questions unanswered. You said there were three tapes in the pack. What's on the other two?"

Dillon heard how one tape was a note to the family. It began the same way the note they found in Covina. If someone was listening to the tape, Crimitin figured he was a dead man. The other tape contained a sort of local diary. They hadn't listened to the entire tape, just the beginning to see what it contained. They wanted Dillon to have the confession as soon as possible.

Everyone seemed satisfied. Dillon gave strict instructions the discovery of the tapes and their contents be kept within their agency. He didn't even want the locals brought into the find until he digested the information. William baulked but acquiesced after Dillon related his concerns over the reported leaks within the local department.

"We can only assume that someone is on the payroll. Our discovery will leak out at the right time." Dillon wanted to know how long it would take to transcribe the tapes. He was particularly interested in the diary tape. Bill assured him the transcript would be on the wires before he went to bed.

"Do you fucken believe that?" William gushed as he spun around in Karl's desk chair. "You were so right about there being tapes with some significant information on them. Let's just hope he names people and places so we can close this puppy down."

"I appreciate your enthusiasm William but I'm not looking for a smokin gun at the end of those tapes. I just hope they lead us further down the path. I'll have to give the young man credit for knowing what he was facing. He knew the men he dealt with were not beyond taking his life. When he was about to close down their game, they eliminated him." Karl retrieved a trio of long necks from his fridge. They toasted their good fortune but all agreed this was just the beginning of a dangerous part of their game.

Christina pulled her laptop from its bag and brought it back to the conference room. Bill was at the keyboard of the room's computer system with Penny poised to take shorthand notes on the tapes verbiage. The confession was first on the recorder. In his own words, Crimitin explained how he became involved with a group of men devoted to the drug trade. He explained their extortion plots and how the threats to his family were the only reason he agreed to take part in their plans. He detailed how he was keeping notes, skimming profits and gathering as much information as he could about the operation to turn over to the DEA. He named Asterfon as his point of contact in Germany. He listed code names for people in Kingdom. He told how he was able to get the dope into Prince Sultan and the money out. At the end, he asked forgiveness from his comrades in the Air Force and from his family.

The second tape was a conglomeration of notes. Contact with his minders, calls to Asterfon, contact with suppliers, trips into the kingdom, the location of additional tapes at Prince Sultan and one of the biggest points, the license plate of a blue Audi used by his minders.

"Bingo," shouted Bill as he heard the license plate number. "Now we've got the bastards by the balls."

"The only problem with having the information is being able to trace the car without tipping off the leak in Hanz's office." Christina began. "We're going to need a bit of luck locating the registered owners with someone working on the inside keeping them informed."

"Not to worry. I'll take care of that matter," Bill assured her. "I've been working on collecting a long list of blue Audi license plates since this thing began. I've had our security folks get me a list of all the registered blue Audis allowed on base and that's a substantial amount. We'll just add this one to the long line and submit it through some devious channels asking for identification on some fictitious problem with crossed communication lines on registration."

They took a break before listening to the last tape. They knew it was going to be the hardest one to transcribe, the one to his parents and family.

After a few minutes, Bill called the ladies back to the conference room for the final tape. It was a heart wrenching discussion of how much he loved his parents and his brother. How he hoped his life would not have been lost in vain, if George stayed in treatment and some day went into the Force. There wasn't a dry eye in the conference room after he bid his parents goodbye and ended the tape. After she pushed the stop button, Christina, Bill and Penny sat in silence for a minute or two while each of them dealt with the sadness of the situation. Finally Bill spoke.

"Christina, let's make a comparison of transcripts and recheck the tapes for anything we might have missed. Penny, please make a duplicate of the last tape before you translate your shorthand notes. I'll check with Dillon but I'm sure he'll want the last one sent off to Crimitin's parents as soon as possible." Without a word in reply, Christina gave the last tape to Penny, installed the first tape in the machine, and pushed the play button. It would take less than an hour to review the tape, make corrections, and get the copy on line to Dillon. In the note attached to the transcript, Bill told Dillon of his intent to send the last tape to the Crimitin family while keeping a copy for their files.

Dillon nodded his head in agreement as he read the note while consuming a single malt and chewing on the butt end of an unlit cigar.

CHAPTER FORTY-EIGHT

Sergeant Johnston walked down the short chute to the colonel's office. Krimshank was on the phone and motioned Johnston into the office. Jerome moved front and center of Krimshank's desk as he assumed an at ease position.

"Thanks for the information Hanz. I'll check with the traffic monitors to see if they have anything on the accident. If the guy gave out a phony address, he must have something to hide. I'm willing to bet he's driving without insurance. Give me the name of your investigator again and I'll pass it along the line."

Krimshank wrote down the name and concluded the call. He picked up the scrap of paper and handed it across the desk to Jerome. "Give that to traffic and have them follow up on the accident. What was it you wanted?"

"Benrod and Durowe are in the front office sir. You want them in here?"

"Nope. Have them cool their heels out there for a while. Are they escorted?"

"Yes sir," Jerome responded.

"Tell the escort to come in here and have them stand at ease in the front office. I'll buzz you when I want them in here."

Jerome left the office and in a moment, the escort was in front of the commander. Krimshank wanted to know what information was passed to the men in the outer office. The escort said he didn't know why they were taken off shift. Krimshank said he would explain later. The escort saluted, performed a perfect about face, and left the office.

Krimshank poured a glass of water from the Czechoslovakian cut crystal decanter he kept on his desk. One of his quirks was keeping water and ice in the decanter. He would use the process of visiting the small fridge in his office to get ice for the decanter as a diversion during tense situations or as a brief thinking period as he mulled over options to dilemmas. He sipped the cold liquid as he pondered his next move. He reviewed the personnel folders of the two men waiting in the front office before calling Jerome. "Have them report in."

First through the doorway was Staff Sergeant Paul N. Benrod. Paul was a member of the security force protecting aerospace assets used by the airlift and fighter wings at Ramstein. Right behind him was Senior Airman David T. Durowe. David was an investigator with the drug interdiction unit. One of the bad apples Krimshank discovered since his arrival. Both men presented themselves to the commander and waited for his return of salute. Krimshank watched the men as they came through the door. He slowly rose from his chair and with both hands gripping the edge of the desk he spoke in a slow concise tone.

"You shitheads are in a deep hole. You may be able to redeem yourself if you pay close attention to what I'm going to say during this interview. If you fail in any of your future work within this squadron, you'll be facing federal charges, a court martial and dishonorable discharge. Stand at ease." Krimshank never returned their salute. The men had stopped about two paces in front of the desk. Krimshank walked slowly to a spot directly in front of the two men and leaned back against the desk crossing his arms on his chest.

"I'm willing to bet if I took you two losers to the clinic right now I could get a positive result for illicit substances. That would be enough to bring you up on charges and process you for disciplinary action. Being members of the security force, you would lose your clearances and your ability to perform your primary duties. Since you would no longer be an asset to the force, you would be processed for discharge at the earliest possible moment. Without the benefit of a trial, you would receive a discharge under less than honorable circumstances. It would affect you for the rest of your sorry lives. Are you following me so far?" Krimshank asked as he leaned toward the two men. Each of them gave the commander an affirmative nod.

"I'm glad we're on the same sheet of music. I have information in my possession that you both used illegal drugs. I'm going to give you a chance to redeem yourselves if you can provide me with some very critical information relating to a case currently under investigation. If your cooperation is deemed successful, I'll make an effort to get you the proper treatment and have you kept in service in some other career field. The rest of the story would be up to you and your desires for redemption." Krimshank stood from his leaning position against the desk. Both men were more than six feet tall so Krimshank looked up at them as he spoke again.

"Any questions?"

Durowe spoke. "I'd like to consult with a lawyer, sir."

Krimshank moved directly in front of the Airman and with the index finger of his right hand, he poked the offender squarely in the chest as he stressed his point. "If you want a lawyer Durowe, I'll get you one but your redemption is over. No fucking lawyer is going to be able to save your ass when I get finished with it. You either take my offer right here and now, or you'll find yourself looking out from the other side of the bars in lockup. Savvy?"

Durowe stiffened as he answered. "Yes sir!"

The commander turned from the two men and went back to his chair. He sat down and pulled the two personnel files to the center of his desk. After reviewing performance reports for the men, he closed the folders and leaned back in his chair.

"Here's the deal. I need your sources. We're trying to confirm some information on another case and your sources may tie into that action. If your information is credible, we can talk about keeping you on the payroll. If you try to bullshit me, I'll take great pleasure in processing you for dishonorable discharges with some very trumped up charges. And let me tell you two scum suckers, I've been around the security game for a long time and I can make trumped up charges as real as I need them to be."

Durowe knew the evidence against the two men was insufficient to have them facing a dishonorable discharge. However, with Krimshank threatening to fabricate charges, he knew their shit was in the wind. He knew of the commander's history and believed the Old Man could make his threats stick.

Benrod began to speak. The colonel cut him off with a wave of his hand. "Durowe, you head back to the waiting room." Durowe saluted, and again, it was not returned. He executed an about face and left the office. Krimshank indicated for Benrod to take a seat in one of the chairs. As he sat down, the commander leaned forward crossing his arms on his desktop and asked, "What's on your mind son?"

The sergeant began a tale of supply and demand filtering through the entire security squadron. Most of his knowledge came first hand from attending parties and concerts. He swore his use was limited to marijuana and only marijuana. His supplier was Durowe. He didn't know any of the other suppliers and considered himself only a casual user.

Once he got going, he couldn't stop. The dates of parties were approximated with attendees from the squadron available when required.

Krimshank just let the man rattle on for as long as he wanted. He knew the time would make Durowe a nervous wreck wondering what Benrod was confessing to the commander. Krimshank knew the information provided by Benrod was reliable. His record was spotless with commendations from past assignments lining the pages of his personnel folder. He felt the man just got in with the wrong crowd after his divorce.

It's a typical scenario; a quality troop goes bad after a traumatic personal crisis. In Benrod's case, he discovered his Korean wife defiling the marital bed with another security force member on a different work shift. It turns out she was just returning to her old habits of providing sexual favors for monetary return.

Benrod met her away from the normal whore mongering bars outside his operational base in Korea. He didn't realize she was just one of the locals trying to land an American for a ticket to the good life. It devastated him. The assignment to Europe was designed to get him away from Asia and the constant reminder of his ex-wife's unfaithfulness. Having been implicated in the use of drugs, Benrod was more than willing to assist the commander in return for leniency. Krimshank would keep him in the dark about his thoughts on punishment until after they closed this aspect of the case.

After Benrod finished, Krimshank continued to incline on his desk for a moment before leaning back in his chair. He gripped the armrests and rocked back and forth a couple of times before addressing the offending sergeant.

"I appreciate your candor, Benrod. All will be taken into consideration as this situation progresses. Now get back to your flight assignment and don't share anything with anyone especially Durowe. Now get out of my face." Benrod quickly rose from the chair, came to attention, saluted, and left the office.

Krimshank opened Durowe's file and scanned the contents once again. He certainly wasn't the same type of individual as Benrod. There wasn't much of consequence in the records to show Durowe's professionalism and dedication to God and Country. His performance reports were good enough to get him promoted but no commendations were listed from any of his previous assignments. Krimshank suspected Durowe volunteered for duty in the drug investigation unit to facilitate his other habits. Once on the inside he could protect himself and his sources. What he didn't expect took place when he dated Airman Zimermon. The colonel closed the record jacket and with elbows on his desk, rested his face in the palms of his hands. He gently shook his head as he thought about how stupid young people can be. He looked up to see Jerome standing in the doorway.

"Ready for Durowe," he asked the colonel.

"Yeah. Send his sorry ass in here." The colonel poured himself another glass of water and waited for Durowe to report in. Again, Krimshank showed no respect to the young man, not returning the salute. Durowe remained at attention while Krimshank read him the riot act about his stupidity and how he wanted to burn his ass for being what Krimshank referred to as one idiotic motherfucker.

After the colonel's tirade concluded, he gave Durowe the redemption he promised. He told him to come up with some names, locations, and dates so they could attempt a tie in with the Crimitin case. He gave him a deadline and dismissed the Airman with a wave of his hand. After he left the office, Krimshank threw both personnel folders into his hold basket. He picked up the phone and called Littlemore. After announcing himself to the administrator, he connected with the maintenance commander.

"Hey colonel. How are things in the world of security?" John asked.

"Just peachy keen," Karl responded sarcastically.

"I just finished talking with two of my sterling employees. Another member of the force busted them for smoking dope during a concert in Frankfurt. One of them works in my drug unit. I can see why this unit failed the inspection and I got the dubious honor of setting this place straight. What have you found?"

Littlemore explained how his random drug sweeps identified a small pool of smokers and one or two cocaine abusers. His first shirt gave him a quick briefing the other day but they weren't ready to move on the offenders until they coordinated with the JAG and the colonel's office.

"We may be able to make some moves very quickly," Krimshank began. He went on to explain his conversations with Durowe and Benrod. Littlemore listened intently as the security commander explained his plan. Having some identified offenders in the maintenance squadron would certainly help the situation. More deals were possible for information leading to the arrest of the pushers and possibly the murderers.

"You can count on our support at this end," John stated.

"Never a doubt in my mind," Karl concluded.

"Give me a couple of days and we'll meet for a strategy session." John agreed and the two commanders bid each other goodbye. John gave Wilber a call on the intercom and when the first shirt came into the office, he received a quick briefing on the situation.

"Sounds great sir. I've been working on the required documents so we won't have to worry about the paperwork push when the shit hits the fan." John thanked his top sergeant and went back to work on the daily reports.

CHAPTER FORTY-NINE

Vinder came through the door of his reception area scanning the contents of a codeword-classified message from one of the operatives in Israel. He was looking for anything to tie his operation into the workings of his counterpart in Israel. His administrator interrupted him.

"Sir?" Vinder looked away from the document. "You had a call from the Prince." Vinder smiled at the message. "And which Prince would that be? There must be hundreds of them."

"THE Prince," his administrator emphasized. Now Vinder knew exactly whom they were discussing.

"His number is on your desk." Vinder thanked her and went into the office. He pulled off the message coversheet, flipped on the switch for his classified shredder, pushed the paper into a slot, which activated the cutting mechanism and cut the water-soluble paper into thousands of tiny paper chips before they fell into a small plastic container with about four inches of water in the bottom. By the end of the day, any documents he read and shredded would be a conglomeration of mush in the plastic container. This mush would be recycled into other paper products. It prevented any reassemble of classified information if they ever left the country in a hurry.

Vinder went to his desk chair and sat down. He picked up the small piece of paper and saw the private mobile phone number for His Royal Highness Prince Muhammud Bin Salah Bin Abdal Azuz. The Prince was head of the Saudi Air Forces and most probably next in line for the throne. However, knowing about Saudi royal accession, no one could be sure who was going to take the top spot until the current ruler died and the in fighting between the top princes sorted out the final standings. There was no clear line of succession like other monarchies. It was a dogfight and the Prince with the most toys at the end of the battle wins the top seat.

Vinder dialed the mobile number on his private line. After several rings, a greeting was heard. "MarHaba."

"Prince Muhammud?" Vinder questioned. "This is Colonel Vinder at the embassy. You called me earlier?"

"Yes I did colonel. I need an appointment with Mr. Reece. When can you arrange it?"

"You name the time and place and I'll get hold of Mr. Reece," Vinder assured the prince. They agreed on first thing the next morning in Vinder's office.

"Shukran," the prince concluded. Vinder rolled to his computer, selected his phone book, and looked up the number for the OSI offices at Eskan. He dialed the number and spoke with Karlotta before patching into Dillon.

"Rufas, how are we doing this morning?" Dillon greeted as he leaned back in his chair and put his feet on the corner of his desk.

"Just fine at the moment, it all depends on what your plans are for tomorrow morning?"

"It just so happens I was going to make a call to your office later today and set up a meeting with you. Why do you ask?" Vinder related the just concluded phone call from the prince.

Dillon listened intently wondering all the time why the prince would want to see him or how he knew about him in the first place. With time and place agreed upon, Dillon let Vinder know what he wanted from him after their meeting with the prince. Vinder listened in silence and made no comment on the request.

After the call finished, Dillon went to Karl's office. "Busy?" he asked coming through the door.

"Never for you," Karl laughed as he turned toward Dillon's spot in front of his desk. Dillon explained the call from Vinder and wondered if Karl possessed any insight to why the prince would want an audience with him.

Karl said he didn't have the slightest idea why a member of the royals would need time from a little old OSI agent out of the backwoods of Florida. Dillon just smiled and thanked Karl for the vote of confidence. Karl agreed to come with Dillon in the morning.

"I'll be able to quiz Mr. Christian like Captain Bligh on some of the jobs we've given him recently. I hope Vinder isn't getting in his way."

"Before you start on Vinder, let me have my time with him," Dillon began. "I need to key in on the Eclipse information. It just isn't what I wanted and I know he's keeping the full story out of our hands." Karl agreed as Dillon left the room.

In the hall, he remembered another question. He came back to the doorway and asked about the Prince Sultan situation.

"William is working that as we speak. He has a couple of reliable folks inside. They'll locate the place Crimitin referred to in his tapes. Once we get those, I'll let you know so we can all listen to them at one time." Dillon agreed with the idea and went back to his office.

∗∗∗

The agents met at the dining facility for breakfast each morning. This morning they would discuss the meeting with Vinder and the prince.

"Just what do you think he wants to talk with you about?" William asked as he poured another cup of coffee from a small round silver carafe.

"I thought about that last night," Dillon replied while scrapping the butter remnants from a small silver wrapper.

"I don't remember either of you mentioning his name and I'm sure if the general wanted me to know the man he would have arranged for a meeting. However, we'll sure know in a couple of hours."

Dillon took a large bite from the three-grain toast he just finished meticulously spreading with strawberry jam. William told both agents he was off to Sultan to meet with one of his contacts. The man found the locker Crimitin mentioned in his tape. William was going to get with the local security forces and cut into the locker. They would have the tapes in the office later that afternoon.

Dillon and Karl thanked William for the good work as they got ready to leave for the embassy. They wanted to ensure enough transit time was available for the trip from Eskan to the Diplomatic Quarters. During the drive, Karl warned Dillon even with an appointment, he would guarantee the prince would be late.

"Don't forget we're working on 'Inshala' time. God willing he'll be there on time. If not, God didn't want him there on time. It's a great system if you're not the one waiting around for someone to show up for a meeting." Dillon just smiled as he watched the passing scenery.

Processing into the building was simplified this time with Vinder pre-announcing them for the morning meeting. The attaché's administrator came to the entrance and escorted the men to Vinder's outer office. Coffee and sweet rolls sat on a silver tray within easy reach of the agents as they took seats on the leather couch. They were told the colonel was in a meeting with the ambassador and would be back to the office as soon as possible. Dillon and Karl sat back to relax since they faced nearly half an hour before the requested appointment time.

Before they could finish their first cup of coffee, they heard a commotion in the hallway. Both men ignored the noise until it became louder and louder. As they looked toward the doorway, a burly man in a military uniform filled the doorframe before stepping into the room. He quickly surveyed the area and moved to one side as a man in an immaculate white thobe and gutra walked in from the hall. Two Marine embassy guards followed closely. Dillon and Karl looked at each other as they stood up from their places on the couch. The newcomer walked directly to their corner of the room.

"Mr. Reece?" he questioned as he approached. Dillon stepped around the coffee table and extended his hand.

"I'm Dillon Reece," he replied as the man reached to shake Dillon's hand.

"I'm Prince Muhammud."

The prince turned toward Karl and extended his hand. "I'm Karl Phobie."

"Pleased to meet you," the prince replied. "Is there somewhere we can talk privately?" he asked in general. Dillon looked at the administrator and received a head nod toward the colonel's office. Dillon extended his arm and ushered the prince toward the open door.

Karl was following close behind but the prince stopped him before he went through the door. "I would like to have this conversation strictly with Mr. Reece," the prince stated.

Karl nodded and turned back toward his seat in the corner. The burly man reached in and closed the door after Dillon entered. He stood squarely in the frame with hands clasped in front of his waist. One of the Marine guards remained near the hallway entrance.

As the door closed behind them, the prince walked to one of the chairs in front of Vinder's desk and sat down. He motioned Dillon to the other chair. After he sat down, Dillon asked, "How can I be of assistance?"

The prince explained how Colonel Mohammod Al-Shqah, mentioned his arrival in Kingdom during one of their meetings. He went on to explain how he conducted an informational search of Dillon's background to ascertain if he would be able to help in a very embarrassing private matter. The report, he was pleased to say, was very positive, and indicated to him a type of experience he would be able to utilize. Dillon nodded in acknowledgement. What followed was a type of history lesson in the line of succession for the house of Azuz.

The man spoke of the infighting following the death of each monarch and how he is seen as the likely successor when the current king dies. Dillon listened intently for some type of hint where he could help the prince solve his dilemma. During the entire conversation, he couldn't see any opening for his type of expertise. As the prince turned to his personal life, Dillon saw the connection.

The prince had three wives. Each arranged marriage designed to strengthen family relationships within the Kingdom. He had 14 children. The oldest was a boy of 31; the youngest was a daughter aged two. There were only 12 living children. Two of his children were killed in a traffic accident while traveling to Dhahran. One of the family's 7-series BMWs ran off the road at an estimated speed of more than 120 miles per hour and disintegrated as it tumbled across the desert floor. Along with his two sons, the son of an investment banker and the son of a Saudi Ground Forces general officer lost their lives. It was a tragedy widely reported in the strictly controlled Saudi press. What wasn't reported in any of the papers nor did it emerge in any of the medical reports was the toxicology report on the driver. His number two son was under the influence of cocaine at the time of the accident.

The prince told Dillon how the family discovered his drug abuse quite by accident. When confronted the boy denied the accusations but when forced to take a blood test, he couldn't hide his habit any longer. What followed was a series of secret treatments outside the Kingdom to help the young man overcome his crutch. The results were a dismal failure as he killed his brother and two close friends.

"Not even my most trusted advisors know the true cause of my anguish. They naturally assume it's related to the loss of my sons. It really goes to the murder of three innocent human beings by a monster I thought was under control. If you're here to work strictly on the murder investigation, I'll leave you to your business; however, if there is another aspect of the case, I want to pledge my full cooperation and the cooperation of my personal security force."

Dillon paused before answering. He didn't want to offend the prince but he also knew he would need some trusted agents once all the pieces fell in place before closing the in Kingdom connections.

"I appreciate your candor. I know how hard it is for people to cope with the loss of loved ones in senseless accidents involving abusers. I can't confirm my involvement with other aspects of our case. We're pursuing several avenues right now and if one of those involves illicit substance activities, I'll be more than happy to accept your offer." The prince rose from his seat and extended his hand. Dillon rose and reached across the gap between the two men. He returned the firm grip of the prince.

"I understand your delicate situation," the prince stated.

"It would be a difficult political position to discuss with our King if the United States were providing an avenue for drugs to be smuggled into the Kingdom. I don't envy your situation. Just know I've promised my support and you can count on my discretion." Dillon thanked him and promised to keep him informed.

They walked toward the door leading to the outer office. Dillon opened it and as he did, the burly man immediately moved to one side. The prince moved swiftly through the door, gave a cursory wave to the other people in the room as he went through the outer door into the hallway and back to the VIP entrance. Dillon came through the door after the prince and was standing just inside the room. He noticed Vinder on the couch next to Karl.

"When I came back to the office and saw burly man in the doorway, I knew the prince arrived early," Vinder said as he moved past Dillon and into his office. He continued to speak as he went around his desk.

"Whatever he told you, it's not connected to any bullshit. He's always been above board with me in any of the situations where we've crossed paths. He's got a grip on who he is and will prove to you, although a royal, he's one smart son of a bitch."

"I got that feeling from our short conversation. He offered assistance for the investigation and I graciously accepted. You never know where we might need some royal assistance in the future," Dillon concluded.

Vinder asked why they wanted to meet with him. Dillon took the opportunity to say how disappointed he was with the information from NSA. "I know they're getting much more than you're giving us. I told you before; there are still a lot of people at the agency who will get me the type of information I can work with. I'll go to them and leave you hanging outside the loop. It's your decision."

Vinder placed both hands on the edge of his desk and was about to stand up when Dillon raised his hand. "And please, don't try to puff yourself up by telling me how important you are or how you'll report me to my superiors. I know your record and how you're on the fast track for stardom. Just remember, your sponsor wouldn't look too favorably on your being a hindrance to an international drug investigation. Just work with me here colonel and we'll all be a lot happier."

Dillon and Karl both stood as he finished. Vinder remained seated. As they left the office, Dillon turned and told the attaché he would be in touch if the information flow didn't improve significantly within the week.

As they stepped into the hallway, Dillon suggested they stop at Christian's office to see how he was doing with his end of the investigation. Compared to Vinder's accommodations, Nelsum lived in a broom closet. Since a DEA agent wasn't standard issue for the Riyadh embassy, they gave him leftovers. As the agents came into the office, Dillon commented, "Holy crapola, you must have to go into the hallway to change your mind."

"It's a bit cramped," Christian agreed. "But I'm out and about most of the day. In fact, I was on my way out the door right now. Asterfon asked me to check on some information he received from our agent in Tel Aviv." When he said that, Dillon and Karl exchanged glances.

Christian put both hands in the air and said, "I know, I know. Just what in the heck does a DEA agent in Israel have to do with our investigation here? I asked him the same thing and he told me the guy worked in Kingdom during the Gulf War and fostered a sneaking suspicion about a particular address in town. The activity surrounding the place garnered more than a passing interest from security forces dispersed around the city. He said they kept their eye on the place as a possible bastion of terrorist activity but nothing ever panned out. With our drug connection, he said this might be a place they use as a distribution center."

Dillon asked if he wanted company on the venture but Christian said he had another errand to run before he made the trip. "I appreciate the offer but it'll be this afternoon before I get out there. I'll give you a call later today with my initial impressions."

⁂

Christian came out of Euromarche, a K-Mart type-shopping establishment, and walked into the parking lot. He opened his trunk and put the packages off to one side of the compartment. He closed the lid and turned toward the Burger King located at one corner of the shopping center. He went into the "singles" section, placed his order, and after it was prepared, went to a table near the window. He set everything up with the proper amount of salt, pepper, and ketchup. He reached into his coat pocket and pulled out a crudely drawn map.

When Asterfon provided the address of the house, Christian had no earthly idea where the place was. He didn't recognize any of the street names and knew he was going to need help finding the place. He went to the drivers' section and sought the assistance of the supervisor. The man worked in Kingdom for nearly 20 years. He was surprised to see where Christian wanted to go.

"Are you sure this is the correct address?" he asked Christian after looking at the e-mail message. "This isn't what you would call the best part of town. It's one of the oldest and occupied by a large number of TCN families."

378

"That's all I have to go on. There's a long story about the place but it's not worth boring you with right now. Can you give me a map?" The supervisor obliged and within a few minutes, he gave Christian the map he now studied while enjoying his lunch.

In Riyadh, a person must navigate with the use of main roads. In this case, Christian would travel down Takhassosi Street toward the "elevated highway". Before getting to the crossroads near the access road, he would make a U-Turn at the signal with the lighting store on the corner and then take a right turn at the "Chicken Restaurant". After that turn, it was a hunt and peck sort of situation. Christian just hoped he would be able to locate the place for a look-see.

As he drove down Takhassosi, he thought back to the conversation with Dillon. He was very interested in the royal connection and hoped to get some addition facts from the other men when he came to them with his information on the house. He made his U-turn at the proper place and drove directly to the next right turn having seen it as he passed on the other side of the street.

The road was a typical three car wide arrangement cut into a single lane with parked trucks, cars, and dumpsters scattered behind the stores facing the main street. He nimbly negotiated his way through the maze. After driving a couple of blocks, the cars thinned out, and the trash was now piled in the streets rather than in dumpsters.

A person needed to approach each intersection cautiously because of the suicidal driving style practiced by many of the Saudis and TCNs. If there isn't a stop sign at the corner, they barrel right through. Christian carefully picked his way along the potholed roadway until he came to one of the landmarks mentioned in the note. That's one down and two to go he thought as he made his way along the new street.

He found the second and third landmarks bringing him to a turn down a street where he was supposed to count down 8 gates on the right. His target was the ninth home on the right. As he made the turn, he noticed a concrete block wall at the end of the street. He slowly drove toward the wall counting the gates cutting through the various walls on his right. There were a few cars parked on the street and sidewalk under the shade of scattered trees. He began his count. One, two, three, four, five, six, and he stopped. He was now within one gate of the block wall. There were only seven homes on the right and only five on the left as he stopped the car, got out, and counted the number of gates he passed.

He walked down the street and looked through one of the many gaps in the hastily constructed wall. He could only see a continuance of the street but nothing else. Since the wall was only about 12 feet high, he pulled his car along side the wall, climbed on the roof, and pulled himself to the top for a better look. What he found was a scattering of homes in various states of disassembly. It appeared someone bought the homes for their convenient location to another piece of property with a new shopping center.

"Well I'll be damned," he lamented aloud as he lowered himself off the wall onto his roof and back to the ground. He opened his door and sat on the edge of his seat with his feet still outside the car. He reached behind the drivers' seat and pulled a pad of paper from the back seat.

As he began to jot a few notes on the pad, he looked up to see one of the local water trucks pull into the street. He silently hoped it wouldn't approach his spot at the end of the cul-de-sac until he finished his note taking. He was becoming allergic to the black diesel fumes belched from their exhaust pipes. He swung his legs inside the car, turned on the ignition, and put the air conditioner on full blast, re-circulate, to cut down the fumes. He pushed in the CD to get a bit of entertainment while he made his notes. It was the last thing he did.

The water truck driver pushed in the clutch and revved the engine. He slowly let the clutch out as he gathered speed. He hit Christian's car directly on the drivers' door. It pressed the car through the wall where 6 feet of concrete blocks collapsed on the roof. The truck pushed through the wall and as Christian's car fell into a small drainage ditch cut into the roadway, the truck followed.

CHAPTER FIFTY

J.R. swung the straps on the air tank over her shoulders as one of her instructors helped adjust the placement. "How's that?" Hetty asked. J.R. bounced the tank around on her back a bit to get it into a comfortable placement. Hetty Cade and her husband Travers were the master instructors for a scuba course taught on the Khamis compound. J.R. traced a solid lead to one of the other part time instructors, so she quickly enrolled in a course for qualification. She figured a trip to the Red Sea would provide her opportunity for additional investigation. This was her last day in the pool before the weekend trip to Al Birk.

Hetty jumped into the pool ahead of J.R. and the lesson began. After about two hours of various trials and tribulations, J.R. was deemed competent enough to join members of the club on an open water dive. It was hard for J.R. to keep from correcting the instructors on several occasions. She'd been diving since her 5th birthday and the restraint shown to the "masters" was saint like. She didn't want to give away anything in her investigation. The class sat in lounge chairs as they cleaned their gear and talked about the weekend trip to the Sea. J.R. would be riding with Hetty, Travers, and the man she hoped would provide her with enough information about the supply of marijuana to begin planning a final sweep.

After work on Wednesday, the caravan of trucks, homemade trailers, and cars headed toward Abha. Once on the outskirts of town, the group turned on the ring road finally approaching the checkpoint before heading down the escarpment. It was a steep drive made more hazardous by the total destruction of bridges along the way. J.R. was fascinated to see the gigantic slabs of reinforced concrete tilting against canyon walls where they were pushed by floodwaters cascading down the narrow gorge after an earthen dam broke. For most of the trip, they negotiated dirt roads with the occasional asphalt or concrete section between bridge remnants.

When they reached the beach, they fixed camp and cooked some dinner. Nothing fancy, just basic camping grub like beans and franks covered with ketchup. One member of the group carried two pressurized containers of home brew. Another guy brought a box of red and white homemade wine. If nothing else, they were going to have enough illegal hooch to keep them busy all weekend. After the cooking and cleaning was finished, J.R. noticed her traveling companion leave camp and wander down the beach. She left to join him.

"Hey Quenton," she called out coming up behind him. She noticed he took the cigarette he was smoking and moved it behind his back. "Where you off to?"

"No where special. Just wanted to get away from the crowd for a bit of quiet time. I love this beach area and always take walks the first night we get here." J.R. asked to join him and he agreed. He still hadn't taken the smoke from behind his back. When he did move his hand, it was empty.

They walked and talked about a wide variety of things. He was in the Air Force for 14 years and took one of the early out programs offered by the Clinton administration. He bummed around for a while spending the bonus money collected from Uncle Sam for leaving the Force without benefit of a retirement check. When the cash ran out, he had to look for an aircraft related spot. Lucky for him, he was able to get on the Saudi program.

J.R.'s cover story was working perfectly. She met Quenton at one of the compound bars. Erpack pointed to him as one of the flight line problem children. J.R. shot pool, soaked in the hot tub; when it wasn't occupied by naked nurses; and just became one of the "guys". She knew not to question anyone too closely until everyone trusted her. She figured Quenton was primed for the taking.

They were on their way back to the campsite when J.R. asked about the demand for marijuana in the area. Quenton stopped and asked why she thought he might know anything about drugs. She told him she felt she could trust him. She wasn't too fond of the local home made hooch and wondered if there was a supply around. She'd been told some of the guys grew their own crop but she needed a point of contact. She hoped Quenton didn't take her question the wrong way.

"I don't want you to think I'm accusing you of using but you seem to know a lot of folks and during my time here I'd like to have another way to relax after work without having to drink this rot gut shit." Quenton laughed and agreed some of the stuff was pretty disgusting. He offered to put her in touch with a guy who made beer like Bud and a red wine with the finesse of Bordeaux. J.R. tried not to show her disappointment.

When they got back to camp most of the group, having finished off a glass or two, were ready for bed. Since there were many things they wanted to accomplish the next day, they suggested everyone head for bed early.

Things got moving the next morning before the sun became visible over the mountains. J.R. volunteered to fix a sumptuous breakfast for their group. Hetty, Travers, and Quenton enjoyed the spread of fruit, hotcakes, scrambled eggs, and sausage. Travers commented he wasn't going to need a weight belt for the morning dive. J.R. noticed Quenton was watching her every move. She couldn't decide if it was a good thing or not.

After cleaning up, their attention turned to open water certification. Other members of the class joined and the shoreline discussions began. Once the instructors were finished, the gang of divers moved into shallow waters. Some of the other class members were a bit shaky getting started. Everyone heard about the drowning that took place right off this particular beach.

One of the lesser-experienced wives was diving with an instructor in rough water. Since the churning water disrupted the view, they decided to head back for the beach. Not being a strong swimmer, she opted to come in submerged while the instructor went to the surface. When he got on shore, he looked back and saw she came up behind him. When he got his gear off, he looked out again to see where she was. It was then he noticed she wasn't moving. He swam back out to help but it was too late. She was dead.

The story, always told to new divers, makes them understand how dangerous the sport can be. Although the Red Sea is probably one of the best spots in the world to dive, it does have its serious side.

The group quickly became comfortable with their abilities and asked question after question of the instructors. Most of the questions didn't have anything to do with their being accustomed to the diving; they wanted to know when they were going to move into deeper waters. After the morning familiarization course was completed and the instructors were feeling confident of their charges abilities, they split into smaller groups each with an instructor for the afternoon dives into deeper water. J.R. managed to get into Quenton's group.

J.R. was a good student listening to all Quenton said before the dive and following his underwater instructions during the dive. As advertised, the area was beautiful. Once the deep-water session was over, Quenton asked if she wanted to visit another spot he knew further up the beach. J.R. eagerly agreed. Quenton said he was watching all of the students and felt J.R. was the most comfortable with the dive. He got the keys for the truck from Travers and headed up the shore.

About 10 minutes later, he pointed to a small outcrop of rock just off the beach. "It's the top of a really interesting hide for fish. The colors are great and it's not too deep. I normally just sit on the bottom and watch the activity." J.R. said it sounded great as they put on their tanks and headed out.

Quenton was not lying when he said it was beautiful. J.R. saw fish and colors she never viewed before. When they finished, they put their gear in the truck. Quenton went up front and sat on the hood. He parked beneath one of the few trees along the beach. He motioned for J.R. to join him. She pulled a bottle of water out of the ice chest and came around front. Quenton held a small plastic container from which he pulled a joint and offered it to his companion.

"Well this is better than I expected," she gushed as she took the well-constructed smoke from Quenton. "Do these yourself?"

"No actually. One of the supervisors in brown section has an oriental wife, I'm not sure what country she's from, but she has a talent for rolling joints. She's one butt ugly bitch but she can make a fine smoking joint." Quenton pulled a lighter out of his bag and offered J.R. a light. She accepted and drew in a long hit. Quenton watched carefully. She new the drill. If you don't use, you probably can't be trusted with information concerning supply. She needed to make it look good. Luckily, she was never asked to use any of the harder drugs.

They sat on the hood of the truck until they finished smoking. The sun was beginning to disappear beyond the horizon. The surface of the Red Sea glistened with the changing hues of sunset. Quenton slid off the hood and held out his hand. As she slid off toward him, he put his hands on her waist and pulled her close. She put her hands on his tanned chest and held him away.

"Whoa Cowboy! Let's not take the sharing of a joint as an open invitation for sex. I may be a fun loving free spirit but I don't ball every guy who gets me in the water. I'm not going anywhere, so there's still time we may take the next step. I've enjoyed the diving and the time I'm spending with you. Don't screw it up by trying to get into my pants!" Quenton looked at her with the blank stare she'd seen so many times before when dealing with pot smokers.

"Can't blame a guy for trying," Quenton replied as he released her waist and stepped back. "Let's get going before they eat all the chow." He turned and got into the truck. J.R. slid into the seat next to him as they headed toward camp.

When they got back, they cleaned their equipment and checked on dinner. Steak on the grill was the cuisine of the evening. Since Travers and

Hetty knew their companions would be back around sunset, they waited dinner. For that nicety, J.R. volunteered to cleanup.

J.R. was up early the next day to watch as sunrise changed the colors of a few scattered clouds. She was sipping her second cup of coffee when Hetty came out of her tent headed for the latrine. She waved to J.R. and went on her way. When she came back, she pulled up a chair and poured herself a cup of the steaming beverage.

The two women began a conversation about the morning dive and the trip back home. To keep up her appearance as a novice, J.R. asked several questions about additional safety precautions and what they might expect to see on the dive. Once Hetty filled her in on details, J.R. went into one of her silent dejected postures. After a couple of minutes, Hetty became interested.

"Something bothering you?" Hetty asked.

J.R. apologized for making it so obvious but she did have something on her mind. She proceeded to tell Hetty about the encounter with Quenton after their dive. She left out the part about smoking a joint but did mention the attempt at physical contact. She recounted how she shut down the attempt but she was concerned she may have caused problems with Quenton.

Hetty told her not to worry. Quenton tries it with every new student, married or single. Sometimes he scored and sometimes he's shut down. J.R. said she was hurt more knowing she was just another piece of fresh meat for the shark. Both of them laughed at the situation and J.R. thanked her for being a sounding board. J.R. figured she might need Hetty's assistance in the future so it was good to foster the sisterhood relationship.

The rest of the group was beginning to stir. Meals were completed and the diving began. J.R. and Hetty dove with a couple of women from one of the other camps. Again, it was just as promised. The weather was beautiful; the water was clear and the sea life abundant. It was a grand morning. After the dives were completed and the equipment cleaned, the groups broke camp for the drive back to Khamis.

When they pulled up to J.R.'s villa, she thanked everyone for the wonderful time and hoped they had more of the same in the future. She leaned over to Quenton and gave him a peck on the cheek. "And a special thanks to you for showing me that special place Thursday evening. I really enjoyed the dive." She gave him a wink as she got out of the truck.

When she came into her villa, she immediately called Dillon. With her roll as administrator, she could access the secure line from her villa. It certainly made keeping in contact with Dillon a lot easier. She could tell Pacman information she wanted and keep the other information close hold.

It was one of Dillon's suggestions when she was getting ready to set up her operation at Khamis. It was wise advice.

"This is Dillon," he answered the secure line in his living room.

"Dillon, J.R. I've got some good news."

"J.R., it's good to hear from you. I've wanted to give you a call on a number of occasions but hesitated each time remembering what you told me when you left. What's the good news?" J.R. began to tell Dillon of her scuba diving activities. Pacman identified the instructor as one of the problem children on the ramp. He was right on target. The man uses and gets his supply from one of the supervisors. She related the butt ugly reference and said she would check that next week. She knew who the supervisors were but hadn't met any of them personally. She planned to use a tour of the flight line as an excuse to meet the players. Dillon agreed it would be an excellent way to ferret out this particular member of the supply chain.

When Dillon asked if she needed any assistance, she said no. He told her of the royal connection. When she was ready to move, he would make contact with the prince and get the names of people he could trust in the area. No one wanted this thing to go bust at the last minute if someone she was counting on for support ended up on the payroll of the suppliers.

CHAPTER FIFTY-ONE

Sidney came into Randy's office with a recently retrieved e-message. "We were right about the key being for a safe deposit box. However, it isn't located in the United States. The manufacture is a company in Germany with clients across Europe. We'll have to get the guys at Ramstein to track down the actual location. I don't think the boss will let one of us go TDY for this," he laughed as he placed the message on Randy's desk blotter.

Randy silently read the message and after finishing, placed it in his top basket. "By the name and location of the firm, I'd be willing to bet it's a small mom and pop operation that's been in business for a hundred years. I don't envy the task of locating the actual box."

"All the more reason for me to make a trip over there," Sidney quipped as he backed out of the office.

"Dream on Moankat," Randy shouted. "You don't even like German wine!" Randy turned to his computer and composed a note to the agents in Germany. He gave them the name and location of the deposit box manufacturer.

After Dillon read his copy of the note, he gave Bill a call to coordinate the process of finding the manufacturing company.

"How far from Ramstein is this place located?" Dillon asked.

"The village is located just outside Frankfurt," Bill said as he ran his finger over the large map of Germany on his office wall. "I'll have Penny give them a call for an exact location but won't let on why we want to visit."

"That would be the best plan of attack at the moment," Dillon agreed. "That way we won't have to worry about security. If we're on site and take what we find with us, we can be on our way to the box before anyone can get a lead on us. You guys did get the key didn't you?"

"Yes we did. They sent it over night while they were looking for the manufacture. We put it with the other stuff in the conference room. That place is beginning to get a bit crowded with all the information we've been accumulating," Bill informed Dillon.

The two men continued to talk for some time. Penny passed by on her way to the coffee bar and with sign language asked Bill if he wanted a cup. He picked up his cup and silently agreed to her offer. When she came back, Bill was still on the line. She figured out who was on the other end and asked Bill to pass along her greetings. Bill did so and asked Penny to have a seat. She dropped into one of the chairs and sipped her coffee as Bill and Dillon concluded their conversation.

"Got a task for you Penny," Bill began. "The key they found in Covina was manufactured by a company in Bad Vibel." He turned to the map and pointed to the location.

"We've got the phone number and address of the place but we need to make a visit to see what we can discover about the box location. We don't want to tip our hand on anything. Give these folks a call to arrange a visit. Give Hanz a call to pick up some support from his department. The company may not want to cooperate with an American investigator but I can guarantee they'll be more forthcoming if we take along a member of the local constabulary." Penny took the piece of paper Bill was handing across the desk.

"Are you sure it's a good idea to get the locals involved?" Penny questioned.

"The truth! NO! Hanz has a leak somewhere in the place and I certainly don't want to tip our hand on anything. Giving him the opportunity to pick a man will keep him in the loop. Tell ya what. I'll give him a call now and arrange for the escort. You give the company a call and find out when they can see us. Make up some story and then let me know what you told them."

Penny left the office as Bill hit speed dial for Hanz at his K-Town office. When connected, Bill was sure to include the phrase they agreed upon to let Hanz know he had something he needed to discuss that couldn't be discussed on the police phone system. They talked about non-critical situations and then disconnected. About 45 minutes later, Bill's private line rang. It was Hanz.

Bill filled him in on details of the situation and asked for some assistance. Hanz said there was a man in the security squadron who would be perfect for the job. When he mentioned Conrad's name, Bill said he knew the man. Hanz told him there was a loose connection between the Germans working security on the base and local law enforcement. He would clear it with Krimshank when they set a firm date. Bill agreed. He asked Hanz to hang on while he checked to see if Penny arranged for a visit. She gave him the information and Bill passed it to Hanz. After their call concluded, Hanz called Krimshank to see if he could pay him a visit. Hanz went back to the office and picked up some folders with information about local accidents before he headed for Krimshank's office.

⚜

Conrad came out his front door resplendently decked out in his formal uniform. When Krimshank told him about the assignment, he was eager to help. They were leaving early enough to miss the majority of commuter traffic around K-Town and by the time they reached the outskirts of Frankfurt, the rush would be over. It was a pleasant drive and Conrad kept Penny amused with stories about working with and around the American forces community. His wife packed a thermos of coffee and provided some sweet rolls for the trip. With this entertainment, the time seemed to fly by and before they knew it, it was time to make the transition from Autobahn to local streets for their approach to the factory.

It certainly was a mom and pop operation. Located on the edge of Bad Vibel, Levi and Olga Scobiehien carved out a profitable little segment of the financial world. As Penny and Conrad were to discover, the boxes, locks and keys manufactured in the Quonset hut type structure attached to the storefront facing a small parking lot, were the highest quality available on the market. Olga was very proud of the family traditions and accomplishments so she offered to provide the pair a guided tour of the facility while Levi researched the key's number and disposition of the locking device.

When they came back to the office, Levi showed them information on the computer screen. He asked if there was anything additional before he printed the data. Penny checked to see if the pertinent information was available. When she was satisfied, Levi printed two copies of the report. He slipped them into a company envelope and gave it to Penny. Since it was getting near time to close for lunch, Olga asked if they wanted to join them in town. The investigators agreed with the offer. Olga picked up her sweater and walked the pair to the parking lot as Levi went to the garage and brought their car around front. Penny put the envelope in her briefcase on the back seat of her car. She then slipped in next to Olga as they were off to lunch.

Christina was returning to the office after paying Dick Famington a visit at headquarters. She was delivering weekly reports to various agencies and stopped by to see if Dick heard from J.R. They both agreed no news was usually good news in this type of situation. She wondered when Penny was due back. She came into the office, threw her purse into a chair in her room, and went to Bill's office. He was busily reading the list of e-mail before he left for the day.

"Have we heard anything from Penny?" Christina asked as she came into the office. Bill said he hadn't heard anything so he buzzed the administrator to see if there were any messages. There were none.

"Let's give her a call and see if we should wait at the office for her great revelation," Bill commented as dialed Penny's cell phone. However, Penny wouldn't be answering. No one would be answering the call unless they happened to be standing close enough to hear the sound of Vivaldi emanating from inside the standard Air Force issue briefcase tilted against the back of the dumpster where it landed after being tossed by a man in a passing car.

Penny and Conrad were finishing the last bit of paperwork with the investigative officer. Thank goodness, she took Conrad with her. When they came back from the village after lunch, they discovered the back passenger window broken out and the office briefcase gone. Conrad made the initial call to the Politzie.

Olga and Levi were more than apologetic. Penny assured them there was nothing of real value in the case other than her cell phone.

"Damn," she exclaimed as she checked her watch to see what time it was. "Can I use your phone?" she asked Olga. Penny was shown the back office phone. She dialed Bill's number and after a single ring, he answered.

"Bill, Penney here. I've got some distressing news." She told him about the information concerning the key and where the lock and box are located. She told him about lunch, the smashed window, and the missing briefcase.

"I tried to give you a call to see if we should wait around the office for you and Conrad. When no one answered, I must admit to an added amount of anxiety. So you and Conrad are OK? You're not off the side of the road in some ditch?"

"We're just fine. We'll be home in a couple of hours. It'll be a drafty ride with the window out. When I get back in town I'll stop by your house with details."

The ride home was a bit drafty but with a makeshift replacement window rigged by Levi, the ride was tolerable. Penny dropped Conrad off at his house and went directly to Bill's. Betty greeted her at the door.

"Penny, it's good to see you," she said as she stepped out of the way to let Penny inside the hall. "Let me take your jacket." Penny handed her the lightweight jacket she was wearing. Betty hung it on one of the hangers attached to a Bavarian coat rack.

"Follow me," Betty said as she headed down the hall. "Bill's in his cubby hole." Bill heard Penny arrive. He was coming out of the office as they approached. He ushered her inside.

"Can I get ya something to drink?" Betty asked as she went toward the kitchen.

"A stiff martini would go good right now," Penny replied as she sat in one of the armchairs. She began telling Bill about finding the information they needed and how they enjoyed the tour of the Scobiehien facility. It was a mom and pop operation of the first degree. Only members of the family worked there and this was one of the selling factors for banks in Europe. Security is guaranteed. When she told him about putting the envelope in her briefcase and locking it on the back seat, Betty interrupted them with a tray of martinis and some snacks. Penny lifted hers and took a long drink.

"Better now?" Bill asked.

"Much better," Penny commented. "When we got back from lunch and saw the window, it was a real shocker for Olga and Levi. They couldn't apologize enough." She continued telling him about the police report and the way they dismissed it as a snatch and grab. It was made worse with Conrad in his dress uniform. The lieutenant, who came on scene after the patrol car, gave Conrad a dressing down. Penny could tell it was a dressing down by the amount of finger pointing done by the lieutenant. Conrad never mentioned a thing about the conversation.

"So the cartel now has the location of the safe deposit box and the key," Bill lamented as he took a sip of his drink.

"You're accurate on the address but wrong about the key," Penny corrected as she reached into her purse and pulled out the safe deposit key. "While we were having lunch in town, I remembered leaving the key in their main office. When we got back and saw the briefcase was gone, I was certainly happy we forgot the key."

"Score one for the good guys," Betty toasted holding her glass up.

"Here, Here!" Penny and Bill joined in.

Leo slammed open the door as he came into the apartment. "This isn't good. Having the address does us no good without the key. You know they'll be watching the bank and have everyone alerted if we try to make

<hr />

a move." He threw the Audi keys on the table, stripped off his jacket and threw it over the back of a dining room chair.

"Want a beer?" he asked walking into the kitchen.

"Yeah, thanks," Garmat replied as he took off his coat and threw it on top of Leos.

"Why wasn't the key in the briefcase? That dumb bitch probably left it inside the building when they left for wherever they went with the owners."

"You think the owners may still have the key?" Leo questioned as he came back to the living room and handed Garmat his beer.

"That's possible but I would tend to doubt they left the key with them. If she didn't leave it there, she put it in her pocket, or that old fart had it. We just got screwed. The boss isn't going to like it. We can tell him we have the address but not the key. Let's see what kind of instructions we get from that news." They flicked on the television and watched the sports channel until they finished their beer. Garmat went in and composed a misleading message trying to deflect some of the heat they knew was coming. The only problem, there was no one else to put the blame on this time.

The only response they got from wherever this message was retrieved and read was a picture of the burning SUV in California and in bold type at the bottom of the page, a warning: THESE BASTARDS FUCKED UP TOO!

CHAPTER FIFTY-TWO

Zainl came into the room where Raj and Abdunn were preparing a delivery. "We got the information from our police contact on the registration of that truck leaving the airport," he said as he handed a small scrap of paper to Raj.

"It tells us just what we expected, it's an RSAF asset. We can conjecture the Americans at Eskan are using it."

Both Raj and Abdunn agreed. They needed to find out if the man here on the murder investigation knew about their connection with the crime. Was there a trail leading to their involvement? They would need to keep up with Dillon's activities and the activities of others he meets.

"On the subject of others, did you take care of the driver?" Raj asked Zainl.

"Not yet," he replied. "He hasn't come in for the rest of his money. We're supposed to meet Friday evening in Bata. I haven't heard from him since the incident. The last time we talked was two days before the embassy guy heard about the house. We arranged to meet the first Friday after the chore was completed. But I'll be surprised if he shows up this week."

<hr/>

Vinder walked into his office and threw the stack of papers he was carrying into his top basket. As he did, he turned back toward the door and called for Zandra. Zandra Daw, long time State Department employee, came into the office. "Yes Sir?" she questioned.

"Give Christian a call and see if he picked up anything on the names I gave him the other day. I had the list here but I must have taken it home and left it there," he finished as he lifted some papers on his desktop searching for the names.

"Will do. Anything else? It's getting near lunch time and I was going to join a few of the ladies in the lunchroom," Zandra finished.

"One more thing. If that pain in the ass Dillon character calls, just tell him I'm unavailable. I haven't got the time to converse with him today." Zandra didn't like fabricating stories for the colonel but knew it was part of the job. She would give Christian a call and then head for lunch.

When his office answering machine picked up, she left a message to give her a call and told him what it was in reference too. She activated her voice mail, picked up her purse, and left the office to join her co-workers for lunch. She wasn't gone five minutes when the phone rang and was answered after the preset two rings. It was one of the deputy under secretaries for something or other located in another part of the embassy. He wanted to talk with the colonel about Christian Nelsum. Please give him a call as soon as possible.

Lunch with the ladies was always interesting. Most of the attendees were long time department employees with varying amounts of experience around the world. They would compare department notes and keep abreast of the latest embassy gossip. One of the subjects for today's discussion was the death of an American in a traffic accident. The lady with the initial information didn't know the person's name.

When Zandra asked if it were a military member, the lady said it wasn't but she knew there was some importance placed on his death because of the interest level generated with the police notification. The subject changed as the ladies moved on to the latest juicy gossip of who was being unfaithful.

On her way back to the office, Zandra took a detour to Christian's cubbyhole to see if he was there. She knocked on the closed door with no answer. She continued on her way back to the office, retrieved her messages, and immediately called Vinder on his cellular when she heard the one from Bernard Lawner, the supervisor of Edwina Wace, the lady with the sketchy lunchtime information about the traffic death of an American citizen.

⚔

Dillon was just coming in his villa when the secure phone began to ring. He kicked the door shut, threw his briefcase on the couch, and sat the plastic bag of snack food on the desk as he picked up. Vinder was on the other end.

394

"Evening colonel," Dillon greeted. "To what do I owe the pleasure?" Vinder told him it wasn't a social call. He continued by telling him Christian was dead. The locals were calling it an accident.

"Where do you want to meet?" Dillon asked. Telling Vinder he wanted to visit the scene with the other agents, Vinder indicated a place and Dillon said they would be there in less than an hour. Forty-five minutes after the call concluded, Dillon, Karl and William were sitting in the designated parking lot waiting for Vinder.

As Vinder pulled into the lot, he flashed his lights to draw their attention. He motioned for them to follow. The police captain briefed him where the accident site was located. He drove directly to the site. He pulled to one side of the narrow street so William could pull along side. Vinder switched on his bright lights and William followed suit.

The men got out of their cars and approached the gap in the concrete block wall. There were blocks scattered around the area with glass and remnants of the embassy issued vehicle lying crumpled in the ditch and on the opposite side. The locals pulled the water truck off the car and discovered Christian's body crushed into one corner of the roof. Vinder was relating the information received from the police captain.

"From what they conjecture, Christian was sitting next to the wall. The water truck came down the street, struck him broadside and drove him through the wall and into this ditch. He didn't stand a chance. The truck followed the car into the ditch and literally flattened it against the other side. An expatriate lives in that house," Vinder said as he pointed to the last house on the right side of the street.

"He heard the crash and came outside his wall to investigate. The truck was still running when he got here but the driver was nowhere around. He didn't know anyone was in the car. He turned off the truck, went back to his house, and called the police. When the first police officer arrived, he just watched from his gate. It wasn't until they pulled the truck off and found Christian's body that he identified himself as the caller. He didn't want to be involved if it were only a traffic accident. When they found the body, he wanted to provide as much information as he could."

"Who owns the truck," Dillon asked.

"It was a private contactor who dealt with some of the outlying areas around Riyadh. The captain didn't indicate they found the owner yet."

"I'm willing to bet the truck was stolen," Karl said as he turned from the ditch.

"I'm sure it was," Dillon added. "They'll probably find some poor unfortunate stuffed inside a blanket and dropped along side a road outside of town. This was a planned execution. It's time to turn up the heat on the suppliers in town and get some answers. I'll begin with getting our hidden Jew off his dead ass and pull the strings on Papa. With their operations in jeopardy, I'm sure they'll be more than willing to help us solve this murder."

Dillon moved to the edge of the ditch and just shook his head as he finished talking. He turned and asked Vinder, "Where did they take the body?

"Since he was identified as an embassy staffer, he was taken to the Air Force hospital."

"Will an autopsy be scheduled?" Dillon wanted to know.

"None by Saudi law. Once we get the body released into our channels, we can have one done if you think it's necessary."

"I do," was the only thing Dillon said as he walked back through the crushed wall toward the car. Karl and William followed in silence. Vinder added nothing as he got into his car and led the way out of the housing maze. None of the men said much on the trip back to Eskan. They all knew their positions in Kingdom just took a substantially more dangerous turn with the elimination of a team member.

As Dillon entered the office early the next morning, he found e-mail from Vinder. He called the embassy on the secure line and got an in-depth briefing on material gathered from the Eclipse system and NSA. Now he needed to arrange for a buy from the pushers.

While Dillon was on the phone, William offered to fetch a cup of coffee. Dillon agreed and threw William his cup. As the call ended, William was bringing the cup into the office. Dillon was reviewing his brief notes.

"Just finished a call from Vinder," he said looking up from the pad. "Our gathering last night must have had some type of positive effect on his willingness to cooperate. He gave me a verbal on Eclipse information and is going to send me e-mail with more details."

"It's shitty he had to be forced into cooperating by a death. I just can't figure out that type of individual," William concluded as he dropped into one of the office chairs. "What's our next move?"

Dillon explained how he wanted to get Buzz involved with setting up a buy from the dealers. They would then have one of them to use as a bargaining chip in dealing with the others. He wasn't sure it would suffice but if they knew their time of prosperity was over in the kingdom, they may give up the names of their outside contacts. At least he hoped it would go down according to plan.

"Sounds solid enough to me. I can't believe the connection between these dealers is tight enough for one of them to protect the others. We should be able to crack them in no time. Do you think they were involved with Christian's death?"

"That would be my first assumption," Dillon responded before he sipped the dark liquid. He put the cup on his desk, clasped his hands behind his head, and leaned back in his chair.

"I've got an idea how to get Buzz involved but I don't want him to tip off the other players in the pleasure palace or along his line of customers. Too much attention will definitely drive this thing the wrong way." Dillon wanted to have someone available to meet Buzz. Since all of them were known on sight, it meant importing another agent. Dillon reached into his briefcase and pulled out a folder marked "Ramstein SPS". He pulled out an e-mail note from Krimshank.

"The boss man of security sent me the name of his new lead agent. I just hope he did a better job picking a top man than his predecessor did. Have Karl contact Krimshank and see if we can use this guy in a sting. We need him here as soon as possible. I'll get with Buzz and arrange a lunchtime meeting with him for tomorrow. We should know about," Dillon paused as he scanned Krimshank's note for the name of the agent. "Here it is, Master Sergeant Carvel F. Povey by then." Dillon wrote the name on a yellow sticky and passed it across the desk to William. As William read the name again, Dillon took a sip of his coffee.

"Povey, don't know the guy. We haven't crossed paths professionally. I'll do some checking with personnel and our channels before we give Krimshank a call." Dillon agreed it was probably a good idea. Don't want to put a guy in a situation where he might feel uncomfortable and blow the operation. If this guy has the experience, they might as well use someone inside the command. William picked up his cup and left Dillon contemplating his next move.

As he left the office, he called to Karlotta for the number of personnel. The fetching administrator said she would get the chief. He stopped long enough for a coffee refill before settling down behind his desk. In a moment, the intercom buzzed. William pushed the flashing button and spoke to the head of Eskan's personnel office. He explained the situation in general terms and asked for their assistance. With the assurance of total cooperation, he thanked the chief and hung up. He went to Karl's office to brief him.

"Sounds like things are beginning to come together," Karl commented after William finished his clarification. The men continued to discuss the situation when Dillon appeared in the doorway. He joined the conversation as they talked about secure meeting locations and the involvement of local law enforcement. The Prince's offer of assistance seemed the best avenue of pursuit. If his security forces were compromised, he probably should discover the problems and deal with them in his own way. The intercom illuminated and Karl pushed the speaker button. Karlotta asked if William was there.

She buzzed his office but got no answer. When Karl said he was; Karlotta transferred the personnel chief.

"Morning chief," Karl greeted. He pushed the speaker button and introduced Dillon to the chief. The information from personnel was very positive. It showed Povey was an experienced investigator recently assigned to the Ramstein office. It appeared Krimshank requested him personally because of a prior working relationship. The sergeant wore three Meritorious Service Medals and his recent promotion to Master Sergeant was earned through the STEP[27] program. He held an undergraduate degree in Criminal Justice backed by an Associate Degree in Law Enforcement. He was a mover and was destined for chief master if past performance was any indicator. All the agents seemed suitably impressed with the man's records.

"Give Krimshank a call while we're all here. We can settle this thing right now and get a meeting set up with Buzz," Dillon directed. Karl pulled the number from his file and called the Ramstein commander. The administrator patched him directly to Krimshank's office.

"Colonel, this is Karl Phobie, Eskan OSI. I have Dillon Reece and my co-worker William Kingston in the office." The colonel greeted other members of the conversation. Dillon took the lead and explained what they needed. Krimshank was hesitant at first.

"I wish you would have called in a week or two. We have some stuff going on right now and Povey is going to be a key player. However, knowing what I do about your investigation, it would probably be a better choice to send him down your way first and then pull the strings up here."

The in Kingdom contingent agreed and arranged to have Povey on the first Kingdom bound flight. Dillon thanked Krimshank for his cooperation and promised an update after Povey arrived.

Once the arrangements for Povey were finalized and a meeting with Buzz arranged, Dillon asked William about the contents of the locker at Sultan. William went back to his office and retrieved the list of items he recovered from the locker. The biggest discovery was the location of the processing house used by the Riyadh connection. All they needed to do was confirm its location and bring the Prince's forces in for a final assault. Things were definitely beginning to gel.

CHAPTER FIFTY-THREE

Sergeant Johnston comes into the office as Krimshank closes the door on his refrigerator. "Whatcha need Jerome?" the commander asks as he steps around the corner of his desk, places the glass of ice water on the silver tray and pulls up his desk chair so he can sit down after he finishes talking with his administrator.

"Povey's here sir," Jerome responded. The commander asked if arrangements for his TDY to Riyadh were final. Jerome said the only thing needed was the command section at USAFE headquarters to complete the signature blocks. Flight arrangements are done and as soon as the jet is airborne, he would make a call to the OSI office in Riyadh to tell them the cargo was loaded and on its way.

"Have him come in," Krimshank instructed. As he finished, he sat in his chair, picked up the ice-filled glass of water and took a sip. In a moment, Povey appeared in front of his desk and reported in with a crisp salute and salutation. Krimshank respectfully returned the salute and asked the sergeant to have a seat. After a bit of small talk about subjects outside the security arena, the commander got down to business.

"I know you've only been here a short time and you're anxious to get your management plan set for the section; however, we need you on a short TDY to assist OSI in closing down a drug connection in Saudi Arabia." Krimshank could tell by the look on Povey's face he was surprised.

"Saudi Arabia sir?" Povey replied in a questioning tone. "And that connection would be?"

Krimshank took his cue and brought the sergeant up to speed on the situation, as he knew it. Povey knew about the murder investigation but wasn't sure how he would be involved. As the commander explained the entire situation, Povey immediately saw the connection between the security forces, the maintenance squadron, and OSI.

Since Krimshank didn't know the full extent of Povey's involvement with the office in Riyadh, he didn't offer any explanations to what the sergeant may do when he arrived. He did have good words about Dillon and his ability to investigate. Povey said he knew of Dillon from an advanced investigation course he attended at OSI headquarters.

"It'll be an honor to work with the man. He's been involved with some very special investigations around the world. Hope I get a chance to pick his brain." Krimshank surmised a brain picking session would be possible if the results were up to Dillon's high standards.

"You can count on my best effort," Povey concluded. Krimshank said he expected nothing less as he turned the conversation to personal issues requiring the squadron's assistance during his absence. Povey was single so there wasn't much. Krimshank got up and came around the desk. Povey stood as the commander offered his hand.

"Do good work for us down there. When you get back, we'll be ready for a big push in the squadron and the flight line. Be ready to transition into one right after your return," Krimshank told the sergeant as he shook his hand.

"I'm looking forward to the challenge," Povey said as the commander led him down the corridor into the front office.

"Jerome," the commander barked out as he came out of the hallway and into view of Johnston's desk.

"What have we got for Sergeant Povey?"

Johnston filled them in on details of the trip. With command approval and involvement, a C-17 Globemaster III diverted into Ramstein from a stateside direct delivery mission to Sultan. The bird was scheduled to arrive later in the evening and depart for Sultan the next day. Clearances and crew rest would determine the exact time of their departure.

Krimshank told Povey to head for home and get his bags packed. They would arrange for transportation to the terminal from his apartment. He shook Povey's hand again before heading back to his office. He went to his desk and dialed John's number. The administrator answered and told the colonel the major was out of the office now. Krimshank asked for a call when he returned. He then turned to his computer and composed a note to Dillon informing him of the plans established for Povey.

When he read the note from Krimshank, Dillon wasn't too pleased with the delay but couldn't complain. Getting notification to Ramstein and getting someone on the way in just over 48 hours was an accomplishment. He would make the initial meeting with Buzz an affair between the two men and their ladies. It would be more of a social visit rather than a business venture. He would arrange for the business meeting after Povey arrived in Kingdom. He picked up his cell phone and called Carmen. She was pleased to hear from him and agreed to accompany him to dinner. She suggested the Al-Khozama hotel. Since Dillon didn't have a clue about fine eating establishments in Riyadh, he agreed to the suggestion and told her he would call back with a time. Since Carmen was the day shift portion of her schedule, she could be ready any time after 6 p.m.

The next call was to Buzz for a change of plans. Dillon arranged to meet the man for lunch but with the delay in Povey's arrival, Dillon thought it would be safer to have the ladies present and the hotel setting sounded like an excellent public place for their conversation. Buzz was cordial but hesitant to change the time and place for their meeting. Dillon was persuasive and they finally agreed to a time. They ended their conversation and Dillon went down the hall to Karl's office.

"Been to the Al-Khozama before?" Dillon asked as he came into the room. Karl said yes but it was only a good meal for an inflated price.

"That's not what I wanted to hear," Dillon moaned. "I agreed to pick up the tab at a meeting with Buzz."

Karl said he thought they were going to meet for lunch. "That's the other part of the story. Povey won't be getting here until sometime tomorrow or the next day. It all depends on when his ride gets into Ramstein. The one good thing about the meeting, I invited Carmen and she agreed."

"You mean your last meeting didn't put her off men for a life time?" Karl laughed.

"Stuff it," was Dillon's response as he left Karl laughing in his office.

William was out scouting the supplier's house location. Dillon made the suggestion William be the first to make a sortie to the house because if there were surveillance in the area, he or Karl could be recognized. As it was, William went dressed in thobe and gutra to blend in a bit more with the local traffic. William reached for his cell phone and called Dillon's number. When answered, he described the site as best he could while trying not to draw much attention to his circling the block. With false beard in place, he even went so far as to get out of the car and consult a piece of paper as if looking for a particular address on the street. He hoped this ploy gave the people he knew were watching him on the cameras mounted at the corner of the subject house a feeling of relief having seen the car pass by the front gate more than once. They didn't talk long as Dillon told William to head back for Eskan. He didn't have to tell him again. William was on his way.

Fogerton replaced the phone's hand piece as he stood up behind his desk, stretched with both arms behind his head and then went to the gray metal filing cabinet wedged into the corner of his office. He pulled open the drawer marked "Current Files" and sifted through the hanging folders until he came to the one with "Investigations" written in pencil along the edge of the manila envelope. He pulled it out and went back behind his desk.

Inside the envelope were several partially completed checklists. These checklists helped keep the maintenance squadron first sergeant abreast of activities taking place with members of the squadron. An investigation could be initiated for any number of reasons. Maintenance malpractice, accident investigations, training, drug sweeps, or a wide range of other situations. The first sergeant learned from his years of work on the line and now as the top enlisted disciplinarian in the squadron, he needed to keep track of the required square filling activities or punishment for offenders was hard to achieve.

He learned that lesson early in his career when he found himself accused of maintenance malpractice in an accident investigation. Luckily, for him, the excellent notes and training records kept by his supervisor saved his ass. He vowed always to keep track of the paperwork, to not only save his own career but also save the careers of those who worked with and for him.

Paper clipped together inside the envelope were several check sheets with a yellow sticky in the center of the first page with the word "SWEEP" printed in red ink. He pulled the note off and read the top sheet. He swiveled around in his high back chair and began to dial the combination for access to the two-drawer safe located under the window overlooking the flight line area. He finished setting the fourth number of the combination, turned over the "CLOSED" sign to "OPEN" and pulled out the top drawer. He scanned to the back of the drawer and pulled out the folder marked "SWEEP". He pushed the drawer shut and spun back to his desk.

Inside the folder were test results and the documents necessary to affect searches of dormitory rooms and locker areas in the squadron. It also included documents for signature when individuals under suspicion are brought in for questioning. Sets of guidelines for questioning were attached to each sheet. If nothing else went right in the squadron, the first sergeant was going to give his best effort to keep the commander out of legal trouble when it came to getting drug offenders into treatment or out of the service. After going over the packages, he left his office and headed for the commander's room.

The major wasn't in so Wilbur pulled one of the spare radios from its credenza-based charger and called the commander on the maintenance net. When there was no answer, he called maintenance control and asked if they knew where the major was located. The controller told him the commander just walked into the room. Fogerton asked for a call on the landline. The controller passed the word and the first sergeant just got back to his office when the administrator passed the call to his office.

"Hey boss, I just wanted to get with you on some of the pressing paperwork associated with the sweep we just conducted," Wilbur told Littlemore. The commander said he would be back to the office within the hour. They would take care of the papers then.

In the front office, Airman Willis is just finishing a note from the SP commander about a situation they need to discuss immediately. He takes the note into the commander's office and puts it on the commander's chair. This position of "honor" is reserved for only the most important of telephone messages. The administrator always checks with the caller to see if they want to have the commander tracked down or if the call can wait until he returns. He has learned the commander considers situations in three categories: CRITICAL, URGENT, and ROUTINE. Critical calls warrant the commander being tracked down and notified of the situation. Urgent calls are placed on the seat of his chair so he sees them as soon as he returns to the office. Routine calls are placed in his basket for return as he gets to them. Krimshank said this was an urgent matter so the note went on the seat.

After John finishes his update on maintenance activity, he drives slowly down the line before returning to his office. As he comes in the back door, he calls for the first shirt to join him. He goes to his small fridge and pulls out a diet soda. He twists off the top and takes a slow swallow of the cold beverage. The first shirt joins him in the office.

"That looks good sir. Mind if I join you?" Naturally, the commander has no objection to his top sergeant joining him in a refreshing beverage. The shirt pulls a non-diet from the shelf and takes a seat in front of the commander's desk. Littlemore has gone around the desk and is finishing the soda before he sits down. He gives the empty can a backhand toss toward a box marked "cans". It bounces off the front edge of the box, does a 180 above the opening, and drops into the empty bottom.

John picks up the note on his seat, reads it, and looks at the sergeant. "What do we have on for discussion?" Fogerton explains the paperwork situation and the drug sweep.

"This note is from Krimshank," John says as he holds up the small piece of paper. "Let's give him a call to see if he has something new to add."

He picks up the handset and pushes the speed dial for "SPS". He announces himself to Jerome and is promptly connected with Krimshank. After routine greetings, John just listens as the security commander explains the current situation with his lead drug investigator and the ongoing work in Riyadh. John does a lot of head nodding and "I see" saying before he gets to ask a question.

"What did you get from that kid Durowe?"

"He was very forthcoming with his information. Should be able to add bits and pieces to the whole picture. We can discuss that when we get ready to move. Anything from the local OSI office?" Krimshank inquires.

John tells him what he has to date but it isn't any more than the security commander already has on file. After a couple more questions about other issues, John bids Krimshank goodbye.

"Well that changes a few things," he says as he leans back in his chair. He proceeds to explain the situation to Wilbur. The first sergeant is not too pleased with the prospect of having to wait but he knows all of this is tied together and they're just one part of the investigation. The two men take the time to go over all the documents making sure everything is ready to proceed once they get the OK from Krimshank and his people. The wait will have one of two effects on those being investigated. One, they'll believe they have beaten the drug test, or, they'll be scared shitless knowing they're probably being processed for immediate discharge.

⚔️

Bill cleared all the identification checks as he approached Ubermann's office. He was in town on another matter and gave Hanz a call to see if the information concerning the car registrations came back from the German motor vehicle department. When Hanz said he received the document, Bill told him he would stop by and pick it up personally. As Bill came within reach of the partially open door, he could hear Hanz on the other side practically screaming in German at the person on the other end of the line. He hesitated before giving a short knock on the door and pushing it open. Hanz saw the door open and motioned Bill into the office. He slipped inside and shut the door behind him. Hanz continued to fire verbal barrages until he slammed the receiver back into its cradle. He gripped the edge of the desk and counted to 10 in German before he looked at Bill.

"Welcome to my world," he sarcastically said as he flopped back into his desk chair.

"I couldn't understand all of it but it doesn't appear you're too pleased with the person on the other end of that line," Bill commented as he leaned back in his seat. "Hope it doesn't involve anyone on the base."

Hanz assured him the matters under discussion with the dunderhead on the other end of the line didn't affect any of the NATO forces unless one of them ran over the mayor's dog. The call was a request for assistance in finding the perpetrator of the heinous crime. Bill sat in silence.

"Your lack of response tells me you find the situation as stupid as I did," Hanz concluded. He spun around in his chair and moved a pile of computer papers off an envelope. He handed the envelope across the desk to Bill.

"Inside is all the information you requested. Hope the needle in the haystack is there."

"Do you think the insiders were suspicious?" Bill asked as he looked inside the envelope at the stack of computer paper.

"I hope not. If they made the connection, we're going to find the Audi burned to a crisp in some field." Bill agreed and stood up to leave. He reached across the desk and shook hands with the investigator.

"Hope your day gets better," Bill commented.

"It won't get any better until I get out of here and open a bottle of Spatlese!" Bill waved goodbye as he walked out of the office.

Once Bill was back on base, he opened his center drawer and pulled out a small slip of paper with the Audi's license plate number scribbled in the middle. Since the numbers were not in alpha or numerical order, he faced scanning each sheet until he came to the one he was looking for. Damn, he muttered. The name and address were not there. The only thing was the name and address of a company in Munich. He knew both would probably be fictitious.

CHAPTER FIFTY-FOUR

Dillon confirmed the times with Carmen for pickup and deliver to the Al-Khozama. Being a major hotel in the center of Riyadh, prayer times were not much of a quandary. They could come and go without too many problems. Since Carmen was a Caucasian, the mutawa, or religious police, didn't pay the couple much attention. White males with Asians drew interest from the roving patrols. The overwhelming feeling of these mobile protectors of virtue was Asian women were all whores no matter what their profession or abilities. It definitely caused problems for some of the expatriates married to Asians.

Dillon set out about an hour before his scheduled pick up of Carmen. He wanted to use the quiet time to sort through the approach he would use with Buzz. He hoped the trump card of Buzz's ethnic background would not be required at this meeting.

Dillon pulled up to the Kingdom City Gate for clearance into the compound after the guard made a call to Carmen's villa. As with most women, she still had a few finishing touches to make before she was ready to leave. She offered Dillon a drink but he declined. If stopped for any reason, he didn't want to have the smell of liquor on his breath.

"I'll take you up on that drink when we get back from dinner," Dillon added to his declination of a beverage.

Carmen stuck her head around the corner and replied, "I'm looking forward to that!"

Dillon stood in the bathroom doorway as Carmen finished her preparations. As she went down the hallway, she pulled off the robe she was wearing and gave Dillon a teasing view of her brightly colored panties and the fact she wasn't wearing a bra.

406

Carmen was out of her bedroom in a moment and grabbed her abaya off the hook in the hallway. Dillon helped her put the garment on as they walked toward the door. They continued their conversation about her work at the hospital as they headed downtown.

The Al-Khozama is located right next to one of the new shopping center/office buildings on Olaya Street. It's one of the "places to be seen" for the expatriate community. Dillon pulled into the small circular drive and allowed a valet to park the Land Cruiser. The door attendant, clad in an immaculate white uniform complete with gloves, greeted them as they stepped into the lobby. It was abuzz with conversations in Arabic and English. Executives from around the world were trying to make deals with Saudis in a wide range of areas. They passed by the smoke filled area and entered the dinning room where Buzz and Lola were waiting. Buzz waved as they came into the room. He rose from his chair as Carmen and Dillon approached their corner table.

"Greetings to you both," Buzz said as he pulled out a chair for Carmen. "You remember Lola," he added as he returned to his seat. Dillon and Carmen both greeted Buzz's companion. The waiter was present immediately with "Saudi Champagne" as the conversation turned to happenings in the community since their last meeting. Buzz asked it Dillon heard about the American killed in the traffic accident. Dillon said he hadn't and asked Buzz to tell him about it. What Buzz related was the story given to the newspapers. Dillon hoped it was all the man knew. Time would tell what his knowledge level was.

The four of them enjoyed the buffet style dinner. Buzz wanted to know if they were going to head for the compound after dinner. Dillon said they were going back to Carmen's place. He had an early meeting and didn't want to face the pleasures of the compound without sufficient recovery time.

After they finished dessert and were waiting for coffee, Dillon asked Buzz to accompany him to the patio area. There was a garden area facing the new office building. Dillon excused himself to the ladies by telling them they needed to talk some boring business stuff. As the two men stepped into the garden area, Dillon got right to the point. He explained how a contractor working for the RSAF made inquiries about a substantial purchase of cocaine. Dillon explained how he tried to put him off but the man was insistent. He worked at one of the remote radar sites and wanted to put in a supply for himself and the others who worked with him.

Buzz stood back from Dillon and feigned surprise. "So why are you coming to me?"

"You know the right people and I don't want to be involved. I'll have the guy make contact with you and you can set up the meeting. I really don't want to know any more." Buzz stared at Dillon trying to detect if he was being told a story or if Dillon was concerned. Dillon on the other hand was putting on a show worthy of a Tony Award.

"Where is this guy now?" Buzz asked.

"He went to Jeddah on a parts run. Said something about the Islamic port. I'm not sure and I don't really care. I told him about the compound and he kept pressuring me about getting some recreational powder. I never made a commitment to him but thought this might be good for you."

Buzz silently studied Dillon's expression and then agreed to make the contacts. He asked Dillon to have the guy get in touch with him when he got back from Jeddah and they would talk. If he felt he could help, he would finalize the arrangements.

Dillon said that's all he could ask for. "I told you before I don't want to be involved with any of the hard stuff and I don't want to have it available for any of the deployed forces. Since this guy is a contractor, I don't give a shit one way or the other." Buzz seemed satisfied as they returned to the dinning room and their companions.

Once coffee was completed and Dillon paid the bill, they walked out of the hotel together. Buzz asked one more time if they wanted to make a trip to the compound. Dillon again declined. When Buzz and Lola got into the back seat of his 600 Series Mercedes, Dillon waved goodbye.

Carmen, standing next to Dillon as they waited for their vehicle, turned and asked, "You have to be back early?"

Dillon smiled and replied, "I've got an early morning meeting at the Kingdom Hospital."

Since Kingdom Hospital was directly next to her compound, Carmen made the connection and gave Dillon a warm smile as she slid into the passenger's seat.

⚔

Dillon reached for Carmen's warm body. It was nowhere on her side of the bed. He opened his eyes and saw her nakedness disappear into the bathroom. He could see the steam gathering along the ceiling tiles and heard sounds of the shower curtain as she pulled it across the tub's threshold. Dillon rolled onto his back and stared at the fan as it turned slowly in the dim morning light. He swung his feet over the side of the bed and scratched himself in all the right places. He stood up, stretched, and walked to the window overlooking Carmen's backyard. Her gardener did a wonderful job in creating a peaceful setting for the hot tub. There were brick walkways, flowerbeds with a wide range of flowering plants and evergreens, a small

408

Japanese style rock garden, and a shaded pond with several large gold fish occupying the bubbling water under the elegantly constructed rock waterfall. He drifted off into thoughts of last night and their use of the tub for recreational activities. He smiled as he turned away from the window and headed for the steam-filled bathroom. He silently pulled one end of the curtain back and stuck his head into the enclosure. Carmen was standing with her back to him rinsing her hair under the showerhead as he admired the curve of her spine and the small tan line on her round hips. Before she could turn around, he pulled his head back from the curtain and called her name.

"What can I do for you Mr. Reece?" she responded.

"Just wondering if a shower came with the room service?" Carmen laughed at the comment and told Dillon there were no additional services provided at this hour of the morning. She did ask for a cup of coffee and some toast. He left the bathroom and went downstairs to the kitchen where the coffee was just finishing its brew cycle.

He reached for the bread sitting on top of the toaster and dropped a couple of slices into the slots. He looked into the fridge and pulled out the margarine and some strawberry jam. He poured two cups, got the fixings for the coffee, and placed them on a small tray beside the margarine and jam. When the toast popped up, he grabbed them, put them on a small plate, and went back upstairs.

As he entered the bedroom, Carmen was just coming out of the bathroom wearing a matching set of deep purple panties and bra. She was rubbing her hair with a large towel. Dillon set the tray down before embracing Carmen. He kissed her gently and bid her good morning before reaching for his cup of coffee. Carmen spread jam only on her toast and watched as Dillon pulled on his pants, stepped into his deck shoes, slid his shirt over his arms, and began to button it. Carmen went to her dressing table and began her makeup routine. Dillon, with coffee cup in hand, picked up his cell phone to check for messages. None appeared pressing so he kept the phone in voicemail mode as he finished his coffee.

"Need a refill?" Dillon asked as he moved toward the doorway. Carmen shook her head in agreement, as she finished chewing the last bite of her toast. Dillon retrieved the pot from the kitchen and poured another cup for both of them. As Carmen finished getting dressed, Dillon wandered down to the living room. It was tastefully decorated with personal items to accent the standard issue furniture for Kingdom City. He drained his coffee and went to the kitchen through the dining room. He met Carmen in the hallway.

"You about ready," he asked. She said she was as she took his cup and put it into the sink with her cup and plate. Dillon returned the jam and margarine to the fridge and headed for the front door. He drove Carmen to the emergency room entrance and said goodbye. No public display of affection to protect her from peering eyes. He left the hospital and picked up the ring road for his trip back to Eskan. He grabbed a quick shower and changed clothes before heading to the office. He greeted Karlotta and put his case on the desk before strolling toward Karl's office.

"Morning," Dillon greeted as he came through the doorway. Karl looked up from his computer and returned the greeting.

"Have you checked the messages on your desk?" he asked as he reached for his cup of coffee. Dillon said he hadn't. "There were about four calls from someone who wouldn't identify himself. They left no messages. Maybe they'll continue the barrage this morning." Dillon asked if the calls were made to the administrative section and Karl said yes. Dillon surmised it would have to do with the investigation but he wasn't sure who would be calling and wouldn't identify themselves. It could be Buzz but there was no reason for him not to leave a number or at least his name.

"Let's hope the information is important enough for the caller to be persistent," Dillon said as he left the room. He went back to his office with a fresh cup of coffee and read the messages neatly arranged on his desk blotter. One of the calls was from Buzz saying everything was in place and he would wait for the customer's call. Dillon went back to Karl's office to fill him in on the details of their meeting.

"Got a note from Buzz. He says the meeting is arranged. All we have to do is put him in touch with the customer," Dillon began as he came into Karl's office.

"Povey will be the perfect front. No one around here knows him and we can get real close to one of the suppliers. Once we have one of them, the others should fall into place rapidly. If they know we want to keep them away from the Saudi authorities and alive, I do believe they'll cooperate quite nicely. We can throw their processing house to the Saudi's as payment for not chopping these guys into pieces."

"I hope that works," Karl commented.

"We can only hope the Prince is true to his word and doesn't play the Saudi game of tell them what they want to hear and then do something completely different."

"I've a good feeling about the guy. He was hurt to the core and I believe all he wants is to cut this line of supply. If we help, I do believe it will be a feather in Uncle Sam's hat and he won't even know why," Dillon laughed as he got up to leave. Before he could push back from the chair, Karl stopped him.

"Let's see what we have on Povey's arrival," Karl said as he punched William's intercom number. When he answered, Karl asked if there was any additional information about Povey. William told him the aircraft was inbound and should be arriving about 1930. He made the same type of arrangements for Povey as he made for J.R. Someone unattached with the office would make the pickup and bring him to Eskan. Dillon went back to his office and after taking care of a few phone calls and some of the boring paperwork, he asked William for a guided tour of the area surrounding the process house.

Not wanting a sighting by security cameras, William kept a one-block distance between their car and the actual house location. Dillon was taking inventory of possible escape routes so he could inform the security forces when they were planning the final assault.

"Pull over under that shade tree," Dillon said as they came around the block for a second time. William pulled to the right side of the street and stopped under the overhanging limbs of a tree growing behind one of the villa walls.

Dillon unsnapped his seatbelt and turned toward William. "What's your assessment of the situation," he asked William. William said he didn't really understand the question.

"Take this as a learning situation. We have a villa with heavy outside surveillance on all sides. We know it's being used to process drugs, and all things being equal, handle a large amount of money. As an investigator, you have to put yourself in their place to understand how they think. It's a never-ending learning process. Just when you believe you have all the angles figured, the bad guys come up with another twist and the learning continues. So put yourself in their place and explain to me how you would handle an assault."

William sat silently for a moment while he pondered his reply. He gave Dillon his best professional opinion on how the place would be fortified for a frontal attack so the best avenue of approach would be heavy equipment from the rear. Dillon sat silently just nodding his head. William continued to express his opinion on how much force would be needed to penetrate the walls and what protection they would need. When he appeared done, Dillon just shook his head and asked William to join him across the street. The men got out and went to the wall of the villa opposite their parked position.

"What do you notice about this wall?" Dillon asked.

"Looks like any of the other white washed block walls on this street," William commented as he stood back and looked at the fence.

"Here's an observation lesson." Dillon began.

"Notice the crack in the white wash running from the top of the fence to the bottom?" William went to the place Dillon was pointing and looked at the modest crack line.

"In all of their fences they have staggered blocks. There wouldn't be a line like this unless they changed building materials. If we scrape away the paint on either side of these lines, I'm willing to bet dinner we have two different types of building material. One will be the normal wall building blocks and the other will be something much lighter."

He picked up a small rock from the sidewalk and scratched at the fence. As he predicted, on one side of the crack was the normal large concrete blocks used for wall building. The other side was a type of red brick normally used for non-load bearing positions in construction work.

William just stood back and looked at the space between the two crack lines. "So," he began. "What we have here is a punch through with something fairly large on the other side of the fence to easily push down the bricks and be on their way down the road."

"Very good cricket," Dillon commented.

"It's probably got a wooden formation on the other side with some type of arrangement to push the wall down without having it come down on top of the vehicle or vehicles."

"Lesson learned," William commented as he stood back to look along the top of the fence line.

"Should we take a look?" Dillon said it wasn't necessary right now but they would make a note for the authorities when the time was right. William shook his head as he walked back to their vehicle. Dillon smiled as he returned to his side. An alternate exit was one of the valuable lessons he learned during his association with J.R.

As they drove back to Eskan, Karl gave them a call wondering when they would be returning. When he found out they were on the way, he asked them to stop by his villa.

As the two men pulled in front of Karl's villa, he came out the door, down the walkway and got into the back seat.

"Got a call from a fellow at the embassy. He doesn't realize I know he's from the embassy but that's another story. Anyway, he thought he was talking to you Dillon. He said Nelsum gave him your name to contact if something should happen to him. Don't ask me why he trusted this guy; he works in the motor pool. When Christian turned up dead, he stayed silent for a while. Said he was scared. Now he's got a friend who may be involved with the situation and he wants to arrange a meeting at Dir'iyyah."

"What's Dir'iyyah?" Dillon asked.

Karl told him it's the old walled city. "People have been living there for years. Mud huts with electricity. Somewhat historically fascinating. He wants to meet there because it's away from the city center and he doesn't have to worry about being recognized."

"Just who the hell is this motor pool guy?" William queried.

"I've no idea but perhaps we can find out when we meet with him. I arranged a time and a place inside Dir'iyyah. Unless you've got some objections, we'll hear what he has to say tomorrow evening." Dillon agreed with the arrangements and asked if there was any other information. None other than Povey was on time. With the business finished, Karl got out and went back to his villa while William dropped Dillon in front of his quarters.

"Give me a call later when you make contact with Povey," Dillon asked William as he was getting out.

"We need to get him an alias and cover story. Then we can contact Buzz and firm up his arrangements." William said he would give him a call as soon as he arrived.

Krimshank pulled a small bottle of water from the fridge, twisted off the top, and tossed it across the room for a direct hit in the wastebasket. Pleased with himself, he walked down the hall into Jerome's office area.

"Anything on Povey getting into Sultan?" he asked as he circled the coffee table and sat down on the well-worn simulated leather couch.

Jerome sifted through the stack of file folders in his distribution baskets and pulled one out. He opened the file and read the top sheet of paper stapled to the left side of the folder.

"When they departed, their estimated time of arrival was 1900 local Saudi time," he confirmed as he took a quick look at the clock hanging above Krimshank's head. "They should be on the ground any minute now."

Master Sergeant Povey was enjoying the ride from Ramstein. The weather was perfect the entire flight and the crew was very accommodating as he shot picture after picture of the magnificent sights passing more than five miles beneath the jumbo cargo aircraft. Even their arrival at Sultan was spectacular. Not the usual haze and muck. A brief rainstorm the day before cleared the air.

He was suitably impressed with the reception committee and their ability to process him into the Kingdom with little or no hassle. He refrained from asking too many questions not wanting to raise much suspicion about his assignment. Since he wasn't sure how long his stay would be, he didn't want anyone he didn't know to have any information about his activities. Without a cover story in place, he didn't want to tip the hand of the investigators currently working the situation.

After making the transition to Eskan, Povey pulled out the slip of paper with the OSI office number scrawled in red ink. He dialed the number from his villa bedroom. He hastily unpacked his hanging clothes and slipped them into the closet. The other stuff could wait until his return from his initial briefing. The phone rang in the deserted office and routed to William's home line. "This is William," was stated into the receiver after only one ring.

"Sir, Sergeant Povey on this end. Just got into the villa."

"Great," was the reaction from William.

"I'll be over in a minute and we'll go meet Agent Reece." Povey asked for enough time to take a quick shower. William said there was time because he wasn't sure where Dillon might be at the moment.

As it was, Dillon was laying out a sketch of the processing house from memory. His ability to recall minute details was paying dividends again. The assault forces would be very happy to have such a diagram when it came time for their final attack.

"Sure," Dillon agreed to the meeting.

"I'll order in pizza. I'm hungry and I'm sure the sergeant hasn't taken time to eat since his arrival." Dillon placed the order and pulled another long neck from the fridge. About 45 minutes passed since his conversation with William. The front door bell rang.

"Good evening gentlemen," Dillon greeted as he stood out of the way so the men could enter the villa. As Povey passed by, Dillon introduced himself. "I'm Dillon Reece."

"Yes sir, I know who you are. I've seen your picture at the academy. It's a pleasure to meet you and have an opportunity to work with you on this investigation."

Dillon laughed and said he hoped the picture wasn't on a wanted poster and their association during this investigation would meet his evidently high expectations.

Before he could close the door, the pizza deliveryman rode up on his specially equipped mountain bike. Dillon went to the desk and pulled out enough riyals for the pizza and tip. He brought the hot pie into the kitchen and collected plates and utensils. William followed him and retrieved three long necks to accompany their late evening snack.

After a couple of bites, Dillon asked Povey about the trip and if the accommodations were satisfactory. The new man was pleased with everything and hoped he met their expectations.

"Krimshank wouldn't send us a dunderhead," Dillon assured the man. "Your part of this activity should be fairly straight forward. I just hope all goes as planned. If not, we don't know what to expect from these guys."

414

He continued to explain how they wanted him to act like a large client making a purchase for a radar site on the Iraqi border. In case Buzz had contact in the ground forces, they would give him another story to tell explaining how the radar story was just a ruse to throw the Air Force off track. Didn't want to take any chances with being discovered laying in a supply for contractors at Sultan.

"From the few times I've dealt with Buzz," Dillon began to relate, "He's been cautious about putting himself on the line. He has a grand empire here and he doesn't want to jeopardize it. We do have a couple of aces up our sleeve and will play them if your initial meeting doesn't go according to plan. "

Dillon said he expected Buzz to want a preliminary meeting with Povey to give himself a warm secure feeling about the stated intentions. "He'll want you on his home turf, so I would say the meet would be at the compound or his villa."

"I'm ready for either place," Povey agreed as he reached for another piece of pizza.

"Need an alias for you. Have any you like to use?" William asked the new member of the investigative team.

Povey asked them not to laugh when he related the name he found most comfortable. Neither man avowed not to chuckle.

"I use Duke Puddefoot most of the time. Duke was a nickname I picked up as a kid and Puddefoot is the name of the county seat where I grew up."

Dillon and William looked at each other and quickly hid behind drinks from their long necks before bursting out in belly laughs.

"That's one we won't soon forget," Dillon agreed. He turned to William and asked him to have the appropriate documents prepared.

"We don't want Buzz to have a chance to ask for an Iqama[28] and Duke here, not to have one." William assured him the document, along with a driver's license, would be ready before the meeting. The men finished the pizza and beer during discussions about the compound, the Kingdom, the status of the investigation and their plans for ending this aspect of their search for the killers.

Before Povey left, Dillon gave him a pack of background information on Sultan. "We'll have business cards made with a phone number that switches back into our offices. Just in case he wants to check on your status." Povey asked about the date and time of the meeting and Dillon told him they would make contact with Buzz tomorrow and see when he wants to meet. Their guess would be the next evening. Povey thanked them for the warm reception.

CHAPTER FIFTY-FIVE

J.R. opened her front door in response to a loud knock. On the red tiled stoop of her villa stood Flavian Ramage, designated maintenance supervisor for the F-15 program at King Khalid. Ramage retired from the Air Force as an E-9. Because he held an unenviable record of forcing his way to the top, he wasn't respected like others who earned the top enlisted rank. None of the maintainers on the line referred to him as "Chief". That designation of respect is reserved for a select group of men who wore the rank proudly and treated their people with esteem. Ramage didn't do it during his career and when he signed on with the Peace program more than 15 years before, he continued his misuse of power. He stepped on people to ingratiate himself to host nation supervisors.

Eventually he was the only one left standing when the top slot opened. He was now firmly entrenched having survived several attempts at eliminating his position for a Saudi. He got the job done but only through fear and intimidation. J.R. was aware of his background and techniques. She would carefully con the man into providing all the information she needed without antagonizing his power position.

"Good morning," J.R. greeted as she stood aside allowing Ramage to step into her villa entryway.

"I'm just finishing up breakfast. Can I get you a cup of coffee?" Ramage agreed to a cup and followed J.R. into the kitchen where they took seats at a small table in the room's center. J.R. poured coffee into their cups placing one in front of Ramage and one next to her plate of three-grain toast.

"I certainly appreciate this tour of the line. It's really the first time I've been around fighters. Most of my work has been with the strategic forces." Ramage just nodded his head as he took a sip of his coffee.

"Is there anything in particular you want to see?" he asked sitting his cup down on the plastic tablecloth. "The boss wasn't too specific."

J.R. explained her cover story. She was sent down to help with the administrative problems discovered when the new administrator arrived. She always liked to get a feel for the business end of the program and not having any experience with tactical aircraft, she wanted to see how they operated on a daily basis. Although the interface between USMTM forces and contract maintenance personnel was limited, she met several of them during visits to compound establishments and while learning to SCUBA dive.

"So you've met some of our folks at the bars?" Ramage grinned as he took another sip of his coffee.

"Got me there," J.R. confessed as she finished off her toast. Ramage explained the maintenance program and the contractual support provided by the expatriates. J.R. sat listening as though really interested in what the bald headed geek said. She didn't respect people who stepped on folks to get ahead. She silently hoped he was involved in the distribution process so she could end his reign. When he reached the bottom of his coffee cup and the end of his explanation, the pair left J.R.'s villa and headed for the air base.

As they drove through the entry control point, Ramage pointed to some of the maintenance facilities on the "compound" side of the base. He turned down one of the access streets and headed for the runway. A pair of British built Tornados lined up at the end of runway waiting for clearance to launch. Ramage pulled up to the red signal light controlling access to the runway overrun crossing point. Until the jets launched, all traffic stopped to prevent damage from afterburner blast generated on takeoff roll. Ramage and J.R. watched as the burners lit up and the fighter-bombers slowly began their roll toward takeoff. They couldn't talk because even with the air conditioner on and the windows rolled up, the din from the four engines powering the two jets was deafening. As the jets broke the bonds of gravity and lifted off the concrete, the signal light turned green and the traffic began to flow across the overrun.

"Those are the noisiest bastards I've ever come across. I don't think US forces have ever had to contend with such a nasty piece of equipment. Even the old F-4 was quieter," he concluded as he shook his head in disapproval of the British product.

"If I had the political clout with an aviation savvy prince, I would convince him to scrap those pieces of shit and go with an entire F-15 fleet. They've got a gold mine of capability with the Eagle but the infighting between royals is staggering when it comes to who has the better toys." They drove on in a moment of silence before Ramage picked up his radio and made a call to determine the location of the maintenance unit supervisor.

As it turned out, the super was in his cubbyhole office. He told Ramage he would meet him outside for the cooks' tour. Ramage pulled in front of the door the super would use to exit the hallway leading to his office. The door pushed open and Olaf Jerningham stepped into the bright sunlight. He raised his hand to shade his eyes as he approached the passenger side window. Ramage activated the window from his control panel.

"Hey Ram, is this the visitor?" he asked while extending his hand through the opening window to greet J.R.

"You're quick as a cat, Oly. That's why we keep you around," Ramage laughed.

"I knew it wasn't for my dashing good looks", the painfully thin man with the Hitler style moustache shot back as he squat down beside the passenger door to talk with his visitors.

Ramage explained what he wanted and Oly agreed to pick up the tour. Ramage needed to get back to the squadron commander's office for a briefing. J.R. thanked Ramage for the ride and the briefing. He replied Oly would drop her off at the USMTM office when they finished. J.R. got out and waved to Ramage as he drove down the taxiway and around the end of the aircraft shelter.

Oly provided J.R. with a comprehensive tour of his facilities. J.R. was suitably impressed by the RSAF setup. When they finished, Oly suggested they visit the other units to meet those supervisors. J.R. readily agreed. She had to get him away from prying ears if she was going to have any chance of making a score. The drives between each unit were too short for J.R. to breech the subject of a buy. She waited until they were in route to her office.

"Does Quenton Blunt work in your unit?" she asked while they were waiting for a pair of Eagles to land.

"Why do you ask," Oly replied with no apparent reaction.

"I went diving with him. I know he works in maintenance but he didn't mention which specific unit he was attached to," J.R. answered without turning her head to look at Oly.

"He showed me some special places to dive and we sat and talked for a while one evening." Oly was silent watching the light change to green and the traffic begin to flow. It was an awkward moment before Oly replied.

"He does work for me. He mentioned your diving venture and said you might give me a call. He didn't declare a personal visit was in the offing."

"Well then let's cut to the chase. I would like to have access to some good stuff while I'm here and he said the shit we smoked while pondering a beautiful Red Sea sunset was provided by your dear sweet loving wife." J.R. turned slightly to get a full view of Oly's reaction. There was none. She strategically left out the reference to "butt ugly bitch". Don't want to piss off the potential salesman if he doesn't consider his wife to be "butt ugly" she thought to herself while waiting for Oly to reply.

"Your story seems to check out. Had some of my friends up north check into just who the fuck you were and they all came up with the same information. I guess we can do some business. You're not connected with the Saudi police and they're the ones I stay away from." J.R. just smiled as she thought about bringing this douche bag down along with his charming wife.

"Just let me know when we can make a connection," she replied to his offer. Oly told her he kept all of his business confined to his compound villa.

"Makes it easier to control," he confidently smiled as they pulled up behind the doublewide trailer used as the USMTM office. J.R. thanked him for all the assistance and said she would be waiting for his call. She'd like to have some before the weekend so she could chill without having to down any of the rotgut stuff they have here. Oly stopped her.

"Don't you active duty types get a ration?" he asked. J.R. reacted fast.

"You're right there. We do have a ration but that's the key word. Ration. I can only have so much of my favorite beverage per month and I go through that in a flash. Work hard, play hard and drink hard. That's always been my motto." There was an uncomfortable silence as Oly digested the information.

"I know how that can be. I had rations in England. That's where I picked up my other recreational activity. It was cheaper to buy a bag to smoke than it was to buy booze off the locals," he commented as he put the car into reverse.

"I'll be in touch." J.R. shut the door and waved as he pulled away to head back toward his maintenance unit. J.R. could only hope he bought the entire story. If he got suspicious, he could throw a wrench into the works. She went inside the building and caught the colonel as he was coming back from the snack bar.

"How was the nickel tour?" he asked dropping the bag of chips on his desk and popping the top on his soda before taking a long pull on the beverage.

"All went as well as could be expected. Made some contacts and met the supervisors. Now all I have to do is play out the line and let the suckers bite." Erpack nodded as though he understood what J.R. was relating.

She kept the fact Jerningham was a supplier away from the colonel for the time being. His maintenance unit was the one most frequently used by the U.S. contingent for training flights. She steered the conversation away from her investigation by commenting on the facilities in the hardened shelters. Erpack bit and they were off on a tangent about how the U.S. Air Force doesn't provide blah, blah, blah......

J.R. wanted to get on line and update Dillon. She listened to Erpack rant for a while and then excused herself for a trip to the latrine. She came back to find Erpack engaged in web surfing so she just slipped past his office and into the admin area. She logged on the secure net and fired off a note to Dillon with all the details.

✳

J.R. didn't have to wait long for Oly to make contact. He stopped by her office the next day and invited her to his villa for some Thai cooking. She agreed to the time and Oly was on his way back to the line. That's where his wife is from, she thought as she kept up her administrative appearance. That evening she readied her evidence collection box and sent a note to Dillon she was headed out to make the buy.

In Riyadh, Dillon's computer was on to watch for just such a message from J.R. He wasn't worried about this buy but he did want her to have some help when she went up against the main suppliers.

The evening was enjoyable despite the underlying reason for her being at Oly's villa. Quenton was accurate with the "butt ugly" reference. Oly's wife was hard to look at. Having spent some time in Thailand during another operation, J.R. knew she was not a typical example of Thai women. Love is blind she laughed to herself as she reached to take the bowl of rice from Lotty.

"I'll have just a bit more of the rice and another spoonful of that fish dish. It's just spicy enough," J.R. complemented as she moved the bowl closer to the side of her plate so she wouldn't drip any of the red sauce on the crochet tablecloth.

After dinner, Oly asked J.R. to follow him into the small storage room off the kitchen. Since he lived in one of the older villas, a small bathroom was adjacent to the storage room. Originally designed as a maid's room, the compound added storage shelves to the room that gave occupants some place to store unused items of any description. Oly pulled a set of keys from his back pocket and unlocked the bathroom door. Inside J.R. could see the window blocked off and the exhaust fan removed. A small humidifier was running in its position under the small sink. Oly installed shelves to facilitate product storage. The toilet was converted into an overstuffed seat with a table pulled down from the opposite wall for the rolling procedure.

"I'm impressed," J.R. commented to Oly as pulled a Havana cigar box off one of the shelves.

"Why thanks. We found this arrangement works really well. We have everything we need within easy reach. When I make a buy Lotty can come in here and have the product ready for purchase in no time at all."

Oly opened the box and pulled out half a dozen joints. He picked up a zip lock bag off another shelf and put the smokes inside. He carefully rolled the bag from the bottom squeezing the air out before sliding his finger across the seal.

"Gave you half a dozen. Should do you for the weekend," he laughed as he handed the baggie to J.R.

"It's been a while since I had enough for a weekend. I've been on the wagon since coming into the Kingdom." J.R. reached into her front pocket and pulled out her Riyals. Oly told her the price, making sure he mentioned the new customer discount she was getting, took the money, and dropped it into the top drawer of a small white cabinet sitting next to the humidifier.

Well done Oly, J.R. said to herself as she backed into the storage room and watched Oly lock the processing room door. Just don't make a deposit of proceeds until I can pay you another visit.

✳

"Shit hot," Dillon exclaimed as he raised his single malt in a salute to the person on the other end of his secure line.

"Should I notify the Prince for assistance?"

"Not right now," she replied.

"I want to play this game a bit longer so he trusts me. I'll be offering him a way out if he rolls over on the main suppliers. Once I have that information and find out where in the hell they are growing this junk, I'll need the Calvary. I would like to have someone down here when I apply pressure for the suppliers." J.R. and Dillon discussed potential tactics and the type of force she expected to need. William would travel south to help with the visit.

"Can I put my trust in this guy?" J.R. asked.

"I believe you'll be suitably impressed. Test him any way you want before you make the move. He's smart and will be an asset. I wouldn't send you a piece of shit. You know that. We'll get him on the way as soon as you give us the word. Don't want to flood the market with new faces. Someone may get suspicious."

"This place doesn't seem to be too nervous about the possibility of getting caught. They must have a good line of protection. They really don't expect the Force to be involved with a possible bust. Erpack came in handy for something."

"Are you going to need some weaponry?" Dillon wanted to know.

"Good suggestion," J.R. agreed.

"Send down a 9MM if you have one. Let William bring what he wants. I don't think the guy is packing but I sure don't want to take a chance. This will be a good bust but I don't want to take it too loosely." Dillon agreed an underestimation of the target could get her killed.

"When the troops move in, I'll have them bring a couple of extra heavies for you and William. Just make sure you keep Erpack away from the final move." J.R. said there wouldn't be a problem with keeping him away from the action. She was playing him like a cheap drum.

Dillon told her what he wanted for a time frame and J.R. agreed her plan would fit those parameters. He told her the timing is driven by his plans to move on the suppliers in Riyadh and get back to Germany for the final sweep.

"Make sure you keep checking your six. Don't let the simplicity of this get in the way. The guys you're dealing with now may be simpletons but the producers have to be a lot more sophisticated to have escaped detection for such a long time. We know they have police protection so keep what you find in our channels until we get the Prince involved."

"Thanks for the pep talk coach. I'll keep myself safe and warm for a return engagement with you."

"I'll keep that in mind," Dillon replied before wishing her the best of luck.

CHAPTER FIFTY-SIX

"You ready," Karl asked as he came into Dillon's office.

"You bet," Dillon responded as he closed the document and shoved the keyboard under his workspace.

"Let me take a leak before we venture down the road. I know there won't be a place to pee out there." Karl went out back and brought the truck round front. Dillon checked with Karlotta as he went out the front door. Karl cranked the air conditioning up to cool the truck as they headed away from Eskan.

"Why did the guy pick this place?" Dillon wondered aloud.

"I really don't know," Karl responded to the unsolicited thought.

"The ruins are on the opposite side of Riyadh. It's a historical place consisting mainly of mud huts protected by an extensive barrier system."

"So it has some relevance to the Saudis?"

"Oh yeah, it was the capital of the first Saudi State. Do you want the full history lesson or just the abridged version?" Karl asked as he brought the truck into the ring road's center lane.

"I guess it depends on how much time we have," Dillon replied. Karl began the abridged version.

"In the mid 18th century, Dir'iyyah was the center of Bedouin society. It could be considered a Commonwealth. All the infighting and other horseshit that kept the country from becoming anything more than a bunch of sheep and camel herders was beginning to be pushed aside. Evidently, the teachings of their Holy book were ignored. This was an attempt to bring the population back to their holy rule of law. It was very close to successful. The society flourished and the tribes began to work together for the good of the whole."

423

"What kind of crap are you handing me," Dillon laughed. "They still can't get along. From what I saw at Khamis, if you aren't one of the in tribes, you don't get the important jobs or the lucrative contracts." Dillon added a verbal emphasis to the words "in tribes".

"There's much truth in your observation but before Dir'iyyah, it was really chaotic. There's been a settlement at the wadi since the mid 15th century, so you see it took them a long time to formulate a plan that seemed to work. Now this isn't to say the time was peaceful. The Saudis were busy conquering tribes in their consolidation move. The Egyptians wanted this land and were willing to strike a deal, which allowed pilgrims to venture to the holy cities but the catch was the Saudis had to give up their claim to the cities. This arrangement seemed to have pluses for both sides. The Egyptians would have the holy cities for the Ottoman Sultan and they would promise not to invade the Najd region. The typical exchange of envoys was made but the Egyptians had other ideas up their sleeve. Muhammad Ali always promised the Sultan the region that included Dir'iyyah. When he made the demand the Saudis relinquish the land between Dir'iyyah and Madinah, he knew they wouldn't agree and it would clear his way for an invasion. That invasion took place somewhere around 1815 or 1816 as the Egyptian forces, under the leadership of Ibrahim Pasha landed at Yanbu. The Iman in Dir'iyyah made some very stupid mistakes militarily. In one battle, his troops were unable to defeat 1500 Egyptians with a force of more than ten thousand camel riders. They planned to cut off the Egyptians by moving against their supply point at Yanbu' but Hasan Pasha, brother of Ibrahim, arrived and prevented the Saudi forces from taking the port."

"Damn Karl, what brought out this need to study history?" Dillon questioned as he held up his hands to stop the dialogue.

"My major in college was history. I always read a bit about the history of the place I'm working. When this guy wanted to meet at Dir'iyyah, I got out the books for a refresher course."

"Please continue," Dillon said as he turned slightly in his seat to get a bit more comfortable.

"Anyway, the hit and run tactics of the Iman weren't working. He was being pushed further and further across the desert. Finally, in early 1818, Ibrahim was ready to move on Dir'iyyah. It took him until September to bring victory. It was one hell of a siege. Being military, we need to sit with a couple of beers and go over this part bit by bit."

"I'm game for that," Dillon agreed. "How much further do we have to go?" They just made a transition from the airport road to another section of the ring road.

"We're on the final leg right now," Karl said.

"So what happened to the Iman?"

"The Turks cut off his head in a public execution. From what I read, it wasn't a pretty sight. After they took off his head, they crushed it in a mortar and stuck what was left of his body up on a pole. His death notice was pinned to the body with a dagger."

"And our bleeding heart liberals say capital punishment is cruel and unusual. Bet you didn't find any of them protesting the Imam's demise!" Dillon concluded as he pointed toward a road sign over the highway.

"You mean they have the ruins signposted?" Karl said the place could be a real tourist spot if they would get their shit together.

"The Saudis just don't seem to give a shit about their history. You don't meet many of them who could tell you one thing or another about where they came from or better yet, where the hell they're going." Karl continued to grumble about the arrogance of the one-time farmers as he brought the truck through the narrow streets approaching a bridge leading to a small parking lot. He pulled in and stopped the truck. Both men got out and began their walk through the dirt streets surrounded by remains of the once proud capital.

"Did this guy mention where he was going to meet us?" Dillon asked.

"No," Karl replied.

"He just said he would meet us here. He specifically mentioned the ruins of Turayf. This was the last place standing after Pasha leveled Dir'iyyah on orders from his dad. We'll just head up toward the Sa'd Palace. It's been rebuilt. If this guy doesn't show, we'll at least have time to take a look at the restoration." They continued to walk the streets sticking their heads into vacant doorways and through partially demolished windows. Dillon commented on the building method of straw and mud.

"Damn lucky it doesn't rain much here," he commented as the men caught sight of the renovated palace. They leaned against a low wall just outside the palace entrance and watched for anyone approaching. Karl continued to give Dillon a history lesson. Karl was taken aback when a Saudi woman, dressed in the long black abaya, came up and stopped a few feet away from the two men.

"Excuse my disguise but I can't take a chance on being photographed with you two," the encased figure stated in a deep manly voice. The shrouded figure began to relate a story about a friend of a friend who may have gotten himself involved too deeply in a very bad situation.

"Let me see if I have this straight," Dillon said when the man finished relating his story.

425

"Your friend was hired by another Indian to push a specific car through a brick wall in order to scare the occupant? Is that what you're trying to make me believe?"

The black-garbed person reiterated the man isn't the killer type. He was paid very well to frighten the driver of the car.

"He wasn't told about a ditch on the other side of the wall. When the truck followed the car into the ditch and crushed it, he panicked and ran from the truck. He hid in Ba'tha for nearly a week. He was supposed to meet the guy who hired him but he was too frightened. He didn't know how the guy would react."

"Where is this Einstein now?" Dillon demanded. He was told the man was hiding in a tailor shop near clock tower. Their conversation ended as they waited for a group of Saudi youth to pass on their way to a soccer field. They gave the black garb a passing look as they kicked their soccer ball down the dusty path. When they were out of earshot, Dillon told the man what they expected.

"This guy is really in deep. However, I happen to have some influence with a royal and will do what I can to help him, if, and it's a big if, he cooperates completely and when we're done with him, he comes into custody. If he doesn't agree with our entire plan, he's on his own. You understand what I'm saying?"

The man was silent as he pondered Dillon's demand. After a brief moment Dillon began, "Hell let's hit the road. This guy just wasted our time and he's beginning to piss me off." The black figure suddenly came to life.

"What do you what him to do?"

"If someone is watching us, we could have been getting a briefing on the city. Unless they are packing around some sophisticated antennas, they don't know what the hell we are discussing. I'm going to drop a few Riyals on you. On one of them is a phone number. You go to a pay phone and call it tomorrow night between the hours of 10 p.m. and midnight. I'll give you further instructions. Meanwhile, keep your friend alive."

Dillon reached into his pocket and counted through his roll of Riyals. He pulled one of his "phone number" riyals out and added it to the other one-riyal notes he selected. He set them on the ledge of the wall and pushed them toward the "woman". He then gave a head nod to Karl and they were on their way back to the truck. "She" picked up the notes, stuffed them into a pocket, and departed the meeting place in the opposite direction as the two agents.

Neither Karl nor Dillon spoke as they briskly walked back to the parking lot. They were on the bridge leading away from the lot before Dillon asked.

"So what do you make of that?" Karl said the story was plausible but not probable.

"Once we get this guy safely on our side of the fence, we should be able to pick his story apart if it's not the truth."

Karl agreed. Dillon explained how he wanted to use the endangered driver to pull out what they hoped was another member of the supply team. If they could get two of them, they would be sure to get the remaining player.

"What we need is a couple of Saudis to make the bust in Ba'tha. I'll make a call to the prince and solicit two of his best. They can dress in thobe and gutra and designate where we want this guy to be. Once they pick him up, we can be wandering in the area. When the shit hits the fan, we can be there to assist if necessary. However, I don't believe they will need our help. We can concentrate on getting the driver out of harms way. Then we can grill him about his story and perhaps save his sorry life."

Karl wasn't too pleased about saving the driver's sorry ass. He put in his two cents for letting the Saudis have him. Dillon agreed but reminded Karl about the purported facts surrounding his involvement.

"If he really didn't know about the ditch and his only job was to scare the driver, then it was an accident gone terribly wrong. I won't go as far as to save him from punishment but I will try to keep his head on his shoulders."

The two agents stopped along the way for some fast food before getting back to Eskan. When they came into the office, they stopped by William's space and tossed an apple pie, his favorite dessert from their stopping place, on the middle of his desk.

"Why thanks gents. How sweet of you to remember. How did the meeting go?" William queried as he pulled open the pie's container and took a large bite from the still warm pastry shell. Dillon gave him a quick briefing as Karl went to get a couple of long necks out of the fridge. William listened intently as they set out their plan for pulling in another member of the supply gang.

"We have to get Povey to make his move on the same date." Dillon began.

"We don't want to scare one of them off. From everything we know; there are only three main players. At least they're the only ones making contact via cell phones copied by Eclipse. If others are involved, we should be able to make a clean bust at the house."

Dillon pulled out his cell phone and dialed the Princes' private line. After a brief explanation of their current situation and an admission there was more to his investigation than the murder, the prince readily agreed to provide two men for the planned action. Dillon said he would get back with the royal to provide time and place for a meeting. He also promised to provide information about the processing house and how they planned to bring in the remaining players. The prince thanked him for his cooperation. Things were beginning to happen at a rapid pace.

Chapter Fifty-Seven

MD picked up as the chirping sound broke the silence of his living room. Oly greeted "doc" as he called him and asked if they could meet. MD agreed to the time and place. Oly dropped the phone in the cradle and rubbed his hands together as he came back into the kitchen where butt ugly was finishing the dinner dishes.

"He agreed to a meeting," Oly gushed grabbing his wife around the waist.

"This could be the beginning of a big score. We could be on the way home with a bucket full of money." Butt Ugly wasn't impressed as she pulled her husband's hands from around her waist.

"I'll withhold judgment until I see the funds hit the bank account," she hissed grabbing a stack of plates to put them back into the cabinet.

The meeting was set for the next day in the compound's central facility. It wasn't unusual for a contractor to meet with the compound's school principal. Oly arrived a few minutes early, poured himself a cup of coffee and grabbed one of the sweet rolls from the display cabinet. He picked a table at the back of the dining facility where he could see the door. He didn't have long to wait as MD came through the door after the short walk from his school office. He too poured a cup of coffee after acknowledging Oly's wave of greeting.

"Good to see you doc," Oly said as MD pulled out his chair and sat down. They talked about other issues briefly before Oly came to the point.

"There's a new Air Force type working with the flyboys. She's in the market for a continued supply and may be able to open up a wide range of potential customers throughout the Kingdom." MD sipped his coffee and listened as Oly continued to explain how he foresaw the expansion working.

When he finished, MD slowly placed his cup into the saucer with its drip-catching napkin.

"Instead of expanding your end of the business," MD began, "Why don't we talk about you taking over the entire operation?" There was no response from Oly. With his cup in mid swing to his lips, he just stared at MD.

"What is that supposed to mean?" he questioned. MD began to explain how he and EB were planning on retirement. It didn't take long for MD to finish his story. After EB made his wishes known, MD did some serious thinking about how to close down and get rid of the workers. When Oly called, he decided to drop this bombshell on him to gage his reaction.

"You gotta be shittin me?" Oly gushed when MD finished. "I never thought you would get out of the business."

"Neither did I," MD confessed, "but when EB wanted out, I guess it all just fell into place. We both have enough cash stashed in various locations to keep us in the style we're accustomed too. I was just going to bury the place but when you called, I thought I'd give you a crack at running the operation."

Oly was quick to agree on a takeover. He wondered about a price but MD said he wouldn't commit until he talked with EB.

"Let me check with EB and I'll get back with you on a timetable for the transaction."

Oly shot the remainder of his coffee and pushed back from the table telling MD he would be waiting for his call. He bolted from the dining facility leaving MD to finish his coffee before returning to his place as principal of the compound school.

⚜

William waited in his seat on the left side of the C-12's single aisle, as the pilot unlatched the door and dropped the steps to the tarmac. The flight from Riyadh was uneventful as the crew gave William a guided tour of the area. Arrangements were made to fly the agent down to Khamis on the "Greater USMTM Transportation System", or GUTS to those in the know, so he could bring along the 9MM for J.R. and a similar piece of weaponry for himself.

As William unbuckled his lap belt and moved toward the opening, he picked up the pair of bags he brought along with his clothes and tossed them out the door to the ramp. He then picked up the gun case and stepped into the cool mountain top air. As he did, a white Chevy Caprice pulled along side the aircraft. J.R. waved to him from the drivers' seat. She popped the

430

trunk and indicated for William to put his gear in back. Once stowed, he got in next to J.R. and introduced himself.

"I'm pleased to make your acquaintance," J.R. responded.

"Let's get back to the office so I can fill you in on some interesting twists to this game."

⁂

Dillon picked up and responded to the caller with a simple "YES". It was the black garbed visitor at Dir'iyyah. Dillon listened for a while and with a brief acknowledgement, he hung up. He picked up a pad a paper from the desk and scratched down a time and location. He pushed the speed dial and waited for a response. When the prince answered, there weren't too many words spoken. The royal promised two of his finest and all he was waiting for was a time and place. Dillon concluded the call and headed for the door to tell Karl and Carvel the news. They were both at the office researching another case dropped into their laps by CENTCOM[29].

As the prince hung up, he pushed a small red button on the intercom system located on the right side of the sumptuous Philippine mahogany desk. He was in his office reviewing programs brought to his attention by members of the public. In Saudi Arabia, many of the high-ranking royals entertain suggestions and requests from members of the pubic at regularly scheduled meetings. The prince just held one of those meetings and was reviewing the programs deemed workable by supporting members of his vast staff. Not more than a minute after depressing the button, a uniformed member of his security staff was at the door. He requested the presence of two particular security personnel. He waited in his office for their arrival.

Karl and Carvel looked up from the stack of files covering the conference table. Since William traveled to Khamis, Carvel was helping in the office until it was time to make his connection. Dillon told them of the phone call and his subsequent conversation with the prince. They nodded in agreement, as they too saw an end for one phase of this operation

It was time to turn Carvel, or Duke Puddefoot, as he's known to Buzz, into a drug-purchasing scoundrel of the first degree. Dillon gave a call to Buzz. Lola answered and cooed a greeting.

"Lola my dear, Dillon on this end. Is Buzz available?" She acknowledged he was and put Dillon on hold as she announced the call to Buzz.

"Greetings Dillon. Let me make the assumption this call is concerning the matter we discussed earlier."

"You are correct, Buzz. I just got a call from the guy and he wants to meet as soon as possible. What's your plan?" Buzz explained how he would meet Duke at his villa. As Dillon heard that, he nodded and gave Carvel thumbs up. Dillon concluded the conversation and explained the particulars to Karl and Carvel.

William listened intently as J.R. explained in detail how she planned the operation to unfold. He was amazed at the structure and how each item of possible failure was contemplated. Dillon was right he thought. She certainly is an amazing investigator.

"Do you have any questions about your part of this operation?" J.R. asked bringing William back from his dream state of admiration.

"No Mam," was the slightly embarrassed response. However, J.R.'s plan didn't include the purchase of the entire operation by Olaf.

CHAPTER FIFTY-EIGHT

Bill was expecting the call from the German motor vehicle division but he wasn't expecting the results. "So the registered owner lives in a post office box in Kaiserslautern?" he asked as he wrote a note on the scratch pad next to his phone.

"Oh," he replied to the caller, "the box is located in Berlin." He took a few more notes as the caller completed passing along the information on the Blue Audi. When Bill was done, he reviewed the notes and left his office to visit with Christina and Penny.

As he passed Penny's office, he signaled her to follow him into Christina's cubby. He told them the findings and asked for any questions. Penny asked if they provided any more information about the owner of the box.

"Nothing more than what I read. We need to get with the folks in Berlin and see what they can tell us."

Christina wanted to know if they were going to bring Asterfon in on their findings.

"Not unless I'm forced to." Bill quickly replied.

"There's just something dubious about that guy and his interest in this case. I know he ties himself in with the victim but I just have an uneasy feeling. Guess that comes from hanging around Dillon too long. His sixth sense is beginning to rub off."

"You wish," Penny chided as she got up to leave the room.

"I'll make contact with security folks at the embassy and have them do a bit of investigation without involving Asterfon. Hope they don't spill the beans by any misplaced sense of loyalty to the agent." Bill agreed with the plan and turned to talk with Christina as Penny left.

433

"With the address in Berlin, there's got to be a local tie." Bill concluded.

With those final words, Bill left the office to give Dillon a call and brief him. He listened intently as Dillon discussed happenings in the Saudi capitol.

"Damn," Bill exclaimed, "sounds like things will be coming to a screeching halt in your arena."

"That's what we're hoping for" Dillon replied.

"I do believe all our problems will be solved in a matter of hours, not days. I know J.R. has her end of the project well in hand and our sting is beginning to take shape"

"Penny asked if you were going to be back for the final push here. I told her there probably wasn't any way we could keep you from being part of the operation."

"You're right there," Dillon agreed.

"I want to see how those responsible for snuffing out such a young life actually look when staring down the business end of a nine mil."

"Let me know what you find on the PO Box," Dillon concluded as he bid farewell to the agent in Germany.

William tucked the weapon into the small of his back in the specially designed holster. J.R. wasn't going to carry any weaponry during this next meeting with Olaf. They were going to meet at one of the local chicken restaurants. As they pulled into the parking lot, Olaf waved from the blue painted concrete steps leading into the facility. J.R. and William climbed the steps and entered an open area with display chillers around the edges.

After introductions, Olaf explained the sequence of events. People picked the type of meat course and their type of drink. The rest of the meal was provided. J.R. and William both picked a couple of skewers crammed with chicken cubes in different sauces. Once selections were made, Olaf led them through an adjoining doorway and up to a booth with old Wild West type barroom swinging doors. They slipped off their shoes and pushed open the doors.

Olaf's wife was inside lounging on the thinly carpeted concrete floor. Around the edge of the area were the ever-present leaning pillows. They're designed to give Saudi family members a place to lean as they ate their meals. As Olaf explained, most Westerners find them uncomfortable and problematic.

During their introductory small talk, there was a knock on the door. Olaf cleared the waiter into their area as he delivered drinks, bread, and dipping substances. When he left, Olaf couldn't contain himself any more.

"I'm going to take over the operation in this area." J.R. could hardly believe what she just heard. All the plans she laid out were just flushed as this dunderhead was going to be the distributor and manufacturer. She must move fast.

"That sounds great for you but why are the current suppliers getting out?" Olaf went into an encapsulated version of why they were closing down shop. J.R. listened intently and began to form another set of plans to get this operation closed down in the next couple of days.

There was another knock on the doors and after Olaf cleared them in, three TCNs descended on the area with plastic sheets, plates, utensils and a roll of paper towels. Once the "table" was set, they left and returned a short time later with everyone's choice of main course, huge bowls of fried rice, more bread, salad items, and more dipping sauce. J.R. and William just stared at the food as the pile began to grow.

After the waiters left, everyone dug in with their hands, as is the custom. The conversation turned away from business and into a tour of the area. When they finished and the waiters rolled everything into the plastic sheeting, J.R. and Olaf settled on a time for their meeting the next day. J.R. was going to force Olaf into taking her to the site where the product was grown. Olaf was very hesitant at first but J.R. was insistent. With visions of grandeur in his head, he agreed to take her but stressed he couldn't guarantee the present operators would be glad to see her.

"Don't worry about them," she stressed trying to ensure the meeting would be kept.

"I'll leave my partner at the house and we can make a quick trip out to the site. Since I've just been extended, I wanted to tell you the amounts of my purchases would be increasing. William is connected to some of the contractors on other Saudi programs. With you taking over the operation, I may want to be an investor. That way I can guarantee my supply will always take precedence over your other clientele." Olaf listened intently, looked over at Lotty, and got a shrug of the shoulders. Her indecision was evident.

"OK," Olaf exclaimed, "I'll give the guys a call and set up a meet for this weekend."

J.R. held up her hand in protest. "Can't wait until the weekend. My friend here has to be back to Taif by tomorrow evening. I've got him on GUTS and you know how pissy those guys get if there's any changes to the schedule."

Olaf knew the statement was true and agreed to try to set up a meet for the next afternoon. They left the restaurant with Olaf and butt ugly heading back for the compound while J.R. took William for a tour of the bustling metropolis of Khamis Mushayt and the greater Abha area. As they drove, J.R. laid out the new plan. With a few minor changes, it seemed to be workable. William would follow Olaf and J.R. when they went to the site. He would remain outside and cutoff any possible escape from the front door. Since they didn't have time to bring in trustworthy assistance, they could only hope there wasn't a back exit to the place.

When they finished the tour, J.R. gave Dillon a call and explained the unexpected glitch. "Sounds like you have the situation covered but I'll give the Prince a call to see what he has in the area to back you up. We know the locals are on the payroll, so we need some outside help. I'm sure he has a summer place in that region and a contingent of guards. Let's hope he trusts them." J.R. agreed to the request for assistance.

She turned to William and explained the circumstances. William confessed he was grateful for any help they could get. "You never know what type of security these guys have. I'd sure hate to run up against some big guns and we're stuck with 9 mils."

"Don't worry too much about the firepower. I don't believe these guys will put up much of a fight. As long as they don't face time in a Saudi jail, I figure they'll come along peaceful enough."

Olaf was busy trying to connect with MD. He knew there would be questions concerning this type of request. With the "partner", he felt secure in getting the transaction completed as soon as possible. When MD returned his call, the request for a meeting the next day was greeted with stony silence. When MD responded, it wasn't exactly what Olaf wanted to hear.

"Just what kind of a lame brained idea is this? You want to bring some outsider to the center of the operation for a tour. Just how fucken stupid do you think we are, you idiot!" Olaf was shocked by the response but tried to put the best spin on it.

"Look, this babe is ready to make some major purchases and may open up some valuable markets for the operation. All I want to do is show her what the fuck we have and be done with it. She can gauge from the size of the operation our ability to produce. Beside, she may want to invest in the venture. She has a partner who can get us to some of the more remote contractor sites in the Kingdom. This is a win win for me." MD didn't answer and the silence irritated Olaf. "You still there?"

"Yeah, I'm still here but I still can't believe what an idiot you are." Olaf wasn't going to get into a pissing contest with MD. He just wanted to get the meeting set and close the deal.

"So are we on for tomorrow?"

MD knew how much EB wanted out and he was ready too.

"Yeah, we're on. Bring the bitch out around five tomorrow afternoon. I'll have EB go out and prep the place before I get there. I have some meetings at the school tomorrow afternoon. They shouldn't take very long. I'll meet you at that gas station near the perimeter road. You know the one?"

Olaf said he knew the one and would be there shortly before five. MD slammed the phone into its desktop cradle. He pressed one of the buttons on his speed dial, after one ring, EB answered. MD explained the situation and what part EB played in the grand scheme of things. EB was immediately annoyed.

"I don't like this plan one bit," EB began, "We have been just fine for all these yeas and now Olaf is going to bring a total stranger into the operation? Does he understand how dangerous that is?"

"I explained my concerns but he seems to trust this bitch and evidently she has a partner who can offer Olaf a significant increase in the amount of business he can muster. We'll bring her out, set the price, and close the deal. You'll be out of the business tomorrow afternoon." EB continued to complain about the situation and MD was gracious enough to listen for a while. After a few minutes, he cut EB off.

"Listen, you have become even more paranoid than before. Just quit your fucken complaining and take care of what I asked. If she is anything other than a potential partner, she won't make it out alive. Neither will Olaf and neither will any of the workers. Just be ready to carry out the plans we have established and all will be well."

Since there was little response from the other end, MD said goodbye and hung up. He would be prepared to react to any eventuality tomorrow evening. He knew EB could be right when it came to J.R. However, just how dangerous could one female admin clerk be? He was soon to find out.

⁂

Ba'tha is a conglomeration of shops located in the oldest section of Riyadh. The third world nationals, the predominant work force in kingdom, frequent it. Westerners only venture there if they are looking for a rock bottom price on practically any manufactured item in the world. If the shop you're in doesn't have the particular piece, the shop owner "knows a man who does." Western women NEVER go without significant escort. The leering eyes of the TCNs are more than some of them can stand.

Dillon pulled the SUV into a miniscule parking area between the gold shops and the fabric section. As was his normal practice, he backed into a slot with only one small Toyota between him and the street. Four-wheel drive LOW would certainly get him up, over the small car, and into the street for a dash to safety if anything happened.

Dillon turned to Karl, "Ready to dance?" With a nod of his head, Karl acknowledged the question and leaned forward in the leather bucket seat so he could reach the 9MM tucked snugly in the small of his back. Dillon took out his piece, disengaged the safety, and returned the weapon to its holster. Both men exited the vehicle and began a slow browsing stroll to the meeting point.

The plan was to have the driver meet the payoff man; the two Saudis move in and arrest both men. The driver thinks he is going to be allowed free passage but Dillon has other ideas. You can't kill a federal agent, by accident or not, and get away free and clear. The guy will spend some time in jail but it will be better living conditions than he has now.

The meet was set for an open area in the maze of shops. In the center of the area was a small fountain. It hadn't worked for years and the "pond" was full of trash and cat feces. The driver was to sit facing the fabric shop with the red awning. Zainl knew him but the Saudis had no idea who they were supposed to be watching. As Dillon and Karl approached the spot, they saw the driver and one of the officers. It was a few minutes before the scheduled meeting time so they slipped into one of the fabric shops across the open area from where the driver was sitting. They didn't have to wait long.

Zainl strolled into the open area as if he owned the world. He knew the driver was scared shitless and he wanted to enjoy the moment. He planned to take him out to his vehicle, dispatch him with an upward cut from the curved Arabian style dagger he carried concealed under his traditional Sri Lankan shirt and leave him for the locals to discover. The police wouldn't be interested, after all it was only one TCN gutted by another TCN. Why should the Saudi government become involved? They would give him a quick Muslim funeral and that would be the end of it.

As Zainl approached, the driver jumped up from his seated position. Zainl was a few steps from him and stopped dead in his tracks. They exchanged words in their native language before the driver began to back away from Zainl. Dillon and Karl watched from the open doorway of the store. Dillon saw one of the Saudis approaching from beside the fountain. The other was behind Zainl. The driver turned to run but Zainl was on him in a flash. The crowd of shoppers casually noticed the confrontation but took no action to intervene. They saw it repeatedly. Probably a dispute about some trivial matter. What they didn't see was the dagger come out of its sheave and with one quick move; it was close to the driver's jugular vein. That's when the Saudi in front of the action spoke. Zainl responded in near perfect Arabic the matter was a private one and the large man shouldn't interfere. When the Saudi persisted, Zainl began to rapidly back out of the square with the dagger still at the driver's throat.

Dillon and Karl left the shop front and were now on the other side of the fountain. Zainl saw them and with one swift move, he sliced the driver's neck from one ear to the other. In the same motion, he pushed the dying man toward the Saudi and turned to run. The Saudi side stepped the driver as blood gushed from the fatal wound. His partially severed head slammed into the brickwork of the fountain before coming to rest on a discarded plastic bag. What Zainl didn't expect was the Saudi strategically located behind him.

When he turned, the knife was in his right hand. The officer grabbed Zainl's right wrist and elbow. With one fluid motion, he snapped Zainl's arm. The knife dropped harmlessly to the ground along with Zainl. The Saudi placed one knee in the small of his back as he brought the good arm and the broken arm behind Zainl's back and secured them with a quick tie. With another swift motion, he picked Zainl up by the scruff of his shirt and drug him from the shopping area.

Dillon arranged to meet the officers outside one of the local hospitals if there were injuries during the bust. Dillon knew there would be injuries just by meeting the two security officers. He looked over to see the other officer wrapping the drivers limp body in a soiled rug. He stuffed the jagged neck wound with some rags to soak up the blood. He slipped a couple of large plastic bags over the rug, swung the completed package onto a small cart sitting outside one of the shops and pushed it toward his vehicle. Without a bit of assistance from Dillon or Karl, the matter was resolved. They returned to their vehicle for the short ride to the appointed hospital waiting room.

⁂

The hair on Carvels arm stood on end as he pushed the illuminated buzzer at the right side of the ornate front door. Before his finger reached the spot, the door swung open and the finely sculptured figure of Lola greeted him.

"Duke, so glad you could make it. Buzz is out by the pool. He wants you to join him there. Can I get you something to drink?" She waited a moment as "Duke" looked around the opulent entry.

"Why yes Mam, you certainly can," he finally responded. "I'll have bourbon and 7." Lola looked in the direction of a neatly dressed TCN and he immediately scurried away to complete the order.

"Follow me," Lola instructed as she turned and walked down the path over the stream. Carvel followed and they were soon approaching Buzz, stretched out on a white plastic lounger.

"Buzz?" Lola interrupted, "Duke's here." Buzz slowly moved his ample frame into a sitting position and removed the small plastic eye protectors. He stood up from the lounge and extended his hand in greeting.

"Duke Puddefoot," Buzz growled as he pumped his visitor's hand.

"Rather unusual name, isn't it?"

"You can blame dad's family for that one. Their original name came from the old country and they were afraid of persecution once they immigrated to America in the mid 1800's. They changed it to something they hoped would be acceptable in their new home." Carvel hoped the irony of a name change was not lost on the Jewish immigrant.

"Come, let's sit and talk," Buzz instructed as they moved toward the small covered area adjacent to the pool. Buzz and Carvel both took seats with their backs to the bushes so they could face the pool area. As they began their "get acquainted" conversation, a couple of staff members arrived with drinks and snacks. They quickly set up the table and silently disappeared. Buzz was prodding with questions he knew the answers for to see if he could slip the buyer up. Carvel was cool and answered each one with the correct story. Since time was running short and one of the suppliers was probably already in custody, Dillon gave Carvel the authority to play the game as he saw fit. The final item to use was the revelation of his Jewish background.

The sparring continued for what Carvel felt was an eternity but was actually less than an hour. Lola gracefully interrupted as she arrived in one of her best thongs to wet herself in the pool and then strategically position her moist frame on a lounger directly across the pool from the two men. Buzz always employed this tactic when talking with "customers". The distraction seemed to work every time. Although it did grab Carvels attention, he was quickly focused again on the subject at hand.

"Look," Carvel began. "I appreciate all the amenities you've provided today but let's get down to the brass balls of my visit. You know I'm in the market and I know all this dancing around the subject has just been a ploy to test my story. I don't have a lot of time to spare. I'm outta here day after tomorrow and I want to have something firmed up before I leave. I don't want to have an intermediary so that's why I agreed to meet with you and get to the inside man. The less people who know about this, the better I feel. I don't fancy spending time in a Saudi jail before meeting the executioner."

With his speech completed, Carvel picked up his drink and sat back in his chair. He didn't have to wait long for a response from Buzz.

Buzz leaned on the table and began a tirade about his business interests, his desire to stay away from the product Carvel was seeking and a myriad of other unrelated subjects. Carvel sat stoically sipping his bourbon and 7. When Buzz finished, he grabbed his drink from the tabletop and flopped back in his chair almost toppling over onto the brick patio.

Carvels training came into play. He pushed back from the table and slowly rose from the chair. He came to where Buzz was sitting and crouched down next to the man's chair. "Thanks for the eloquent speech Buzz but it don't mean didly squat to me. I want you to make the connection I need and I want you to make it now. I would hate having to notify the family Barak back in the mother country of their relative's untimely demise in a Saudi prison."

The look on Buzz's face was one Carvel would remember for the rest of his career. "That's right Lumir, we know who you are and will use the information against you if you don't come across with some assistance at this very moment."

Carvel stood, pulled up the bottom of his shirt, and exposed the weaponry he brought to the game. "And please, don't get any ideas of calling in outside assistance. You'll be the first to go."

Buzz sat in stunned silence for a moment before any words came out of his mouth. "Fuck" was all he said.

"That's very resourceful of you," Carvel replied.

"Just who are you and what is going to happen to me after this meeting?"

"Who I am and where I come from are unimportant to you at this particular moment in time. All we want is your cooperation and you'll be able to continue your life of pleasure in the magic kingdom. Cross us and it will all come crashing down around your ears."

"You mother fuckers sure have a closed system," Buzz began as he stood up and shot the remainder of his drink.

"I tried to find out just who you were but came up with blanks or stories you have confirmed at each and every turn."

"I'll take that as a semi complement." Carvel replied. "What's next on the agenda?"

Buzz motioned him to follow as they headed for the house. Buzz wasn't the violent type although he did know people who were. He was quite used to the lifestyle he established and didn't want to jeopardize anything. He was resigned to the fact this man and his other connections could easily end everything with one phone call. For them to operate as they are, they required some royal connections higher up the food chain than his. It was best just to make the link and stand out of the way.

"I set up a meet at a juice bar in Kingdom Mall. There's always a lot of activity and he won't be able to escape since what you want to do is bring him over from the dark side." Buzz chuckled as he opened the door and stepped inside. Carvel didn't let him out of his sight since he used his trump card to ensure cooperation. It didn't take Buzz long to change into some casual clothes. He led Carvel out the front door and started to walk toward his vehicle.

"I'll drive," Carvel began, "I'm sure you can find a ride home after all of this is over." Buzz just nodded his head and climbed into the SUV. The gates opened and they were off to the meet with Abdunn.

Dillon peered into the plastic bag which contained items removed from Zainl's pockets. The royal officer brought them to Karl and Dillon as they sat in the rather disgusting waiting room of the hospital. Zainl was having the damage to his arm repaired before he met the interrogation of Dillon and Karl. There wasn't much in the bag just a set of keys, a cell phone, 300 Saudi Riyals and his Iqama. "Not much to show for such an elaborate operation," Karl commented as he took the baggie from Dillon.

"I'm sure the home base is replete with all the items they need for business," Dillon countered as he looked over to where the Saudi officer was standing in a doorway of the small emergency room.

"We need to give the prince a call to tell him this portion of the situation has been completed. He has some of his security force ready to move on the compound as soon as we give the word. To stay out of the corrupted sections of the police force, he enlisted the help of a friend and his brigade of troops from outside the city limits. They are in route as we speak. Should be here by later this evening. That's when we'll make the move on the villa. Should be an interesting bust. However, all the credit will be heaped on the locals. Don't want any publicity for our end of the game."

Karl agreed and pulled his phone out of the small leather holder attached to his belt. "Wonder who this is?" he queried as he looked at the number displayed on the face of the phone. He pressed the receive button and greeted the caller.

"J.R. How's business in your section of the kingdom?" Karl listened for a moment and then responded.

"Yeah, he's right here with me. He said he didn't carry his cell phone on operations and we just finished pulling in one of our targets." He paused again as he listened to comments from J.R.

"Sure, here he is," he replied as he handed the phone to Dillon. J.R. explained where they were in the close down of operations at Khamis. Dillon was a bit concerned about her making a trip to the farm but knew J.R. wouldn't put herself in harms way. He felt better knowing she had backup. As they finished their conversation, Dillon handed the phone back to Karl.

"Things are beginning to move at a rapid pace on all fronts. J.R. is going to have the Khamis operation closed down by tomorrow afternoon. We have one of the supply trio and Carvel is moving in on another one. The Prince has the Calvary headed for the main compound and we are about to get some details on just who is running this operation."

CHAPTER FIFTY-NINE

Christina came into the office dragging one of those old style 18-inch wide computer sheets. She was haphazardly pulling the perforated edges off the copy as she scanned the print on each sheet. Bill looked up as she entered the room.

"The car is really registered to an Encyclopedia sales company headquartered in Düsseldorf. They have the PO Box here in K town but that's about it." She looked over the top of the page and waited for his reaction.

"So what do you guess? They make contact with the American community in this vicinity through mail messages sent by the leader of the pack?" Bill queried as he picked up the cola can and took a sip of the fizzy liquid.

"That would be my guess," Christina replied as she carefully folded the computer printout into one neat pile.

"All we have to do is get a handle on who is making the pickup, find out their connection to the local constabulary and we're moving toward closing this whole thing down." She sat in one of the chairs facing Bill's desk and clasped her hands behind her head.

"Makes a body feel good to see all of this come together. Any word from our amigo down range?"

"None in a few days," Bill puzzled. "Let's give him a call to check on his situation and we'll give him our details. You know he's going to want this closed out as soon as he gets back." Christina agreed and left the office for a soda. Bill held his empty can up and shook it from side to side indicating his desire for a refill. Bill punched up the office number and waited for an answer. When Karlotta answered, Bill asked for Dillon.

"He's out right now Bill. Do you want him to give you a call when he returns?"

"That's fine Karlotta. When do you expect him?" Karlotta told Bill what she knew about Dillon's plan for the day. It was just enough to give Bill the information he needed. He knew the Ba'tha plan and the coinciding plan for Carvel. He just hoped both of them came off without a hitch. He knew better than to try Dillon's cell phone. He knew Dillon never carried the instrument when he was on an operation. Christina came into the room just as he was hanging up.

"So what's the news?" she asked setting Bill's soda on the coaster placed near the edge of his blotter.

"Dillon and Karl are out on the bust of the first player in the cartel. From what Dillon told me the other day, Carvel was making a simultaneous bust on another troika member. That will leave only one player and they have some royal assistance to trap him. If all goes well and we can get him back up here, we should be able to cave this thing in by end of the week." Both of them smiled as they gave a mock salute with their sodas.

Bill, Christina, and Penny setup surveillance of the subject post office box with the assistance of the security squadron. Luckily, the box was located at the front of the main post office building in K Town. All they had to do was watch and wait for someone to use the box and they made their connection. They didn't have to wait long.

Detective Ramsay Brandt pulled out the file drawer of his dilapidated wooden desk in the murder investigation section of the K Town police department. He poured about three fingers of vodka into his coffee cup before heading to the brew pot in the kitchen. There he filled the remaining space with coffee. It was a vile concoction but one that kept the severely alcoholic officer functional enough to work on a daily basis. He leaned against the tile counter and slowly sipped the steaming liquid. As several members of the department came into the room, he greeted each one with a raised glass and a hearty "prost!" Most members of the force knew about his problem but ignored it because he was functional during the day. None of them wanted to have him out on a serious investigation where he would need to be their backup but he did have excellent powers of observation and those always came in handy at a murder scene.

When he finished his midmorning booster, Ramsay closed his desk and locked the main drawer. He signed out on the board and left the building.

Since he hadn't paid a visit to the post office in a couple of days, he thought it would be a good time since the weather was fine and the walk was short. When he got to the appointed location, he pulled out his key chain and unlocked the box. He peered inside to see one letter. He pulled it from the box and pushed the door shut pulling his key out of the lock in one motion.

Across the street, members of the surveillance team were busily collecting the sights and sounds of their targeted visitor. As Ramsay pulled the envelope open and read the contents, he made it too easy for the collection team. Because of the poor lighting in the building, he turned his back toward the window and held the letter up high enough for the cameras to record every letter on the page. It was a simple task since the only words were "CALL ME" in bold face and a phone number. It wasn't one immediately recognized by the team. They quickly entered it into the computer system on the other side of the van as they watched their target leave the post office and head back for his office. The front seat passenger left the van and followed at a discrete distance. Penny reached into her pocket, pulled out her cell phone, and called Bill. When he answered, all she said was, "The Beagle has landed." Cute code for a successful mission.

Back inside the van, the designated phone number was being processed through the million's of phone connections in Europe. A hit finally appeared in the guise of a Satellite Phone owned by a leasing company in Berlin.

As Penny got back into the passenger's seat, the other member of the team said, "This is going to be too easy. All we have to do is input this number into the system and give it a time frame to watch. It should be able to pick up the call in a matter of nanoseconds. We can trace the conversation, the location, and time of the call. Ain't technology great?"

"It's great when it works." Penny countered. "Let's get this show back to the base and make the necessary arrangements to get the text of his phone call." In anticipation of a break, all the necessary clearances were granted to get information from NSA on phone calls for lines designated by the team of agents. With Dillon's connections, it was an easy task. This was the first time the Ramstein team used this type of surveillance in an investigation.

When Bill received the "Beagle" call, he immediately up channeled a request for satellite coverage. When Penny called with the number, he forwarded it to the appropriate authorities at NSA who contacted the watch team responsible for the particular area. They set the number into the watch list and waited for a hit. It was almost instantaneous.

The conversation was recorded about an hour before between a number in K Town and the satellite phone. The location of the satellite phone was a bit murky but with a little more work, they could pin down the location within 500 meters. Since the only request was for the conversation, the analysts didn't request any location information.

One of the duty analysts tore the multi-page paper from the printer and made the proper distribution. The top copy went into a small folder sent to the duty officer in the front cubicles of the operations center. There, the document was scanned, turned into a JPEG file and sent over the CIPER net to the requesting office. Penny, Bill, and Christina awaited the results. When the nice lady inside Bill's computer announced "You Have Mail", he keyed in his password and brought the file up on screen.

"Well I'll be hooked," Bill exclaimed as he read the conversation. There's his name in black and white. I knew there was something a bit strange about that guy." Penny and Christina nodded in agreement and went back to their seats in front of Bill's desk.

"We need to get the name of the dirty cop and put a tap on his line to see if there are any other connections in the area," Penny suggested.

"All ready in the works," Bill confirmed. "I gave Hanz a call when this whole thing about the post office box came up and he has the order already in hand. All we have to do is give him the name. With the photos we have, he'll be able to get the tap in place without having to arouse suspicion in the department."

"But there's got to be another leak in the area. This one guy couldn't be the only source of information. Some of the information came from the base. We need to check with the colonel to see if his investigation has turned up any downtown links." Bill agreed with Christina's assessment of the situation. He would give Krimshank a call to check.

The ladies left Bill's office as he called the security commander. He was disappointed at the news. The only information he was getting was on low-level suppliers and occasional users. Nothing significant. Krimshank listened intently to the new information Bill provided. He was pleased the investigation was progressing so well on the OSI side of the house. He only wished his side of the equation were providing more assistance.

"Don't worry about that," Bill consoled. "I'm sure this current line of findings will lead us to the killers and in turn, to the kingfish. We have one name; now all we have to do is pull in the line and hope the other fish get stuck on the trouble hooks."

"Nice fishing analogy Bill. How long have you been waiting to use that one in a sentence?" Krimshank laughed as they bid each other goodbye. Bill picked up his soda and drained the remaining liquid. He tossed the can into the recycle bin and turned to give Hanz a call. With the standard array of deception, they arranged for a brief meet. Bill picked up the photos and a transcript of the recorded conversation. It was then out the door for a meeting with Hanz.

Bill picked one of the tables near the back of the gasthaus. He ordered a glass of Spatlese and after its arrival, sat back to watch the gathering crowd of afternoon shoppers as they stopped in to imbibe before heading home for the day. It wasn't long before Hanz showed in the doorway. After seeing where Bill was sitting, he stopped by the bar, put in his order and headed for the table. Bill rose from the bench seat to greet him.

"Hanz," Bill began, "it's been a while since we had the opportunity to talk. Hope this is the last time we have to use these tactics. I do believe we found the leak in your office."

"I sure hope so," Hanz replied. "It gets very frustrating when you have to sneak around your own office to make things happen without fear of someone stirring the pot." He watched as Bill pulled a set of photos from the envelope. He handed them to Hanz who immediately recognized the man in the photos.

"That's Detective Second Class, Ramsay Brandt. I believe he hangs his hat in the murder investigation area right now. Got a serious alcohol problem. Great investigative skills but once he's outside the job, he's nothing more than a drunk. I've never seen him impaired enough to cause problems at work but none of the other investigators will work with him on dangerous cases for fear of his not being able to back them up when the going gets tough."

"I've seen that on our side of the house too." Bill commented. "If they keep their nose clean on the job, the higher ups usually don't throw them out on their ass."

Bill and Hanz talked about the tap and when it would be in place. Since the order was already in hand, Hanz could have some specialists from outside the department initiate the tap in less than 24 hours. Bill was happy. Since the activity down range was beginning to peak, he knew Dillon would want to have all the "ducks in a row" when he came back to Ramstein.

"Let me show you a bit of information you may or may not be surprised to read." Bill teased as he pulled the transcript out of the same folder. Hanz took the document and began to read. When he got to one particular section, he paused.

"Isn't that," he began.

"That's him alright," Bill interrupted.

CHAPTER SIXTY

J.R. and William checked their weapons and gathered the extra clips they hoped wouldn't be necessary on this operation. They would leave the compound separately. J.R. showed William where the meeting place was and he picked out a waiting spot. J.R. was going to meet Olaf at the station and leave her car in the lot. Olaf would drive from there.

William left the compound and picked up a loaner car from the dealership. He turned his SUV in for service to ensure the standard Air Force issue SUV wouldn't be recognized by the principal or the potential owner of the operation. At the appointed time, J.R. drove out the gate and down snake road for what she hoped would be a simple bust.

In the meantime, EB made his way to the fields. He disengaged the tracking weapons and drove down the dusty road. As he approached, Kinkaid came out of the shaded area next to the shack and waved a greeting. A couple of the workers were in between the crops attending to some gathering weeds. They paid no attention to the visitor. When EB got out of the car, Kinkaid waited for the dust to settle before he approached and offered a verbal greeting.

"So we may have a new owner. It's better to know there will be someone taking over rather than having to eliminate the entire operation." Kinkaid began as they walked back toward the shack.

"I don't know if it's a good idea or not." EB began. "You know how tricky this thing has been to keep working. I just don't like the idea of bringing someone in and selling them the whole thing and then...." Kinkaid held up his hand and asked EB to stop.

"MD made up the mind and that's about all we say. I'll get books out to show them." Kinkaid said as he turned toward the shack. EB set about picking up the place as if expecting the Queen of Sheba. MD knew he would be paranoid about the situation and he figured getting EB out to the fields would only serve one purpose; too keep him out of his way.

With thobe and gutra in place, William wrapped the extra cloth across his face to hide the fact he had no facial hair. Depending on what sect of Islam you profess to follow, the scraggier the beard, the better practitioner of the faith you could claim to be. However, the Birkenstocks on his feet were a dead give away if anyone was inclined to notice.

He pulled the loaner SUV into a small alleyway across the street from the gas station. Olaf was right on time. MD arrived a few minutes after the appointed time. William watched as they exchanged greetings. J.R. had to leave her purse in her vehicle as she got into Olaf's truck. MD turned on the cross road and started out of town. Olaf and J.R. followed as William picked up the trail a few hundred feet behind the others.

Olaf and J.R. could see MD was on the phone as he traveled. After a few kilometers, he put on his right blinker and left the paved surface. Olaf and J.R. followed. William pulled off to the left, and waited a few minutes until he felt the others progressed far enough down the dirt trail that he could safely follow without being detected. He found a place to pull the SUV off the dusty path and under a scrub tree. He hoped it wouldn't be a long wait.

J.R. watched as MD left his vehicle and activated the switching mechanism to move the barrier and shut off the guns. Of course, she didn't know about the guns but she did notice he manipulated two switches as he coded in the sequence to override the lockout. As they drove down the remaining portion of the access road, she noticed the topography. No wonder they had it so good. It was a tough place to get in to and a tougher place to leave. She knew William was in the right place. There just couldn't be another way out of this place.

As they pulled into a wide spot in the road, J.R. noticed the buildings and the fields of product in various stages of growth. MD backed his vehicle under a small camouflaged tarpaulin next to one of the shacks. He rolled down the window and lit a cigar before walking toward Olaf and J.R. They got out of their SUV and wandered toward one of the crop rows. EB was nowhere in sight.

"Shit, MD. I had no idea." Olaf gasped as he fingered one of the multipoint leaves.

"Not many people would," MD replied, "or we couldn't stay in business. This bowl presented the best possible place to set up operations. It wasn't easy but we did have some assistance from the local constabulary. That's why we're so successful. They don't mess with us and we keep them supplied with product and funds. It's a win win for all concerned."

"So what's the protection like on the edge of this place?" J.R. inquired.

"It's all automatic. Intruder devices, weapons, the lot. State of the art. Of course, you only get the occasional Bedouin wandering into the area. Even then, the stupid bastards don't know what they're looking at. We've collected a few at the back of the fields. However, we kept with their religious beliefs and put them in the ground before sunset. Just a part of being a good neighbor." MD laughed aloud at his inhumane joke.

J.R. kept looking for the other Expat before she made any move toward bringing them down. She didn't have to wait much longer. MD waved to EB as he came from between one of the rows at the far end of the area.

"EB," MD began, "You know Olaf and this is..."

"Just call me Jay," J.R. offered as she stepped forward to shake EB's hand. "This is quite an operation you have going here. I can see this is really something worth putting some money in to so I can keep Olaf in business."

EB didn't offer much of a response. He just stared past J.R. to MD. That didn't give the agent much of a warm fuzzy feeling. She let go of his hand and walked past him toward one of the shacks. As she did, Kinkaid came out and introduced himself. He ushered J.R. and Olaf into the shack and showed them the books. MD and EB stayed on the outside and were deep in conversation when J.R. and Olaf came out of the shack.

"So, what do you think of our little operation?" MD asked as he butted out the cigar on one of the large stones in the area.

Olaf began to gush as J.R. maintained her position near the shack. She was about to make her move but needed to notify William. She reached into her shirt pocket, pulled out the Palm, and scribbled a couple of notes on the scratch pad. MD came to see what she was doing. As he did, J.R. hit the send button and beamed the message to William. The units were tied to a military satellite with nearly instantaneous transmit and delivery capability.

"Excuse me," MD shouted as he tried to grab the unit out of J.R.'s hands. "No fucken notes taken here missy." J.R.'s reactions were much quicker than the principal as she moved the unit out of his reach and into her back pocket. In the same motion, she retrieved her weapon from the small of her back and positioned it under MD's ample jowls before he knew what happened.

"I don't think you understand the situation," she hissed as MD backed toward the other stunned individuals.

"The game is over." As she spoke the words, she heard the gravelly sounds of footsteps behind her. As she sidestepped, Kinkaid completed the swing of the shovel. It glanced off J.R.'s left shoulder but with enough force to knock her off balance. She stumbled and was on the way to the ground when she got off a shot at Kinkaid. He dropped in a heap. As J.R. hit the ground, she rolled and was on her feet again as EB made a run for the fields. She fired once and brought him down with a hit to the back of his thigh. Olaf was standing with his hands raised above his head but MD was making a run for his vehicle. With a quick double squeeze of the trigger, she blew out both front tires. MD stopped, raised his hands, and slowly turned to face J.R.

"I TOLD YOU NOT TO TRUST ANYONE," EB screamed as he withered in pain where he fell to the ground. J.R. motioned for Olaf to give him a hand. She knew the maintainer was no real threat. She looked toward the road to see a cloud of dust rapidly approaching. Luckily, for William, they hadn't reconnected the surveillance system and he took a free ride into the farm. He slid to a stop, jumped from the cab, and following the head nod of J.R., went to secure EB and Olaf.

"Sorry I have to spoil your plans for retirement." J.R. apologized as she pulled MD's hands around behind him and secured them with a quick tie.

"Fuck you bitch," was the only reply.

It took them a while to find the actual farm workers. Kinkaid told them to stay hidden no matter what happened. He knew the plans MD and EB held for them and if things went sour, as they certainly did, he knew they would be murdered. As it was, he was the only one to die. J.R. and William loaded the group into the back of the SUV and before they left the farm, they called the number Dillon provided as the only trusted agent in the area. J.R. told the man she had a delivery to make and that was all he needed to hear. Dillon arranged with the Prince to have a pickup made just outside the main gate of the compound. J.R. would turn over the offenders and be done with the situation. Dillon told her not to worry about their fate. J.R. knew exactly what that meant. Swift justice and a shallow grave.

When all the processing was completed, J.R. dropped William off at his villa and drove the short distance to her abode. She pulled a long neck out of the fridge and sat down to compose a note to Dillon. He received the note sent to William so he knew the operation was going down. He just had to wait until the next communication from J.R.

As she took a long pull from the bottle, she opened her mail and sent a quick note to Dillon. It simply stated success and not to bother her for a few hours. She was going to soak the severely bruised shoulder in a hot tub and then catch a few winks before calling to provide a full report. She could only hope he reviewed his email before calling her to "check in".

The results of the afternoon's handiwork severely affected the training mission at Khamis. From human resources to operations director, the guilty pleas came from across the entire gamut of personalities and positions. Anyone could see why the head shed didn't want a drug-testing program instituted. He would have lost nearly half the work force in one sweep. The incompetent HR "manager' rolled over on a host of offenders in various aspects of illegal hooch distilling to a prostitution ring run by one of the old time mama sans from Thailand.

Since Olaf and Butt Ugly were only small players in the general scheme of things, J.R. arranged to have them processed with others discovered from the confessions of the ops director and the HR clown. They were turned over to military authorities for processing. Since their support came from a military contract, she thought it was only fair.

⁂

The Kingdom complex is an impressive edifice on the Riyadh skyline. Offices, a 5-star hotel, conference centers, and a mall to rival any in the United States were all part of the setup. Carvel pulled the SUV into the underground parking area and slipped into a slot near one of the many entrances. He followed Buzz up the escalator to the main floor. He was very impressed with the sights greeting him. He could have been in any mall back home except for the men in dresses and the women encased in black.

Buzz was drifting to the right side of the mall. He turned in a small cafeteria area surrounded by boutique type stores. In the center was a juice bar under the canopy of a large tree. Buzz showed no sign of acknowledgement as he approached a table in the corner. Abdunn rose slightly as they approached. Carvel indicated for Buzz to take the chair closest to the railing. It was opposite "ROM". Carvel pulled one of the extra chairs to the end of the table so he could keep both of the men in sight and at arms length. Buzz made the introductions.

"ROM, I'd like you to meet Duke Puddefoot." Carvel firmly grasped the tiny brown hand extended by the Bangladeshi native. They exchanged pleasantries and got down to business. Buzz assured ROM he completed a body search of Duke so he wasn't wired for sound.

"I've got to hand it to Buzz," Carvel began, "he wasn't too keen on setting up this meeting. I really had to do some fancy talking. I guess my ability to reach back and touch the inner man really paid off in this case. He's dead set against what I want to accomplish and I respect that. However, I do have a growing clientele and they have the ability to consume great quantities of powder, if you know what I mean," he finished with a wink.

Buzz began to excuse himself but Carvel was adamant he stick around. "Don't be in such a hurry to leave. I promise not to set up any buys in your presence so you can maintain your objections to this despicable business. Let's just enjoy the drinks and we can part company later." They continued

453

to discuss matters other than supply and demand. About half an hour passed when Carvel suggested they adjourn the meeting.

"Where are you parked?" Carvel asked ROM.

"I'm down by Debenems." ROM replied.

"We parked at the other end. Tell ya what, let's go down to my vehicle and I'll get you some other numbers to contact." ROM was hesitant but Buzz nodded his head in agreement.

The trio rose from the table and after paying the bill at the central cash register, left the bar, and headed for the escalator. As they made the transition from one down unit to another, Carvel noticed ROM put his right hand into his pants pocket. Now this isn't an unusual move for a man but when you leave it there, it's not a good thing.

As they pushed open the glass doors leading to the parking lot, Carvel maneuvered Buzz in between himself and ROM. As they got closer to the SUV and out of the watchful eye of a dozen drivers sitting around waiting for their masters, Carvel made his move.

They were just coming from between parked cars when Carvel violently pushed Buzz into ROM. Both men lost their balance but the wiry little man quickly regained his footing and with a quick move put the butterfly knife in his right hand. Buzz crumpled to the ground in a heap as he hit his head on a mirror, fender, and concrete stoop. He was out.

Carvel placed his weapon in his left hand as he tried to tell the little man the game was finished. If he didn't want to face the executioner, he'd best drop the knife and come along peaceable like. ROM did not intend to come quietly. As Carvel finished speaking, he lunged at the bigger man taking a wild swing with the knife. Carvel easily sidestepped the lunge and with one swing of his right hand, he broke ROM's jaw in two places and with a left hand follow through, he knocked the supplier out with the butt of his gun.

Knowing the commotion would draw attention, he quickly drug the dealer to the back of the SUV, opened the door and unceremoniously tossed him in the back. He secured his hands with a quick tie and shut the back door and window. The smoked glass prevented anyone from seeing inside the vehicle. He then quickly returned to Buzz. Although he was missing a couple of teeth and carried a nasty bump on his forehead, Carvel knew he would survive.

After getting Buzz into the front seat of the SUV and warding off the gathering crowd, he slipped out of the parking garage and onto the main street. He phoned Dillon and gave him the news. The second piece of the puzzle was in place. Only one remained.

"Did Hanz ever call back with information about the guy in the murder section?" Bill asked as he pushed back his chair and headed for the salad bar.

"Not that I know of," Penny replied. The office adjourned to the club for a spot of lunch before trying to close in on the murderers. The information provided by the motor vehicle department, coupled with the discovery of the inside man at police headquarters; put them on the verge of bringing in the perpetrator's. They needed to be careful not to tip their hand too soon for fear of making the men into a pair of runners instead of a pair in cuffs. They knew there was one other player with inside information. They weren't too sure if it was inside the cop squadron, or inside headquarters in K-Town. There were about to lay out a plan to see where the information flowed. When they had the trail confirmed, they would be ready for Dillon's return and the final push.

"I've been working on the report through HQ which should make it into our friends' hands." Christina began.

"It's sufficiently juicy to warrant his interest but not too involved to get any of our people up the line concerned with follow-up. If anything, they will make a call to you (pointing toward Bill with her fork) and when that happens, we can improvise what we want to tell them. After all, the other leak may be in our chain."

Bill said the message traffic and phone messages would be easy enough to track. If the leak were in their chain, it would be known very soon. They changed the conversation to other cases pending in the office and when they all finished lunch, each returned to their current workload. Christina was to finish the report and pass it along the intelligence lines. She reestablished a watch on the post office but this time it wasn't quite as elaborate as before. Just some bystanders watching for the police insider to make a pick up. Penny was coordinating a collection of possible inside candidates in the cop squadron. Krimshank was being more than helpful. Bill coordinated the watch inside K-Town police headquarters with Hanz. They were set to spring the plan.

Christina came down the hall into Bill's office. "Here's the release. This really should do the job." Bill took the document and reviewed the contents.

"Just spicy enough," he commented, handing the document back to Christina. "Get it on the line." With those directions, Christina returned to her office and put the message into cyberspace. Now the waiting game began.

⁂

Dillon put down the phone and clapped his hands together. "Two down, one to go," he exclaimed. "Let me give the Prince a call to find out where the cavalry is located at the present time. We can move right now if they're in the vicinity." Karl reached for the phone sitting on the table next to him. He tossed the cell to Dillon.

"Say Howdy for me," Karl laughed as Dillon dialed the number.

When the prince answered, Dillon quickly briefed him on their activities both locally and at Khamis. The prince listened politely and after Dillon's question about the outside forces, the prince informed him the troops were assembled at one of his palaces and were ready to move with little notice. Both men agreed the time was now. Dillon explained where the villa was located and asked where he could meet the force commander. Prince Abdal Azuz told him where the palace was located and that he would meet him there. He wanted to be in on the final push. Dillon could not disagree.

When Dillon disconnected, he briefed Karl on the conversation. "Sounds good to me," Karl responded. "No time like the present."

The Princes "home" sat on the edge of a cliff overlooking a lush green wadi. As they pulled up to the gate, the guard came to the drivers' window and demanded to know what their business was. When he read the name on the identification papers, he immediately indicated for an unseen person to open the gates. The gold encrusted metal and glass units swung slowly open to reveal a fountain more than 30 feet high cascading streams of floodlit water into a basin more than 50 feet wide. Behind the water display, an ornately decorated covered driveway brought visitors to the palace entrance. In the center of the covered drive was a chandelier more than 20 feet in length. Dillon pulled the SUV in front of the doors. Before he could open his door, a uniformed guard was there, with a sweeping bow, opened the door, and indicated for Dillon and Karl to follow another uniformed guard around the side of the building.

Karl poked Dillon as they followed their caretaker, "Shit, I was kinda hopin we could get inside this joint!"

Dillon nodded in agreement, as they continued to follow the man down a driveway leading away from the front of the house and into a grove of date palm trees. As they drew closer, they could hear the sound of engines running and orders given in Arabic. The guard made a stop at the first

456

uniformed person he came to. With a bow, he indicated there were visitors behind him. The prince turned around and warmly greeted the two men. He was resplendent in a crisp military style uniform of unknown allegiance. There were numerous medals (full size) and ropes hanging from epaulets on the shirt. Dillon had to contain himself from laughing aloud. However, he followed Karl's lead and simply offered his hand in greeting with a slight bow. After exchanging the required pleasantries, they turned to business.

The prince was eager to show the two men what he was able to assemble. It was quite impressive. Moreover, none of it belonged to the Kingdom. The prince held it all privately. As this was explained, Dillon couldn't help but wonder what evil plan the prince schemed for the next king. Since the present monarch was in failing health and the princes were positioning themselves for the show of force, which would ultimately lead to the election of the next ruler, Dillon could see how this type of arms cache would come in handy during a struggle for power in the void following the kings' death. However, there was no time to postulate on what might be. There were other matters to contemplate.

The prince introduced the commander of the force to Dillon and Karl. He was a full colonel in the prince's guard. A Sandhurst graduate, he earned the respect of the prince by his actions during Gulf War I. The men walked through the lines of vehicles and back to the entrance of the grove.

"Well it's about time," Dillon commented. The prince waved his right hand. The gesture resulted in the lights of a Humvee coming on and the vehicle lurching forward to where the men were standing. In a gesture right out of a "B" movie, the prince turned toward the assembled group and pumped his fist up and down in the warm night air. The final push in Riyadh was on.

⁂

The distribution clerk brought the morning read file into the office and laid it on the desk. The man behind the desk picked up the folder and scanned the listing of messages included in the file. One peaked his attention. He lifted the tab where the message was located and read the note. He put his initials in the designated space for his office and threw the file into the out basket. He turned to the computer, typed a quick note in 24 pt bold face, printed the document, and pulled it from the tray. He reached into his briefcase and took out a preaddressed stamped envelope. He folded the note, slipped it into the envelope, and returned the document, now securely sealed inside the envelope, to his briefcase. When work was over for the day, he would slip the envelope into the mail slot located in the lobby of his building and wait for the results. With mail service like it was in Germany, he could expect a call from the intended recipient within three days.

⚜

Once again, Rajmohamed picked up the cell phone and dialed Abdunn's number. It wasn't like him not to answer. They had a disagreement about who was going to meet the new customer but Abdunn insisted on making first contact through his "good friend" Buzz. Actually, all Abdunn wanted was to pull in an invite to "the compound" for some white girl sex. Buzz worked a deal with Papa Good on two other occasions when Abdunn came through with some product on short notice. All he wanted for the favor was an invite for some pleasure seeking. Buzz made it happen and Abdunn certainly wasn't one to forget such an evening.

Raj scrolled through the number listing on his phone and selected HD's number. He was greeted with the Arabic announcement "the number could not be reached at this time". He puzzled as he threw the phone on a pile of papers at one side of his desk. He continued to jot notes in his logbook before returning to the processing area. He wanted to check the status of deliveries scheduled for the next day. He casually passed by the room holding their surveillance equipment without giving it a second glance. If he would have been more attentive, his advance warning time would have been enhanced.

A few blocks away, the small tracked vehicle was off loaded. The driver and lone gunner mounted up for their drive through the gate. A reconnaissance pass was made after a full briefing from Dillon. The front of the vehicle was specially modified to provide maximum opening capability on gates and doors. If there were blocking mechanisms inside the area, and in this case, there was, the tracks would carry the unit over a barrier more than four feet high. Titanium plates surrounding his position on top of the unit with a swiveling turret capable of 360 degrees of rotation protected the gunner. It was a masterful piece of equipment Dillon imagined would come in handy during the coup attempt he felt was pending. The only problem Dillon could see was the tracks. They hadn't been noise protected. When the unit fired up, it was relatively noiseless. Nothing more than a normal diesel engine. A bit of clattering but nothing significant. However, when the unit moved off down the road, the tracks shook the ground. Dillon held up his hands to halt the unit.

"Change of plans," he began as walked toward the prince.

458

"I would imagine this group has noise sensors mounted at each corner of the compound. When this unit approaches, it's going to set off every alarm they have. We need to position the men before the gates come crashing down and then bring this thing in at the last possible moment. Please explain to all, this guy has cameras mounted everywhere. We just have to hope he isn't watching the monitors as we approach." The prince explained the situation in Arabic although all of the leaders understood English. After a few instructions to squad leaders, the troops moved out for their assault positions.

The prince, Dillon and Karl jumped into the Humvee and were off down one of the side streets for another angle of approach. It took just a few minutes for the forces to set up. The commander of the force then gave the notice to the track driver to make his approach as rapidly as possible. As the unit got within one block of the villa, every light in the place came on. The street was bathed in bright white light. Inside the compound extra barriers popped into place and an audible alarm sounded in the surveillance room. Raj ran to the doorway and peered at the screens. Now he knew why no one was answering their phones. He was the only one left.

As the tracked unit came screeching around the corner toward the gate, Raj was sprinting down the stairs and out into the escape room. He wasn't going to put up a fight by himself. It was a matter of survival now. As he reached the door of the concrete building, he heard the front gates crash open under the assault of the vehicle. He then heard the sound of machine gun fire as the turret-mounted twin 50s raked the front of the house. The tracks gripped the blocking unit and crawled over the top in one jolting movement. As it did, the 50's blew out all the windows on the second floor. It stopped just in front of the entrance and waited for the following troops to gather. As they came through the shattered gateway, they noticed there was no return fire. They were literally by themselves in the flood lit parking area. The tracked unit then pushed into the front door as support elements swept into the downstairs area.

Raj pushed open the door inside the other villa. He stopped to listen for gunfire. There was none. He knew the troops discovered the lack of a security force inside the walls. They probably breeched the front of the house and were now combing the rooms looking for anyone and anything they could find. He pushed open the back door and sprinted the few yards to one of the vehicles. He picked up the keys from the floorboard and brought the vehicle to life. He dropped the gearshift into low 4WD and plowed his way through the wall. Once through the veneer, he swung the truck to the right for his planned escape route. As he did, the bright lights of several vehicles blocking his retreat greeted him. He slammed on the brakes and waited for the small arms barrage to begin. However, it didn't happen.

After only a few seconds, Raj dropped the shifter into reverse and headed for the other end of the street. It was the last thing he would do. The prince, along with Dillon and Karl, were positioned just waiting for such an opportunity. With a small squeeze on the trigger, the prince launched an RPG in the direction of the rapidly approaching vehicle. It slammed home with the resulting explosion lifting the vehicle off the ground and dropping it on a parked Lexus. The men shielded their faces from the searing heat created by the fireball. It was all over in a matter of minutes. From the gathering of troops outside the villa, until the destruction of the retreating supplier, not more than 15 minutes elapsed. The Prince pulled his satellite phone from one of the cargo pockets on his uniform and called the local fire brigade. He then motioned for Dillon and Karl to follow him as they retreated to the safety of the Humvee. Once inside the prince turned to thank the men for their assistance.

"This has been a very grand day for my family and members of our community." The prince began.

"The loss of a child cannot be redeemed by the liquidation of evil doers. I can only hope the plague that stuck my country can be brought under control. We have eliminated only one avenue of supply. However, as my God is my witness, I will dedicate myself to searching out and severely punishing anyone who deals in this type of death."

As he finished, he nodded to the driver and they were away from the scene before any of the locals arrived. The militia dispersed in such a manner the only sign of their brief assault was the demolished gate, the façade of the villa riddled with bullet holes and the tracked vehicles distinctive trail of chewed up asphalt.

The prince's Humvee swept through the gates of his palace and up to Dillon's SUV. The prince again thanked both men for their assistance and offered to entertain them for the evening. Dillon was quick to decline the royal invite. The prince said the invite stood whenever they wanted to avail themselves of the opportunity. It was an invitation never to be kept. Once the men left the palace, the pace for getting back to Germany and the final sweep for the murderers would rapidly increase.

⚜

Ramsay opened the box and pulled the envelope from the narrow slot. He shook the contents down to one end and haphazardly ripped off the other dropping the detached portion of the envelope to the tile floor of the post office. He read the contents of the letter, folded it in half and stuck it into his back pocket. He left the building and walked to one of the local fast food operations for a bit of lunch. The message sender could wait until his lunch break was over, he thought to himself as he stepped into the establishment.

All of this activity was being noted and relayed to agents at Ramstein. They in turn made calls to other surveillance units to activate the monitoring systems recently installed to capture the communications resulting from the letter. Once Ramsay finished his lunch, he returned to his office and called the message sender. Penny went to one of the collection points to listen in on the conversation between the two parties. The information passed was exactly what they wanted. It would flush out the other player. This was the final setup for an all out move on the cartel.

⁂

Dillon tied up the loose ends resulting from his visit to Riyadh. He paid another visit to Papa Good's compound with Carmen and met with Buzz to ensure his full cooperation in keeping matters under his hat. He didn't want to have his Jewish background pop up in the face of a royal. If Buzz wanted to stay in kingdom, Dillon knew this tidbit of information would keep him firmly entrenched on their side. Carvel played his cards well and Dillon made a special note to get with Krimshank and thank him for the excellent choice. He knew the drug section of the cop squadron would be in excellent hands once Carvel eliminated the dead wood and instituted his own game plan.

Dillon arranged for Carvel to head back for Ramstein on the rotator out of Prince Sultan. The lovely Karlotta made Dillon's travel arrangements. He was scheduled on the Oh Dark Thirty Lufthansa flight to Frankfurt. He was glad he didn't have to travel in and out of the kingdom very often. The connecting flight for all the major European cities left the Saudi capitol in the middle of the night.

Karlotta looked up from her computer screen as Dillon entered the office. "Your tickets are on the desk in your office," she cooed as Dillon passed her on his way to the coffee pot. He gave her a wink of thanks as he moved down the hall. After pouring a cup, he went to see Karl.

"Any news from that asshole Vinder?" he asked while taking a seat in one of the office chairs.

"Not a word," Karl replied as he closed the folder on his desk and tossed it into the out basket. "You would think he would be first in line to provide

461

congratulations on bringing this thing to a close. After all, one of the victims in this whole thing was a federal agent working under his direct supervision. It just doesn't make much sense."

"Well it's not something I'm going to worry about," Dillon replied as he got up to leave the office.

"We should have this pile of shit swept into one bag in a matter of days after I get back to Germany. They've put most of the ducks into a single row for us to blast out of the preverbal pond."

He raised his mug in salute. Once back in his office, he picked up the ticket and slipped it into his briefcase. He signed on the computer and checked his email. Nothing of significance so he logged out for the final time. All his working files were transferred to a CD and put into boxes containing the hard copy reports and investigation information. It was shipped back with Carvel for safekeeping in the Ramstein archives. As he was leaving the office, he stopped to give Karlotta a warm farewell.

Before he could put the key in the lock of his villa, the door swung open to reveal J.R. in a bathrobe. Dillon stopped in his tracks. "Aren't you going to come in?" she asked.

"For a second, I thought I had the wrong place," Dillon replied as he stepped through the doorway tossing his briefcase to the floor, kicking the door shut with his foot as he took the lovely lady into his arms. He held her tight as she whispered in his ear,

"You know how horny I get after a successful mission!" That was all Dillon needed to hear. He pulled the robe from her shoulders and swept her into his arms. Hell, there were several hours before the pickup for his ride to the airport. What better way to spend the rest of the afternoon.....

CHAPTER SIXTY-ONE

Dillon came through the doors from customs and looked for a sign with his name on it. When he found out what time his plane arrived in Frankfurt, he made Bill promise to send a driver and not bother about coming to pick him up. They were going to need a full day of work to bring this "collection" to a climax. He spotted a blue sign with white block letters, REECE. He waved to the man who hurried to assist with Dillon's luggage. When they stepped into the crisp air outside the terminal, Dillon took a deep breath. Much better to smell the city than the dust and pollution of Riyadh. It was good to be back in civilization.

They walked to where the low profile was parked in the maze of slots surrounding the terminal. Dillon helped as the driver placed his kit in the trunk. Dillon got into the back seat for a brief combat nap on the way to Ramstein. He wanted to be fresh for the meetings and knew once he arrived; a shower and shave would set him right for the day. He gave Bill a quick call to let him know he'd arrived and was on the way. He then settled back and let the driver weave his way out of the terminal area and on the autobahn for K-Town.

Bill took the call and told Dillon they would be ready when he got to the office. In fact, there was little he needed other than a briefing on status. With Dillon closing the operation in Kingdom, the players on this end were prime for picking. The only long pole in the tent was the man outside K-Town. They needed a plan to get him away from his sanctuary and out in the open.

Bill stuck his head into the hallway and shouted to the other agents, "Dillon's on the ramp. Should be here in a couple of hours."

Both unseen agents acknowledged the news. Bill went into the coffee room and poured the last cup from the pot. He took the time to fix another while he was thinking about the moves they were going to make.

On the other side of town, Ramsay was adding a bit of fortification to his first cup of coffee. He pulled the phone close to the edge of his desk and dialed his other contact number. The information he received was distressing. There might be a problem with the supply and he wanted to see if there was any Air Force information available. The phone rang once before the other insider answered. Ramsay passed the information and listened as his counterpart said it would take a couple of days to collect the real story. Ramsay hung up as the trace was completed. Since neither man suspected they were being watched, the direct line they used was an easy one to trace.

Hanz arranged for the tap to have an automatic trace coupled to the number. When the location flashed on the screen of the surveillance team, one of the agents picked up the phone and called Hanz. It was only a matter of minutes before he knew the exact location of the other player. As he read the name, he just shook his head. It was one name he never thought would be tied into this type of activity.

From his vantage point atop the forested hilltop, one of the security team members peered through the high-powered binoculars at their target. Garmat and Leo were just getting ready to leave the house. As they got into the Audi, Leo stopped before opening the driver side door. His cell phone evidently was ringing. The team couldn't hear the conversation. It wasn't a long call because Ramsay didn't have much to tell them except there was a question about supply and they were checking on the situation. If there were anything to pass along later in the day, he would give them a call. The men backed out of the drive and were on their way. A radio call to the other teams would have them picked up as they came out of their street. The hilltop team could warm up with a thermos of coffee brought to them by their relief crew. Neither team knew their portion of this game would end later in the day.

⁂

"Good morning Mary," Dillon greeted the receptionist as he came through the front door and into the office area.

"Good morning to you stranger," Mary responded as she turned her cheek to Dillon for a quick kiss.

"We were beginning to think you didn't like us any more."

"Not true, not true," Dillon assured her as he headed down the hall. Bill, Christina, and Penny were out of their offices to offer their greetings and

464

congratulations on closing down the Riyadh operation. Once the hugging and congratulatory slaps on the back were done, they all filled their coffee cups and headed for the conference room. Once inside, it was all business.

Dillon listened to the progress reports and op plans for gathering the bad guys. He didn't like the sequence they were proposing and offered an alternative. The first to fall would be the K-Town detective.

Bill and Dillon arrived at K-Town's police department just before noon. Hanz got them through the security checks and into his office. Once there, he was briefed on their plan of action. Dillon called Krimshank to see if the fourth member of the group was contacted. When the security commander confirmed the man was in route, Dillon confirmed the availability of the Security force SWAT. Hanz nodded in agreement when asked if all coordination was done on his side of the house. A joint maneuver was planned for just after dark or just after the men returned home in the evening. Dillon told Krimshank they would be at the house, so it was up to him to bring in the kingpin.

"Don't worry about my end of the game," Krimshank told Dillon. "It'll be a pleasure hanging this guy out to dry. I just hope he resists so I can bang on his ass for a while."

"Just remember to leave enough for the Justice Department," Dillon cautioned as they concluded their conversation. It was time to begin the takedowns.

Dillon gave a quick call to Christina and cleared her for the second portion of the equation. When he hung up, he joined Bill and Hanz in the hallway.

"Homicide is up that flight of stairs," Hanz stated as he pointed to a set of stairs at the other end of the hallway.

"He knows all of us so there may be a problem if we all come in together. There's one other exit. We should have that one covered too."

The three men moved into position. With everyone in the building armed, they didn't want to risk gunplay. They were confident of being able to take him down with little or no resistance. Hanz noticed Ramsay look up from his dilapidated desk when he walked in the door. Hanz walked past where Ramsay sat and went into the homicide lieutenant's office. When Bill entered the other door, Ramsay was busy refilling his coffee cup with hooch from his file drawer. It was only when he brought the mug to his lips he saw the Ramstein OSI officer in his space.

Since Bill was a few feet away, Ramsay quickly stood up and backed toward the coffee room. The only other exit was through that room and down a fire escape. As he was backing toward the door, Hanz came out of the lieutenant's office and called Ramsay's name. As he did, Ramsay pulled the snub-nosed 38 from its shoulder holster and aimed it in Hanz's direction. Hanz and the lieutenant retreated into the office as Bill took shelter behind one of the building support columns.

There were two other homicide officers in the room. It was a simple matter for them to ascertain who the bad guy was in this drama sequence. Ramsay turned to run out the escape door. As he did, Bill and one of the other officers fired single shots. One of them hit Ramsay in the shoulder; the other hit him in the back of the thigh. He crashed into the door knocking it from its hinges smashing on to the landing. Dillon placed the barrel of his 9MM to the man's forehead. "Don't even think about it," were the only instructions Dillon gave as the wounded man released his grip on the 38.

Dillon looked to see Hanz, Bill, the lieutenant and the other homicide officers standing in the now open doorway. "Call the paramedics," the lieutenant ordered. "We don't want to lose him now."

⁂

Christina turned off the ignition and sat motionless as she pondered what was about to happen. Of all the people in the security forces, this was the last person she would have suspected. She checked the weapon in her bag and got out of the car. She pushed open the gate to the impound lot and walked toward the shack. Conrad heard the gate squeak. He came out of the shack to greet his visitor.

"Christina, my dear sweet girl," Conrad gushed as he held his arms out to embrace the agent. Christina held up her arms to hold him back.

"This isn't a social visit Conrad. I'm here to ask you to come along to the security desk." Conrad's expression was one of puzzlement.

"My dear. What is this all about?"

"Don't make this any harder than it is," Christina told the old man.

"We have you on tape talking with Ramsay at K-Town police headquarters. We also have a trace to your phone in the shack. Didn't you think after the airman was murdered you would eventually come under suspicion? Were you so comfortable with your inside work you didn't believe we would eventually catch you out? At this moment, Ramsay is being taken into custody on a charge of complicity to murder. That's what you're being charged with."

Conrad hung is head as he realized the game was over. His years of supplementing the meager retirement benefits offered by both the US and German governments wasn't nearly enough. He'd gone into the information business to help. When it became so lucrative, he was hooked. Christina signaled the two airmen with her to come and take Conrad to the security

466

desk. She was sure Krimshank would have a few words for him before they turned him over to Hanz.

Christina sighed as she watched the little man walk away. This was one of the hardest things she ever dealt with. Now she must tell his wife. She pulled the gate closed behind her, ran the chain through the loops in the fence, and secured the padlock. By this time, the security team placed Conrad in the back of the cruiser and was ready to leave. Christina waved them off as she got back into her vehicle for the long ride to Conrad's house.

⁂

First Lieutenant Xavier Cockcroft, a graduate of the US Military Academy at West Point, opened the door to the ready room. As the door swung open, a voice inside called the room to attention. Members of his security team snapped to where they stood.

"As you were," Xavier ordered. The men and women returned to their previous activities. Senior Master Sergeant Denman Endicott greeted the team leader.

"Evenin Boss. Just a few minor adjustments and we're ready for the show."

"Sergeant Endicott, this is Special Agent Reece, Dillon Reece. He's the one responsible for making tonight's activity possible."

"Now hold on lieutenant. I like to think of my work as a team effort. There were many people involved in this investigation. It was multi-faceted and I might add, multi-cultural."

"Oh I know Agent Reece. I saw," the sergeant began when Dillon cut him short.

"Please don't say you saw my picture at the academy!" The sergeant was quiet for a brief moment.

"Anything you say sir," he began again.

"I saw this picture on a wanted poster in the stag bar located right near the academy." Dillon just shook his head and reached for the sergeant's outstretched hand.

"It's a pleasure to meet you Agent Reece. I'm looking forward to the activities of this evening."

"Thanks Den," the lieutenant replied.

"We've still got some time left before we have to be on station," he concluded as he looked at his watch.

"I just pulled the latest information on the pair. Seems to be a straightforward takedown. Our only instructions are to bring them in alive. The commander was VERY adamant. He didn't say they must be in perfect condition, just alive," he smiled as Denman shook his head in acknowledgement.

"I get the picture sir. Shake and bake without the deep fryer."

The lieutenant moved across the room to where his gear was stored and made a check. Denman was responsible for the boss's gear. The lieutenant knew the equipment would be in tiptop shape. The inspection was really a formality. After a few minutes, the lieutenant called the group to gather round a white board hanging at one end of the room. He grabbed a blue marker from the tray and began the final briefing.

"This seems to be fairly straightforward. The house has two exits. One leads to the street, the other leads into the back yard which is terraced up to the neighbors backyard," the lieutenant finished the simple drawing and turned toward the group.

"Our instructions are to bring them in ALIVE. The commander stressed this repeatedly. Xavier made eye contact with each team member. He knew their capabilities and he wanted to instill in them the desires of command. When he assured himself the instruction was received and understood, he returned to his briefing.

Mavis, I want you up here watching the rear."

"Roger that sir," Technical Sergeant Mavis Benter responded to the instructions.

"Gareth, you and Naomi will be in front of the place. There's a small brick wall to use as a shield. Naomi can watch the walkway leading from the front door and you can position by the driveway in case they have the Audi in the garage. Most of the time they leave it on the street. Don't see why they would change anything tonight. We have closed down all their information sources, so they're on their own." Technical Sergeant Gareth Retup and Master Sergeant Naomi Snaith echoed they acknowledgement of orders and their placement at the scene.

"Ben," the lieutenant began again,

"I want you and your heavy artillery, right down at this point in the road," the boss indicated a spot on the white board which would equate to approximately two houses down from the scene of the action.

"If all else fails, you can take any action necessary to make escape impossible."

"Roger that sir," Master Sergeant Benedict Zeal replied patting the butt end of a very large caliber weapon lying on the table next to him.

"Any questions?"

"Agent Reece, do you have anything to add?" Dillon just wished the men and women good luck.

"OK then." The lieutenant shouted. "Mount up!"

The group moved away from the briefing board and gathered their gear. It was just after sunset and the specially designed Expeditions were waiting in the parking lot. First stop would be the observation point. Once there, they would make contact with the local constabulary with the job of closing down all in vicinity activity. They even took the precaution of asking neighbors to be their guest at a local watering hole while the action took place.

When they arrived on scene, the subjects of their attention were not home. It was more than an hour before the now infamous Blue Audi pulled in front of the house. Leo and Garmat parked the car on the street as normal. The lieutenant gave thumbs up to the others as he watched the men open the front door and head into the house. It was now time to position the troops.

With silent hand signals, the group moved down the hill and into their assigned positions. The lieutenant and Denman boarded one of the trucks and headed for their position directly in front of the driveway, slightly angled down the hill. Once everyone was in position, Xavier picked up the satellite phone mounted on the truck's dashboard. He dialed the house number. Leo picked up.

"Yeah," was the only thing he said into the receiver.

"Is this Garmat?" the lieutenant questioned.

"No. This is Leo. Garmat isn't here. What can I do for you?"

"It's very simple sir, this is Lieutenant Ebenezer Ever, security team commander in charge of the detachment with the awesome responsibility of bringing you two scumbags in for questioning."

"Sure fuckhead. Just what kind of a joke is this?" Leo screamed into the phone.

"No joke sir," the lieutenant assured the man.

"We have control of the house and to show you what I mean by control, let me cut off the lights." The lieutenant gave Denman a nod and he pushed a small red button on the detonator controlling a small explosive charge set in the power box. A "crew" from the local power authority installed the explosive device just the other day. As the small detonation took place, the house went dark. Each member of the team switched to night vision. There was silence on the other end of the line.

"Leo. Leo, are you there?" the team leader questioned.

"Fuck you," was the only reply as the line went dead. As the back door flew open, Mavis laid down a few rounds, which shattered the glass door and splintered the trellis holding a few bunches of Riesling grapes. Garmat and Leo retreated inside the house.

"You should have fucken known they would have the back covered." Garmat screeched at Leo.

469

"Shut the fuck up. Let's take the truck." With those instructions, both men moved to the garage area. Inside was a well-equipped SUV with reinforced doors and windows. The men figured they may have to face a firefight some day but they weren't expecting the team they now faced.

Leo jumped into the drivers' seat with Garmat strapping in to the passenger side. He opened a port on the window and stuck the barrel of a short-barreled shotgun through the hole. Leo had a similar port but figured he would have to drive more than shoot. He was right.

Gareth heard the truck fire up inside the garage. He turned to the lieutenant and signaled something was taking place in the garage. Before he could duck down again, the SUV burst through the aluminum door and down the short driveway. Gareth steadied his weapon on the retaining wall and opened up on the driver's side door. The reinforcement worked for a while but the shear amount of firepower overwhelmed the protection. Leo grimaced as a round cut through the door, passed through his knee and lodged in the seat under his thigh. He caught sight of the larger SUV parked at a slight angle to his route of escape. He swung the truck violently to the left. Garmat pumped off two rounds, which hit nothing.

As the bad guys blew through the garage door, Denman dropped the transmission into four-wheel drive low. As the opposing force pulled in front of his vehicle, he slammed his foot on the accelerator and pushed the cattle catcher welded to the frame of his truck into the side of the escaping duo. Gareth jumped onto the retaining wall as the back end of the criminal's vehicle swung his way and into the front of the Audi. However, Leo held enough momentum to squeeze through the pile-driving hit. He accelerated down the street only to be met by Zeal's suppressing fire into the front wheels, engine block, and radiator. The hood flew up blocking Leo's view causing him to lose control and smash into a light standard. The street fell silent except for the hiss of steam escaping the shattered engine block.

⚜

"John, good to see you," Krimshank greeted as the major entered the security forces command office.

"Good to see you Karl. I'm glad we're about to shut this thing down," John replied as he took a seat opposite Krimshank's desk.

"Can I get you a frosty beverage?" Karlton asked as he opened the door to his fridge.

"No thanks. I'll have celebratory toddies at the club after this meeting is concluded." Krimshank pulled a bottle of fizzy water from the shelf

470

and kicked the door shut. He went back behind the desk and began an explanation of what took place during the day.

"You mean that nice little old man at the impound lot?" John asked in surprised tones.

"That's him. Conrad was the base insider. He kept the dude at K-Town informed on happenings involving their operation. That's why they could operate so freely. If we got close, they shut down. When the heat was off, they were in business again. I'm sure the former head guy in my own drug unit had something to do with the whole operation but he's gone now and with a new guy in town, I'm sure the squadron will clean up very nicely." As he finished speaking, the buzzer on his desk announced a message from Jerome.

"Sir, your visitor is here."

"Send him in," the commander replied.

Krimshank came around the edge of his desk and offered his hand to the man entering his office. "Agent Asterfon, what a pleasure to see you on such short notice. Please, have a seat." Asterfon shook the colonel's hand and then turned to the major.

"Cornelius Asterfon, Special Agent, DEA, from the Embassy."

"Glad to meet you. I'm John Littlemore, maintenance commander here at Ramstein." John replied to the introduction.

"So what's so damn important you needed to have me here in person at this time of the day?" Asterfon questioned as he made himself comfortable in the other chair in front of Krimshank's desk. The commander opened a folder on his desk, pulled out a pair of pictures, and tossed them on the desk in front of Asterfon.

"Either of those two look familiar?" Krimshank asked the agent. Asterfon looked fleetingly at the photos, sat back in his chair, and told the other two men he never saw those men before.

"Are they involved in the investigation?"

"Not any more," Krimshank replied. "There are now the guests of K-Town's finest after a brief stop at our humble facilities here at Ramstein." Asterfon was silent as the beads of sweat broke out on his forehead.

"If that's all you have, please let me admonish you for telling me you had something of significance needing my personal attention. This is shit and I'm offended you would waste my precious time on something so trivial." Asterfon rose from his chair and gripped the edge of Krimshank's desk.

"We don't consider it a trivial matter," Dillon said as he stepped into the office.

"Let me give you another couple of pictures to ponder." Dillon tossed surveillance photos of Leo and Garmat on the desk.

"I just took a call from out takedown team; both of those individuals are in custody. A bit the worse for wear but they will be able to stand trial for the murder of Airman First Class William Calhoon Crimitin the Third.

✳

Following the arrest of Asterfon, everyone involved with the case met for a discussion of events. It turned in to a type of grandiose after actions report. Everyone was able to review the operation and learn from each phase.

The Blue Audi contained cotton and latex gloves used when Leo and Garmat searched Crimitin's apartment. They also found traces of mud on the inside of each wheel well matching the dirt at the top of the hill. The boys were even stupid enough to leave the boots they wore tossed in a corner of the garage. They never expected to have those boots tie them to the time and location of Crimitin's death. With the fingerprints lifted from the drinking glass and the other bits and pieces, it was an easy case for trial.

With all the assembled evidence against them, Leo and Garmat were willing participants in placing all the other arrestees into their proper position within the cartel. They naturally hoped it would keep them away from the United States and a certain death penalty.

Conrad and Ramsay also planned to turn states evidence in return for reduced sentences. Asterfon was sent back to the United State to face federal charges in addition to the life sentence he faced in Germany. On our side of the Atlantic, he faced the death penalty.

Dillon threw his suit bag on top of his case in the trunk of the car. The driver closed the trunk as Dillon turned to the farewell committee. John, Bill, Christina, and Penny all came to the Cannon to say goodbye. Dillon went down the line and thanked each one of them for their excellent work.

"I told you when I got here I was just part of the team. An outside set of eyes and values. I'm glad we all worked so well together."

As he came to John, the maintainer grasped his friends hand and pulled him close. "I'm sure the Crimitin family is happy this all came to a successful end. At least they know the reasons behind their son's activities."

Dillon waved to all as the low profile pulled out of the drive. There was just one other matter to take care of.

472

CHAPTER SIXTY-TWO

Dillon looked out the window and watched the Jetway move slowly into position outside the exit door as his flight to Zurich ended. He stepped into the cool evening air of the Swiss capitol. A steward for the Swiss airline directed him to baggage claim and the rental car agencies. Christina booked a room at the ArabellaSheraton Neues Schloss. Since he was headed for an office of Union Bank of Switzerland, it was an easy walk from the hotel. It also offered off street parking, a decent watering hole, and 24-hour room service making his brief stay more pleasurable.

A room on the top floor with a corner balcony opened to Dillon as the bellman explained the amenities. Dillon listened haphazardly and tipped the man handsomely for his briefing. After the man left, Dillon stepped on the flowerpot-adorned balcony. He could see Lake Zurich just off to his right. It was a beautiful sight but one he wished young Airman Crimitin was able to enjoy. He wasn't sure where the crew chief stayed when he made visits to Zurich for deposits into his Swiss account but was sure the young man appreciated the beauty of the city.

The next morning, Dillon rose early and enjoyed a leisurely breakfast before taking his complementary newspaper down to the lakeshore. He picked a bench where he could watch the activity along the walkway. Just before eight, he threw the paper into a trash bin and headed up General-Guisan-Quai to where it met Bahnhofstrassa at a complicated main intersection. Typical of European cities, there were several streets meeting in one central location. He gingerly crossed each street until he was on the correct corner. He didn't have very far to go until he was outside number 45. The bank opened at precisely 0815.

Dillon surveyed the bank's interior and located the security box entrance. He calmly approached the clerk at a modestly appointed desk and asked for assistance in gaining entrance to box 09134. The clerk scanned the computer screen after entering the box number. "Mr. William Crimitin the Third?" the clerk questioned.

"No Mam, I'm William Crimitin Junior." The clerk scrolled down the screen a bit and located the information she needed.

"Here you are, if you would just sign this card for a verification of signature and let me see one form of picture ID." Dillon took the 3 by 5 card pushed across the desk by the clerk and signed the name of William Crimitin Jr. in perfectly matching strokes of those left by Airman Crimitin in the locker at Sultan. Once done, he reached into his coat pocket and pulled out the recently procured tourist passport in the name of William Crimitin Jr. The clerk made a copy of the document, compared the signatures, and asked Dillon to follow her down a short hallway to the entrance of the safety box room. After they entered, the clerk used her key for one of the locks and took the other key from Dillon. She slid the key into the lock and after a bit of struggling, the door opened.

"When you're finished, just push that button on the wall," she said before exiting.

Dillon waited until she disappeared down the hall before pulling the long metal box from its cubbyhole in the wall. He went to a table set up for customers' convenience and lifted the lid. Inside were stacks of US dollars in various denominations. Evidently, the young Airman wasn't too fussy when he skimmed off the top. Most were 100-dollar bills but there were a few piles of 50s and even a few 20s. He set about counting the funds.

Dillon transferred all the cash to the oversized briefcase he purchased just for this purpose. He locked the case and returned the box to its hole in the wall. He pushed the buzzer and waited for the young clerk to meander down the hall. Dillon signed out of the area and left the bank. He again walked up Bahnhofstrasse until he was outside number 72. This next branch of Union Bank of Switzerland was to be his new branch.

Dillon sat in front of the "new accounts" desk and waited for the dapper man in the grey business suit to finish with his current customer. Once pleasantries were exchanged, Dillon said he wanted to open an account, have ATM cards issued and sent to an address in the United States. The account manager said all was possible.

"Would there be a charge for use of an ATM outside of Switzerland?" Dillon asked.

"That all depends on the size of the account and the number of withdrawals per month. How much did you want to deposit? The man asked. Dillon set the case on the edge of the desk, snapped open the locks, and lifted the lid.

"Six Hundred Seventy Five Thousand, Seven Hundred and Twenty US dollars," Dillon replied.

True to the professionalism of Swiss bankers, the man behind the desk didn't flinch. He simply thanked Dillon, slid some paperwork across the desk asking Dillon to complete the forms, and took the briefcase to the teller line for verification. He waited until the head teller returned the case with a tape of the addition process completed as the machines counted the bills. Exactly like Dillon said. USD675,720.00. The man returned to his seat behind the desk with the tally and a receipt for the amount on deposit in the new account.

"Is there anything else you need?" Dillon asked as the man scanned the documents presented for identification.

"No Mr. Crimitin that should just about do it. The cards should arrive in about two week's time. If you need to access your cash before that time, all you have to do is give us a call and we can authorize a transfer of funds to a stateside bank with no problems at all."

"That won't be necessary. I'm not going to be in California for at least a month. But I appreciate the information," Dillon responded as he rose and reached across the desk to shake the man's hand.

As Dillon left the bank, he paused and drew in a deep breath. Not exactly legal, he thought but this is what the boy wanted and this is what he's going to get. The money was now available to his family in Azusa. The family could move into a better neighborhood or out of California all together. The notes to his family stated those facts exactly. Dillon would package everything they collected over the term of the investigation and send it along to the family. Once he got back to Florida, he would call the family and offer his condolences.

When he arrived back at the hotel, he went immediately to his room and made a quick phone call to the embassy. He then stretched out on the bed for a combat nap. His flight back to Frankfurt and then on to Atlanta didn't leave until the next day. He wanted to ensure he had sufficient time to conclude all of his business before he left the city.

Dillon awoke to the sound of knocking at his door. He peered through the lens and saw a bellman outside the room. He swung the door open and saw a note on a small silver tray held in the man's right hand. As Dillon reached for the note, the bellman's left hand swung from behind his back. In an automatic reaction, Dillon blocked the man's emerging arm with his and brought his right foot up into the counterfeit bellman's groin. The blocking motion knocked the small caliber silencer fitted pistol from the man's grip.

It dropped harmlessly to the carpeted floor as Dillon rendered the assailant unconscious with a double-fisted blow to the back of the man's neck. He crumbled in a heap.

Dillon quickly picked up the piece and drug the man inside his room. He hogtied him with curtain tiebacks, straightened his shirt, put on his coat, and left the room. He casually strolled through the bar and lobby area and into the street. He returned to his morning paper reading bench location along the river walkway and sat down. He was there less than an hour before a visitor arrived. Without looking, he greeted the new bench warmer.

"Sonta, Sonta, Sonta. Did you really believe I was foolish enough to fall for the fake message from the bellman routine?"

"Did you open the door?" Sonta queried.

"Yes, Yes I did. But only to rearrange his gonads." Dillon turned, placed one arm along the back of the bench, and looked at his one time lover.

"I guess I was just too vulnerable at the time we met. You really did a number on me."

Without looking at Dillon, Sonta replied, "So when did you put my identity together?"

"It did take some time but all the traffic we picked up and the lack of leadership led me to believe the true kingpin of the operation was outside the august group we were tracking. The man you killed had an address book with six names. One by one, I was able to associate each name with someone we brought down. Asterfon was an oddball. He did cause some questions as we went through this whole operation. However, when it was all talked out, I still had one name. Then things began to bother my senses. Your phone calls and notes were too well informed. The note in Paris, the phone call at the terminal in Germany? How did you know when to call? Reason, you were in Germany. You weren't in Florida. It would have been the middle of the night. It really didn't sink in until I started putting it all together. You knew too much about me during the first days of our relationship. I was flattered but then it all made sense." Dillon paused and watched for any reaction. There was none. Sonta just sat staring at the lake.

Dillon continued to explain how the team pieced together the many trails found in the maze of electronic messages, fake identifications and threats issued to members of the cartel. When it was all presented to the investigators, one small item tied Sonta, or Charmain Collyns as she was know to her parents, into the whole operation. At one point, she changed email providers. Dillon mentioned a number of returned emails before she contacted him with a new address. Unbeknownst to her, a tracer cookie lodged on the hard drive of one of the computers located in the processing villa in Riyadh. When all the information was decoded, Dillon recognized an email address. That's all it took.

As Dillon finished, Charmain turned slowly to face him. As she brought her right hand into view, Dillon noticed the large pistol cupped in her slim fingers.

"I'm sorry it comes down to this. I didn't want to be the one to end your excellent career. The more I learned about your abilities, the more I knew if my operation was going to be successful, you had to be eliminated. I was going to take care of it in Florida after abusing your body a few hundred times. Then that dumb kid decided to turn in the very lucrative Saudi market. When that call came in, I wasn't prepared. I knew damn good and well none of the boneheads I had working for me were capable of making things happen. Seeing how you've thoroughly decapitated my operation, I wanted to get some of the money back before having you killed."

"I moved the money," Dillon flatly stated.

"I know. I watched," she replied.

"We had you pegged for elimination when you came out of the bank and back to the hotel. When you went to the second bank, we were puzzled. When you came out minus the case, we knew we were screwed. That's when I came up with the bellman ploy trying to take you out without my involvement. When you fucked that up, it came down to this."

Dillon just looked into her eyes. As she pulled back the trigger, she didn't hear the sniper's rifle crack sending a fast round into her forearm shattering the bones and tearing the arm nearly in two. Her gun fired but the bullet missed Dillon's midsection grazing his thigh as he fell off the bench and on to the concrete path.

As Charmain reacted to the situation, she stood up clutching her dangling right arm. The police sniper brought her down with a round to the back of her thigh. She collapsed on the bench and then on the path next to Dillon. As Dillon stood up holding his hand over his wounded thigh, the special team he notified with help from the Embassy DEA agent surrounded the prone kingpin of the Saudi connection.

After the paperwork was done, the wounds bandaged and the assault teams departed, Dillon limped down the street toward the hotel on his bandaged leg. Maybe he would spend another couple of days in Zurich.

ENDNOTES

[1] Old Man -- Term of endearment for commanding officer

[2] CIF -- California Interscholastic Federation

[3] C-141 -- "Starlifter" Long time workhorse for Air Force long range logistics delivery

[4] crew chief -- Person responsible for the basic maintenance of the Starlifter

[5] Combat nap -- Short duration, maximum effect

[6] TDY -- Temporary Duty Assignment

[7] ADC -- Area Defense Counsel Air Force's Public Defender

[8] UCMJ -- Uniform Code of Military Justice The basis for all legal action in any US Military force

[9] JAG -- Judge Advocate General

[10] BDU -- Battle Dress Uniform

[11] USAFE -- United States Air Forces in Europe

[12] MICAP -- Mission Capability

[13] ETD -- Estimated Time of Departure

[14] dash 60 -- Electrical Ground Power Unit

[15] DEA -- Drug Enforcement Agency

[16] INCO -- In Country

[17] USMTM -- United States Military Training Mission

[18] NATO -- North Atlantic Treaty Organization

[19] AFRTS -- Armed Forces Radio and Television Service

[20] FMS -- Foreign Military Sales

[21] PSPO -- Peace Sun Project Officer

[22] DSN -- Defense Switched Network

[23] MWR -- Morale, Welfare and Recreation

[24] KKMC -- King Khalid Military City

[25] AFIT -- Air Force Institute of Technology

[26] PMEL -- Precision Measurement Equipment Laboratory

[27] STEP -- Stripes To Exceptional Performers -- An accelerated promotion system.

[28] Iqama -- Identification document required of all foreign workers in Saudi Arabia

[29] CENTCOM -- Central Command

Printed in the United States
43261LVS00003B/13-30

9 781420 876192